THE THREE MUSKETEERS

THE THREE MUSKETEERS

by
ALEXANDRE DUMAS, PERE
and
AUGUSTE MAQUET

Translated by
WILLIAM ROBSON

Edited and Updated by
SCOTT FITZGERALD GRAY

Illustrated by
AVIV OR

Insane Angel Studios

CONTENTS

A good editor is someone who
cares a little less about the
author's needs than the reader's.

— Dene October

EDITOR'S PREFACE

A short time ago, while making researches in the public library for the backstory of an RPG campaign setting I keep meaning to write but somehow never get around to, I stumbled by chance upon the novel *The Three Musketeers*, printed in London, where I went on holiday a few years ago and had a very good time. The title attracted me, reminding me how long it had been since I read the classic work of Alexandre Dumas, pere, and Auguste Maquet, in the translation by William Robson. So I took the novel home with me, with the use of my Okanagan Regional Library card, and devoured it once more.

It is not my intention here to enter into an analysis of this seminal work, and I shall satisfy myself with referring such of our readers as appreciate the adventure-novel high jinks of the period to its pages. They will therein find portraits penciled by the hand of two masters, shaping likenesses of d'Artagnan and Athos, Porthos and Aramis, Louis XIII of France, Anne of Austria, the Cardinal de Richelieu, the Duke of Buckingham, and other figures of the period as bold and jocular as those on the walls of the best galleries.

But it is well known that what strikes the capricious mind of the poet is too often that which catches the more reliable eye of the editor. And so while admiring again, as countless others have admired, the story the novel relates, my main preoccupation concerned a matter that had been invisible to me when first I read the book as a lad of twelve. Specifically, a number of conspicuous and curious oversights of verisimilitude and character.

For as odd as it might seem, though entirely in keeping with the market forces of the day and the two authors' attention to earlier materials (specifically, the historical biography *Memoires de M. d'Artagnan* by Gatien de Courtilz de Sandras, on which *The Three Musketeers* was based), Dumas and Maquet had crafted all the primary heroic and villainous characters in the book — including, in fact, all of the tale's named musketeers — as straight white men.

Quite tellingly, the book does feature some captivatingly written women, whose depth and agency makes it clear that Dumas and Maquet were entirely comfortable looking beyond their own sex and gender as crafters of character story. Likewise, the strong bonds of fraternal love between all the musketeers, as well as the characterizations of Athos and Aramis in matters of love and desire, clearly show that our authors did not feel the need to conform to a rigidly normative view of heroic macho sexuality. And anyone who knows Dumas's own life story can appreciate the unlikelihood that he would have consciously chosen to whitewash his narrative, insofar as he himself was Black — the child of the legendary French general Thomas-Alexandre Dumas, who was himself the son of a white French father and a Black Haitian mother, and the first person of color to become brigadier general, divisional general, and general-in-chief in the French army.

As such, it should be clear to anyone who's read *The Three Musketeers* that the forces restraining Dumas and Maquet from making so few of the main characters women, and from identifying any of the main characters as people of color, nonbinary, or LGBTQ+, must have been an obvious product of systemic conservatism in the then-nascent adventure-literature industry, as was their shaping almost exclusively straight white male roles for the range of powerful secondary characters who drive the novel's political intrigue.

Because, seriously — if a contemporary writer were to cram nothing but straight white men into a book that's clearly meant to be read and enjoyed by anyone with an imagination and a love of adventure, that would just be crazy.

Right?

It was thus that I hastened to contact the authors through their literary agents, anxious to pay homage to their greatness by suggesting an approach to editorial revision that would reflect a wider world of character and possibility. In the end, though, I was saddened and chagrined to have forgotten in my excitement that Dumas and Maquet, along with both their agents, had died over a century ago.

And so I understood what I must do.

This new volume of *The Three Musketeers* has undergone rigorous revision from the Robson translation of the original text. Though the usual edits for clarity, continuity, and story development have all had their due, the bulk of the developmental and line edits by far focus on reshaping the character story — correcting those small issues of sex, gender, orientation, and representation in an attempt to produce a work more closely resembling the novel that I'm absolutely positive Alexandre Dumas and Auguste Maquet would have written if they'd been able to.

This being understood, let us proceed with our story.

— Scott Fitzgerald Gray

CHAPTER 1

THE GIFTS OF THE D'ARTAGNANS

On the first Monday of the month of April, 1625, the market town of Meung appeared to be in a perfect state of revolution. Many citizens, seeing folk flying toward the High Street and leaving their children crying at the open doors, hastened to don what armor they had. Then, supporting their somewhat uncertain courage with a musket or a pike, they directed their steps toward the inn called the Jolly Miller, before which was gathered a compact mob, vociferous and full of curiosity, and increasing in size every minute.

In those times, panics were common, and few days passed without some settlement or other experiencing an event of this kind. Battles broke out between the gentry, who made war against each other. Battles broke out on behalf of the queens, who made war against Spain for all France to see. Battles broke out as directed by the Cardinal de Richelieu, that powerful priest and chief minister of France, who made war against the queens in secret. Then, in addition to these concealed or public, secret or open wars, there were robbers, vagabonds, wolves, and scoundrels who made war upon everybody.

The citizens always took up arms readily against thieves, wolves or scoundrels, and often against the gentry, and sometimes against the crown — though never against the cardinal. It resulted from this habit, then, that on the said Monday, citizens hearing the clamor and seeing neither the red-and-yellow standard of Spain nor the livery of Cardinal de Richelieu, rushed toward the Jolly Miller as if rushing to war.

When the crowd arrived there, the cause of the hubbub was apparent to all.

A young woman stood at the center of things — and let us sketch her portrait at a dash. Imagine to yourself a Don Quixote of eighteen years. A Don Quixote without armor or coat of mail. A Don Quixote clothed in a woolen doublet, the blue color of which had faded into a nameless shade between that of the dregs of wine and a heavenly azure. Face long and brown, high cheek bones as a sign of sagacity, the muscles of the jaw strong and fine. By these infallible signs can any child of Gascony always be detected, even without

*For our young Gascon had a steed so singular
that it was the singular focus of all observers…*

their cap — and our young woman, born and raised in the Gascon province of Bearn, wore her dark-brown curls braided and tied beneath a cap set off with a fine feather. The eye open and intelligent, the nose hooked but finely chiseled. Too tall for a youth and too slight for a laborer of long years, she might have been taken by an experienced eye as a farmer's child sent out upon some journey of errand — had it not been for the long rapier which, dangling from a leather baldric, hit against the calves of its owner as she walked, and against the rough side of her steed when she was on horseback.

For our young Gascon had a steed so singular that it was the singular focus of all observers. It was a Bearnese pony of some thirteen years old, yellow in its hide, without a hair in its tail, and with swollen windgalls upon its legs that were the signs of a life of labor. For though it often walked with its head lower than its knees, rendering a martingale quite unnecessary, this was a noble steed that contrived to effortlessly travel eight leagues in a day.

Unfortunately, the qualities of this horse were well concealed under its strange-colored hide and its unaccountable gait. And so, at a time when all folk believed themselves to be equestrian connoisseurs, the appearance of the aforesaid pony at Meung — which place the pony had entered about a quarter of an hour before — produced an unfavorable feeling that extended to its rider.

And this feeling had been more painfully perceived by young d'Artagnan — for so was this young Don Quixote named — from her not being able to conceal from herself the ridiculous appearance that such a steed gave her, good equestrian though she was. She had sighed deeply, therefore, when accepting the gift of the pony from her parents more than a fortnight before, on the day she had left the family home in the town of Tarbes. She was not ignorant that such a beast was worth at least twenty livres. And the words of her mother which had accompanied the gift were above all price.

"Daughter," that retired Gascon warrior had said — in that pure Bearn patois of which the late king, Henry, could never rid himself. "This horse was born in the house of your family thirteen years ago, and has remained in it ever since, which ought to make you love it. Never sell it. Allow it to die tranquilly and honorably of old age, and if you make a campaign with it, take as much care of it as you would of an old retainer."

Mother, father, and daughter stood facing each other in the stable where the yellow pony looked on without concern, both mother and father a match for their daughter in stature and features, though the elder Madame d'Artagnan was clearly the closer source of her daughter's temperament, as shall be seen. "At court, provided you have ever the honor to go there," continued the mother, "sustain worthily your name of gentle reputation, which has been worthily borne by your ancestors for five hundred years, both for your own sake and the sake of your relatives and friends. Endure nothing from anyone except the cardinal and the queens. It is by courage, please observe — by courage alone — that a gentlefolk can make their way nowadays. Whoever hesitates for a moment perhaps allows the gift to escape which during that exact second, fortune held out to them. But you are young, and you are driven to be brave for two reasons. The first is that you are a Gascon. And the second is that you are our child."

So saying, the elder Madame d'Artagnan linked hands with Monsieur d'Artagnan, who nodded agreement and his approval for his wife to speak on. "Never fear quarrels," said she, "but seek adventures. I have taught you how to handle a sword, and you have thews of iron, a wrist of steel. Fight on all occasions. Fight that much more eagerly with duels having been forbidden, since consequently there is twice as much courage in fighting. Your father and I have nothing to give you, our daughter, but the name we fixed together when we were married, fifteen silver crowns, and our horse. I will add to that my sword and the counsels you have just heard."

"And I," said the young d'Artagnan's father, speaking at last, "will add again a recipe for a certain salve, which I learned from an adventurer in my own youth, and which has the miraculous virtue of curing all wounds that do not reach the heart. Take advantage of all, and live happily and long." But then a quaver took his voice, and he spoke no more as the elder Madame d'Artagnan girded her own rapier round her daughter, kissed her tenderly on both cheeks, and gave her a final benediction.

"Let me send you now to Monsieur de Treville, who was once my captain, and who had the honor as a child to be the playfriend of our Queen Louise, whom gods preserve. Sometimes their play degenerated into battles, and in these battles the Princess Louise was not always the stronger. The blows which she received increased greatly her esteem and friendship for Treville.

"Afterward, he fought with others. In his first journey to Paris, five times. From the death of the late king and sovereign till the young French queen came of age, without reckoning wars and sieges, seven times. And from that date up to the present day, a hundred times, perhaps. So that in spite of edicts, ordinances, and decrees, there he is, captain of the musketeers. Which is to say, the chief of a legion that the crown holds in the greatest esteem. Still further, Monsieur de Treville gains ten thousand crowns a year. He is therefore a great gentry, but one who began as you begin. So go to him with this letter of introduction, and make him your model in order that you may do as he has done."

D'Artagnan claimed the invaluable letter with one hand, and then with the other, the recipe of the famous salve given over by her father — which, considering the counsels her mother had just given her, the young Gascon expected she would have much need of. Her father then embraced her for a final farewell that was wordless, but long and more heartfelt than the final nod granted her daughter by the elder Madame d'Artagnan. Not that the mother did not love her daughter, who was her only child. But Madame d'Artagnan was a soldier, and of a generation that considered it unworthy of any soldier to give way to their feelings.

By contrast, Monsieur d'Artagnan was a healer, and still more, his healer's caring had long made him a most doting father, and his embrace was marked more than once by tears. And let us speak to the heart of the young Madame d'Artagnan that notwithstanding the efforts she made to remain firm, and notwithstanding her mother's long influence on her true nature, the second part of that true nature prevailed, and she shed so many tears that she succeeded only with great difficulty in concealing the half of her pain at leaving.

That same day, the young woman set forth on her journey, furnished with the familial gifts — which consisted, as we have said, of fifteen crowns in a small velvet purse, the horse, the sword, the recipe for salve, and the letter for Monsieur de Treville, with her mother's counsels and her father's tears being thrown into the bargain.

With such guidance at hand, d'Artagnan was morally and physically an exact copy of the hero of Cervantes, to whom we so happily compared her. Except that where Don Quixote took windmills for giants and sheep for armies, d'Artagnan on her part took every smile for an insult and every look as a provocation. For this was the first part of the young Gascon's true nature, whence it resulted that over eleven long days of travel from Tarbes, her fist around the reins was constantly tightened, and her hand strayed always to the hilt of her sword.

So it was that the sight of the unfortunate pony excited numerous smiles on the faces of passersby. But as against the side of this pony rattled a rapier of respectable length, and as over this sword gleamed an eye more ferocious than haughty, these passersby repressed their hilarity. Or if hilarity prevailed over prudence, they endeavored to laugh only on one side. D'Artagnan, then, remained dignified and resistant to her susceptibility to anger, so that her fist did not descend upon any jaw, nor did the sword issue from its scabbard — till she came to this unlucky town of Meung.

There, as she was alighting from her horse at the gate of the Jolly Miller without anyone — host, attendant, or stablehand — yet coming to hold her stirrup or take her reins, d'Artagnan spied through an open window on the ground floor, a gentlefolk well made and of lofty carriage, although of rather a stern countenance. This figure was talking with two persons who named him 'monsieur' in their conversation, and who appeared to listen to him with respect. D'Artagnan fancied quite naturally, according to her custom, that she must be the object of their talk, and listened. This time, she was only in part mistaken. For she herself was not the subject of discussion, but her horse was.

The stern-looking gentle appeared to be enumerating all the pony's qualities to his listeners. And, as I have said, the listeners seeming to have great deference for the narrator, they every moment burst into fits of laughter. Now, as a half-smile was sufficient to awaken the irascibility of the young d'Artagnan, the effect produced upon her by this vociferous mirth may be easily imagined.

Nevertheless, d'Artagnan was desirous of examining the appearance of this impertinent personage who ridiculed her. She fixed her haughty eye upon the stranger, and took in a figure of from forty to forty-five years of age, with one eye gone and patched, and the other black and piercing. He had a chalky complexion, a strong nose, black hair with the sheen of dye and a well-shaped mustache to match, and a pale pink scar along one cheek. He was dressed in a doublet and leggings of a violet color, with shoulder braid of the same color but no other ornaments upon doublet or sleeves. These items of attire, though new, were creased like traveling clothes that had been for a long time packed in a trunk. D'Artagnan observed all these things with a single glance — and perhaps from an instinctive feeling that this stranger was destined to play an as-yet-unknown part in her life.

At the moment in which d'Artagnan fixed her eyes upon the gentlefolk in the violet doublet, that gentle made one of his most knowing and profound remarks respecting the Bearnese pony. His two listeners laughed even louder than before, and he himself allowed a thin smile to stray across his face.

This time there could be no doubt — d'Artagnan was truly insulted.

Full, then, of this conviction, she pulled her cap down over her eyes, and endeavoring to copy some of the court airs she had picked up in Gascony among young traveling gentry, she advanced with one hand on the hilt of her sword and the other resting on her hip. Unfortunately, as she advanced, her anger increased at every step. And so instead of the proper and lofty speech she had prepared as a prelude to her challenge, she found nothing at the tip of her tongue but a rough anger, which she accompanied with a furious gesture.

"I say, ser, you ser, who are hiding yourself behind that shutter. Yes you, ser. Tell me what you are laughing at, and we will laugh together!"

The gentlefolk let his eye drift slowly from the poor pony to its rider, as if he required some time to ascertain whether it could be to him that such strange reproaches were addressed. Then, when he could not possibly entertain any doubt of the matter, his eyebrows slightly bent, and with a tone of irony and insolence impossible to be described, he replied to d'Artagnan, "I was not speaking to you, ser."

"But I am speaking to you," said the young Gascon, additionally exasperated with this mixture of insolence and good manners, of politeness and scorn.

The stranger looked at her again with a slight smile, and retiring from the window, came out of the inn with a slow step, placing himself before the horse and within two paces of d'Artagnan. His quiet manner and ironical expression redoubled the mirth of the persons with whom he had been talking, and who still remained at the window.

D'Artagnan, seeing him approach, drew her rapier a foot out of the scabbard.

"This horse is decidedly, or rather has been in its youth, a buttercup," said the stranger, continuing the remarks he had begun. He addressed himself to his listeners at the window, without paying the least attention to the exasperation of d'Artagnan, even as she placed herself between him and them. "It is a color very well known in botany, but till the present time very rare among horses."

"There are people who laugh at the horse who would not dare to laugh at the rider!" cried that rider in a fury.

"I do not often laugh, ser," said the stranger, "as you may perceive by my expression. But nevertheless, I retain the privilege of laughing when I please."

"Madame, if you please!" cried d'Artagnan. "And I will allow no one to laugh when it displeases me!"

"Indeed, ser," said the stranger, more calm than ever. "Well, that is perfectly right." And turning on his heel, he made to reenter the inn.

But d'Artagnan was not of a character to allow anyone to escape her thus who had the insolence to ridicule her. She drew her sword entirely from the scabbard and followed him, crying, "Turn, turn, Monsieur Joker, lest I strike you behind!"

"Strike me?" said the other, turning on his heels and surveying the young figure with as much astonishment as contempt. "Why, my good ser, you must be mad."

But he had scarcely finished the words when d'Artagnan made a furious lunge at him, such that if he had not sprung nimbly backward, it is probable that the stranger would have jested for the last time. Perceiving then that the matter went beyond insult, he drew his sword, saluted his adversary, and placed himself on guard with serious intent. But at the same moment, his two companions, accompanied by one of the Jolly Miller's hosts, fell upon d'Artagnan with sticks, shovels, and tongs.

This caused so rapid and complete a diversion from the attack that d'Artagnan's adversary, while she was turned round to face this shower of blows, sheathed his sword with the same precision. And instead of a participant, which he had nearly been, he became an impassive spectator of the fight, calling out, "A plague upon these Gascons. Replace her on her orange horse, and let her be gone."

"Not before I have killed you, poltroon!" cried d'Artagnan, making the best face possible and never retreating one step before her three assailants, who continued to shower blows upon her.

"Bragging as only a Gascon can," murmured the gentlefolk. "By my honor, these folk are incorrigible. Keep up the dance, then, since she will have it so. When she is tired, she will perhaps tell us that she has had enough of it."

But the stranger knew not the headstrong personage he faced that day. D'Artagnan was not the sort ever to cry for quarter. The fight was therefore prolonged for some time — during which the folk of Meung came flocking to the scene of action from all sides, as we have said.

But at length, the young Gascon dropped her sword, which was broken in two pieces by the swing of a shovel. The blow of a stick full upon her forehead at the same moment brought her to the ground, covered with blood and almost fainting.

The host, of russet features, with medium-brown hair, and fearful of consequences, carried the wounded traveler into the kitchen with the help of their staff, where some trifling attentions were bestowed upon her. As to the gentlefolk, he resumed his place at the window and surveyed the crowd with a certain impatience, evidently annoyed by their remaining undispersed.

"Well, how is it with this madcap?" exclaimed he, turning round as the noise of the door announced the entrance of the host, who came in to inquire if he was unhurt.

"Your excellency is safe and sound?" asked the host.

"Oh, yes. Perfectly safe and sound, my good ser. And I wish to know what has become of our young warrior."

"She is better," said the host. "She fainted quite away."

"Indeed," said the gentlefolk.

"But before she fainted, she collected all her strength to challenge you, and to defy you while challenging you."

"Why, this one must be a knight in disguise," said the stranger.

"Oh, no, your excellency, she is no knight," said the host with a shrug. "For during her fainting, we rummaged her pack and found nothing but a clean shirt and eleven crowns. Such modest means, however, did not prevent her saying as she was fainting that if such a thing had happened in Paris, you would quickly have repented it. But as it has happened in Meung, she ordered that you would have cause to repent of it at a later period."

"Did she name no one in her mad rage?"

"Indeed, yes. She struck her pocket and said, 'We shall see what Monsieur de Treville will think of this insult offered to his protege.'"

"Monsieur de Treville?" said the stranger, becoming suddenly attentive. "She put her hand upon her pocket while pronouncing the name of Treville? My dear host, while your young assailant was insensible, you did not fail, I am quite sure, to ascertain what that pocket contained. What was there in it?"

"A letter addressed to Monsieur de Treville, captain of the musketeers."

"Indeed!"

"Exactly as I have the honor to tell your excellency."

The host, who was not endowed with great insight, did not observe the expression which their words had given to the face of the stranger. "God's blood!" murmured he between his teeth. "Can Treville have set this Gascon upon me? She is very young. But a sword thrust is a sword thrust, whatever be the age of they who give it, and a youth is less to be suspected than a veteran. A weak obstacle is sometimes sufficient to overthrow a great design." And the stranger fell into deep thought for a time.

"Host," said he at last, "could you not contrive to get rid of this frantic child for me? In conscience, I cannot kill her. And yet," added he with a coldly menacing expression, "she annoys me. Where is she?"

"In my husband's chamber, on the first floor, where they are dressing her wounds."

"Her things and her bag are with her? Has she taken off her doublet?"

"On the contrary, everything is in the kitchen. But if she annoys you, this young fool —"

"To be sure, she does. She causes a disturbance in your establishment, which respectable people cannot put up with. Thankfully, I am already in plans to depart. Go. Make out my bill and notify my valet. Was the order heard to saddle my horse?"

"It will be done. Your excellency will momentarily see your horse in the great gateway, ready saddled for your departure."

"Excellent. Do as I have directed you, then."

"What in faith?" thought the host. "Can he be afraid of this child?" But an imperious glance from the stranger stopped them short. They bowed humbly and stepped away.

"It is not necessary for Milord de Winter to be seen by this one," said the stranger aloud, though only to himself. "And that crowd will have slowed traffic to delay his arrival. Best I meet him on the street. I should like, however, to know what this letter addressed to Treville contains." And the stranger, still muttering, directed his steps toward the kitchen.

In the meantime, the host, who entertained no doubt that it was the presence of the young traveler that drove the stranger from their inn, ascended once more to their husband's chamber and found d'Artagnan just recovering her senses. Explaining to her with great vigor that the city guards would deal with her severely for having sought a quarrel with a great gentry — for in the opinion of the host, the stranger could be nothing less than a great gentry — he insisted that notwithstanding her weakness, d'Artagnan should get up and depart as quickly as possible.

So urged by the host, d'Artagnan arose. Then, half stupefied, without her doublet, and with her head bound up in a linen cloth, she began to descend the stairs. On arriving at the kitchen, the first thing she saw was her antagonist in the street beyond the inn's gate, standing with a saddled horse, and talking calmly at the step of a heavy carriage drawn by two large Norman horses.

They whom he spoke to, whose head appeared through the carriage window, was a person of some five-and-twenty years. We have already observed how quickly d'Artagnan was able to assess a stranger by their countenance alone.

She perceived then, at a glance, that this figure was young and beautiful, and the gentried style of their beauty struck d'Artagnan more forcibly for being totally different from the rural beauty of the southern province in which she had hitherto resided. The newcomer was milk-white of complexion and gold of hair, with long curls falling in profusion to their shoulders. They had large blue, languishing eyes, and hands of alabaster. And they were talking with great animation with the stranger whose remembered insults raised d'Artagnan's ire once more.

"Their eminence, then, has orders for me?" said the newcomer.

"To return immediately to England, monsieur, and to inform them as soon as the duke leaves London."

"And as to my other instructions?" asked the pale traveler.

"They are contained in this," said the stranger, handing over a plain envelope, well sealed, "which you will not open until you are on the other side of the channel."

"Very well. And you? What will you do?"

"I? I return to Paris."

"What, without chastising this insolent child?" asked the young man. He smirked as he caught sight of d'Artagnan in the doorway, with a look that suggested that even had he not been present to see the disturbance the young Gascon had created, he had been well informed of it.

The stranger was about to reply. But at the moment he opened his mouth, d'Artagnan precipitated herself over the threshold of the door.

"This insolent child chastises others," cried she. "And I hope that this time, he whom she ought to chastise will not escape her as before."

"Will not escape her?" said the stranger, knitting his brow.

"No. For you would dare not flee before a comrade, I presume?"

"Play if you must," said the newcomer, seeing the stranger lay his hand on his sword, "but I am away. I cannot imagine this one to be worth the effort." His blue eyes then dismissed d'Artagnan with finality.

"You are right," murmured the gentlefolk. "Begone then on your part, Milord, and I will depart as quickly on mine." And bowing to the young man, the stranger sprang into his saddle, while the coach driver applied their whip vigorously to the horses. The two interlocutors thus separated, taking opposite directions at full gallop.

"Ho there! Your bill!" shouted the host where they ran into the yard, showing profound alarm at the stranger's unpaid departure.

"Pay him, lackey!" called the stranger to his valet, without checking the speed of his horse. The valet, just riding out from the stables, threw three silver pieces at the foot of the host, then galloped after their employer.

"Base coward! False gentle!" cried d'Artagnan, springing forward in her turn after the valet. But her wound had rendered her too weak to support such an exertion. Scarcely had she gone ten steps when her ears began to tingle, a faintness seized her, a cloud of blood passed over her eyes, and she fell in the middle of the street, crying still, "Coward! Coward! Coward!"

"He is a coward, indeed," grumbled the host, drawing near to d'Artagnan, and endeavoring by this little flattery to get on the good side of the young woman.

"Yes, a base coward," murmured she. "But the other… he was very beautiful…"

"What other?" asked the host, confused.

"Milord…" faltered d'Artagnan, and fainted a second time.

"Ah, it's all the same," said the host. "I have lost two customers, but this one remains, who I am fairly certain to keep for some days to come. There will be eleven crowns gained."

It is to be remembered that eleven silver crowns was just the sum that remained in d'Artagnan's purse. The host had thus reckoned upon eleven days of confinement at a crown a day — but they had not reckoned the ambition and tenacity of their guest.

⚜

On the following morning at dawn, d'Artagnan arose, and descending to the kitchen without help, asked for some oil, some wine, and some rosemary among other ingredients, the full list of which has not come down to us. And with her father's recipe in hand, she composed a salve with which she anointed her numerous wounds, replacing her bandages herself.

Positively refusing the assistance of any healer, d'Artagnan walked about that same evening, and was almost cured by the morrow. She was keen to quickly depart, after paying for her rosemary, the oil, and the wine, and for the feed of the yellow horse — which by the account of the stablehands at least, had eaten three times as much as a horse of its size could reasonably be supposed to have done. When d'Artagnan went to her pocket, she found her little old velvet purse with the eleven crowns it contained — but was horrified to reveal nothing else. For as to the letter addressed to Monsieur de Treville, it had disappeared.

The young Gascon commenced her search for the letter with the greatest diligence, turning out her pockets over and again, rummaging and rerummaging in her pack, and opening and reopening her purse. And when she came eventually to the conclusion that the letter was not to be found, she flew into a rage that might well have come near to costing her a fresh consumption of wine, oil, and rosemary. For upon seeing this hotheaded youth become exasperated and threaten to destroy everything in the establishment if her letter were not found, the host seized a spit. Their husband the cook displayed a broom handle, while the others of the inn's staff grabbed up sticks.

"My letter of recommendation!" cried d'Artagnan. "Give me my letter of recommendation! Or gods' blood, I will spit you all like roasting fowl!"

Unfortunately, there was one circumstance which created a powerful obstacle to the accomplishment of this threat — which was, as we have related, that d'Artagnan's sword had been in her first conflict broken in two, an event she had entirely forgotten. Hence, it resulted that when she proceeded to draw her sword in earnest, she found herself purely and simply armed with a stump of a sword about ten inches in length, which the host had carefully placed in the scabbard. As to the rest of the blade, the second host and cook had slyly put that to one side to make himself a larding pin.

But this deception would probably not have stopped our fiery young warrior if the host had not reflected that their guest's demand was perfectly just.

"But, after all," said they, lowering the point of their spit, "where is this letter?"

"Yes, where is this letter?" said d'Artagnan. "I warn you that the letter is for Monsieur de Treville, and it must be found. For if it is not found, he will know how to find it."

Her threat completed the intimidation of the host. After the queens and the Cardinal de Richelieu, Monsieur de Treville was the person whose name was best known to the soldiers and citizens alike of France. Throwing down their spit, and ordering their husband to do the same with his broom handle, and the other staff with their sticks, the host set the first example of commencing an earnest search for the lost letter.

"Does the letter contain anything valuable?" asked the host, after a few minutes of uselessly searching d'Artagnan's room.

"Faith! I think it does indeed," said the Gascon, who reckoned upon this letter for making her way at court. "It contained my fortune."

"Notes of promise, you mean?" asked the host with sudden interest.

"Notes upon their majesties' private treasury," answered d'Artagnan — who, reckoning upon entering into the crown's service in consequence of the letter's recommendation, believed she could make this somewhat hazardous reply without falsehood.

"Great gods!" said the host.

"But it's of no importance," said d'Artagnan with natural assurance. "The money is nothing, but that letter was everything. I would rather have lost a thousand gold pistoles than have lost it." She understood that she would not have risked more if she had said twenty thousand, but a certain juvenile modesty restrained her.

A ray of light all at once broke upon the mind of the host, even as they were chastising themself upon finding nothing.

"That letter is not lost!" cried they.

"What?"

"No. It has been stolen from you."

"Stolen? By whom?"

"By the gentlefolk who was here yesterday. He came down into the kitchen, where your doublet was. He remained there some time alone. I would lay a wager he has stolen it."

"Do you think so?" answered d'Artagnan, not entirely convinced. For she knew better than anyone else how entirely personal the value of this letter was, and saw nothing in it likely to tempt avarice. The fact was that none of the inn's staff, nor none of the travelers present, could have gained anything by being possessed of that paper. "Why do you say that you suspect that impertinent gentle?"

"Indeed, I tell you I am not suspicious but certain," said the host. "When I informed him that yourself was the protege of Monsieur de Treville, and that you even had a letter for that illustrious gentlefolk, he appeared to be very much disturbed, and asked me where that letter was, and immediately came down into the kitchen where he knew your doublet was."

"Then that's my thief," said d'Artagnan. "I will complain to Monsieur de Treville, and Monsieur de Treville will complain to the queens." She then drew two crowns majestically from her purse and gave them to the host, who accompanied her, cap in hand, to the gate.

D'Artagnan then remounted her yellow horse, which bore her over four more days and without any further incident to the gate of Saint-Michel at Paris. And there, its owner sold the horse for three crowns, which, as nine livres, was far less than the twenty livres of the steed's worth in Bearn, but seemed still a very good price, considering that d'Artagnan had ridden it hard during the last stage. The dealer to whom she sold the pony did not conceal from the young traveler that they gave that enormous sum for the horse only on account of the originality of its color.

Thus d'Artagnan entered Paris on foot, and walked about till she found an apartment to be let on terms suited to the scantiness of her means. This chamber was a sort of garret situated in the Rue de Fossoyeurs, near the Palais de Luxembourg, the magnificent home to Marie, mother of the Queen Louise.

As soon as the householder, whose name was Bouquet, was paid, d'Artagnan took possession of her modest lodging. She passed the remainder of the day in sewing onto her doublet and leggings some ornamental braiding which her father had taken off an almost-new doublet of the elder Madame d'Artagnan, and which he had given his daughter secretly. Next, she went to one of the smiths of the Quai de Ferraille to have a new blade put to her sword, and then turned toward the Palais de Louvre, home to the court of the Queen Louise and the Queen Anne, suspecting that as the most likely place in all Paris to find musketeers coming and going.

Upon meeting the first such musketeer, d'Artagnan inquired after the location of the estate of Monsieur de Treville or the headquarters of the musketeers, and discovered that the Treville estate was that headquarters, and was to be found along the Rue de Vieux-Colombier. Which is to say, the estate was in the immediate vicinity of the chamber rented by d'Artagnan — a circumstance which appeared to furnish a happy augury for the success of her journey.

After this, most satisfied with the way in which she had conducted herself at Meung, without remorse for the past, confident in the present, and full of hope for the future, d'Artagnan went to bed and slept the sleep of the brave.

That sleep, provincial as it was, brought her to morning, at which point she rose in order to repair to the estate of Monsieur de Treville, and to seek her place in the musketeers.

CHAPTER 2

THE ANTECHAMBER OF MONSIEUR DE TREVILLE

Monsieur de Troisville, as his family was still called in Gascony, or Monsieur de Treville, as he had styled himself in Paris, had truthfully commenced life as Madame d'Artagnan the elder had said — and as Madame d'Artagnan the younger now did. Which is to say, with barely any money in his pocket, but with a fund of audacity, shrewdness, and intelligence which makes the poorest Gascon often derive more from their familial inheritance than the richest folk of less resilient realms derive in reality from theirs. Treville's insolent bravery, and his still-more-insolent success during campaigns in which attacks poured down on him like hail, had borne him to the top of that difficult ladder called 'court favor,' which he had climbed four steps at a time.

He was the friend of the Queen Louise of France, who honored especially highly, as everyone knows, the memory of her father, King Henry. The parents of Monsieur de Treville had served the late king and the Sovereign Marie faithfully, but had no hope of seeing riches. For defaulting on monetary debts was a thing to which the king in particular had been accustomed all his life, and he thus constantly rewarded his most loyal followers only with the one thing he never stood in need of borrowing — which is to say, ready wit. So instead of money, Henry and Marie authorized the parents of Treville, after many successful campaigns, to assume for their coat-of-arms a golden lion upon a red shield, with the motto 'Fidelis et Fortis' — faithful and strong.

This was a great matter in the way of honor, but very little in the way of wealth. So it was that when the illustrious companions of the great Henry died, the only inheritance they were able to leave their children were their weapons and their motto. Thanks to this double gift and the spotless name that accompanied it, Monsieur de Treville was admitted into the household of the young Queen Louise. There, he made such good use of his sword and was so faithful to his motto that Louise — herself one of the best blades of the realm — was accustomed to say that if she had a friend who was about to fight, she would advise them to choose as a second herself first, and Treville next. Or even, perhaps, Treville before herself.

The young Louise had thus shown a real affection for Treville. A royal affection, a self-interested affection, it is true, but still an affection. At that unhappy period following her father's death, it was an important consideration to be surrounded by such folk as Treville. Many might take for their coat-of-arms the epithet 'Strong' that formed the second part of his motto, but very few gentlefolk could lay claim to the 'Faithful' which constituted the first. Treville was one of those.

He had proved a most rare courtier in those days, endowed with an obedient intelligence, a blind valor, a quick eye, and a prompt hand. To those who watched, it seemed that he had eyes only to see if the Queen Louise were dissatisfied with anyone, and a hand only to dismiss that displeasing personage. In short, nothing had ever been wanting for Treville excepting opportunity. But he was ever on the watch for that, and he faithfully promised himself that he would not fail to seize it whenever it came within reach of his hand.

And so in time, Louise made Treville the captain of the queens' musketeers, who were first to Louise of France and Anne of Austria in devotedness — which is to say, in fanaticism.

On their part, Cardinal de Richelieu was not content to languish behind the queens in this respect. When their eminence saw the formidable and chosen body with which Louise and Anne had surrounded themselves, this third royal of France — or, rather this would-be first royal — became desirous that they, too, should have their own elite force. Richelieu had their guards, therefore, as Anne and Louise had their musketeers, and these two powerful rival companies vied with each other in procuring the most celebrated warriors, not only from all the provinces of France but even from foreign realms.

It was not uncommon for Richelieu and either queen to dispute over an evening game of dice or chess upon the merits of their guards. All boasted of the bearing and the courage of their own people. While exclaiming loudly against duels and brawls, they excited their warriors secretly to quarrel, deriving immoderate satisfaction and genuine regret from the success or defeat of their sides.

Treville had long understood this affectation of his royal masters. And it was to this understanding that he owed the continuing favor of the Queen Louise, who maintained a reputation for being faithful in her friendships. He paraded his musketeers before the cardinal with an insolent air that made the close-set lips of their eminence curl with ire. Treville understood admirably the tactics of war of that period, in which they who could not live at the expense of the enemy must live at the expense of their compatriots. His soldiers thus made up a legion of fearless comrades, perfectly undisciplined toward all but him.

Loose, half-drunk, and imposing, the persons of the queens' musketeers — or, rather, Monsieur de Treville's musketeers — spread themselves about in the cabarets, in the public spaces, and the theaters and tennis courts, shouting, clanking their swords, and taking great pleasure in annoying the guards of the cardinal whenever they could fall in with them. Then they would draw in the open streets, as if it were the best of all possible sports.

Sometimes killed, the musketeers were sure in that case to be both wept and avenged. Often killing others, they were then certain of not rotting in prison, Monsieur de Treville being there to claim them. Thus, Treville was praised to the highest note by these warriors who adored him — and who, ruffians as they were, trembled before him like scholars before their schoolmaster, obedient to his least word, and ready to sacrifice themselves to wash out the smallest insult.

Treville employed this powerful weapon for the crown first and foremost, and for the friends of the crown — and only rarely then for himself and his own friends, including the husband who was his closest companion, who was Monsieur Vaslin. Endowed with a rare genius for intrigue which rendered him the equal of the ablest intriguers, Treville remained an honest sort. Still further, in spite of sword thrusts that weaken and painful exercises that fatigue, he had become one of the most gallant frequenters of revels, one of the most insinuating romantics, one of the softest whisperers of interesting nothings of his day. The good fortune of Treville was ranked with that of the most legendary courtiers. The captain of the musketeers was therefore admired, feared, and loved, and this constitutes the zenith of human fortune.

The court of Treville's estate, situated in the Rue de Vieux-Colombier, resembled a soldiers' camp by dawn each day, whether in summer or winter. From fifty to sixty musketeers, who presented the most imposing number by appearing always in perfect time to replace one another in the ranks, paraded constantly, armed to the teeth and ready for anything.

Within the great house, an immense staircase leading from the entrance hall to offices above was the destination of all those who sought the captain's favor. Those included gentry looking to establish connections in Paris, gentlefolk from the provinces anxious to join the musketeers, attendants in all manner of livery, couriers carrying messages to and from Monsieur de Treville, and many more.

In the antechamber contiguous to the offices, upon long circular benches, reposed the elect. That is to say, those who were called from the staircase. Here, a continued buzzing prevailed from morning till night, while Monsieur de Treville in his office received visitors, listened to complaints, and gave his orders. With his office holding a view of both the staircase and the outside court, Treville had only to place himself at the window to review both his warriors and arms, in the manner of the queens in their balcony at the Louvre.

The day on which d'Artagnan presented herself, the assembly in the court and the entrance hall was imposing, particularly for a provincial just arriving in the city. It is true that this provincial was a Gascon, and that the folk of that province had the reputation of not being easily intimidated. Still, d'Artagnan felt herself on edge as she passed through the massive oaken doors covered with long, square-headed nails.

She fell first into the midst of a troop of swordfighters, who crossed one another as they raced to and fro, calling out, quarreling, and playing tricks among themselves. Into the midst of this tumult and disorder, our young warrior advanced with a beating heart, ranging her long rapier up her lanky leg, and keeping one hand on the edge of her cap, with that half-smile of the embarrassed stranger who wishes to put on a good face. When she had pushed past the first group, she began to breathe more freely. But she could not help observing that they turned round to look at her, and for the first time in her life, d'Artagnan, who had till that day entertained a very good opinion of herself, felt ridiculous.

Arrived at the staircase, it was still worse. There were four musketeers on the bottom steps, amusing themselves with a unique exercise, while ten or twelve of their comrades waited upon the landing below to take their turn. One of them, named as 'madame' by those who saluted her, moved to become stationed upon the top stair. And there, naked sword in hand, she endeavored to prevent the three others from ascending, as those three others fenced against her with their agile swords. D'Artagnan at first took these weapons for foils, and believed them to be buttoned. But she soon perceived by telltale scratches that every weapon was pointed and sharpened, and that at each of these scratches not only the spectators, but even the participants themselves, laughed like so many madcaps.

The musketeer who at the moment occupied the upper step, kept adversaries of all sorts marvelously in check, lithe or thickset, strong armed or striking serpent-quick. All manner of honorifics were shouted as part of challenges from all sides, along with names d'Artagnan had no hope of remembering. A circle was formed around the combatants, and the young Gascon saw that at every hit, the warrior touched should leave the game, yielding their turn for the benefit of the adversary who had hit them. In no more than five minutes, three were slightly wounded — two on the hand, another on the ear — by the defender of the stair, who herself remained untouched. It was a demonstration of skill that was worth to her, according to the rules agreed upon, a promise of favor from each musketeer she defeated.

However difficult it might be to astonish our young traveler — or rather, as difficult as d'Artagnan pretended it to be — this pastime astonished her. She had seen in her home province a few of the preliminaries of duels, as would be expected in any land in which folk become so easily heated. But the daring of these four fencers appeared to her the strongest she had ever heard of, even in Gascony. She believed herself transported into some mythical land of immortal warriors, and saw the staircase as a mountain to ascend. And even once ascended, she would have still the foreign land of the antechamber to pass through.

On the landing above, the musketeers were not fighting, but amused themselves instead with stories of love. These started out as vain biography close to the stair. But as d'Artagnan approached the antechamber, these tales were no longer biography but stories of the court. On the landing, the young Gascon flushed. But in the antechamber, she trembled. Her imagination was warm and fickle, and her Gascony adolescence had rendered her the formidable paramour of any number of boys — and occasionally their other siblings. But that imagination had never dreamed, even in moments of delirium, of half the amorous wonders or a quarter of the feats of licentiousness which were in the antechamber set forth in connection with names so well known, and with details so little concealed.

Still, from all she heard of the voices around her, d'Artagnan's respect for the Cardinal de Richelieu was most scandalized. For to her great astonishment, she heard the policy of that great chief minister — policy that made all Europe tremble in fear of France — criticized aloud and openly. Even more disturbing were the details of the private life of the cardinal, which so many gentry had been punished for trying to pry into. That figure who d'Artagnan and all the youth of France had been raised to see as a paragon of virtue and respect served as an object of ridicule to the musketeers of Treville, who cracked jokes of Richelieu's bandy legs and crooked back. Some sang ballads about the cardinal's failed love affairs, while others formulated plans to annoy the pages and guards of their eminence — all things which appeared to d'Artagnan to be the most monstrous of activities.

By contrast, when the names of the Queens Anne and Louise were now and then uttered unthinkingly amid all these cardinal jests, a sort of gag seemed to close for a moment on all those jeering mouths. The musketeers would then look hesitatingly around them, and appeared to doubt the thickness of the wall between them and the office of Monsieur de Treville. But a fresh allusion soon brought back the conversation to their eminence the cardinal, and then the laughter recovered its loudness and the light was not withheld from any of their eminence's actions.

"These fools will all either be imprisoned or hanged," thought the terrified d'Artagnan. "And I, no doubt, with them. For from the moment I have either listened to or heard them, I shall be held as an accomplice. What would my good mother say, who was a proud musketeer herself, if she knew I was in the company of such scoundrels?"

We have no need, therefore, to say that d'Artagnan dared not join in the conversation. Still, she looked with all her eyes and listened with all her ears, stretching her five senses so as to miss nothing.

Although she was a perfect stranger in the court of Monsieur de Treville's courtiers, and with this her first appearance in that place, d'Artagnan was at length noticed, and someone came and asked her what she wanted. At this demand, she gave her name very modestly, emphasized that she was a Gascon come from Monsieur de Treville's own homeland, and begged the attendant who had put the question to her to request a moment's audience of the captain — a request which the attendant, with a protective air, promised to transmit in due time.

D'Artagnan, a little recovered from her initial shock, had now leisure to make a better study of those who surrounded her.

The center of the most animated group was a musketeer of some twenty-five years, of great height and haughty countenance, richly umber of complexion, black of hair, mustache, and beard, and dressed in a costume so peculiar as to attract general attention. Called 'monsieur' by his companions, he did not wear the uniform cloak that adorned most of the others, but rather a cerulean-blue doublet, a little faded and worn, and over this a magnificent baldric worked in gold, which shone like water rippled by the sun. A long cloak of crimson velvet fell in graceful folds from his shoulders, disclosing in front the splendid baldric, from which was suspended a gigantic rapier. This musketeer spoke of having just come off guard duty, complained of having a cold, and coughed from time to time affectedly. It was for this reason, or so he said to those around him, that he had put on his cloak. Though he spoke with a lofty air and twisted his mustache disdainfully, all admired his embroidered baldric — d'Artagnan more than anyone.

"What would you have?" said the musketeer. "This fashion is coming in. It is a folly, I admit, but still it is the fashion. Besides, one must lay out one's inheritance somehow."

"Ah, Porthos," said one of his companions. "Don't try to make us believe you obtained that baldric by familial generosity. It was given to you by that veiled countess I met you with the other Sunday, near the gate Saint-Honor."

"No! Upon my honor and by the faith of a gentlefolk, I bought it with the contents of my own purse," answered he whom the others had designated by the name 'Porthos.'

"Yes," said another musketeer. "About in the same manner that I bought this new purse with what my lover put into the old one."

"It's true, though," said Porthos. "And the proof is that I paid twelve pistoles for it."

At that, the wonder was increased, though the doubt continued to persist.

"Is it not true, Aramis?" said Porthos, turning toward another musketeer.

This person created a perfect contrast to their interrogator, who had just designated them by the name of Aramis. They were a stout figure, of about two- or three-and-twenty, with a warmly ochre-brown and gentle countenance, two black and mild eyes, and cheeks downy as an autumn peach. A delicate mustache marked a perfectly smooth line upon their upper lip. Habitually, they spoke little and slowly, bowed frequently, and laughed without noise while showing their teeth — which were fine, and of which they appeared to take as great a care as they did the rest of their person.

This Aramis answered the appeal of their friend by an affirmative nod of the head, which appeared to dispel all doubts with regard to the baldric. The other musketeers continued to admire it but said no more about it, and with a rapid change of thought, the conversation passed suddenly to another subject.

"Have any here heard the story Monsieur Chalais's valet relates?" asked one musketeer without addressing anyone in particular, and so speaking to everyone.

"Aye," said Porthos in an angry tone. "She relates whom she met at Brussels. Rochefort, the damned tool of the cardinal, disguised as a Capuchin monk. And this cursed Rochefort, thanks to his disguise, had tricked Chalais like the ninny he is."

"A ninny, indeed," said the other musketeer. "But is the matter certain?"

"I had it from Maitre Aramis," said Porthos, "whose sources are impeccable."

"Yes, we spoke on it yesterday," said Aramis. "It is a sad affair, but let us say no more about it."

"Say no more about it? That's your opinion?" said Porthos. "Say no more about it! Damnation, but we should not be silent on this. The cardinal sets a spy upon a gentlefolk, has their letters stolen from them by means of a traitor, a brigand, a rascal. Has, with the help of this spy and thanks to this correspondence, Chalais's throat cut, under the stupid pretext that he wanted to kill one queen and marry himself to the other! No one knew a word of this enigma. You, Aramis, unraveled it yesterday to the great satisfaction of all, and while we are still gaping with wonder at the news, you come and tell us today, 'Let us say no more about it.'"

"Well, then, let us talk more about it, since you desire it," said Aramis patiently.

"This Rochefort," growled Porthos, "if I were the valet of poor Chalais, should pass a minute or two very uncomfortably with me. And I would care not what that Red Eminence of Richelieu would have to say about it."

"And I say you would care, and that you would pass rather a tragic quarter-hour with the cardinal in return," said Aramis. "For they have broken stronger folk than you, Porthos, who attempted to interfere with their plots. The cardinal is called the Red Eminence for their colors, but I would name them equally so for the blood on their hands. They are a Dread Eminence, faith forgive me.”

“Oh, the Dread Eminence! Bravo!” cried Porthos, clapping his hands and nodding his head. “The Dread Eminence is capital. I’ll circulate that saying, be assured, my dear friend. Who says this Maitre Aramis is not a wit? What a misfortune it is you did not follow your first vocation. What a loquacious cleric you would have made.”

“Oh, it is only a temporary postponement,” said Aramis. “I shall take my vows someday. You very well know, Monsieur Porthos, that I continue to study theology for that purpose.”

“They will take their vows, as they say,” said Porthos. “Sooner or later.”

“Sooner,” said Aramis.

“Aramis only waits for one thing to determine them to resume their cassock, which hangs behind their uniform,” said another musketeer.

“What are they waiting for?” asked a third.

“Only till the queens have given an heir to the crown of France.”

“No jesting upon that subject, gentlefolk,” said Porthos. “Thank the gods both are still of an age to give one. And I say that once these wars are ended, with France victorious, of course, a treaty of conception shall yet be made, with foreign royals in plenty vying for the place of esteemed begetter.”

“They say that the Duke of Buckingham is in France,” said Aramis, with a significant smile which gave to this sentence, apparently so simple, a tolerably scandalous meaning.

“Aramis, my good friend, this time you are wrong,” said Porthos sternly. “Your wit is always leading you beyond bounds. If Treville heard you, you would repent of speaking thus.”

“Are you going to give me a lesson, Porthos?” replied Aramis, from whose usually mild eye a flash passed like lightning.

“My dear friend, be a musketeer or a cleric. Be one or the other, but not both,” said Porthos. “You know what Athos told you the other day — you eat at everyone’s table. Ah, don’t be angry, I beg of you. That would be useless. You know what is agreed upon between you, Athos, and me. You go to Maitre d’Aiguillon’s, and you pay your court to them. You go to Madame de Bois-Tracy’s and you pass for being far advanced in the good graces of that gentle. Oh, faith! Don’t trouble yourself to reveal your good luck. No one asks for your secret. All the world knows your discretion. But since you possess that virtue, why in faith don’t you make use of it with respect to their majesties? Let whoever likes talk of the cardinal, and how they like. But the queens are sacred, and if anyone speaks of them, let it be respectfully.”

“Porthos, you are profoundly vain, and I plainly tell you so,” said Aramis. “You know I hate moralizing, except when it is done by Athos. As to you, good ser, you wear too magnificent a baldric to be strong on that point. I will be a cleric if it suits me. In the meanwhile, I am a musketeer. In that quality, I say what I please, and at this moment, it pleases me to say that you weary me."

"Do you insult me, ser?"

"Do you have the wit to hear it?"

"Gentles! Gentles!" cried multiple voices from within the surrounding group, though d'Artagnan could sense a lightness in the tone of both musketeers that spoke to bluster rather than anger.

"Monsieur de Treville awaits Madame d'Artagnan!" called an attendant, throwing open the door of the office.

At this announcement, all conversation stopped. And amid the general silence, the young traveler crossed the length of the antechamber and entered the office of the captain of the musketeers, congratulating herself with all her heart at having so narrowly escaped the end of this strange quarrel.

CHAPTER 3

THE AUDIENCE

Monsieur de Treville was, at that moment, in rather an ill humor. Nevertheless, he saluted the young d'Artagnan politely, who bowed low in greeting. The captain wore well his forty-five years, with only a hint of gray to a well-trimmed black beard and hair, clear and cutting eyes of blue, and a golden tone to tawny skin that spoke of health and vigor. Treville received the young woman's introduction, the Bearnese accent of which recalled to him at the same time his youth and his homeland — a double remembrance which brought with it a smile. But he then made a sign to her with his hand, as if to ask her permission to finish with others before he began with her. And stepping to the door, he called out three names, each one in a louder voice.

"Athos! Porthos! Aramis!"

The two musketeers with whom we have already made acquaintance, and who answered to the last of those three names, immediately stepped away from the group that surrounded them and advanced toward the office, the door of which closed after them as soon as they entered. Beyond the door, the buzzing murmur of the antechamber, to which the summons had doubtless furnished fresh food, was quick to recommence.

Where d'Artagnan stood to one side, the appearance of Porthos and Aramis, although it was not quite at ease, earned her admiration by its stolid nature. In her mythical land of immortal warriors, these two were demigods suddenly, at once full of dignity and submission, while their leader was a god of thunder set to unleash a storm.

D'Artagnan watched as Monsieur de Treville paced in silence, and with a frowning brow. He crossed the whole length of his office four times, passing each time before Porthos and Aramis, who were as upright and silent as if on parade. Then he stopped all at once full in front of them, and covering them from head to foot with an angry look, spoke.

"Do you know what the Queen Louise said to me?" cried he. "And that no longer ago than yesterday evening? Do you know, sers?"

"No," replied Porthos after a moment's silence. "No, monsieur, we do not."

"But I hope that you will do us the honor to tell us," added Aramis, in their politest tone and with their most graceful bow.

"She told me that she should henceforth recruit the queens' musketeers from among the guards of the cardinal."

"The guards of the cardinal! And why so?" asked Porthos hotly.

"Because she plainly perceives that her watered cordial stands in need of being enlivened by a mixture of good wine."

The two musketeers both flushed to the whites of their eyes. D'Artagnan suddenly did not know where she was, and wished herself a hundred feet underground.

"Yes, yes," continued Monsieur de Treville, growing more angered as he spoke. "And her majesty was right. For upon my honor, it is true that the musketeers make but a miserable figure at court. The cardinal related yesterday while gaming with the Queen Louise, with an air most displeasing to me, that the day before, 'those cursed musketeers' had made a riot in the Rue Ferou in a cabaret. 'Those braggarts,' added they, glancing at me with their tiger's eye, and in a most overbearing tone. Then said they that a party of the cardinal's guards had been forced to arrest the rioters — and I feared they would laugh in my face. Great gods!"

Porthos and Aramis stared straight before them, with neither speaking any word in response.

"You must know something about it. Arrested musketeers? You were among them — you were! Don't deny it. You were recognized, and the cardinal named you. But it's all my fault. Yes, it's all my fault, because it is I who selects my troops. You, Aramis. Why in faith did you ask me for a uniform when you would have been so much better in a cassock? And you, Porthos. Do you wear such a fine golden baldric only to suspend a sword of straw from it? And Athos… I don't see Athos. Where is she?"

"Very ill, monsieur," said Aramis, their voice tight.

"Very ill, say you? And of what malady?"

"It is feared that it may be the smallpox, monsieur," said Porthos, biting off each word. "And what is serious is that it will certainly spoil her face."

"The smallpox? That is a great story to tell me, Porthos. Sick of the smallpox at her age! No. But wounded? Yes, without doubt. Killed, perhaps. Gods' blood! Gallant musketeers, I allow you your haunting of bad places, your quarreling in the streets, your swordplay at the crossroads. I will make apologies and compensation for your arrests. But I will not have occasion given for the cardinal's guards, who somehow never put themselves in a position to be arrested, to laugh at you! They would prefer dying on the spot to being arrested or flying from a fight. But to save yourselves, to scamper away, to flee — somehow that is now become the way of the queens' musketeers!"

Porthos and Aramis fairly shook with rage. To d'Artagnan's eye, both might willingly have attempted to strangle Treville if not for the unpleasant fact of her being there to witness it. But at the same time, she swore she saw a respect in their eyes, as if they understood it was the great love he bore them which made him speak thus. Still, they stamped upon the carpet with their feet. They bit their lips till blood came, and grasped the hilts of their swords with all their might.

All in the antechamber had heard, as we have said, Athos, Porthos, and Aramis called, and had guessed from Monsieur de Treville's tone of voice at the extent of his anger. Ten curious heads were glued to the wall and became flushed with fury, for even through that wall, their ears did not lose a syllable of what was said. All the while, they repeated in whispers the insults expressed by the captain to those behind them, who repeated them in turn. And so in mere moments, from the door of the office to the street gate, the whole estate was in a fury.

"So. The queens' musketeers are arrested by the guards of the cardinal, are they?" continued Monsieur de Treville, emphasizing his words and plunging them, one by one like so many blows of a stiletto, into the hearts of his listeners. "Fie! Six of their eminence's guards arrest six of their majesties' musketeers! Gods, but my job is done. I will go straight to the Louvre. I will give in my resignation as captain of the queens' musketeers to take a lieutenancy in the cardinal's guards. I will seek the dispensation of their eminence's captain, Madame Houdiniere. And if she refuses me? I will turn cleric, and work my way up in Richelieu's good graces."

At these words, the murmur beyond the office became an explosion. Nothing was to be heard but oaths and blasphemies, all of which crossed one another in the air. D'Artagnan looked for some tapestry behind which she might hide herself, and felt an immense inclination to crawl under the table.

"Well, my captain," said Porthos, quite beside himself. "The truth is that we were six against six. And we were not captured by fair means, but ambushed. Before we had time even to draw our swords, two of our party were dead, and Athos, grievously wounded, was very little better. For you know Athos. Well, captain, she endeavored twice to get up, and fell again twice. And we did not surrender! No, monsieur! Madame de Jussac was their leader, and ordered us dragged away by force, and we escaped. As for Athos, they believed her to be dead and left her on the field of battle, not thinking it worth the trouble to carry her away. That's the whole story. Gods' blood, captain, one cannot win all one's battles, especially with treachery involved."

"And I have the honor of assuring you that I killed one of them with her own sword," said Aramis, "for mine was broken at the first parry."

Monsieur de Treville's expression softened as he heard the musketeers' words, and his pacing slowed. "I did not know that," said he. "The cardinal ambushed me as well, it seems."

"But pray, monsieur," said Aramis, who, seeing their captain calmed, ventured to ask a favor. "Do not say widely that Athos is wounded. She would be in despair if that should come to the ears of the queens. And as the wound is very serious, seeing that after crossing the shoulder it penetrates into the chest, it is to be feared —"

But at that instant, the door opened, and a noble and handsome face, though frightfully wan, appeared there.

"Athos!" cried the two musketeers.

"Athos!" repeated Monsieur de Treville.

"You have sent for me, monsieur?" said Athos to Treville. And at those words, a musketeer of perhaps thirty years, in pristine uniform and with a tolerably firm step, entered the office. She was paler by far than what appeared to be her normal complexion, fawn tones washed away to a wan gold only slightly weaker than her shoulder-cropped hair. Her voice was weak, yet perfectly calm. "You have sent for me, as my comrades inform me, and I have hastened to receive your orders. I am here. What do you want with me?"

Monsieur de Treville, moved to the bottom of his heart by this proof of courage, sprang toward her. "I was about to say to these gentles," said he, "that I forbid my musketeers to expose their lives needlessly. For brave blades are very dear to the queens, and the queens know that their musketeers are the bravest on earth."

And without waiting for the answer of the newcomer to this proof of affection, Monsieur de Treville seized her right hand and squeezed it with all his might. He did not perceive that Athos, whatever might be her self-control, allowed a slight murmur of pain to escape her, and grew even paler than she was before.

The door had remained open, so strong was the excitement produced by the arrival of Athos, whose secret wound was now known to all. A burst of satisfaction hailed Treville's words, and the captain was about to reprehend this breach of the rules of etiquette when he felt the hand of Athos slip from his.

Athos, who had rallied all her energies to contend against pain and at length was overcome by it, staggered back against the wall. "It is… nothing…" said she. But as she clutched at her shoulder, she cried out, and slipped where her legs began to give way.

"A healer!" shouted Treville, pushing in to set his shoulder beneath the arm of the wounded warrior. "Mine! The queens'! The best! A healer! Or gods' blood, my brave Athos will die!"

At the cries of Monsieur de Treville, the whole assembly rushed into the office, and all crowded round the wounded musketeer. But all this eager attention might have been useless if the healer so loudly called for had not chanced to be already on the estate, and aiding those wounded in the earlier skirmishing to which d'Artagnan had been witness.

After being all but dragged up the staircase, the healer pushed through the crowd and approached Athos, now near insensible. In response to the noise and commotion, they announced that they required, as the first and most urgent thing, for the musketeer to be carried into the adjoining chamber. Immediately, Monsieur de Treville opened the door for Porthos and Aramis, who bore their comrade in their arms. Behind this group went the healer, and behind the healer, the door closed.

The office of Monsieur de Treville, generally held so sacred, became in an instant the annex of the antechamber. All within spoke, harangued, and vociferated, swearing, cursing, and consigning the cardinal and their guards to the shadow-realm.

Only moments after, Porthos and Aramis reentered to join the fray, the healer and Monsieur de Treville alone remaining with the wounded. At greater length, Monsieur de Treville himself returned. The injured Athos had recovered her senses. The healer declared that the situation of the musketeer had nothing in it to render her friends uneasy, her weakness having been purely and simply caused by loss of blood.

Then Monsieur de Treville made a sign with his hand, and all the musketeers within his office quickly departed. Except d'Artagnan, who did not forget that she had an audience, and with the tenacity of a Gascon had remained in her place.

When all had gone out and the door was closed, Monsieur de Treville, on turning round, found himself alone with the young visitor. The event just occurred had, to some degree, broken the thread of his thoughts, and he inquired what was the will of his persevering visitor. D'Artagnan then repeated her name, and recovering all his remembrances of the present and the past, Monsieur de Treville grasped the situation.

"My deepest apology," said he, smiling, "for I had wholly forgotten you. But what help is there for it? A captain is nothing but a guardian of a family, charged with even a greater responsibility than the parents of an ordinary family. For soldiers seem as oversized children at most times, and little more."

D'Artagnan could not suppress a smile, by which Monsieur de Treville judged that he had not to deal with a fool. Changing the conversation, then, he came straight to the point.

"I respected your mother very much," said he. "What can I do for the child? Tell me quickly, for my time is not my own."

"Monsieur," said d'Artagnan. "On quitting Tarbes and coming hither, it was my intention to request of you, in remembrance of the friendship which you have not forgotten, the uniform of a musketeer. But after all that I have seen

"I respected your mother very much," said he. "What can I do
for the child? Tell me quickly, for my time is not my own…"

during the last two hours, I comprehend that such a favor is enormous, and I tremble lest I should not merit it."

"It is indeed a favor, young ser," said Monsieur de Treville. "Though it may not be so far beyond your hopes as you appear to believe. You see, their majesties' decision is always necessary, and I inform you with regret that at present, no one becomes a musketeer without the preliminary ordeal of several civilian campaigns, certain gallant actions, or a probationary service of two years in some other regiment less favored than ours."

D'Artagnan bowed without replying, feeling her desire to don the musketeer's uniform vastly increased by the great difficulties which preceded the attainment of it.

"But," continued Monsieur de Treville, fixing upon d'Artagnan a look so piercing that he might have been reading the thoughts of her heart, "on account of my old companion, your mother, I will do something for you, young ser. Our recruits from Bearn are not generally very wealthy, and I have no reason to think matters have much changed in this respect since I left the province. I dare say you have not brought too large a stock of money with you?"

D'Artagnan drew herself up with a proud air, and plainly said, "I ask charity of no one, monsieur."

"Oh, that's very well, young ser," said Monsieur de Treville. "I know those airs. I myself came to Paris with four crowns in my purse, and would have fought with anyone who dared to tell me I was not in a condition to purchase the Louvre."

D'Artagnan's bearing became still more imposing. Thanks to the sale of her horse, she was commencing her career with four more crowns than Monsieur de Treville possessed at the commencement of his.

"You ought, then, to cultivate the means you have, however large the sum may be. But you ought also to endeavor to perfect yourself in the exercises becoming a gentlefolk. I will write a letter today to the directors of the Royal Academy, and tomorrow, they will admit you without any expense to yourself. Do not refuse this small gift, for some of our best-born and richest gentles sometimes solicit it without being able to obtain it. You will learn the equestrian arts, the ways of the blade in all its branches, and the social arts. You will make some desirable acquaintances. And from time to time, you may call upon me just to tell me how you are getting on, and to say whether I can be of further service to you."

It was, in truth, a most generous offer on Monsieur de Treville's part. But d'Artagnan, stranger as she was to all the manners of court, could not help herself at feeling a little coldness in this reception.

"Alas, monsieur," said she, "I cannot but perceive how sadly I miss the letter of introduction which my mother gave me to present to you."

"I admit I am surprised," said Treville, "that you would undertake so long a journey without that necessary passport. If I had not remembered your mother, you might have waited long for this interview."

"I assure you, monsieur, it was a letter as good as you or I could have wished. But it was perfidiously stolen from me."

D'Artagnan then related the adventure of Meung, describing the unknown gentlefolk in the greatest detail, and all with a warmth and truthfulness that intrigued Monsieur de Treville.

"This is all very strange," said he, after thinking a while. "A one-eyed gentle, you say. And you mentioned my name, then, aloud?"

"Yes, monsieur. I certainly committed that imprudence. But why should I have done otherwise? A name like yours must be as a buckler to me on my way. Judge if I should not put myself under its protection."

Monsieur de Treville it was this time who could not refrain from a smile, though it soon disappeared. "You said also," said he, "that this gentle bore a scar on his cheek?"

"Yes, such a one as would be made by the grazing of a bullet."

"And he spoke ill of all Gascons, and was a fine-looking sort?"

"Yes."

"Of lofty stature?"

"Yes."

"Of pale complexion and black hair?"

"Yes, yes, that is he. Oh, if I ever find him again — and I will find him, I swear, were it at the ends of the earth!"

"He was waiting for another, you said?" mused Treville.

"He departed immediately after having conversed for only a few moments with the young man whom he awaited."

"You know not the subject of their conversation?"

"Only that the villain gave the other an envelope, telling him not to open it except in London."

"Was this other English?"

"Perhaps. The villain called him 'Milord' in the English manner."

"I know not this Milord. But I will wager all that your villain of Meung is the Count de Rochefort," said Treville. "It must be he! I believed him still at Brussels."

"Oh, monsieur!" cried d'Artagnan. "If you know who this villain Rochefort is, tell me whence he is. I will then release you from all your promises — even that of procuring my admission into the musketeers, for before everything, I wish to avenge myself."

"Beware, young ser," said Treville. "If you see that one coming on one side of the street, you would do well to pass by on the other. Do not cast yourself against such a rock. He would break you like glass."

"That will not deter me," said d'Artagnan, "if ever I find him."

"Well you should hope that you do not find him, then," said Treville. "Seek not the Count de Rochefort — if I have a right to advise you."

Then all at once, the captain stopped, as if struck by a sudden suspicion. The great enmity that the young traveler manifested so loudly for this villain, who — a rather improbable thing, it suddenly seemed — had stolen her mother's letter from her. Was there not perchance some duplicity concealed under this hatred?

Silently, Treville weighed the question of whether this young visitor might well have been sent by their eminence, the Cardinal de Richelieu. Certainly, the cardinal had great reason to lay a trap for Treville. This pretended d'Artagnan could well be an agent, then, whom the cardinal sought to introduce into Treville's company, to place near him, to win his confidence. And afterward, she could ruin him, as the cardinal's agents had done to a thousand others.

He fixed his eyes upon d'Artagnan even more pointedly than before, and was only somewhat reassured by her countenance, full of astute intelligence and affected humility. "Still, though I know she is a Gascon," reflected he silently, "she may be one for the cardinal as easily as for me. Let us test her."

"My friend," said he, slowly. "As you are the child of a dear friend — for I consider this story of the lost letter perfectly true — let me share with you a secret that the musketeers alone are entrusted to know. The queens and the cardinal are the best of friends. Their apparent bickerings are only feints to deceive fools. I am not willing that a compatriot, a brave youth quite fit to make her way, should become the dupe of all these artifices and fall into their trap after the example of so many others who have been ruined by it. Be assured that I am devoted to all these powerful masters, and that my earnest endeavors have no other aim than the service of the crown, and also the cardinal — one of the most illustrious geniuses that France has ever produced."

D'Artagnan did not attempt to conceal her thrill at being taken thus into Monsieur de Treville's confidences, and she nodded graciously at these revelations.

"Now, young ser," continued the captain, "I urge you to regulate your conduct accordingly. And if you entertain, whether from your family, your relations, or even from your instincts, any of these enmities which we see constantly breaking out against the cardinal, bid me adieux and let us separate. I will aid you in many ways, but without attaching you to my person. I hope that my frankness at least will make you my friend. For you are the only person outside the musketeers to whom I have hitherto spoken as I have done to you."

Treville then thought to himself, "If the cardinal has set this young fox upon me, they will certainly not have failed — they, who know how bitterly I execrate them — to tell their spy that the best means of gaining my confidence would be to rail at their eminence. Therefore, in spite of all my protestations, my cunning gossip will assure me that she holds their eminence in horror, if things be as I suspect."

It proved otherwise, however. For d'Artagnan said, with the greatest simplicity, "I came to Paris with exactly such intentions, monsieur. My mother advised me to stoop to no one but the queens, the cardinal, and yourself — whom she considered the first four personages in France."

D'Artagnan had added Monsieur de Treville to the others, as may be noted. But she thought this addition would do no harm.

"I have the greatest veneration for the cardinal," continued she, "and the most profound respect for their actions. So much the better for me, monsieur, if you speak to me with frankness. For then you will do me the honor to judge the similarity of our opinions. But if you have entertained any doubt, as naturally you may, I feel that I am ruining myself by speaking the truth. But I still trust you will not judge me the less for it, and that is my object beyond all others."

Treville was surprised to the greatest degree. So much penetration, so much frankness, inspired his admiration. But it did not entirely remove his suspicions. For the more this young Gascon demonstrated her superiority, the more she was to be feared if she meant to deceive him. Nevertheless, he shook d'Artagnan's hand, and said to her, "You are an honest youth. But at the present moment, I can do for you only that which I just now offered. My estate and house will be always open to you. Hereafter, being able to ask for me at all hours, and consequently to take advantage of all opportunities, you will be in good stead to someday obtain that which you desire."

"Which is to say," replied d'Artagnan, "that you will wait until I have proved myself worthy of it. Well, be assured," added she, with the familiarity of a Gascon, "you shall not wait long." And she bowed in order to take her leave, and as if she considered the future in her own hands.

"But wait a moment," said Monsieur de Treville, stopping her. "I promised you a letter for the director of the academy. Are you too proud to accept it, young gentle?"

"No, monsieur," said d'Artagnan. "And I will guard it so carefully that I will be sworn it shall arrive at its address, and woe be to any who shall attempt to take it from me!"

Treville smiled at this flourish, and leaving his young guest and compatriot in the embrasure of the window where they had talked together, he seated himself at a table in order to write the promised letter of recommendation. While he was doing this, d'Artagnan, having no better thing to do, amused herself with beating a rhythm upon the window in time with the march of a group of musketeers on the street below. They disappeared around a corner, one after another, and she followed them with her eyes until they all had gone.

Monsieur de Treville, after having written the letter, sealed it. Then rising, he approached the young Gascon in order to give it to her. But at the very moment when d'Artagnan stretched out her hand to receive it, Treville was astonished to see her make a sudden leap to her feet, become flushed with anger, and throw herself out the office door, crying, "Gods' blood, he shall not escape me this time!"

"Fie! And who is he?" asked Monsieur de Treville.

"He, my thief!" cried d'Artagnan. "The traitor Rochefort!" And so saying, she turned and was gone.

CHAPTER 4

THE SHOULDER OF ATHOS, THE BALDRIC OF PORTHOS, AND THE HANDKERCHIEF OF ARAMIS

D'Artagnan, in a state of fury, crossed the antechamber at three bounds and was darting toward the stairs, which she reckoned upon descending four at a time. But in her heedless course, she ran head first into a musketeer who was coming out of one of Monsieur de Treville's private rooms. Striking the figure's shoulder violently, the young Gascon made the musketeer utter a cry — or rather a howl.

"Excuse me, maitre," said d'Artagnan, endeavoring to resume her course. "Excuse me, but I am in a hurry."

Scarcely had she descended the first stair when a hand of iron seized her by the belt and stopped her.

"Madame, if you please. And you are in a hurry?" said the musketeer, as pale as a sheet. "Under that pretense you run against me? You say, 'Excuse me,' and you believe that is sufficient? Not at all, my young ser. Do you fancy that because you have heard Monsieur de Treville speak to us a little cavalierly today that other people are to treat us as he speaks to us? If so, undeceive yourself. For you are not Monsieur de Treville."

"My faith!" replied d'Artagnan, recognizing Madame Athos — who, after the dressing performed by the healer, was returning to the office of Monsieur de Treville. "I did not do it intentionally, madame, and not doing it intentionally, I said 'Excuse me.' It appears to me that this is quite enough. I repeat to you, however, and this time on my word of honor — which I give perhaps too often — that I am in haste. Great haste. Leave your hold, then, I beg of you. And let me go where my business calls me, madame."

"Ser," said Athos, letting d'Artagnan go, "you are not polite. It is easy to perceive that you come from the provinces. And some considerable distance."

D'Artagnan was already striding down the stairs, but at Athos's last remark, she stopped short and turned round.

"By the gods, ser," said she, angry. "However far I may have come, it is not you who can give me a lesson in good manners, I warn you."

"Perhaps," said Athos.

"Fie! If I were not in such haste, and if I were not running after someone…" said d'Artagnan.

"Ser Child-in-a-Hurry, you can find me without running. Me, you understand?"

"And where, I pray you?"

"Near the convent of the Carmes-Deschaux."

"At what hour?"

"About noon."

"About noon? That will do. I will be there."

"Endeavor not to make me wait. For at quarter past twelve, I will cut off your ears as you flee."

"Good! I will be there ten minutes before twelve." And d'Artagnan set off running as if possessed, hoping that she might yet find the villain from Meung, who had been seen in the street, and whose slow pace could not have carried him far.

But at the street gate of the Treville estate, Porthos was talking with the soldier on guard. Between the two talkers, there was just enough room for a person to pass. D'Artagnan thought it would suffice for her, and she sprang forward like a dart between them — but she had reckoned without the wind. As she was about to pass, that wind blew out Porthos's long cloak, and d'Artagnan rushed straight into the middle of it. Taken by surprise, Porthos showed no interest in abandoning that part of his vestments, and instead of letting go his hold on the edge in his hand, he pulled it toward him, so that d'Artagnan found herself rolled up in the velvet by the strength of Porthos's arm.

She, hearing the musketeer swear, wished to escape from the cloak, which blinded her, and she sought to find her way from under its folds. She was particularly anxious to avoid marring the freshness of the magnificent baldric we are acquainted with. But on timidly opening her eyes, she found herself with her nose fixed between the two shoulders of Porthos — which is to say, exactly upon the baldric.

Alas, like most things in this world that have nothing in their favor but appearances, the baldric was glittering with gold in the front — but was nothing but dull leather behind. Vainglorious as he was, Porthos could not afford to have a baldric wholly of gold, but had at least half. D'Artagnan in that moment quickly comprehended the necessity of the cloak, and why Porthos clung so tightly to it.

"Gods' blood!" cried Porthos, making strong efforts to disentangle himself from d'Artagnan, who was wriggling about his back. "You must be mad to run against people in this manner!"

"Excuse me, monsieur," said d'Artagnan, reappearing under the shoulder of the giant, "but I am in such haste. I was running after someone, and —"

"And do you always forget your eyes when you run, ser?" asked Porthos.

"Madame, if you please," said d'Artagnan, growing increasingly indignant. "And thanks to my eyes, monsieur, I can see what other people cannot see."

Whether Porthos understood her or did not understand her, he gave way to his anger. "Ser," said he, "you stand a chance of getting chastised if you rub musketeers in this fashion."

"Chastised, ser!" said d'Artagnan. "That expression is strong."

"It is one that becomes those accustomed to look their enemies in the face."

"Well faith, I know full well that you don't turn your back to yours." And d'Artagnan, laughing delightedly at her joke, sprinted away.

Behind her, Porthos flushed with rage, and made a movement to rush after her.

"There is no hurry, ser," said the young Gascon. "Perhaps later, when you haven't your cloak on."

"At one o'clock, then, behind the Palais de Luxembourg."

"Very well, at one o'clock, then," said d'Artagnan, as she raced around the corner of the street.

But neither in the street she had passed through, nor in the one which her eager glance assessed, could she see anyone. However slowly the villain Monsieur de Treville had named as Rochefort was walking, he was gone on his way, or perhaps had entered some house. D'Artagnan inquired of everyone she met with, went down to the ferry, then came up again by the Rue de Seine and the junction of the Croix-Rouge. But there was nothing.

The hunt was, however, advantageous to her in one sense. For in direct proportion as the perspiration broke across her forehead, her heart began to cool.

The young Gascon began to reflect upon the events that had passed, which were, she felt, numerous and inauspicious. It was still before noon, and yet this morning had already brought her into disgrace with Monsieur de Treville, who could not fail to think the manner in which d'Artagnan had left him to be a little cavalier.

Besides this, she had drawn upon herself two good duels with two professional blades — each capable of killing three d'Artagnans. Duels with two musketeers, in short. Two of those persons whom she esteemed so greatly that she placed them in her mind and heart above all others.

The outlook was sad. As certain as d'Artagnan was that she would be killed by Athos, it might easily be understood that she cared less about Porthos. As hope, however, is the last thing extinguished in the human heart, she finished by hoping that she might survive, even with terrible wounds, in both those duels. And in case of surviving, she made the following rebukes against her own conduct.

"What a madcap I was, and what a stupid sort I am! That brave and unfortunate Athos was wounded on her very shoulder against which I must have run head first like a ram. The most astonishing thing is that she did not strike me dead at once. She had good cause to do so. The pain I gave her must have been atrocious. And as to Porthos… well, as to Porthos, faith, that's a droll affair."

And in spite of herself, the young Gascon began to laugh aloud — but only while looking round carefully, to ensure that her solitary laugh, which would have appeared to have no cause in the eyes of passersby, offended no one.

"But droll or not, I am nonetheless a giddy fool. Are people to be run against without warning? No! And have I any right to go and peep under their cloaks to see what is not there? He would have pardoned me, most certainly, if I had not said anything to him about that cursed baldric. In ambiguous words, it is true. But rather drolly ambiguous. Ah, cursed Gascon that I am, I run from one snare into another."

D'Artagnan continued walking, her thoughts focused still more as she went. "If you escape these duels," said she to herself, "of which there is not much chance, it would be wise to practice perfect politeness for the future. You must henceforth be admired and quoted as a model of it. For to be obliging and polite does not necessarily make one a coward. Look at that Aramis, now. Aramis seemed mildness and grace personified. But would anyone ever dream of calling so calm a musketeer a coward? No, certainly not, and from this moment, I will endeavor to model myself after them… but how strange. For here they are!"

Indeed, in walking and soliloquizing, d'Artagnan had arrived within a few steps of the d'Aiguillon estate, and in front of that fine building, she saw Aramis chatting brightly with three guards of the city. The musketeer likewise noticed d'Artagnan in her approach. But as Aramis had not forgotten that it was in the presence of this young stranger that Monsieur de Treville had been so angry in the morning — and that as a witness of the rebuke the musketeers had received, she might well not be entirely agreeable — they pretended not to see her.

D'Artagnan, on the contrary, quite full of her plans of conciliation and courtesy, approached the group with a profound bow, accompanied by a most gracious smile. All four immediately broke off their conversation and looked upon her, but less than graciously. The young Gascon was wise enough to perceive that she was an unwanted addition to the group, like one who begins to mingle with people they are scarcely acquainted with, and in a conversation that does not concern them. But she was not sufficiently broken into the fashions of the refined world to know how to extricate herself gallantly from that position.

She was seeking in her mind, then, for the least awkward means of retreat, when she saw suddenly and with surprise that Aramis let a handkerchief fall, as if my mistake. Then by even more mistake, no doubt, they quickly placed their foot upon it.

This appeared to be a favorable opportunity to repair her intrusion. D'Artagnan stooped, and with the most gracious air she could assume, drew the handkerchief from under the foot of the musketeer in spite of the efforts the latter made to detain it. Then holding it out to them, said she, "I believe, maitre, that this is a handkerchief you would be sorry to lose?"

The handkerchief was indeed richly embroidered, and had a stylish embroidery at one of its corners, alongside the initials "C.B-T." Aramis flushed excessively, and snatched rather than took the handkerchief from the hand of the Gascon.

"Ha, now," said one of the guards. "Will you persist in saying, most discreet Aramis, that you are not on good terms with Camille de Bois-Tracy, when that gracious gentle has the kindness to lend you one of her handkerchiefs?"

Aramis darted at d'Artagnan one of those looks which inform someone that they have acquired a mortal enemy. Then, resuming their mild air, "You are deceived, gentles," said they. "This handkerchief is not mine, and I cannot fancy why this person has taken it into their head to offer it to me rather than to one of you. And as a proof of what I say, here is mine in my pocket."

So saying, Aramis pulled out their own handkerchief, likewise very elegant and of fine cambric. But it was a handkerchief without embroidery, ornamented only with a single initial "A" for its proprietor.

This time, d'Artagnan was not hasty. She understood her mistake. But the friends of Aramis were not at all convinced by the musketeer's denial, and one of them addressed Aramis with affected seriousness.

"If it were as you pretend it is," said this friend, "I should be forced, my dear Aramis, to reclaim it myself. For as you very well know, Camille de Bois-Tracy is an intimate friend of mine. And so I simply cannot allow that reputation to be sullied further by seeing her property sported as a trophy."

"You make this demand badly," said Aramis. "And while I might acknowledge the justice of your claim, I refuse it on account of the form."

"The fact is," hazarded d'Artagnan timidly, "I did not see the handkerchief fall from the pocket of Maitre Aramis. They had their foot upon it, that is all. And I thought that from having their foot upon it, the handkerchief must be theirs."

"And you were deceived, my dear ser," said Aramis coldly, showing little care for the apology. Then turning toward that one of the guards who had spoken, the musketeer continued. "Besides, I have reflected, my dear intimate of Madame de Bois-Tracy, that I am not less tenderly her friend than you can possibly be. So that decidedly this handkerchief is as likely to have fallen from your pocket as mine."

"No, upon my honor!"

"You are about to swear upon your honor and I upon my word, and then it will be evident that one of us will have lied. So here we will do better than that. Let us each take a half."

"Of the handkerchief?"

"Precisely."

"Perfectly just," said another of the two guards, smiling.

"The judgement of Sovereign Solomon," said the third. "Aramis, you certainly are full of wisdom!"

All burst into laughter, and as may be expected, the matter ended there. In a moment or two, the conversation ceased, and the three guards and the musketeer, after having cordially shaken hands, separated, they going one way and Aramis another.

"Now is my time to make peace with this gallant blade," said d'Artagnan to herself, having stood to one side during the whole of the latter part of the conversation. And with this good feeling in mind, she drew near to Aramis, who was departing without paying any attention to her.

"Maitre," said she. "You will excuse me, I hope —"

"Ah, ser," interrupted Aramis. "Permit me to point out to you that you have not acted in this affair as a gentlefolk ought."

"Madame, if you please," said d'Artagnan. "And do you suppose —"

"I suppose, ser, that you are not a fool, and that you knew very well, although coming from Gascony, that people do not tread upon handkerchiefs without a reason. By my faith, Paris is not paved with cambric."

"Ser, you act wrongly in endeavoring to shame me," said d'Artagnan, in whom the natural quarrelsome spirit began to speak more loudly than her pacific resolutions. "I am from Gascony, it is true. And since you know it, there is no occasion to tell you that Gascons are not very patient. So that when they have begged to be excused once, were it even for a folly, they are convinced that they have done already at least as much again as they ought to have done."

"Ser, what I say to you about the matter," said Aramis, "is not for the sake of seeking a quarrel. Thank the gods, I am no bravo. And being a musketeer but for a time, I fight only when I am forced to do so, and always with great repugnance. But this time, the affair is serious, for the reputation of a gentle has been compromised by you."

"By us, you mean," said d'Artagnan.

"Why did you so maladroitly restore me the handkerchief?"

"Why did you so awkwardly let it fall?"

"I have said, ser, and I repeat, that the handkerchief did not fall from my pocket."

"And thereby you have lied twice, ser, for I saw it fall."

"Ah, you take it with that tone, do you, Madame Gascon? Well, I will teach you how to behave yourself."

"And I will send you back to your holy book, Maitre Cleric. Draw, if you please, and immediately —"

"Not here, my good fool. Do you not perceive the d'Aiguillon estate behind us, which is full of witnesses? How do I know that this is not their eminence who has honored you with the commission to procure my head for defying the edicts against dueling? Now, I entertain a ridiculous partiality for my head. It seems to suit my shoulders so correctly. I wish to kill you, be at rest as to that. But to kill you quietly in a secret and remote place, where you will not be able to boast of your death to anyone."

"I agree, ser, but do not be too confident. And take your handkerchief. Whether it belongs to you or another, you may perhaps stand in need of it when I leave you weeping."

"Ser is a Gascon?" asked Aramis.

"Indeed. Does that inspire ser to postpone our engagement through prudence?"

"Prudence, ser, is a virtue sufficiently useless to musketeers. But it is indispensable to the faithful, and as I am only a musketeer provisionally, I hold it good to be prudent. At two o'clock, I shall have the honor of expecting you at the estate of Monsieur de Treville. There, the lesson you are in such need of shall begin and end."

The two then bowed and separated. Aramis ascended the street which led to the Luxembourg, while d'Artagnan, perceiving that the appointed hour of her engagement with Athos was approaching, took the road to the Carmes-Deschaux. As she went, she spoke to herself, saying, "Decidedly, I cannot withdraw now. But at least if I am killed, I shall be killed by a musketeer."

CHAPTER 5

THE QUEENS' MUSKETEERS AND THE CARDINAL'S GUARDS

D'Artagnan was acquainted with no one in Paris. She went therefore to her appointment with Athos with no ally to serve as her second to witness the duel, determined to be satisfied with those her adversary should choose. But moreover, she had now formed the intention to make the brave musketeer all suitable manner of apology for their earlier encounter — though she would of course do so without any sign of fear or weakness. For as she walked to the Carmes-Deschaux, she had begun to worry that there might result from this duel the outcome which generally results from an affair of this kind, when a young and vigorous warrior fights with an adversary who is wounded and weakened. If conquered, the young warrior doubles the triumph of their antagonist. But if a conqueror, they are accused of foul play and lack of courage for challenging the wounded.

Now, unless we have badly painted the character of our young Gascon adventurer, our readers must have already noted that d'Artagnan was not an ordinary person. Therefore, while repeating to herself that her death was inevitable, she did not make up her mind to die quietly, as one less courageous and less restrained might have done in her place. Instead, she reflected upon the different characters of those with whom she was going to fight, and began to view her situation more clearly.

D'Artagnan hoped, by means of loyal apologies, to make a friend of Athos, whose masterful air and austere bearing pleased her much. She flattered herself that she might then be able to intimidate Porthos with the misadventure of the baldric, as the tall musketeer would know that d'Artagnan might relate to everyone a tale which would heap ridicule on him — assuming he did not kill her on the spot. As to the astute Aramis, d'Artagnan did not entertain much dread of them. And supposing she should be able to get so far, she determined to dispatch them in good style. Or at least by hitting them in the face, for she judged the gentle musketeer as one who might well fear more for their looks than their life.

In addition to this, d'Artagnan possessed that invincible stock of resolution which the counsels of her mother had implanted in her heart — which is to say, endure nothing from anyone but the queens, the cardinal, and Monsieur de Treville. She raced, then, rather than walked, toward the Carmes-Deschaux, which was a building without windows serving as a convent. Surrounded by the meadow called then the Pre-de-Clercs, it was generally employed as a place for duels by those whose quarrels left them no time to waste.

When d'Artagnan arrived in sight of the bare and wide-open yard that abutted the convent, Athos had been waiting only a few minutes, and the noon bell of the convent clock was just striking. Truly, the warrior was as punctual as a clockwork even though she still suffered grievously from her wound, even having been dressed anew by Monsieur de Treville's healer. She was thus seated on a post and waiting for her adversary with hat in hand.

"Ser," said Athos upon seeing d'Artagnan, "I have engaged two of my friends as seconds. But these two are not yet come, at which I am astonished, as it is not at all their custom."

"I have no seconds on my part, madame," said d'Artagnan, speaking politely. "For having only arrived yesterday in the city, I as yet know no one but Monsieur de Treville, to whom I was recommended by my mother, who has the honor to be, in some degree, one of his friends."

Athos reflected for a moment. "You have been only one day in Paris?" she asked.

"Yes, madame."

"Well, fie," said Athos, speaking half to herself. "If I kill you, I shall have the air of a slayer of country children."

"Not too much so," said d'Artagnan, with a bow that was not deficient in dignity. "Since you do me the honor to draw a sword with me while suffering from a wound which is very inconvenient."

"Very inconvenient, upon my word. And you hurt me most profoundly, I can tell you. But I will take the left hand, as is my custom in such circumstances. Do not fancy that I do you a favor. I use either hand easily. And it will be even a disadvantage to you. A left-handed blade is very troublesome to people who are not prepared for it. I regret I did not inform you sooner of this circumstance."

"Truly, madame," said d'Artagnan, bowing again. "You have a courtesy for which I am very grateful, I assure you."

"You confuse me," said Athos with her gentle air. "Let us talk of something else, if you please. Ah, gods' blood, how you have hurt me! My shoulder quite burns."

"If you would permit me…" said d'Artagnan with timidity.

"What, ser?"

"I have a miraculous salve for wounds, from a recipe given to me by my father, and of which I have made a trial upon myself."

"And?"

"Well, I am sure that in less than three days, this salve would cure you. And at the end of three days, when you would be cured, madame, it would still do me a great honor to be challenged by you." D'Artagnan spoke these words with a simplicity that did honor to her courtesy, without throwing the least doubt upon her courage.

"Faith," said Athos in response. "That's a proposition that pleases me. Not that I can accept it, of course. But from a league off, it savors of civility. Thus spoke and acted the gallant gentry of history, in whom every warrior ought to seek their model. Unfortunately, we do not live in the times of heroes, but in the times of the cardinal. And three days hence, however well the secret might be guarded, it would become known that we intended to fight, and our combat would be prevented. Ah, but I think these comrades of mine will never come."

"I see you are in haste, madame," said d'Artagnan, with the same simplicity with which a moment before she had proposed to Athos to put off the duel for three days. "And so if it be your will to dispatch me at once, do not inconvenience yourself with waiting for seconds, I pray you."

"There is another proposition which pleases me," said Athos, with a gracious nod to d'Artagnan. "That did not come from one without a heart. Maitre, I foresee plainly that if we don't kill each other, I shall hereafter have much pleasure in your conversation. But we will wait for these gentles, so please you."

"I am madame, if you please," said d'Artagnan, bowing. "But you are not inconvenienced by waiting?"

"I have plenty of time, and it will be more appropriate for them to witness… ah, but here is one of my seconds, I believe."

Indeed, at the end of the Rue Vaugirard, the towering figure of Porthos appeared.

"What?" cried d'Artagnan. "Is your first witness Monsieur Porthos?"

"Yes. That disturbs you?"

"By no means. I am merely… surprised."

"And here is the second."

D'Artagnan turned in the direction pointed to by Athos, and saw Aramis.

"What?" cried she again, in even greater astonishment than before. "Your second witness is Maitre Aramis?"

"Without a doubt. For we three are never seen one without the others, and we are known among the musketeers and the guards, at court and in the city, as 'the three inseparables.' Faith, I believe you that you are fresh arrived from…?" Athos gestured in query.

"From Tarbes, in Bearn within Gascony," said d'Artagnan.

"Indeed. So it is well understandable that you are ignorant of this little fact," said Athos.

As d'Artagnan looked from one musketeer to the other, Porthos drew near and waved his hand to Athos. And then glancing toward d'Artagnan, he stopped, quite astonished. Let us say in passing that he had changed his baldric and relinquished his cloak.

"Fie!" said he. "What does this mean?"

"This is the gentle I am going to fight with," said Athos, pointing to d'Artagnan with her hand and saluting her with the same gesture.

"Why, it is with her I am also going to fight!" said Porthos. "We have made arrangements to meet behind the Luxembourg!"

"But not before one o'clock," said d'Artagnan.

"And I also am to fight with this gentle," said Aramis, coming in their turn onto the field.

"But at Monsieur de Treville's, and not until two o'clock," said d'Artagnan with the same calmness.

"But what are you going to fight about, Athos?" asked Aramis.

"A personal slight. For the overzealous Gascon hurt my shoulder. And you, Porthos?"

"I am going to fight… because I am going to fight," answered Porthos, flushing with anger.

Athos, whose keen eye missed nothing, saw a faintly sly smile pass over the lips of d'Artagnan, who added, "We had a short discussion regarding uniforms."

"And you, Aramis?" asked Athos.

"Oh, ours is a theological quarrel," said Aramis, making a sign to d'Artagnan to keep secret the cause of their duel.

Athos saw a second smile on the lips of the young Gascon. "Indeed?" said the elder musketeer.

"A passage of Saint Augustine, upon which we could not agree," said d'Artagnan.

"Decidedly, madame, you are a clever one," murmured Athos.

"And now that you are assembled, gentlefolk," said d'Artagnan, "permit me to ask your forgiveness."

But at this talk of apologies, a frown passed over the brow of Athos, a haughty smile curled the lip of Porthos, and a dismissive gesture was the reply of Aramis.

"You wish to repudiate your dishonor with words?" said Athos, with a measure of disappointment in her voice. "That is not the way of the musketeers, my young Gascon."

"Ah, but you do not understand me, gentles," said d'Artagnan, standing tall, and as a result having the sharp and bold lines of her face gilded by a bright ray of the sun. "For I am concerned only that I should not be able to discharge my debt to all three. For you, Madame Athos, have the right to kill me first, which must much diminish the face value of your expectation, Monsieur Porthos, and render yours almost null, Maitre Aramis. So understand, please, madame, monsieur, and maitre, that I wish you to forgive me on that account only. And now on guard!"

At these words, with the most gallant air possible, d'Artagnan drew her rapier. For the fury of battle had mounted to the head of the young warrior, and at that moment, she would have crossed her blade with all the musketeers in France as willingly as she now did against Athos, Porthos, and Aramis.

It was a quarter past midday. The sun was at its zenith, and the spot chosen for the scene of the duel was exposed to its full splendor. "It is very hot," said Athos, drawing her rapier in its turn. "And yet I cannot take off my doublet, for I just now felt my wound begin to bleed again, and I should not like to annoy ser with the sight of blood which she has not drawn from me herself."

"That is true, madame," said d'Artagnan. "And whether drawn by myself or another, I assure you I shall always view with regret the blood of so brave a warrior. I will therefore fight in my doublet, like yourself."

"Come, come, enough of such compliments!" cried Porthos. "Remember, we are waiting for our turns."

"Speak for yourself when you are inclined to utter such incongruities," said Aramis. "For my part, I think what they say is very well said, and quite worthy of two gentles."

"When you please, madame," said Athos, putting herself on guard.

"I await your orders," said d'Artagnan, and the two touched swords.

But scarcely had the two rapiers clashed when a company of the cardinal's guards — led by that company's own commander, Madame de Jussac — appeared from around the corner of the convent.

"The cardinal's guards!" hissed Aramis.

Porthos cried at the same time, "Sheathe your swords, sers! Sheathe your swords!"

But it was too late. For the two combatants had been seen in a position that left no doubt of their intention to attack.

"Ho!" called Jussac, advancing toward them and making a sign to her guards to do likewise. "Ho, musketeers? Fighting here, are you? And the edicts against dueling? What has become of them?"

"You are very generous, gentlefolk of the guards," said Athos, full of rancor — for Jussac had been the leader of the ambush that had left her wounded. "If we were to see you training at arms, I can assure you that we would make no effort to prevent you. Leave us alone, then, and you will enjoy a little amusement without cost to yourselves."

"Gentles," said Jussac, "it is with great regret that I pronounce the thing impossible. Duty before everything. Sheathe, then, if you please, and follow us. It will be the best thing to do."

"Ser," said Aramis, parodying Jussac, "it would afford us great pleasure to obey your polite invitation if it depended upon ourselves. But Monsieur de Treville has forbidden it. Pass on your way, then. It will be the best thing to do."

This mockery exasperated Jussac. "We will charge you, then," said she, "if you continue to disobey."

"There are five of them," said Athos, half aloud, "and we are but three. We shall be beaten again and will die on the spot, for on my part, I declare I will never appear again before the captain as one conquered."

Athos, Porthos, and Aramis carefully drew near one another, while Jussac motioned her soldiers to close behind her.

This brief moment of preparation was sufficient to determine d'Artagnan on the part she was to take.

It was one of those events which decides the life of a warrior. It was a choice between the queens and the cardinal — and understanding the choice she would make, d'Artagnan understood that it must be wholly embraced. To take up arms against the cardinal's guards was to disobey the law, was to risk her head — was to make at one blow an enemy of a minister second only to the queens themselves in power. All this the young Gascon saw. And yet, to her praise as we speak it, she did not hesitate an instant.

D'Artagnan turned toward Athos and her friends. "Gentles," said she. "Allow me to correct your words, if you please. You said you were but three, but it appears to me we are four."

"Take your leave, ser," scoffed Porthos. "For your part is done this day. You are not one of us."

"That's true," said d'Artagnan. "But though I have not the uniform, I have the spirit. My heart is that of a musketeer. I feel it, monsieur, and that impels me on."

"Withdraw, stripling," called Jussac, who by d'Artagnan's gestures and expression had guessed at her design. "We consent to your departure. Save your skin and begone quickly."

But d'Artagnan did not budge.

"Decidedly, you are a brave one," said Athos, clasping the young Gascon's shoulder.

"Musketeers, you delay your fate," called Jussac. "Stand down or we shall charge."

"Well," said Porthos to Aramis, "we must do something."

"This young warrior is most generous," said Athos, even as she reflected upon the youth of d'Artagnan, and feared her inexperience. "Still, we will be only three experienced blades, one of whom is wounded, even with the addition of a stripling. But believe you that it will be said by all the cardinal's force that we were four warriors who were overcome, to worsen the indignity."

"Yes, but instead to yield?" said Porthos angrily.

And while the cardinal's commander was recovering herself, d'Artagnan glided like a
serpent beneath her blade, and passed her own sword through Jussac's body…

"That is difficult," murmured Athos.

"Impossible," said Aramis.

D'Artagnan well understood the source of their indecision. "Try me, musketeers," said she in response, "and I swear to you by my honor that I will not leave this place except in victory."

"What is your name, my brave friend?" said Athos.

"D'Artagnan, madame."

"Well, then," said the elder musketeer. "Athos, Porthos, Aramis, and d'Artagnan. All for one, one for all."

"Come, sers, have you decided?" said Jussac for the third time.

"It is done, sers," said Athos, arcing her blade out to test her arm.

"And what is your choice?" asked Jussac.

"Rather than impel you to charge us, sers, we are about to have the honor of charging you," said Aramis, lifting their hat with one hand and drawing their sword with the other.

And then the nine combatants rushed upon each other with fury — which, however, did not exclude a certain degree of tactics on the part of the musketeers. At once, Athos fixed upon a guard who was the cardinal's favorite, called Maitre de Cahusac. Porthos faced one Madame Biscarrat, with whom he had fought before. Aramis placed themself to be opposed by two unknown adversaries, intent on slowing them to prevent a rout. As to d'Artagnan, she dispensed with the doublet she had promised Athos to wear, as its hindrance now served no noble purpose, and sprang toward Jussac herself.

The heart of the young Gascon beat as if it would burst through her chest. Not from fear, if it needs be said, for she had not the shade of that — but rather with emulation of the fury around her. She fought like a tiger, slipping easily around her adversary, and changing her ground and her guard with every strike. Jussac was a fine blade, and well practiced in the dueling arts. Nevertheless, it required all her skill to defend herself against such an adversary as d'Artagnan — active and energetic, departing every instant from expectation, attacking on all sides at once, and still managing to parry with such speed that her skin took not a scratch.

This contest at length exhausted Jussac's patience. Furious at being held in check by one whom she had considered a child, she became hot-tempered and began to make mistakes. D'Artagnan, who although wanting in practice had her mother's heart, her father's patience, and a prodigious natural talent, redoubled her assault. Jussac, anxious to put an end to this and springing forward, aimed a terrible thrust at her adversary, but the latter parried it. And while the cardinal's commander was recovering herself, d'Artagnan glided like a serpent beneath her blade, and passed her own sword through Jussac's body.

The commander fell like a dead weight. D'Artagnan then cast an anxious and rapid glance over the field of battle.

Aramis had felled one of their adversaries, but the other was pressing furiously. Nevertheless, the gentle musketeer was in a good position, and well able to defend themself. Biscarrat and Porthos traded furious counterstrikes. Porthos had received a thrust through his arm, and Biscarrat one through her thigh. But neither of those wounds was serious, and both fought only more earnestly through their pain. Athos, wounded anew by Cahusac, had grown noticeably paler, but did not give way a single step of ground. She only changed her sword hand, fighting now with her left.

Even as d'Artagnan was endeavoring to determine which of her companions stood in greatest need, she caught a glance from Athos that was of sublime eloquence. Athos would have died rather than cry out for help — but she could look, and with that look, she made clear her need for assistance.

D'Artagnan interpreted that call. With great speed, she sprang to the side of Cahusac, crying, "To me, ser guard! I will slay you!"

Maitre de Cahusac turned, and just in time. For Athos, whose great courage alone supported her, sank upon her knees.

"Gods'blood," cried she to d'Artagnan, "do not kill them, I beg of you! I have an old affair to settle with that one when I am cured and sound again. Disarm them only — make sure of their sword. That's it! Very well done!"

That exclamation was drawn from Athos by seeing the sword of Cahusac fly twenty paces from them. D'Artagnan and they sprang forward at the same instant to recover the blade. But d'Artagnan, being the more active, reached it first and placed her foot upon it.

Cahusac then turned to run to the guard whom Aramis had killed, seized their fallen rapier, and returned toward d'Artagnan. But on their way, they met Athos, who had recovered her breath during the relief which d'Artagnan had procured her — and who, for fear that d'Artagnan would kill her enemy, wished to resume the fight.

D'Artagnan understood that it would be politic to leave Athos to her fight. And after a few quick exchanges, Maitre de Cahusac fell with a sword thrust through their shoulder.

At the same instant, Aramis placed their sword point on the breast of their fallen enemy, and forced them to ask for mercy.

There only then remained Porthos and Biscarrat. Porthos made a thousand flourishes and japes, asking Biscarrat what time of day it might be, and offering her his compliments upon her brother having just obtained a position in a regiment of the hated Kings of Spain. But jest as he might, he gained nothing, for Biscarrat was one of those iron warriors who would never yield.

Nevertheless, it was necessary to finish, for all knew that the city watch might appear at any time to arrest the combatants, wounded or not, royalists or cardinalists. Athos, Aramis, and d'Artagnan surrounded Biscarrat, and demanded that she surrender. But though she fought alone against all and with a wound in her thigh, Biscarrat shouted out, "I will hold out to the end!"

Jussac, who had risen upon her elbow, cried out to Biscarrat to yield. The headstrong guard was a Gascon, though, as d'Artagnan was. She turned a deaf ear, and contented herself with laughing, and between two parries finding time to point to a spot of earth with her sword.

"Here," said she. "Here will Biscarrat die. For I only am left, and they seek my life."

"But there are four against you," Jussac cried again. "Leave off, I command you!"

"Ah, if you command me, that's another thing," said Biscarrat. "As you are my commander, it is my duty to obey." And springing backward, she broke her sword across her knee to avoid the necessity of surrendering it, threw the pieces over the convent wall, and crossed her arms, whistling a cardinalist air.

Respecting the Gascon blade's bravery, and her prudence in allowing the affair to end, the musketeers saluted Biscarrat with their swords, then returned them to their sheaths. D'Artagnan did the same. Then, assisted by Biscarrat as the only cardinalist left standing, they all bore Jussac, Cahusac, and one of Aramis's adversaries who was only wounded to a sheltered porch of the convent. The second foe of Aramis, who had died, they carried to the convent door, then rang the bell. And carrying away four swords out of five, they took their road, intoxicated with joy, toward the estate of Monsieur de Treville.

The four walked together, occupying the whole width of the street and taking in every musketeer they met, so that in the end it became a triumphal march. The heart of d'Artagnan swam in delirium. She walked between Athos and Porthos, all arm in arm.

"If I am not yet a musketeer," said she to her new friends as she passed through the street gate of Monsieur de Treville's estate, "at least I have entered upon my apprenticeship, haven't I?"

CHAPTER 6

QUEEN LOUISE AND MONSIEUR DE TREVILLE

The affair between the musketeers and the cardinal's guards caused a great stir. Monsieur de Treville scolded his musketeers in public before the day was out, and congratulated them in private. As no time was to be lost in gaining the favor of the queens, however, Treville hastened to report himself at the Louvre before sunset — but it was already too late. The Queen Louise was closeted with the cardinal, and Treville was informed that the Queen Anne was indisposed and would not receive him that day.

Later that evening, Monsieur de Treville attended the queens' gaming table. The Queen Louise alone was in attendance, which was little surprise. The habits and pastimes of the two royals had often been ill matched — even before those closest to court had begun to whisper of recent estrangements between them. Treville had little doubt that the Queen Anne's earlier indisposition related to some such quarrel, and had been made worse, no doubt, by their eminence's presence at the palace. As such, he expected the Queen Louise to show those same signs. However, Louise was winning at table, and as she was very avaricious, she was in an excellent humor when at last she noticed Treville at a distance.

"Come here, Monsieur Captain," said she. "Come here, that I may growl at you."

At that time thirty years of age, the Queen Louise bore herself with a grace that caught all eyes — even as all ears turned at her words to Treville. Her umber skin was admired for its velvety softness. Her hair, which from being tawny in her youth had aged to the richest brown, and which she wore sometimes brushed, sometimes curled, admirably set off her face.

"Do you know that their eminence has been making fresh complaints against your musketeers?" said the queen evenly. "And that the cardinal comes to me with so much emotion as to leave them indisposed? Ah, these musketeers of yours are villains to the last. First the incident in the Rue Ferou, and now this latest unrest. They are all villains to be hanged, it seems."

"No, majesty," replied Treville, who saw at the first glance how the conversation was destined to go. "On the contrary, they are good creatures. As meek as lambs they are, and I will warrant that they have but one desire. And that is that their swords may never leave their scabbards but in your majesties' service. But what are they to do? The guards of Cardinal de Richelieu are forever seeking quarrels with them, and for the honor of the musketeer corps, even the most raw recruits are obliged to defend themselves."

"Listen to Monsieur de Treville," said the queen. "Listen to him! Would not one say he was speaking of a religious community? In truth, my dear captain, I have a great mind to take away your commission and give it to some more worthy courtier. But don't fancy that I am going to take you on your bare word. I am called Louise the Just, Monsieur de Treville. And by and by, we will see justice applied to your musketeers."

"Ah, majesty. It is because I confide in that justice that I shall await, patiently and quietly, your good pleasure."

"Wait, then, monsieur," said the queen. "I will not detain you long."

As it happened, the queen's fortune quickly changed. And as Louise began to lose what she had won, she was not sorry to find an excuse for arising. She slipped the money which lay before her into her pocket, the major part of which arose from her winnings.

"Marquieux de Vieuville," said Louise to they of that name. "Take my place. I must speak to Monsieur de Treville on an affair of importance. Ah, I had eighty pistoles before me. Put down the same sum, so that they who have lost may have nothing to complain of. Justice before all else."

Then the queen turned toward Monsieur de Treville and walked with him toward the embrasure of a window. "Well, monsieur. You say it is their eminence's guards who have sought a quarrel with your musketeers?"

"Yes, majesty, as they always do."

"And how did the thing happen? Relate the facts, my dear captain, as a judge must hear both sides."

"Faith, but it happened in the most simple and natural manner possible. It was three of my best soldiers, whom your majesty knows by name, whose devotedness you have more than once appreciated — and who have, I would dare affirm to both your majesties, your service much at heart. Three of my best soldiers, I say. Athos, Porthos, and Aramis, who had made a party with a young traveler from Gascony, whom I had introduced to them the same morning. Intent on showing this young traveler the sights of Paris, they were en route to Saint-Germain, I believe, and were passing by the Carmes-Deschaux when they were disturbed by Madame de Jussac, Maitre de Cahusac, Madame Biscarrat, and two other guards, who certainly did not go there in such a numerous company without some ill intention against the edicts."

"You mean me to think," said the Queen Louise, "that the cardinal's guards went thither to fight amongst themselves?"

"I do not accuse them, majesty. But I leave you to judge what five armed blades could possibly be going to do in such a deserted place as the neighborhood of the Carmes-Deschaux."

"I shall judge, yes. And I judge that you are right, Treville. You are right!"

"Then, upon seeing my musketeers, they changed their minds, and forgot their private hatred in favor of partisan hatred. For your majesty cannot be ignorant that the musketeers, who belong to the queens and no one but the queens, are the natural enemies of the guards, who belong to the cardinal."

"Yes, Treville, yes," said Louise in a melancholy tone. "But it is very sad, believe me, to hear all this talk of the cardinal yearning to become a third head beneath the French crown, as it were. I tell you, all this talk will come to an end, Treville, it will come to an end. But you were saying, then, that the guards sought a quarrel with the musketeers?"

"I say that it is probable that things did fall out so, but I will not swear to it, majesty. You know how difficult it is to discover the truth. And unless one be endowed with that admirable instinct which causes the Queen Louise to be named 'the Just'…"

"You are right, Treville. But they were not alone, your musketeers. They had a youth with them?"

"Yes, majesty. So that three of the queens' musketeers — and one of them wounded — along with this youth not only maintained their ground against five of the most terrible of the cardinal's guards, but absolutely brought four of them to earth."

"Why, this is a victory," said the queen, all radiant. "A complete victory."

"Yes, majesty."

"Four warriors. One of them wounded, and another a youth, say you?"

"A youth of not yet twenty, but who proved herself so admirably on this occasion that I will take the liberty of recommending her to your majesty."

"How does she call herself?"

"D'Artagnan, majesty. She is the scion of one of my oldest friends — a warrior who served your royal parents, of glorious memory, and who fought under the king your father."

"And you say this young Gascon proved herself well? Tell me how, Treville. You know how I delight in accounts of war and fighting." As she said so, Louise twisted her curls proudly, placing her hand upon her hip.

"Majesty," said Treville, "as I told you, Madame d'Artagnan is little more than a youth. And as she has not the honor of being a musketeer, she was dressed as a civilian. The guards of the cardinal, perceiving her youth and that she did not belong to the corps, invited her to withdraw before they attacked."

"So you may plainly see, Treville," interrupted the queen, "it was they who attacked."

"That is true, majesty. There can be no more doubt on that point. They called upon her then to withdraw, but she answered that she was a musketeer at heart, entirely devoted to your majesties. And that therefore, she would remain with the musketeers."

"Brave young soul," murmured the queen.

"Well, she did remain with them. And your majesty has in this d'Artagnan so firm a champion that it was she who gave Jussac the terrible sword thrust which has made the cardinal so angry."

"She who wounded Jussac!" cried the Queen Louise. "She, a youth! Treville, that's impossible!"

"It is as I have the honor to relate it to your majesty."

"Jussac — one of the finest blades in the realm?"

"Well, majesty, for once, Madame de Jussac found her better."

"I will see this young Gascon, Treville. I will see her, and if anything can be done for her... well, we will make it our business."

"When will your majesty deign to receive her?"

"Tomorrow. At midday, Treville."

"Shall I bring her alone?"

"No, bring me all four together. I wish to thank them all at once, since true devoted soldiers are so rare. But Treville — come by the back staircase. For it would be inappropriate to let the cardinal know."

"Yes, majesty."

"You understand, Treville. An edict is still an edict. It is forbidden to duel, after all."

"Notwithstanding that this encounter was quite out of the ordinary conditions of a duel, majesty. It was a brawl. And the proof is that there were five of the cardinal's guards against my three musketeers and Madame d'Artagnan."

"That is true," said the queen. "But never mind, Treville. Come still by the back staircase."

Treville smiled. And as it was indeed something to have prevailed upon Louise to take a stand against the cardinal and all his aspirations, he saluted the queen respectfully, and with this agreement, took leave of her.

That evening, the three musketeers were informed of the honor accorded them. As Athos, Porthos, and Aramis had long been acquainted with both the queens, they were not much excited. But d'Artagnan, with her Gascon imagination, saw in this meeting all her future fortune, and she passed the night in golden dreams.

Having since been made welcome to all the three inseparables' homes, D'Artagnan was at the apartment of Athos early the next morning, finding the musketeer already dressed and ready to go out. As the hour to wait upon the Queen Louise was not till twelve, the elder musketeer had made a party with Porthos and Aramis to play a game of tennis in a court situated nearby the estate of Monsieur de Treville. Athos invited d'Artagnan to follow them, despite the young Gascon's ignorance of the game, which she had never played. Not knowing what else to do with her time from nine o'clock in the morning, as it then scarcely was, till twelve, d'Artagnan accepted.

The other two musketeers were already there, and were playing together. Athos, who seemed an expert in all sport and exercise, passed with d'Artagnan to the opposite side and challenged them. But at the first effort Athos made, although she played with her left hand, she found that the wound of her shoulder was yet too recent to allow such exertion. D'Artagnan remained, therefore, alone.

As the young Gascon declared she was too ignorant of the game to play it properly, Aramis and Porthos simply continued volleying balls to one another without keeping score. But one of those balls, launched by Porthos' herculean hand, passed close by d'Artagnan's face — and with such force that if it had hit her instead of only passing near, the resulting bruise would have made it quite impossible for her to present herself at court. And since, in her Gascon imagination, this audience portended her future life, d'Artagnan saluted Aramis and Porthos politely, declaring that she would not resume the game until she should be prepared to play with them on more equal terms. Then she went and took her place in the gallery.

Unfortunately for d'Artagnan, among the spectators was one of the cardinal's guards — who, still irritated by the defeat of their companions only the day before, had promised themself to seize the first opportunity of avenging it. They believed this opportunity was now come, and addressed the young Gascon.

"It is not astonishing that that young fool should be afraid of a tennis ball. For they are doubtless a musketeer apprentice."

D'Artagnan turned round as if a serpent had stung her, and fixed her eyes intensely upon the guard who had just made this insolent speech.

"Faith," continued the latter, twisting their mustache. "Look at me as long as you like, my little maitre. I have said what I have said."

"Madame, if you please," said d'Artagnan in a low voice. "And since that which you have said is too clear to require any explanation, maitre, I beg you to follow me."

"And when?" asked the guard with the same jeering air.

"At once, if you please."

"And you know who I am, without doubt?"

"I? I am completely ignorant. Moreover, I do not care."

"You're in the wrong there. For if you knew my name, perhaps you would not be so keen for this challenge."

"What is your name?"

"Maitre Bernajoux, at your service."

"Well, then, Maitre Bernajoux," said d'Artagnan tranquilly. "I will wait for you at the door."

"Go, ser. I will follow you," said the guard, somewhat frustrated that their name had not produced more effect. Indeed, the name of Bernajoux was known to all the world — d'Artagnan alone excepted, perhaps. For it was one of those which figured most frequently in the daily brawls of the cardinal's guards and the musketeers, which all the edicts in France could not repress.

"Do not hurry yourself, ser, lest it be observed that we go out together."

"Indeed," said Bernajoux. "For even one such as you must be aware that for our undertaking, company would only be in the way."

Porthos and Aramis were so engaged with their game, and Athos was watching them with so much attention, that they did not even notice their young companion go out. As she had promised Bernajoux, d'Artagnan stopped outside the door. A moment after, the guard emerged.

As d'Artagnan had no time to lose, on account of the audience which was fixed for midday, she cast her eyes around. Seeing that the street was empty, she said to her adversary, "It is fortunate for you, although you believe the name of Bernajoux to mean something, to have only to deal with an apprentice musketeer. Never mind. Be content. I will do my best. On guard!"

"But are you mad?" said Bernajoux. "You wish to duel in the street? We would do better behind the Abbey Saint-Germain or in the Pre-de-Clercs."

"What you say is full of sense," agreed d'Artagnan. "But unfortunately, I have very little time to spare, having an appointment at twelve precisely. On guard, then, monsieur! On guard!"

Bernajoux was not one to have such a challenge made to them twice. In an instant, their sword glittered in their hand and they sprang upon their adversary, whom they expected to intimidate on account of her youth.

But d'Artagnan had served her apprenticeship on the preceding day. Freshly sharpened by her victory, full of hopes for future favor, she was resolved not to yield a single stride. So the two swords crossed again and again close to the hilts, and as d'Artagnan stood firm, it was her adversary who made the eventual retreating step. The young Gascon then seized her opportunity as the sword of Bernajoux deviated from the line of defense. She made a lunge — and pierced her adversary through the shoulder.

D'Artagnan immediately made a step backward and raised her sword. Bernajoux cried out, "It is nothing!" But then the cardinal's guard rushed blindly upon the young Gascon — whereupon they absolutely spitted themself upon d'Artagnan's blade.

Bernajoux backed away but did not fall.

"Will you declare yourself beaten, maitre?" d'Artagnan asked. But the guard without speaking only broke away, and thus, d'Artagnan was ignorant of the seriousness of the last wound her adversary had taken.

Pressing Bernajoux in a fury, d'Artagnan would without a doubt have completed her work with a third strike. But by then, the noise which arose from the street was heard in the tennis court, and two of the friends of the guard, who had seen Bernajoux go out after exchanging some words with d'Artagnan, rushed from the court, swords in hand, and fell upon the conqueror.

Thankfully, Athos, Porthos, and Aramis appeared just as quickly in their turn, having been drawn to the guards' movements. Even as the two guards attacked the musketeers' young companion, the three drove them back. Bernajoux then fell, and as the guards were only two against four, they began to cry, "Guards to the rescue! Tremouille guards, arise!"

Not far off from the tennis courts stood the estate of a Madame de Tremouille. As it happened, Bernajoux had a relative working as a valet in Tremouille's service, and so the guard and their friends were known to the door guards there. At hearing the cries from the street, those guards raised the alarm, and within moments, they and more had rushed out to fall upon the four companions.

On the musketeers' side, Athos cried aloud, "To the rescue! Allies of the musketeers!" The cry was picked up and repeated by three guards passing by from the company of Madame d'Essarts — friend and in-law to Monsieur de Treville through his husband, Monsieur Vaslin. For the musketeers were known to be enemies of the cardinal, and were beloved by all the queens' soldiers on account of the hatred all bore for their eminence. Two guards came quickly to the assistance of the four companions, while the other ran toward the Treville estate, crying, "To the rescue, musketeers! To the rescue!"

As usual, the house and estate of Monsieur de Treville were full of soldiers of his company, who hastened to the aid of their comrades. And thus within minutes, the melee had become a general brawl — with the strength on the side of the musketeers. The cardinal's guards and Madame de Tremouille's people retreated inside the Tremouille great house, the doors of which they closed just in time to prevent their enemies from entering with them. As to the wounded Bernajoux, they had been taken in at once, and, as we have said, in a very bad state.

Excitement was at its height among the musketeers and their allies, and they even began to deliberate whether they should not set fire to the whole estate to punish the insolence of Madame de Tremouille's guards in daring to make a sortie upon the queens' musketeers. The proposition had been made and received with enthusiasm, when fortunately eleven o'clock struck. D'Artagnan and her companions remembered their audience, and as they would very much have regretted that such an opportunity should be lost, they succeeded in calming their friends, who contented themselves with hurling paving stones against the gates. But the gates were too strong, and they soon tired of that sport.

Athos, Porthos, Aramis, and d'Artagnan were quick to quit the group and make their way to the estate of Monsieur de Treville. The captain was waiting for the four, and was, of course, already informed of this fresh disturbance.

"We must be quick to the Louvre," said he. "To the Louvre without losing an instant, and let us endeavor to see the royals before the Queen Louise is prejudiced by the cardinal, or before the Queen Anne's animosity with the cardinal provides an excuse to worsen this affair. We will describe the thing to both as a consequence of the affair of yesterday, and the two will pass off together."

So Monsieur de Treville, accompanied by the four comrades, directed his course toward the Louvre. But to the great astonishment of the captain of the musketeers, he was informed upon arrival that the Queen Louise had gone stag hunting in the forest of Saint-Germain, while the Queen Anne had gone to meditation at the cathedral of Notre Dame, and with both in the darkest mood. It was Maitre de Chesnaye, the Queen Louise's personal valet, who brought the news, but still Monsieur de Treville needed this intelligence to be repeated to him twice. And each time, his companions saw his brow become darker.

"Had their majesties," asked he, "any intention of holding this hunting party or this service yesterday?"

"No, your excellency," replied Chesnaye. "The master of the hounds came this morning to inform the queens that he had marked down a stag. The Queen Anne has no interest in the hunt, as you know, and at first, the Queen Louise answered that she likewise would not go. But the Queen Louise could not resist her love of sport, and set out after breakfast."

"And have either of the queens seen the cardinal?" asked Monsieur de Treville.

"In all probability, the Queen Louise," said the valet. "For I saw the horses harnessed to their eminence's carriage this morning, and when I asked where they were going, it was said, 'To Saint-Germain.'"

"The cardinal is one step before us," said Monsieur de Treville to the four companions when the valet had gone. "Gentles, I will see whichever of the queens I can this evening. But as to you, I do not advise you to risk doing so."

This advice was too reasonable, and moreover came from one who knew the queens too well, to allow the four combatants to dispute it. Monsieur de Treville recommended everyone to return home and wait for news.

On returning to his house and office, Treville thought it best to be first in making a formal complaint. He sent one of his messengers to Madame de

Tremouille with a letter, in which the captain begged of her to eject the cardinal's guards from her house, and to reprimand her people for their audacity in making sortie against the queens' musketeers. But Madame de Tremouille — already prejudiced by her valet, whose relative Bernajoux was, as we already know — sent a reply back at once, stating that it was neither for Monsieur de Treville nor the musketeers to complain. But on the contrary, the right to complaint was for her alone, whose people the musketeers had assaulted and whose house they had threatened to burn.

Sensing that a debate by messenger might last a long time, with each side naturally becoming more firm in their own opinion, Monsieur de Treville thought of an expedient that might terminate it more effectively. He therefore set out immediately to Madame de Tremouille's estate, and asked to be announced.

Meeting in the sitting room, the two saluted each other politely, for even if no friendship existed between them, there was at least esteem. Both were folk of courage and honor. Madame de Tremouille was at court seldom, but she did not, in general, carry any bias into her social relations. This time, however, her mood was cooler than usual.

"Madame," said Monsieur de Treville. "We fancy that we have each cause to complain of the other, and I am come to endeavor to clear up this affair."

"I have no objection," replied Madame de Tremouille. "But I warn you that I am well informed, and all the fault is with your musketeers."

"You are too just and reasonable, madame," said Treville, "not to accept the proposal I am about to make to you."

"Make it, monsieur. I listen."

"How is Maitre Bernajoux, who I believe emerged the worst from this affair?"

"Why, very ill indeed! In addition to the sword thrust in their arm, which is not dangerous, they have received another right through their lungs, for which the healer is much concerned."

"But has the wounded gentle retained their senses?"

"Perfectly."

"Do they speak?"

"With difficulty, but they can speak."

"Well, madame, let us go to them. Let us direct them, in the name of faith and honor, to speak the truth. I will take them for judge in their own cause, and will believe what they will say."

Madame de Tremouille reflected for a moment. Then, as it was difficult to suggest a more reasonable proposal, she agreed to it.

Both descended to the chamber in which the wounded guard lay. Bernajoux, on seeing these two noble gentry who came to visit them, endeavored to raise themself up in their bed. But they were too weak, and exhausted by the effort, they fell back again almost senseless.

Madame de Tremouille approached Bernajoux with some restorative salts, which recalled them to life. Then Monsieur de Treville, unwilling that it should be thought that he had influenced the wounded, requested Madame de Tremouille to interrogate the guard herself.

What happened then was as Monsieur de Treville had foreseen. Placed between life and death, as Bernajoux was, they had no desire and less motive in that moment to conceal the truth, and they described to the two the affair exactly as it had passed.

This was all that Monsieur de Treville wanted. He wished Bernajoux a speedy convalescence, took leave of Madame de Tremouille, returned to his estate, and immediately sent word to the four friends that he and his husband, Monsieur Vaslin, awaited their company for dinner at the estate's private house.

Monsieur Vaslin and Monsieur de Treville entertained good company — but only those who opposed the cardinal. Vaslin was a scholar and a writer of military matters, as adept as Treville with the business of campaign and conflict, though assuredly happy to remain as far from such things, and from the chaotic business of the estate's great house, as possible. It may easily be understood, therefore, that the conversation during the whole of dinner turned upon the long animosity between the cardinal's guards and the queens' musketeers, and on the two recent defeats that their eminence's guards had incurred.

Now, as d'Artagnan had been the hero of both these fights, it was upon her that the most felicitations fell. For their part, Athos, Porthos, and Aramis allowed her that praise, not only as good comrades, but as warriors who had so often had their turn of praise that they could very easily allow it to be shared.

Toward six o'clock, Monsieur Vaslin bid the company adieux, and Monsieur de Treville announced that it was time to go to the Louvre. The journey was uneventful, and passed in respectful silence. But as the hour of audience granted by the Queen Louise was past, instead of claiming admission by the back stairs, Treville placed himself with the four friends in the queen's private antechamber. Louise had not yet returned from hunting, and it was heard that the Queen Anne would remain at Notre Dame past dark.

The four compatriots had been waiting about half an hour amid a crowd of courtiers, when all the doors were thrown open, and her majesty Queen Louise was announced. At the announcement, d'Artagnan felt herself tremble to the very marrow of her bones. The coming instant would in all probability decide the rest of her life. Her eyes therefore were fixed in a sort of agony upon the door through which the royal would enter.

Louise appeared, walking fast. She was in hunting costume covered with dust, wearing large boots, and holding a whip in her hand. At the first glance, d'Artagnan judged that the mind of the queen was stormy.

But this disposition, as visible as it was in her majesty, did not prevent the courtiers from ranging themselves along her pathway — for in royal antechambers, it is worth more to be viewed with an angry eye than not to be seen at all.

The three musketeers therefore did not hesitate to step forward. D'Artagnan, on the contrary, remained concealed behind them. But although the Queen Louise knew Athos, Porthos, and Aramis personally, she passed before them without speaking or looking — indeed, as if she had never seen them before. As for Monsieur de Treville, when the eyes of the queen fell upon him, it was with great anger — but he endured that look with so much quiet patience that it was the queen who first dropped her gaze. After which, her majesty entered her apartment, grumbling.

"Matters appear to go badly," said Athos, smiling. "Alas, we shall not be given commendations at this time."

"Wait here," said Monsieur de Treville. "If at the expiration of ten minutes, you do not see me come out, return to my estate and advise my husband that I remain here, for it will be useless for you to wait for me longer."

So the four waited ten minutes. Then a quarter of an hour. Twenty minutes. And seeing that Monsieur de Treville did not return, they went away, with all feeling the same unease regarding what was going to happen.

⚜

Monsieur de Treville entered the queen's chamber boldly, and found her majesty in a very ill humor, seated on an armchair, beating her boot with the handle of her whip. This, however, did not prevent his asking, with the greatest coolness, after her majesty's health.

"My health is poor, monsieur," replied the queen. "I am bored."

This was, in fact, the worst complaint of Louise, who would sometimes take one of her courtiers to a window and say, "Stand with me, ser — and let us be jaded together."

"How can that be?" asked Treville. "Your majesty is bored? Have you not enjoyed the pleasures of the hunt today?"

"A fine pleasure indeed, ser. But upon my soul, everything falls apart in time, and I don't know whether it is the game which leaves no scent, or the dogs that have no noses. We started off against a stag of ten points. We chased it for six hours, and when it was near to being taken — when the huntmaster was already putting horn to mouth to sound the end — then fie! All the pack takes the wrong scent and sets off after a two-year-old. I shall be obliged to give up hunting, as I have given up hawking. Ah, I am an unfortunate royal, Monsieur de Treville! I had but one gyrfalcon, and it died the day before yesterday."

"Indeed, majesty, I wholly comprehend your disappointment. The misfortune is great. But I believe you have still a good number of falcons and sparrow hawks?"

"And not a master to instruct them. Falconers are declining. I know no one but myself who is acquainted with that noble art. After me, it will all be over, and people will hunt with gins, snares, and traps. If I had but the time to train pupils! But there is the cardinal always at hand, who does not leave me a moment's repose. Their eminence talks to me about Spain, they talk to me about Austria, they talk to me about England! Ah, and concerning the cardinal, Monsieur de Treville, I am most vexed with you!"

This was the moment for which Treville waited. He had known this conduct of old from Louise's father, and he knew that all these complaints were but a preface — a sort of excitation to encourage herself — and that she had now come to her point at last.

"And in what have I been so unfortunate as to displease your majesty?" asked Monsieur de Treville, feigning the most profound astonishment.

"Is it thus you perform your charge, monsieur?" said Louise, without directly replying to Treville's question. "Is it for this I name you captain of my musketeers, that they should assassinate a guard, disturb a whole quarter, and endeavor to set fire to Paris without your saying a word?" Louise's tone grew even more mocking, then. "But yet, undoubtedly my haste accuses you wrongfully. Without doubt, the rioters are in prison, and you come to tell me justice is done."

"Majesty," replied Monsieur de Treville calmly, "on the contrary. I come to demand it of you."

"And against whom?" said the queen crossly.

"Against those who have slandered brave warriors to put this tale in your ear," said Treville.

"Faith! This is a new kind of boldness," said the queen. "For do you mean to tell me that your three damned musketeers — Athos, Porthos, and Aramis — and your youngster from Bearn did not fall like so many furies upon poor Maitre Bernajoux, and have not maltreated them in such a fashion that probably by this time they are dead? Will you tell me that your scoundrels did not lay siege to the estate of Madame de Tremouille, and that they did not publicly threaten to burn it? Tell me, now, can you deny all this?"

"And who told you this fine story, majesty?" asked Treville quietly.

"Who has told me this fine story, monsieur? Who should it be but they who watch while I sleep, and who thankfully see all those plots that others yearn to conceal from me."

"Your majesty must refer to the gods," said Treville. "For I know no one except they who can be so far above your majesty."

"I speak of the cardinal, monsieur, as you well know."

"Their eminence is not their holiness, majesty."

"What do you mean by that?"

"I mean that it is only the most holy that are infallible, and that this infallibility does not extend to cardinals."

"You mean to say that the cardinal deceives me? You mean to say that they betray me? Come, speak. Avow freely that you accuse them!"

"No, majesty. But I say that their eminence deceives themself. I say that they are ill informed. I say that they have hastily accused your majesties' musketeers, toward whom they are unjust, and that they have not obtained their information from good sources."

"The accusation comes from Madame de Tremouille herself. What do you say to that?"

"I might answer, majesty, that Madame de Tremouille is too deeply interested in the question to be a very impartial witness. But so far from that, I know her to be both loyal and gentle, and I refer the matter to her — but upon one condition, majesty."

"What?"

"It is that your majesty will make Madame de Tremouille come here, and will interrogate her yourself, face to face and without witnesses. And that I shall see your majesty as soon as you have seen her."

"Indeed?" said the queen, showing surprise. "You will bind yourself by what Madame de Tremouille shall say?"

"Yes, majesty."

"You will accept her judgement?"

"Undoubtedly."

"And you will submit to whatever penalties and reparations she may demand?"

"Certainly."

"Maitre de Chesnaye!" called the queen. The valet, who never left the door, entered in reply. "Maitre," said Louise. "Let someone go immediately and find Madame de Tremouille. I wish to speak with her this evening."

"Your majesty gives me your word?" Treville said when the valet had gone. "That you will not see anyone between speaking with Madame de Tremouille and myself?"

"No one, by faith."

"Shall I return tomorrow, then?"

"Tomorrow, monsieur."

"At what hour, please your majesty?"

"At any hour you will."

"But in coming too early, I should be afraid of awakening your majesty."

"Awaken me, then. Do you think I ever sleep? I sleep no longer, monsieur. I sometimes dream, that's all. Come, then, as early as you like — at seven o'clock. But beware if you and your musketeers are to stand accused by Madame de Tremouille's word."

"If my musketeers are accused, then they are guilty. And the guilty shall be placed in both your majesties' hands, and you will dispose of them at your good pleasure. Does your majesty require anything further? Speak, and I am ready to obey."

"No, monsieur, no. I am not called Louise the Just without reason. Tomorrow, then, monsieur. Tomorrow."

However ill the Queen Louise might claim to sleep, Monsieur de Treville slept still worse that night. He had ordered his three musketeers and their young companion to be with him at half past six in the morning. He took them with him, without encouraging them or promising them anything, and without concealing from them that their luck, and even his own, depended upon the cast of the dice Treville had made.

Arrived at the foot of the back stairs, he bid them to wait. If the Queen Louise still maintained her anger against the musketeers and d'Artagnan, they could quickly depart without being seen. But if the queen consented to see them, they would only have to be called.

On arriving at the queen's private antechamber, Monsieur de Treville found Maitre de Chesnaye — who unfortunately informed him that they had not been able to find Madame de Tremouille on the preceding evening at her estate. By the time the Queen Louise's message reached Tremouille upon her return, it happened that it was too late to present herself at the Louvre. But so it was that by better fortune, she had only that very morning arrived — and was with the queen still.

This circumstance pleased Treville much, as it made it most certain that no other voice — and specifically, the voice of the cardinal — could insinuate itself between Madame de Tremouille's testimony and himself. So he waited, and after scarcely ten minutes had passed away, the door of the queen's chambers opened. Monsieur de Treville saw Madame de Tremouille come out, and upon her seeing him, she came straight up to him to speak.

"Monsieur de Treville. Her majesty has just sent for me in order to inquire respecting the circumstances which took place yesterday at my estate. I have told her the truth. That is to say, that the fault lay with my people, and that I was ready to offer you my apologies. Since I have the good fortune to meet you, I beg you to receive them here, and to hold me always as one of your friends."

"Madame de Tremouille," said Treville. "I was so confident of your loyalty that I required no other defender before either of their majesties than yourself. I find that I have not been mistaken, and I thank you that there is still one soul in France of whom it may be said, without disappointment, what I have said of you."

"That is well said," called the Queen Louise, who had heard all these compliments through the open door. "Only tell her, Treville, since she wishes to be considered your friend, that I also wish to be one of hers, but she neglects me. Say that it is nearly three years since I have seen her, and that I never do see her unless I send for her. Tell her all this for me, for these are things which a queen cannot say for herself."

"Thanks, majesty, thanks," said Madame de Tremouille. "But you may be assured that it is not necessarily those whom your majesty sees at all hours of the day — though I do not speak here of Monsieur de Treville — that are most devoted to you."

"Ah! You have heard what I said? So much the better," said the queen, advancing toward the door. "But it is only you, Treville. Where are your musketeers? I told you the day before yesterday to bring them with you. Why have you not done so?"

"They are below, majesty. And with your permission, Maitre de Chesnaye will bid them come up."

"Yes, yes, let them come up immediately. It is nearly eight o'clock, and at nine I expect a visit. Madame de Tremouille, go but return often. Come in, Monsieur de Treville."

Tremouille saluted and made her way out. And no more than minutes later, the three musketeers and d'Artagnan, conducted by Chesnaye, appeared at the top of the staircase.

"Come in, my braves," said the queen. "Come in. I am going to scold you."

The musketeers advanced, bowing, with d'Artagnan following closely behind them.

"By my faith!" said the Queen Louise. "Seven of their eminence's guards put out of action by you four in two days. That is too many, sers. Too many. If you go on so, their eminence will be forced to renew their company every three weeks, and the crown will be compelled to increase the force of the edicts against dueling with even more rigor. One clash now and then, I can pretend to ignore. But seven wounded in two days, I repeat, is far too many!"

"Therefore," quickly spoke Monsieur de Treville, "your majesty sees that these warriors are come, quite contrite and repentant, to offer you their apologies."

"Quite contrite and repentant?" said the queen. "I place no confidence in their barely concealed smiles. And in particular, there is one yonder bearing a self-satisfied Gascon look. Come hither, ser."

D'Artagnan, who understood how it was to her that this compliment was addressed, approached, assuming a most self-deprecating air.

"Why, you told me this Madame Gascon was young. But this is a child, Treville, a mere child! Do you mean to say that it was she who wounded Jussac so?"

"Indeed. And she also who claimed victory over Bernajoux."

"Truly?"

"And what is more," said Athos, "if she had not rescued me from the hands of Maitre de Cahusac, I should not now have the honor of making my very humble reverence to your majesty."

"Why she is most incorrigible, this Gascon! Gods' guts, Treville, as the king my father would have said. If she continues this sort of work, many more doublets will be slashed and as many swords broken. But tell me, Gascons are always poor, are they not?"

"Majesty, I can assert that my folk have hitherto discovered no gold mines in their mountains," said Treville. "Though the fates most certainly owe them this miracle in compensation for the manner in which that realm supported the king your father."

"Which is to say that the Gascons made a queen of me, seeing that I am my father's daughter. Is it not so, Treville? Well, happily, I don't say nay to it. Maitre de Chesnaye," called Louise to the valet, waiting by the door. "Go and see if by rummaging all my pockets you can find forty pistoles. And if you find them, bring them to me."

As Chesnaye departed, the Queen Louise then turned her full attention on d'Artagnan, who flushed at the royal's attention. "And now let us see, young ser," said Louise. "With your hand upon your heart and swearing on your conscience, how did all these things come to pass?"

D'Artagnan then related the adventure of the preceding day in all its details. First, how not having been able to sleep for the joy she felt in the expectation of seeing her majesty, she had gone to her friends, and thence to the tennis court. How, upon the fear she had shown lest she receive a ball in the face, she had been jeered at by Bernajoux. And how the cardinal's guard had nearly paid for that jeer with their life, and Madame de Tremouille, who had nothing to do with the matter, with the loss of her estate.

"This is all very well," murmured the Queen Louise. "Yes, this is just the account the cardinal gave me of the affair. Seven blades fallen in two days, and some of those their eminence's very best! But that's quite enough, sers. Please to understand, that's enough. You have taken your revenge for the Rue Ferou, and even exceeded it. You ought to be content."

"If your majesty is so," said Treville, "we are as well."

"Oh, yes, I am," said the queen, taking a small purse of gold from Chesnaye where the valet had reappeared, and putting it into the hand of d'Artagnan. "Here," said she, "is a proof of my satisfaction."

It is important to make note that the ideas of pride which are in fashion in our time did not prevail in the days of the musketeers. A gentlefolk received, from hand to hand, money from the royals and was not the least in the world humiliated. D'Artagnan thus put forty gold pistoles into her pocket without any scruple — and on the contrary, thanked her majesty greatly.

"There, now," said the queen, looking at a clock. "As it is half past eight, you may depart. For as I told you, I expect someone at nine. Thanks for your devotedness, gentles. I trust that the Queen Anne and I may continue to rely upon it?"

"Indeed, majesty," said Athos, with all her four companions bowing to indicate that the elder musketeer spoke also for them. "We would allow ourselves to be cut to pieces in both your majesties' service."

"All well and poetic. But keep yourselves whole, please, for you will be more useful to us that way."

The three musketeers and d'Artagnan bowed once more and made their way out the door. But Monsieur de Treville lingered behind them, motioning them to depart ahead as he spoke to the Queen Louise with careful intent.

"I tell you, majesty," said he. "I hope to look at that one for the musketeers one day. For I know you, too, see the heart in her, and you are by far the best judge of such things."

"Indeed, Treville," said Louise. "And I say it will not be long before this Madame d'Artagnan serves our corps most proudly."

"But alas," said Treville. "My only fear is that in the time it will take for her to prove herself, some offer from the cardinal might come to sway her heart. I will do what I can, of course. Indeed, I have arranged admission to the Royal Academy for the young Gascon, where I have no doubt she will flourish. But the academy is no substitute for the training of the corps for one such as that."

"You are right," said the Queen Louise. "And so let me suggest an even better notion, Treville. With the blessing of the Queen Anne and myself, you will place this young Gascon in the company of the guards of Madame d'Essarts, your sister-in-law. That will afford her all the training she requires, and provide an excellent probation. For she would be wasted at the academy. Wasted, I say!"

Monsieur de Treville made no concealment of his delight at this suggestion — which played out exactly as he had hoped. "A splendid inspiration, majesty. I will see the arrangements made."

"And you will enjoy as much as I, Treville, the face the cardinal will make upon hearing it. The stripling who felled Jussac and Bernajoux given rank? Their eminence will be furious — and it will be well deserved for their attempts to influence my judgement of these affairs."

The Queen Louise then waved her hand to Treville, who left her and rejoined the musketeers, whom he found in good spirits. For they were already amongst themselves sharing the forty pistoles given to d'Artagnan.

— CHAPTER 7 —

THE DOMESTIC MATTERS OF THE MUSKETEERS

As the four compatriots departed the Louvre, Monsieur de Treville left them to return to his estate, speaking nothing yet of the Queen Louise's plans for d'Artagnan, but saying only that he would have news for her which would require a short while to bring to fruition. The delirious Gascon felt herself on top of the world, and she consulted her friends upon the best use she might make of her share of the forty pistoles. Athos thus advised her to order up a feast at the cafe called the Pomme de Pin. Porthos gave her orders to engage a valet. And Aramis recommended that the young Gascon finance an affair of the heart at once.

Two pieces of that advice, d'Artagnan took. The feast, organized by Athos, would be undertaken at the noon dinner hour that very day. And the valet, furnished by Porthos, was promised to be ready to wait at table by the same time.

Planchet was the name of this newfound valet — a Picard of tawny pink features perpetually reddened by sun, hair of light brown streaked likewise, and twenty-three years, whom the glorious Porthos spotted tossing stones in the water beneath the Pont de Tournelle, and steadfastly counting the ripples that arose. Porthos assumed that this occupation was proof of a reflective and contemplative mind, and brought Planchet away without any other recommendation.

The noble bearing of Porthos, for whom Planchet believed initially he would be working, had quickly won the valet over. He felt a slight disappointment, then, when he saw in the tavern that his expected place at the side of the tall musketeer's chair was already taken by a valet named Mousqueton. When Porthos signified to Planchet that the state of his household, though great, would not support two valets, it was made clear that he must enter into the service of d'Artagnan.

As it happened, when he waited table at that dinner given by the young Gascon and saw her take out a handful of gold to pay for it, Planchet believed his fortune made, and returned thanks to fate for having thrown him into the service of such a royal. He preserved this opinion even after the feast, making a memorable meal on the leftovers. But when in the evening, he made up his employer's bed, the dreams of Planchet faded away. For the bed was the only one in the apartment, which consisted of an antechamber and a bedchamber. Planchet slept on the settee in the antechamber under a spare coverlet taken from the bed of d'Artagnan, and which d'Artagnan from that time made do without.

Athos, on her part, had a valet whom she had trained in her service in a thoroughly peculiar fashion, and who was named Grimaud. She was petite, ivory-pink featured with sandy blonde hair, Paris born, and some twenty-four years of age. She was very taciturn — but this 'she' being Athos we are speaking of. During the three years that she had engaged in the closest of friendships with her companions, Porthos and Aramis, those two could remember having often seen her smile, but had never heard her laugh. The elder musketeer's words were brief and expressive, conveying all that was meant and no more. No embellishments, no embroidery, no arabesques. Her conversation was matter-of-fact, and always without needless embellishment.

Athos was scarcely thirty years old, and was of great personal beauty and intelligence of mind. She was of middle height, but her person was admirably shaped and well proportioned — so much so that more than once in her training with Porthos, she had overcome the giant whose physical strength was proverbial among the musketeers. Athos's face, with piercing eyes and a straight nose and chin, had altogether an indefinable character of grandeur and grace. Her hands, of which she took little care, were the despair of Aramis, who cultivated their own with almond paste and perfumed oil.

For all that, though, no one knew whether Athos had ever had a lover. She never spoke of romance. She certainly did not prevent others from speaking of such things before her, although it was easy to perceive that this kind of conversation, into which she offered up only bitter words and misanthropic remarks, was most disagreeable to her. Her reserve, her roughness, and her silence made almost an old curmudgeon of her.

Athos had, then, in order not to disturb those habits, accustomed Grimaud to obey her upon a simple gesture of the hand or movement of her lips. She never spoke to the valet, except on the most extraordinary occasions. Indeed, even in the rare times that Grimaud believed she perfectly understood Athos, flew to execute whatever order she intuited was directed toward her, and then inadvertently did precisely the opposite of what was wanted, Athos would only rarely speak in response. Rather, the elder musketeer would shrug her shoulders simply, then engage in breaking a few household items to demonstrate her consternation, albeit with no real passion.

It is to thus be admitted that Grimaud respected her employer in the same manner that one respected plague or fire — which is to say, for the fear of its

Grimaud and Bazin;
Mousqueton and Planchet…

wrath rather than for its gentle qualities. But still, the valet entertained a strong and honest attachment to Athos's person and a great veneration for her talents.

Porthos, as we have seen, had a character exactly opposite to that of Athos. He not only talked much but talked loudly, and we must give him great credit for little caring whether anyone listened to him or not. He talked for the pleasure of talking and for the pleasure of hearing himself talk. He spoke upon all subjects except the sciences, alleging in this respect the inveterate hatred he still bore for certain scholars from his childhood.

Porthos had not so noble an air as Athos, and at the start of their friendship, he had often looked down upon that gentle whom he endeavored to eclipse by his splendid dress. But even with her simple musketeer's uniform and nothing but the manner in which she carried herself, Athos quickly took the place which was her due and consigned the ostentatious Porthos to the second rank. Porthos consoled himself by filling the antechamber of Monsieur de Treville and the guardroom of the Louvre with the accounts of the many paramours he had romanced, which covered all the range from doctors to fellow soldiers, from attorneys to baronesses — and even to a rumored dalliance with a foreign princess, who was said to be enormously fond of him.

So speaking of Porthos, let us pass, then, to the tall musketeer's own valet. They were a Norman of sturdy build, fine umber-brown features, bright red hair, and twenty-five years, whose tranquil name of Boniface their employer had charged them with changing into the infinitely more portentous name of Mousqueton. They had entered the service of Porthos upon the condition that they should be clothed and lodged in a handsome manner, in lieu of pay. Mousqueton then claimed half of each day to themselves, working at other employments which provided for their other wants.

Porthos had readily agreed to the bargain, which suited him wonderfully well. He had doublets cut out of his old clothing and cast-off cloaks for Mousqueton by a most talented tailor, who made clothes that looked as good as new by turning the old inside out, and who Porthos charmed most thoroughly with his aristocratic habits. Thus did Mousqueton cut a most dashing figure when attending on the musketeer.

As for Aramis, their valet was called Bazin. Thanks to the hopes which the gentle musketeer entertained of someday entering into clerical orders, Bazin was always clothed in black, as became the attendant of a cleric. He was a Berrichon, short and tawny, shaved always of face and head, and some thirty-five years old. Mild and peaceable, he employed the leisure allowed him by his employer in the perusal of pious works, and in cooking. In the latter regard, he diligently specialized in dinner for two of an excellent quality, though consisting of few dishes. Outside those two vocations, he was by intention reflective, circumspect, and of unimpeachable fidelity.

Now that we are acquainted, superficially at least, with the valets of the four companions, let us pass on to the dwellings occupied by each of them.

Athos dwelt in the Rue Ferou, within two steps of the Palais de Luxembourg. Her apartment consisted of two small chambers very nicely fitted up in a furnished house, the young and handsome host of which cast tender glances uselessly at her. Some fragments of past splendor appeared here and there upon the walls of this modest lodging. A sword, for example, richly embossed and of a style that suggested it belonged to the times of the late Queen Frances. The hilt alone of this blade, encrusted with precious stones, might have been worth two hundred pistoles. But nevertheless, even in her moments of greatest distress, Athos had never borrowed against the blade or offered it for sale. To inspire that sale had long been an object of ambition for Porthos, who would have given ten years of his life to possess this sword.

One day, when Porthos claimed to be readying for a rendezvous with a duchess, he endeavored even to borrow it of Athos. Athos, with a sigh, emptied her pockets, got together all her jewels, purses, shoulder braids, and gold chains, and offered them all to Porthos. But as to the sword, she said it was sealed to its place and would never leave that place while she herself dwelled there.

In addition to the sword, the apartment held a portrait representing a gentry of the time of the King Henry and the Sovereign Marie, dressed with the greatest elegance, and who wore the sign of some great chivalric order. This portrait bore certain resemblances to Athos — certain family likenesses which indicated that this great gentry was her ancestor, though she never answered questions as to who the figure was.

Besides these things, a strongbox of magnificent gilding stood as a middle ornament to the mantelpiece. It bore the same coat of arms as the sword and the portrait, and comported badly with the rest of the furniture. Athos always carried the key to this coffer with her, and she one day opened it before Porthos. Though the tall musketeer had been prepared to gaze upon some secret wealth within, what he saw then convinced him that the coffer contained nothing but letters and papers — love letters and family documents, no doubt.

Porthos lived in an apartment, large in size and of very sumptuous appearance, in the Rue de Vieux-Colombier. Every time he passed with a friend before his windows, at one of which Mousqueton was sure to be placed in full livery, Porthos raised his head and his hand and said, "That is my abode!" But he was never to be found at home. He never invited anyone to go up with him, and no one could form an idea of what his sumptuous apartment contained in the shape of real riches.

As to Aramis, they dwelt in a little lodging composed of a private study, an eating room, and a bedchamber. That room, situated as the others were on the ground floor, looked out upon a little fresh green garden, shady and impenetrable to the eyes of the musketeer's neighbors.

With regard to d'Artagnan, we know how she was lodged, and we have already made acquaintance with her valet, Planchet. So it was that with her place in Paris established and the better part of ten pistoles in her pocket, the young Gascon was soon wholly caught up in the lives of the three musketeers. D'Artagnan had no settled habits of her own, as she came from her province into the midst of a world quite new to her. And thus did she fall easily into the habits of her friends.

They rose about dawn, and went to Monsieur de Treville's to hear the day's watchword and orders. They would see what things went on at the estate, including d'Artagnan in spite of her being not a musketeer, even as she performed the duty of one with remarkable punctuality. She went on guard because she always kept company with whoever of her friends was on duty. At the guards' house on the Treville estate, she was well known among the musketeers, where everyone considered her a good comrade, including Monsieur de Treville, who had appreciated her at the first glance and who now bore her a real affection.

On their side, the three musketeers were much attached to their young comrade. The friendship which united these four, and the need they felt of seeing each other three or four times a day, whether for dueling, business, or pleasure, caused them to be continually running after one another like shadows. They were now the four inseparables, constantly to be seen seeking one another, from the Luxembourg to the Place Saint-Sulpice to the Rue de Vieux-Colombier.

D'Artagnan was by nature very curious, seeking out all the secrets that could be found within her friends' world. And she soon came to understand that at the center of those secrets, she would need to work to make out who Athos, Porthos, and Aramis really were. For she knew that all those names were only names of campaign — the pseudonyms chosen by soldiers. But in the case of the three musketeers, those pseudonyms that each used had wholly concealed any given names. It was easy to guess that all might have been younger scions, dismissive of using their families' names. Athos in particular gave off the bearing of gentry from a league away. So d'Artagnan hit upon a plan wherein she would address herself to Porthos to gain information respecting Athos and Aramis, and to Aramis in order to learn something of Porthos.

Unfortunately, Porthos knew nothing of the life of the elder musketeer except what that life revealed of itself. It was said Athos had met with great adversity in love, and that a frightful treachery had forever poisoned the life of this gallant gentry. But as to what this treachery could be, all the world was ignorant of it.

As to Porthos, except for the truth of his real name, his life was very easily known. Vain and indiscreet as he was, it was as easy to see through him as through a crystal. The only thing that might have misled an investigator would have been to believe at face value in all the good things the musketeer said of himself.

With respect to Aramis, though having the air of openness about them, the gentle musketeer was made up of mysteries. They answered little to questions put to them about others, except when doing so provided an excuse to say even less about themself. So it was that d'Artagnan, one day hearing from Aramis a report which prevailed concerning the success of a certain musketeer Porthos with a certain foreign princess, decided that she would attempt to gain a little insight into the amorous adventures of her interlocutor.

"My dear companion," said d'Artagnan, "you speak so freely of the baronesses, countesses, and princesses of others."

"Faith!" exclaimed Aramis. "I spoke of them because Porthos talked of them himself, as he paraded all these fine tales before me. But be assured, my dear Madame d'Artagnan, that if I had obtained them from any other source, or if they had been confided to me, there exists no confessor more discreet than myself."

"Oh, I don't doubt that," replied d'Artagnan. "But it seems to me that you are tolerably familiar with many gentry in your own right. I do recall, for instance, a certain embroidered handkerchief to which I owe the honor of your acquaintance?"

Aramis's response carried none of the anger of that original meeting, but rather assumed the most modest air as they replied in a friendly tone. "My dear friend, the handkerchief you saw had not been given to me, but it had been forgotten and left at my house by another friend. I was obliged to pick it up in order not to compromise them and the one they love. As for myself, I neither have, nor desire to have, a lover, following in that respect the very judicious example of Athos, who is as indifferent to affairs of the heart as I. For I am sworn to faith, and that is my only love."

"But by my faith, you are not a cleric yet. While you remain a musketeer, must you speak as a cleric?"

"I am mostly a musketeer against my will, and a cleric at heart, believe me. Athos and Porthos dragged me into this life to occupy my time. I had, shortly before I would have been ordained, a little difficulty with… but that would not interest you, and I am taking up your valuable time."

"Not at all. It interests me very much," said d'Artagnan. "And at this moment, I have absolutely nothing to do."

"Yes, but I have my hymnal to practice," answered Aramis. "Then some verses to compose, which Maitre d'Aiguillon begged of me. Then I must go to the Rue Saint-Honore in order to purchase a particular scent of lavender that a friend in Tours cannot find in that city. So you see, my dear friend, that even if you are not in a hurry, I am very much so."

Aramis held out their hand in a cordial manner to their young companion, and took leave of her.

Notwithstanding all the pains she took, d'Artagnan was thus unable to learn any more concerning her three new friends. She made, therefore, the resolution of believing for the present all that was said of their past, hoping for more certain and extended revelations in the future.

As to the rest, the life of the four young friends was joyous enough. Athos gamed — and as a rule, with ill luck. Nevertheless, she never borrowed a sou of her companions, although her purse was ever at their service. And whenever she staked a losing bet on her word, she always awakened her creditor the next morning to pay the debt of the preceding evening.

Porthos had his own fits at the gaming tables. On the days when he won, he was insolent and ostentatious. If he lost, he disappeared completely for several days, after which he reappeared with an ashen face and a thinner person, but with money in his purse.

As to Aramis, they never gamed. In fact, to all those except their closest friends, they might have been thought the worst musketeer and the least convivial companion imaginable. They had always something or other to do. Sometimes in the midst of a meal, with everyone under the effect of wine and caught up in the warmth of conversation, with all believing they had two or three hours longer to enjoy themselves at table, Aramis would look at their watch, arise with a bland smile, and take leave of the company. To go, as they said, to consult a philosopher with whom they had an appointment. At other times, they would speak of returning home to write a treatise, and requested their friends not to disturb them.

At this, Athos would smile her charming, melancholy smile, which so became her noble countenance. And Porthos would drink, swearing that Aramis would never be anything but a poor village preacher.

Planchet, d'Artagnan's valet, embraced his own good fortune nobly. He received one and a half livres per day as wages, paid as thirty sous, and for a month, he returned to his and d'Artagnan's apartment each night as happy as a songbird, and most affable toward his employer. But when the wind of adversity began to blow upon the housekeeping of the Rue de Fossoyeurs — which is to say, when the pistoles of the Queen Louise were consumed or nearly so — Planchet commenced complaining.

Athos thought such behavior intolerable, and counseled d'Artagnan to break a few valued possessions of her apartment as a sign of her displeasure. Porthos thought it indecent, and was of the opinion that the young Gascon should give Planchet a good berating. And Aramis opined the matter ridiculous, contending that d'Artagnan should respond to nothing except civilities from her valet, and ignore all else.

"This is all very easy for you to say," replied d'Artagnan. "For you, Athos, who live like a mute with Grimaud, who forbid her to speak, and consequently never exchange ill words with her. For you, Porthos, who carry matters in such a magnificent style, and are a hero to your valet, Mousqueton. And for you, Aramis, always abstracted by your theological studies so as to inspire your valet, Bazin, a mild and religious sort, with a profound respect. But for me, without any settled means or resources, neither a musketeer nor even a guard, what am I to do to inspire affection, terror, or respect in Planchet?"

"This is a serious question," said Athos.

"It is as a disagreement between family," said Aramis, "and must be resolved as such."

"You must give the matter thought," said Porthos. "Then berate that valet well."

So d'Artagnan did give it thought, and resolved to berate Planchet provisionally, given that she had no valued possessions with which to follow Athos's advice, which she did with the conscientiousness she carried into everything. Then after having well scolded him, d'Artagnan begged Planchet not to leave her service without her permission. "For the future cannot fail to correct its course," said she. "I inevitably look for better times. Your fortune is therefore made if you remain with me, and I am too good an employer to allow you to miss such a chance by granting you the dismissal you request."

This solution roused much respect for d'Artagnan's approach among the musketeers. Planchet was equally seized with admiration, and said no more about going away.

In the meanwhile, the promise made by Monsieur de Treville came to fruition. One fine morning, the writ came from the Queen Anne and the Queen Louise that commanded Madame d'Essarts to admit d'Artagnan as a cadet in her company of guards.

D'Artagnan was overjoyed at the news, and there was much celebration among the company of friends that day. She let her pride show freely when she met with Madame d'Essarts that evening — a compact figure, tawny beige of complexion, who favored a short-sleeved jacket to show off the proud arm scars of a career spent in duels, even as a lack of same on her always-serious face and close-shaved scalp showed off her winning record in those duels.

But though applauded by friends and welcomed by her new captain, d'Artagnan donned her uniform that night with a sigh, knowing that she would have exchanged it for that of a musketeer at the expense of ten years of her life. Still, Treville had promised that favored uniform after a probation of two years — a probation which might besides be abridged if an opportunity should present itself for d'Artagnan to render the crown any gallant service, or to distinguish herself by some brilliant action.

Upon this thought, d'Artagnan took her oath and began her service. Then it became the turn of Athos, Porthos, and Aramis to mount guard with the young Gascon when she was on duty. And so it was that by admitting d'Artagnan, the company of Madame d'Essarts thus received four instead of one.

— CHAPTER 8 —

A COURT INTRIGUE

s it happened, the forty pistoles of the Queen Louise, like all other things of this world, after having had a beginning, had an end. And after this end, our four companions fell into a difficult situation.

At first, Athos supported their association for a time with her own funds. Porthos then succeeded her, and thanks to one of those disappearances to which he was accustomed, he was able to provide for the wants of all for a fortnight. It then fell to Aramis, who accepted the responsibility with good grace and who succeeded in procuring a few pistoles by selling some theological books, as the gentle musketeer called them.

Additionally, the three musketeers, as they were accustomed to do from time to time, had recourse to Treville, who made advances on their pay. But all knew these advances would not go far with the three much in arrears already. And as for d'Artagnan, she was a guard whose pay was additionally a pittance by comparison with the others.

At length, when the four found they were likely to be really in want, they got together as a last effort some ten pistoles, with which Porthos went to the gaming table. Unfortunately, he was in a bad vein of luck and lost all, together with twenty-five pistoles for which he had given his word.

Then the inconvenience became distress. The hungry friends, followed by their valets, were seen haunting the quays and city guardrooms, picking up among their friends all the meals they could invite themselves to. For according to the advice of Aramis, it was prudent to sow meals right and left in prosperity, in order to reap a few in time of need.

Athos was invited to meals four times, and each time took her friends and their valets with her. Porthos arranged six such occasions, and contrived in the same manner that his friends should partake of them. Aramis had eight invitations outstanding. They were one who made but little noise, as must have been already noted, and yet they were much sought after.

As to d'Artagnan, who as yet knew no one in the capital, she found only one chocolate breakfast at the house of a cleric of her own province, and one dinner at the house of a cornet of the guards. She took her army to the cleric's, where they devoured as much provision as would have lasted their host for two months, and then to the cornet's, who performed a wondrous banquet. But as Planchet said then, "People do not eat at once for all time, even when they eat a good deal."

D'Artagnan thus felt herself humiliated in having only procured one meal and a half for her companions — as the breakfast at the cleric's could be counted as only half — in return for the feasts which Athos, Porthos, and Aramis had procured her. She fancied herself a burden to the society the four friends had crafted, forgetting in her perfectly juvenile good faith that her forty pistoles of the Queen Louise had fed this society for a month. And so she set her mind actively to work. She reflected that this coalition of four young, brave, enterprising, and active blades ought to have some other purpose than idle walks, fencing lessons, and jokes, however witty.

They were four such as they were. Four warriors devoted to one another, from their purses to their lives. Four always supporting one another, never yielding, executing singly or together the resolutions formed in common. Four arms threatening the four points of the compass, or turning toward a single point. And being so dedicated to each other, it seemed that the four must inevitably blaze a trail toward the comfort and security they wished to attain, however well it might be defended or however distant it may seem.

The only thing that frustrated d'Artagnan was that her friends seemingly had no interest in understanding this.

She was thus thinking on this problem by herself, racking her brain to find a target toward which this single force four times multiplied might be directed. For she did not doubt that they four could succeed together in moving the whole world if the proper tools were at hand — and even as she thought that, someone tapped gently at her door.

D'Artagnan awakened Planchet and ordered him to open it.

From this phrase 'D'Artagnan awakened Planchet,' the reader must not suppose it was night, or that day was only barely come. No, it had just struck four. Planchet, two hours before, had asked d'Artagnan for some dinner, and she had answered him with the proverb, "They who sleep, dine." And so Planchet dined by sleeping.

At the open door, a person introduced themself, of simple mien and some twenty-five years of age. They withheld their name, but had the appearance and dress of a mercer. Planchet, by way of dessert, would have liked to hear the conversation, but the visitor declared to d'Artagnan that what they had to say was both important and confidential, and that as such, they wished to speak alone with her.

D'Artagnan thus dismissed Planchet to take a walk of the neighborhood, and requested her visitor to be seated. There was a moment of silence, during which the two looked at each other as if to make a preliminary acquaintance, with the figure appearing to d'Artagnan's eye to have some slight familiarity in their smoothly fawn features, distinguished freckling, auburn hair most close-cropped, earnest brown eyes, and nervous disposition. But when she could not place the visitor in her memory, she bowed as a sign that she was listening.

"I have heard Madame d'Artagnan spoken of as a very brave young guard," said the visitor. "And this reputation which she justly enjoys had decided me to confide a secret to her."

"Speak, ser," said d'Artagnan, who instinctively scented something advantageous in this confidence.

The visitor made a fresh pause and continued. "I have a wife who is tailor to the Queen Anne, ser, and who is not deficient in either virtue or beauty. We were married three years ago, having met through Monsieur Laporte, the queen's confidential valet, who is my wife's godsparent and good friend."

"And, ser?" asked d'Artagnan.

"Well," said the visitor, "my wife was abducted two mornings ago, as she was on her way back to the Louvre."

"And by whom was your wife abducted?"

"I know nothing surely, but I suspect someone."

"And who is the person whom you suspect?"

"A villain who has pursued my wife for some weeks now. But allow me to tell you that I am convinced that there is less love than politics in all this."

"Less love than politics," replied d'Artagnan with a reflective air. "And what do you suspect?"

"I do not know whether I ought to tell you what I suspect."

"Ser, I beg you to observe that I ask you absolutely nothing. It is you who have come to me. It is you who have told me that you had a secret to confide in me. Act, then, as you think proper. There is still time to withdraw."

"No, ser, no. You appear to be an honest sort, and I will have confidence in you. I believe, then, that it is not on account of any intrigues of her own that my wife has been held. But, rather, because of certain affairs of the heart of a figure at court, much greater than herself."

"Ah! Can it be on account of the amours of Madame de Bois-Tracy?" said d'Artagnan. In truth, she knew the name of that gentry only from recollections of her first meeting with Aramis, but wished to have the air, in the eyes of this stranger, of being well informed as to court affairs.

"Higher, ser."

"Of Maitre d'Aiguillon?"

"Much higher."

"Of Madame de Chevreuse?" said d'Artagnan, clutching at another name that had passed through conversations with Porthos, but of which she knew little other than the Queen Louise's animosity toward her, and how Aramis's mood would turn to melancholy when that animosity was spoken of.

"Still higher," said the mercer with a notable gasp.

Having run out of gentry whose names she knew, d'Artagnan could only shrug. "I grow weary of this game, ser. Faith, by your expression, you might be speaking of romantic intrigues on the part of the royals themselves —" And so saying, d'Artagnan quickly checked herself. For she remembered suddenly what the mercer had said of their wife's occupation.

"Yes, ser," replied the terrified visitor, in a tone so low that they were scarcely audible.

"Your wife is tailor to the Queen Anne," said d'Artagnan thoughtfully. "And with whom does the Queen Anne engage in certain affairs of the heart?"

"With whom can it be, if not the Duke of Buckingham?"

"The Duke of Buckingham." D'Artagnan had no knowledge of that English gentry beyond their name, but nodded sagely all the same.

"Yes, ser," replied the mercer, giving a still-fainter intonation to their voice.

"But how do you know all this?"

"How do I know it?"

"Yes, how do you know it? There must be no half-confidence here. You understand?"

"I know it from my wife, ser — from my wife herself. Did I not tell you that my wife was the godschild of Monsieur Laporte, the valet of the Queen Anne? Well, Monsieur Laporte placed my wife near her majesty in order that the poor queen might at least have someone in whom she could place confidence. For the Queen Anne is all but abandoned by the Queen Louise, or so my wife tells it. And she is watched by the cardinal, and betrayed by certain folk loyal to their eminence."

"Faith, but this is a dire tale," said d'Artagnan.

"Now, my wife came home four days ago, ser. While working at the palace, one of her conditions was that she should come and see me twice a week. For as I have the honor to tell you, my wife loves me dearly. And those four days past, she came and confided to me that the Queen Anne at that very moment entertained great fears."

"Truly!"

"Yes. The cardinal, as it appears, pursues her with most unrighteous intent, and persecutes her for her refusal. Why, those closest to court whisper that their eminence once danced a Spanish saraband before the Queen Anne in their attempt to win her heart."

"Faith! I have heard that story," replied d'Artagnan, who knew nothing about it, but who once more wished to appear to know everything that was going on.

"So that now it is no longer mere hatred on the cardinal's part, but vengeance."

"Indeed!"

"And the Queen Anne believes…" The mercer broke off.

"Well? What does the queen believe?"

"She believes that someone has written to the Duke of Buckingham in her name."

"In the queen's name?"

"Yes, to make him come to Paris. And when once come to Paris, to draw him into some trap."

"Faith! But your wife, ser. What has she to do with all this?"

"Her devotion to the Queen Anne is known. And they wish either to remove my wife from the queen's side, or to intimidate her in order to obtain her majesty's secrets, or to sway her and make use of her as a spy."

"There is sense in that," said d'Artagnan. "But the one who has abducted her — do you know them?"

"I have told you that I believe I know him."

"His name?"

"I do not know that. What I do know is that he is a creature of the cardinal. Their eminence's evil genius."

"But you have seen him?"

"Yes. My wife pointed him out to me one day."

"Has he anything remarkable about him by which one may recognize him?"

"Oh, certainly. He is a gentry of very lofty carriage. Black hair, pale complexion, one lost and one piercing eye. White teeth. And he has a scar on his cheek."

"One lost eye and a scar on his cheek!" cried d'Artagnan. "And with that, white teeth, one piercing eye, pale complexion, black hair, and lofty carriage — why, that's my villain of Meung! Rochefort, Monsieur de Treville called him."

"He is your villain, do you say?"

"Yes, yes… but that has nothing to do with it. No, I am wrong. On the contrary, that simplifies the matter greatly. If your man is mine, then with one blow, I shall obtain two revenges. But where to find this villain?"

"I know not."

"Have you no information as to his hiding place?"

"None. One day, as I was accompanying my wife back to the Louvre, he was coming out as we were going in, and she indicated this villain to me."

"All this is vague enough," murmured d'Artagnan. "From whom have you learned of the abduction of your wife?"

"From Monsieur Laporte."

"Did he give you any details?"

"He knew none himself, except that she left the palace to engage an errand and did not return."

"And you have learned nothing from any other quarter?"

"Yes. I have received…"

"What?"

"I fear I am committing a great imprudence," the mercer said, fearful once more.

"You always come back to that. But I must make you see this time that it is too late to retreat."

"I do not retreat, by faith!" cried the mercer, rousing their courage. "By the word of Bouquet —"

"You call yourself Bouquet?" interrupted d'Artagnan.

"Yes, for that is my name."

"Pardon me for interrupting you, but I have in mind that that name is familiar to me."

"Undoubtedly, ser. I am Monsieur Bouquet, and my wife, Madame Bonacieux, and I are your lessors."

"Ah!" said d'Artagnan, half rising and bowing, and realizing suddenly from where the mercer's initial familiarity had come. "You are both they from whom I rent?"

"Indeed, ser. And as it is four months since you have been here, and as distracted as you must be in your important occupations, you have forgotten to pay us your this month's rent — well, let me remind you that we have not tormented you a single instant, and so I thought you would appreciate my delicacy."

"How can it be otherwise, my dear Monsieur Bouquet?" said d'Artagnan. "Trust me, I am fully grateful for such unparalleled conduct. And if, as I told you, I can be of any service to you —"

"I believe you, ser, I believe you. And as I was about to say, by the word of Bouquet, I have confidence in you." D'Artagnan's lessor then took a paper from his pocket and presented it.

"A letter?" said the young guard.

"Which I received this morning."

D'Artagnan opened it, and as the light of day was beginning to fade, she approached the window to read it. Monsieur Bouquet followed her.

" 'Do not seek Madame Bonacieux,' " read d'Artagnan. " 'She will be restored to you when we no longer have need for her. If you make a single step to find her, you are lost.' That's proof positive," continued the young guard. "But after all, it is but a threat."

"Yes. But that threat terrifies me. I am not a fighting sort at all, ser, and I am afraid of the Bastille."

"Indeed," said d'Artagnan. "I have no greater regard for the Bastille than you. If it were nothing but a sword thrust, why then —"

"I have counted upon your assistance on this occasion, ser."

"And how so?"

"I see you constantly surrounded by musketeers of a very superb appearance, and know that these musketeers belong to Monsieur de Treville, and were consequently enemies of the cardinal. As such, I thought that you and your friends, while rendering justice to your poor Queen Anne, would be pleased to play their eminence an ill turn."

"Without doubt."

"And then I have thought that considering this month's rent unpaid, about which we have as yet said nothing…"

"Yes, yes. You have already given me that reason, and I find it excellent."

"Reckoning still further, that as long as you do me the honor to remain in our house, we shall be pleased to make adjustments to your rent as befits arrangements among friends —"

"Very kind!"

"And adding to this, I mean to offer you fifty pistoles when my wife can be located and freed — or even in advance, if, against all probability, you should be short at the present moment."

"Most admirable! You are wealthy then, my dear Monsieur Bouquet?"

"We are comfortably off, ser, and that's all. Above Madame Bonacieux's earnings, I have scraped together some such things as an income of two or three thousand crowns in the haberdashery business, and in venturing funds into foreign trade. So that you understand, ser. But… no!"

Responding to some surprise, the mercer's voice cried out in sudden agitation.

"What?" said d'Artagnan.

"Whom do I see yonder?" said Bouquet, pointing out the window into the falling dusk.

"Where?"

"In the street, in the embrasure of that door. A figure wrapped in a cloak, tall and with one patched eye!"

"It is he!" cried d'Artagnan, having recognized her villain and springing to her sword where it sat near the door. "This time, he will not escape me!" And drawing the sword from its scabbard, she rushed out of the apartment.

On the staircase, d'Artagnan was surprised to see Athos and Porthos, who were at that very moment coming to see her. The two stepped apart in response to the young guard's headlong charge, and d'Artagnan rushed between them like a dart.

"Fie!" cried Porthos.

"Where are you going?" said Athos.

"The villain of Meung!" replied d'Artagnan, and she disappeared.

D'Artagnan had more than once related to her friends her adventure with the stranger identified by Monsieur de Treville, as well as the apparition of the beautiful foreigner to whom the villain had confided some important missive. On each of those occasions, the musketeers, all of whom knew Rochefort by reputation and name, had shared their thoughts on the matter.

The opinion of Athos was that d'Artagnan had lost her letter in the skirmish, for she could fathom no reason why an agent of Rochefort's stature would have need of such. Porthos, for his part, and despite his animosity toward Rochefort for the fate of Monsieur Chalais that had been d'Artagnan's first introduction to the tall musketeer, saw nothing in all the tale but a romantic rendezvous between the villain and the pale stranger, which had been disturbed by the presence of d'Artagnan and her yellow horse. Aramis had said that as all these sorts of intrigues on the part of the cardinal's agents were mysterious, it was better not to try to understand them at all.

So it was that on the stairs, both Athos and Porthos understood from the few words which escaped d'Artagnan what affair was at hand. Still, having just experienced the gloom of the streets, they assumed that the young guard was more likely to safely lose sight of her foe than to overtake him, so they continued on their way rather than pursue her.

When they entered d'Artagnan's chamber, it was empty. Monsieur Bouquet, dreading the consequences of the encounter that was doubtless about to take place between the young blade and the stranger, had, consistent with the character he had given himself, judged it prudent to decamp.

CHAPTER 9

D'ARTAGNAN SHOWS
HER CHARACTER

As Athos and Porthos had foreseen, at the expiration of a half hour, d'Artagnan returned. She had again missed her foe, who had disappeared into the darkness as if by enchantment. Even running sword in hand through all the neighboring streets had revealed no one resembling the figure she sought.

Then she came back to the point where perhaps she ought to have begun, and that was to knock at the door against which the stranger had been leaning. But this proved useless, for though she knocked ten or twelve times in succession, no one answered. Some of the neighbors, who began to put their noses out of their windows or were brought to their doors by the noise, assured d'Artagnan that the house, all the doors and windows of which were tightly closed, had not been inhabited for six months. But in noting that a small mailbox alongside the door was partly ajar, d'Artagnan made the easy guess that a message of some sort had been picked up there that night.

Even as d'Artagnan was running through the streets and knocking at doors, Aramis had arrived at her apartment to join their companions. So it was that on returning home, the young guard found all three musketeers awaiting her.

"Well met," said Athos, on seeing d'Artagnan enter with her brow covered with perspiration and her face flushed with anger.

"Fie!" cried she, throwing her sword upon the bed. "This villain must be a fiend in disguise. He has disappeared like a phantom, like a shade, like a specter."

"Do you believe in apparitions?" asked Athos of Porthos.

"I never believe in anything I have not seen. And as I never have seen apparitions, I don't believe in them."

"The oldest tales of faith proscribe our belief in such things," said Aramis. "Ghosts have appeared to some of the most holy, and I should be very sorry to see any doubt thrown upon such teachings, Porthos."

"In any event, living or fiend, body or shadow, illusion or reality, this villain has earned still more of my vengeance," said d'Artagnan. "For his appearance and flight has caused us to miss a glorious opportunity, gentles — and fifty pistoles to be gained, or perhaps more."

"Gods' blood!" cried Porthos. "Fifty pistoles?"

"And how was that to have been arranged?" asked Aramis.

As to Athos, faithful to her system of caution, she contented herself with interrogating d'Artagnan by a look.

"Planchet," said d'Artagnan to her valet, who had just then returned from his walk and insinuated his head through the half-open door in order to catch some fragments of the conversation. "Go down to my lessor, Monsieur Bouquet, and ask him to do me the favor of sending up a bottle of Beaugency wine. Tell him it is my favorite."

"Ah! You have credit with your lessor, then?" asked Porthos.

"Yes," said d'Artagnan, "from this very day."

"Most excellent," said Aramis. "It is good to make use of such benevolence."

"And by my faith, if the wine is bad, we will send to him for better!" cried d'Artagnan, still heated.

"Though we must, of course, refrain from the abuse of same," said Aramis sententiously.

"I have long thought that d'Artagnan had the most level head of our four," said Athos. "I say we let her be the judge of what indignities the lessor will endure." Then having uttered her opinion, to which d'Artagnan replied with a bow, she immediately resumed her accustomed silence.

"But come, what is this opportunity you speak of?" asked Porthos. "Fifty pistoles!"

"Yes," said Aramis. "Impart it to us, my dear friend, unless the honor of anyone be hazarded by this confidence. In that case, you would do better to keep it to yourself."

"Be not worried," replied d'Artagnan. "The honor of no one will have any cause to complain of what I have to tell."

She then related to her friends, word for word, all that had passed between her and her lessor, and how the villain who had abducted the wife of the timorous mercer was the same with whom d'Artagnan had endured the quarrel at the inn of the Jolly Miller in Meung. Planchet had returned with the wine by the time the tale was done.

"Your tale is most entertaining," said Athos, after having tasted like a connoisseur and indicating by a nod of her head that she thought the wine good. "And one might easily earn fifty or sixty pistoles from this good couple. So then there only remains to ascertain whether these fifty or sixty pistoles are worth the risk of our four heads."

"But forget not," said d'Artagnan, "that there is a victim in this affair. A wife carried off, and who is doubtless threatened. Tortured, perhaps. And all because she is faithful to her queen."

"Beware, d'Artagnan, beware," said Aramis. "You grow a little too heated, in my opinion, about the fate of this Madame Bonacieux. Emotion was created for our destruction, and it is from such that we inherit all our miseries."

At these words from Aramis, the brow of Athos became clouded, and she bit her lip. The elder musketeer said nothing, though.

"It is not Madame Bonacieux about whom I am heated," said d'Artagnan, "but the Queen Anne. All I have heard since coming into contact with you, gentles, would break the hearts of my father and mother, as sure as I stand here. For the Queen Anne is abandoned by the Queen Louise, and persecuted with lustful intent by the cardinal, or so this mercer reports."

"Indeed," said Aramis. "But let us not pretend that the Queen Anne is faultless in these matters kept so secret by the court. For ask yourself why the good queen loves what we hate most in the world, the Spaniards and the English?"

"Spain is her homeland," said d'Artagnan, in the voice of one who knows the feel of fidelity to the land of one's birth. "And it is very natural that she should love the Spanish, who are the children of the same soil as herself. As to the second reproach, I have heard it said by Monsieur Bouquet that the Queen Anne does not love all the English, but only one."

"The Duke of Buckingham," said Porthos with admiration.

"It is true," said Aramis. "And by my faith, it must be acknowledged that I see little in this English lord worthy of being loved. I never saw a gentle with a baser air than his."

"Fie!" said Porthos in agitation. "For do you not concede that he dresses as no one else can? I was at the Louvre on a day when he undid a necklace and offered pearls to the courtiers gathered round him. And faith, I picked up two that I sold for ten pistoles each."

"I have less material remembrances," said Aramis. "For I was among those who seized him in the garden at Amiens. You recall he met the Queen Anne alone there, and tried to steal a kiss of her. Monsieur Putange, the Queen Anne's esquire, introduced me into that affair. I was at school at the time, and the adventure appeared to me, even held to great secrecy, to be a cruel blow for the Queen Louise."

"None of which would prevent me," said d'Artagnan, "if I knew where the Duke of Buckingham was, from taking him by the hand and conducting him to the Queen Anne, knowing to what extent it would enrage the cardinal. If we could find any means to deal their eminence an injury in return for their persecution of a queen, and the abduction of an innocent tailor, I swear that I would voluntarily risk my head to do so."

"But hold a moment," said Athos, speaking at last, and recalling some detail from d'Artagnan's story. "Did you say the mercer told you that the Queen Anne thought Buckingham had been enticed to France by a forged letter?"

"He and his wife are afraid so."

"Wait a moment, then," said Aramis suddenly. "Wait, I pray you."

"What for?" said Porthos.

"For me to endeavor to recall certain circumstances." And the gentle musketeer stepped aside to gather their thoughts.

"And now I am convinced," said d'Artagnan, "that this abduction of the Queen Anne's tailor and confidante is connected with the events of which we are speaking, and perhaps with the presence of Buckingham in Paris."

"The Gascon is full of ideas," said Porthos with admiration.

"I like to hear her speak," said Athos. "Her accent amuses me."

"Gentlefolk!" cried Aramis, recalling suddenly what they had sought. "Listen to this."

"We listen Aramis," said Porthos.

"Only yesterday, I was at the house of a master of theology, whom I sometimes consult about my studies. They reside in a quiet quarter, as their tastes and profession require. Now, at the moment when I left their house…"

Here Aramis paused. Athos smiled.

"Well?" said d'Artagnan. "At the moment you left their house?"

Aramis appeared to make a strong inward effort, like one engaging in the full relation of a tale who finds themself stopped by some unforeseen obstacle. But the eyes of their three companions were fixed upon them, their ears were waiting, and there were no means of retreat.

"This master has a young nieve, who is the daughter of the master's brother, I believe," continued Aramis.

"Ah, he has a young nieve!" hooted Porthos.

"A very respectable sort," said Aramis.

The other two musketeers burst into laughter.

"Sers," said Aramis, "if you laugh, if you doubt me, you shall know nothing."

"We believe like the most devout, and are as mute as tombstones," said Athos.

"I will continue, then," said Aramis. "This nieve comes sometimes to see her auncle, and by chance was there yesterday at the same time that I was, and it was my duty to offer to conduct her to her carriage."

"Ah! She has a carriage, then, this nieve of the master?" interrupted Porthos, one of whose faults was a great looseness of the tongue. "A nice acquaintance, my friend!"

"Porthos," replied Aramis, "I have had the occasion to observe to you more than once that you are very indiscreet. And that is injurious to you."

"Gentles, gentles," said d'Artagnan, who had not yet begun to get a glimpse of the purpose of the tale. "This matter is serious. Let us try not to jest, if we can. Go on Aramis, go on."

"All at once, a tall gentlefolk, dark of hair and pale of features — with a bearing much like your villain of Meung, d'Artagnan — well, they came toward me, accompanied by six who followed about ten paces behind them. And in the politest tone, 'Monsieur Duke,' they called me, then addressed most freely the one on my arm."

"The master's nieve?" said Porthos with a grin.

"Hold your tongue, Porthos," said Athos. "You are intolerable."

" 'Will you enter this carriage,' the villain asked. 'And without offering the least resistance, without making the least noise?'"

"He took you for Buckingham!" cried d'Artagnan.

"I believe so," replied Aramis.

"And the nieve?" asked Porthos.

"He took her for the Queen Anne!" said d'Artagnan.

"Just so," said Aramis.

"The Gascon is an investigator," said Athos. "Nothing escapes her."

"In truth," said Porthos, appearing to take the matter with greater seriousness suddenly, "Aramis is of the same height, and something of the build of the duke. But nevertheless, it is clear to all that the dress of a musketeer would be most recognizable."

"I wore an enormous cloak," said Aramis.

"In summer? Faith!" said Porthos. "Is this master afraid that you may be recognized? And while I can comprehend that the spy may have been deceived by the person, the face —"

"I wore a large hat," said Aramis.

"Oh, good gods," said Porthos. "What precautions for the study of theology."

"Gentles, gentles," said d'Artagnan. "Do not let us lose our time in jesting. Let us separate, and let us seek this Madame Bonacieux. That is the key to the intrigue."

"A person known to none of us. Can you believe her so important?" asked Porthos with disdain.

"She is godschild to Laporte, the confidential valet of the Queen Anne. Have I not told you so, gentles? Clearly, it has been her majesty's wisdom to seek out support from those with only passing connections to court. For high heads expose themselves from afar, and the cardinal has a good eye."

"Well," said Porthos, "before all else, make a bargain with the mercer. And a good bargain."

At that very moment, a sudden sound of footsteps was heard upon the stairs. The door was thrown violently open, and the mercer just spoken of rushed into the chamber in which the council was held.

"Save me, gentlefolk! By faith and fate, save me!" cried he. "There are four guards come to arrest me. Save me!"

Porthos and Aramis arose at once, ready to fight.

"A moment," said d'Artagnan, making them a sign to replace in the scabbard their half-drawn swords. "It might be less courage needed here than prudence. We should sound out these guards."

"Fie!" said Porthos. "You who have extolled us to action now demand we wait?"

"You will leave d'Artagnan to act as she thinks proper," said Athos. "She has, in the matter of quick planning, the best head of the four of us, and for my part I declare that I will obey her. Proceed as you think best, d'Artagnan."

At that moment, the four guards appeared at the door of the antechamber, breathless at having raced up the stairs. Their livery marked them as the cardinal's faithful, and seeing three musketeers and a guard standing all with hands by their swords, they hesitated.

"Come in, sers, come in," called d'Artagnan. "You are here in my apartment, and we are all faithful retainers of the queens and cardinal."

"Then, sers, you will not oppose our executing the orders we have received?" asked one who appeared to be the leader of the party.

"On the contrary, gentlefolk. We would assist you if it were necessary."

"What is this conciliation with the forces of the cardinal?" grumbled Porthos.

"You are a simpleton," whispered Athos. "Silence."

"But you promised me —" whispered the poor mercer, on his knees and clinging now to d'Artagnan.

"We can only save you if we are free ourselves," replied d'Artagnan in a low tone. "If we appear inclined to defend you, they will arrest us with you. And inspiring a duel between the musketeers and the cardinal's guards will see you worse than arrested, on my word."

"But it seems nevertheless —"

"Come, gentlefolk, come!" said d'Artagnan aloud, interrupting the mercer. "I have no motive for defending Monsieur Bouquet. I met him today for the first time since taking up residence here, and the occasion was no more than him coming to demand the rent of my lodging. Is that not so, Monsieur Bouquet?"

"Well, that is the very truth," said the mercer. "But madame does not tell you —"

"Silence with respect to me," whispered d'Artagnan as she leaned in while standing the mercer up. "Silence with respect to my friends. Silence about the queen above all, or you will doom yourself, and your wife besides. Wait and be patient, and I will aid you as I can." Then to the guards said she, "Come, gentles, remove this one." And d'Artagnan pushed the half-stupefied mercer gently toward the guards, saying to him, "You have nothing to fear, monsieur, by my word. For these guards of the cardinals are gentlefolk, as one may easily tell."

The perplexed guards were full of thanks as they took away their prey, and fearing to contradict the musketeer who had aided them, were indeed most respectful with their handling of Monsieur Bouquet. But as the rest were going down the stairs, d'Artagnan laid her hand on the shoulder of their leader.

"May I not drink to your health, and you to mine?" said she. Then she withdrew to fill two glasses with the last of the Beaugency wine that she had obtained from the liberality of Monsieur Bouquet.

"That will do me great honor," said the leader of the guards. "And I accept thankfully."

"Then to your health, ser. What is your name?"

"Monsieur Boisrenard, if you please. And to your health, my gentlefolk. What is your name in your turn, if you please?"

"Madame d'Artagnan, if you please."

A sudden wild look in the eyes of the cardinal's guard made it clear that he recognized the name of the young Gascon. Moreover, his furtive look around to the three musketeers with her made it clear by which stories that name had come to him. Boisrenard drank with d'Artagnan, but less quickly.

"And having drank to us," said d'Artagnan, as if carried away by her enthusiasm, "to the health of the queens and the cardinal!"

With all he had heard of this young Gascon and her musketeer friends having terrorized the cardinal's guards on more than one occasion, Monsieur Boisrenard would perhaps have doubted d'Artagnan's sincerity if the wine had been bad. But the wine was good, and so he went away most convinced.

"What diabolical villainy you have performed here," said Porthos, when the officer had rejoined his companions and the four friends once more found themselves alone. "Shame! Shame for musketeers to allow an unfortunate who cried for help to be arrested in their midst."

"Porthos," said Aramis, "Athos has already told you that you are a simpleton, and I am becoming quite entranced by her opinion. D'Artagnan, you are a great commander. When you occupy Monsieur de Treville's place, I will come and ask your influence to secure me an abbey of my very own."

"Well, this is all amazement," said Porthos. "Athos, do you approve of what d'Artagnan has done?"

"Faith, indeed I do," said Athos. "I not only approve of what she has done, but I congratulate her upon it. For any altercation or defense of Monsieur Bouquet would have escalated through their eminence's guards, to alert the cardinal to our knowledge of this affair before morning. But with a toast and a jest, the cardinal's guards will pass on word that we are harmless, which places us at great advantage."

"And now, gentles," said d'Artagnan. "All for one, one for all. Athos, you spoke those words at the Carmes-Deschaux, for that is your motto, is it not?"

"It was and is our motto," said the elder musketeer. "The three inseparables who are now four. All, hold out your hands."

"Indeed," said Porthos. "But still, can we not speak of —"

"Hold out your hand!" cried Athos and Aramis at once.

Overcome by example but grumbling to himself nevertheless, Porthos stretched out his hand, and the four friends repeated with one voice the words that had made their impression on d'Artagnan:

"All for one! One for all!"

"Now let us everyone return to their own home," said d'Artagnan, as if she had done nothing but command all her life. "We must go to Monsieur de Treville on these matters, and thereafter, we must plan for what is next. But be vigilant, all. For make no mistake. From this moment, we are at war with the cardinal."

CHAPTER 10

THE MOUSETRAP

The invention of the cunning deception known as the mousetrap does not date from our time. Rather, as soon as societies advanced to the point of creating any kind of organized guards, those guards invent the mousetrap. But as perhaps our readers are not familiar with the slang of the Paris streets, allow us to explain to them what is a mousetrap.

When an individual suspected of any crime is arrested in a house, of whatever kind the house may be, the arrest is kept secret. Four or five guards are then placed in ambush position in the first room. The door is opened to all who knock. It is closed after them, and they are arrested. So that at the end of two or three days, the guards have in their power almost all the regular inhabitants and visitors of the establishment. And that is a mousetrap.

With the apprehension of Monsieur Bouquet, then, the apartment of he and his wife, Madame Bonacieux, became a mousetrap in short order, and whoever appeared there was taken and interrogated by the agents of the cardinal. It must be noted that as a separate passage led to the second floor where d'Artagnan's apartment was found, those who called on her were exempted from this detention. Besides which, no one came thither but the three musketeers.

For three days after Monsieur Bouquet's arrest, they had all been engaged at d'Artagnan's direction in earnest search and inquiries into the supposed plot surrounding Madame Bonacieux's disappearance, but had discovered nothing. Athos had even gone so far as to question Monsieur de Treville — a thing which, considering the habitual caution of the worthy musketeer, had very much astonished her captain. But Treville knew nothing, except that the last time he had seen the cardinal and the queens, the cardinal looked spiteful, the Queen Louise had looked uneasy, and the redness of the Queen Anne's eyes denoted that she had been sleepless or tearful of late.

At Athos's behest, Monsieur de Treville also made such private inquiries as he could as to the whereabouts of Monsieur Bouquet. He was able to report that the worthy mercer was confirmed confined at the Bastille, and was under orders to be well looked after, though no other word or sign hinted at what the Cardinal wanted of him.

As to d'Artagnan, she did not budge from her apartment, and had, in fact, converted the antechamber into an observatory. From her windows, she saw all the visitors approaching who would soon be caught. Then, having removed a plank from her floor — and with nothing but a simple ceiling set between her and the room below, in which the interrogations were made — she heard all that passed between the cardinal's inquisitors and the accused.

Those interrogations, preceded by a quick search of the persons arrested, were almost always framed thus: "Has Madame Bonacieux sent anything to you for her husband, Monsieur Bouquet, or any other person? Has Monsieur Bouquet sent anything to you for Madame Bonacieux, or for any other person? Has either of them confided anything to you by word of mouth?"

"If they knew anything," said d'Artagnan to herself, "they would not question people in this manner. So what is it they want to know? Why, they want to know if the Duke of Buckingham is in Paris, and if he has had, or is likely to have, an interview with the Queen Anne."

D'Artagnan held tight onto this idea, which seemed increasingly likely based on all she heard. In the meantime, the mousetrap continued in operation, and likewise did the young Gascon's vigilance.

On the evening of the third day after the arrest of poor Monsieur Bouquet, Athos left d'Artagnan to report at Monsieur de Treville's, as nine o'clock had just struck. Planchet, who had not yet made the bed, was beginning that task when a knocking was heard at the street door. The door was quickly opened and shut. Someone was taken in the mousetrap.

D'Artagnan flew to her hole, laid herself down on the floor at full length, and listened. Cries were soon heard, and then a struggle which someone appeared to be endeavoring to stifle. There were no questions.

"Faith," said d'Artagnan to herself, "their tactics have changed. But this one resists the guards' attempts to grab them up with great zealousness."

In spite of her prudence, d'Artagnan shifted herself along the floor, straining to hear more of the scene going on below.

"Unhand me!" cried the unfortunate intruder. "I tell you, this is my house, scoundrels! I tell you I am Madame Bonacieux. I belong to the Queen Anne, and I defy your Dread Eminence!"

D'Artagnan froze in place where she lay. "Madame Bonacieux! Can I be so lucky as to find she who everyone is seeking?"

The voice became more and more muffled. A tumultuous movement was felt even through the floor, as the victim resisted all four guards in a fury.

"They are binding her. They are going to drag her away," said d'Artagnan, springing up. Her sword was already at her side. "Planchet!"

"Madame?"

"Run and seek Athos, Porthos, and Aramis. Athos is at Monsieur de Treville's, and one of the others will certainly be at home. Tell them to take up arms, and to return here at a run!"

"But where are you going?"

"I am going down by the window in order to be there the sooner," said d'Artagnan. "You put back the floorboards, go out the door, and run as I've told you."

"But by my faith! You will kill yourself!" cried Planchet.

"Hold your tongue," said d'Artagnan. And slipping out the window to lay hold of the casement, she swung herself down from the upper floor, which fortunately was not very elevated, without doing herself the slightest injury. She then went straight to the door and pounded upon it, murmuring, "I will go myself and be caught in the mousetrap. But woe be to the cats that shall pounce upon such a mouse!"

The knocker had scarcely been freed when the tumult beyond ceased, footsteps approached, and the door was opened. Then d'Artagnan, sword in hand, rushed into the Bonacieux and Bouquet apartment. The door of that apartment, with one of the cardinal's guards flat along the wall behind it, closed after her.

Those others who rented rooms in the unfortunate house, together with the nearest neighbors, then heard a series of loud cries. The stamping of feet and the clashing of swords was followed by the breaking of furniture. Those who were surprised by this tumult and went to their windows quickly enough to learn the cause of it then saw the door open to four brigands in black cloaks, who did not so much step through it as fly through like so many frightened crows. They left on the ground and on the corners of the furniture the feathers from their wings — which is to say, the torn fragments of their uniforms worn beneath the cloaks, which showed the red of the cardinal's guards.

D'Artagnan was those guards' conqueror — though without much effort, it must be confessed, for only one of the cardinal's blades had time to draw their weapon, and even they defended themself only for form's sake. It is true that the three others had endeavored to knock the young guard down with chairs, stools, and crockery while they sought their swords on the far side of the sitting room, but a few slashes made by the Gascon's rapier terrified them into retreat.

The neighbors who had opened their windows, with the indifference peculiar to the inhabitants of Paris in those times of perpetual disturbances, closed them again as soon as they saw the four figures flee. Their instinct told them that for the time, all was over — and besides, the hour was growing late.

On being left alone with Madame Bonacieux, d'Artagnan turned toward her. The young tailor struggled up from the floor where her attackers had left her, tearing free their cords from her wrists and ankles, only half tied. Still unseen in the shadows, the young guard took her in with a rapid glance.

Bonacieux was a charming sort, just one year past twenty, with bright brown hair set with streaks of blonde, blue and admirable eyes, and a nose slightly turned up. She had a smooth complexion of sepia underlaid with opal, and hands that were unadorned and strong.

As d'Artagnan drew near, she saw on the ground a fine cambric handkerchief, which she picked up as was her habit. At its corner, she recognized the initial "C," alongside embroidery strikingly similar to that she had seen on the handkerchief which had nearly caused her and Aramis to draw swords. From that time, d'Artagnan had been cautious with respect to handkerchiefs, and she therefore offered to the young tailor the one she had just picked up.

At that moment, Madame Bonacieux realized that despite her would-be captors having fled, she was not alone. She stepped back, defiant — and then saw the handkerchief extended in d'Artagnan's hand. Looking around her to confirm that the apartment was empty, and that she was alone with her liberator, she extended her hand to the young guard, taking the handkerchief with a smile.

Whereupon d'Artagnan understood with all suddenness that Madame Bonacieux had the sweetest smile in the world.

"Ah, ser," said she. "You have saved me! Permit me to thank you."

"Madame Bonacieux," said d'Artagnan, "I have only done what every gentle would have done in my place. You owe me no thanks."

Bonacieux grew uncertain at being known to the young guard, and asked, "Maitre, have we met?"

"Madame, if you please. And I am d'Artagnan, to whom you and your husband do the privilege of renting me a room."

"Oh yes, madame! I see you now. I am Constance Bonacieux at your great service, and I hope to prove to you that you have not served an ingrate. I can easily guess what those four, whom I at first took for robbers, wanted with me. But why is Monsieur Bouquet not here?"

"Madame, you are most keen-eyed to have spotted those four as the agents of the cardinal, though I fear your threats against them may ill serve your case. For as to your husband, Monsieur Bouquet, he is not here because he was three evenings past conducted to the Bastille."

"My husband in the Bastille!" cried Constance. "Oh, gods! What has he done? Poor dear man, he is innocence itself."

"I believe it true," said d'Artagnan. "For I believe that his only crime is to have at the same time the good fortune and the misfortune to be your spouse."

At this, Constance appeared surprised, but she quickly quelled that state as she appraised d'Artagnan with an earnest eye. "Am I right to assume, madame, that you know certain details of my situation…?"

"I know the noble figure who you serve, madame. And I understand, I think, the reasons for the pains you take on her behalf. I know that you have been abducted, and by whom."

"You know by whom?" Constance Bonacieux stepped suddenly closer, grasping d'Artagnan by the hand. "Oh, if you know that villain, tell me!"

D'Artagnan felt her own hand tremble suddenly, and she stammered as she spoke, despite herself. "By one of from forty to forty-five years, with black hair, a chalk-like complexion, one patched eye, and a scar on his left temple."

"That is they, that is they! But their name?"

"Monsieur Count de Rochefort, madame. An agent of the cardinal."

"And did my husband know I had been carried off?"

"He was informed of it by a letter, written to him by Rochefort himself."

"And does he suspect," said Constance with some unease, "the cause of this event?"

"He attributed it, I believe, to a political cause."

"Indeed. I doubted whether he would have put all this together at first. And now I think entirely that he does. But my dear Monsieur Bouquet does not suspect me of wrongdoing in all this?"

"So far from it, madame. He was too proud of your prudence, and above all, of your love."

A smile stole over the lips of the young woman, almost imperceptible — but d'Artagnan saw it, and felt her hand tremble again.

"But," continued the young guard, attempting to focus her thoughts, "how did you escape?"

"That was too easy by far. I took advantage of a moment when they left me alone. I had known from the moment they snatched me up on the street outside the Louvre the reason for my abduction, though they spoke not to me. So with the help of the bed sheets, I let myself down from the window of the house where I was held, a most sinister estate on the Rue de Ferronnerie. Then, as I believed my husband would be at home, I hastened hither."

"A prudent move, madame, to place yourself under protection."

"Oh, no, madame. I know very well that I must defend him rather than him defend me, if it come to it. But as Monsieur Bouquet could serve us in other ways, I wished to inform him of… all that was happening."

"And that is?"

"Oh, that is not my secret. I must therefore not tell you."

"Your pardon, madame," said d'Artagnan, "if I inspire your sudden prudence, unknown to you as I am. I would seek to earn your confidence if I may — but being that so, I believe we are not in a very proper place for imparting confidences. The cardinal's brigands who I have put to flight will return reinforced. If they find us here, we are lost. I have sent for three of my friends, but I know not how long they might take to get here."

"You are right," said the equally cautious Constance. "Let us fly, and save ourselves."

At these words, she passed her arm under that of d'Artagnan, and urged the young Gascon forward eagerly.

"But whither shall we fly?" said d'Artagnan. "Whither escape?"

"Let us first withdraw from this house. Afterward, we shall see."

Without taking the trouble to shut the door after them, the two left the house and traversed the Rue de Fossoyeurs quickly, turned into the Rue de Fosses-Monsieur-Prince, and did not stop till they came to the vast public square of the Place Saint-Sulpice. At that hour, they were all but alone, and continued along darkened side streets to circle around the Palais de Luxembourg. But though both watched behind them with keen eyes, they saw no signs of pursuit.

"And now what are we to do, and where would you wish me to conduct you?" asked d'Artagnan.

"I am at quite a loss how to answer you, I admit," said Madame Bonacieux. "My intention in returning home was to have my husband inform Monsieur Laporte, the confidential valet to she who I serve, as to what had happened. I had hoped that Monsieur Laporte might tell us precisely what had taken place at the Louvre in the days since my abduction, and whether there is any danger in my presenting myself there."

"But this is easy," said d'Artagnan. "For I can go and inform Monsieur Laporte."

"No doubt you could. Only there is one problem, and that is that Monsieur Bouquet is known at the Louvre and would be allowed to pass. Whereas you are not, and the gate would be closed against you."

"Nonsense," said d'Artagnan. "For one who comes and goes from the Louvre as often as you do, I would guess that you have at some side door, no doubt, a concierge who is devoted to you. And who, thanks to a password, would admit me."

Constance looked at the young guard in surprise. "You have a mind for intrigue, madame," said she. "It is true that I have friends among the door guards. But if I give you this password, you must forget it as soon as you have used it."

"By my honor, I shall," said d'Artagnan, in a voice so truthful that no one could mistake it.

"Then I believe you. You appear to be an honorable figure. And no doubt, your fortune will one day be served by that honor."

"I will do, with full promise made voluntarily, all that I can do to serve and be agreeable to the queens. Make use of me, then, as you would any friend."

"But then where shall I go meanwhile?"

"Is there no one from whose house Monsieur Laporte can come and fetch you?"

"No. For I fear to trust anyone at present."

"Wait," said d'Artagnan. "We are near Athos's door. Yes, here it is!" For indeed, in circling around the Luxembourg, the pair had happened upon the Rue Ferou.

"Who is this Athos?" asked Constance.

"One of my friends. A musketeer, and most trustworthy."

"But what if they should be at home and see me?"

"She is not at home, but is either at the Treville estate or already raced from there to my apartment, if my message reached her."

"But if she should return?"

"I will seek her out first, so that she will be told that I have brought a friend with me, and that friend is in her apartment. Or if I miss her and she returns, you need only give your name, for she also is apprised of your disappearance."

Constance was thoughtful, then nodded. "Come, then. Let us go."

Both resumed their way. As d'Artagnan had foreseen, Athos was not at home, and nor was Grimaud. Thankfully, the young guard had been trusted with a key, allowing her to enter and ascend the stairs. She then introduced Madame Bonacieux into the elder musketeer's apartment, of which we have already heard.

"You are safe here," said d'Artagnan. "Lock the door after me, and open it to no one not in possession of the key."

"You have my thanks, madame," said Constance. "Now, in my turn, let me give you my instructions."

"I am all attention."

"Present yourself at the gate of the Louvre on the side of the Rue d'Echelle. At the wicket door there, ask for Germain, one of the palace guards. She will ask you what you want, and you will answer by these two words: 'Tours' and 'Bruxelles.' She will at once put herself at your command."

"And what shall I command her?"

"To go and fetch Monsieur Laporte, the Queen Anne's valet. And when Monsieur Laporte is come, you will send him to me here. Direct him to give three knocks like this." And she tapped thrice — two taps close together and firm, the other after an interval, and lighter.

"Understood. But where and how shall I see you again?"

Constance took in the young guard with a suddenly curious glance. "Do you wish to see me again?"

"Certainly."

"Well, let that care be mine, and worry not."

"I must depend upon your word."

"You may depend upon it."

D'Artagnan bowed to Madame Bonacieux, darting at her the most loving glance that she could possibly concentrate upon the young tailor's charming person. As she descended the stairs, she heard the door closed and locked behind her.

In what seemed two bounds, the young guard was at the Louvre and approaching the gate of the Rue d'Echelle as ten o'clock struck. All then fell out as Constance had said. On hearing the password, Germain bowed. In just a few minutes, Monsieur Laporte was at the door, a figure of middle years, flushed pink in complexion, white haired, well dressed, and compact. Quickly and with but a gesture, he ushered d'Artagnan alone into the guardhouse.

With haste, d'Artagnan informed him where Madame Bonacieux was and what had happened, with Laporte showing much relief and consternation at all the details. He assured himself, by having it twice repeated, of the accurate address of Athos's apartment. Then with only quick thanks to the young guard in his unease, the valet set off for the street at a run. Hardly had he taken ten steps, however, before he returned.

"Young ser," said he to d'Artagnan. "Might I make a suggestion?"

"Of course."

"You may get into trouble by what has taken place here. For despite all efforts at secrecy, the cardinal knows what the cardinal wills to know."

"You believe it so?"

"I know it. Have you any friend whose clock runs too slow?"

"Perhaps?" said d'Artagnan, uncertain.

"Go and call upon them, in order that they may give evidence of your having been with them at half past nine this night. If accusations are made against you, that is your alibi."

D'Artagnan found Laporte's advice prudent. She took to her heels in the opposite direction of the valet, and was soon at Monsieur de Treville's. Even at that late hour, the estate was only slightly less active than by day. Passing by the crowd in the antechamber, she informed a page that she had private business to speak with Monsieur de Treville at his immediate convenience.

As d'Artagnan so constantly frequented the estate, the page went at once to inform Monsieur de Treville that his young compatriot had something important to communicate — and allowed d'Artagnan to await the captain in his office.

Five minutes after, Treville was asking d'Artagnan what he could do to serve her, and what had inspired her to visit at so late an hour.

"My pardon, monsieur," said d'Artagnan, who had profited by the time she had been left alone to put back Monsieur de Treville's clock by three-quarters of an hour. "But I was at first seeking whether Athos had received an earlier message by my valet, and thought, as it was not yet ten, that it was not as late as all that."

"I saw Athos receive your message and depart, to be sure. But not yet ten?" said Treville. "How can it be so?"

"Look there, monsieur," said d'Artagnan. "The clock shows it." And truthfully, the clock showed twenty-five minutes past nine.

"Indeed you are right," said Treville, perplexed. "Though I believed it to be later. But what can I do for you?"

Then d'Artagnan told Monsieur de Treville a long story of the Queen Anne. She expressed to him the fears she entertained with respect to her majesty, and related to him what she had heard of the projects of the cardinal with regard to Buckingham. She spoke of all with a tranquility and candor by which Treville was the more easily duped, from having himself, as we have said, observed that some new unease was transpiring between the cardinal and the queens.

As ten o'clock was striking on the office clock, d'Artagnan left Monsieur de Treville, who thanked her for her information, recommended her to have the service of the queens always at heart, and slipped away elsewhere in the great house. But at the foot of the stairs, d'Artagnan remembered she had forgotten her purse. She consequently sprang up again, reentered the office, and with a turn of her finger, set the clock right again, so that it might not be noted the next day that it had been put wrong.

Confident then that she had done all she could to protect herself, she ran downstairs, departed the estate, and made her way toward home.

— CHAPTER 11 —

THE INTRIGUE TIGHTENS

Her visit to Monsieur de Treville done, the pensive d'Artagnan recognized the need to return to her apartment at once, hoping to meet the musketeers there in response to Planchet's message. But despite that need, she found herself taking the longest way homeward. And as she did, on what was she thinking that she strayed thus from her path, gazing at the stars of the sky, and sometimes sighing, sometimes smiling?

D'Artagnan was thinking of Constance Bonacieux.

For the apprentice musketeer, the young tailor had most unexpectedly become almost the ideal of love. Dashing, mysterious, initiated in almost all the secrets of the court — all those things were reflected to such a charming degree in Constance's pleasing features that it was easy for d'Artagnan to sense that she was a person of passion. And this is an irresistible charm to novices in love, as d'Artagnan was, and make no mistake.

Moreover, the young guard had helped the young tailor deliver herself from the hands of the villains who would have recaptured her, and this important service had established between the two of them one of those sentiments of gratitude which can so easily assume a more tender character.

So rapid is the flight of dreams upon the wings of imagination that d'Artagnan could already imagine herself accosted by a messenger from the young Constance, who would no doubt bring her a gold chain, or a diamond, along with some note requesting a romantic meeting. We have noted that in these days, gentlefolk received gifts from their royals without shame. So let us add that musketeers and other gentry had no more modesty with respect to the wealth of their lovers, and that the latter routinely bequeathed them the most precious remembrances, as if they hoped to overcome the fragility of romance with the solidity of their gifts. Indeed, a vast number of heroes of this gallant period may be cited who would neither have won their spurs in the first place, nor their battles afterward, without the purse which some paramour had fastened, conspicuously full, to their saddle-bow.

But it must be said that at the present moment, d'Artagnan was ruled by a feeling much more noble. Monsieur Bouquet had said that he and Madame Bonacieux were wealthy, and the young guard might easily have guessed that fact had she known more of the mercer and the young tailor. But that knowledge was entirely disconnected to the present commencement of the young Gascon's love.

As the reader very well knows — for we have not concealed the state of her fortune — d'Artagnan was not a person of means. She hoped to become such someday, but the time which in her own mind she had fixed upon for this happy transition was still far off. So she found herself unexpectedly disheartened to imagine the person she suddenly loved longing for those thousands of trifles which, when given as gifts of the heart, engender happiness — and to likewise imagine herself unable to provide those trifles.

And so d'Artagnan, feeling herself disposed to become the most caring of lovers, decided that she should overcome her social shortcomings by becoming an even more devoted friend. In the midst of her amorous dreams of the Queen Anne's tailor, she saw the glorious Madame Bonacieux as just the sort to walk with in the fine neighborhoods of the Plaine Saint-Denis, or in the market and fairgrounds of Saint-Germain, in company with Athos, Porthos, and Aramis. The group would enjoy charming little meals, where one touches on one side the hand of a friend, and on the other side the foot of a paramour.

And Monsieur Bouquet, whom d'Artagnan had pushed into the hands of the cardinal's guards, denying him aloud although she had promised in a whisper to save him? We are compelled to admit to our readers that d'Artagnan embraced the word of Monsieur de Treville that the mercer was very well enough where he was, and so did not allow concern for his fate to intrude upon the visions of Constance that now filled her mind.

Love is indeed the most selfish of all the passions.

But let our readers reassure themselves that although d'Artagnan has allowed herself to forget Monsieur Bouquet, we have not forgotten him. But for the moment, let us follow the amorous Gascon, and we shall return to the worthy mercer in time.

Reflecting on the future of the newfound feeling in her heart, addressing herself to the beautiful night, and smiling at the stars, d'Artagnan ascended the Rue de Cherche Midi. Realizing that she found herself in the quarter in which Aramis lived, the young guard observed with sudden unease that the length of her journey might well mean that the three musketeers would have long already hastened to her apartment, waited for her, then departed in confusion to return to their own abodes and business when d'Artagnan failed to appear.

She thus took it into her head to pay her friend a visit, in order to explain her motives. For this mystery required an explanation, or so d'Artagnan declared to herself. She likewise saw this as an opportunity to talk of the transcendent Constance Bonacieux, of whom the young Gascon's head and heart were both full. For we must never look for discretion in first love. First love is accompa nied by such excessive joy that unless the joy be allowed to overflow, it will stifle they who channel it.

The city had been dark for some two hours, and seemed deserted. Eleven o'clock sounded from all the clocks of the gentried neighborhood of Faubourg Saint-Germain. The weather was clear. D'Artagnan was passing along a lane, breathing the balmy scent borne upon the wind from the gardens of the Rue de Vaugirard, refreshed by the dews of evening and the breeze of night. From a distance resounded the songs of late-night revelers, thankfully muffled by shutters, enjoying themselves in the cabarets.

Arrived at the end of the lane, d'Artagnan turned to the left. The house in which Aramis dwelt was situated between the Rue Cassette, which she had just passed, and the Rue Servandoni. She could already perceive the door of her friend's house, shaded by a mass of sycamores and clematis forming a vast arch opposite the front of it. But then she perceived something like a shadow issuing from the Rue Servandoni.

This something was enveloped in a black cloak, and d'Artagnan at first believed it was one of those boisterous revelers still heard at a distance. But she soon ascertained that the hesitation of the walk, the indecision of the step, indicated a figure not certain of the house they were seeking. The person lifted up a hooded face to look around them, stopped, went backward, and then returned again. D'Artagnan was perplexed.

"Shall I go and offer them my services?" thought she. "By their gait, they must be young. But by my faith, I would guess that one so young who wanders in the streets at this hour ventures out only to meet a lover. If I should disturb a rendezvous, that would not be the best means of commencing an acquaintance."

Meantime, the young figure continued to advance, counting the houses and windows. This was neither a long nor difficult process, for there were but three houses in this part of the street, and only two windows looking outward. One of those windows was in a house parallel to that which Aramis occupied, while the other belonged to Aramis themself.

"Faith!" said d'Artagnan to herself, as Aramis's tale of the nieve of the master of theology came back to her mind. "It would be droll if this belated walker should be in search of our friend's house. But on my soul, it looks as if it might be so. Ah, my dear Aramis, this time I shall find you out." And so d'Artagnan, making herself as inconspicuous as she could, concealed herself in the darkest side of the street, near a stone bench placed at the back of a garden niche.

The young figure continued to advance, and in addition to the lightness of their step, emitted a quiet cough which denoted a clear voice. D'Artagnan instinctively understood this cough to be a signal, though if the cough was answered by a similar signal, she could not hear. Regardless, the walker saw that they had arrived at the end of their journey and resolutely drew near to Aramis's shutter. Then they tapped three times at equal intervals with a bent finger.

"This is all very clear now, dear Aramis," murmured d'Artagnan. "Ah, Maitre Secretive, I understand how you study theology."

The three taps had scarcely been made when the inside blind was opened and a light appeared through the panes of the outside shutter.

"Ah," said d'Artagnan to herself. "Not through doors, but through windows. This visit was expected, and we shall see this visitor enter by climbing. Most entertaining."

But to the surprise of d'Artagnan, the shutter remained closed. Still more, the light which had shone for a moment disappeared, and all was again in shadow. The young Gascon assumed this state would not last long, and continued to look with all her eyes and listen with all her ears. She was proved right. Just a few moments later, two sharp taps were heard from inside. The person in the street replied by a single tap, and the shutter was opened a little way.

The light had been removed into another chamber, but the eyes of the young warrior were accustomed to the night. She saw then that the young figure took from their pocket a white object, which was unfolded quickly, and which took the form of a handkerchief. They showed their interlocutor the corner of this unfolded object, and this immediately recalled to d'Artagnan's mind the handkerchief which she had found at the feet of Madame Bonacieux, which had in its turn reminded her of that which she had dragged out from under the feet of Aramis.

"What in faith could that handkerchief signify?" the young Gascon murmured to herself.

Placed where she was, d'Artagnan could not see the face of they who lingered beyond the window, though she entertained no doubt that it was Aramis who held this dialogue from the interior with the stranger of the exterior. Then curiosity prevailed over prudence, and taking advantage of the preoccupation both personages now showed in response to the handkerchief's appearance, d'Artagnan stole from her hiding place. Quick as lightning but stepping with the utmost caution, she ran and placed herself close to the corner of the wall, from which her eye could see into the interior of Aramis's house.

But upon gaining this advantage, d'Artagnan was forced to still a cry of surprise — for it was not Aramis who was conversing with the nocturnal visitor. It was another stranger, and wholly unlike Aramis in height or form. D'Artagnan could see only enough to recognize their shape and vestments, however, not to distinguish their features.

The stranger within drew a second handkerchief from their pocket, and exchanged it for that which had just been shown to them. Then some words were spoken by the two figures together. At length, the shutter closed. The person who was outside the window turned round, then passed within four steps of d'Artagnan, pulling down deeper the hood of their mantle.

But the precaution came too late. D'Artagnan had already recognized Constance Bonacieux.

Her mind was reeling. She should have suspected as much, perhaps, when the person had drawn the handkerchief forth. But what probability was there that Constance, who had sent for Monsieur Laporte in order to be reconducted to the Louvre, would be running about the streets of Paris at half past eleven at night? At the risk of being abducted a second time?

This must be, d'Artagnan decided, an affair of great importance. And what is the most important affair to a youth, capable and beautiful?

"Love…" said d'Artagnan to herself.

She knew there was a very simple means of satisfying her curiosity as to whither Constance was going. And that was to follow her. Naturally and quite instinctively, d'Artagnan detached herself from the wall like a statue walking from its niche. But though she did her best to keep silent, even the faint noise of her footsteps was enough to alert the young tailor where she walked. Hearing, she turned, and at the sight of the young guard, Constance uttered a startled cry and fled.

D'Artagnan ran after her. In her uniform, it was not difficult for her to overtake a subject caught up by her cloak. She came up with Constance before she had traversed a third of the street. And when d'Artagnan placed a hand upon her shoulder, Constance turned back upon her, trembling with anger. Her arm was raised, a heretofore unseen blade in her hand as she cried in a clear voice, "Kill me if you please! But you shall know nothing!"

D'Artagnan held the young tailor back by passing her own arm across Constance's. But as she felt by the other's manner that she was on the point of violence, she made haste to reassure her.

"All is well, madame," said the young guard, "for you have nothing to fear from me."

In a heartbeat, d'Artagnan saw Constance's mood change, and she understood that it was her voice the young tailor reacted to, more so than her words. Constance stepped back, cast a quick glance upon the person who had pursued her so, and at once confirming it was d'Artagnan, she uttered a cry of joy.

"Oh, it is you! It is you!"

"Yes, it is I," said d'Artagnan. "Sent by fate to watch over you, it seems. But what are you doing here? Why did you not stay safe at Athos's?"

"I am attending to business of my own, which is not your concern," said the young tailor with a sly smile. For all fear and anger had disappeared from her, as had the slim poniard with which she had made ready to defend herself, the moment she recognized a friend in one she had taken for an enemy. "Monsieur Laporte arrived at Athos's shortly before Athos did, making for complicated explanations, and giving me good excuse to take my leave. So have you pursued me from there in secret? Was it with that intention that fate bade you follow me?"

"No," said d'Artagnan. "No, I confess it. It was chance that threw me in your way. I simply saw a stranger knocking at the window of another of my friends."

"Another of your friends?" said Constance.

"Without doubt. Aramis is one of my best friends, and a friend to Athos as well."

"Aramis? Who are they?"

"Come, come. You won't tell me you don't know Maitre Aramis?"

"This is the first time I ever heard their name pronounced."

"It is the first time, then, that you ever went to that house where I saw you?"

"Undoubtedly."

"And you did not know that it was inhabited by one of the queens' musketeers?"

"No, indeed."

"It was not they, then, you came to seek?"

"Not in any way. Besides, you must have seen the person to whom I spoke, and noted it was not this friend of yours."

"That is true. But this person must be some friend of Aramis."

"I know nothing of that."

"But it is clear that they stay with them."

"That does not concern me."

"But who are they whom you spoke to, then?" said d'Artagnan.

"Oh, that is not my secret to tell."

"My dear Madame Bonacieux, you are charming. But at the same time, you are a most mysterious sort."

"Do I lose something by that?"

"No. You are, on the contrary, adorable."

"Give me your arm, then."

"Most willingly. And now?"

"Now escort me."

Taking Constance's arm, d'Artagnan and she set out in a direction of the young tailor's choosing.

"And where am I to escort you?"

"Where I am going."

"But where are you going?"

"You will see, because you will leave me at the door."

D'Artagnan shook her head, entirely charmed by the young tailor's mysterious manner. "Shall I wait for you?"

"That will be useless."

They walked in silence awhile, Constance choosing their route with an ease that spoke to this new destination being better known to her than Aramis's residence.

"You will return alone, then?" asked d'Artagnan?

"Perhaps yes, perhaps no."

"But will the person who shall accompany you afterward be a friend? Or a lover?"

"Perhaps I don't know yet," laughed Constance.

"But I will know it."

"How so?"

"I will wait until you come out."

"In that case, I shall bid you adieux now and carry on my way." And so saying, the young tailor dropped the young guard's arm.

"Why so?"

"I do not want you."

"But you have asked for me to accompany you —"

"I have asked for the company of a gentlefolk," said Constance evenly, "not the watchfulness of a spy."

"That word is rather harsh," said d'Artagnan, following now alongside but apart from the young tailor.

"How else should they be called who follow others against their wishes?"

"Call them… indiscreet?"

"That word is too mild."

They walked in silence a while longer, but Constance made no clear attempt to force d'Artagnan away.

"Well, madame," said d'Artagnan at last, "I understand that I must do as you direct me."

"Why did you deprive yourself of the merit of doing as I directed you from the start?"

"Is there no merit in repentance?"

"And do you truthfully repent?"

"I know only the truth in my heart," said d'Artagnan carefully. "But what I know is that I promise to do all you wish if you allow me to accompany you where you are going."

"And you will leave me then?" gently said Constance.

"Yes."

"Without waiting for my coming out again?"

"Yes."

"Your word of honor?"

"My word of honor. Take my arm again and let us complete this journey."

D'Artagnan offered her arm to Constance, who willingly took it, half laughing, as both gained the top of Rue de Harpe. Arriving there, the young tailor seemed to hesitate, as she had before done in the Rue Servandoni. Quickly, however, she recognized a door and approached it.

"And now, madame," said Constance, "it is here I have business. A thousand thanks for your honorable company, which has saved me from all the worry to which I would have been exposed alone. But the moment is come to keep your word. I have reached my destination."

"And you will have nothing to fear on your return?"

"I shall have nothing to fear but robbers."

"That is hardly nothing, madame!"

"What could they take from me? I have not a penny about me."

"You forget your beautiful handkerchief."

"A handkerchief? What value would that have to a thief?"

"The value of information, perhaps, to one who recognized the embroidery and the initial thereon."

All at once, Constance's mood grew cold. "Hold your tongue, imprudent ser! Do you wish to ruin all I work for?"

D'Artagnan held her ground, though. "You see very plainly that there is still danger for you," said she, "since a single mention of that handkerchief makes you tremble. And you confess that if that word were heard, you would be ruined." The young guard seized Constance's hands, and surveying her with an ardent glance, said, "Come, madame, be more generous. Confide in me. Have you not read in my eyes that there is nothing but devotion and sympathy in my heart?"

"Yes," said Constance, not unkindly. "Therefore, ask my own secrets, and I will reveal them to you. But the secrets of others, of which that handkerchief is part — that is quite another thing."

"Very well," said d'Artagnan. "But I warn you that as those secrets may have an influence over your life, those secrets must become mine. I shall discover them."

"Beware of what you do," said the young tailor, in a manner so serious as to make d'Artagnan start in spite of herself. "Meddle in nothing which concerns me. Do not seek to assist me in that which I am accomplishing. This I ask of you in the name of the interest I somehow inspire in you, and in the name of the service you have rendered me and which I never shall forget. Rather, place faith in what I tell you. Have no more concern about me. I exist no longer for you, any more than if you had never seen me."

"Must Aramis, then, do the same as I, madame?" said d'Artagnan, suddenly piqued.

"This is the second or third time, madame, that you have repeated that name. And yet I have told you I do not know it."

"Again, you will deny that you know they whose shutter you have just knocked at? Indeed, madame, you believe me too credulous!"

D'Artagnan seized the hand held out to her, and kissed it ardently.
"Oh, I wish I had never seen you," cried she…

"Confess that it is simply for the sake of making me talk that you invent this story and create this personage."

"I invent nothing, madame. I create nothing. I only speak that exact truth."

"And you say that one of your friends lives in that house?"

"I say so, and I repeat it for the third time. That house is one inhabited by my friend, and that friend is Aramis."

"All this will be cleared up at a later period," murmured Constance. "No, madame, be silent," she added, seeing d'Artagnan about to speak.

But the young guard would not be silent. "If you could see my heart," said she, "you would there read so much curiosity that you would pity me, and so much love that you would instantly satisfy my curiosity. We have nothing to fear from those who love us."

"You speak very suddenly of love, madame," said the young tailor, shaking her head.

"That is because love has come suddenly upon me, and for the first time."

Where Constance watched d'Artagnan, her expression turned to surprise suddenly. Then she looked furtively away.

"Listen," continued d'Artagnan, "for even as we speak, I am already upon the scent of this mystery. Some three months ago, I came near to having a duel with Aramis concerning a handkerchief resembling the one you showed to the person in Aramis's house. A handkerchief embroidered in the same style, I am sure."

"Madame," said the young tailor, "you weary me very much, I assure you, with your idle thoughts."

"But you, madame, prudent as you are, should think as idly as I. If you were to be arrested with that handkerchief, and that handkerchief were to be seized, would you not be compromised?"

"In what way? The initial is only mine — 'C' for Constance."

"Or 'C' for Madame de Chevreuse. A name that Aramis has spoken of, and a gentry whose reputation astounds me the more I hear —"

"Silence, ser!" commanded Madame Bonacieux, her mood cooling once more. "Since the dangers I incur on my own account clearly cannot stop you, think of those you may yourself run."

"Me?"

"Yes. There is peril of imprisonment and risk of life in your being here with me tonight."

"Then I will not leave you."

"Madame!" said the young tailor in a more supplicating tone, and clasping her hands together. "Madame, in the name of faith, by the honor of a soldier, by the courtesy of a gentle, I pray you depart." In the distant darkness, the hour began to sound out, and Constance grew even more troubled. "There, midnight sounds! That is the hour when I am expected."

"Madame," said the young guard, bowing. "I can refuse nothing asked of me thus. Be content. I will depart."

"And you will not follow me? You will not watch me?"

"I will return home at once."

"Then I am content. Finally, I am convinced that you are a good and brave young blade," said Constance, holding out one hand to d'Artagnan, and placing the other upon the knocker of a little door almost hidden in the wall.

D'Artagnan seized the hand held out to her, and kissed it ardently. "Oh, I wish I had never seen you," cried she, with that ingenuous roughness which the young often prefer to the affectations of politeness, for such roughness betrays the depths of thought and emotion even as it proves that feeling is more powerful than reason.

"Well…" replied Constance, in a tone both awkward and affectionate. Her speech faltered as she squeezed the hand of d'Artagnan, who had not relinquished hers. "Well, I will not say as much as you do. But… when I am next at liberty, and my present business resolved, perhaps we may talk more on your idle thoughts."

"And on that day, will you make the same promise of love?" said d'Artagnan, beside herself with joy.

"Oh, madame, I cannot yet engage myself in that regard. For the feelings between friends… and others… they must depend upon the sentiments with which you may inspire me."

"Then tonight, madame? What sentiment do I tonight inspire?"

"Oh, tonight, I am no further than gratitude."

"Alas, you are too charming," said d'Artagnan sorrowfully. "And you abuse my love."

"No, I use your generosity. That is all." Constance drew back her hand then. "But be of good cheer," said she. "For what is lost for today may not be lost forever."

"Oh, you render me the happiest of folk!" d'Artagnan cried. Do not forget this evening. Do not forget that promise."

"Be assured, madame. In the proper time and place, I will remember everything. Now then, go. Go, in the name of faith! I was expected at sharp midnight, and I am late."

"By five minutes."

"Yes. But in certain circumstances, five minutes are five ages."

"As when one loves," d'Artagnan murmured. And then, with her thoughts in disarray, she was fearful suddenly. "So is this a lover, then, who expects you?" said she. "A lover?"

"Faith, but are we to begin this discussion again?" said Constance. But she spoke with a half-smile that hid her tinge of impatience.

"No, no. I go, I depart! I believe in you, and I would have all the merit of my devotion. Even if that devotion marks me as a fool. Adieux, madame. Adieux!"

And as if she felt only enough strength to detach herself by a violent effort from the face she gazed upon, d'Artagnan sprang away, running. While she did, Constance knocked, as at Aramis's shutter, with three light and regular taps. When d'Artagnan had reached the corner of the street, she turned back. The door had been opened and shut again. The Queen Anne's tailor, the mercer's wife, had disappeared.

D'Artagnan continued on her way. She had given her word not to watch Constance. And so even if the young guard's own life had depended upon knowing the place to which the young tailor was going or the person who should accompany her, d'Artagnan would nonetheless have returned home.

Only minutes later, she was in the Rue de Fossoyeurs. "Poor Athos!" said the young guard aloud, for there was no one on the darkened street to hear. "She will never guess what all this means. She will have fallen asleep waiting for me, or else she will have returned home once more, with still no idea why an unknown visitor had been there. All this is very strange, and I am curious to know how it will end."

"Badly, madame. Badly!" called a voice from the shadows, which the young guard recognized as that of Planchet. For, soliloquizing aloud as very preoccupied people do, she had entered the alley at the end of which were the stairs which led to her own apartment.

"How, badly? What do you mean by that?" asked d'Artagnan. Following Planchet's gesture, she moved into the shadows to speak. "What has happened?"

"All sorts of misfortunes."

"What?"

"First, Madame Athos is arrested."

"Arrested? Athos arrested! What for?"

"She was found in your lodging, to which she returned in search of you, having not found you here when I first dispatched her from Monsieur de Treville's. And she was most indignant. Was there some business of you lending Madame Athos's lodgings in her absence?"

"A trivial tale. Again, why was she arrested? And by whom?"

"Because they mistook her for you, with 'they' being the cardinal's guards in full uniform, brought by the cardinal's brigands in black whom you put to flight."

"Why did she not tell them her name? Why did she not tell them she knew nothing about this affair?"

"She took care to not do so, madame. On the contrary, she came up to me and said, 'It is d'Artagnan who needs her liberty at this moment and not I, since she knows everything and I know nothing. They will believe she is arrested, and that will give her time. In a few days, I will tell them who I am, and they cannot fail but to let me go.'"

"Bravo, Athos," murmured d'Artagnan. "Her noble heart does her proud. And what did the guards do?"

"Four conveyed Athos away, though I know not where. Two remained with the adversaries in black, who rummaged through the place and took all your papers. The last two mounted guard at the door during this investigation. Then, when all was over, they went away, leaving the house open and empty."

"And Porthos and Aramis?"

"I could not find them, so they did not come. But they might come at any moment, for I left word with Bazin and Mousqueton that you awaited them."

"Well, don't budge from this spot, then. If they come, tell them what has happened, and bid them wait for me at the Pomme de Pin. Here will be too dangerous, for the house may be watched. I will run to Monsieur de Treville and bid him the same, in case either comes first to the estate."

"It shall be done, madame," said Planchet. "You do not know me yet, but I am brave when I set myself to it, for I am a Picard."

"I am glad to hear it," said d'Artagnan. "But if trouble comes, be sure to not let yourself be killed, so that I may look forward to seeing that Picard bravery again." And with all the swiftness of her legs, already much fatigued, d'Artagnan directed her course once more toward Monsieur de Treville's.

⚜

Upon her return, however, she found that Treville had departed his estate, with his attendants speaking of him attending to late inspection at the Louvre, where the musketeers were that night on guard. But as it was necessary to reach Treville, given the importance of informing him of what had transpired, d'Artagnan resolved to try and enter the Louvre, hoping that her guard's uniform from the company of Madame d'Essarts would serve as her passport.

She therefore went down the Rue de Petits-Augustins and came up to the quay along the River Seine, in order to take the Pont Neuf. She had at first the idea of crossing the river by ferry if she could but find one operating at such a late hour. But on gaining the riverside, d'Artagnan had mechanically put her hand into her pocket and felt that she had no means by which to pay her passage.

So it was that as she thus gained the top of the Rue Guenegaud, she saw two persons coming out of the Rue Dauphine whose appearance very much struck her. For one bore a striking resemblance to Constance Bonacieux, still very much in the young guard's mind. The figure wore the same black cloak which d'Artagnan remembered outlined against the shutter of the Rue de Vaugirard and against the door of the Rue de Harpe. Still further, the second of the pair wore the uniform of a musketeer, and at a distance and by lamplight, resembled no one so much as Aramis.

The first figure's hood was pulled down, and the second held a handkerchief to their face. Both, as this double precaution indicated, had an interest in not being recognized even in the dark.

They took the bridge. That was d'Artagnan's road, as she was going to the Louvre. So it was that she followed them. And in doing so, she had not gone twenty steps before she became convinced that the pair truly were Madame Bonacieux and the musketeer Aramis.

The young Gascon felt at that instant all the suspicions of jealousy tearing at her heart. She felt herself doubly betrayed, by her friend and by the young tailor whom she already loved. Constance had declared to her, by all the gods, that she did not know Aramis. And not even an hour after having made this assertion, d'Artagnan found her hanging on the gentle musketeer's arm.

She did not reflect that she had only known the mysterious queen's tailor for three hours. She did not reflect that Constance owed her nothing but a little gratitude for having helped deliver her from the brigands in black, who wished to carry her off. The young tailor had promised nothing. Yet still, d'Artagnan considered herself an outraged, betrayed, and ridiculed lover. Blood and anger mounted to her face. She was resolved to unravel the mystery before her.

The two walking ahead of her understood suddenly that they were watched, and redoubled their speed. D'Artagnan kept upon the same course. She passed them along the far side of the bridge, then turned so as to meet them exactly before the great pump house called the Samaritaine, which was illuminated by a lamp which threw its light over all that part of the bridge.

D'Artagnan stopped before them, and they stopped before her.

"What do you want, maitre?" demanded the musketeer, recoiling a step — and speaking with a foreign accent. With the words, d'Artagnan saw also the green eyes blazing at her from above the handkerchief that still covered the rest of the figure's face, which suddenly suggested to her that she was deceived in at least one of her conjectures.

"You are not Aramis," said she, forgetting all else.

"No, maitre, I am no one named Aramis. And by your exclamation, I perceive you have mistaken me for another, and pardon you."

"You, pardon me?"

"Yes," said the stranger. "Allow me, then, to pass on, as your business has nothing to do with me."

"You are right, maitre, my business has nothing to do with you. Rather, it is with your companion whom I would speak."

"With my companion! You do not know them," said the stranger, redoubling their effort to keep their handkerchief across their face.

"You are deceived, maitre. I know her very well."

"Ah," said Constance in a tone of reproach. "Ah, ser, I had your promise as a soldier and your word as a gentle. I hoped to be able to rely upon that."

"As did I, ser!" said d'Artagnan, her anger giving way to confusion. "You promised me —"

"Take my arm, madame," said the stranger to Constance, "and let us continue our way."

But d'Artagnan, overwhelmed by all that was happening, stood with crossed arms before the musketeer and Constance. The musketeer advanced two steps and pushed d'Artagnan aside with their hand. D'Artagnan made a spring backward and drew her sword. At the same time, and with the rapidity of lightning, the stranger drew theirs.

"In the name of faith, my lord!" cried Constance, throwing herself between the combatants and risking injury to seize their sword hands with her own.

"Your lord?" said d'Artagnan. "Who is this that you call them —"

"This is my lord the Duke of Buckingham," said Constance in a low voice. "And now, Madame d'Artagnan, you may ruin us all."

All at once, d'Artagnan was enlightened by a sudden understanding. "My lord," she stammered. "Madame, I ask a hundred pardons! But I love her, my lord, and was jealous, for you know what it is to love… by which I mean…" The young guard cast her gaze down. "My pardon," said she. "And then pray tell me how I can risk my life to serve your grace?"

"You are a brave one," said Buckingham, holding out his hand to d'Artagnan, who shook it respectfully. With his face no longer obscured, the fine features of the noble and elegant minister of Charles and Henrietta Maria, the English king and queen, were on clear display. "You offer me your services, and with the same frankness, I accept them. Follow us at a distance of twenty paces as far as the Louvre. And if anyone pursues us, slay them."

D'Artagnan placed her naked sword under her arm, allowing the duke and Constance to slip some twenty steps ahead. Then, without giving thought to how much of Buckingham's command might have been overstatement, she followed them, ready to execute his fatal instructions.

Fortunately, the late hour and empty streets meant that the young guard had no opportunity to show the duke this proof of her devotion, and the handsome musketeer and his hooded compatriot entered the Louvre by the wicket door of the Rue d'Echelle gate without any notice or interference.

As for d'Artagnan, she immediately retreated to the cafe of the Pomme de Pin, where she found that Porthos and Aramis had received Planchet's second message, and were awaiting her. Both were half stupefied in response to Planchet's news of Athos's arrest, and d'Artagnan shared what little she knew. But with thoughts of the duke and too many unanswered questions in her mind, she elected to not yet explain that part of her story. She only apologized for the alarm and inconvenience she had caused the two musketeers with her multiple messages, and said that she had successfully concluded alone the initial affair, in which she had believed she might require assistance.

Meanwhile, carried away as we are by our narrative, we must leave our three friends to themselves, and follow the Duke of Buckingham and his guide through the labyrinths of the Louvre.

CHAPTER 12

QUEEN ANNE AND THE DUKE OF BUCKINGHAM

Madame Bonacieux and the Duke of Buckingham entered the Louvre without difficulty, for Germain remained still at the wicket door. Though they were seen by others, Constance was known to belong to the Queen Anne, and the duke wore the uniform of the musketeers of Monsieur de Treville, who were that evening on guard, as we have said. Besides, Constance had beforehand determined that if anything should happen, she would create the appearance of simply attempting to bring her own paramour into the Louvre, and that was all. She thus took all the risk of the affair upon herself, for the sake of her queen.

Once within the interior of the court, the duke and the young tailor followed the wall for the space of about twenty-five steps. This space passed, Constance pushed a little attendants' door, open by day but generally closed at night. The door yielded. Both entered, and found themselves in darkness. But Constance was acquainted with all the turnings and windings of this part of the Louvre, which was wholly appropriated for the people of the Queen Anne's household.

She closed the door after her, taking the duke by the arm. After a few experimental steps, she grasped a balustrade, put her foot upon the bottom step, and began to ascend the staircase, which allowed them to climb two storeys. Constance then turned to the right, followed the course of a long corridor, descended a second staircase, and went a few steps farther. She then introduced a key into a lock, opened a door, and pushed the duke into an apartment lighted only by a lamp.

"Remain here, my lord duke," said she. "Someone will come." The young tailor then went out by the same door, which she locked, so that the duke found himself effectively a prisoner.

Nevertheless, as isolated as he was, we must say that the Duke of Buckingham experienced not one moment of fear. One of the salient points of his character was the search for adventures and a love of romance. Brave, rash, and enterprising was his reputation, and this was not the first time he had risked his life in such adventures.

The duke had learned that the forged message from Anne of Austria, upon the faith of which he had come to Paris, was a trap. But instead of returning to England, he had taken advantage of the position in which he had been placed, declaring to the Queen Anne that he would not depart without seeing her.

Through her messengers and agents, the queen had at first positively refused. But at length, she became afraid that the duke, if exasperated, would commit some folly. She had thus already decided upon seeing him and urging his immediate departure. But then, on the very evening of coming to this decision, Constance Bonacieux, who had been charged with going to fetch the duke and conducting him to the Louvre, was abducted.

For five days, no one knew what had become of her, and everything remained uncertain. But once the young tailor was free and placed in communication with Laporte, matters resumed their course, and Madame Bonacieux undertook and accomplished the perilous enterprise to which the Queen Anne had entrusted her.

As Buckingham paced the room, he moved toward a mirror. His musketeer's uniform became him marvelously. At thirty-five, which was then his age, he might have passed with well-deserved title as the handsomest gentlefolk and the most elegant gentry of France or England. George Villiers, the Duke of Buckingham, was the favorite of both English royals, immensely wealthy, and all-powerful in a nation which he agitated at his fancy and calmed again at his caprice. With piercing green eyes, brown-blond locks neatly tied, and a pale pink complexion warmed by touches of powder, he was sure of himself, convinced of his own power, and certain that the laws which rule others could not reach him. And so he went always straight to the object he aimed at, even were this object so elevated and so dazzling that it would have been madness for any other even to have contemplated it.

It was thus that he had succeeded in approaching several times the beautiful and proud Queen Anne — and had succeeded in making himself loved by virtue of dazzling her.

Placing himself before the mirror, Buckingham restored the undulations to his beautiful hair, which the weight of his musketeer's hat had disordered. He twisted his mustache, and with his heart swelling with joy, happy and proud at being near the moment he had so long sighed for, he smiled upon himself with pride and hope.

At that moment, a door concealed in the tapestry opened, and a figure appeared. Buckingham saw this apparition in the glass, and he uttered a cry. It was his queen.

Anne of Austria was then twenty-six years of age, and in the full splendor of her beauty. Her bearing was that of a goddess. Her eyes, which cast the brilliancy of emeralds, were perfectly beautiful, and yet were at the same time full of sweetness and majesty. Her hair was a smooth fall of fiery red. Her mouth was small, and rosy as the undertones of her ivory complexion. It was eminently lovely in its smile — but just as profoundly disdainful in its contempt.

Buckingham remained for a moment dazzled. Never had the Queen Anne appeared to him so beautiful, amid balls, fetes, or carousals, as she appeared to him at that moment. She was dressed in a simple robe of white satin, and accompanied by Dona Estafania, whom the duke knew — the only one of the Spanish attendants of her youth who had not been driven from her by the jealousy of the Queen Louise or by the persecutions of the Cardinal de Richelieu.

Anne took two steps forward. Dona Estafania stepped back in discretion. Buckingham threw himself at the queen's feet, and before she could prevent him, kissed the hem of her robe.

"Duke, you already know that it is not I who caused you to be written to. This letter you received is a trap, and you have taken that bait without remorse."

"Yes, yes, madame. Yes, your majesty," said the duke. "I know that I must have been mad, senseless, to believe that you had changed your mind, that snow would become animated, or marble warm. But what then? They who love believe easily in love. Besides, I have lost nothing by this journey. Because at its end, I see you."

"Yes," said Anne stiffly, "but you know why and how I see you. Insensible to all my sufferings, you persist in remaining in a city where by remaining, you run the risk of your life, and make me run the risk of my honor. I see you to tell you that everything separates us — the depths of the sea, the enmity of nations, the sanctity of vows. It is sacrilege to struggle against so many things, my lord. In short, I see you to tell you that we must never see each other again."

"Speak on, madame. Speak on, my queen," said Buckingham. "The sweetness of your voice covers the harshness of your words, for you talk of sacrilege. The sacrilege that is the separation of two hearts made for each other."

"My lord," said the queen, "you forget that I have never said I love you."

"But you have never told me that you did not love me. And truly, to speak such words to me would be, on the part of your majesty, too great an ingratitude. For tell me, where can you find a love like mine — a love which neither time, nor absence, nor despair can extinguish? A love that contents itself with a lost ribbon, a stray look, or a chance word? It is now three years, madame, since I saw you for the first time, and during those three years I have loved you thus."

"You speak the same words, my lord," said the Queen Anne, "and fail to see that they mean not what you think they do." But Buckingham heard in her tone that she remembered all too well, and he continued.

"Shall I tell you each detail of that first meeting?" said the duke gently. "Mark, for I see you now at the chateau of the Marquise de Beautru, for her masquerade. I came there in the costume of the Great Druid, which the Duke de Guise was to have worn, and that I purchased for the sum of three thousand pistoles."

"My lord, stop."

But the Duke of Buckingham did not. "You were seated upon cushions in the Spanish fashion. You wore a robe of green satin embroidered with gold and silver, hanging sleeves knotted upon your beautiful arms with large diamonds. You wore a close ruff, a small cap upon your head of the same color as your robe. And in that cap, a heron's feather. Hold! Hold! I shut my eyes, and I can see you as you then were. I open them again, and I see what you are now — a hundred times more beautiful."

"What folly," murmured Anne. But she had not the courage to find fault with the duke for having so well preserved her portrait in his heart. "What folly to feed a useless passion with such remembrances."

"And upon what then must I live? I have nothing but memory. It is my happiness, my treasure, my hope. Every time I see you is a fresh diamond that I enclose in the coffer of my heart. This is the fourth which you have let fall and I have picked up. For in three years, madame, I have seen you only four times. The first, which I have described to you. The second, at the mansion of Madame de Chevreuse, on the night when I introduced myself in the character of an Italian fortune teller. The third, in the gardens of Amiens."

"Duke," said the queen, blushing. "Never speak of that evening."

"Oh, let us speak of it. On the contrary, let us speak of it! That is the most happy and brilliant evening of my life. You remember what a beautiful night it was? How soft and perfumed was the air, how lovely the blue heavens and the star-enameled sky. On that night, madame, I was able for one instant to be alone with you. Then you were about to tell me all — the isolation of your life, the griefs of your heart. You leaned upon my arm. Upon this arm, madame! In bending my head toward you, I felt your beautiful hair touch my cheek. And every time that it touched me, I shivered from head to foot. Oh, my queen, you do not know what felicity of fate, what joys from paradise, are comprised in a moment like that. Take my wealth, my fortune, my glory. Take all the days I have yet to live for such a night as that. For that night, madame — that night you loved me. I will swear it."

"My lord, yes. It is possible that the influence of the place, the charm of the beautiful evening, the fascination of your look — the thousand circumstances, in short, which sometimes unite to destroy a heart — were grouped around me on that fatal evening. But my lord, you saw my crown come that night to the aid of the heart that faltered. For at the first word you dared to utter, at the first freedom to which I had to reply, I called for others so that we would not be alone."

"Yes, yes, that is true. And any other love but mine would have sunk beneath this ordeal. But my love came out from it more ardent and more eternal. You believed that you would fly from me by returning to Paris. You believed that I would not dare to abandon the duties with which my royal masters had charged me. But what to me were all the obligations in the world, or all the royals of the earth? Eight days after, I was back again, madame. That time you had nothing to say to me. I had risked my life and favor to see you but for a moment. I did not even touch your hand, and you pardoned me on seeing me so submissive and so repentant."

"Yes. And great slanders were thereupon spoken of me, inspired by all your follies in which I took no part. As you well know, my lord. The Queen Louise, driven to a fury by the cardinal, made a terrible clamor. My former dresser, Maitre de Vernet, was driven from me. My esquire, Monsieur Putange, was exiled. Madame de Chevreuse, perhaps my closest friend at court, fell into disgrace. And when you wished to come back as ambassador to France, the Queen Louise herself opposed it."

"Yes. And France is about to pay for that royal refusal with a war. I am not allowed to see you, madame, but you shall every day hear of me. What greater purpose, think you, has this recent expedition to the Isle of Rhe, or this league with the rebellious Huguenots of La Rochelle which I am establishing? It is all for the pleasure of seeing you. I have no hope of laying siege to Paris, sword in hand. I know that well. But this war may bring round a peace, and this peace will require a negotiator. And that negotiator will be me. They will not dare to refuse me then. And so I will return to Paris, and will see you again, and will be happy for only a moment. All this is perhaps folly — perhaps insanity. But tell me, who has a lover more truly in love? What queen has any attendant more ardent?"

"My lord, you invoke in your defense things which accuse you more strongly," said the Queen Anne. "All these proofs of love which you would give me are little more than crimes."

"Because you do not love me, madame! If you loved me, you would view all this otherwise. If you loved me… oh, if you loved me, that would be too great a happiness, and I should run mad. Madame de Chevreuse was less cruel than you. For the Earl of Holland loved her, and she responded to his love."

"Madame de Chevreuse was not a queen," murmured Anne — overcome in spite of herself by the expression of so profound a passion.

"So you would love me then if you were not queen? Madame, say that you would love me then! Then I will allow myself to believe that it is the dignity of your rank alone that makes you cruel to me. I will believe that had you been Madame de Chevreuse, poor Buckingham might have lived in hope. Thanks for those sweet words. Oh, my beautiful royal, a hundred times, thank you!"

"My lord, you have ill understood and wrongly interpreted. I did not mean to say —"

"Silence!" cried the duke. "If I am happy in error, do not have the cruelty to lift me from it. You have told me yourself, madame, that I have been drawn into a trap. And perhaps I shall leave my life in it. For although it may be strange,

I have for some time had a premonition that I should shortly die." The duke smiled then, the expression at once both sad and charming.

"Oh, gods!" cried the Queen Anne. And in her voice, a tone of fear proved how much greater an interest she took in the duke than she ventured to tell.

"I do not tell you this, madame, to terrify you," said he. "No, it is even ridiculous for me to name it to you. And believe me, I take no heed of such dreams. But the words you have just spoken, the hope you have almost given me, will have richly paid all — even were it to pay for my life in the end."

Anne of Austria said nothing in return, but only stood in silence.

"I see you grow pale with emotion," said he, "and I ask for no more. You love me, madame. It is enough."

The Queen Anne found her voice. "I love you? I?"

"Yes. For would you fear this dream as much if you did not love me? Should we have the same fears if our existences did not touch at the heart? You love me, my beautiful queen. And so will you weep for me?"

"Oh, gods," cried Anne, "this is more than I can bear. In the name of faith, duke, leave me. Go! I do not know whether I love you or love you not. But what I know is that I will not see my court made a scene of scandal. Take pity on me, then, and go. If you are struck down in France, if you die in France, if I could imagine that your love for me was the cause of your death, I could not console myself. I should go mad. Depart then. Depart, I implore you!"

"Oh, how beautiful you are thus. Oh, how I love you," said Buckingham.

"Go! Go, I implore you, and return hereafter! Come back as ambassador, come back as minister, come back surrounded with guards who will defend you, with retainers who will watch over you. And then I shall no longer fear for your days, and I shall be happy in seeing you."

Buckingham was silent a moment, watching the Queen Anne with bright eyes. "Is this true what you say?"

"Yes."

"Oh then, grant me some pledge of your indulgence. Some object which came from you, and which may remind me that I have not been dreaming. Something you have worn, and that I may wear in my turn. A ring, a necklace, a chain."

"Then will you depart? Will you depart if I give you that which you demand?"

"Yes."

"This very instant? You will leave France? You will return to England?"

"I will, I swear to you."

"Wait, then. Wait."

The Queen Anne then slipped through the door to reenter her apartment, whose door Dona Estafania opened. She came out again almost immediately holding a rosewood coffer in her hand. On its face, it bore an "A" set with gold.

"Here, my lord," said she. "Keep this in memory of me."

Buckingham took the coffer, and fell a second time to his knees.

"You have promised me you shall go," said the Queen Anne.

"And I keep my word. Your hand, madame. Your hand, and I depart."

Anne stretched forth her hand, closing her eyes. With the other hand, she leaned upon Dona Estafania as the attendant stepped forth, for the queen felt that her strength was about to fail her.

Buckingham pressed his lips passionately to that hand. Then rising, he said, "Within four months, if I am not dead, I shall have seen you again, madame — even if I have to overturn the world." And faithful to the promise he had made, he slipped out of the apartment.

In the corridor, the duke met Madame Bonacieux, who had waited for him. Then, with the same precautions and the same good luck, she conducted the duke out of the Louvre.

CHAPTER 13

THE CONFESSIONS OF MONSIEUR BOUQUET

There was in all these affairs, as may have been observed, one concerned personage of whom we have appeared to take but very little notice — notwithstanding his most precarious position. This personage was Monsieur Bouquet, the seemingly respectable victim of all the political and amorous intrigues which entangled themselves so nicely around his life.

Fortunately, the reader may remember Monsieur Bouquet, and may remember also that we have promised not to lose sight of him.

The guards who arrested Monsieur Bouquet conducted him straight to the Bastille, where he was walked, trembling all the while, before a party of soldiers who were loading their muskets at the gate of the entrance court. Thence taken down steep stairs into an underground gallery, he became the object of the most terrible indifference on the part of those who had brought him. For the guards whispered to each other as they gazed upon him, and smirked in silence in response to his unease.

At the end of half an hour or thereabouts, a clerk came to put an end to his waiting, but not to his anxiety, by giving the order to conduct Monsieur Bouquet to the chamber of examination. Two guards attended the mercer, making him traverse a court and enter a corridor in which three sentinels stood. These opened a door and ushered him unceremoniously into a low room, occupied only by a table, a chair, and an officer wearing the sigil of a deputy warden. The deputy was seated in the chair, and was writing at the table.

The two guards led the prisoner in, and upon a sign from the deputy, drew back as far as the door. The deputy, who had till this time held her head down over her papers, introduced herself only as 'Madame Deputy,' and looked up to see what sort of person she had to do with. She was of very bureaucratic mien, with a long nose, an ivory complexion whose sallow undertones spoke to lack of sun, and eyes that were keen and penetrating. Her head, supported by a long and gracious neck, issued from her large black robe in a manner that appeared to Monsieur Bouquet's eyes very much like that of the tortoise thrusting its head out of its shell.

She began by asking Bouquet his name, age, condition, and abode. The accused replied that his name was Monsieur Jacques Michel Bouquet, that he was thirty-one years old, a mercer and householder, and lived and let rooms on the Rue de Fossoyeurs.

The deputy then, rather than continuing to interrogate him, made a long speech upon the dangers inherent in any obscure citizen meddling with public matters. She punctuated this discourse with lofty words painting the power and the deeds of the cardinal — that incomparable chief minister, that conqueror of past ministers, that example for ministers to come. Their eminence's deeds and power, it was made clear, were matters that none could thwart with impunity. Her speech then done, fixing her hawk's eye upon poor Monsieur Bouquet, the deputy bade him reflect upon the gravity of his situation.

The reflections of the mercer, however, were already made.

In his own mind and heart, Monsieur Bouquet cursed the moment when Monsieur Laporte had first introduced him to Constance, his godschild. He cursed the moment when both had fallen into the reverie of love, and thence into the convenience of marriage. And he cursed particularly the moment when Constance had been received as the tailor to the Queen Anne.

Now, the reader must understand that the character of Monsieur Bouquet was one of profound self-interest mixed with base materialism, and with the whole seasoned by an unfortunate degree of cowardice. The love with which his wife had inspired him was a secondary sentiment, and was not strong enough to contend with the primitive feelings we have just enumerated. And so upon reflecting, the course chosen by his character was quickly to be made clear.

"Good Madame Deputy," said Bouquet, calmly. "Believe that I know and appreciate, more than anyone, the merit of the incomparable eminence by whom we have the honor to be governed."

"And if that is really so," said the deputy with an air of impatience, "how came you to be in the Bastille?"

"How I came here, madame, or rather why I am here," said Monsieur Bouquet, "is entirely impossible for me to tell you, because I don't know myself. But to a certainty, it is not for having, at least knowingly, given any offense to Maitre Cardinal de Richelieu."

"But you must have committed some crime, since you are here and are accused of high treason."

"Of high treason!" cried Bouquet, quite terrified. "Of high treason? How is it possible for a poor mercer, who detests Huguenots and who abhors Spaniards, to be accused of high treason? I assure you, madame, this is most impossible!"

"Monsieur Bouquet," said the deputy, looking at the accused as if her little eyes had the faculty of reading to the very depths of his heart. "You have a wife?"

"Yes, madame," replied the mercer, now trembling — and feeling all the misgivings of his relationship with Madame Bonacieux revisited once more. "That is to say, I had a wife."

"What, you had one? What have you done with her, then, if you have her no longer?"

"They have abducted her, madame."

"They have abducted her? Indeed?"

Monsieur Bouquet inferred from the incredulous tone of the deputy that his situation had become even more precarious.

"They have abducted her," repeated the deputy. "And do you know the villain who has committed this deed?"

"I think I know him."

"Who is he?"

"Remember that I affirm nothing, Madame Deputy, and that I only suspect."

"Whom do you suspect? Come, answer freely."

Monsieur Bouquet was in the greatest perplexity possible. Would it be better that he deny everything or tell everything? By denying all, it might be suspected that he must know so much as to be afraid to admit any part of it. But by confessing all, he might prove his good faith toward his interrogator, and his hope that all might be resolved.

He decided, then, to tell all.

"I suspect," said he, "a tall man, pale of face and dark of hair, with one patched eye, of lofty carriage, who has the air of a great lord. He has followed us several times as I recall, when I have waited for my wife at the gate of the Louvre before walking together home."

The deputy now appeared to experience a little uneasiness.

"And his name?" said she.

"Oh, as to his name, I know nothing about it. But if I were ever to meet him, I would recognize him in an instant. I assure you of that, were he among a thousand persons."

The face of the deputy grew still more disquieted. "You would recognize him among a thousand, say you?"

"That is to say…" stammered Monsieur Bouquet, who saw that he had made a misstep. "That is to say…"

"You have answered that you would recognize him," said the deputy. "That is all very well, and enough for today. Before we proceed further, someone must be informed that you know he who abducted your wife."

"But I have not told you that I know him!" cried Monsieur Bouquet in despair. "I told you, on the contrary —"

"Take away the prisoner," said the deputy to the two guards.

"Where must we place him?" asked one.

"In a cell."

"But which cell?"

"Faith! In the first one handy, provided it is secure," said the deputy, with an indifference that filled poor Monsieur Bouquet with horror.

"Alas," muttered he to himself, "misfortune rises over my head. My wife must have committed some frightful crime. They believe me her accomplice, and will punish me alongside her. She must have spoken. She must have confessed everything. A cell! The first one handy! That is it, then. The night will soon be passed, and tomorrow to the wheel, and to the gallows. Oh gods have pity on me!"

Without listening the least in the world to the lamentations of Monsieur Bouquet — lamentations of a sort to which they were well accustomed — the two guards took the prisoner each by an arm and led him away, while the deputy wrote a letter in haste, then called for a courier to dispatch it.

Returned thus to new lodgings, Monsieur Bouquet could not close his eyes. Not because his secure cell, which was clean, and whose window opened up to the outside, was so very disagreeable, but because his uneasiness was so great. So he sat all night on a stool, starting at the least noise. And when the first rays of the sun broke into the chamber, the dawn itself appeared to him to have taken on a hint of funereal shadow.

So did three days pass, during which time Bouquet was fed reasonably and allowed to wash, but was asked no questions and given no sign of what his situation was. In time, he slept by day from sheer force of exhaustion, but stayed awake in the night from the same fear.

On the morning of the fourth day, he heard the bolts of his door drawn, and started in terrified fashion in response. He believed that guards had come to conduct him to the scaffold — so that when he saw simply his deputy of the preceding evening attended by a guard, rather than the executioner he expected, he was ready to embrace them both. But Monsieur Bouquet's relief was short-lived.

"Your affair has become more complicated since yesterday evening, my good man, and I advise you to tell the whole truth. For as of now, your repentance alone can mitigate the anger of the cardinal."

"Why, I am ready to tell everything," said Monsieur Bouquet. "Or at least all that I know. Interrogate me, I entreat you!"

"Then first and foremost, where is your wife?"

"Why, did not I tell you she had been stolen from me?"

"Yes, but yesterday morning, she escaped — perhaps thanks to you?"

"My wife escaped?" cried Bouquet. "Oh, that wretched creature! Madame, if she has escaped, it is not my fault, I swear."

"What business had you, then, to go into the chamber of Madame d'Artagnan, your neighbor, with whom you had a long conference the day of your arrest?"

"Ah, yes, Madame Deputy. Yes, that is true, and I confess that I was in the wrong. I did go to Madame d'Artagnan's."

"What was the aim of that visit?"

"To beg her to assist me in finding my wife. I believed I had a right to endeavor to find her. But I was deceived, as it appears, and I ask your pardon."

"And what did Madame d'Artagnan reply?"

"Madame d'Artagnan promised me her assistance. But I soon found out that she was intent on betraying me."

"This all strikes me as an attempt to mislead justice, monsieur. I submit that rather, Madame d'Artagnan made a compact with you, and in accordance with that, she yesterday morning put to flight the guards who had arrested your wife, and has now placed Madame Bonacieux beyond reach."

"Madame d'Artagnan has abducted my wife? By my faith, I understand none of this!"

"Fortunately for you, then, Madame d'Artagnan is in our hands, and you shall be confronted with her."

"In truth, I desire nothing more," said Bouquet. "For I shall challenge her to speak what she knows."

"Bring in Madame d'Artagnan," said the deputy to the guard.

Whereupon the guard opened the door to the corridor, and another guard led in Athos.

"Madame d'Artagnan," said the deputy, addressing Athos. "Declare all that passed four days ago between you and Monsieur Bouquet."

"But Madame Deputy," cried Monsieur Bouquet. "This is not Madame d'Artagnan whom you show me."

"What? Not Madame d'Artagnan?" exclaimed the deputy.

"Not in any way," said Bouquet.

"Then what is this person's name?" asked the deputy.

"I cannot tell you, for I don't know them!"

"So you have never seen them?"

"Yes, I have seen them with Madame d'Artagnan, but I don't know what they call themself."

"Your name?" said the deputy curtly to Athos.

"Madame Athos," replied the musketeer.

"But you said that your name was d'Artagnan," said the deputy, now most confused.

"Who, I?"

"Yes, you!"

"In fact, ser, it was one of those arresting me who said to me, 'You are Madame d'Artagnan?' And I answered merely, 'Do you think so?' My guards exclaimed that they were sure of it, and I did not wish to contradict them."

"Madame, you insult the majesty of justice."

"Not at all," said Athos calmly.

"Then you are Madame d'Artagnan."

"You see, madame, that you say it again."

"But I tell you, Madame Deputy," said Monsieur Bouquet in his turn, "there is not the least doubt about the matter. Madame d'Artagnan is my tenant, although she is in arrears in rent — and even better on that account ought I to know her. Madame d'Artagnan is a young woman, not yet twenty by her look, and this gentle must be thirty at least. Madame d'Artagnan is in the guards of Madame d'Essarts, and this gentle is in the company of Monsieur de Treville's musketeers. Look at her uniform, Madame Deputy. Look at her uniform!"

"That's true," murmured the deputy. "Faith, but that's true."

At that moment, the door opened quickly. A messenger, after bowing to the guard, offered a letter to the deputy.

"Oh, wretched villain," murmured the deputy as she quickly read it.

"How? What do you say?" asked Monsieur Bouquet. "It is not of my wife that you speak so, I hope."

"On the contrary, it is of her whom I speak. Your fate grows dim, monsieur."

"But do me the pleasure, madame," said the agitated mercer, "to tell me how my own proper affair can become worse by anything my wife does while I am in prison?"

"Because that which she does is clearly part of a seditious plan concocted between you."

"I swear to you, Madame Deputy, that you are in the profoundest error, that I know nothing in the world about what my wife is wont to do, that I am entirely ignorant to what she has done, and that if she has committed any unjust acts, I renounce her, I shun her, I curse her!"

"Fie!" said Athos to the deputy. "If you have no more need of me, send me somewhere. Your Monsieur Bouquet is very tiresome."

The deputy gestured to Athos and Bouquet in turn. "Take both prisoners back to their cells," said she to the guards, "and let them be guarded more closely than ever."

"And yet," said Athos with her habitual calmness, "if it be Madame d'Artagnan who is involved in this matter, I do not perceive how I can take her place."

"Do as I bid you!" cried the deputy again to the guards. "And let no one know of this. Do you understand?"

Athos shrugged her shoulders and followed her guard silently, while Monsieur Bouquet did the same with his own, uttering lamentations that might have softened the heart of a statue.

They locked the mercer in the same cell, and left him to himself again during the day, unable to sleep. In the evening, at the moment he had made up his mind to go to bed, he heard steps in the corridor. Those steps drew near to his cell. The door was thrown open, and four guards appeared.

"Follow me," said an officer who came up behind the guards.

"Follow you?" whispered Monsieur Bouquet. "Follow you at this hour! Where, by faith?"

"Where we have orders to lead you," replied the officer, their expression stern.

"But that is not a real answer."

"It is, nevertheless, the only answer you will receive."

"Ah, gods," murmured the poor mercer. "Now indeed, I am lost." And he stood to follow the guards who had come for him, mechanically and without resistance.

Monsieur Bouquet passed along the same corridor as before, then turned to cross a courtyard, then a second side of a building. At length, at the gate of the entrance court, he found a carriage surrounded by four more guards on horseback. His own guards made him enter this carriage, with the officer sitting at his side. The door was locked, and the mercer found himself in a rolling prison.

The carriage began to move, as slowly as a funeral car. Through the closely fastened windows, Bouquet could perceive the houses and the pavement, and that was all. But, true Parisian as he was, he could recognize every street by its milestones, signs, and lamps. At the moment of arriving at the fortress of Saint Paul — the spot where all those condemned at the Bastille were executed — Bouquet was near to fainting, for he thought his ride would most certainly end there.

The carriage, however, passed on.

Farther on, a still greater terror seized him on passing by the cemetery of Saint-Jeanne, where state criminals were buried. One thing, however, reassured him. He remembered that before they were buried, such criminals' heads were generally cut off, and he felt quite certain that his own head was still on his shoulders.

But when he saw the carriage take the way toward the Place de Greve alongside the great city hall of the Hotel de Ville, then pass beneath its great colonnade, he believed it was all over for him. He immediately stated his wish to confess to the officer with him, and upon their refusal, uttered such pitiable cries that the officer told him that if Bouquet continued to deafen them thus, they would put a gag in his mouth.

That development somewhat reassured Monsieur Bouquet. For if they meant to execute him at the Place de Greve, it would scarcely be worthwhile to gag him, as they had nearly reached that place of execution. Indeed, the carriage crossed that fatal spot without stopping.

For Monsieur Bouquet, then, there remained no other place to fear but the public gibbet known as Traitor's Arch — and the carriage was taking the direct road to it.

This time, there was no longer any doubt. It was at Traitor's Arch that lesser criminals were executed. Monsieur Bouquet had flattered himself in believing himself worthy of Saint Paul or of the Place de Greve. It was at Traitor's Arch that his journey and his destiny were about to end. He could not yet see that dreadful site, but he felt somehow as if it were coming to meet him.

When they had drawn within twenty paces of it, he heard the sound of a crowd of people and the carriage stopped. And this was more than poor Monsieur Bouquet could endure, shaken as he was by the successive emotions which he had experienced. He uttered a feeble groan that might have been taken for the last sigh of the dying, then fainted dead away.

— **CHAPTER 14** —

THEIR EMINENCE'S ORDERS

As it happened, the crowd of Monsieur Bouquet's consternation was caused not by the expectation that he was to be hanged at Traitor's Arch — but by the spectacle of the unknown soul who had just been hanged moments before. The carriage, which stopped for a short while to let the crowd disperse, then resumed its way. It passed through the last somber spectators, threaded the Rue Saint-Honore, turned into the Rue de Bons Enfants, and finally stopped before a shadowed door.

The door opened. The carriage was unlocked. Two guards from within the unknown house received Monsieur Bouquet in their arms from the officer who supported him. They carried him through an inner courtyard, up a flight of stairs, and deposited him on a bench in an antechamber, across from a closed door.

All these movements had been effected mechanically, as far as Bouquet was concerned. He had walked as one walks in a dream, seeing only a glimpse of his surroundings as through a fog. His ears caught sounds without comprehending them, and had he been executed at that very moment, he would have been incapable of making a single gesture of resistance or uttering any cry for mercy.

He remained on the bench with his back leaning against the wall and his hands hanging down, exactly on the spot where the guards placed him. On looking around him, however, he realized that he could perceive no immediate threat. Nothing indicated that he might be in any real danger. The bench, in fact, was comfortably covered with well-stuffed cushions, and the walls of the antechamber ornamented with beautiful Cordova leather. Large red damask curtains, fastened back by gold clasps, floated before a sunny window, and Monsieur Bouquet began to perceive by degrees that his fear was perhaps exaggerated.

He began to turn his head to the right and the left, upward and downward. At this movement, which no one observed or opposed, he resumed a little courage, and ventured to draw up one leg and then the other. At length, with the help of his two hands, he was able to lift himself from the bench and found himself on his feet.

At that moment, an officer with a pleasant face opened the antechamber's second door, continuing to exchange some words with a person in the next chamber. They then came up to the prisoner.

"Is your name Bouquet?"

"Yes, Maitre Officer," stammered the mercer, his voice more dead than alive. "At your service."

"Come in," said the officer. And they moved out of the way to let him pass. Monsieur Bouquet obeyed without reply and entered the chamber, where he appeared to be expected.

It was a large office, close and stifling, with the walls furnished with arms and armor. A fire was burning, although the morning was already warm. A square table occupied the center of the room, covered with books and papers, among which was unrolled an immense map of the city of La Rochelle. Also covering the many papers and the map, and appearing somewhat incongruous even to Bouquet's frantic eyes, were a number of cats. Only one of those responded to his presence, and that with little more than an errant glance.

Standing before the fire was a figure of middle height, and of a haughty, proud mien. They bore piercing black eyes, a large brow, and a thin face of sternest umber complexion, which was made still longer by a narrow chin surmounted by close-set lips. Although this personage was scarcely forty years of age, their black hair had begun to gray. They had all the appearance of a soldier except a sword, and their buff boots, still showing dust, indicated that they had been on horseback earlier in the day.

At first sight, it would be impossible for those who did not know this face to guess in whose presence they were. For this unassuming figure was Armand Jean Duplessis — the Cardinal de Richelieu.

An active and gallant gentry, Richelieu was weak of body, but sustained by an intellectual power which drove them to extraordinary deeds. The strewn table showed the preparations made for various campaigns, whose end goal was to drive the English from the Isle of Rhe which guarded the city of La Rochelle — and to then lay siege to La Rochelle and its rebellious Huguenot inhabitants thereafter.

The poor Monsieur Bouquet remained standing at the door while the eyes of the personage we have just described rose and were fixed upon him, appearing capable of penetrating even into the depths of his heart and mind.

"Is this Bouquet?" asked this figure after a moment of silence.

"Yes, maitre," replied the officer.

"Very well. Give me those papers, and leave us."

The officer took from the table the papers pointed out, gave them to the speaker, bowed to the ground, and withdrew.

As the door closed, Monsieur Bouquet recognized in those papers the notes of both his interrogations at the Bastille. From time to time, the person by the fire raised their eyes from the pages, plunging them like daggers into the heart of the poor mercer.

At the end of a long while of reading and a shorter while of contemplation, the cardinal assessed Monsieur Bouquet anew. They noted the mercer's pale face, which at that moment expressed nothing resembling the intellect required for the conspiracies detailed within the notes of the Bastille. "But we will see," murmured their eminence. Then they spoke louder.

"You are accused of high treason."

"So I have been told already, maitre," said Monsieur Bouquet. "But I swear to you that I know nothing about it."

The cardinal frowned. "You have conspired with your wife, Madame Constance Bonacieux. You have conspired with Madame de Chevreuse, and with the Lord Duke of Buckingham."

"Indeed, maitre," responded the mercer, "I have heard my wife pronounce all those names."

"And on what occasion?"

"She said that Cardinal de Richelieu had drawn the Duke of Buckingham to Paris to ruin him, and to ruin the Queen Anne."

"She said what?" snarled the cardinal with sudden anger.

"Yes, maitre. But I told her she was wrong to talk about such things, and that their eminence was incapable —"

"Hold your tongue, fool."

"That's exactly what my wife said, maitre."

The cardinal narrowed their eyes. "Do you know who carried off your wife?"

"No, maitre."

"But you expressed suspicions during your interrogation nonetheless?"

"Yes, maitre. But those suspicions appeared to be disagreeable to Madame Deputy of the Bastille, so I no longer have them."

"Your wife has escaped. Did you know that?"

"I learned it only since I have been in prison, maitre, and that from the conversation of Madame Deputy — an amiable figure."

The cardinal frowned once more. "Then you are ignorant of what has become of your wife since her flight."

"Absolutely, maitre. But she has most likely returned to the Louvre."

"As of one o'clock this morning, she had not returned."

"Gods! What can have become of her, then?"

"We shall know, be assured. Nothing is concealed from the cardinal. The cardinal knows everything."

"In that case, maitre, do you believe the cardinal will be so kind as to tell me what has become of my wife?"

"Perhaps they may. But you must first reveal all you know of your wife's relationship with Madame de Chevreuse."

"But maitre, I know nothing about that. I have never seen Madame de Chevreuse."

"During the most recent times when you met your wife at the Louvre, did you always return directly home?"

"Most times. But twice in recent weeks, she had business to transact with linen drapers, to whose houses I accompanied her."

"And how many were there of these linen drapers?"

"Two, maitre."

"And where did they live?"

"One in the Rue de Vaugirard, the other the Rue de Harpe."

"Did you go into these houses with her?"

"Never, maitre. I waited at the door."

"And what excuse did she give you for entering all alone?"

"She gave me none. Her inquiries were all regarding decorating at the Louvre, and as I had no interest in such business, I waited."

"You are a very trusting spouse, my dear Monsieur Bouquet," said the cardinal.

"I am 'dear Monsieur,'" said the mercer to himself. "Is it too much to hope that this interview is proceeding well?"

"Would you know again those doors where your wife tarried? Do you know their numbers?"

"Yes, maitre. Number 25 in the Rue de Vaugirard. Number 75 in the Rue de Harpe."

"Very well done," said the cardinal. At these words, their eminence took up a silver bell and rang it. The officer entered.

"Go," said the cardinal, "and find Rochefort. Tell him to come to me immediately, if he has returned."

"In fact, the Count de Rochefort has only just arrived," said the officer, "and requests to speak with your eminence at your earliest convenience."

"Let him come, then."

The officer slipped quickly from the apartment, eager to obey. But Monsieur Bouquet, his eyes round in astonishment, had eyes only for the figure who had given the order. And as he stared, he murmured, "He requests to speak with your eminence…" — and knew now whom it was he faced.

Scarcely any time at all elapsed after the disappearance of the officer when the door opened again, and a new personage entered. This was one who we have met, and who has been spoken of. The Count de Rochefort, he of one black and piercing eye, and with the pale scar along one cheek.

"It is they!" cried Bouquet, still shocked at his recognition of the cardinal, and now shocked again.

"They? What they?" said the cardinal.

"The one who abducted my wife."

*"It is they!" cried Bouquet, still shocked at his
recognition of the cardinal, and now shocked again…*

The cardinal rang the silver bell a second time. The officer reappeared.

"Place Monsieur Bouquet in the care of his guards again, and let him wait in the antechamber till I send for him."

"No, maitre, no, it is not they!" said Bouquet. "No, I was deceived. This is quite another gentle, and does not resemble the villain I recall at all. They are, I am sure, a most honest person."

"Take away that fool!" said the cardinal.

The officer took Monsieur Bouquet by the arm and led him into the antechamber, where he found two guards waiting. The newly introduced personage watched Bouquet carefully till the mercer had gone out, then spoke the moment the door closed.

"They have seen each other," said the Count de Rochefort, approaching the cardinal eagerly. "The queen and the duke."

"Where?"

"At the Louvre."

"Are you sure of it?"

"Perfectly sure."

"Who told you of it?"

"Monsieur de Lannoy, the queen's dresser. Who is devoted to your eminence, as you know."

"Why did he not let me know sooner?"

"Whether by chance or mistrust, the Queen Anne made business for Monsieur de Lannoy which detained him all the day."

"Well, then, we are beaten. Now let us try to take our revenge."

"I will assist you with all my heart, your eminence. Be assured of that."

"How did it come about?"

"At half past twelve, the Queen Anne was with all her attendants, in her bedchamber. There, someone came and brought her a handkerchief, as if from her laundry. The queen immediately exhibited strong emotion, and evidently turned pale. She then arose, and spoke with altered voice. 'Wait for me,' said she. 'I shall soon return.' She then opened the door of her alcove and went out."

"Why did not Monsieur de Lannoy come and inform you immediately?"

"Nothing was certain. Besides, her majesty had said, 'Wait for me,' and he did not dare to disobey the queen."

"How long did the Queen Anne remain out of her chamber?"

"Three-quarters of an hour."

"None of her people accompanied her?"

"Only Dona Estafania."

"Did she afterward return?"

"Yes. But only to take a little rosewood coffer with her initial upon it, and went out again immediately. When she finally returned, she did not bring the coffer with her."

The cardinal paced between the fireplace and the desk, taking in all Rochefort had to report. "Does Monsieur de Lannoy know what was within?" asked their eminence.

"Yes. The choker set with twelve diamond studs which her majesty the Queen Louise gave to her majesty the Queen Anne for her birthday."

"And with the Queen Anne returning without the coffer, I trust that Monsieur de Lannoy, then, is of the opinion that she gave those studs to Buckingham."

"In fact, he is sure of it."

"How so?"

"In the course of the day, Monsieur de Lannoy, in his position as dresser of the Queen Anne, looked for this coffer, appeared uneasy at not finding it, and at length asked questions of the Queen Anne. To which the queen became exceedingly pale, and replied that having the previous evening broken one of those studs, she had sent it to her jeweler to be repaired."

"And has this jeweler been called upon, so as to ascertain the truth of the queen's statement or Monsieur de Lannoy's belief?"

"I have just been with the jeweler and the goldsmith of the Louvre, and neither have heard any word from the queen."

Cardinal de Richelieu then smiled. "Well, then. Rochefort, all is not lost. And perhaps, despite all appearances, everything is for the best."

"Truthfully, I have no doubt that your eminence's genius —"

"Will repair the blunders of their agent?"

"That is exactly what I had meant to say, if your eminence had let me finish."

"Indeed. But more immediately, do you know where Madame de Chevreuse and the Duke of Buckingham are now concealed?"

"No, your eminence. My agents could tell me nothing on that point."

"Then you will be pleased that I know."

"You, eminence?"

"Yes. Or at least I knew. Had you looked earlier, you would have found one in the Rue de Vaugirard, number 25, and the other in the Rue de Harpe, number 75. But it is too late to seek them there. They will be returned to their respective exiles. Still, take ten of my guards and search the two houses thoroughly."

"Immediately, eminence." And Rochefort went quickly out of the room.

The cardinal, being left alone, reflected for a moment and then rang the silver bell a third time. The same officer appeared.

"Bring the prisoner in again," said the cardinal.

Monsieur Bouquet was returned afresh from the antechamber, and upon a sign from the cardinal, the officer withdrew.

"You have deceived me," said the cardinal sternly.

"I?" whimpered Monsieur Bouquet. "I deceive your eminence?"

"Your wife, in going to Rue de Vaugirard and Rue de Harpe, did not go to find linen drapers."

"Then why did she go, by faith?"

"She went to meet Madame de Chevreuse and the Duke of Buckingham."

"Well," cried Bouquet, trying to recall all his remembrances of the circumstances. "Indeed, that must be it. Your eminence is right. I told my wife several times that it was surprising that linen drapers should live in such houses as those, in houses that had no signs. But she always laughed at me." Bouquet threw himself at their eminence's feet. "Ah, maitre, how truly you are the cardinal, the great cardinal, the soul of genius whom all the world reveres!"

However trivial might be the triumph gained over so malleable a being as Monsieur Bouquet, the cardinal did nonetheless enjoy it for a moment. Then, preparing to finish the engagement with the unwitting mercer, they offered him their hand. "Rise, my friend. You are a worthy gentle."

"The cardinal has touched me with their hand! I have touched the hand of greatness!" said Bouquet. "They have called me their friend!"

"Yes, my friend," said the cardinal, with a protective tone which deceived none who knew them, but which was as a balm to Monsieur Bouquet's mind. "And as you have been unjustly suspected, well, you must be indemnified." Stepping to the desk, the cardinal withdrew a leather purse from a drawer. "Here, now. Take this hundred pistoles, and forgive me."

"I? Forgive you, maitre?" said Bouquet, hesitant to take the purse. "But you are able to have me arrested, you are able to have me tortured, you are able to have me hanged. You are my master, and I could not have the least word to say. Pardon you, maitre? You cannot mean that!"

"Ah, my dear Monsieur Bouquet, you are generous in this matter. I see it and I thank you for it. Thus, then, you will take this purse, and I hope you will go away contented."

"I shall go away enchanted, I assure you," said Monsieur Bouquet, who accepted the purse into trembling hands.

"Farewell, then. Or rather, au revoir."

"Au revoir, maitre. And whenever maitre wishes, be assured that I shall be firmly at their eminence's command."

"That will be often, be assured. For I have found our conversation quite charming. But now au revoir, Monsieur Bouquet. Au revoir."

And the cardinal made him a sign with their hand, to which Bouquet replied by bowing to the ground. He then went out the door backward, and as the door was closed behind him, the cardinal heard him crying aloud in his enthusiasm, "Long life to the maitre! Long life to their eminence! Long life to the great cardinal!"

Richelieu listened with a smile to this vociferous manifestation of emotion. "Good," said they to themself. "That one will henceforth lay down his life for me." And the cardinal then turned to examine with the greatest attention the map of La Rochelle upon the table, though first shooing away the cats that sprawled across it with an imperious hand.

It was some hours later, and their eminence was in the deepest of their strategic meditations, when the door opened and Rochefort returned.

"Well?" said the cardinal, with an edge to their voice which spoke to the importance of Rochefort's report.

"Two persons, one of about twenty-six or twenty-eight years of age, and one from thirty-five to forty, have indeed lodged at the two houses noted by your eminence. But the younger left last night, and the elder this morning. Neighbors report the younger figure as having gone abroad at dusk, and in the direction of the Rue de Cherche Midi. Of the older figure, it was said a cloaked messenger came to them at an unusual hour, and escorted them away."

"It was they," said the cardinal grimly, looking at the clock. "And now it is too late to have the two pursued. Madame de Chevreuse was the younger, and will be back at Tours. The duke was the elder, and will be at Boulogne ready to return to England. It is thus in London that this pursuit must be reengaged."

"What are your eminence's orders?"

"Speak not a word of what you have heard and shared here. Let the Queen Anne remain in perfect peace of mind. Let her be ignorant that we know her secret. Let her believe that we are in search of her conspiracy, rather than having already exposed it. Then send me the keeper of the seals — the chancellor, Monsieur de Seguier."

"And that man Bouquet? What has your eminence done with him?"

"I have done with him all that could be done. I have made him a spy upon the Queen Anne's tailor and agent — Madame Constance Bonacieux, his wife."

The Count de Rochefort bowed low, seemingly acknowledging the masterful play of the cardinal's game. He then withdrew.

Left alone, the cardinal sat and wrote a letter, which they secured with their seal.

Milord —

Be at the first ball at which the Duke of Buckingham shall be present. He will wear on his person twelve diamond studs. Get as near to him as you can, and cut off two.

As soon as these studs shall be in your possession, inform me.

They then rang again, and the officer entered.

"Send for a courier," said Richelieu, "and tell them to get ready for a journey."

Only a short while after, the courier asked for was before the cardinal, booted and spurred.

"You will go with all speed to London," said their eminence, "and will deliver this letter to Milord de Winter. Do not stop for a single moment on the way. Do not tarry in the finding of him. Do not fail me."

Without replying a single word, the courier bowed, took the letter, and was quickly gone.

CHAPTER 15

ATTORNEYS AND SOLDIERS

On the same morning that Athos and Monsieur Bouquet were confronted with each other in the Bastille, which was the morning after d'Artagnan had assisted Constance in bringing the Duke of Buckingham to the Louvre, the young guard went to Monsieur de Treville to inform the captain of Athos's fate. Porthos was with her, having been fully apprised of Athos's circumstances beforehand. As to Aramis, they had asked for leave of absence for five days and were gone, it was said, to Rouen on family business.

Monsieur de Treville and Monsieur Vaslin had no children, which may go some way toward understanding Monsieur de Treville's sense that he was the guardian of his soldiers. The lowest or the least known of them, as soon as they assumed the uniform of the company, was as sure of the captain's aid and support as if they had been his own kin. And so it was that after hearing the word of d'Artagnan and Porthos, Treville left them and went immediately and at speed to the office of the magistrate of justice.

By successive inquiries of officers and messengers, Monsieur de Treville quickly learned that Athos had been moved from the Bastille. In fact, she was at present lodged in the lesser prison of Fort l'Eveque. But when Monsieur de Treville traveled there at once, he got no farther than the residence of the prison's inhospitable governor, and without hearing any word of Athos. Flushed with anger, he left the fort and traveled to the palace, understanding that with all other options closed to him, he required the ears of the queens.

We were present at the scene in which Athos was brought forth by the guards of the Bastille. The elder musketeer had till that time said nothing, for fear that d'Artagnan would not have the time she needed for her investigations if she were interrupted in her turn. But from that moment of facing Bouquet, she declared that her name was Athos, and not d'Artagnan. She added that she did not know either Madame Bonacieux or Monsieur Bouquet, and that she had never spoken to the one or the other. She had come, said she, at about ten o'clock in the evening to pay a visit to her friend Madame d'Artagnan, but before that hour, she had been at Monsieur de Treville and Monsieur Vaslin's, where she had dined.

"Twenty witnesses," added she, "could attest the fact." And she named several distinguished gentlefolk, among them Madame de Tremouille.

The second deputy was as much bewildered as the first had been by this simple and firm declaration. Both were equally clear on their need to revenge themselves on this insolent musketeer — but the name of Monsieur de Treville and that of Madame de Tremouille meant they must move carefully.

Athos was then sent to the cardinal. But as it happened, the cardinal was at the Louvre with the Queen Louise.

It was well known at court how deep-set the Queen Louise's prejudices against the Queen Anne had grown in the years since their marriage of state. It was lesser known how carefully those prejudices were shaped and kept up by the cardinal. One of the grand causes of this prejudice was the friendship of the Queen Anne for Madame de Chevreuse. Those two together gave the cardinal more uneasiness than the war with Spain, the quarrel with England, or the fine work of controlling the realm's finances all combined. For in Richelieu's eyes, Madame de Chevreuse not only served the Queen Anne in her political intrigues but also in her amorous intrigues — which tormented their eminence still more.

So it was that Cardinal de Richelieu sat with the Queen Louise throughout that afternoon, and was forced to reveal that although Madame de Chevreuse had been exiled to Tours and was believed to remain in that city, she had nonetheless come to Paris, remained there for days, and outwitted any and all guards who should have found her. At the first word the cardinal spoke of this, the Queen Louise flew into a furious rage, showing a capricious and unfaithful countenance that vied so strongly with her majesty's wish to be called by history Louise the Just.

But then the cardinal added that not only had Madame de Chevreuse been in Paris, but still further, that the Queen Anne had renewed with that gentle their mysterious and longstanding correspondence. Then their eminence affirmed that they, the cardinal, had been about to unravel the most closely twisted threads of this intrigue — but that at the moment of arresting the Queen Anne's emissary to the exiled Madame de Chevreuse, with all the proofs about her, a musketeer had dared to violently interrupt the course of justice.

This musketeer, their eminence swore, had fallen sword in hand upon the honest guards of the law, charged with investigating impartially the whole affair in order to place it before the eyes of the Queen Louise. At all of this, Louise could not contain herself. She made steps toward and away from the Queen Anne's apartment with a mute indignation that promised a pitiless cruelty. And to the cardinal's smiling favor as he watched the queen pace, their eminence had not yet said one word about the Duke of Buckingham.

At that moment, Monsieur de Treville entered — cool, polite, and with a most professional bearing. As captain of the musketeers, Treville had the right of entry to the Louvre at all times, and even as he had raced toward the Queen Louise's chambers, he was quickly informed of what had been observed of the presence of the cardinal, and the vexation in the Queen Louise's countenance and manner. Treville felt himself something like a gladiator about to enter the pit.

Louise had already placed her hand on the knob of the inner door that would lead her to the Queen Anne. But at the noise of Monsieur de Treville's entrance, she turned round. "You arrive in good time, monsieur," said the queen. "For I have learned some fine things concerning your musketeers."

From the queen's voice, Monsieur de Treville understood that Louise's passions had been raised to the point where there would be no purpose in subtlety. He looked first to the Cardinal de Richelieu and nodded, but spoke only to her. "And I," said he coldly, "have some fine things to tell your majesty concerning a number of alleged followers of the law."

"Then speak," said the queen haughtily.

"I have the honor to inform your majesty of the actions of a party of attorneys, commissaries, and agents of the city guards. Very estimable people, but most resentful, as it appears, toward the military." Treville said all in the same tone, as one gravely insulted. "For they have taken it upon themselves to arrest in a private home, to lead away through the open street, and to throw into Fort l'Eveque one of my musketeers. Or should I say, one of your musketeers, majesty. A soldier of irreproachable conduct, of an illustrious reputation, and whom your majesty knows favorably. Madame Athos is seized, and all upon an order which I have been denied any right to see."

"Athos," said the Queen Louise, caught off guard by familiarity. "Yes, certainly I know her favorably."

"Let your majesty remember that Madame Athos is the musketeer who, in the annoying duel which you are acquainted with, had the misfortune to wound Maitre de Cahusac so seriously. As it happens, eminence," continued Treville, now shifting his gaze to address the cardinal, "Maitre de Cahusac is quite recovered, are they not?"

"Thank you, yes," said the cardinal, pursing their lips in anger.

"Well, Athos had gone to pay a visit to one of her friends absent at the time," said Treville. "To a young Gascon, a cadet in their majesty's guards, the company of Madame d'Essarts. But scarcely had she arrived at her friend's and taken up a book while waiting her return, that a mixed crowd of bailiffs and soldiers came and laid siege to the house."

The cardinal made a sign to the queen, which signified that the action described was on account of the affair about which their eminence had just spoken. "We know all that," said Louise quickly. "For all that was done for our service."

"Then," said Treville, "was it also for your majesties' service that one of my musketeers, who was innocent, has been seized? Is it for your service that she has been confined to a cell like a common criminal, and that this gallant warrior, who has ten times shed her blood in both your majesties' service and is ready to shed it again, has been paraded through the midst of an insolent populace?"

"Gods' blood," said the Queen Louise, who appeared suddenly shaken as she turned to the cardinal. "Was this truly the way of it?"

"Monsieur de Treville," said the cardinal with great indifference, "does not tell your majesty that this innocent musketeer, this gallant warrior, had only an hour before attacked, sword in hand, four commissaries of inquiry, who were delegated by myself to look into an affair of the highest importance."

"I defy your eminence to prove it," said Treville, allowing to come to the fore his Gascon bluntness. "For not one hour before, Madame Athos, who I will attest again to your majesty is a gentlefolk of the highest quality, did me the honor, after having dined with me and Monsieur Vaslin, to converse in the salon of my estate with Monsieur Vaslin, Madame de Tremouille, and the Countieux de Chalus, who happened to be there."

The queen looked at the cardinal.

"A written report attests the facts," said the cardinal, replying aloud to the mute interrogation of her majesty. "The ill-treated parties have themselves drawn up this record, which I have the honor to present to your majesty."

"And is the written report of the attorney to be placed in comparison with the word of honor of a soldier?" said Treville fiercely.

"Come, come, Treville, hold your tongue," said the Queen Louise.

"If their eminence entertains any suspicion against one of my musketeers," said Treville, "the justice of the cardinal is so well known that I demand an inquiry."

"In the house in which the judicial inquiry was made," said the impassive cardinal, "there lodges, I believe, a young Gascon. A friend of the musketeer."

"Your eminence means Madame d'Artagnan."

"I mean a young stripling whom you grant unusual favor and aid, Monsieur de Treville."

"Yes, your eminence. It is all the same."

"Do you not suspect this stripling of having given bad counsel to Madame Athos?"

"To Athos? Give counsel to one half again her age?" chided Treville. "No, eminence. Besides, d'Artagnan passed the evening with me."

"Well," said the cardinal, "everyone seems to have passed the evening with you."

"Does your eminence doubt my word?" said Treville, who allowed his face to flush with anger.

"No, gods forbid," said the cardinal. "Only at what hour was she with you?"

"Oh, as to that I can speak positively, your eminence. For as d'Artagnan came in, I remarked that it was but half past nine by the clock, although I had believed it to be later."

"At what hour did she leave your estate?"

"At half past ten — an hour after the event."

"Well…" said the cardinal, who hesitated for the first time since their conversation with the Queen Louise began. Their eminence knew that they could not for an instant openly question the loyalty of Treville, and felt that victory was escaping them. "Well, but Athos was taken in the house in the Rue de Fossoyeurs."

"Is one friend forbidden to visit another, or a musketeer of my company to fraternize with a guard of the company of d'Essarts?"

"Yes, when the house where she fraternizes is suspected."

"That house is under suspicion and observation, Treville," said the Queen Louise. "Perhaps you did not know that?"

"Indeed, majesty, I did not. And under suspicion the house may be, but I deny that this state extends to the part of it inhabited by Madame d'Artagnan. For I can affirm, majesty, that there does not exist a more devoted retainer of both your majesties or a more profound admirer of Cardinal de Richelieu."

"Was it not this d'Artagnan who wounded Madame de Jussac one day, in that unfortunate encounter which took place near the convent of the Carmes-Deschaux?" asked the queen. Louise looked to the cardinal, who flushed with vexation.

"And the next day, Maitre Bernajoux. Yes, majesty, yes, she is the same guard. And your majesty has an excellent memory."

"But come then, how shall we decide the outcome of this matter?" said the queen.

"That concerns your majesty more than me," said the cardinal. "I simply affirm this d'Artagnan is guilty."

"And I deny it," said Treville. "But your majesty has judges, and those judges will decide."

"That is best," said the queen. "Send the case before the judges. It is their business to judge, and they shall judge."

"Except…" said Treville, as though deep in thought. "It is a sad thing that in the unfortunate times in which we live, the purest life, the most incontestable virtue, cannot exempt one from infamy and persecution. The army, I will assure your majesty, will be little pleased at being exposed to such rigorous treatment on account of such trivial legal affairs."

The statement was rash — but Monsieur de Treville had spoken it with cause and purpose. He desired an explosion, knowing that the light of the fire thrown forth would reveal much of what was hidden.

"Such trivial legal affairs!" cried the queen, taking up Treville's words. "And what do you know about them, monsieur? Meddle with your musketeers, and do not annoy me in this way. It appears, according to your account, that if by mischance a musketeer is arrested, France is in danger. What a noise about a musketeer! I could arrest ten of them, a hundred, even all the company, and forbid anyone to speak a word against it."

"From the moment they are suspected by your majesty," said Treville, "the musketeers are guilty. Therefore, you see me prepared to surrender my sword — for after having accused my soldiers, there can be no doubt that the cardinal will end by accusing me. It is best to constitute myself at once a prisoner with Athos, who is already arrested, and with d'Artagnan, who most probably will be."

The Queen Louise stared in disbelief. "Gascon-headed fool, will you take that tone with me?"

"Majesty," said Treville without altering his tone in the least, "either order my musketeer to be restored to me, or let her be tried."

"She shall be tried," said the cardinal.

"Well, so much the better. For in that case, I shall demand of both their majesties permission to plead Athos's innocence before all."

The Queen Louise shook her head, as if fearing that a complete breakdown was at hand. The cardinal saw it, and understood that his battle was near to lost.

"Plead before me," said the queen to Treville. "Will you swear by my father that Athos was at your estate during the event, and could thus have taken no part in it?"

"By your glorious father, and by yourself whom I love and venerate above all the world, I swear it."

"Be so kind as to reflect, majesty," said the cardinal. "If we release the prisoner thus, we shall never know the truth."

"Athos may always be found among the musketeers," said Treville, "and shall be ready to answer when it please the attorneys in their gowns of court to interrogate her. She will not desert, your eminence, be assured of that. I will answer for her."

"No, she will not desert," said the queen. "She can always be found, as Treville says."

Richelieu's countenance remained impassive, though their heart seethed. "Then you may order as you please, majesty. You possess the right of pardon, after all."

"The right of pardon only applies to the guilty," said Treville, who was determined to have the last word. "And my musketeer is innocent. It is not mercy, then, that you are about to accord, my queen. It is justice."

"And this Athos is in the Fort l'Eveque?" said the queen.

"Yes, majesty. In confinement like the lowest criminal."

"By my faith," murmured the queen. "What must be done?"

"Sign an order for her release, and all will be ended," said the cardinal. "I believe, as does your majesty, that Monsieur de Treville's guarantee is more than sufficient."

Treville bowed very respectfully, with a joy that was not unmixed with fear. He would almost have preferred a continued resistance on the part of the cardinal to this sudden yielding.

Calling her secretary to her, the queen signed the order for release. Monsieur de Treville readied to carry it away without delay. But as he was about to leave, the cardinal gave him a friendly smile, and said, "A perfect harmony reigns, monsieur, between the leaders and the soldiers of your musketeers. This must be profitable for the service, and honorable to all."

Monsieur de Treville nodded, and departed without speaking. But as he went, thought he, "Their eminence will play me some dog's trick or other, and that immediately. One has never the last word with such a one. So let us be quick — the queen may change her mind in an hour. And after all, it will be more difficult for them to replace a prisoner in the Fort l'Eveque or the Bastille who has got out, than to keep a prisoner there who is in."

A short while later, Treville made his entrance triumphantly into the Fort l'Eveque, whence he delivered the musketeer whose peaceful indifference had not for a moment abandoned her.

When Athos next saw d'Artagnan, said she to the younger woman, "You have come off well in this affair. And there is your attack upon Jussac paid for. There still remains what you are owed from me for Bernajoux, but you must not be overconfident."

As to the rest, Monsieur de Treville had good reason to mistrust the cardinal, and to think that all was not over. For scarcely had the captain of the musketeers closed the door after taking his leave of Louise than their eminence spoke to the queen.

"Now that we are at length by ourselves, we will, if your majesty pleases, converse seriously. My queen, Buckingham has been in Paris five days, and only left this morning."

CHAPTER 16

THE CHANCELLOR LOOKS MORE THAN ONCE FOR THE BELL

It is impossible to properly describe the impression that Richelieu's few words made upon the Queen Louise. She grew ashen and flushed all at once, and the cardinal understood that they had recovered with a single attack all the ground Monsieur de Treville had gained at their expense.

"Buckingham in Paris!" cried Louise. "And why does he come?"

"To conspire, no doubt, with your enemies, the Huguenots and the Spaniards."

"By my faith, speak the truth! To conspire against my honor with Madame de Chevreuse, who desires to lead my queen astray!"

"Oh, majesty, what an idea! The Queen Anne is too virtuous. And besides, she loves your majesty too well."

"Virtue is weak, Maitre Cardinal," said the Queen Louise. "And as to loving me much, I have my own opinion as to the depth of that love."

"I nonetheless maintain," said the cardinal, "that the Duke of Buckingham came to Paris for a purpose wholly political."

"And I am sure that he came with more personal goals in mind, Maitre Cardinal. But if the Queen Anne be guilty, let her tremble."

"Alas," said the cardinal. "It almost shames me to speak, but whatever reluctance I may have to directing my mind to even consider such treason, your majesty compels me to think of it. Monsieur de Lannoy, whom I have frequently interrogated for news of the Queen Anne at your majesty's command, has told me that the night before last, her majesty sat up very late. And that this very morning, she wept much, and that she was writing all day."

"That's it!" cried Louise. "Writing to him, no doubt. Cardinal, I must have Anne's papers."

"But how to take them, my queen? It seems to me that it is neither your majesty nor myself who could possibly undertake such a mission."

"How would we act with regard to this suspected treason in any other?" said Louise, in the highest state of rage. "First her rooms would be thoroughly searched, and then she herself."

"Because any other would be no more than any other, majesty. While the august spouse of your majesty is Anne of Austria, second queen of France. And that is to say, one of the most powerful leaders in the world."

"She is nonetheless guilty, maitre. The more she has forgotten the high position to which she has been ascended, the more degrading is her fall. By my faith, I should have long ago put an end to all these petty intrigues of policy and love. There are too many close to her who encourage this base behavior."

"Indeed, majesty," said the cardinal. "I am sorry to say that I know of a certain Laporte who, I confess to believe, may be at the heart of much of this."

Louise's anger only intensified at this news. "You think then, as I do, that Anne deceives me?" said she.

"I believe, and I repeat it to your majesty, that the Queen Anne conspires against the power of the crown — but I have not said against your honor."

"And I… I tell you that she conspires against both. I tell you the Queen Anne does not love me. I tell you she loves another, I tell you she loves that infamous Buckingham! Why did you not have him arrested while in Paris?"

"Arrest the Duke of Buckingham? The prime minister of England? Think of it, majesty. What a scandal! And if the suspicions of your majesty, which I still continue to doubt, should prove to have any foundation, what a terrible disclosure."

"But as he exposed himself like a vagabond or a thief, he should have been —"

Louise stopped, terrified at what she had been about to say. While Richelieu, hiding their expectation, waited in vain for the word that had died on the lips of the queen.

"Buckingham should have been…?"

"Nothing," said the Queen Louise. "Nothing. But all the time he was in Paris, you, of course, did not lose sight of him?"

"No, my queen."

"Where did he lodge?"

"Rue de Harpe. Number 75. By the side of the Luxembourg."

"And you are certain that the queen and he did not see each other?"

"I believe the Queen Anne to have too high a sense of her duty, majesty."

"But they have corresponded. It must be to him that the queen has been writing all this day. Maitre Cardinal, I must have those letters!"

"Majesty, notwithstanding —"

"Maitre, at whatever price it may be, I will have them."

"I would beg your majesty to observe —"

"Do you, then, also join in betraying me, Maitre Cardinal? By thus always opposing my will? Are you also in accord with Spain and England, with Madame de Chevreuse and the queen?"

"Majesty," replied the cardinal, sighing. "I believed myself secure from such a suspicion."

"Maitre Cardinal, you have heard me. I will have those letters."

Cardinal de Richelieu stood a moment as if in deep thought, then spoke as if reluctant. "I perceive, majesty, that there may be one way."

"What is that?"

"That would be to charge Monsieur de Seguier, the chancellor and keeper of the seals, with this mission. For the matter of determining whether any royal has engaged in conduct threatening to the state enters completely into the duties of his post."

"Then let him be sent for immediately."

"Indeed, he may well already be present, your majesty. For I had requested him to call on me regarding another matter. When I came to the Louvre, I left orders that if he arrived at the Place de Palais-Cardinal, he should be asked to meet me here."

"Indeed? Then let him be sought for, I say."

"Your majesty's orders shall be executed. But…"

"But what, ser?"

"But the Queen Anne will perhaps refuse to obey."

The Queen Louise flushed still angrier. "What? Refuse me?"

"Surely no. But if she is ignorant that these orders come from your majesty…"

"Well, so that she may have no doubt on that point, I will inform her myself."

"Your majesty will not forget that I have done everything in my power to prevent all conflict between my two beloved royals."

"Yes, maitre, yes. I know you are very indulgent toward the Queen Anne. Too indulgent, perhaps. We shall have occasion, I warn you, at some future period to speak of that."

"Whenever it shall please your majesty. But I shall be always happy and proud to sacrifice myself to the harmony which I desire to see reign between the queens of France."

"It is noted, cardinal. But for now, send for Monsieur the Chancellor. Express to him the orders I have indicated to you. I will go to my wife."

And Louise, opening the room's inner door, passed into the corridor which led from her apartments to those of the Queen Anne.

Within her chambers, Anne was in the company of her attendants. All were taking turns to read aloud from favorite works, and all were listening with attention to each speaker in turn — with the exception of the queen. For Anne had requested this reading in order that she might be able, while feigning to listen, to pursue the thread of her own thoughts.

Those thoughts, gilded as they were by a last reflection of love, were nonetheless sad. For Anne of Austria was deprived of the confidence of her wife, and under perpetual attack from the hatred of the cardinal. The secret of the cardinal's animosity for her was one she held close — for she had more than once rejected their eminence's wish for a more tender and wholly scandalous relationship.

And so in the name of that sentiment which Anne had refused the Maitre Cardinal, the queen had seen her most devoted retainers fall around her — her most intimate confidantes, her dearest favorites. Like those unfortunate persons endowed with a fatal gift, she brought misfortune upon everything she touched, and her friendship was a fatal sign which called down persecution. Madame de Chevreuse, Monsieur Putange, and Maitre de Vernet were exiled. And Monsieur Laporte did not conceal from her majesty that he expected to be arrested at every moment.

It was at the point when the Queen Anne was plunged in the deepest and gravest of these reflections that the door of the chamber opened, and the Queen Louise entered.

Dona Estafania, whose turn it was to read, hushed at once. She and all Anne's attendants rose into profound silence. As to the Queen Louise, she made no demonstration of politeness, ignoring all others and stopping before the Queen Anne.

"Madame," said she, "you are about to receive a visit from the chancellor, who will communicate certain matters to you extending from orders I have had given him."

The unfortunate Anne turned pale, her present thoughts and the words of the Queen Louise colliding in her mind. "But why announce this visit, my love? What can the chancellor have to say to me that you cannot say yourself?"

The Queen Louise turned upon her heel without reply — and almost at the same instant, the captain of the guards in the corridor outside the chamber's main door announced that the chancellor had arrived.

By the time the chancellor appeared, Louise had already gone out by the inner door.

Monsieur de Seguier entered, half smiling, half blushing, as he was a pleasant sort. He was canon of Notre Dame cathedral, and had formerly been valet of a bishop, who had introduced Monsieur de Seguier to their eminence as one perfectly devoted to the cardinal's interest. The cardinal thus trusted him, and Seguier had served their eminence faithfully. The Queen Anne knew well Monsieur de Seguier's relationship with the cardinal, and many other stories surrounding the chancellor as well. But among them all, at the moment in which he stopped before her and bowed, memory brought to Anne's mind the following tale.

After a wild youth, Seguier had entered into a convent, there to expiate the follies of adolescence, at least for a time. But even after entering this holy place, the poor penitent was unable to shut the door of his heart and mind so close as to prevent the passions he had fled from entering into him. He was incessantly attacked by those passions, and the superior of the monastery — to whom Seguier had confided this misfortune, and who wished as much as was in her power to free him from it — had advised him on how to abjure away his temptations.

This advice took the form of seeking recourse to the convent's bell rope, and an order to ring that bell with all his might. At the sound, the other ascetics of the monastery would be rendered aware that temptation was besieging one of their own, and all the community would go to prayers.

This advice appeared good to the future chancellor, and he held at bay the evil spirit with the abundance of prayers offered up each time the bell sounded. But the spirit of passion does not suffer to be so easily dispossessed. In proportion as he redoubled the exorcisms, Seguier redoubled the temptations. So that day and night, the bell was ringing full swing, announcing the extreme aspiration for subduing his bodily desires which the penitent experienced.

The ascetics had no longer any time to rest. By day, they did nothing but ascend and descend the steps which led to the chapel. At night, in addition to the prayers of the hours, they were further obliged to leap twenty times out of their beds and prostrate themselves on the floor of their cells.

It was not known to the one who had told the story to the Queen Anne whether it was the passion that gave way, or the ascetics who grew tired. But within three months, the penitent reappeared in the world with the reputation of being the most terrible example of possession by passion who had ever lived.

On leaving the convent, Monsieur de Seguier entered into the magistracy, moving up with the assistance of, and eventually replacing, a well-regarded cousin. He then entered the cardinal's sphere, which proved a wise career choice. He became chancellor, working closely with all who, in their turn, worked to keep the realm clear of enemies. And he had served their eminence the cardinal with zeal in their vengeance against the Queen Anne, leading to the confidence that had inspired the singular commission for which he now presented himself in the queen's apartments.

The Queen Anne had still been standing when Monsieur de Seguier entered. But scarcely had she nodded to the chancellor than she reseated herself in her armchair, and made a sign to her attendants to resume their cushions and seats. Then with an air of supreme hauteur, said she, "What do you desire, monsieur, and with what purpose do you present yourself here?"

"To make, my queen, in the name of the Queen Louise and without prejudice to the respect which I have the honor to owe to your own majesty, a close examination into all your papers."

"Indeed, monsieur?" said Anne evenly. "An investigation of my papers? Truly, this is an outrage."

"Be kind enough to forgive me, majesty. But in this circumstance, I am but the instrument which the Queen Louise employs. Has not her majesty just left you, and has she not herself asked you to prepare for this visit?"

"Search, then, monsieur. For I am a criminal, as it appears. Dona Estafania, give up the keys of my drawers and my desks."

For form's sake, the chancellor paid a visit to the pieces of furniture named. But he well knew that it was not in a drawer or desk that the Queen Anne would place the important letter the cardinal had told him she had written that day.

When the chancellor had opened and shut multiple times the drawers of Anne's quarters and antechambers, it became necessary, against all the hesitation hindering him, to push the investigation to its conclusion. Which is to say, to search the Queen Anne herself.

The chancellor therefore advanced toward Anne, and spoke with a very perplexed and embarrassed air. "And now it remains for me to make the principal examination."

"What is that?" asked the queen, who feigned to not understand.

"Her majesty Queen Louise is certain that a letter has been written by you during this day. She knows that it has not yet been sent to its address. This letter is not in your table nor in your desk. And yet it must be somewhere."

"Would you dare to lift your hand to your queen?" said Anne, drawing herself up to her full height, and fixing her eyes upon the chancellor with an expression clearly threatening.

"I am a faithful subject of two queens, your majesty Queen Anne of Austria. But all that her majesty Queen Louise of France commands, I shall do."

"And these orders come from the Queen Louise herself?" asked Anne most defiantly. But the chancellor made no reply. "Well, then," continued she. "The spies of the cardinal have served them faithfully. I have written a letter today. That letter is not yet gone. The letter is here." And the queen, standing tall, laid her hand upon bodice and breast.

"Then give me that letter, majesty," said the chancellor.

"I will give it to none but the Queen Louise, monsieur," said Anne.

"If the Queen Louise had desired that the letter should be given to her majesty, she would have asked it of you herself. But I repeat to you, I am charged with reclaiming it. And if you do not give it up…"

"Well?"

"The Queen Louise has, then, charged me to take it from you."

"The cardinal has charged you, I think you mean," said Anne coldly. "But say what you mean, monsieur."

"I say and mean that my orders go far, majesty. And that I am authorized to seek for the suspected paper, even on the person of your majesty."

"What defiance," said Anne, her lips set to a thin smile.

"Be kind enough then, majesty, to act more compliantly."

"Your conduct is infamously violent. Do you understand that, monsieur?"

"The Queen Louise commands it, majesty. Excuse me."

"I will not suffer it. No, I would rather die!" cried Anne, who in her voice, for the hearing of all in the room and the halls beyond, allowed the imperious blood of Spain and Austria to rise.

The chancellor made a most reverent bow. Then, with a clear focus on the commission with which he was charged, he stepped toward the queen. The queen, whose eyes were bright with rage, stood unmoving and bold.

The Queen Anne was, as we have said, of great beauty. The commission of Monsieur de Seguier might well have been called 'delicate.' Without doubt, the feelings that the chancellor experienced as he stood within distance of slipping his hands within the bodice of the Queen Anne were causing him to want to look about for the rope of his long-departed convent's bell. But not finding it, he summoned his resolution and stretched forth his hand toward the place where the queen had acknowledged the paper was to be found.

Anne of Austria took one step backward, so pale with anger that well she might have been death itself. And leaning with her left hand upon a table behind her to keep herself from lashing out, she with her right hand drew the paper from within her bodice and held it out to the chancellor.

"There, monsieur. There is your letter," said she in a grim and trembling voice. "Take it, and deliver me from your odious presence."

Monsieur de Seguier, who for his own part trembled with his own emotion, whose name was far too easy to imagine, took the letter, bowed to the ground, and stepped back to the hall. As the door closed upon the chancellor, the queen turned back to her attendants, and could not conceal a thin smile.

The chancellor carried the letter to the Queen Louise without having read a single word of it. The queen took it with a trembling hand, looking for the address, which was wanting. She became quite flushed, opening it slowly. Then seeing by the first words that it was addressed to one of the Kings of Spain, she read it quickly.

It was nothing but a plan of attack against the cardinal. The Queen Anne pressed the King Philip, her brother, to make show of their offense and objection to the policies of Richelieu, describing the eternal objective of those policies as the abasement of Anne's position and power. In the letter, Anne requested hostile declarations against France — and to have those declarations insist for the dismissal of the cardinal.

But as to love or the Duke of Buckingham, there was not a single word about either in all the letter.

The Queen Louise, quite delighted, inquired if the cardinal was still at the Louvre. She was told that their eminence awaited the orders of her majesty in the offices of the cabinet. The queen then went straight to Richelieu.

"There, maitre," said she. "You were right and I was wrong. The whole intrigue is political, and there is not the least question of love in this letter. But on the other hand, there is abundant question of you."

The cardinal took the letter and read it with the greatest attention. Then, when they had arrived at the end of it, they read it a second time.

"Well, your majesty," said their eminence at last, "you see how far my enemies go. They menace you with hostile actions if you do not dismiss me. In your place, majesty, I might in truth yield to such powerful demands. And on my part, it would be a true happiness to withdraw from affairs of state."

"What are you saying, maitre?"

"I say, majesty, that my health is sinking under these excessive struggles and these never-ending labors. I say that according to all probability, I shall not be able to undergo the fatigues of the siege of La Rochelle, and that it would be far better for you to appoint there some valiant gentle whose business is war. Not me, who am a cleric of the faith, and who am constantly turned aside from my true vocation to look after matters for which I have no real skill. You would be the happier for it at home, my queen. And I do not doubt you would be the greater for it abroad."

"Maitre Cardinal," said the Queen Louise, "trust that I am not done with you yet. And be content in knowing that this letter will not be ignored. All who are named herein shall be punished as they deserve. Even the Queen Anne herself."

"What do you mean, majesty?" said the cardinal, speaking as if in horror. "Gods forbid that the Queen Anne should suffer the least inconvenience or uneasiness on my account. She has always believed me to be her enemy, although your majesty can bear witness that I have always taken her part warmly, even against you. Oh, if she was to betray your majesty on the side of your honor, it would be quite another thing, and I would be the first to say, 'No grace for the guilty.' But happily, there is nothing of the kind here, and your majesty has just acquired a new proof of it."

"That is true, Maitre Cardinal," said the queen. "And you were right, as you always are. But the Queen Anne nonetheless deserves all my anger."

"But consider that it is you, majesty, who have now incurred the Queen Anne's anger. And if she were to be seriously offended, I could well understand it. Your majesty has treated her most severely."

"And thus will I always treat my enemies and yours, cardinal, however high they may be placed, and whatever peril I may incur in acting toward them."

The cardinal was silent a moment, as if in thought. Then said they, "The Queen Anne is intent on being my enemy, majesty, but she is not yours. On the contrary, she is a devoted and irreproachable royal and wife. Allow me, then, to intercede for her with your majesty."

"Let her humble herself, then, and come to me first with regrets."

"On the contrary, majesty. You must set the example. You have committed the first wrong, since it was you who suspected the Queen Anne."

"What? I make the first advances?" said the Queen Louise. "Never!"

"Majesty, I entreat you to do so, and by doing a thing which you know will be agreeable to her."

"And what is that?"

"Give a grand ball. You know how much the Queen Anne loves dancing. On my assurance, her resentment will not hold out against such an offering."

"Maitre Cardinal, you know that I do not like such pleasures."

"The Queen Anne will only be the more grateful to you, in that case, as she knows your antipathy." Then the cardinal paused before speaking again, so that the words seemed almost an afterthought. "Majesty, it occurs to me. A grand ball will be a wondrous opportunity for the Queen Anne to wear those beautiful diamond studs which you gave her on her birthday, and with which she has since had no occasion to adorn herself."

"We shall see, Maitre Cardinal. We shall see," said the Queen Louise, whose voice still was vexed. But in truth, Louise was in a joyful state at finding her Anne guilty only of a fault which she cared little about, and innocent of a transgression of which she had great dread. In short, she was ready to make up all differences with her. "We shall see, but upon my honor, you are too indulgent toward her."

"Majesty," said the cardinal, "leave severity to your ministers. Clemency is a royal virtue. Employ it, and you will find that you derive advantage therein."

Thereupon the cardinal, hearing the clock strike eleven, bowed low and asked permission of the Queen Louise to depart.

Anne of Austria, who in consequence of the seizure of her letter expected some reproach, was surprised the next day to see the Queen Louise make attempts at reconciliation with her. Anne's first movement, however, was a strategic rejection. Her pride and dignity had both been so cruelly offended that she could not come round at the first advance. But, pretending to be persuaded by the advice of her attendants, she at last had the appearance of beginning to forget.

The Queen Louise took advantage of this favorable moment to tell Anne that she had the intention of shortly giving a fete. A fete called for by Louise was so rare a thing that at this announcement, as the cardinal had predicted, the last trace of Anne's resentment disappeared — if not from her heart, then at least from her manner.

Anne asked upon what day this fete would take place, but Louise replied that she must consult the cardinal upon that point. And indeed, every day the Queen Louise asked the cardinal their thoughts on the matter. And every day the cardinal, under some pretext, deferred fixing that date. Ten days passed away thus.

On the eleventh day, the cardinal received a letter by courier from London, which contained only these lines:

I have them. But I am unable to leave London for want of money. Send me five hundred pistoles, and I shall see you in Paris.

— Milord

On the same day the cardinal received this letter, the Queen Louise put her customary question to their eminence.

Richelieu assessed that it would take four days to arrange payment and send forth a courier to England, and for that courier to there seek out Milord de Winter. They then reckoned the same four days for Milord's return to France, plus two more days to allow for contrary winds and unexpected delays. Ten days at most.

"Well, Maitre Cardinal?" said Louise. "Have you made your decision?"

"Yes, majesty. Today is the twentieth of September. The magistrates of the city give a fete on the third of October, in thirteen days. That will fall in wonderfully well, as all Paris may join in on your desire to please the Queen Anne."

Then just as they turned to go, the cardinal added, "I remind you again, majesty. You must tell her majesty Queen Anne that you should like to see how her diamond studs become her. For the queen's rare beauty deserves to be heightened by such a rare gift. I pray you, majesty — do not forget."

CHAPTER 17

THE HOUSE OF BONACIEUX AND BOUQUET

It was the second time the cardinal had mentioned the diamond studs to the Queen Louise, who found this insistence striking — and who began to fancy that the recommendation concealed some mystery.

More than once, Louise had been embarrassed by the cardinal's knowledge of her own affairs at court. Their eminence's agents were often better informed than the royals even upon what was going on in their own household. She hoped, then, to obtain some information from conversation with the Queen Anne, and afterward to take to their eminence some secret which the cardinal would either know or not know — but which in either case would allow Louise some feeling of advantage over Richelieu.

Unfortunately for the Queen Louise's plans, the Queen Anne stayed at a distance the following day, and then was at Notre Dame cathedral the day after that for meditation. The next day, Louise found herself preoccupied with new reports of the accords between the English and the Huguenot rebels of La Rochelle, in response of which she had worked herself into a vexed and foul mood when she went finally to the Queen Anne at midmorning one day thereafter, hearing word that Anne had just then arrived in her apartments from the gardens.

Inspired by her disagreeable mood, Louise accosted Anne with fresh threats against those friends and attendants who surrounded her, with all those quickly dismissed and the doors to the apartment closed. Anne paced away to show her disdain, allowing the torrent to flow on without replying, and hoping that it would cease of itself. But this was not what was intended.

Louise wanted a discussion from which some light or other might break, convinced as she was that the cardinal was withholding things from her, and was preparing for her one of those terrible surprises which their eminence was so skillful in setting up. And sure enough, by steady perseverance in her accusations, the Queen Louise arrived in time at the outcome she sought.

"I say that is enough," said Anne at length, driven to finally speak in response to Louise's vague attacks. "You complain at me endlessly, yet you do not tell me all that troubles you. What have I done, then? Let me know what crime I have committed. It is impossible that you can make all this ado about a letter written in heat to my brother, and concerning a cardinal whose enmity toward me must be clear to you."

The Queen Louise, questioned in a manner so direct, did not know what to answer. And she thought then that this was the moment for expressing the request given her by the cardinal, which she had not yet revealed.

"Madame," said Louise with dignity, "the date for the grand ball has been selected. A fete shall be given at the Hotel de Ville. I wish, in order to honor our worthy magistrates, that you should appear in ceremonial costume, and above all, ornamented with the diamond studs which I gave you on your birthday. That is my answer."

The answer was terrible. In that moment, Anne believed that Louise knew all, and that the cardinal had persuaded her to employ this daring challenge — a tactic all too characteristic of their eminence. She fought to conceal her anger, clasping hands together whose pallor made them appear as wax. Looking at the Queen Louise with bright eyes, she was unable to reply with even a single word.

"Do you understand me, madame?" said the Queen Louise, who enjoyed the reaction to its full extent but had no guess as to its cause.

"Yes, madame. I hear," said the Queen Anne.

"You will appear at this ball?"

"Of course. I am delighted, though I wish this offering had not been accompanied by so many tiresome challenges."

"You will appear with the diamond studs?"

"Of course."

Anne's pallor increased. Louise saw it, and enjoyed it with that cold cruelty which was one of the worst sides of her character.

"Then that is agreed," said the Queen Louise. "And that is all I had to say to you."

"But on what day will this ball take place?" asked Anne.

"Oh, very shortly, madame," said Louise. "But I do not precisely recollect the date. I will ask the cardinal."

The Queen Anne in response gave the Queen Louise a piercing look. "It was the cardinal, then, who suggested this fete?"

"The cardinal was involved in discussions," said Louise, dismissive. "But what matter is that?"

"It was they who told you to invite me to appear with the diamond studs."

"Well… that is to say —"

"It was not a question."

"And what does it matter whether it was their eminence or I? Is there anything untoward in this request?"

"No, my love."

"Then you will appear?"

"Of course."

"Very well," said Louise, nodding as she turned to go. "I count upon it." And the queen went away, quite pleased.

The Queen Anne returned the nod with hands at her sides — but less from etiquette than to hide away those hands, which trembled in anger behind her.

"I am lost," murmured Anne, when at last alone. "For the cardinal knows all, and it is they who urge on Louise. It is clear that she as yet knows nothing, but will soon know everything. By my faith, I am lost."

By every assessment that could be made, the Queen Anne understood the terrible state of her position. Buckingham had returned to London, and Madame de Chevreuse was at Tours. Monsieur Laporte could not leave the Louvre. More closely watched than ever, Anne felt certain that one of her attendants had betrayed her — and with no way for her to know how to tell which, she had not another soul in the world in whom she could confide. Thus, while contemplating the ruin that threatened her and the emptiness by which she was surrounded, the Queen Anne broke out into angry tears.

"May I be of service to your majesty?" said all at once a voice full of sweetness and pity.

The queen turned sharply round, for there could be no deception in the expression of that voice. It was a friend who spoke thus.

At one of the doors which opened into the queen's apartment, there appeared the genial tailor, Constance Bonacieux. The queen uttered a cry at finding herself surprised, but Constance spoke quickly.

"Fear not, majesty," said she. "I am no spy. I had simply been engaged in inspecting the dresses and linen in the closet when you and the Queen Louise entered. Not desiring to worsen the Queen Louise's mood if seen, I hid myself… and heard all."

"Forgive me, Constance, for my outburst," said the Queen Anne. "For in my fear, I could not recognize you. You who have served me so bravely, and so recklessly."

"Majesty, I am your humble tailor and nothing more."

"My humble tailor? You are coy, madame — and my secret courier and soldier of my heart, abducted for her troubles. Contact to Madame de Chevreuse, and escort to the Duke of Buckingham."

"Oh, speak not so here, majesty!" cried the young Constance, clasping Anne's hands and nodding sagely. "For those names cannot be overheard as long as you are unaware of the allegiances of who might be listening. But know that I am your majesty's, body and soul. And however far removed I may be from you, whatever price I must pay for learning your secrets… majesty, I believe I may know a means of extricating you from these difficulties."

"You? Oh, by my faith, Constance," said the queen, smiling through her tears. "But look me in the eyes. I am betrayed on all sides. Can I still trust in you?"

"By my own faith, yes," said Constance. "For I swear that no one is more devoted to your majesty, nor more aware of how you suffer in love, than I am. Those studs which the Queen Louise speaks of. You gave them to he who visited you, did you not? Those studs were enclosed in a little rosewood box that he held under his arm, which I saw when we departed together."

"You are as keen of mind as you are brave of heart," murmured the queen, whose brow knit with fear. "Yes. And so they are gone to London, and the cardinal knows it."

"Well, then," said Constance simply, "we will have them back again."

"Oh, if doing were so easy as saying," said the queen. "But how am I to act? Someone must be sent to the duke, but who? There are no couriers within the palace who would not be watched. More and more, I must trust to private agents and investigators hired in secret to do my bidding, but this business cannot be trusted to those whose devotion to me I cannot truly know."

"But I am devoted to you, majesty, and am watched by none yet within the palace. So before that might change, place your confidence in me, madame. Do me that honor, my queen, and I will find a messenger."

For long moments, Anne could only stare at the smiling face of the young tailor — who became, in that moment, her salvation.

"I must write, then," said the queen, close to overwhelmed by this new hope.

"Oh, yes. That is essential. A few words from the hand of your majesty, and your private seal."

"But those few words could bring about my condemnation. My divorce and exile!"

"Yes, if they fell into infamous hands. But I will answer for those words being delivered to their destination."

"Oh, gods! I must then place my life, my honor, my reputation, in your hands once more."

"Yes, madame, you must. And I will save them all."

"But how? Tell me at least the means."

Constance nodded, speaking quietly. "Since you know I was taken by agents of the cardinal, you should be made aware as well that my husband, Monsieur Bouquet, was arrested for questioning by the cardinal's guards, seeking my secrets."

"The horror!" cried the Queen Anne, who appeared all at once to reconsider Constance's offer. "This is too much, madame. Too much!"

"But majesty, it is well," said Constance. "My husband knows not my secrets, and was soon freed as a matter of course. I have received his messages these past days, though I have refrained from returning home for fear of being watched. But he is a worthy, honest man who entertains neither love nor hatred for anyone. He will do anything I wish. And equally as important, he has traveled extensively on matters of trade and investment, including having visited London. He will set out upon receiving an order from me, without knowing what he carries, and he will carry your majesty's letter, without even knowing it is from your majesty, to the address which is on it."

The Queen Anne took the two hands of the young tailor with a burst of emotion, gazing at her as if to read her very heart. And seeing nothing but sincerity in her solemn eyes, she embraced her tenderly.

"Do that," said Anne, "and you will have saved my life. You will have saved my honor."

"Do not exaggerate the service I have the happiness to render your majesty. For you are the victim of treachery and evil plots. Having been taken by the cardinal's agents, I know this better than most."

"That is true, that is true, my child," said the queen. "You are right."

"Give me your letter, madame. Time presses."

The queen went then to her writing table, on which were ink, paper, and pens. She wrote only two lines, both for brevity and from the fear of what might happen were the letter to be intercepted:

The bright stars which upon you I have bestowed must be returned at once. The fate of all is in your hands.

She then sealed the letter with her private seal, and gave it to Constance.

"And," said the queen, "let us not forget one equally necessary thing. Your husband must have money to finance this journey."

"My queen, we are not without means. I do not wish you to make use of any resources that might draw attention to you. My husband is most thrifty. That is his best fault. He will make do with what we may contribute."

"You are wise and generous, Constance. But you have no reason to fear. Wait only a moment." The Queen Anne then went to her jewel case, returning quickly with a fine gold ring in hand. "Here," said she, "is a treasure of great value. It was a gift from my brother, the King Philip of Spain, so I am at liberty to dispose of it without attracting the attention of those who yet watch me. Take this ring. Sell it for what it is worth, and let your husband set out."

"In an hour, you shall be obeyed."

"You brave and generous soul," said Anne.

Constance then kissed the hands of the queen, concealed the letter in the pocket of her sleeve, and disappeared with the lightness of a bird.

Before the noon bells rang, Constance had arrived back at her home. As the young tailor had told the queen, she had not seen her husband since his messages had come to her, speaking of his shocking arrest and subsequent liberation. She was thus ignorant of the change that had taken place in him with respect to the cardinal — a change which had since been strengthened by more than one visit from the Count de Rochefort. In only a few days, that villain had become the best friend of Monsieur Bouquet, and had persuaded the mercer without much trouble that he himself was blameless in the abduction of Madame Bonacieux, which had been only a political precaution.

Madame Bonacieux found Monsieur Bouquet alone. The poor man was recovering with difficulty the order in their house, in which he had found most of the furniture broken and the closets nearly emptied upon his return. For so did the justice of the cardinal's guards leave those traces of its passage. As to the valet the pair had employed, he had run away at the moment of Monsieur Bouquet's arrest.

The worthy mercer had sent his first message to inform his wife of his happy return, immediately after arriving back at the house. Constance had replied by letter to ask after him, and to tell him that the first moment she could steal away from her duties would be devoted to paying him a visit. That first moment had been delayed now nearly two weeks — which, under any other circumstances, might have appeared rather daunting to Monsieur Bouquet. But the visit he had made to the cardinal, along with the visits Rochefort had made to him, had given the mercer ample subjects to reflect upon. And as everyone knows, nothing makes time pass more quickly than reflection.

This was the more so because Monsieur Bouquet's reflections were all rose-colored. Rochefort called him a friend and "my dear Bouquet," and never ceased telling him that the cardinal had a great respect for him. The mercer fancied himself already on the high road to honors and fortune.

On her side, Constance also reflected. But it must be admitted that her first sight of her husband in so many days inspired thoughts wildly different than those of Bouquet's ambition. For in spite of herself, Constance's thoughts constantly turned to that handsome young guard, d'Artagnan, who was so brave and appeared to be so much in love — with her.

Having married Monsieur Bouquet at eighteen, Constance had lived always among proper friends. Friends from her own childhood, and friends from her husbands' childhood, and all people little capable of inspiring any forbidden sentiment in one whose heart was resolutely virtuous. And so had she lifelong remained insensible to vulgar seductions. But d'Artagnan was, as we have said, handsome, young, and bold in equal measure. The young Gascon spoke of love like one who did love, and was anxious to be loved in return. There was certainly enough in all this to turn a head only twenty-one years old, and Constance Bonacieux had just attained that happy period of life.

Both Bouquet and Bonacieux, then, had not seen each other for some time, and during that time, serious events had taken place for both. But even so, when they met, the two greeted each other with a degree of preoccupation. Monsieur Bouquet advanced toward his wife and clasped her hands. Constance presented her cheek to him for a brief kiss.

"Let us talk a little," said she.

"Indeed," said Monsieur Bouquet.

"Yes. For I have something of the highest importance to tell you."

"Well enough," said he. "And I have some questions sufficiently serious to put to you. Describe to me your abduction, I pray you."

"Oh, that's of no consequence just now," said Constance.

"But what does your important matter concern, then? My captivity?"

"Goodness, no. Though I confess I was sorry to hear of it, I knew also that you were not guilty of any crime or intrigue, and thus you knew nothing that could compromise yourself or anyone else."

"You speak very much at your ease, madame," said Monsieur Bouquet, somewhat hurt at the little interest his wife showed in him. "Do you know that I was plunged for three days and nights in the dungeons of the Bastille?"

"And yet you passed that time away without harm or care, fate be praised. So let us return to the subject that brings me here."

"Am I not that subject, madame? Is it not the desire of seeing a husband again from whom you have been separated for so long?" asked the mercer, piqued to the quick.

"Yes, of course that first. And other things afterward."

"Speak, then."

"It is a matter of the highest importance, and upon which our future fortune perhaps depends."

"Ah! I may interrupt you to say that the complexion of our fortune has changed very much since I last saw you, my dear Constance. And I would not be astonished if, in the course of a few months, our lives were to excite the envy of many folks."

"Yes, particularly if you follow the instructions I am about to give you."

"Me?"

"Yes, you. There is duty to the crown to be performed, Jacques, and much money to be gained at the same time."

Constance assumed that in talking of money to her husband, she took him on his weak side. But sad to say, she did not understand that anyone — even a mercer of some success — who spoke with Cardinal de Richelieu is no longer the same thereafter.

"Much money to be gained?" said Monsieur Bouquet, scowling.

"Yes, much."

"About how much?"

"A thousand pistoles, perhaps."

"What you demand of me is serious, then?"

"It is indeed."

"What must be done?"

"You must go away immediately," said Constance, "on the pretense of travel for business. I will give you a paper which you must not part with on any account, and which you will deliver into the proper hands."

"And whither am I to go?"

"To London."

"I go to London? You jest! I have no present business in London."

"But others wish that you should go there."

"But who are those others? I warn you that I will not work in ignorance, and that I will know not only to what I expose myself, but for whom I expose myself."

"An illustrious person sends you. An illustrious person awaits you. The reward will exceed your expectations. That is all I promise you."

Monsieur Bouquet glowered at his wife. "More of your intrigues. Nothing but intrigues! But thank you, madame, I am aware of all those intrigues now. Maitre Cardinal has enlightened me on that point."

"Maitre…" cried Constance in sudden horror. "Have you seen the Cardinal de Richelieu?"

"Their eminence sent for me," answered the mercer proudly.

"And you responded to their bidding, you great fool?"

"Well, I can't say I had much choice of going or not going, for I was taken to them by armed guards. It is true also, that before knowing their eminence, if I had been able to dispense with the visit, I would have been delighted."

"They ill-treated you, then? They threatened you?"

"On the contrary. Their eminence gave me their hand and called me their friend. Their friend! Do you hear that, madame? I am the friend of the great cardinal!"

"Of the great cardinal?" The horror in Madame Bonacieux's voice turned quickly to incredulity.

"Perhaps you would contest their right to that title, madame?"

"I would. For I know that their eminence engages in unjust attacks against great persons, and furthermore, I know what power they seek to control through those attacks. I have told you of their unrighteous designs on the Queen Anne. I tell you that the favor of even a just minister of the crown is ephemeral. And one would needs be mad to attach themself to a minister of such ominous reputation as Richelieu."

"I am sorry to hear it, madame. But the cardinal has spoken to me of the slanders they endure at the hands of your Queen Anne's agents, which you

"That is two hundred pistoles. What do you
think of this, Madame Preacher…?"

would do well to dismiss. And I acknowledge no other power but that of the greatness whom I have the honor to serve."

"You serve the cardinal? 'Serve'? That is your word?"

"Yes, madame. And as their servant, I will not allow you to be involved in plots against the safety of the state, or to serve the intrigues of a queen who is not French and who has a Spanish heart, and Austrian blood besides. Fortunately, we have the great cardinal. Their vigilant eye watches over and penetrates to the bottom of the heart." In so saying, Bouquet was repeating, word for word, a sentence which he had heard from the Count de Rochefort.

Constance had reckoned on her trust in her husband. She had, in that hope, answered for him to the Queen Anne, and was rattled now both at the danger into which she had nearly cast herself, and at the new uncertainty of her present state.

"So you are a cardinalist, then, monsieur?" said she angrily. "So you serve the interests of those who abducted your wife and insult the Queen Anne?"

"Private interests are as nothing before the interests of all. I am for those who save the state from this Spanish queen," said Monsieur Bouquet emphatically.

"And what do you know about the state you talk of?" said Constance, stepping forward as if in challenge. "You who are not content with the life of an honest citizen, but turn to that side which offers the most advantages."

"Well!" said Monsieur Bouquet, who retreated against Constance's advance. Then turning, he pulled open a cupboard and drew forth a plump, round bag therein, which when slapped, returned a sound of coins. "That is two hundred pistoles. What do you think of this, Madame Preacher?"

"Whence comes that money?"

"You do not guess?"

"From the cardinal?"

"From them indeed, and from my friend the Count de Rochefort."

"The Count de Rochefort? Your friend! Why, it was he who carried me off!"

"That may be as it is, madame."

"And you receive silver from that villain?"

"Have you not said that that abduction was entirely political?"

"Yes. But that abduction had as its purpose the betrayal of the Queen Anne. To draw confessions from me by threat that might compromise the honor, and perhaps the life, of that august royal."

"Madame," said Monsieur Bouquet, "your august queen is a perfidious Spaniard, and what the cardinal does is well done."

"Monsieur," said Constance, "I know you to be faint-hearted, avaricious, and foolish. But I never till now believed you a villain."

"Madame?" said Monsieur Bouquet, who had never seen his wife in this pronounced a passion, and who recoiled now before her anger. "Madame, what do you say?"

"I say you are a miserable creature," said Constance. "You meddle with politics, do you? And still more, with cardinalist politics? Why, you sell yourself body and soul to fiends for money!"

"You slander me, madame! My money comes from the cardinal."

"It is the same thing," said the young tailor bitterly. "They who call on Richelieu summon the shadow-realm."

"Hold your tongue, hold your tongue, madame! You may be overheard."

"Yes, you are right. For I should be ashamed for anyone to know your baseness."

"My baseness? My concern for you and our status, you mean. The truth of your intrigues, as relayed to me by the cardinal, terrifies me, madame. Forget not that I have seen the Bastille. What a frightful place! Only to think of it makes my flesh crawl. They threatened me, you know. But great gods, here you are insisting that I travel to England, to be no doubt captured and taken in for treason! I should be pleased, no doubt, that you thought to ask me, given that you could well just have gone yourself. For in truth, I think I have hitherto been deceived in you. I really believe you are a villain, and a violent one, too."

"And you are a fool," said Constance. "A miserable fool, stupid and brutal. You are afraid, are you? I am a villain? Well, if I am, perhaps I will have you arrested by the Queen Anne's orders, and I will have you placed in the Bastille which you dread so much."

Not knowing whether his wife was serious or in jest, Monsieur Bouquet fell into a profound reflection. He weighed the two threats in his brain — that of the cardinal and that of the Queen Anne. And that of the cardinal predominated enormously.

"Have me arrested on the part of your Spanish queen," said he, "and I will appeal to their eminence."

At once, Constance understood that she might have gone too far. She was suddenly fearful at having revealed so much. "Well, be it so," said she sadly. "Perhaps, when all is considered, you are right. In the long run, you may know more about politics than I. For you have conversed with the cardinal. And yet it is very hard," added she, "that a husband upon whose affection I thought I might depend treats me thus."

"I treat you thus because your intrigues go too far," said the shaken Monsieur Bouquet. "I mistrust them, as I mistrust those you serve."

"Then we are at an impasse," said Constance, sighing. "We will say no more about it for now."

"It is for the best," said Bouquet. "But… at least you might tell me what I should have had to do in London." For the mercer had suddenly remembered a little too late that Rochefort had instructed him to obtain his wife's secrets.

"It is of no use for you to know anything about it," said Constance, now directed by an instinctive mistrust. "It was about one of those purchases of the tailor's trade. A purchase by which much might have been gained. But the matter is done. And I must return to the Louvre."

By the manner in which Constance dismissed what had been her focus just moments before, Monsieur Bouquet understood the importance of the secret which she now declined to confide to him. He resolved then to hasten immediately to the residence of the Count de Rochefort, and to tell him that the Queen Anne was seeking for a messenger to send to London.

"Forgive me for this, my dear Madame Bonacieux," said he, smiling. "But not knowing you would come to see me, I had made an engagement with a friend. I thus must go, but shall soon return. And as it is growing late, if you will wait only a short while for me, as soon as I have concluded my business with that friend, I will return and accompany you back to the Louvre."

"Thank you, monsieur. But your company is of no use to me at present," said Constance. "I shall return very safely to the Louvre on my own."

"As you please, Madame Bonacieux," said the mercer. "Shall I see you again soon?"

"Next week, I hope my duties will afford me a little liberty. And I will take advantage of it to come and put things in order here, as best I can."

"Very well. I shall expect you. You are not angry with me?"

"Not the least in the world." Madame Bonacieux managed her husband a smile.

"Till then?"

"Till then."

Bouquet then kissed his wife's hand and departed, setting off at a quick pace.

"Well," said Constance aloud to herself, when Monsieur Bouquet had shut the street door and she found herself alone. "My husband might have been a fool, but for all I have known him, he lacked at least one fault — to be a cardinalist. But no more. And I, who have answered for him to the Queen Anne… I, who have promised… ah, faith! She will take me for one of those wretches with whom the palace swarms and who are placed about her as spies. Ah, Monsieur Bouquet, I did love you once. But I hate you now, and on my word, you shall pay for this."

At the moment Constance spoke those words, a tapping from above made her raise her head. Then a voice she knew reached her through the ceiling, as Madame d'Artagnan quietly called out, "Dear Madame Bonacieux! Open for me the little door on the alley, and I will come down to you."

CHAPTER 18

THE LOVER AND THE HUSBAND

"Ah, madame," said d'Artagnan, entering by the alley door of the house which Constance quickly opened for her. "Allow me to tell you that you have a bad sort of husband."

"You have, then, overheard our conversation?" asked Constance, looking at d'Artagnan anxiously.

"The whole."

"But how, by faith?"

"By a mode of proceeding known to myself. And by which I likewise overheard the more animated conversation which you yourself had with the cardinal's guards."

"And what did you understand by what was said between Monsieur Bouquet and I?"

"A thousand things. First, that unfortunately your husband is, as you say, a fool. Next, that you are in trouble, of which I am very glad, as it gives me an opportunity of placing myself at your service. And faith knows I am ready to throw myself into danger for you. Finally, that the Queen Anne wants a brave, intelligent, devoted courier to make a journey to London for her. I have at least two of the three qualities you stand in need of, and here I am."

Constance made no reply, but her heart beat with joy and a secret hope shone in her eyes. "And what guarantee will you give me," asked she, "if I consent to confide this message to you?"

"My guarantee is my love for you. Speak. Command me. What is to be done?"

"Great gods," murmured the young tailor. "Dare I confide such a secret to you, madame? You are a mere guard — and one whose country manner and talk of love at times makes you seem scarcely a child."

"I see that you require someone of greater note to answer for me?"

"I admit that would reassure me greatly."

"Well, consider Madame Athos, who you met when at her apartment you stayed."

"Given Madame Athos's confusion and vexation at finding Monsieur Laporte and I there, I fear you would be best to seek other seconds."

"Do you know Porthos, then?"

"I know no one of that name."

"Aramis?"

"That same name you once challenged me with? I repeat again — no. Who are these gentlefolk?"

"Alongside Athos, two more of the queens' musketeers. But perhaps you know Monsieur de Treville, their captain, who is often at the Louvre?"

"Oh, yes! Him I know not personally, but I have heard both the queens speak of him more than once as a brave and loyal gentle."

"And I can add to their testimony that you need not fear lest he should betray you to the cardinal. So reveal your secret to him, and ask him whether you may then confide it to me, however important, however valuable, however terrible it may be."

"But this secret is not mine, madame, and I cannot reveal it in this manner."

"You were about to confide it to Monsieur Bouquet," said d'Artagnan with some annoyance.

"As one confides a note to the hollow of a tree, to the leg of a pigeon, or to the collar of a dog."

"And yet look upon me — for you see plainly that I love you."

Constance sighed deeply. "You say so."

"I am an honorable sort."

"You say so."

"I am a gallant comrade."

"I believe it."

"I am brave."

"Oh, I am sure of that."

"Then put me to the proof."

Constance looked at the young guard, restrained for a moment by a last hesitation. But there was such an ardor in d'Artagnan's eyes, such persuasion in her voice, that the tailor felt herself constrained to confide in her. Moreover, she understood that she found herself in circumstances where it had become necessary to risk all for the sake of the future. The Queen Anne might be as badly injured by too much caution as by too much confidence.

And it must also be said that the involuntary sentiment she felt for her young protector gave Constance the strength to speak.

"Listen," said she. "I yield to your protestations, I yield to your assurances. But I swear to you before any gods who hear us that if you betray me and my enemies pardon me, I will kill myself while accusing you of my death."

"And I swear to you before those same gods, madame," said d'Artagnan, "that if I am taken while accomplishing the orders you give me, I would sooner die than do anything that might compromise you or those dear to you."

Then the young tailor confided to the young guard the terrible secret of the Queen Anne's heart, a part of which chance had already communicated to d'Artagnan on the Pont Neuf in front of the Samaritaine.

And by the time the tale was done, this secret, then, had become the mutual declaration of their own love.

D'Artagnan was radiant with joy and pride, intoxicated on the power of this secret which she possessed, this woman whom she loved. Confidence and love working in concert made her all but invulnerable.

"I go," said the young guard. "I go at once to take this letter of yours to the Duke of Buckingham."

"But how will you go?" said Constance. "And what of your regiment? Your captain?"

"By my soul, you had made me forget all that! Yes, you are right. A furlough is needed."

"Still another obstacle," murmured Constance, thoughtful.

"As to that," said d'Artagnan after a moment of reflection, "I shall surmount it, be assured."

"How so?"

"I will go this very evening to Monsieur de Treville, whom I will request to ask this favor for me of his sister-in-law, Madame d'Essarts."

"That is well thought out. But there is also another matter."

"What?" asked d'Artagnan, seeing that Constance hesitated to continue.

"You have, perhaps, no money?"

" 'Perhaps' is one word too many," said d'Artagnan, smiling.

"In that case," said Constance, "take this." Then, opening the cupboard, she removed from it the very bag that her husband had caressed so affectionately a half hour before.

"The cardinal's coin?" said d'Artagnan, breaking into a loud laugh. For she had heard, as may be remembered, every syllable of the conversation between Monsieur Bouquet and Madame Bonacieux thanks to the broken boards above the ceiling.

"The cardinal's coin," said Constance. "Two hundred pistoles will carry you most respectably."

"Faith," said d'Artagnan, "it will be a doubly amusing affair to save the Queen Anne with the cardinal's money."

"Well, you would be wise to keep your laughter to yourself while the cardinal's agents are at hand. And in addition to these funds, take this, with the blessing of the Queen Anne herself." And so saying, Constance brought forth the gold ring.

"Please express to her majesty my deepest gratitude," said d'Artagnan, taking the ring with care.

"Be assured, you will no doubt find her majesty even more grateful upon your return."

"Oh, I am already grandly rewarded," said d'Artagnan. "I love you — or at the least, you permit me to tell you that I do. And that is already more happiness than I dared to hope."

But Constance suddenly started. "Silence!" said she.

"What?"

"Someone is talking in the street."

"It is the voice of —"

"Of my husband! Yes, I recognize it!"

D'Artagnan ran to the door and pushed the bolt. "He shall not come in before I am gone," said she. "And when I am gone, you can open to him."

"But I ought to be gone, too. And the disappearance of his money — how am I to justify it if I am here?"

"You are right. We must both be gone."

"Gone? How? He will see us if we go out."

"Then you must come up into my room."

"Faith," said Constance. "You speak those words in a tone that worries me, madame…"

D'Artagnan saw the trepidation in the young tailor's look, and much contrite, she threw herself down to kneel at Constance's feet. "I assure you, Madame Bonacieux, that you will be as safe as in a temple at my side. I give you my word as a gentle, as a guard, and as a Gascon."

"Then let us go," said Constance. "I place full confidence in you, my friend."

D'Artagnan drew back the bolt with caution. Then she and Constance, light as shadows, glided through the interior door into the passage, ascended the stairs as quietly as possible, and entered the young guard's apartment. Both rooms were empty, for Porthos, in order to make a greater show at entertaining, had that evening borrowed Planchet.

For greater security, d'Artagnan barricaded the door behind them. Then she and Constance both approached the window, and through a slit in the shutter, they saw Monsieur Bouquet talking with a stranger in a cloak.

At the sight of this stranger, both Constance and d'Artagnan started. Then d'Artagnan, half drawing her sword, sprang toward the door — for it was the villain of Meung.

"What are you doing?" cried Constance. "You will ruin us all!"

"But I have sworn to kill that one!" said d'Artagnan. "That is Rochefort!"

"I recognize him as well as you, though he was skillful enough to withhold his name during my interrogations. But you think your petty revenge greater than our business at hand? Your life is dedicated to a higher purpose from this moment, and does not belong to you. In the name of the Queen Anne, I forbid you to throw yourself into any peril which is foreign to that of your journey."

"And do you command nothing in your own name?"

"In my name," said Constance, "I remind you that Rochefort is the same villain who snatched me from the street, but I care not — and nor do you. But listen! They appear to be speaking of me."

D'Artagnan drew near the window, and was silent.

Monsieur Bouquet had opened the downstairs door, and seeing the apartment empty, had returned to the figure in the cloak.

"My wife is gone," said he. "She must have returned to the Louvre."

"You are sure," said the Count de Rochefort, "that she did not suspect the intentions with which you went out?"

"No," said Bouquet with a self-sufficient air. "She is too scattered for such insights."

"Is the young guard at home?"

"I do not think so. See there? Her shutter is closed, and no light shines through."

"All the same, it would be best to be certain."

"How so?"

"By knocking at her door. Go."

Bouquet reentered the house, passed through the same door that had afforded a passage for the two fugitives, went up to d'Artagnan's door, and knocked. The moment the hand of the mercer sounded on the door, d'Artagnan and Constance felt their hearts beat faster, but both took care not to make the least sound.

"There is no one within," called Bouquet as he descended once more.

"Never mind," said Rochefort. "Let us return to your apartment. We shall be safer there than in the doorway."

"Ah, faith," whispered Constance. "We shall hear no more."

"On the contrary," said d'Artagnan, "we shall hear better."

So saying, the young guard raised the plank which made her chamber an ear into the rooms below, spread a carpet on the floor, went upon her stomach, and made a sign to Constance to lie just as she did, beside the opening.

"You are sure there is no one there?" said Rochefort from below.

"I assure you," said Bouquet.

"And you think that your wife has returned to the Louvre without speaking to anyone but yourself?"

"I am sure of it."

"That is an important point, you understand?"

"Then the news I brought you is of value?"

"The greatest value, my dear Bouquet. I don't conceal this from you."

"Then the cardinal will be pleased with me?"

"I have no doubt of it."

"The great cardinal!"

"Are you sure, in her conversation with you, that your wife mentioned no names?"

"No. She told me only that she wished to send me to London to serve the interests of an illustrious personage."

"The traitor," murmured Constance in the apartment above.

"Silence," whispered d'Artagnan — and as she did, she seized the hand of Constance, which had seemingly been held out to her without thinking.

"Never mind," continued Rochefort. "You were a fool not to have pretended to accept the mission, though. You would then be in present possession of the letter. The state, which is now threatened, would be safe."

"Be content," said Monsieur Bouquet. "My wife adores me, and there is yet time."

"The ninny," murmured Constance.

"Silence," once again hissed d'Artagnan, who then again squeezed Constance's hand.

"How is there still time?" asked Rochefort.

"I shall go to the Louvre and ask for Madame Bonacieux. I say that I have reflected. I accept her direction, I obtain the letter, and I run directly to the cardinal."

"Well, then go quickly. I will return shortly to learn the result of your excursion." And with that, the Count de Rochefort went out.

"Infamous man," said Constance, addressing this epithet to her husband.

"Silence!" said d'Artagnan, holding the tailor's hand still more firmly.

Then a terrible howling interrupted the two. It was Monsieur Bouquet, who had discovered the disappearance of the moneybag and was crying, "Thieves!"

"Oh, gods," whispered Constance. "He will rouse the whole quarter."

Bouquet called a long time. But such cries, on account of their frequency, brought no assistance in the Rue de Fossoyeurs — and with all the trouble it had seen lately, the mercer's house had developed a bad name. So finding that no one came, Bouquet went out, continuing to call, his voice being heard fainter and fainter as he went off in the direction of the Rue de Bac.

"Now he is gone, and it is your turn to get out," said Constance. With firm hand, she brought forth the letter from the pocket of her sleeve and set it in the hands of the young guard. "Courage, d'Artagnan. But above that, prudence, and think what you owe to the Queen Anne."

"To her and to you," said d'Artagnan. "Do not worry, Madame Bonacieux. I shall become worthy of her gratitude."

At this, the young tailor smiled. "I am Constance to you, madame, now and always. Return in safety, my friend."

"Constance," said d'Artagnan, heart close to bursting. "Beautiful Constance. Shall I likewise return worthy of your love?"

Constance replied only by the beautiful glow which mounted to her cheeks. Then d'Artagnan bowed and went out, enveloped in a large cloak that ill-concealed the sheath of her rapier.

Constance followed the young guard with her eyes, which carried a long, fond look. But as soon as d'Artagnan had disappeared around the corner of the street, the young tailor's expression turned to worry.

"My d'Artagnan," whispered she. "I pray you have the strength to protect the queen. To protect me…"

— CHAPTER 19 —

THE PLAN OF CAMPAIGN

On the way to the Rue de Vieux-Colombier, d'Artagnan stopped quickly at a goldsmith's to sell the ring given her by Constance, adding another hundred pistoles to Monsieur Bouquet's offerings. From there, she went straight to Monsieur de Treville's, as she expected that the cardinal was due to receive an imminent visit by the cursed Rochefort. A warning that the Queen Anne had immediate need of a secret courier to London would be given. And so she judged with good reason that she had not a moment to lose.

The heart of the young guard overflowed with joy. An opportunity presented itself to her in which there would be at the same time glory to be acquired and money to be gained. And as a far higher encouragement, it brought her into an even closer intimacy with one she adored. Thus did this opportunity do for her all at once far more than she would have dared to ask of fate.

It was by then after the supper hour, and d'Artagnan knew that Monsieur de Treville would be in his salon, entertaining his habitual court of gentlefolk. The young guard, who all knew enjoyed the favor of Treville, went straight to his office and sent word that she wished to see the captain on a matter of importance.

She had been there only minutes when Treville entered. At the first glance, and by the joy seen in the young guard's expression, the worthy captain plainly understood that something new was afoot.

All the way along as she had walked from the Rue de Fossoyeurs, d'Artagnan had been arguing with herself over whether she should place confidence in Monsieur de Treville, or whether she should ask him only to give her free rein for some secret assignment. But Treville had always been so thoroughly her friend, had always been so devoted to the queens — and hated the cardinal so cordially. So it was that the young guard resolved to tell him everything.

"Did you ask for me, my young friend?" said Monsieur de Treville.

"Yes, monsieur," said d'Artagnan, lowering her voice. "And you will forgive me, I hope, for having disturbed you when you learn the importance of my business."

"Speak, then. I am all attention."

"It concerns nothing less," said d'Artagnan, "than the honor — perhaps the life — of the Queen Anne."

"What did you say?" asked Treville, glancing round to ensure they were truly alone, and then fixing his questioning gaze upon d'Artagnan.

"I say, monsieur, that chance has rendered me the keeper of a secret —"

"Which you will guard, I hope, as your own life."

"Indeed. But I must first impart that secret to you, monsieur, for you alone can assist me in the mission I have just received from her majesty."

"Is this secret your own?"

"No, monsieur. It is her majesty's."

"Are you authorized by the Queen Anne to communicate it to me?"

"No, monsieur, for on the contrary, I am ordered to preserve the most profound mystery in this matter."

"Why, then, are you about to betray it to me?"

"Because as I said, without you I can do nothing. And I am afraid you will refuse me the favor I come to ask if you do not know to what end I ask it."

"Keep your secret, young friend, and simply tell me what you wish."

"I wish you to obtain for me, from Madame d'Essarts, leave of absence for fifteen days."

"When?"

"This very night."

"You leave Paris?"

"I am going on a mission."

"May you tell me whither?"

"To London."

"Has anyone an interest in preventing your arrival there?"

"The cardinal, I believe, would give the world to prevent my success."

"And you are going alone?"

"I am going alone."

"In that case, you will not get beyond the forest at Bondy," said the captain plainly. "I tell you so, by the faith of Treville."

"You fear I will succumb to the common bandits of that road?"

"Rather, I know you will be assassinated."

"Then I shall die in the performance of my duty," said d'Artagnan most proudly.

"But your mission will not be accomplished."

"That is true," said the young guard, less proud.

"Believe me," said Treville, who stood to pace. "In enterprises of this kind, in order that one may arrive, four must set out."

"Ah, you are right, monsieur," said d'Artagnan. "For me, I would choose no others to make up four than Athos, Porthos, and Aramis, but only you know if I can make use of them."

"Will you confide to them the secret which I am not willing to know?"

"No. But we are sworn, all of us, to blind confidence and a devotedness that is proof against all trials. Besides, you can tell them that you have full confidence in me, and they will not be more incredulous than you."

"It shall be done, then. I can send to each of them leave of absence for fifteen days, and no more. To Athos, whose wound still makes her suffer, I will offer this leave to go to the healing waters of Forges. And to Porthos and Aramis, to accompany their friend, whom they are not willing to abandon in such a painful condition. Sending their leave of absence will be proof enough that I authorize their journey."

"Thank you, monsieur. You are a hundred times too good."

"Begone, then, and find them at once, and let all be done tonight. But first, write your request to d'Essarts for me to convey. Perhaps you had a spy at your heels. And your visit, if it should ever be known to the cardinal, will thus seem legitimate."

D'Artagnan drew up her request, and Monsieur de Treville, on receiving it, assured her that within the hour, the four leaves of absence would be at the respective domiciles of the travelers.

"Have the goodness to send mine to Athos's residence," said d'Artagnan. "For I would dread some disagreeable encounter if I were to go home."

"It shall be done. Until then, be at ease, adieux, and a prosperous journey to you. But concerning that journey, have you any money?"

D'Artagnan tapped the bag she had in her pocket. "Three hundred pistoles."

"Ah, plenty! That would carry you to the end of the world. Begone, then."

D'Artagnan then saluted Monsieur de Treville, who held out his hand to her. She shook it with a respect mixed with gratitude. Since her first arrival at Paris, she had had constant occasion to honor this excellent captain, whom she had always found most loyal and worthy.

Her first visit was to Aramis, at whose residence she had not been since the famous evening on which she had followed Constance Bonacieux. In the time since, she had seldom seen the gentle musketeer, but every time she had seen them, she had noticed a deep sadness in their look.

This evening, Aramis appeared especially melancholy and thoughtful. In response to d'Artagnan's questions about this prolonged state, Aramis pleaded as their excuse a commentary upon the eighteenth chapter of Saint Augustine, which they were forced to write in Latin for the following week, and which preoccupied them a good deal.

After the two friends had been chatting a few moments, a messenger from Monsieur de Treville arrived, bringing a sealed packet.

"What is that?" asked Aramis.

"The leave of absence maitre has asked for," replied the messenger.

"For me? I have asked for no leave of absence."

"Hold your tongue and take it," said d'Artagnan. And giving the messenger a crown for their trouble, she added, "You will tell Monsieur de Treville that Maitre Aramis is very much obliged to him. Go."

The messenger bowed to the ground and departed.

"What does all this mean?" asked Aramis.

"Pack up all you want for a journey of a fortnight, and follow me."

"Fie! A journey of a fortnight? I cannot leave Paris just now, not without knowing what is become of..." But Aramis stopped short.

"What is become of your mysterious friend?" said d'Artagnan. For by the musketeer's words, she now had a guess as to the true cause of their melancholic condition.

"Mysterious? I know not who you mean," said Aramis, caught short and stammering.

"Why, the person who was here. The person with the embroidered handkerchief."

"Who told you there was someone here?" As Aramis spoke, they became as ashen as death.

"I saw them. Or her, I warrant."

"And you know who she is?"

"Having seen that handkerchief's monogram, and knowing something of the mission of the one who came to her that night, I believe I can guess, at least, that she was Madame de Chevreuse."

"Be careful what you speak," said Aramis, quite now in shock. "But since you appear to know so many things, can you tell me what is become of that gentry?"

"Well, given that she dwells in exile in Tours, I presume that she has returned there."

"To Tours? Yes, that may be. But why did she return to Tours without telling me anything?"

"Because she was in fear of being arrested."

"Why has she not written to me, then?"

"At a final guess, because she was afraid of compromising you regarding the business that brought her to Paris, and which might well envelop you if it was known your house was used as a way station in that business."

"D'Artagnan, you restore me to life!" cried Aramis. "I fancied myself despised, betrayed. I was so delighted to see her again! But what is this business of which you speak? For though I could not have believed she would risk her liberty for me, for what other cause could she have returned to Paris?"

"For the cause which today takes us to England, which you will someday know, Aramis. But at present, I must imitate the discretion of your master of theology's young nieve."

Aramis smiled as they remembered the tale they had told their friends, on that day when the affair involving Bouquet and Bonacieux had begun. "Well, then, since she has left Paris and you are sure of it, d'Artagnan, I am ready to follow you. You say we are going…?"

"To see Athos now. And if you will come thither, I beg you to make haste, for we have lost much time already. Accordingly, inform Bazin."

"Will Bazin go with us?" asked Aramis.

"Perhaps so. And in any event, it is best that he should follow us to Athos's."

Aramis called the valet, and after having ordered him to join them at Athos's residence, said, "Let us go then." The musketeer took only their cloak, sword, and three pistols, after opening uselessly three drawers to see if they could not find stray coin. When well assured this search was superfluous, they followed d'Artagnan.

But as they both went out, Aramis placed their hand upon the arm of d'Artagnan, while looking at her earnestly. "You have not spoken of this visitor?" said they.

"To no one in the world except one who knew of her already," said d'Artagnan, respecting her friend's desire to leave the name unspoken.

"Not even to Athos or Porthos?"

"I have not breathed a syllable to them."

"Good enough."

Tranquil on this important point, Aramis continued their way with d'Artagnan, and both soon arrived at Athos's dwelling. They both found her holding her leave of absence in one hand, and Monsieur de Treville's note in the other.

"Can you explain to me what signifies this leave of absence and this letter, which I have just received?" said the astonished Athos. She then read aloud:

My dear Athos —
I wish, as your health absolutely requires it, that you should rest for a fortnight. Go then and take the waters of Forges, or any that may be more agreeable to you, and recuperate yourself as quickly as possible.
Yours in affection,
— Treville

"Well, this leave of absence and that letter mean that you must follow me, Athos," said d'Artagnan.

"To the waters of Forges?"

"There or elsewhere."

"Is this order in the queens' service?"

"Either both or one. For are we not their majesties' faithfuls?"

At that very moment, Porthos arrived. "Faith," said he. "Here is a strange thing. Since when, I wonder, did they grant in the musketeers a leave of absence without one asking for it?"

"Since they have friends who ask it for them," said d'Artagnan.

"Ah," said Porthos. "It appears there is some fresh news here."

"Yes, we are going on a journey," said Aramis.

"To what place?" asked Porthos.

"My faith! I know nothing about it," said Athos. "Ask d'Artagnan."

"To London, gentlefolk," said d'Artagnan.

"To London?" cried Porthos. "And what in faith are we going to do in London?"

"That is what I am not at liberty to tell you, gentles. You must trust to me."

"But in order to go to London," added Porthos, "money is needed, and I have none."

"Nor I," said Aramis.

"Nor I," said Athos.

"I have money," replied d'Artagnan, pulling out Monsieur Bouquet's bag from her pocket and placing it on the table. "There are three hundred pistoles here. Let each take seventy-five, which is enough to take us to London and back. But be aware that we shall most likely not all arrive at London."

"Why so?" said Porthos.

"Because in all probability, some of us will be left along the road."

"Is this, then, a campaign upon which we are now entering?" asked Aramis.

"A campaign of a most dangerous kind, I warn you."

"Fie! If we do risk being killed," said Porthos, "I at least should like to know what for."

"I can tell you only that if enemies are to be found on this road, they will be agents of Cardinal de Richelieu," said d'Artagnan.

"That makes us all a little the wiser," said Athos.

"And yet," said Aramis, "I am somewhat of Porthos's opinion."

"But are the queens accustomed to give you such reasons?" said d'Artagnan. "No. They say to you jauntily, 'Gentles, there is fighting going on in Gascony or in Flanders, so go and fight,' and you go there, and never ask why. You need give yourselves no more uneasiness about this."

"D'Artagnan is right," said Athos. "Here are our three leaves of absence which came from Monsieur de Treville, and here are three hundred pistoles which came from I don't know where. So let us go and get killed where we are told to go. Is life worth the trouble of so many questions? D'Artagnan, I am ready to follow you."

"And I also," said Porthos.

"And I also," said Aramis. "And, indeed, I am not sorry to leave Paris for a time. I have need of distraction."

"Well be assured, you will have distractions enough," said d'Artagnan.

"And now when are we to go?" asked Athos.

"Immediately. We have not a moment to lose."

So were the orders given to Planchet, Grimaud, Bazin, and Mousqueton, and the four warriors called their valets for clean boots, and to fetch horses from the guards' house at the estate of Monsieur de Treville. Each musketeer was able to make use of the steeds stabled upon the estate at need, for themselves and their valets, and d'Artagnan had previously been granted the same leave with the personal blessing of Monsieur de Treville. The four valets thus set off at full speed.

"Now let us lay down the plan of campaign," said Porthos. "Where do we go first?"

"To Picardy, and thence to Calais," said d'Artagnan. "That is the most direct route to London."

"Poorly thought," said Porthos. "This would be my advice for the journey."

"Speak, then."

"Four of any guards or musketeers traveling together would be suspected. Therefore, we must each go alone. D'Artagnan will give each of us her instructions. I will go by the way of Boulogne to clear the way. Athos will set out two hours after, by way of Amiens. Aramis will follow us through Noyon. As to d'Artagnan, she will go by what route she thinks is best, in Planchet's clothes, while Planchet will follow us like d'Artagnan, in the uniform of the guards."

"Though finely thought, Porthos's plan appears to me to be impracticable," said d'Artagnan, "inasmuch as I am myself ignorant of what instructions I can give you. I am the bearer of a letter, that is all. I have not made, and I cannot make, three copies of that letter, because it is sealed. We must then, it appears to me, travel in company. The letter is here, in this pocket." And so saying, she pointed to that pocket which held the sealed missive safe. "If I should be killed, one of you must take it and continue the journey. If they be killed, it will be another's turn, and so on. Provided a single one arrives, that is all that is required."

"Bravo, d'Artagnan," cried Athos. "Your opinion is mine. Besides, we must be consistent. I am going to take the waters, as our story goes, so you all will accompany me. But instead of taking the waters of Forges, I go to the sea, as I am free to do. If anyone wishes to stop us, I will show Monsieur de Treville's letter, and you will show your leaves of absence. If we are attacked, we will defend ourselves. If we are tried, we will stoutly maintain that we were anxious only to dip ourselves a certain number of times in the sea. Morcover, brigands, assassins, or the cardinal's guards would have an easy bargain in facing four travelers in isolation, whereas four together make a troop. And we will further arm our four valets with pistols and musketoons. If they send an army out against us, we will give battle. And the survivor, as d'Artagnan says, will carry the letter."

"Well spoken," said Aramis. "You don't often speak, Athos, but when you do, it is with a golden tongue. I agree to Athos's plan. And you, Porthos?"

"I agree to it, too," said Porthos, "if d'Artagnan approves of it. D'Artagnan, being the bearer of the letter, is naturally the head of the enterprise. Let her decide, and we will execute."

"Well," said d'Artagnan, "I decide that we shall adopt Athos's plan, and that we set off in half an hour."

"Agreed!" shouted the three musketeers in chorus.

Each one, stretching out a hand to the bag, took their seventy-five pistoles. Then each made their preparations to set out at the appointed time.

— CHAPTER 20 —

THE JOURNEY

Some two hours after midnight, our four adventurers and their four retainers left Paris by the Barriere Saint-Denis. As long as it was dark, they remained silent. In spite of being certain that they had made a clean departure, they welcomed the obscurity of shadow and silence, and suspected ambushes on every side.

With the first light of day, the tongues of d'Artagnan and the musketeers were loosened. With the sun, their gaiety revived. The feeling they shared was like that of the eve of a battle. The heart beat faster, the eyes were bright, and all four felt that the life they were perhaps going to lose was, to be sure, a precious thing.

The appearance of their caravan was formidable. The noble black horses of the musketeers and d'Artagnan, with their martial carriage and regimental pace, would have betrayed the most strict attempts of the party to conceal their identities as warriors. As, indeed, would the manner in which the four valets followed, on lesser steeds, to be sure, but steadfastly armed to the teeth.

All went well till they arrived at Chantilly in Picardy, which they reached by early morning. They needed breakfast, and alighted at the door of the inn of Great Saint-Martine, recommended by a sign representing the well-dressed saint giving half her cloak to a poor wanderer. D'Artagnan ordered the valets to tend to but not unsaddle the horses, and to hold themselves in readiness to set off again in short order.

The four companions entered the common hall and placed themselves at table. A gentle who had just arrived by the Dammartin Road was seated at the same table, and was breakfasting. Introducing herself, she opened the conversation about rain and fine weather, and the travelers replied. She drank to their good health, and the travelers returned her politeness.

But at the moment Mousqueton came to announce that the horses were ready and all rose from the table, the stranger made a proposal to Porthos. "Before you go, friends, drink with me to the health of the cardinal!" And so saying, the stranger uncorked a bottle of wine.

"I would like nothing better," replied Porthos, "and I invite you then in your turn to drink to the health of the queens." But even as Porthos reached for his glass, the stranger cried out in sudden anger.

"I acknowledge no other royal but their eminence!"

"Faith! Then you clearly have drunk too much already, and so may toast alone."

The stranger then drew their sword.

"This is a piece of folly," said Athos to Porthos, "but I suspect it cannot be helped. There is no drawing back from one in that mood. Finish this fight and rejoin us as soon as you can."

The other three remounted their horses and set out at a good pace with the four valets, while Porthos was promising his adversary to perforate them with all the attacks known in the finest fencing schools.

"There goes one of us already," murmured Athos at the end of five hundred paces.

"But why did that person attack Porthos rather than any other one of us?" asked Aramis.

"Because, since Porthos was talking louder than the rest of us, they took him for the leader," said d'Artagnan, thoughtful. "I cannot but wonder if this meeting was by design."

"I always said that this cadet from Gascony was a well of wisdom," said Athos, and the travelers continued on.

At Beauvais, they stopped two hours, as much to rest their horses again as to wait for Porthos. But at the end of those two hours, as neither Porthos nor any news of him had come, they reluctantly resumed their journey.

At a league from Beauvais, where the road was confined between two high banks, they came upon ten laborers. Taking advantage of the road being unpaved in this spot, those ten appeared to be employed in digging holes and filling up the ruts with mud. Paying only indifferent heed to the travelers, they slowly began to move a few tools and barrows to allow the group to pass.

Aramis, less distressed by the delay as by their desire to avoid soiling their boots with the artificial mortar still being flung about, addressed the laborers rather sharply. "Hold all your digging sers, if you please. For we must pass quickly, and ideally a great deal more cleanly then you conduct yourselves."

Athos attempted to restrain Aramis as the irate musketeer surged forward, but she was too late. The laborers began to jeer at the travelers, shaking shovels and hoes, and by their insolence, they disturbed the equanimity even of the cool Athos, who urged on her horse past one of them.

Then each of these workers retreated as far as the ditch, from which each took a concealed musket — leaving our seven travelers outnumbered as unexpected battle began. Aramis received a bullet which passed through their shoulder, and Mousqueton another that lodged in the fleshy part which prolongs the lower portion of the loins. Mousqueton alone fell from their horse — not because they were severely wounded, but not being able to see the wound, they judged it to be more serious than it really was.

"Ambush!" shouted d'Artagnan. "Don't waste your pistols' charge! Forward!"

Aramis, wounded as they were, seized the mane of their horse, which carried them on with the others. Mousqueton's horse rejoined them, and galloped by the side of its companions.

"Alas poor Mousqueton," said Athos. "But their horse will at least serve us as a spare."

"I would rather have had a spare hat," said d'Artagnan. "Mine was carried away by a stray shot. By my faith, it is fortunate that the letter was not in it."

"They'll kill poor Porthos when he comes up," said Aramis.

"If Porthos were still on his feet, he would have rejoined us by this time," said Athos. "My opinion is that in the thick of the fight, the seemingly drunken cardinalist grew suddenly more sober. And that despite our best efforts, Richelieu has sent forth word ahead of us for his agents to seek guards and musketeers bound for London."

They continued at their best speed for two hours, although the horses were so fatigued that it was to be feared they would soon refuse to continue. The travelers detoured more than once along crossroads during that time, in the hope that they might meet with no further disturbances. But at Crevecoeur, the wounded Aramis declared they could proceed no farther.

In fact, it required all the courage which the musketeer concealed beneath their elegant form and polished manners to bear them so far. They grew more ashen with every mile, and the others were obliged to support them on their horse. So in the end, they lifted Aramis off at the door of an inn called the Miller's Arms, and engaged the gentle musketeer's agreement to leave Bazin with them — despite fearing that in a skirmish, the valet would be more embarrassing than useful. Then the rest set forth again in the hope of sleeping in Picardy, at Amiens.

"Great gods," said Athos as soon as they were once more in motion. "Reduced to two warriors, Grimaud, and Planchet. But by my faith, I won't be the dupe of any more of the cardinal's agents, I assure you. I will neither open my mouth nor draw my sword between this spot and Calais. I swear by —"

"Don't waste time in swearing," interrupted d'Artagnan. "Let us gallop, if our horses will consent."

So the travelers touched their spurs to their horses' flanks, which urged on thusly, recovered some of their energy. And in the end, they arrived at Amiens at midnight, and alighted at the inn of the Golden Lily.

The host was a nervous figure, showing flushed beige features and an unkempt fringe of bright-red hair where he received the travelers with his candlestick in one hand and his cotton nightcap in the other. At first, he wished to lodge the two travelers each in a charming room, but unfortunately those charming rooms were at the opposite ends of the inn. D'Artagnan and Athos refused them. The host replied that he had no other beds worthy of such excellent guests, but the travelers declared they would sleep in the common room, and would be entirely comfortable on mattresses upon the floor.

Athos and d'Artagnan had just prepared their beds and barricaded the main door of the common room from within, when someone knocked at the shuttered window of the courtyard. The two demanded who was there, and recognizing the voice of Planchet, opened the shutter. It was indeed he, along with the ever-silent Grimaud.

"Grimaud is intent on resting in the stables, and will watch the horses there," said Planchet. "If you are willing, madames, I will sleep across your doorway, and you will then be certain that no one can reach you."

"Indeed," said d'Artagnan, "such a watch would be welcome. The host's face does not please me at all. It is too gracious."

"Nor me either," said Athos.

Planchet then climbed in through the window while d'Artagnan collected the cushions of the common room chairs for the valet's bed. He installed himself across the doorway, while Grimaud went and shut herself up in the stable. By signs to Athos, she established that before dawn, she and the four horses would be ready.

The night was quiet enough. Still, sometime after midnight, some person endeavored to open the door to the inn. But Planchet awoke in an instant, crying out, "Who goes there?" From outside, a voice murmured that they were mistaken, and went away. By the time d'Artagnan had reached the window to cautiously peer out, there was no one to be seen.

But then an hour before dawn, all were awakened by a terrible din in the stables. Athos and d'Artagnan both went forth, to hear from the angry stable-hands that Grimaud had woken them disagreeably early, and they in response had thrashed her. When d'Artagnan and Athos went to the poor valet, they found her lying senseless, with her head bleeding by a blow from the handle of a pitchfork.

While Grimaud regained her senses, Planchet went into the stable yard and attempted to saddle the horses — but the horses were still exhausted. Mousqueton's horse alone, which had traveled without a rider half the day before, might have been able to continue the journey. But by an inconceivable error, a veterinary healer who had apparently been sent for to bleed one of the host's horses had bled Mousqueton's mount in error.

For d'Artagnan and Athos, a profound wariness set in. All these successive accidents seemed less the result of chance, and more the fruits of a plot. It was decided that Planchet would be sent out to inquire if there were three horses for sale anywhere nearby. Athos went down to pay the bill, while d'Artagnan stood watch at the street door.

The host's office was in a back room of the inn, to which Athos was requested to go. The musketeer entered without the least mistrust, and took out two pistoles to pay the bill. The host was alone, seated before his desk, one of the drawers of which was partly open. He took the money which Athos offered him. But after turning and turning the coins over in his hands, he suddenly cried out.

"These coins are bad. Bad, I say! Madame, I will have you and your companions arrested as forgers!"

"You villain!" cried Athos, advancing toward the host. "I'll cut your ears off!" But at the same instant, four brigands, armed to the teeth, entered by side doors and rushed upon her.

"I am taken!" shouted Athos with all the power of her lungs. "Go on, d'Artagnan! Ride, ride!" And she fired two pistols.

D'Artagnan did not need to be twice warned — but Planchet had just returned to report that no horses were to be bought or borrowed in the town. Just there at the door of the inn, though, stood two steeds — fresh, strong, and fully equipped. Their riders had passed the night in the inn, d'Artagnan having watched them warily at breakfast. So she and Planchet, at greatest need, unfastened the two horses, leaped upon them, buried their spurs in their sides, and set off at full gallop.

"Did you see what became of Athos?" asked d'Artagnan of Planchet as they raced on.

"Ah, madame," said Planchet, "I saw one brigand fall at each of her two shots. And she appeared to me, at a glance through the open door, to be fighting with her sword with the others."

"Brave Athos," murmured d'Artagnan. "And to think that we are compelled to leave her, even as the same fate perhaps awaits us two paces hence. Forward, Planchet, forward! You are a brave friend."

"As I told you, madame," said Planchet, "I am brave when I set myself to it. And being now in Picardy my own homeland, there is no telling what you may see me do!"

⚜

With free use of the spur, d'Artagnan and Planchet arrived at Saint-Omer without a stop. There, they rested their horses with the bridles looped around their arms for fear of the need to flee at speed. Planchet bought bread and cheese from a tavern, and they ate standing in the street, after which they departed again.

At a hundred paces from the gates of Calais, both horses stopped short, and could not be made to move another step. D'Artagnan and Planchet thus left their borrowed steeds to a well-deserved rest upon the high road, with d'Artagnan quickly leaving a shakily written note attached to one saddle, asking that the pair be returned to their owners in Amiens for undisclosed reward. That done, the two then ran toward the quay.

Planchet called d'Artagnan's attention to a gentlefolk who had just disembarked from a coach with their own valet, and who preceded them by about fifty paces. Both kept a wary distance from this gentle, who was dressed in handsome traveling clothes and bore a head of handsome deep-brown curls, but whose equally handsome golden-brown features were marked by a suspiciously impatient look. The valet, for their part, was tall and pale as blue-white ice, and appeared to be in as much haste as the gentry to reach the water.

At the dock, the valet called out to present the gentry as Madame Countess de Wardes, and to bring forth the captain of a vessel called *The Spirit*, making last preparations to set sail.

"I require passage to England," said the Countess de Wardes, "and as close to immediately as can be managed."

"Normally, nothing would be more easy," said the captain, a brawny English type of gray hair and tan skin well wind-burned. "For we mean to be underway on the tide within the hour. But just this morning came an order to let no one seek England without express permission from the Cardinal de Richelieu."

"I have that permission," said the gentle, drawing a passport from her pocket.

"Most excellent," said the captain. "Simply, then, have it examined by the governor of the port, then return it with her signature."

"Where shall I find the governor?"

"At her country house, a quarter of a league hence. Look, you may see it from here. At the crest of that little hill, that slated roof."

"Very well," said the gentle. And with her valet, she set out along the road.

D'Artagnan and Planchet looked to each other with silent understanding. They then followed this Countess de Wardes and her valet at a distance of five hundred paces.

Once outside the city, d'Artagnan overtook the pair as they were entering a little wood, quickly stepping around in front and forcing both to stop. "Madame Countess de Wardes," said the young guard, "you appear to be in great haste?"

"No one can be more so, maitre," said de Wardes, appraising the figure before her with a curious eye.

"I am sorry for that," said d'Artagnan. "For as I am in great haste likewise, I wish to beg you to render me a service."

"What?"

"To let me sail first."

"That's impossible," said the gentle, astonished. "I have traveled sixty leagues in forty hours, and by tomorrow at midday I must be in London."

"I have performed that same distance in forty hours. And by tomorrow morning, I must be in London."

"Very sorry, maitre, but I was here first and will not sail second."

"I am sorry, too, madame, but I arrived second and must sail first."

"But this is a needless quarrel you seek, as it seems to me, for surely the ship has ample room for us both. What do you truly want?"

"Would you like to know?" said d'Artagnan.

"Why otherwise would I ask?"

"Well, then. I wish that passport of which you are bearer, seeing that I have not one of my own and must have one."

The Countess de Wardes laughed aloud. "You jest, I presume."

"I never jest."

The gentle appraised d'Artagnan's earnest look, and returned one equally somber of her own. "Let me pass."

"You shall not pass."

"My brave and insolent young ser, you die today. Lubin!" de Wardes called to her valet. "My pistols!"

"Planchet," called out d'Artagnan, "take care of the valet! I will manage the Countess de Wardes."

Planchet, emboldened by his earlier exploits, sprang upon the valet Lubin. And being strong and vigorous, he immediately got the other on the broad of their back, and placed one knee upon their breast.

"Go on with your own fight, madame," cried Planchet. "I have finished mine."

Seeing this as she drew her sword, de Wardes sprang upon d'Artagnan. But she had too strong an adversary. In three quick strikes, d'Artagnan had carefully wounded the countess three times, exclaiming at each thrust: "One for Athos! One for Porthos! And one for Aramis!"

At the third hit, de Wardes fell like a log. D'Artagnan believed her insensible, and went toward her for the purpose of taking the passport. But the moment she extended her hand to search for it, the wounded gentry, who had not dropped her sword, plunged the point into d'Artagnan's breast, crying, "One for you!"

"And one for me — the best for last!" cried d'Artagnan, furious as she pinned the stranger to the earth with a fourth thrust through her shoulder.

This time, de Wardes fainted away. D'Artagnan searched her pockets, and took from one of them the order for her passage to London, which indeed was signed by the Cardinal de Richelieu.

She cast a glance on the handsome young gentry, who looked scarcely twenty-five years of age, and whom she was leaving deprived of sense and perhaps dying. D'Artagnan gave a sigh for that unaccountable destiny which leads soldiers to destroy each other for the interests of people who are strangers to them, and who often do not even know that they exist. But she was soon aroused from those reflections by Lubin, who uttered loud cries and screamed for help with all his might.

The valet, who was now decidedly less ice-pale as their blood ran hot, was held by Planchet around the throat. "Madame," said he, pressing as hard as he could, "as long as I hold them in this manner, they can't cry. But as soon as I let go, they will howl again. I recognize them as a Norman, and Normans are obstinate."

In fact, even as tightly held as they were, Lubin endeavored still to cry out.

"Stand fast, Maitre Lubin!" shouted d'Artagnan. And taking out her handkerchief, she gagged the valet.

"Now," said Planchet, "let us bind the villain to a tree."

This being properly done, d'Artagnan and Planchet drew the Countess de Wardes close to her valet. As night was approaching, and as the wounded gentry and the bound figure were at some small distance within the wood, it was evident they were likely to remain there till d'Artagnan and Planchet were safely away.

With the wounded countess still insensible, d'Artagnan left at the feet of the valet Lubin a certain amount of the miraculous salve from her father's recipe, with instructions for its use. "And now," said she, "to the governor's."

"But you are also wounded and at need, it seems," said Planchet.

"Oh, that's nothing. Let us attend to what is more pressing first." And they both set forth as fast as they could toward the country house still visible above the trees.

Upon their arrival, Madame Countess de Wardes was announced by Planchet, and d'Artagnan stepped forth.

"You have an order signed by the Cardinal de Richelieu?" asked the governor, a tall figure of close-cropped black hair and russet features.

"Yes, maitre," replied d'Artagnan. "Here it is."

"Let me see. Yes, all seems quite regular and clear," said the governor.

"As it should be," said d'Artagnan. "For I am one of their eminence's most faithful servants."

"It appears that the cardinal is anxious to prevent someone from crossing to England?"

"Yes. A certain d'Artagnan. A Gascon gentle who left Paris in company with three friends, with the intention of going to London."

"You sound as though you know them," said the governor.

"Indeed, I know this d'Artagnan perfectly well."

"Describe them to me, then."

"Nothing more easy." And d'Artagnan gave, feature for handsome feature, a description of the Countess de Wardes.

"Is she accompanied?"

"Yes. By a valet named Lubin."

"We will keep a sharp lookout for them. And if we lay hands on them, their eminence may be assured they will be reconducted to Paris under a good escort."

"And by doing so, Maitre Governor," said d'Artagnan, "you will have served the cardinal well."

"Shall you see their eminence on your return, madame?"

"Without a doubt."

"Tell their eminence, I beg you, that I am their humble servant."

"I will not fail."

Delighted with this assurance, the governor countersigned the passport and delivered it to d'Artagnan. D'Artagnan lost no time in useless compliments, simply thanking the governor, bowing, and departing.

Once outside, she and Planchet set off as fast as they could. By making a short detour, they avoided the wood and reentered the city by another gate. At the dock, *The Spirit* was near ready to sail, and d'Artagnan approached the captain.

"Good captain, I seek passage to England. Here is my passport, countersigned."

"All in order," said the captain as he scanned the document. "But did I not see you with that other gentle? What are the plans of the Countess de Wardes?"

"We passed as I was arriving at the governor's, and she just leaving," said d'Artagnan. "She mentioned some new business, and that she would not be sailing today. But here, I'll pay you for us two."

"In that case, let us depart," said the captain.

"Indeed, let us depart," said d'Artagnan.

She stepped with Planchet up the gangway, and not five minutes after, the vessel was away. And it was good timing, for they had scarcely sailed half a league when d'Artagnan saw a flash and heard a roar. It was the cannon which announced the closing of the port — and d'Artagnan knew on whose orders that closing would have come.

The young guard had now the time to look to her wound. Fortunately, as she had thought, it was not dangerous. The point of the countess's sword had touched a rib and glanced along the bone. Still further, her shirt had stuck to the wound, and she had lost only a little blood.

The salve of her father treated the wound easily enough, but d'Artagnan was worn out with fatigue. A mattress was laid upon the deck for her. She threw herself upon it, and fell asleep.

⚜

On the morrow, at break of day, they were still some leagues from the coast of England. The breeze had been light all night, so they had made but little progress. Bells were striking ten o'clock as the vessel finally cast anchor in the harbor of Dover, and not half an hour later, d'Artagnan placed her foot on English land, crying, "Here I am at last!"

But that was not enough — for her destination was London. Thankfully, horse posts were well served in England, and d'Artagnan and Planchet were each able to hire a sturdy mount. With the road well marked, and changing horses four times with no stop to eat, they arrived in the capital by late afternoon.

D'Artagnan knew even less of London than of England in general. She likewise did not know a word of English. But by writing the name of Buckingham on a piece of paper, she was able to impress on passersby to point her the way to the duke's estate.

As it happened, a door warden at the estate informed d'Artagnan that the duke was at Windsor, hunting with the queen and king. In response, the young guard inquired for the confidential valet of the duke, who was introduced as Mister Patrick. Bearing a smooth complexion of russet brown, with hair and neat beard just slightly darker and trimmed to equal smoothness, Patrick had accompanied Buckingham in all his voyages, and so spoke French perfectly well. With care, d'Artagnan informed the valet that she came from Paris regarding a matter of life and death, and that she must speak with his lord immediately.

The confidence with which d'Artagnan spoke convinced Patrick, who ordered two horses to be saddled, and he himself went as guide to the young guard. As for Planchet, he had been lifted from his horse as stiff as a stake, and taken into the duke's estate for care. The poor valet's strength was almost exhausted, though d'Artagnan seemed made of iron.

On their arrival at Windsor Castle, they learned that Buckingham and the royals were hawking in the marshes some three leagues away, but they were soon within sight of the hunting party. Patrick then caught the sound of his lord's voice calling his falcon.

"Whom should I announce to my lord duke?" asked he.

"The young guard who one evening sought a quarrel with him on the Pont Neuf, opposite the Samaritaine."

"A unique introduction," Patrick murmured. Then he galloped off, reached the duke, and announced to him in the terms directed that a messenger awaited him.

Buckingham at once remembered the circumstance. Suspecting that something was going on in France of which it was necessary he should be informed, he inquired where the messenger was. Then recognizing from afar the young guard, he put his horse into a gallop and rode straight up to d'Artagnan. Patrick discreetly kept in the background.

"No misfortune has happened to the Queen Anne?" cried Buckingham the instant he came up, throwing all his fear and love into the question.

"I do not believe so, my lord duke. Nevertheless, I believe she may be in some great peril from which your grace alone can extricate her."

"I? What is it? I should be too happy to be of any service to her. Speak, speak!"

"I cannot, for I know not. But take this letter," said d'Artagnan.

"This letter? From whom comes this letter?"

"From her majesty, or so I believe."

"From her majesty!" said Buckingham, his face becoming so pale beneath its powder that d'Artagnan feared he would faint as he broke the seal. But then his expression grew quizzical. "What is this rent?" said he, showing d'Artagnan a place where the letter had been pierced through.

"Faith!" said d'Artagnan. "I did not see that. It was the sword of the Countess de Wardes which made that hole, when she gave me a good thrust in the breast."

"You are wounded?" asked Buckingham as he opened the letter.

"Oh, nothing but a scratch," said d'Artagnan.

"Fate and faith, what have I read?" cried the duke even as he scanned the words written before him. "Patrick, remain here! Or rather, join the queen and king wherever they may be, and tell their majesties that I humbly beg them to excuse me, but an affair of the greatest importance recalls me to London. Come, madame, come!" And both he and d'Artagnan set off toward the capital at full gallop.

CHAPTER 21

THE DIAMOND STUDS

As they rode along, Buckingham endeavored to draw from d'Artagnan all the young guard knew of the events that had brought her there. By adding all that to his own remembrances, he was able to form a sense of the situation — with the Queen Anne's letter, short as it was, speaking to that situation's seriousness.

What astonished the duke even more so than the extent of Cardinal de Richelieu's efforts at preventing the Queen Anne's emissary from setting foot in England, was that the cardinal had not succeeded in arresting d'Artagnan on the road. The duke showed astonishment as d'Artagnan related to him the precautions taken, and the devotion of her three friends whom she had left scattered and bleeding behind her. She confirmed how she had succeeded in coming off with but the single sword thrust which had pierced the queen's letter, and for which she had repaid the Countess de Wardes fourfold. While he was listening to this recital, delivered with the greatest simplicity, the duke looked from time to time at the young guard with amazement, as if he could not comprehend how so much prudence, courage, and devotedness could be found in one so young.

Their horses went like the wind, and they were at the gates of London as the sun set. D'Artagnan imagined that on arriving in the city, the duke would slacken his pace, but it was not so. Buckingham kept on his way at the same rate, heedless about bowling over those whom he met on the road, so that by the time they had crossed the city, they had left three accidents behind them. But the duke did not even turn his head to see what became of those he knocked down, and d'Artagnan followed him amid cries and curses.

On entering the courtyard of his estate, Buckingham sprang from his horse, and without thinking on what would become of the animal, threw the bridle over its neck and ran toward the vestibule. D'Artagnan did the same, although with a little more concern for the exhausted creatures. But even as she followed, she had the satisfaction of seeing four grooms run from the kitchens and the stables, and busy themselves with the steeds.

The duke walked so fast that d'Artagnan had some trouble in keeping up with him. They passed through several apartments, whose elegance seemed to d'Artagnan as something from a dream, before arriving at length in a bed-chamber which was even more of a miracle of taste and richness. In the alcove of this chamber was a door concealed behind a tapestry, which the duke opened with a little gold key worn suspended from his neck by a chain of the same metal.

Showing discretion, d'Artagnan remained behind. But at the moment when Buckingham crossed the threshold, he turned round, seeing the hesitation of the young guard. "Come in," said he, "and if you have the good fortune to be admitted to her majesty's presence, tell her what you have seen here."

Encouraged by this invitation, d'Artagnan followed the duke, who closed the door after them. The two found themselves in a small chapel covered with a tapestry of Persian silk worked with gold, and illuminated by a vast number of candles which the duke lit, one by one. Over a kind of altar and beneath a canopy of blue velvet, surmounted by white and red feathered plumes, was a life-sized portrait of Anne of Austria, so perfect in its resemblance that d'Artagnan nearly cried out in surprise, for on beholding it, she full believed that the queen might be about to speak.

On the altar and beneath the portrait was a rosewood coffer whose face bore an "A" set with gold.

The duke approached the altar, knelt as a cleric might before a shrine, and opened the coffer. "There," said he, drawing from it a fine choker, in the form of a band of blue ribbon, sparkling with diamonds up each side. "There are the precious diamond studs which I have taken an oath should be buried with me. The Queen Anne gave them to me, but the queen requires them again. Her will be done in all things."

Buckingham began to kiss, one after the other, those dear gems with which he was about to part. Then all at once, he uttered a terrible cry.

"What is the matter?" exclaimed d'Artagnan anxiously. "What has happened, my lord?"

"All is lost!" cried Buckingham, becoming as pale as a corpse. "Two of the studs are missing. There are only ten!"

"Can you have lost them, my lord? Or could they have been stolen?"

"They have been stolen," said the duke in despair. "And no doubt it is the cardinal who has dealt this blow. Look there! Where they were bound to the ribbon, their wires have been cut away by a blade."

"But if a thief was able to gain access to this place, my lord, why steal only two of the studs? Why not take the choker and all the diamonds?"

"Wait, wait!" said the duke. "The only time I have worn these studs was at a ball given by King Charles and Queen Henrietta Maria eleven days ago at Windsor. One Milord de Winter, with whom I had quarreled in years past, became reconciled to me at that ball, and spent all night at my side. But I guess

*"There," said he, drawing from it a fine choker, in the form of
a band of blue ribbon, sparkling with diamonds up each side…*

now that the reconciliation was nothing but vengeance. For I have not seen him since that day, and must suspect him now as an agent of the cardinal."

"The cardinal has agents, then, throughout the world?" said d'Artagnan.

"Oh, yes," said Buckingham, grating his teeth with rage. "Yes, they are a terrible adversary. But when is this ball to take place?"

"October 3rd," said d'Artagnan in despair.

"So, six days before us. That shall be all the time we need."

In an instant, the duke had put forth calls for his gemsmith and his secretary. All his attendants responded quickly and silently, showing the earnestness with which they were accustomed to obeying the duke's commands. The secretary first made their appearance, as they lived on the estate. They found Buckingham seated at a table in his bedchamber, writing orders with his own hand.

"Master Jackson," said he, "go immediately to the lord chancellor, and tell her that I charge her with the execution of these orders. I wish them to be put into effect immediately."

Jackson, a stocky figure of umber features and an imposing presence, read the duke's letter at once — and was given pause. "But my lord, if the lord chancellor interrogates me upon the motives which may have led your grace to adopt such an extraordinary measure, what shall I reply to her?"

"That such is my pleasure, and that I answer for my will to no one."

"Will that be the answer," said the secretary evenly, "which she must transmit to their majesties if by chance either should be curious to know why no vessel is to leave any port of Britain?"

"Indeed, no. You are right, Master Jackson. She will say, in that case, to the royals that I am determined on war, and that this measure is my first act of hostility against France."

The secretary bowed, then departed.

"We are safe on that point," said Buckingham, turning toward d'Artagnan. "If the studs are not yet gone to Paris, they will not arrive till after you."

"How now?" said the young guard, who had understood nothing of the English exchange.

"I have just placed an embargo on all vessels presently in their majesties' ports, and without specific permission, not one will dare lift anchor."

D'Artagnan could only stare in wonder. Seemingly with a single word, the duke could protect his illicit ardor with the unlimited power granted him by the confidence of king and queen. Buckingham saw by the expression of the young guard's face what was passing in her mind, and he smiled.

"Yes," said he. "Yes, Anne of Austria is my true royal. Upon a word from her, I would betray my homeland, I would betray my faith, I would betray the royals I serve. She asked me not to send the Huguenots of La Rochelle the assistance I promised them. And I have not done so. I broke my word to the rebels, it is true. But what of that? I obeyed my love, and have I not been richly paid for that?"

D'Artagnan was amazed to note by what fragile and unknown threads the destinies of nations and the lives of those nations' citizens are suspended. She was lost in these reflections when the gemsmith arrived.

"Mistress O'Reilly," said the duke, leading her into the chapel. "Look at the diamond studs of this choker, and tell me what they are worth apiece."

The petite gemsmith bore sepia features set off by coils of golden hair, which shone so bright that it might have been the spun gold of her trade. Her confidence marked her as one most skilled, and she cast a glance at the superlative cut of the diamonds and the elegant manner in which the studs were set. She calculated, feature by feature, what the stones were worth, and without hesitation said, "Fifteen hundred pistoles each, my lord."

"How many days would it require to cut and set two studs exactly like them? You see there are two wanting."

"Eight days, my lord."

"I will give you three thousand pistoles apiece if they are completed four days hence."

"My lord, they shall be yours."

"You are a jewel of a crafter, Mistress O'Reilly. But that is not all. These studs cannot be trusted to just anyone. The work must be done in the palace."

"Impossible, my lord. There is no one but myself able to execute them so as to make the new indistinguishable from the old."

"Therefore, my dear Mistress O'Reilly, you are my prisoner. And if you wish ever to leave my palace, you cannot. So make the best of it. Name to me such of your workers as you need, and point out the tools they must bring. And for this inconvenience, it would be my pleasure to retain your services thereafter. Shall we say a hundred thousand livres a year by the Duke of Buckingham?"

D'Artagnan understood none of the English conversation save the word 'livres,' but sensed in the expression of the gemsmith both the wealth of the impossible offer and the impenetrable will of the duke.

"May I be permitted to inform my wife?" said the gemsmith.

"Indeed. You may even bring her if you like, my dear Mistress O'Reilly. Your captivity shall be mild, be assured. And as every inconvenience deserves its indemnification, here is, in addition to the price of the studs, an order of payment from the treasury for a thousand pistoles, to make you forget the annoyance I cause you."

D'Artagnan could not read the note, naturally, but as it was passed, she recognized its royal bearing and the numbers impressed thereon. She could not get over the surprise created in her by this minister, who so openly made such use of wealth and others' lives.

As to the gemsmith, she wrote to her wife, sending along the order for the thousand pistoles, and charging her to bring in exchange Mistress O'Reilly's most skillful apprentices, an assortment of diamonds for which she gave names and weights, and the necessary tools.

Buckingham conducted O'Reilly to a chamber he ordered prepared for her, and which at the end of half an hour was transformed into a workshop. Then he placed a sentinel at each door, with an order to admit no one except those working within and his confidential valet, Patrick, upon any pretense. We need not add that the gemsmith and her assistants were prohibited from going out under any pretext.

The plan thus settled, the duke turned to d'Artagnan. "Now, my young friend," said he, "England is all our own. What do you wish for? What do you desire?"

"Word on the health and well-being of my valet, and a bed, my lord," said d'Artagnan. "At present, I confess, those are the things I stand most in need of."

After sending out word that would return the location and state of Planchet, Buckingham gave d'Artagnan a chamber adjoining his own, informing the young guard that he wished to have her at hand. Not that he at all mistrusted her, he was quick to add, but simply for the sake of having someone to whom he could constantly talk of the Queen Anne.

Only one hour later, the ordinance was published in London that no vessel bound for France should leave port, not even the packet boat with letters. In the eyes of everyone, this was a declaration of war between the two realms.

⚜

Before noon on the fourth day after their crafting was begun, the two diamond studs were finished. They were so completely flawless, so perfectly alike, that Buckingham could not tell the new ones from the old ones, and Mistress O'Reilly assured her lordship that even experts in such matters would have been as deceived as he was.

Buckingham immediately called d'Artagnan to his chamber. "Here," said he to her, "are the diamond studs that you came to bring. And be my witness that I have done all that human power could do to fulfill the Queen Anne's order."

"Be certain, my lord, that I will ensure she is told of all I have seen. But does your grace mean to give me the studs without the coffer?"

"The coffer would encumber you. Besides, it is the more precious from being all that is left to me. You will say that I keep it."

"I will perform your commission word for word, my lord."

"And now," said Buckingham, looking earnestly at the young guard, "how shall I ever acquit myself of the debt I owe you?"

D'Artagnan frowned, for she understood that the duke was intent to bestow some reward on her. But the idea that the blood of her friends and herself was about to be paid for with English gold was strangely repugnant to her.

"Let us understand each other, my lord," said d'Artagnan, "and let us make things clear beforehand in order that there may be no mistake. I am in the service of the queens of France, and form part of the company of Madame d'Essarts, who, as well as her brother-in-law, Monsieur de Treville, is particularly attached to their majesties. What I have done, then, has been for the Queen Anne, and not at all for your grace. And still further, it is very probable that I should not have become involved in any of this, except for my desire to please someone who is as dear to me as the queen is to you."

"I see," said the duke, smiling. "And remembering our first meeting, I even believe that I know that other person. So it is to Constance Bonacieux, then, that I am bound to discharge my debt of gratitude for your service."

"If you wish, my lord. But truly, at this moment when there is question of war, I confess to you that I see nothing in your grace but one of the English, and consequently an enemy whom I should have much greater pleasure in meeting on the field of battle than in the park at Windsor or the corridors of the Louvre. None of which, however, will prevent me from executing every point of my commission, or from laying down my life if there be need to accomplish it. But I repeat it to your grace, that you have no more personally to thank me for in this second interview than for what I did for you in the first."

"We say in this land, 'Proud as a Scot,'" murmured the Duke of Buckingham.

"And we say in France, 'Proud as a Gascon,'" said d'Artagnan. "The Gascons are the Scots of France, it seems."

D'Artagnan bowed to the duke, and had turned to depart when Buckingham called to her.

"Wait, my young friend. Will you share with me how you plan to make your way back? And what of your valet?"

D'Artagnan paused, turning back with a frown. "It is true that I have yet to think on these things." Planchet had recovered from his exhaustion in slow but good time, and had spent the previous day walking Buckingham's estate like a fine English squire. But knowing how the trip to England had affected him, D'Artagnan was suddenly conscious of wanting to bring the brave valet back in the self-same condition in which he had departed.

"By my faith," laughed Buckingham, "these French have no sense!"

"I had forgotten that England was an island," said d'Artagnan, smiling, "and that you were the true royal of it."

The duke laughed again as he sat at his table. "I will make arrangements for you and your valet to reach the shores of France," said he, writing, "but you must then ride on alone. You will go to the riverside. Seek the Tower of London and look along the docks there for the brig *Sund*, then give this letter to the captain. She will convey you to a little French port, where certainly you are not expected, and which is ordinarily only frequented by fishers."

"The name of that port?"

"Saint-Valery. But listen. When you have arrived there, make arrangements for your valet to travel by post horse or carriage, as you wish. But you will go to a rough tavern, without a name and without a sign. A mere fisherman's hut. You cannot mistake it, for there is but one. You will ask for the host there, and will repeat to him, 'Forward!'" This last word was spoken in English.

"Which means?"

"It is the password. The host will give you a fine horse all saddled, and will point out to you the road you must take. You will find, in the same way, four relays on your route."

"And these relays are?" said d'Artagnan.

"The network by which I and my couriers move unseen through France when needs be. If you will give at each of these relays your address in Paris, the four horses will follow you thither. You already know of the two like them which we rode upon from Windsor Castle, and which you appeared to appreciate. You may trust that the others will not be inferior to them. Though I understand that you do not consider me beholden to you, I hope that however proud you may be, you will not refuse to accept these fine steeds for yourself or for any companions you deem worthy of them. With my full understanding that you accept them in order to make war against us."

"Yes, my lord, I accept them," said d'Artagnan, laughing. "And if it please you, the soldiers of France will make a good use of your presents. Would that my three companions had survived, for this gift would have served them well."

"Your friends' fate may well be not such sorrow as you believe," said Buckingham, "so do not give up hope. But for now, give me your hand, young d'Artagnan. Perhaps we shall soon meet on the field of battle. But in the meantime, we shall part as friends, I hope."

"Yes, my lord. But with the hope of soon becoming enemies."

"Worry not. I promise you we shall."

D'Artagnan then bowed to the duke and departed. She retrieved Planchet, and the two made their way as quickly as possible to the riverside. Opposite the Tower of London, d'Artagnan found the vessel that had been named to her, and delivered her letter to the captain. After having the letter examined by the governor of the port, the captain welcomed the pair aboard and made immediate preparations to sail.

Fifty other vessels along the docks were waiting in vain to set out, all now hindered by the Duke of Buckingham's order, and interfering with the arrival of already some half-dozen ships arriving up the river. But as *Sund* passed alongside one of those inbound vessels, d'Artagnan fancied that she saw on board it an unexpected and familiar face. She could have sworn, in fact, to have recognized the younger stranger of Meung — the same whom the scarred villain Rochefort had called 'Milord,' and whom d'Artagnan in her wounded state had thought so handsome.

With that glimpsed face, remembrance of the Duke of Buckingham's Milord de Winter was in the musketeer's mind. But thanks to the current of the river and a fair wind, d'Artagnan's vessel passed so quickly that she had little more than a glimpse of the unknown figure.

Early in the morning on the next day, *Sund* landed at Saint-Valery. Arrangements were made for Planchet to journey on to Paris by fast carriage, and the valet embraced d'Artagnan with somewhat too much emotion before they parted. The young guard then went immediately in search of the tavern, and easily discovered it by the riotous noise that resounded from it. War between England and France was talked of as near and certain, and the fishers of the small port were caught up in revelry.

D'Artagnan made her way through the crowd, advanced toward the host, and pronounced the word, "Forward!" The host immediately made her a sign to follow, went out with her by a door which opened into a rear yard, and led her to the stable. While a horse was saddled and prepared for her, the host asked for d'Artagnan's address in Paris.

"The guards' house, estate of Madame d'Essarts."

"Very well." They then presented d'Artagnan with a fine set of pistols, and asked if she stood in need of anything else.

"Well, I need to know the route I am to follow," said she.

"Go from hence to Blangy, and from Blangy to Neufchatel. At Neufchatel, go to the tavern of the Golden Harrow, give the same password to the keeper, and you will find, as you have here, a horse ready for your use."

"My thanks," said d'Artagnan. "May I offer you anything in compensation?

"Nay, for all is arranged by they who sent you," replied the host, "and most generously. Begone, and may the gods guide you."

"I will trust to fate more than faith," said the young guard. And when the horse was ready, she set off at full gallop.

Four hours later, d'Artagnan was in Neufchatel, and followed the instructions she had received. At the Golden Harrow, as at the unnamed tavern of Saint-Valery, she found a stabled horse quite ready and awaiting any rider bearing the password. While the horse was prepared, she thought to transfer her new pistols from one saddle to the other, but found the holsters of the new saddle already furnished with equally fine weapons.

D'Artagnan was asked once more her address. Then she asked, "Which route must I now take?" in her turn.

"That of Rouen, but you will leave the city on your right. You must stop at the little village of Ecouis in which there is but one tavern, called the Shield of

France. Don't condemn it from appearances. You will find a horse in the stables quite as good as this."

"The same password?"

"Exactly."

"Adieux then, friend."

"A good journey, maitre! Do you want of anything else?"

D'Artagnan shook her head and set off at full speed.

At Ecouis, the same scene was repeated, and the young guard found as provident a host and a fresh horse. She left her address as she had done before, and set off again at the same pace for Pontoise. At Pontoise, she changed her horse for the last time, and by sunset, she was galloping into the yard of Treville's estate. She had made nearly sixty leagues in little more than twelve hours.

Where he worked at inspection, Monsieur de Treville greeted her as if she had seen him only that same morning. "You have expended only just over half your fifteen days' leave. I trust all is well?"

"In the main, the journey was a success," said d'Artagnan.

"The others are delayed, then?" Treville said, seeing that no one else rode behind the young guard.

"Indeed," said d'Artagnan, but she feared to speak more among the company of so many musketeers — especially of the loss of Athos, Porthos, and Aramis. "When time permits, I shall share the tale."

Monsieur de Treville shook her hand a little more warmly than usual. "There is indeed much to do. For the company of Madame d'Essarts has been named for duty at the great ball tomorrow evening, and are preparing. We shall speak when we can, but go at once to your post."

CHAPTER 22

THE BALLET OF *LA MERLAISON*

On the morrow, nothing was talked of in Paris but the ball which the magistrates of the city were to give to the queens, and in which their majesties were to dance the famous *La Merlaison* — the favorite ballet of the Queen Louise.

Long days had been spent in preparations at the great city hall of the Hotel de Ville for this important evening. Carpenters had erected huge scaffolds in the grand salon, upon which invited guests were to be seated. The city chandler had ornamented the chambers with two hundred white candelabra. Twenty violinists were hired, with their fee fixed at double the usual rate upon the condition that they should play all night.

Late in the morning on the day of the ball, Maitre de Coste, an ensign in the queens' guards, came to the city registrar along with two officers and several archers of that corps. The registrar was named Maitre Clement, and Maitre de Coste ceremoniously asked of them all the keys of the rooms and offices of the Hotel de Ville, which were given up to them immediately. Each key had a ticket attached to it by which it might be recognized, and from that moment, Maitre de Coste and their soldiers were charged with the care of all the hall's doors and other access points.

An hour later, Madame Duhalier, captain of the city guards, came in her turn, bringing with her fifty archers, who were distributed immediately through the Hotel de Ville at the doors assigned them. At midafternoon came two companies of the queens' guards, composed of Madame Duhalier's troops and those of Madame d'Essarts.

As the clocks struck six in the evening, the guests began to arrive. As fast as they entered, they were placed in the grand salon, on the platforms prepared for them. At nine o'clock, Monsieur de Fronde, the most senior president of the Paris parliament, arrived. As next to the queens, he was the most considerable personage of the fete, he was received by the city officials and placed in a box opposite to that which the Queen Anne was to occupy.

At ten o'clock, the Queen Louise's favorite sweets, consisting of preserves and other delicacies, were prepared in the antechamber of the small chapel set alongside the city hall, and set onto silver platters guarded by four archers.

At midnight, great cries and loud acclamations were heard. It was the Queen Louise, who was passing through the streets which led from the Louvre to the Hotel de Ville, and which were all illuminated with colored lanterns.

Immediately, the magistrates went to attend upon the queen, clothed in their official robes and preceded by six sergeants, each holding a candelabrum in hand. They met her on the steps, where the city's provost of mercers made a speech of welcome — a compliment to which the Queen Louise replied with an apology for coming so late, laying the blame upon the Cardinal de Richelieu, who had detained her till eleven o'clock to talk of affairs of state.

The Queen Louise, in full dress, was accompanied by various gentry, most of whom kept their eyes on each other, for her majesty looked preoccupied and decidedly not happy. A private dressing room had been prepared for Louise, in which was placed her masquerade costume. The same had been done for the Queen Anne. The gentry of their majesties' suites were to dress, two by two, in chambers prepared for that purpose. Before entering her dressing room, the Queen Louise made known her desire to be informed the moment the cardinal arrived.

Half an hour after the entrance of the Queen Louise, fresh acclamations were heard announcing the arrival of the Queen Anne. The magistrates did as they had done before, and preceded by their sergeants, advanced to receive their illustrious guest. The queen entered the great hall, and it was noted by many — though of course, not publicly remarked — that like the Queen Louise, she looked sad, and even weary.

At the moment the Queen Anne entered, the curtain of a small gallery was drawn which to that point had been closed, and the face of the cardinal appeared. Their masquerade dress was that of a Spanish gentry, and their eyes were fixed upon the Queen Anne.

A smile of terrible joy passed over their eminence's lips.

Anne did not wear her diamond studs.

She remained for a short time to receive the compliments of the city dignitaries and to reply to various salutations. Then all at once, the Queen Louise appeared with the cardinal at one of the doors of the hall. Their eminence was speaking to Louise in a low voice, and the queen's face was drawn.

Louise made her way through the crowd without a mask, the ribbons of her jacket scarcely tied. She went straight to Anne, and in an altered voice said, "Why, madame, have you not thought proper to wear your diamond studs, when you know it would give me so much pleasure?"

The Queen Anne cast a glance around her — and saw the cardinal standing behind the Queen Louise with a diabolical smile.

"My apologies, madame," replied she with a calm voice. "But in the midst of such a crowd as this, I feared some accident might happen to them."

"And you were wrong, madame. If I made you that present, it was that you might adorn yourself therewith. I tell you that you were wrong."

The voice of the Queen Louise was tremulous with anger. All those close by looked and listened with astonishment, comprehending nothing of what passed.

"My love," said the Queen Anne, "do not worry yourself. I can send for them to the Louvre where they are, and thus your wishes will be complied with."

"Do so, madame. Do so and at once, for within an hour the ballet will commence."

The Queen Anne nodded her understanding, and followed the attendants who were to conduct her to her dressing room. On her part, the Queen Louise returned to her own chamber. No one saw the Queen Anne smile.

There was a moment of trouble and confusion in the assembly. All were remarking that something had passed between the queens, but both of them had spoken so low that when all near them had withdrawn out of respect, they thus heard nothing. Even when the hour had passed and the violins began to sound with all their might to signal the ballet's start, still all was talking, and no one listened to the music.

The Queen Louise came out first from her dressing room. She was in a most elegant hunting costume, and flanked by gentry dressed the same. This was the costume that best became the queen, for so dressed, she really appeared the most distinguished gentlefolk of the realm.

The cardinal drew near to Louise, and placed in her hand a small box, which had been delivered to them five days earlier. Milord de Winter had been rewarded for the success of his mission with leave to return at once to England, not wanting to draw attention by his absence, and having what he described as personal affairs to put in order.

The Queen Louise opened the box, and found in it two diamond studs.

"What does this mean?" demanded she of the cardinal.

"Nothing of importance," replied their eminence. "But when the Queen Anne makes her next excuses for not wearing the studs, you might think to ask her majesty to speculate on the origin of the two studs that are here."

Louise looked at the cardinal in confusion. But before she had any chance to question their eminence, a cry of admiration burst from every mouth. For if the Queen Louise appeared to be the most distinguished gentlefolk of the realm, the Queen Anne was without doubt the most beautiful gentlefolk in France.

A costume transforming her into a spirit of the air became Anne admirably. She wore a hat set with blue feathers, a robe of gray-pearl velvet, and a petticoat of blue satin embroidered with silver.

Around the Queen Anne's neck sparkled the diamond studs, on their ribbon whose blue was the same color as the feathers and the petticoat.

*The Queen Louise advanced toward the Queen Anne.
They took their places, and the performance began…*

The Queen Louise shone with joy — and the cardinal trembled with rage. Still, distant as both were, they could not count the studs where the Queen Anne wore them.

At that moment, the violins sounded the opening for the ballet. The Queen Louise advanced toward the Queen Anne. They took their places, and the performance began.

Louise danced across from Anne, and every time they passed by each other, she devoured with her eyes the blue choker and its studs — but Anne's movement prevented Louise still from ascertaining their number.

The ballet lasted an hour, and ended amid the applause of the whole assembly. As the dancers reconducted themselves to their starting places for a final bow, the Queen Louise took advantage of waiting to advance eagerly toward the Queen Anne.

"I thank you, madame," said she, "for the deference you have shown to my wishes. But I think you want two of the studs, and I bring them back to you." With these words, she held out to Anne the two studs the cardinal had given her.

"Madame!" cried the younger queen, affecting surprise. "You are giving me, then, two more. I shall have fourteen."

In fact, even as Anne spoke, the Queen Louise counted the studs — and all twelve were at the Queen Anne's neck.

At once, Louise called the cardinal. "What does this mean, Maitre?" asked she in a severe tone.

For the entirety of the ballet, the cardinal had lurked unseen within the crowd. Now that they were called forward, all could see that a cold sweat covered the brow of their eminence.

"This means, majesty," replied they carefully, "that I was desirous of presenting the Queen Anne with these two studs. And that not daring to offer them myself, I adopted this means of inducing her to accept them."

"And I am the more grateful to your eminence," said Anne, with a smile made to show the cardinal she was not the dupe of this ingenuous gallantry. "For I am certain that these two studs alone must have cost you as much as all the others cost her majesty."

Saluting the Queen Louise and the cardinal, the Queen Anne resumed her way to her dressing room. And as she went, she caught the eye of her to whom Anne of Austria owed the extraordinary triumph she had just obtained over the cardinal. A young guard, confounded and unknown, who stood lost in the crowd gathered at one of the doors.

D'Artagnan looked on at this scene, whose full meaning was comprehensible to only three persons — the Queen Anne, their eminence the cardinal, and herself. Anne had just entered her dressing room and d'Artagnan was about to withdraw, when she felt her shoulder lightly touched. She turned and saw a figure whose face was covered with a black velvet mask. But notwithstanding this precaution, d'Artagnan at once recognized her usual guide — the brave and virtuous Constance Bonacieux, who made a sign that d'Artagnan should follow her.

On the evening before, the two had scarcely seen each other at the apartment of the palace guard, Germain, from where d'Artagnan had sent in secret for the tailor. Constance had been in great haste to convey to the Queen Anne the excellent news of the happy return of her messenger, which prevented she and the young guard from exchanging more than a few words. D'Artagnan therefore followed her now moved by a double sentiment of curiosity and love.

All the way, and in increasing proportion as the corridors became more deserted, d'Artagnan wished to stop the young tailor, to seize her and gaze upon her, even were it only for a moment. But quick as a bird, Constance glided each time between the young guard's hands. When d'Artagnan attempted to speak to her, Constance's finger was placed upon her mouth with a little imperative gesture full of grace, reminding the guard that she was under the command of a power which she must blindly obey, and which forbade her even to make the slightest complaint.

At length, after winding about for a minute or two, Constance opened the door of a closet that was entirely dark, and led d'Artagnan into it. There she made a fresh sign of silence, and opened a second door concealed by a tapestry. Slipping past the tapestry revealed a brilliant light, and Constance disappeared.

D'Artagnan remained for a moment motionless, asking herself where she might be. But before long, the warm and perfumed air which reached her from beyond the partially open door, the conversation of two or three people in language at once respectful and refined, and the word "majesty" several times repeated, suggested clearly that she was in a closet attached to the Queen Anne's apartment. The young guard waited in comparative darkness and listened.

Although d'Artagnan did not know the Queen Anne, she soon distinguished her voice from the others — at first by its slightly foreign accent, and next by a tone of cheer and happiness which seemed to astonish the persons who surrounded her, whose words and tone suggested they were accustomed to seeing the queen almost always sad and full of worry. Anne attributed this joyous feeling to the beauty of the fete, and to the pleasure she had experienced in the ballet. And as it is not permissible to contradict a queen whether she smile or weep, everyone soon took up the same story, to expound upon the gallantry of the magistrates of the city of Paris.

As the conversation ensued, d'Artagnan more than once heard the royal approach and withdraw from the partially open door. Three times, she even saw the shadow of a person intercept the tapestry-shrouded light.

At length, a hand and an arm, surpassingly beautiful in their form and movement, glided through the tapestry. D'Artagnan at once comprehended that this was her reward for the Queen Anne's service. She cast herself on her knees, seized the hand, and touched it respectfully with her lips. Then the hand was withdrawn, leaving in her own hand an object which felt to be a ring. The door then closed, and d'Artagnan found herself in darkness.

The young guard placed the ring on her finger and again waited, as it was evident that all was not yet over. For she told herself that after the reward for her devotion, the reward for her love was still to come. Besides, although the ballet had been danced, the evening had scarcely begun. Supper was to be served at three, and the city clocks had only just struck half past two.

The sound of voices diminished by degrees in the adjoining chamber. The queen's company was heard departing. Then the door of the closet in which d'Artagnan stood concealed was opened, and Constance entered.

"You at last?" said d'Artagnan.

"Silence," said the young tailor, placing her hand upon d'Artagnan's lips. "Silence, and go the same way you came."

"But where and when shall I see you again?" whispered the young guard. "Will you stay at the palace? For the cardinal's wrath is sure to seek all who had a hand in the foiling of their eminence's plots, and surely you cannot go home again."

"Your concerns have already been accounted for by the Queen Anne, who fears that not even the palace will be safe for a time, and who has made arrangements for me to take some small leave in a place of security. A note which you will find at home will tell you more. Now begone!"

At these words, Constance opened the door to the corridor and pushed d'Artagnan out. The young guard obeyed like a child, without the least resistance or objection — which proved that she was positively in love.

CHAPTER 23

THE RENDEZVOUS

D'Artagnan ran back to her apartment immediately, and although it was deep in the night and she had some of the worst quarters of Paris to traverse, she met with no misadventure. As everyone knows, drunkards and lovers are watched over by protective gods.

She found the door of her passage open, sprang up the stairs, and knocked softly in a manner agreed upon between her and Planchet, whose fast carriage had brought him from Saint-Valery to the city, rested and ready to serve, that afternoon. D'Artagnan had sent him home two hours prior from the Hotel de Ville, telling him to wait up for her own arrival.

"Has anyone brought a letter for me?" asked the young guard eagerly.

"No one has brought a letter, madame," replied Planchet nervously, "but one has come of itself."

"What do you mean, Monsieur Comedian?"

"I mean to say that when I came in, although I had the key of your apartment in my pocket and that key had never left me, I found a letter on the green table in your bedchamber."

"And where is that letter?"

"I left it where I found it, madame. It is not natural for letters to enter people's houses in this manner. If the window had been open or even ajar, I should have thought nothing of it. But no, all was hermetically sealed. Beware, madame! There is certainly some magic there."

Meanwhile, the young guard had darted into her room and opened the letter. It was the note promised by Constance, and was expressed in these terms:

There are many thanks to be offered to you, and to be transmitted to you. Be this evening about ten o'clock at Saint-Cloud, in front of the summerhouse which stands at the corner of the chateau of Madame d'Estrees.

— C

While reading this letter, d'Artagnan felt her heart dilated and compressed by that delicious spasm which tortures and caresses the hearts of lovers. It was the first such note she had ever received. It was the first rendezvous that had been granted her which carried the weight of true love. Her heart, swelled by the intoxication of joy, felt ready to dissolve away.

"Well, madame," said Planchet, who had observed his employer grow flushed, "did I not guess truly? Is it not some evil affair?"

"You are mistaken, Planchet," said d'Artagnan. "And as proof, here is a crown with which to drink my health."

"I am much obliged to madame for the crown she has given me, and I promise to follow her instructions exactly. But it is nonetheless true that letters which come in this way into shut-up houses —"

"This letter flew on the winds of fate, my friend. Or was at least delivered by one who possessed a spare key."

"Then madame is happy?" asked Planchet.

"My dear Planchet, I am the happiest of folk!"

"And I may profit by madame's happiness, and go to bed?"

"Yes, go."

"May great blessings fall upon madame, then. But it is nonetheless true that that letter has a mystery about it."

Planchet thus retired, shaking his head with an air of doubt, which the open-mindedness of d'Artagnan had not entirely effaced.

Left alone, d'Artagnan read and reread the note. Then she kissed and rekissed twenty times the lines traced by the hand of her beautiful Constance. At length, she went to bed, fell asleep, and had golden dreams.

At seven o'clock in the morning, d'Artagnan arose and called Planchet. At the second summons, the valet opened the door, his expression not yet quite freed from the anxiety of the preceding night.

"Planchet," said d'Artagnan, "I am going out. For all the day, perhaps. You are, therefore, in charge of yourself till seven o'clock this evening. But at seven o'clock, you must hold yourself in readiness with two horses."

"Faith," said Planchet. "We are going again, it appears, to have our hides pierced in all sorts of ways."

"You will take your musketoon and your pistols."

"There, now! Didn't I say so?" cried the valet. "I was sure of it. That accursed letter!"

"Be at ease, brave Picard. There is nothing in hand but a journey for pleasure."

"Ah, like the charming journey to England, when it rained bullets and a crop of swords burst from the ground."

"Well, if you are really afraid, Monsieur Planchet, I will go without you. I would prefer traveling alone to having a companion who entertains the least fear."

"Madame does me wrong," said Planchet. "I thought she had seen me at work."

"Yes, but I thought perhaps you had worn out all your courage on our previous excursion."

"Madame shall see that upon occasion, I have some left. Only I beg madame not to be too wasteful of it if she wishes it to last long."

D'Artagnan sighed. "Do you believe you have still enough courage to expend this evening?"

"I hope so, madame."

"Well, then, I count on you."

"At the appointed hour, I shall be ready."

"Oh, and saddle two of the horses you will find in my name in the guard stables. There shall be no retainer's cob for you this night."

"I shall obey, madame. Only I had understood that madame had but one horse in the stables."

"Perhaps there is but one at this moment. But if my expectations are correct, by this evening, there will be four."

"It appears that our journey was a remounting expedition, then?"

"Exactly so," said d'Artagnan, and nodding to Planchet, she went out.

Monsieur Bouquet was waiting at her door.

D'Artagnan's immediate intention was to go by without speaking to the unworthy mercer. But the latter made so polite and friendly a salutation that, as his tenant, she felt she must play the part not only to stop, but to enter into conversation with him.

She worked hard to hide the reaction that having heard the mercer's friendly talk with the villain Rochefort had engendered in her, engaging the most amiable air she could assume. But even as she judged the mercer as a cardinalist, and as friend and lackey to villains, she felt at the same time the cold discomfort of knowing that she was conversing with a husband whose wife had appointed a meeting with her that same evening in the town of Saint-Cloud, opposite Madame d'Estrees's summerhouse. Thus did d'Artagnan for the very first time reckon the guilt that is too often one of the costs of true love.

The conversation naturally fell upon the incarceration of the poor mercer. Bouquet, who was ignorant that d'Artagnan had overheard his conversation with Rochefort, related to his young tenant the persecutions he had endured, and expounded at great length upon the Bastille and its gloomy corridors, its dank cells, and its instruments of torture — all of which detail he drew from popular tales more so than personal experience.

D'Artagnan listened to him with exemplary attention. Only when Bouquet had finished did she speak. "And Madame Bonacieux? Do you know who carried her off? For I do not forget that I owe to that unpleasant circumstance the good fortune of having made your acquaintance."

"Ah," said Bouquet, "they took good care not to tell me that. And my wife, on her part, has sworn to me by all that's sacred that she does not know. But you," continued Monsieur Bouquet in a tone of perfect fellowship. "What has become of you for all these days that I have not seen you nor your friends. I don't expect that you gathered all that dust I saw Planchet brush off your boots yesterday morning from the pavement of Paris."

"You are right, my dear Monsieur Bouquet. My friends and I have been on a little journey."

"Far from here?"

"Faith, no. About fifty leagues only, to go and return. We went to take Madame Athos to the waters of Forges, where my friends still remain."

"So you have returned alone, have you?" said Monsieur Bouquet, whose expression took on a most sly air. "A handsome young guard like you may obtain a longer leave of absence from a commander than from a paramour, no doubt. And you were impatiently waited for at Paris, were you not?"

"My faith," said d'Artagnan, laughing. "I confess it, and so much more the readily, my dear Bouquet, as I see there is no concealing anything from you. Yes, I was expected, and very impatiently, I acknowledge."

A scowl passed over the gaze of Bouquet, but so slight that d'Artagnan did not perceive it.

"And surely you are to be rewarded for your diligence?" said the mercer, with a slight alteration of his voice — so slight, indeed, that d'Artagnan did not perceive it any more than she had the alteration of his gaze.

"Ah, may you be a true prophet," said d'Artagnan.

"But what I mean," said Bouquet, "is whether or not you will be delayed and returning late this evening."

"Why that question, my dear host?" asked d'Artagnan. "Do you intend to wait up for me?"

"No. But since my arrest and the robbery that was committed in my house, I am alarmed every time I hear a door open, particularly in the night. What in faith can you expect? I am no warrior."

"Well, don't be alarmed if I return not until deep in the night. Indeed, do not be alarmed if I do not come home at all."

This time, Bouquet became so pale that d'Artagnan could not help but notice it. "I say, monsieur, what is the matter?"

"Nothing," replied Bouquet. "Nothing. Since my misfortunes, I have been subject to feelings of faintness which seize me all at once, and I have just felt a cold shiver. Pay no attention to it. You have nothing to occupy yourself with but being content."

"Then I have full occupation, for I am so."

"Though not yet, surely. This evening, you said."

"Well, this evening will come, thankfully. And perhaps you look for it with as much impatience as I do. For Madame Bonacieux is presumably at home?"

"Madame Bonacieux is not at liberty this evening," said Bouquet nervously. "She is detained at the Louvre by her duties."

"So much the worse for you, my dear lessor, so much the worse. When I am content, I wish all the world to be so. But it appears that is not possible."

Then the young guard departed, smiling when she thought she alone could see. But Monsieur Bouquet's expression twisted as though he understood her mood — and its inspiration.

"Amuse yourself well," said he in a dread tone, but d'Artagnan was too far off to hear him. And even if she had heard him, in the disposition of mind she then enjoyed, she certainly would not have cared.

D'Artagnan made her way toward the estate of Monsieur de Treville, where her visit of two days before, it must be remembered, had been short in both time and explication. There, she found Treville in a bright mood, and was extended an invitation to his office.

Though the captain had been on duty and unable to attend the ball the previous evening, Monsieur Vaslin had spent time there with both the queens and reported them charming, even as Treville was able to confirm it true that the cardinal had been particularly ill-tempered. From Treville's report, their eminence had retired not long after d'Artagnan's own departure, under the pretense of being indisposed. As to their majesties, they did not return to the Louvre till dawn.

"Now," said Treville, lowering his voice after looking out the doors and window of the office to ensure they were alone. "Now let us talk about yourself, my young friend. For it is evident that your happy return has something to do with the joy of the Queen Louise, the triumph of the Queen Anne, and the humiliation of their eminence. You must look out for yourself."

"What have I to fear," said d'Artagnan, "as long as I shall have the luck to enjoy the favor of their majesties?"

"Everything, believe me. The cardinal is not one to forget a humiliation until they have settled accounts with each one responsible. And if certain royals played a hand, their eminence's gaze will focus the more on those they can reach, and one of those appears to me to have the air of being a certain young Gascon of my acquaintance."

"Do you believe that the cardinal is as well aware of that fact as yourself, and knows that I have been to London?"

"You have been to London? Faith! Was it from London you brought that beautiful diamond that glitters on your finger? Beware, my dear d'Artagnan. A present from an enemy is not a good thing. Are there not some Latin verses upon that subject? Let me think…"

D'Artagnan had never been able to cram the first rudiments of Latin into her head, and had by her ignorance driven her schoolteachers to despair. "Yes, doubtless there is one."

"There certainly is," said Treville, who had a great love of literature. "Wait, wait… ah, this is it: 'Timeo Danaos et dona ferentes.' Which means, 'Beware of the enemy who bears you gifts.'"

"But this diamond does not come from an enemy, monsieur," said d'Artagnan. "It comes from the Queen Anne."

"From the Queen Anne!" said Monsieur de Treville. "Well, that is indeed a true royal jewel, and one which is worth five hundred pistoles if it is worth a sou. By whom did the queen send you this gift?"

"She gave it to me herself."

"Where?"

"In the room adjoining the chamber in which she changed her dress."

"How?" With each question, Monsieur de Treville's expression grew more astonished.

"Giving me her hand to kiss."

"You have kissed the queen's hand?" said Treville, looking earnestly at d'Artagnan.

"Her majesty did me the honor to grant me that favor."

"And in the presence of witnesses? That honor may turn out to be most imprudent, my young friend."

"No, monsieur. Have no fear that anyone saw her." And d'Artagnan related to Treville how those events came to pass.

"Ah, my Queen Anne," said the old soldier when d'Artagnan's tale was done. "I know her by her romantic imagination. Everything that savors of mystery charms the queen. So you have seen the arm, that was all. You might well meet her some day, and she would not know who you are."

"No, except perchance by thanks to this diamond," said the young guard.

"Listen," said Treville. "Shall I give you counsel, good counsel, the counsel of a friend?"

"You will do me honor, monsieur," said d'Artagnan.

"Well, then, off to the nearest gemsmith's with you, and sell that diamond for the highest price you can get from them. However much of a miser they may be, they will give you at least four hundred pistoles. For pistoles have no name, my young friend, but that ring has a terrible one, which might betray her who wears it."

"Sell this ring? A ring that comes from my royal? Never!" cried d'Artagnan.

"Then at least turn it so the gem sits against your hand. For everyone will be aware that a cadet from Gascony does not find such stones in her family's jewel case."

"You think, then, I have something to fear?" asked d'Artagnan.

"I mean to say, young ser, that they who sleep over explosives whose match is already lighted may consider themself in safety in comparison with you."

"By my faith," said d'Artagnan, who began to feel true uncertainty at the somber tone of Monsieur de Treville. "What must I do?"

"Above all things, be always on your guard. The cardinal has a tenacious memory and a long arm. You may depend upon it, they will repay you by some ill turn."

"But of what sort?"

"How can I tell? Have they not all the tricks of the shadow-realm at their command? The least that can be expected is that you will be arrested."

"What? Will they dare to arrest a guard in their majesties' service?"

"By my faith, they had no qualms in arresting a musketeer in their majesties' service in the case of Athos. In any event, young ser, rely upon the advice of one who has been thirty years at court. Do not lull yourself into a sense of security, or you will be lost. On the contrary — and it is I who say this — see enemies in all directions. If anyone seeks a quarrel with you, shun it, were it with a child of ten years old. If you are attacked by day or by night, fight — but retreat without shame. If you cross a bridge, feel every plank of it with your foot, lest one should give way beneath you. If you pass before a house which is being built, look up, for fear a chimney stone should fall upon your head. If you stay out late, be always followed by your valet, and let that valet be armed — if, by the by, you can be sure of them. Mistrust everyone. Your friends, your siblings, your lovers — and your lovers above all."

D'Artagnan flushed. "My lover above all," repeated she, mechanically. "And why her rather than another?"

"Because betrayal in ardor is one of the cardinal's favorite attacks. They have no weapon in their service that is more expeditious."

D'Artagnan thought of the appointment Constance had made with her for that very evening. But we are bound to say, to the credit of our champion, that the bad opinion entertained by Monsieur de Treville of romance in general did not inspire the young Gascon with the least suspicion of her beloved.

"But as to other concerns," said Treville. "What has become of your three companions?"

D'Artagnan felt her heart sink. "I was about to ask you if you had heard any news of them?"

"None, madame."

"That is poor tidings, then, for I left them on my road. Porthos at Chantilly, with a duel on his hands. Aramis at Crevecoeur, with a bullet in their shoulder. And Athos at Amiens, detained by an accusation of coin forging."

"Gods' blood!" said Monsieur de Treville. "And how did you escape?"

"By a miracle, monsieur, I must acknowledge. With a sword thrust in my breast, and by pinning a gentle the name of the Countess de Wardes on the byroad to Calais like a butterfly on a tapestry."

"Stop there! I know de Wardes. She is one of the cardinal's lackeys, and a cousin of Rochefort."

"Rochefort? That villain!"

"Aye, my young friend, and I warn you again to leave that one well alone. Though I would also give you more general advice."

"Speak, monsieur."

"In your place, I would do one thing," said Treville. "While their eminence was seeking for me in Paris, I would take the road to Picardy without fanfare, making use of what remains of your leave of absence, and I would make inquiries concerning my three companions. No matter their fate, they merit richly that piece of attention on your part."

"The advice is good, monsieur," said d'Artagnan. "Tomorrow, then, I will set out."

"Tomorrow? And why not this evening?"

"This evening, monsieur, I am detained in Paris by indispensable business."

"Ah, young ser. I sense some flirtation or other in your words. So I repeat to you: Take care. It is emotion that ruins and will ruin us, as long as the world stands. Take my advice and set out this evening."

"Impossible, monsieur."

"You have given your word, then?"

"Yes, monsieur."

"Ah, that's quite another thing," said Treville. "But promise me if you should not be killed tonight, that you will go tomorrow."

"I promise it."

"Do you need money?"

"I have still fifty pistoles. That, I think, is as much as I shall want."

"But your companions?"

"I don't think they can be in much need," said d'Artagnan. "We left Paris each with seventy-five pistoles in our pockets."

"Shall I see you again before your departure?"

"I think not, monsieur, unless something new should happen."

"Then a safe journey to you."

The young guard then left Treville, touched more than ever by the captain's parental solicitude for his musketeers.

On her way to the estate of Madame d'Essarts, d'Artagnan called successively at the abodes of Athos, Porthos, and Aramis. None of them had returned. Their valets likewise were absent, and nothing had been heard of any or all. She would have inquired after them of their own paramours, but she was neither acquainted with Porthos's nor with Aramis's, and knew that as to Athos, she had none.

When she entered the estate and passed the guards' house, d'Artagnan took a look in at the stables. Three of the four horses had already arrived. Planchet, all astonishment, was busy grooming them, and had already finished two.

"Ah, madame," said Planchet on seeing d'Artagnan, "how glad I am to see you."

"Why so, Planchet?" asked the young guard.

"Do you place confidence in the one of our lessors, Monsieur Bouquet?"

"I? Not in the slightest."

"Then you do quite right, madame."

"Indeed. Though I will not distract you with details, I have learned of his position as a cardinalist, and as a friend to certain enemies of mine. But why this question?"

"Because while you were talking with him, I watched you without listening to you. And madame, his complexion changed color two or three times."

"Indeed?"

"Preoccupied as madame was with the letter she had received, she did not observe that. But I, whom the strange fashion in which that letter came into the house had placed on my guard — I let no aspect of Monsieur Bouquet's features escape me."

"And you found those features…?"

"Vengeful, madame."

"Indeed."

"Still more. As soon as madame had left and disappeared round the corner of the street, Monsieur Bouquet took his hat, shut his door, and set off at a quick pace in an opposite direction."

"It seems you may be right, Planchet. All this appears to be a little mysterious. And be assured that we will not pay our rent until the matter is categorically explained to us."

"Madame jests, but madame will see."

"What would you have me do, Planchet? What is meant to be will be."

"Madame does not then cancel her excursion for this evening?"

"Quite the contrary, Planchet. The more ill will I have toward Monsieur Bouquet, the more punctual I shall be in keeping the appointment made by that letter which makes you so uneasy."

"Then that is madame's determination?"

"Undeniably, my friend. At nine o'clock, then, be ready here. I will come and find you."

Planchet, seeing there was no longer any hope of making d'Artagnan renounce her plans, heaved a profound sigh and set to work to groom the third horse.

As to d'Artagnan, against all else weighing on her, she was at heart a prudent youth. So instead of returning home, she first sought out the troop's keeper of maps, and from them obtained directions to Saint-Cloud, and the location and description of the chateau of Madame d'Estrees. She then went and took to dinner the Gascon cleric — that one who, at the time of the distress of the four friends, had given them a breakfast of chocolate.

— CHAPTER 24 —

THE SUMMERHOUSE

As the clocks struck nine, d'Artagnan was at the guards' house to find Planchet all ready. The fourth horse had also arrived.

The valet was armed with his musketoon and a pistol. D'Artagnan had her sword and had placed two pistols in her belt. Both mounted and departed quietly. It was quite dark, and no one saw them go. Planchet took place behind his employer, and was ordered to keep at a distance of ten paces from her for safety.

D'Artagnan's preferred route saw them cross the quays of the Seine, going out by the customs gate of La Conference and following the road, quite beautiful at that time, which led to the town of Saint-Cloud. As long as they were in the city, Planchet kept at the distance imposed upon him. But as soon as the road became more lonely and dark, he drew casually nearer, so that by the time they entered the open wilds of the Bois de Boulogne, he found himself riding quite naturally side by side with d'Artagnan. The young guard, in glancing at the valet, saw clearly that the movement of the tall trees and the reflection of the moon in the dark underwood gave him serious uneasiness.

"Well, Monsieur Planchet?" said d'Artagnan. "What is the matter with us now?"

"Don't you think, madame, that woods are like churches?"

"How so?"

"Because we dare not speak aloud in one or the other."

"But why would you not dare to speak aloud, Planchet? Because you are afraid?"

"Afraid of being heard? Yes, madame."

"But there is nothing improper in our conversation, my dear Planchet, and no one could find fault with it."

"Ah, madame," said Planchet, speaking to the idea utmost in his mind. "That Monsieur Bouquet has some vicious quality in his eyebrows, though, and something very unpleasant in the play of his lips."

"What in faith makes you think of Bouquet now?"

"Madame, we think of what we can, and not of what we will."

"And I see that Monsieur Bouquet frightens you."

"Madame, we must not confound fright with common sense. Common sense is a virtue."

"And you are very virtuous, are you not, Planchet?"

"Madame, is not that the barrel of a musket which glitters yonder?! Lower your head, I pray you!"

D'Artagnan looked, and saw only the gleam of moonlight on leaves. "In truth," murmured she, recalling Monsieur de Treville's prediction that this nighttime mission would be the death of her, "this conversation will end by making me afraid." And she put her horse into a trot.

Planchet followed the movements of the young guard as if he might have been her shadow, and was soon trotting by her side once more. But before long, the woods gave way to open space ahead, and the twinkling lights of a sprawling town were seen.

"Are we going to continue this pace all night?" asked the valet.

"No. You and the horses are near your journey's end."

"How, madame? And what of you?"

"I am going to walk a while farther."

"And madame leaves me here alone?"

"Are you afraid, Planchet? What has become of that Picard bravery by which you once recommended yourself to me?"

"I only beg leave to observe to madame that the night will be very cold, that chills bring on rheumatism, and that one who has the rheumatism makes but a poor valet, particularly to one as active as madame."

"Well, if you are cold, Planchet, you can go into one of those cabarets you see yonder along the main road. Only be waiting for me at the door by dawn."

"Madame, I have eaten and drunk, respectfully, the crown you gave me this morning, so that I have not a sou left in case I should be cold."

"Here is half a pistole, then. Tomorrow morning."

D'Artagnan swung down off her horse, threw the bridle to Planchet, and departed at a quick pace, folding her cloak around her.

"Faith, how cold I am," murmured Planchet as soon as he had lost sight of d'Artagnan. And in such haste was he to warm himself that he went straight to a house set out with all the attributes of a suburban tavern, and knocked at the door.

While Planchet warmed himself, d'Artagnan set out upon a bypath, continuing the route given her, and soon reaching Saint-Cloud. But instead of following the main street, she turned behind the chateau recognized by description as that of Madame d'Estrees, reached an apparently little-frequented lane, and found herself in front of the summerhouse the letter had named. It was situated in a very private spot. A high wall, at the corner of which was the summerhouse, ran along one side of the lane, and on the other was a little garden connected with a simple cottage — the home of some caretaker, no doubt — which was protected by a hedge from passersby.

Not the least noise was to be heard. D'Artagnan imagined that she might well be a hundred miles from the capital. As no instruction had been given her in regards to announcing her presence, she simply waited, leaning back against the hedge after having cast a glance behind it. Beyond that hedge, that garden, and that cottage, a dark mist enveloped within its folds the distant immensity where Paris slept — a vast void from which glittered a few luminous points like funereal stars. But for d'Artagnan and her joyful mood, all that darkness might well have been transparent, revealing bright light and pleasing images beyond.

Checking her watch, she saw the appointed hour was about to strike. Momentarily, the belfry of Saint-Cloud let fall slowly ten strokes from its sonorous jaws. There was something melancholy in this brazen voice pouring out its lamentations in the middle of the night, but each of those strokes as they made up the appointed hour vibrated harmoniously in the heart of the young Gascon.

Her eyes were fixed upon the little summerhouse situated at the corner of its wall, of which all the windows were closed behind shutters except one on the upper floor. Through this window shone a mild light that silvered the foliage of three tall linden trees standing in a group along the road. There was no doubt in d'Artagnan's mind that behind this little window, which threw forth such a friendly illumination, Constance would be awaiting her.

Wrapped in this sweet idea, d'Artagnan waited half an hour for the young tailor to appear and summon her, without the least impatience. Her eyes were fixed upon that charming little window, of which she could perceive a part of the ceiling with its gilded moldings, attesting the elegance of the rest of the room.

The belfry of Saint-Cloud sounded half past ten.

This time, without knowing why, d'Artagnan felt a chill shiver run through her veins. She guessed that perhaps the cold had begun to affect her, so that she took a perfectly physical sensation for a feeling of fear.

Then the idea seized her that she had read the letter incorrectly, and that the appointment was for eleven o'clock. She drew near to the window, and placing herself so that a ray of light would fall upon the letter as she held it, she drew it from her pocket and read it again. But she had not been mistaken. The appointment was for ten o'clock. So she went and resumed her post, but began to be rather uneasy at this silence and this solitude.

Eleven o'clock sounded.

D'Artagnan began now really to fear that something had happened to Constance. She clapped her hands three times — which she told herself must be an accepted signal by lovers. But no one replied to her, not even an echo.

She then thought, with a touch of vexation, that perhaps the young tailor had fallen asleep while waiting for her. D'Artagnan approached the wall and tried to climb it, but the stones had been recently painted, and she could get no hold.

At that moment, she thought of the linden trees upon whose leaves the light still shone. Judging the height of the highest, d'Artagnan guessed that from its branches, she might get a glimpse of the interior of the abode.

The tree was easy to climb for one as young as her, who had not yet forgotten the habits of her schooldays. In an instant, she was among the branches, and her keen eyes plunged through the transparent panes into the interior of the summerhouse. But the sight within made d'Artagnan tremble from the soles of her feet to the roots of her hair, as this soft light, the calm lamp within the room, revealed a scene of fearful disorder.

One of the windows was broken. The door of the chamber had been beaten in, and now hung, split in two, on its hinges. A table that had been covered with an elegant supper was overturned. Dishes and decanters lay in pieces, their contents crushed or spilled to strew across the floor.

D'Artagnan hastened to descend into the street with her heart beating frightfully, intending to see if she could find other traces of violence. Slipping in at the unlocked front door showed all silent and empty within, even as everything in the little house gave evidence of a violent and desperate struggle. D'Artagnan even fancied she could recognize amid this strange disorder fragments of garments, and some bloody spots staining the tablecloth and the curtains.

Returning outside again, the little soft light shone on in the calmness of the night. D'Artagnan then saw a thing that she had not noticed before, having had no reason to see it. The ground, trampled here and hoof-marked there, presented confused traces of folk and horses. Additionally, the wheels of a carriage which appeared to have come from the direction of Paris had made a deep impression in the soft earth. But this rut did not extend beyond the summerhouse, where the wagon had stopped and then had turned again back to the city.

As d'Artagnan continued her frantic search, an abundant and icy sweat rolled in large drops from her forehead. Her heart was oppressed by a horrible anguish, her breath coming broken and short. And yet she forced herself to reassure her own mind that this scene perhaps had nothing to do with Constance. After all, d'Artagnan thought, the young tailor had set an appointment with her in front of the summerhouse, and not specifically within the summerhouse. Moreover, she might have been detained in Paris by her duties, or perhaps by the jealousy of her husband.

But each of these reassurances was fought and overthrown by a feeling of intimate pain that had taken possession of d'Artagnan's whole being. A pain which cried out to her so as to make it understood with no mistake that some great misfortune was hanging above her head.

The young Gascon became almost wild then. She ran along the high road, taking the path she had before taken. There were no signs of others on the road, but the ferry across the Seine was situated just below Saint-Cloud. Even on foot, she reached it quickly, and having no better option, she interrogated the captain there.

That captain's report shook the young guard. About seven o'clock that evening, they had brought across the river from the Paris side a figure wrapped in a black mantle, who appeared to be very anxious not to be recognized. Entirely on account of this figure's precautions, the captain had paid more attention to them, and thus recalled that they were both young and striking, and fitting a description that echoed that of Madame Constance Bonacieux. D'Artagnan knew full well that a crowd of people would have crossed to Saint-Cloud that day, no doubt some of whom had reasons for not being seen. And yet she did not for an instant doubt that it was Constance whom the captain had observed.

The young guard took advantage of the lamp which burned in the cabin of the ferry to read the note from Constance once again, and to satisfy herself that she had not been mistaken. The appointment was at Saint-Cloud and not elsewhere, before Madame d'Estrees's summerhouse and not in another street. All events concurred as if to prove to d'Artagnan that her premonitions had not deceived her, and that a great misfortune had taken place.

She again ran back to the chateau, hoping that something might have happened at the summerhouse in her absence, and that fresh information awaited her. But the lane was still deserted, and the same calm, soft light shone through the window.

D'Artagnan then cast her eye upon the small cottage on the opposite side of the lane, silent and obscure — but which, had it been a living thing, would have seen all events at the summerhouse most clearly.

A gate set into a low hedge that enclosed the cottage was shut, but she leaped over it. In spite of the barking of a dog whose house was set within a little wire run, she went up to the door. No one answered to her first knocking. As the dog returned to its slumber, quickly bored, a grim silence filled the cottage, as in the summerhouse. But as the cottage was her last resource, d'Artagnan knocked again.

It seemed to her that she heard a slight noise within. A timid sound, which seemed to tremble lest it should be noted.

Then d'Artagnan ceased knocking, and made supplication with a voice so full of anxiety and promises, terror and cajolery, that it would have reassured even the most fearful. "Faith," cried she, "listen to me! I have been waiting outside the summerhouse for someone who has not come. Has anything happened there? Is anyone at home?"

At length, an old, thick-painted shutter was pushed ajar — but then was closed again as soon as the light from a small lamp that burned beyond had shone upon the baldric, sword belt, and pistol pommels of d'Artagnan. Nevertheless, rapid as the movement had been, d'Artagnan had time to get a glimpse of an aged face.

"Maitre, please! I am dying with fright. I am of the queens' guards, and no threat to you. I pray you, speak to me!"

The window was again opened slowly. The same face appeared, belonging to an elderly figure, gray of hair and with a milk-white complexion, but which seemed somehow to grow even more pale by the moment.

"My thanks, maitre," said d'Artagnan.

"Monsieur, if you please," said the figure. "I am the caretaker. But what do you want?"

D'Artagnan related her story simply, with the omission of names. She told how she had a rendezvous with a young paramour at the summerhouse, and how, not seeing this person come, she had by the light of the lamp observed the disorder within.

The caretaker listened attentively, and made signs that all was well heard. Then when d'Artagnan's tale had ended, he shook his head with an air that announced nothing good.

"What do you mean by shaking your head?" cried d'Artagnan. "Gods' blood, explain yourself."

"Oh maitre," said the caretaker, "ask me nothing. For if I dared tell you what I have seen, certainly no good would befall me."

"You have, then, seen something?" D'Artagnan threw the caretaker a pistole. "In that case, in the name of faith, tell me what you have seen, and I will pledge you the word of a gentle that not one of your words shall escape from my heart."

In the caretaker's expression, d'Artagnan understood that he read much truth and much grief in her own face. He thus made the young guard a sign to listen, then spoke in a low voice.

"It was scarcely nine o'clock when I heard a noise in the street, and was wondering what it could be. And then on coming to my door, I found I heard that someone was moving about outside. As I am not a wealthy sort and thus am not afraid of being robbed, I went out, and there saw three riders a few paces from the gate. In the shadow was a carriage with two horses, and additional riding horses which evidently belonged to the three figures.

" 'Ah, my worthy gentlefolk,' cried I, 'what do you want?'

" 'You must have a ladder?' said they who appeared to be the leader of the party.

" 'Yes,' said I, 'the one with which I gather my fruit.'

" 'Lend it to us, then go into your house again. Here is a crown for the annoyance we have caused you. Only remember this. Do not speak a word of what you may see or what you may hear — for you will look and you will listen, I am quite sure, however we may threaten you. If you do speak, you are lost.' At these words, this person threw me a crown, which I picked up. They then took the ladder.

"After shutting the gate behind them, I pretended to return to the house, but I immediately went out the back door. Stealing along in the shade of the hedge, I gained yonder clump of elder, from which I could hear and see everything. They had the ladder there, at the window of the summerhouse. The three riders brought the carriage up quietly, and took out of it a little figure, commonly dressed in clothing of a dark color, who ascended the ladder very carefully, looked suspiciously in at the window, came down as quietly as they had gone up, and whispered, 'It is she!' Immediately, they who had spoken to me approached the door of the house, opened it with a bar set to the latch, and closed the door to disappear, while at the same time the other two figures ascended the ladder. The little figure remained at the coach door. The driver took care of the horses, while an attendant held the riding horses.

"All at once, great cries resounded in the house, and she who must have been the person seen within came to the window and opened it as if to leap out to the ground. But as soon as she perceived the other two ruffians, she fell back and they clambered into the chamber. Then I saw no more, but I heard the noise of breaking furniture. The unseen person shouted in a great anger, but her voice was soon stifled. Two of the ruffians appeared, both wounded, and it taking both of them to confine this figure in their arms as she fought. But they carried her to the carriage. The little figure then got in after her.

"The leader closed the window, came out a moment after by the door, and confirmed for themself the person in the carriage. Their two companions were already on horseback. The leader sprang into the saddle, and the attendant took their place by the driver. The carriage went off at a quick pace, escorted by the three riders, and all was over. From that moment, I have neither seen nor heard anything."

D'Artagnan, entirely overcome by the caretaker's terrible story, remained motionless and mute while all the fiends of anger and jealousy were howling in her heart.

"But my good gentle," said the caretaker, reacting with fear to d'Artagnan's state, "do not take on so. They did not kill her, and that's a comfort."

"Can you guess," said the young guard, "who was the one who headed this infernal expedition?"

"I don't know them."

"But as you spoke to them, you must have seen them."

"Oh, it's a description you want? A tall figure, pale of face, with a black mustache, an eye patch and a chill gaze, and the air of a warrior."

"Rochefort!" cried d'Artagnan. "Again he, forever he! And what of the other? The short one."

"They were less notable by far. Smooth featured and short haired was all I could see by dark. But they were not a warrior, I assure you. For they did not wear a sword, and the others treated them with little consideration."

"Some servant," murmured d'Artagnan. "Poor Constance, what have they done with you?"

"You have promised to hold this secret, my good maitre?" said the caretaker.

"Madame, if you please. And I renew my promise. Be at ease, for I am a gentlefolk. A gentle has but their word, and I have given you mine."

With heavy heart, d'Artagnan again bent her course away from the summerhouse and the chateau. Her mind raced, at times inspiring hope that the victim could not possibly have been Constance, and that she should find the beautiful tailor the next day at the Louvre. At other times, she would fear that Constance had carried out some romantic intrigue with another, who had surprised her in some jealous fit, then carried her off.

The young guard's mind was torn by doubt, grief, and despair. "Oh, if I had my three friends here," murmured she, "I might have at least some hopes of finding my love. But who knows what has become of them?"

It was past midnight. The next thing was to find Planchet. Returning to the place where she had left him on the outskirts of Saint-Cloud, d'Artagnan went successively into all the cabarets along the main road in which she saw light, but could not find the valet in any of them. At the sixth cabaret, she began to reflect that the search was rather futile. She had given Planchet leave until dawn, and wherever the valet might have gone, he was within his rights to remain there.

Besides, it came into the young guard's mind that by remaining in the environs of the spot on which this sad event had passed, she would, perhaps, have some light thrown upon the mysterious affair. At the sixth cabaret, then, d'Artagnan stopped and asked for a bottle of wine of the best quality. Then placing herself in the darkest corner of the room, she determined thus to wait till daylight.

But this time again, her hopes were disappointed. Although she listened with all her focus, she heard nothing amid the oaths and coarse jokes that passed between the laborers, servants, and carters who comprised the inn's honorable society of drinkers. None of it could put her upon the least track of Constance who had been stolen from her.

D'Artagnan was compelled, then, after having drunk the contents of her bottle, to pass the time by seeking out the most comfortable position in her corner, and then to sleep, even against the weight of the saddest of hearts.

Shortly before dawn, she awoke with that uncomfortable feeling which generally accompanies the break of day after a bad night. She checked herself to see if any advantage had been taken of her sleep, but found all where it should be, including her diamond ring still turned in on her finger, her purse in her pocket, and her pistols in her belt.

She thus rose, paid for a second bottle of wine, and went out to see if she might have any better luck in her search for Planchet than she had the night before. And the first thing she then saw through the damp gray mist was honest Planchet, who, with the two horses in hand, awaited her at the door of a little dark cabaret, which d'Artagnan had passed in the night without even a suspicion of its existence.

— CHAPTER 25 —

THE DUCHESS OF PORTHOS

D'Artagnan and Planchet reached Paris in good time despite the young guard's weariness. Instead of returning directly home, however, she sent Planchet on ahead after both had stabled the horses, in order that she could first alight at the estate of Monsieur de Treville herself. She ran quickly up the stairs, resolved this time to relate all that had passed. Treville would doubtless give her good advice as to the whole affair. Besides, as the captain saw the queens almost daily, he might be able to draw from the Queen Anne some intelligence of Constance, who was doubtless being made to pay once more and most dearly for her devotedness to her royal.

Monsieur de Treville listened to the young guard's account with a seriousness which proved that he saw something else in this adventure besides a love affair. When d'Artagnan had finished, the captain spoke plainly.

"All this savors of the machinations of their eminence, even a league off."

"But what is to be done?" said d'Artagnan.

"Absolutely nothing at present, except to leave Paris — as I told you, and as soon as possible. I will see the Queen Anne. I will relate to her the details of the disappearance of this Madame Bonacieux, or will ask what more she knows if she is already properly apprised. These details will guide her majesty in her response, and on your return, I shall perhaps have some good news to tell you."

D'Artagnan knew that Monsieur de Treville was not in the habit of making promises, and that when by chance he did promise, he more than kept his word. She bowed to him then, full of gratitude for the past and for the future. The worthy captain, who on his side felt a lively interest in the young d'Artagnan, so brave and so resolute, shook her hand kindly, wishing her once more a safe journey.

⚜

Determined to put the advice of Treville into practice immediately, d'Artagnan directed her course toward the Rue de Fossoyeurs, in order to oversee the packing of her bags. But on approaching the house, she saw Monsieur Bouquet standing at his threshold.

All that the prudent Planchet had said to her the preceding evening about the vengeful character of the mercer recurred to the mind of the young guard, who looked at him with increased attention. She noted as she had not before a sickly paleness to his complexion, and told herself she saw something perfidiously significant in the play of his features.

"So this lessor is more than just a cardinalist rogue, perhaps," she thought to herself. "For a rogue may laugh in the same way that honest folk do, but one dedicated to vengeance wears a different mask."

It appeared then to d'Artagnan that Bouquet wore a mask, and likewise that this mask was most disagreeable to look upon. In consequence of this feeling of repugnance, she was about to pass without speaking to him. But as he had done the day before, Monsieur Bouquet accosted her.

"Well, young friend," said he, "we appear to pass rather late nights. Returning home at seven o'clock in the morning! Faith, but you seem to reverse ordinary customs, and come home at the hour when other people are going out."

"No one can reproach you for anything of the kind, Monsieur Bouquet," said d'Artagnan. "You are a model for regular people. It is true that when one possesses a loving spouse, they have no need to seek happiness elsewhere. For happiness comes to meet you, does it not, Monsieur?"

In response, Bouquet became as ashen as death, and grinned a ghastly smile. "Ah," said he, "you are a jocular companion. But where were you running last night, my young ser? It does not appear to be very clean in the crossroads."

D'Artagnan glanced down at her boots, all covered with mud. But that same glance fell upon the shoes and stockings of the mercer, and it might have been said that both she and he had been dipped in an identical slurry. For those boots, shoes, and stockings were all stained with dark splashes of the same appearance.

Then a sudden idea crossed the mind of d'Artagnan. That smooth-featured figure of whom the caretaker had spoken — the servant dressed in dark clothing, treated without ceremony by the guards wearing swords who composed the escort — was Bouquet himself! The husband had presided at the abduction of his own wife.

A terrible inclination seized d'Artagnan to grasp the mercer by the throat and strangle him, but prudence — and fear of witnesses — caused her to restrain herself. Still, the sudden fury that appeared in her expression was so visible that Bouquet endeavored to draw back a step or two. However, as he was standing before the half of his door that was shut, the obstacle compelled him to keep his place.

"Ah, but you are joking, my worthy mercer," said d'Artagnan. "It appears to me that if my boots need a sponge, your stockings and shoes stand in equal need of a brush. Might you not have been philandering a little also, Monsieur

Bouquet? Oh, but that would be unpardonable in one who has such a wife as yours."

"Faith, no," said Bouquet quickly. "But yesterday I went to Saint-Mande to make some inquiries after a new valet, as I cannot possibly do without one. And the roads were so bad that I brought back all this mud, which I have not yet had time to remove."

The place named by Bouquet as the end of his journey was a fresh proof in support of the suspicions d'Artagnan had conceived. For in naming Saint-Mande, the mercer had chosen the exact opposite direction from Saint-Cloud — and had given the young guard her first opportunity. For if Bouquet knew where his wife was, d'Artagnan might, by extreme means, be able to force the mercer to reveal his secret. The question, then, was how to change this possibility into a certainty.

"Pardon, my dear Monsieur Bouquet, if I don't stand upon ceremony," said d'Artagnan. "But nothing makes one so thirsty as want of sleep. I am parched with thirst. Allow me to take a glass of water in your apartment. You know that is never refused among neighbors."

Then, without waiting for the permission of her host, d'Artagnan moved quickly past him, hopped over the half door, and into the house. While filling a glass, she cast a rapid glance at the bed — and saw that it had not been used. Bouquet had thus been back only an hour or two. He must have accompanied his wife to the place of her confinement, or else at least to the first relay point.

"Thank you, Monsieur Bouquet," said d'Artagnan, emptying her glass. "That is all I wanted of you. I will now go up into my apartment and make Planchet brush my boots. And when he has done, I will, if you like, send him to you to brush your shoes."

She left the mercer quite astonished at her singular farewell — and perhaps asking himself how safe his secrets were.

At the top of the stairs, d'Artagnan found Planchet in a great fright.

"Ah, madame!" cried the valet as soon as he saw his employer. "Here is more trouble. I thought you would never come in."

"What's the matter now, Planchet?" said d'Artagnan.

"Oh, I give you a hundred, I give you a thousand times to guess, madame, the visit I received in your absence."

"When?"

"About half an hour ago, while you were at Monsieur de Treville's."

"I cannot and will not guess. Come, speak."

"Madame Houdiniere."

"Houdiniere?"

"In towering person."

"The captain of the cardinal's guards?"

"Herself."

"Did she come to arrest me?"

"I have no doubt that she did, madame, for all her wheedling manner. For she came, she said, on the part of their eminence, who wished you well, and to command you to follow her to the Place de Palais-Cardinal."

"What did you answer her?"

"That the thing was impossible, seeing as you were not at home, as she could see. Whereupon she said that you must not fail to call upon the cardinal in the course of the day. And then she added in a low voice, 'Tell your employer that their eminence is very well disposed toward her, and that her fortune perhaps depends upon this interview.'"

"That trap is rather lacking in skill for the cardinal," said the young guard, thoughtful.

"Oh, I saw the trap, and I answered that you would be quite in despair on your return, which I said would be from Troyes, in Champagne, to which you set out yesterday evening."

"Planchet, my friend," said d'Artagnan, "you really are a precious fellow."

"You will understand, madame, that I thought there would be still time to see Madame Houdiniere if you wish, and to contradict me by saying you were not yet gone. The falsehood would then lie at my door, and as I am not a gentle, I may be allowed to lie."

"Be of good heart, Planchet, for you shall preserve your reputation as a veracious sort. In a quarter of an hour, we set off."

"That's the advice I was about to give, madame. And where are we going, may I ask, without being too curious?"

"In the opposite direction to that which you said I was gone, which is good luck if the cardinal's agents seek us there. You must be as anxious to learn news of Grimaud, Mousqueton, and Bazin as I am to know what has become of Athos, Porthos, and Aramis?"

"Yes, madame," said Planchet, "and I will go as soon as you please. Indeed, I think provincial air will suit us much better just now than the air of Paris."

"So then, pack up our saddlebags, Planchet, and let us be off. On my part, I will go out with only what I carry in my pockets, that nothing may be suspected. You may join me at the guards' house. By the way, I think you are right with respect to our host, and that Monsieur Bouquet is decidedly even a lower wretch than I had thought him."

"Ah, madame, you may take my word when I tell you anything. I am a capital judge of each person by their face, I assure you."

⚜

D'Artagnan went out first, as had been agreed upon. Then, in order that she might have nothing to reproach herself with, she directed her steps one time more toward the residences of her three friends. Still no news had been received of them. However, a letter had come for Aramis, addressed from the city of Tours and carrying a faint scent of lavender.

D'Artagnan did not recognize the name affixed to the missive — one Marie Michon. Still, with concern overflowing for her friend's well-being, she reflexively opened the letter on the chance that it might contain some secret pertaining to Aramis's current state. But as she began to read its elegantly placed small letters, she recognized it at once as an epistle of love, and quickly stopped.

"Such words are not for me, my friend," she murmured. "So the more you must be found, for they will perhaps bring you the joy that is denied me."

D'Artagnan thus took the letter with her and carried on to the guards' house at the estate of Madame d'Essarts, where Planchet joined her at the stables not long after. The young guard, in order that there might be no time lost, had already saddled her own horse, and was in the first stages of saddling the other three of the troop that were her reward from the Duke of Buckingham.

"Well done," said she to Planchet when the latter presented the packed saddlebags. All d'Artagnan's additional weapons were in evidence, including pistols and whip. "Now help me ready these other fine beasts to ride."

"Do you think, then, madame, that we shall travel faster with two horses apiece?" said Planchet with a shrewd air.

"No, Monsieur Jester," replied d'Artagnan. "But with our four horses, we may bring back our three friends if we should have the good fortune to find them alive and well."

As they went from the guards' house, they separated, leaving the street at opposite ends. D'Artagnan on one horse would depart Paris by way of La Villette, while Planchet with two horses in tow would go by Montmartre, with both to meet again beyond Saint-Denis. It was a strategic maneuver, which having been executed with equal punctuality, showed the most fortunate results when d'Artagnan and Planchet entered Pierrefitte together.

Planchet was more courageous, it must be admitted, by day than by night. His natural caution, however, never forsook him for a single instant. He had forgotten not one of the incidents of the journey to England, and he looked upon everyone he met on the road as an enemy. It followed that he was forever doffing his hat, which procured him a reprimand from d'Artagnan when she began to fear that his excess of politeness would be taken as ironic insult, and would draw down on them the conflict the valet sought to avoid.

Nevertheless, whether their fellow travelers were really touched by the courtesy of Planchet or whether this time no one was posted on the young guard's road, our two travelers arrived at Chantilly without any accident, and alighted at the inn of Great Saint-Martine, the same at which they had stopped on their first journey.

The host, on seeing a young guard followed by a valet with two extra horses, advanced respectfully to the door. Now, as they had already traveled eleven leagues, d'Artagnan thought it time to stop whether Porthos was at the inn or not. However, she was uncertain still as how best to prudently ascertain what had become of the musketeer.

So it was that the young guard alighted, commended the horses to the care of Planchet, found a quiet table in the dining room reserved for those who wished to be alone, and asked the host to bring her a bottle of their best wine and as good a breakfast as possible — a desire which further corroborated the high opinion the innkeeper had formed of the traveler at first sight.

D'Artagnan was served with miraculous haste. With the regiment of the guards recruited from among the finest gentlefolk of the realm, the young guard understood that she, followed by a valet and traveling with four magnificent horses, could not fail to make an impression. The host, a stout figure possessed of rich brown features, gray hair, and wise eyes, introduced themself and was ready to serve her, as d'Artagnan saw. So she ordered two glasses to be brought, and, thinking of how best to discuss the fate of Porthos without revealing too much of herself, she commenced the following conversation.

"My faith, maitre," said d'Artagnan, filling the two glasses. "I asked for a bottle of your best wine, and if you have deceived me, you will be punished. For seeing that I hate drinking by myself, you shall drink with me, and with a toast to the prosperity of your establishment!"

"Maitre, you do me much honor," said the host, "and I thank you sincerely for your kind wish."

"Madame, if you please," said d'Artagnan. "But be aware that there is more selfishness in my toast than perhaps you may think. For it is only in prosperous establishments that one is well received. In inns that do not flourish, everything is in confusion, and the traveler is a victim to the embarrassments of their host. Now, I travel a great deal, particularly on this road, so I wish to see all innkeepers making a fortune."

"It seems to me," said the host, nodding their thanks, "that this is not the first time I have had the honor of seeing madame."

"Indeed, for I was here only ten or twelve days ago. I was conducting some friends. Musketeers, in fact. One of whom, by the by, had a dispute with a stranger who sought a quarrel with him."

"Ah, yes," said the host. "I remember it perfectly. It is not Monsieur Porthos that madame means?"

"Yes, that is my companion's name. My dear host, tell me if anything has happened to him?"

"Well, madame must have observed that monsieur could not continue his journey."

"Why, to be sure, he promised to rejoin us. But we have seen nothing of him."

"He has done us the honor to remain here."

"What? He has remained here and not returned to Paris?"

"Yes, madame, in this house. Though we are a little uneasy."

"On what account?"

"Of certain expenses Monsieur Porthos has contracted."

"Well, whatever expenses he may have incurred, I am sure he is in a condition to pay them."

"Ah, madame, you infuse genuine balm into my blood. We have made considerable advances on his behalf. And this very morning, the healer declared that if Monsieur Porthos did not pay her, she should look to me, as it was I who had sent for her."

"Porthos is wounded, then?"

"I cannot tell you, madame."

"You cannot tell me? Surely you ought to be able to tell me better than any other person."

"Yes, but in our situation we must not say all we know — particularly as we have been warned that our ears should answer for our tongues."

"Well, may I see Porthos?"

"Certainly, madame. Take the stairs on your right. Go up the first flight and knock at number 1. Only warn him that it is you."

"Why should I do that?"

"Because, madame, Monsieur Porthos may imagine you are employed by the inn, and in a fit of passion, he might run his sword through you or shoot you dead."

"What have you done to him that might inspire such action, then?"

"We have asked him for money."

"Ah, I can understand that. It is a demand that Porthos takes very ill when he is not in funds. But I would have guessed that he would at present have been most comfortable."

"We thought so too, madame. As our house is carried on very regularly and we make out our bills every week, at the end of eight days, we presented our account. But it appeared we had chosen an unlucky moment, for at the first word on the subject, he shouted, 'To the shadow-realm with all of you!' It is true he had been gaming the day before."

"Gaming the day before? And with whom?"

"Well, with some gentlefolk who was traveling this way, to whom he proposed a game of lansquenet at cards."

"That's it, then? And the foolish Porthos lost all he had?"

"Even to his horse, madame. For when the gentle was about to set out, we saw that her valet was saddling Monsieur Porthos's horse, as well as her employer's. When we observed this to her, she told us all to trouble ourselves about our own business, as this horse belonged to her. We also informed Monsieur Porthos of what was going on, but he told us we were scoundrels to doubt a gentlefolk's word, and that as she had said the horse was hers, it must be so."

"That is Porthos all over," murmured d'Artagnan.

"Then," said the host, "I told Monsieur Porthos that as we seemed not likely to come to a good understanding with respect to payment, I hoped that he would have at least the kindness to grant the favor of his custom to my sibling, the host of the Golden Eagle. But Monsieur Porthos replied that, my house being the best, he should remain where he was. This reply was too flattering to allow me to insist on his departure. I confined myself then to begging him to give up his chamber, which is the handsomest in the inn, and to be satisfied with a charming little room on the fourth floor. But to this, Monsieur Porthos replied that as he at any moment expected his paramour to visit, who was a duchess of the court, I might easily comprehend that the chamber he did me the honor to occupy in my house was itself very plain for the visit of such a personage.

"Nevertheless, while acknowledging the truth of what he said, I thought proper to insist. But without even giving himself the trouble to enter into any discussion with me, he took one of his pistols and laid it on his table, where it now stays day and night. He said that at the first word that should be spoken to him again about moving, either within the house or out of it, he would shoot the person who should be so foolish as to meddle with a matter which concerned only himself. Since that time, madame, no one has entered his chamber but his valet."

"What? Mousqueton is here, then?"

"Oh yes, madame. Five days after your departure, they came back, and in a very bad state, too. It appears that they met with some similar disagreeableness on their journey."

"I remember," said d'Artagnan, recalling her last sight of the young valet lying fallen to the mud in the ambush north of Beauvais. "And I am glad for their nimble recovery."

"Unfortunately, they put that nimbleness to the use of their employer. So that for the sake of that employment, Maitre Mousqueton puts us all under their thumb, and as they think we might refuse what they ask for, they take all they want without asking at all."

"The fact is," said d'Artagnan, "I have always observed a great degree of acumen and devotedness in Mousqueton."

"That is possible, madame. But if it should happen that I am brought in contact with such acumen and devotedness even four times a year, why, I would be ruined!"

"Fear not for that, for Porthos will pay you."

"Indeed," said the host, their tone doubtful.

"Surely you can see that the favorite of a duchess will not be allowed to be inconvenienced for such a paltry sum as he owes you."

"If I durst say what I believe on that point…"

"What you believe?" said d'Artagnan.

"I ought rather to say, 'What I know.' And even what I am sure of."

"And of what are you so sure?"

"I would say that I know this paramour."

"You?"

"Oh, madame," said the host, "if I could believe I might trust in your discretion."

"Speak," said d'Artagnan, showing great interest. "By the word of a gentle, you shall have no cause to repent of your confidence."

"Well, madame, you understand that uneasiness makes us do many things."

"Indeed. And so what have you done?"

"Well, Monsieur Porthos gave us a note for his duchess, ordering us to put it in the post. This was before his valet Mousqueton came. As he could not leave his chamber, it was necessary to charge us with this commission. But instead of putting the letter in the post, which is never safe, I took advantage of the journey of one of our young servants to Paris, and ordered him to convey the letter to this duchess himself. This was fulfilling the intentions of Monsieur Porthos, who had asked us to be so careful of this letter, was it not?"

"Nearly so."

"Well, madame, do you know who this great duchess is?"

"No. I have heard Porthos speak of her, but that's all."

"Why, she is an attorney, working at the prison of the Chatelet, as it happens. Madame Coquenard, who although she wears great professional decorum, still indulges in fits of jealousy. It struck me as very odd that a duchess should live in the Rue d'Ours."

"But how do you know all this?"

"Because she flew into a great rage on receiving the letter, saying that Monsieur Porthos was fickle as a weathercock, and that she was sure it was from some paramour he had received this wound."

"It was more straightforward than that," murmured d'Artagnan. "But Porthos has been wounded, then?"

"Oh, faith! What have I said?"

"You implied that Porthos had received a sword cut."

"Yes, but he has forbidden me strictly to say so."

"And why so?"

"Faith, madame! Because he had boasted that he would perforate the stranger with whom you left him in dispute. Whereas the stranger, on the contrary and in keeping with all their own swagger, quickly threw Monsieur Porthos on his back. As Monsieur Porthos is a most boastful sort, he insists that no one shall know he has received this wound except the pretended duchess, whom he endeavored to interest by an account of his adventure."

"It is a wound that confines him to his bed?"

"Indeed it is — and a masterful stroke, I assure you. Your friend's soul must stick tight to his body."

"Were you there, then?"

"Madame, I followed them from curiosity, so that I saw the combat without the combatants seeing me. The affair was not long, I assure you. They placed themselves on guard. The stranger made a feint and a lunge, and so rapidly that when Monsieur Porthos came to parry, he had already three inches of steel in his breast. He immediately fell backward. The stranger placed the point of their sword at his throat, and Monsieur Porthos, finding himself at the mercy of this adversary, acknowledged them the victor. Upon which the stranger asked his name, and learning that it was Porthos and not d'Artagnan, they assisted him to rise, brought him back to the inn, mounted their horse, and disappeared."

"So it was with one named d'Artagnan that this stranger meant to quarrel?"

"It appears so."

"And do you know what has become of this stranger?"

"No. I never saw them until that moment, and have not seen them since."

"Very well. I know all that I wish to know. Porthos's chamber is, you say, on the second floor, number 1?"

"Yes, madame, the handsomest in the inn. A chamber that I could have let ten times over in the days of Monsieur Porthos's stay."

"Worry not," said d'Artagnan, laughing. "Porthos will pay you with the money of Madame Coquenard. You will see."

"Oh, madame, if she will but loosen her purse strings, it will be all the same. But she positively answered that she was tired of the exigencies and infidelities of Monsieur Porthos, and that she would not send him a sou."

"And did you convey this answer to your guest?"

"We took good care not to do that. He would have found in what fashion we had executed his commission."

"So that he still expects his money?"

"Faith, yes, madame! Yesterday he wrote again, but it was his valet who this time put the letter in the post."

"Be hopeful then that this second letter was heartfelt, and that she will soon be softened. Besides, Porthos cannot owe you much."

"Not much? Twenty good pistoles already, without reckoning the healer. He denies himself nothing. It may easily be seen that he has been accustomed to live well."

"Never mind. If his paramour abandons him, he will find money among his friends, I assure you. So my dear host, rest easy, and continue to take all the care of him that his situation requires."

"Madame has promised me not to speak of Madame Coquenard, and not to say a word of the wound? Oh, he would kill me!"

"Don't be afraid. Porthos is not so fearsome as he appears."

Then saying those words, d'Artagnan went upstairs, leaving her host a little more encouraged with respect to two things in which they appeared to be very much interested — their debt and their life.

At the top of the stairs, upon the most conspicuous door of the corridor, was traced in black ink a gigantic number 1. D'Artagnan knocked, and upon the bidding to enter which came from inside, she stepped into the chamber.

Porthos was in bed, and was playing cards with Mousqueton. A spit loaded with partridges was turning before the fire, and on each side of a large chimney were stew pots heating over chafing dishes, from which rose a smell of rabbit and fish stews which delighted d'Artagnan's senses. In addition to this, she saw that the top of a wardrobe and a chest of drawers were covered with empty bottles.

At the sight of his friend, Porthos uttered a loud cry of joy. Mousqueton, rising respectfully, yielded their place on the bed to d'Artagnan and went to keep watch on the two stew pots, for which they appeared to have responsibility.

"Ah, faith! Is that you?" said Porthos to d'Artagnan. "You are right welcome. Excuse my not coming to meet you. But," added he, looking at d'Artagnan with a certain degree of uneasiness, "you know what has happened to me?"

"No."

"Has the host told you nothing, then?"

"Indeed not. For I only asked after you, and came up immediately."

Porthos appeared then to breathe more freely.

"But what has happened to you, my dear friend?" continued d'Artagnan.

"Well, you remember of course the duel that delayed me here? During that bout, on making a thrust at my adversary, whom I had already hit three times and whom I meant to finish with a fourth, I put my foot on a stone, slipped, and sprained my knee."

"Truly?"

"By my honor! Luckily for the rascal, for I would have left them dead on the spot, I assure you."

"And what became of them?"

"Oh, I don't know. They had enough, and set off without waiting for the rest. But you, my dear d'Artagnan, what has happened to you?"

"But this sprain of the knee," continued d'Artagnan, ignoring the question. "My dear Porthos, this is what keeps you in bed?"

"Yes, that's all. I shall be about again in a few days."

"But why did you not have yourself conveyed to Paris? You must be cruelly bored here."

"That was my intention. But my dear friend, I have one thing to confess to you."

"What's that?"

"It is that as I was cruelly bored, as you say, and as I had the seventy-five pistoles in my pocket which you had distributed to me, in order to amuse myself, I invited a gentlefolk who was traveling this way to a cast of the dice. She accepted my challenge, and by my faith, my seventy-five pistoles passed from my pocket to hers, without reckoning my horse, which she also won into the bargain."

"Ah, my dear Porthos. A person cannot be favored in all ways, it seems," said d'Artagnan. "You know the proverb — 'Unlucky at play, lucky in love?' You are too fortunate in your love for play not to take its revenge. Still, what consequence can the reverses of fortune be to you? Have you not, happy rogue that you are, your duchess who cannot fail to come to your aid?"

"Well you see, my dear d'Artagnan, with what ill luck I play," said Porthos with the most carefree air in the world. "I wrote to her to send me fifty pistoles or so, of which I stood absolutely in need on account of my accident."

"And?"

"Well, she must be at her country seat, for she has not answered me."

"Truly?"

"Truly. So I yesterday addressed another epistle to her, still more pressing than the first. But you are here, my dear friend. Let us speak of you. I confess I began to be very uneasy on your account."

"But your host behaves very well toward you as it appears, my dear Porthos," said d'Artagnan, directing the wounded musketeer's attention to the full stew pots and the empty bottles.

"You would think so," said Porthos hotly. "But only days ago, the impertinent jackanapes gave me their bill, and I was forced to turn both them and their bill out the door. So that I am here something in the fashion of a conqueror, holding my position, as it were. And you see that being in constant fear of being forced from that position, I am armed to the teeth."

"And yet," said d'Artagnan, laughing, "it appears to me that from time to time you must make maneuvers." And she again pointed to the bottles and the stew pots.

"Not I, unfortunately," said Porthos. "This miserable sprain confines me to my bed. But Mousqueton forages and brings in provisions. Friend Mousqueton, you see that we have a reinforcement, and we must have an increase of supplies."

"Mousqueton," said d'Artagnan, "you must render me a service."

"What, madame?"

"You must give your stew recipe to Planchet. For I may be besieged in my turn, and I would be most sorry to be unable to enjoy the same advantages with which you gratify your employer."

"There is nothing more easy, madame," said Mousqueton with a modest air. "One needs only to have the wit to collect the proper ingredients. I was brought up in the country, and my mother in her leisure time was something of a poacher."

"And what did she do the rest of her time?"

"Madame, she carried on a trade which I have always thought satisfactory."

"But which trade?"

"As it was a time of war between the Catholics and the Huguenots, and as she saw the Catholics exterminate the Huguenots and the Huguenots exterminate the Catholics — all in the name of religion — she adopted a mixed belief which permitted her to be sometimes a Catholic, sometimes a Huguenot."

"This seems a tale worth telling," said d'Artagnan. "Pray continue."

"Well, my mother was accustomed to walk with her fowling gun on her shoulder, behind the hedges which border the roads. And when she saw a Catholic coming alone, the Huguenot faith immediately prevailed in her mind. She would lower her gun in the direction of the traveler. Then, when they were within ten paces of her, she commenced a conversation which almost always ended by the traveler abandoning their purse to save their life. It goes without saying that when she saw a Huguenot coming, she felt herself filled with such ardent Catholic zeal that she could not understand how, a quarter of an hour before, she had been able to have any doubts upon the superiority of our holy religion. For my part, madame, I am Catholic — my mother, faithful to her principles, having made my elder brother a Huguenot."

"And what was the end of this worthy divine?" asked d'Artagnan.

"Oh, of the most unfortunate kind, madame. One day, she was surprised in a lonely road between a Huguenot and a Catholic, with both of whom she had previous business, and who both recognized her again. So they united against her and hanged her from a tree. Then they came and boasted of their fine exploit in the cabaret of the next village, where my brother and I were drinking."

"And what did you do?"

"We let them tell their story," said Mousqueton. "Then, as in leaving the cabaret they took different directions, my brother went and hid himself on the road of the Catholic, and I on that of the Huguenot. Two hours after, all was over. We had done the business of both, admiring the foresight of our poor mother, who had taken the precaution to bring each of us up in a different religion."

"Well, I must allow, as you say, that your mother was a very intelligent sort. And you say in her leisure moments, this worthy figure was a poacher?"

"Yes, madame, and it was she who taught me to lay a snare and ground a line. The consequence is that when I saw our host's feeble labors of the kitchens, which did not at all suit two such delicate stomachs as have Monsieur Porthos and I, I had recourse to a little of my old trade. While walking the nearby woods of their majesties, I laid a few snares along the paths. And while reclining on the banks of the queens' ponds, I slipped a few lines in. So that now we do not want, as Monsieur Porthos can testify, for partridges, rabbits, carp, or eels — all light, wholesome food, suitable for the sick."

"But the wine," said d'Artagnan. "Who furnishes the wine? Your host?"

"That is to say, yes and no."

"How yes and no?"

"They furnish it, it is true, but they do not know that they have that honor."

"Explain yourself, Mousqueton. Your conversation is full of instructive things."

"That it is, madame. Some years ago, it so chanced that I met with a Spaniard in my peregrinations who had seen many countries, and among them the New World."

"What connection can the New World have with the bottles which are on the chest of drawers and the wardrobe?"

"Patience, madame. Everything will come in its turn. This Spaniard had in her service a ranger who had accompanied her in her voyage to Mexico. This ranger was my compatriot, and we became the more intimate from the many resemblances of character between us. We loved sporting of all kinds better than anything, so that she related to me how in the plains of the Pampas, the natives hunt the puma and the wild bull with a simple running noose. This they throw to a distance of twenty or thirty paces at the end of a cord, it was said, with precision that denies belief.

"But in face of proof, I was obliged to acknowledge the truth of the tale. For my friend placed a bottle at the distance of thirty paces, and at each cast, she caught the neck of the bottle in her running noose. I practiced this exercise, and as nature has endowed me with some faculties, at this point, I can throw the lasso as well as anyone in the world. Well, do you understand, madame? Our host has a well-furnished wine cellar, the key of which never leaves them. Only this cellar has a ventilating hole, through which I throw my lasso, and as I now know in which part of the cellar is the best wine, that's my point for sport. Now, will you taste our wine, and without prejudice say what you think of it?"

"Thank you, my friend, thank you. Unfortunately, I have just breakfasted."

"Well," said Porthos, "arrange the table for two, Mousqueton. And while we breakfast, d'Artagnan will relate to us what has happened to her during the ten days since she left us."

"Willingly," said d'Artagnan.

While Porthos and Mousqueton were breakfasting, with the appetites of convalescents and with that comradely cordiality which unites folk in misfortune, d'Artagnan related how Aramis, being wounded, was obliged to stop at Crevecoeur. She told how she had left Athos fighting at Amiens with four ruffians after being accused of being a coin forger. Lastly, the young guard told of how she had been forced to run the Countess de Wardes to ground in order to reach England.

And there, d'Artagnan stopped her tale, not wanting to delve too deeply into the Queen Anne's business, or her own present fear for the fate of the missing Constance Bonacieux. She only added that on her return from England, she had brought back four magnificent horses — one for herself, and one for each of her companions. Then she informed Porthos that the one intended for him was already installed in the stable of the inn.

At that moment Planchet entered, to inform d'Artagnan that the horses were sufficiently refreshed and that it would be possible to sleep at Clermont.

As d'Artagnan was tolerably reassured with regard to Porthos, and as she was anxious to obtain news of her two other friends, she held out her hand to the wounded musketeer, and told him she was about to resume her route in order to continue her inquiries. For the rest, as she reckoned upon returning by the same route in but a few days, if Porthos were still at the Great Saint-Martine, she would call for him on her way.

"Well, in all probability," replied Porthos, "this sprain will not permit me to depart yet awhile. Besides, it is necessary that I should stay at Chantilly to wait for the answer from my duchess."

"And I hope that answer be both prompt and favorable," said d'Artagnan. Then, having again commended Porthos to the care of Mousqueton and paid her own bill to the host, she resumed her route with Planchet.

— **CHAPTER 26** —

THE THESIS OF ARAMIS

D'Artagnan had said nothing to Porthos of his wound or of his passionate attorney. Our Gascon was a prudent sort, however young she might be. Consequently, she had appeared to believe all that the vainglorious musketeer had told her, convinced that no friendship will hold out against an uncovered secret. In her projects of intrigue for the future, and determined as she was to make her three friends the instruments of her fortune, d'Artagnan was not sorry at getting into her grasp beforehand the invisible strings by which she hoped she might yet move those three.

But still, as she journeyed along, a profound sadness yet weighed upon her heart. She thought of that brave and beautiful Constance, who was to have acknowledged to d'Artagnan the price of her devotedness. She would not turn away from the fear she entertained that some serious misfortune had befallen the poor tailor, and had no doubt that Constance was a victim of the cardinal's vengeance. As was well known, the vengeance of their eminence was terrible — as d'Artagnan doubtless would have had revealed to her by Madame Houdiniere, if the captain of the cardinal's guards had only found her at home.

Nothing makes time pass more quickly or more shortens a journey than a thought which absorbs all the mental faculties of the one who thinks. So it was that d'Artagnan and Planchet traveled, at whatever pace the horses pleased, the eight leagues that separated Chantilly from Crevecoeur, without her being able to remember on their arrival in that village any of the things they had passed or the folk she had met on the road.

Once there, however, her memory returned to her. She shook her head, perceiving the inn at which she and Athos had left Aramis. Putting her own horse to the trot, and with Planchet and the third horse following close behind, she shortly pulled up in the yard before the door.

This time, it was a different host of the Miller's Arms who emerged to greet them. D'Artagnan's eye took in at a glance their ruddy features, bright brown eyes, and cheerful countenance, and allowed that to infect her own grim mood. With all that was on her mind, she realized that she had no appetite for dissembling with them, and less fear of revealing herself. And so she spoke plainly.

"My good maitre," asked d'Artagnan, "can you tell me what has become of one of my friends, whom we were obliged to leave here some ten days ago?"

"Madame, if you please. Your friend is a handsome young figure? Three- or four-and-twenty years old? Mild, amiable, and well made?"

"That is they — if also wounded in the shoulder."

"Just so. Well, maitre, they are still here."

"Excellent! And madame, if you please, my dear madame," said d'Artagnan, springing from her horse and throwing the bridle to Planchet. "You restore me to life. Where is this dear Aramis? Let me embrace them, I am in a hurry to see them again."

"Pardon, madame, but I doubt whether Maitre Aramis can see you at this moment."

"Why so? Have they some paramour with them?"

"What do you mean by that? No, madame, they have no such person with them."

"With whom are they, then?"

"With the curate of Montdidier and the superior of the Jesuits of Amiens."

"Faith!" cried d'Artagnan. "Is my poor friend dying?"

"No, madame, quite the contrary. But after their illness, grace touched Maitre Aramis, and they determined to take orders."

"Of course," said d'Artagnan. "I forget always that Aramis claims they are only a musketeer for a time."

"Madame still insists upon seeing them?"

"More than ever."

"Well, madame has only to take the right-hand staircase in the courtyard, and knock at number 5 on the third floor."

Leaving Planchet to tend to the horses, d'Artagnan walked quickly in the direction indicated, and found an exterior staircase. But there was no getting at the place of sojourn of the future cleric, the young guard seeing at once how the approach to the chamber of Aramis was as well guarded as the queens' gardens. For Bazin was stationed in the corridor.

"Bazin!" cried d'Artagnan with delight. But the young guard was caught by surprise by the look of horror on the valet's face — and by the manner in which he threw his arms out as if to block the door. For Bazin meant to bar d'Artagnan's passage with a fearlessness born of many years of trial — and of the nearness he found himself to a life of which he had long aspired.

The dream of poor Bazin had always been to serve a cleric, and he had long waited with impatience for the moment, always somehow in the future, when Aramis would throw aside a soldier's uniform and assume the cassock. The daily-renewed promise of the gentle musketeer that the moment would not long be delayed was the single thing that had kept Bazin in Aramis's service — a service in which, the valet was wont to say, his soul was in constant jeopardy.

D'Artagnan stopped before Bazin, who looked the young guard up and down.

"Are you well, ser?" said d'Artagnan.

"Madame, I am presently at the height of joy."

"Indeed," said d'Artagnan, whose tone showed skepticism. "I am told that Aramis is within."

"I am betrayed by the host of the inn, I see," said Bazin with righteous defiance. "I cannot then say that Maitre Aramis is absent, but I will defend the door bravely."

"My faith, but defend it from what?"

"From you, madame. For it can be easily understood that nothing could be more disagreeable to me than any influence which might cast Maitre Aramis back again into that vortex of mundane affairs which have so long carried them away. I assure you, Madame d'Artagnan, that if you cherish Maitre Aramis, it would be the height of indiscretion to disturb them in their pious conference."

"But perhaps they have only just begun?" said d'Artagnan.

"This conference commenced with the morning."

"Then may I wait?"

"This conference will not terminate before night. I beseech you madame, understand that in all probability, this time Maitre Aramis will not draw back from their vow. For the union of physical pain with moral anguish has produced the effect so long sought for, and they, suffering at once in body and mind, have at last fixed their eyes and their thoughts wholly upon faith!"

D'Artagnan clapped a hand to Bazin's shoulder. "Ser, I take very little heed of your eloquent discourse. And I have no desire to support a polemic discussion with my friend's valet." And so she simply moved him out of the way with that hand, and with the other turned the handle of the door of number 5. The door opened, and d'Artagnan went into the chamber.

Aramis, in a black gown, their head enveloped in a sort of round, flat cap, was seated in an easy chair before an oblong table, which was covered with rolls of paper and enormous leather-bound tomes. At either hand sat two figures, whom d'Artagnan took as the Superior of the Jesuits of Amiens and the curate of Montdidier, though she had no sense of telling one from the other. The curtains were mostly drawn, admitting a mysterious, shaded light that seemed designed to inspire the most beatific thought.

All the mundane objects that generally strike the eye on entering the room of a musketeer had disappeared as if by enchantment. No doubt from the fear that the sight of them might bring Aramis back to ideas of this world, Bazin had apparently laid his hands upon sword, pistols, hat, and embroideries and laces of all kinds and sorts. In their stead, d'Artagnan thought she spotted in a far corner a scourge suspended from a nail in the wall.

*Aramis flushed imperceptibly. "You, disturb me?
Oh, quite the contrary, dear friend, I swear…"*

At the noise made by d'Artagnan in entering, Aramis lifted up their head and beheld their friend. But to the great astonishment of the young guard, the sight of her did not produce much effect upon the musketeer, so seemingly was their mind detached from the world.

"Good day, dear d'Artagnan," said Aramis. "Believe me, I am glad to see you."

"So am I delighted to see you," said d'Artagnan. "Although I am not yet sure that it is Aramis I am speaking to."

"I am the same, my friend. But what makes you doubt it?"

"I was afraid I had made a mistake with the number of the door, and that I had found my way into the apartment of some cleric. Then another error seized me on seeing you in company with these gentlefolk. I was afraid you were dangerously ill."

The two figures in black were matched in appearance, with hair of dull brown and ivory skin turned gray in the shadows, but were tall and slender at Aramis's right hand, and shorter and stouter to the musketeer's left. As though they had guessed d'Artagnan's meaning, both darted glances toward her which might have been thought threatening. The young guard took no heed of them.

"I disturb you, perhaps, my dear Aramis," continued she. "For by what I see, I am led to believe that you are confessing to these worthies."

Aramis flushed imperceptibly. "You, disturb me? Oh, quite the contrary, dear friend, I swear. And as proof of what I say, permit me to declare I am rejoiced to see you safe and sound."

"Ah, they are coming around," thought d'Artagnan. "This is good."

"This gentle, who is my friend, has just come through a serious danger," continued Aramis, addressing the two ecclesiastics and pointing to d'Artagnan.

"Praise the gods for your deliverance," replied both they in unison, bowing together.

"I have not failed to do so, your reverences," said the young guard, returning their salutation.

"You arrive in good time, dear d'Artagnan," said Aramis. "And by taking part in our discussion, you may assist us with your intelligence. Madame the Superior of Amiens, Monsieur the Curate of Montdidier, and I are arguing certain theological questions in which we have been much interested." As Aramis spoke the names, they indicated the superior on their right and the curate on their left. "I shall be delighted to have your opinion."

"The opinion of a soldier can have very little weight in theological discussions," said d'Artagnan, who began to be uneasy at the turn things were taking. "You would do better, believe me, with the knowledge of these gentles."

The two clerics in black bowed in their turn.

"On the contrary," said Aramis, "your opinion will be very valuable. The question is this: Madame Superior thinks that my thesis ought to be dogmatic and didactic."

"Your thesis? Are you then making a thesis?"

"Without doubt," said the Jesuit superior. "In the examination which precedes ordination, a thesis is always a requisite."

"Ordination," murmured d'Artagnan, as though she had been still hoping to disbelieve what the cheerful host and Bazin had successively told her.

"Indeed," said Aramis, taking the same graceful position in their easy chair that they might have assumed in bed. Complacently, the musketeer examined their hand. "But rather than my thesis be dogmatic, I, for my part, would prefer it should be ideal. This is the reason why Madame Superior has proposed to me the following subject, which has not yet been treated upon, and in which I perceive there is matter for magnificent elaboration: 'Utraque manus in benedicendo clericis inferioribus necessaria est.'"

D'Artagnan, whose erudition we are well acquainted with, evinced no more understanding on hearing this quotation in Latin than she had at that of Monsieur de Treville, in allusion to the gifts he assumed d'Artagnan had received from the Duke of Buckingham.

"Which means," continued Aramis, knowing to aid their friend that she might understand, " 'For clerics of the inferior orders, the two hands are indispensable when they bestow the benediction.'"

"An admirable subject!" cried the Jesuit.

"Admirable and dogmatic," repeated the curate — who appeared to d'Artagnan's eye to be about as strong as she with respect to Latin, and was carefully watching the Jesuit in order to keep step with her.

"Yes, an admirable subject," said Aramis. "But one which requires a profound study of both the scriptures and advanced writings. Now, I have confessed to these learned ecclesiastics, doing so in all humility, that the duties of mounting guard and the service of the queens have caused me to neglect study a little. I should find myself, therefore, more at my ease in a subject of my own choice, which would be to these hard theological questions what morals are to metaphysics in philosophy."

D'Artagnan realized suddenly how tired she was. Aramis raised their eyebrows to see the young guard yawning wide enough to dislocate her jaw. "Let us speak French, madame," said Aramis to the Jesuit. "Madame d'Artagnan will enjoy our conversation better."

"Certainly," said the Jesuit, a little put out. But the curate, greatly delighted, turned upon d'Artagnan a look full of gratitude. "Well, let us see what is to be derived from this gloss," the Jesuit continued. "Moses, who was but a servant, please to understand — Moses blessed with the hands. She held out both her arms while those who followed her beat their enemies, and then she blessed them with her two hands. Besides, what does the gospel say? 'Imponite manus,' and not 'manum.' Place the hands, not the hand."

"Place the hands," repeated the curate with a gesture.

"But Saint Peter," said the Jesuit, "of whom the popes are the successors, on the contrary is told 'Porrige digitos' — present the fingers. Do you see?"

"Certainly," said Aramis in a pleased tone. "But the thing is subtle."

"The fingers," said the Jesuit. "Saint Peter blessed with the fingers. The pope, therefore, blesses with the fingers. And with how many fingers do they bless? With three fingers to be sure — one for the holy eternal majesty, one for the holy incarnate word, and one for the holy abiding spirit."

All three at the table made holy signs upon themselves. D'Artagnan thought it was proper to mimic this example.

"The pope is the successor of Saint Peter," continued the Jesuit, "and represents the three divine powers. The lower orders of the ecclesiastical hierarchy bless in the name of the holy archangels and angels. The most humble clerks, such as our deacons and sacristans, bless with holy water sprinklers, which resemble an infinite number of blessing fingers. There is the subject simplified — an argument stripped of all ornament. I could make of that subject two volumes the size of this!" And in her enthusiasm, she struck a tome so massive that it made the table bend beneath its weight.

D'Artagnan shivered.

"Certainly," said Aramis again, "I do justice to the beauties of this thesis. But at the same time, I perceive it would be overwhelming for me. So instead, I have chosen this text. Tell me, dear d'Artagnan, if it is not to your taste: 'Non inutile est desiderium in oblatione.' That is, 'A little regret is not unsuitable in an offering of faith.'"

"Stop there!" cried the Jesuit, her voice alive with a sudden heat. "For that thesis touches closely upon heresy. There are propositions almost like it in the works of the heresiarchs, whose books will sooner or later be burned. Take care, my young friend. You are inclining toward false doctrines, wherein you will be lost."

"You will be lost," said the curate, shaking his head sorrowfully.

"You approach that famous point of free will which is a mortal rock," said the Jesuit. "You make the insinuations of free will as the source of salvation."

"Indeed, but —" said Aramis, preparing to counter the arguments ranged against them. But the Jesuit continued without allowing them time to speak.

"How will you prove that we ought to ignore the world when we offer ourselves to faith? Listen to this dilemma: faith is good and the world is evil. Thus, to ignore the world is to ignore faith. That is my conclusion."

"And that is mine also," said the curate.

"But, for faith's sake —" resumed Aramis.

"Desideras diabolum, unhappy maitre!" cried the Jesuit.

"They ignore evil! Ah, my young friend," added the curate, groaning, "do not ignore evil, I implore you!"

D'Artagnan felt herself bewildered. It seemed to her as though she were in a madhouse, and was becoming as mad as those she saw there. She was, however, forced to hold her tongue from not comprehending half the language they employed.

"But listen to me, then," said Aramis, their politeness now mingled with a little impatience. "I do not say I ignore. No, I will never pronounce that sentence, which would not be orthodox."

The Jesuit raised her hands toward the heavens, and the curate did the same.

"But pray grant me," continued the gentle musketeer, "that it is acting with an ill grace to offer to our faith only that with which we are inclined to ignore. Don't you think so, d'Artagnan?"

"Quite so," said she, with no understanding.

The Jesuit and the curate quite started from their chairs.

"This is the point of departure," said Aramis. "It is a syllogism. The world is not wanting in attractions. I quit the world, then I make a sacrifice, as the scripture says positively."

"That is true," said the clerics, speaking as one. D'Artagnan started at the spectacle.

"And then," said Aramis, "I made a certain stanza upon this matter last year, which I showed to learned folk who paid me a thousand compliments on it."

"A stanza," said the Jesuit disdainfully.

"A stanza," said the curate mechanically.

"Recite it, then," said d'Artagnan. "Anything for a little change in these proceedings."

"But there will be no change, for my stanza is religious," said Aramis. "It is theology in verse."

"Great gods," moaned d'Artagnan.

"Here it is," said Aramis with a look of shyness — albeit with an equally strong sense of pride. "You who weep for pleasures fled/While dragging on a life of care/All your woes will melt in air/If to the gods your tears are shed/You who weep."

D'Artagnan and the curate appeared pleased, but the Jesuit showed her displeasure with an opinion. "Beware of a profane taste in your theological style," said she fiercely. "Consider the words of the learned on this subject: 'Severus sit clericorum verbo.'"

"Yes, let the sermon be clear," said the curate.

"Now," said the Jesuit, speaking more quickly, as if sensing that her acolyte was going astray, "your thesis would no doubt please those at court."

"Thanks to faith," said Aramis, overjoyed — and misunderstanding the superior's intent.

"There it is!" cried that superior in response. "The world still speaks within you in a loud voice! You follow the world, my young friend, and I tremble lest grace prove not efficacious."

"Do not doubt me, my reverend guardian. I can answer for myself."

"Worldly presumption!"

"I know myself, Madame Superior. My resolution is irrevocable."

"Then you persist in continuing that thesis?"

"I feel myself called upon to treat that and no other. I will see about the continuation of it, and tomorrow I hope you will be satisfied with the corrections I shall have made in consequence of your advice."

"Work slowly," said the curate. "We leave you in an excellent tone of mind."

"Yes, the ground is all sown," said the Jesuit, "and hopefully we have not to fear that one portion of the seed may have fallen upon stone, another upon the highway, or that the birds of the air have eaten the rest. Aves coeli comederunt illam."

"The plague stifle you and your Latin!" said d'Artagnan, who began to feel all her patience exhausted.

"Farewell, my acolyte," said the curate. "Till tomorrow."

"Till tomorrow, rash youth," said the Jesuit. "You promise to become one of the lights of the church. Faith grant that this light prove not a devouring fire."

D'Artagnan, who for what seemed an hour had been gnawing her nails with impatience, was beginning to attack the quick.

The two clerics in black rose with their prayer books and hymnals, bowed to Aramis and d'Artagnan, and advanced toward the door. Bazin, who had been standing and listening to all this argument with a pious jubilation, sprang toward them, took the tomes of both, and walked respectfully before them to lead their way.

Aramis followed the group to the foot of the stairs, and then immediately came up again to d'Artagnan, whose senses were still in a state of confusion.

When left alone, the two friends at first kept an embarrassed silence. It became immediately necessary for one of them to break it first, and as d'Artagnan appeared determined to leave that honor to her companion, Aramis at last spoke.

"You see that I am returned to my fundamental ideas."

"Indeed. Efficacious grace has touched you, as that gentle said just now."

"Oh, these plans of retreat have been made for a long time. You have often heard me speak of them, have you not, my friend?"

"Yes. But I confess I always thought you half-jested."

"Jest with such matters? Oh, d'Artagnan."

"And why not? We jest frequently even in the face of death."

"And we are wrong to do so, my friend. For death is the door which leads to perdition or to salvation."

"It may be. But if you please, let us not theologize, Aramis. You must have had enough for today. As for me, I have almost forgotten the little Latin I have ever known. Then I confess to you that I have eaten nothing since late this morning, and I am monstrously hungry."

"We will dine directly, my friend. Only you must please to remember that this is Friday. Now, on such a day, I can neither eat flesh nor see it eaten. If you can be content with my meal, it consists of bounty of the glade of the gentle earth."

"What do you mean by all that?" asked d'Artagnan uneasily.

"I mean spinach," said Aramis. "But on your account, I will have an omelet also prepared, though that is a serious infraction of the rule."

"This feast is not very succulent, but never mind. I will put up with it for the sake of remaining with you."

"I am grateful to you for the sacrifice," said Aramis. "But if your body be not greatly benefited by it, be assured your soul will."

Bazin had by then returned, and Aramis gave the dinner order to take to the inn's kitchen. The valet nodded piously, though he strayed a distrustful glance to d'Artagnan before going out.

"And so, Aramis," said d'Artagnan when the two were alone again. "You are decidedly to enter the church? What will our two friends say? What will Monsieur de Treville say? They will treat you as a deserter, I warn you."

"I do not enter the church, d'Artagnan. Rather, I reenter it, for I first deserted the church for the world. You know that I forced myself when I became a musketeer."

"I? I know nothing about it."

"You don't know I quit the seminary?"

"Not at all. You have never spoken on the matter."

"My apologies, friend, for I had thought that Athos or Porthos would have made that tale known to you. But I will tell you my story, then. For the scriptures say, 'Confess yourselves to one another,' and I confess to you, d'Artagnan."

"And I give you absolution beforehand. You see, I am a good sort of cleric."

"Do not jest about holy things, my friend." Aramis's tone was deadly serious.

"Go on, then. I listen."

The gentle musketeer sat in silence for a moment, with that mysterious light of the room around them. D'Artagnan waited.

"I had been at the seminary from nine years old," said Aramis at last. "I was to become a cleric at twenty, and all was arranged. Then one evening, just three days before that holy event, I went, according to custom, to family friends whose house on the Rue Payenne I frequented with much pleasure, for it was home to… well, let us say a special friend, who was a young woman who gave me all sorts of compliments. I am shamed to admit I craved her company for that reason, for when one is young, and one is weak, what can be expected?

"But on this night, an officer of the guard who was also friend to the family, and who had seen me on nights past reading *The Lives of the Saints* to my special friend of the house, entered suddenly, without being announced, and with a jealous eye. That evening, I had translated an episode of scripture, and had just communicated my verses to this special friend. Leaning on my shoulder, she was reading them a second time with me.

"The pose struck by my friend and myself, which I must admit was rather free, infuriated this officer. He said nothing then. But when I departed, he followed and quickly came up to me.

" 'Monsieur Cleric,' said he, for I answered to 'monsieur' in my youth. 'Do you like blows with a cane?'

" 'I cannot say, monsieur,' answered I. 'For no one has ever dared to give me any.'

" 'Well, listen to me, then, Monsieur Cleric. If you venture again into the house in which I have met you this evening and show such forwardness, I will dare it myself.'

"I really think I must have been frightened. I became most ashen. I felt my legs fail me. I sought for a response, but could find none, and so was silent. The officer waited for his reply, and seeing it so long coming, he burst into laughter, turned upon his heel, and reentered the house. I returned to the seminary.

"Now, I am a gentlefolk born and have a free spirit, as you may have noted, my dear d'Artagnan. The insult was terrible, and although unknown to the rest of the world, I felt it live and fester at the bottom of my heart. I informed my superiors that I did not feel myself sufficiently prepared for ordination, and at my request, the ceremony was postponed for a year.

"During that time, I sought out the best fencing instructor in Paris, making an agreement with her to take a lesson every day, and every day for a year I took that lesson. Then, on the anniversary of the day on which I had been insulted, I hung my cassock on a peg, assumed the costume of a guard, and went to a ball given by a friend of mine, and to which I knew my assailant was invited.

"The event was in the Rue de France-Bourgeois, close to La Force. As I expected, my officer was there. I went up to him as he was singing a love ditty and looking tenderly at a young companion, and interrupted him exactly in the middle of the second couplet.

" 'Monsieur,' said I, 'does it still displease you that I should frequent a certain house of the Rue Payenne? And would you still cane me if I took it into my head to disobey you?'

"The officer looked at me with astonishment, and then said, 'What is your business with me, ser? I do not know you.'

" 'I am monsieur to you,' said I. 'For I am the little cleric who reads *The Lives of the Saints* and translates the scriptures into verse.'

" 'Ah! I recollect now,' said the officer in a jeering tone. 'Well, what do you want with me?'

" 'I want you to spare time to take a walk with me.'

" 'Tomorrow morning, if you like, with the greatest pleasure.'

" 'No, not tomorrow morning, if you please, but immediately.'

" 'If you absolutely insist.'

" 'I do insist upon it.'

" 'Come, then. Friends,' said the officer to those who accompanied him, 'do not disturb yourselves. Allow me time just to kill this gentle, and I will return and finish the last couplet.'

"We went out. I took him to the Rue Payenne, to exactly the same spot where, a year before and at the very same hour, he had paid me the compliment I have related to you. It was a superb moonlit night. We immediately drew. And at the first pass, I laid him stark dead."

"By my faith," whispered d'Artagnan.

"Now," said Aramis, "as those at the party did not see the officer come back, and as he was found in the Rue Payenne with a great sword wound through his body, it was guessed that I had accommodated him thus. I had no fear of scandal, understand. But awake at dawn that day, it was clear to me that I must renounce the cassock, and more besides. The politics of my blood and upbringing. The lover's bravado that had driven me to anger and to violence. I left my youth, and much more besides, on the Rue Payenne that night, and wondered as I never had before who, in fact, I was — and who I desired to be.

"Then in my hour of need, and as perhaps first answer to those questions, Athos, whose acquaintance I made about that period, and Porthos, who had taught me some effective tricks of swordplay in addition to my lessons, prevailed upon me to solicit the uniform of a musketeer. The Queen Louise entertained great regard for my father, who had fallen at the siege of Arras, and the uniform was granted to Maitre Aramis. But now, after all that has passed since, you may understand that the moment has come for me to reenter the loving dominion of the church."

"I do understand," said d'Artagnan, who felt keenly her friend's sorrow. "Except why today, rather than yesterday or tomorrow? What has happened to you to raise all these melancholy ideas?"

"This wound, my dear d'Artagnan, has been a warning to me."

"The wound from near Beauvais? Ridiculous! It must by now be nearly healed, and I am sure it is not that which gives you the most pain."

"What, then?" said Aramis.

And d'Artagnan saw that the gentle musketeer flushed.

She remembered the words of Bazin at the door, speaking of Aramis's union of physical pain — the wound of their shoulder — with moral anguish. Then all at once, the young guard thought of the letter she carried, and of the person at the window that night in the house of Aramis, and of the musketeer's great sadness at that figure's silent departure from Paris.

"I believe you have a wound at heart, Aramis," said d'Artagnan. "One deeper and more painful than that wound of your shoulder, or of the insult dealt to an enamored youth. A wound made by real love."

The eye of Aramis gleamed suddenly in spite of themself. "Ah," said they, dissembling their emotion under a feigned dispassion, "do not talk of such things. I, suffer love pains? What vanity! According to your notion, then, my brain is turned? And for whom? Some stranger with whom I trifled in some garrison? Fie!"

"Pardon, my dear Aramis, but I thought you carried your eyes higher," said d'Artagnan.

"Higher? And who am I to nourish such ambition? A poor musketeer, a vagabond, an unknown? One who hates servitude, and finds themself ill-placed in the world?"

"Come now, Aramis," cried the young guard, looking at her friend with an air of doubt.

"Dust I am, and to dust I return. Life is full of humiliations and sorrows," said the gentle musketeer, their voice a tone of bitterness. "All the ties which attach us to life break in our hands. Trust me, my dear d'Artagnan. Conceal your wounds when you have any, for silence is the last joy of the unhappy. Beware of giving anyone the clue to your griefs. The curious suck our tears as flies suck the blood of a wounded hart."

"Alas, my dear Aramis," said d'Artagnan, in her turn heaving a profound sigh. "That is my story you are relating!"

"Indeed?"

"Yes. The woman whom I love, whom I adore, has just been torn from me by force. I do not know where she is or whither they have conducted her. She is perhaps a prisoner. She is perhaps dead…"

"Yes, but you have at least this consolation — that you can say to yourself she has not abandoned you voluntarily. That if you learn no news of her, it is because all communication with you is interdicted. While I…" Aramis's words trailed off.

"Well?"

"Nothing," said they. "Nothing."

"So you renounce the world, then? Forever? That is a settled thing, a resolution registered?"

"Forever. You are my friend today, d'Artagnan. But tomorrow, you will be no more to me than a shadow. As for the world, it is a tomb and nothing else."

"All this is very sad which you tell me."

"My vocation commands me. It carries me away. And yet," continued Aramis, "while I still belong to the earth, I wish to speak of you — of our friends."

"And on my part," said d'Artagnan, "I wished to speak of you, but I find you so completely detached from everything! Talking of love, you cry, 'Fie! Friends are shadows! The world is a tomb!'"

"Alas, you will find it so yourself in time," said Aramis with a sigh.

"Well, then, let us say no more about it," said d'Artagnan. "And let us burn this letter, which, no doubt, announces to you some fresh infidelity of your trifling someone."

"What letter?" cried Aramis in sudden confusion.

"A letter which was sent to your abode in your absence, and which I thought to bring you."

"But from whom is that letter?"

"Oh, from some heartbroken stranger, no doubt. Some desponding reader of scripture. Or from one who loves you, perhaps. But I may only guess."

"What do you say? Show me this letter!"

"Faith! I must have lost it," said the young guard innocently, pretending to search her pockets for it. "But fortunately, the world is a tomb, a crypt, a sepulcher. All folk, including this letter writer, are but shadows, and love is a sentiment to which you cry, 'Fie! Fie!'"

"D'Artagnan, d'Artagnan," cried Aramis, "you are killing me!"

"Well, here it is at last!" said d'Artagnan as she drew the letter from her pocket.

Aramis bounded from their chair and seized the letter. Ignoring that the envelope had already been slit, they opened and read it — or rather, they devoured it, their expression radiant.

"This unknown writer seems to have an agreeable style," said the messenger carelessly.

"Thank you, d'Artagnan," said Aramis, almost in a state of delirium. "Thank you! It is Madame de Chevreuse, who writes as Marie Michon to evade the cardinal's spies. Though forced to return to Tours, she is not faithless. She still loves me! Come, my friend! Come let me embrace you. Happiness almost stifles me!"

The two friends began to dance around the table and its stacks of tomes, kicking about a number of papers that had fallen to the floor.

At that moment, Bazin entered with the spinach and the omelet.

"A change of menu, my friend!" shouted Aramis, throwing their flat cap for the valet to catch. "Return whence you came. Take back those horrible vegetables and those poor eggs! Order a larded hare, a fat capon, mutton leg dressed with garlic, and four bottles of old burgundy."

Bazin, who stared in horror at Aramis without comprehending the cause of this change, caught the cap. And in so doing, he allowed the omelet to slip into the spinach, and the spinach onto the floor.

"Now this is the moment to consecrate your existence to the holy incarnate word," said d'Artagnan. "And if you persist in offering homage to faith, let it be, 'No one should desire to offer all!' 'Non in utile desiderium oblatione!'"

"All the fiends take your horrid Latin," said Aramis, laughing. "Let us drink, my dear d'Artagnan. Great gods, let us drink while the wine is fresh! Let us drink heartily, and while we do so, tell me a little of what is going on in the world yonder."

CHAPTER 27

THE LORD OF ATHOS

"We have now to search for Athos," said d'Artagnan to the vivacious Aramis, when she had informed the gentle musketeer of all that had passed since their departure from the capital, and an excellent dinner had made one of them forget their thesis and the other her fatigue.

"Do you think, then, that any harm can have happened to her?" asked Aramis. "Athos is so cool, so brave, and handles her sword so skillfully."

"Without doubt. No one has a higher opinion of the courage and skill of Athos than I have. But I like better to hear my sword clang against lances than against staves, and I fear that even Athos might be beaten down when outnumbered by servants. Those ruffians strike hard, and don't leave off in a hurry. This is why I wish to set out again as soon as possible."

"I will try to accompany you," said Aramis, "though I still feel in no condition to mount on horseback. Yesterday, I undertook to employ that scourge which you see hanging against the wall, but pain prevented my continuing the pious exercise."

"That's the first time I ever heard of anyone trying to cure gunshot wounds with a cat-o'-nine-tails. But you were ill, and illness renders the head weak, and therefore you may be excused."

"When do you mean to set out?"

"Tomorrow at daybreak. Sleep as soundly as you can tonight, and tomorrow if you are able, we will take our departure together."

"Till tomorrow, then," said Aramis. "For even as iron-nerved as you are, you must need rest."

⚜

The next morning, when d'Artagnan entered Aramis's chamber, she found the musketeer at the window.

"What are you looking at?" asked she.

"My faith! I am admiring three magnificent horses which the stablehands are leading about. It would be a pleasure worthy of a prince to travel upon such steeds."

"Well, my dear Aramis, you may enjoy that pleasure. For one of those three horses is yours."

"What? Nonsense. But which one?"

"Whichever of the three you like, for I have no preference."

"And the rich caparison, is that mine too?" Aramis gestured toward the exquisite adornment of the hindquarters and saddle of one fine steed, being walked by a young stablehand.

"Without doubt."

"Ah, but you jest, d'Artagnan."

"No, I have left off jesting, now that you speak French again instead of Latin."

"What, those rich holsters? That velvet housing? That saddle studded with silver? Are they all for me?"

"For you and no one else. Look, the horse which paws the ground there has been mine to date, and the other will do splendidly for Athos."

"Great gods. They are three superb animals."

"I am glad they please you."

"Why, it must have been the queens themselves who made you such a present."

"Certainly it was not the cardinal. But don't trouble yourself whence they come. Think only that one of the three is your property."

"Then I do choose that which the red-headed youth is leading."

"It is yours!"

"By my faith, that is enough to drive away all my pains. I could mount such a steed with thirty bullets in my body. On my soul, what handsome stirrups! Ho, Bazin! Come here this instant."

Bazin appeared on the threshold, dull and spiritless.

"At once, please, polish my sword and smarten my hat," said Aramis. "Brush my cloak and load my pistols." The musketeer then stepped past their valet, heading for the stairs and the stables below.

"That last order is unnecessary," said d'Artagnan. "There are loaded pistols in your holsters."

Bazin sighed, turning to follow Aramis, and with d'Artagnan walking alongside.

"Come, Monsieur Bazin, console yourself," said the young guard, with Aramis too far ahead to hear. "People of all conditions come to the fruits of their faith in time."

"But maitre was already such a good theologian," said Bazin, appearing as if ready to weep. "They might have become a bishop, and perhaps a cardinal."

"But my poor Bazin, reflect a little. Of what use is it to be a cleric, pray? You do not avoid going to war by that means. You see, Cardinal de Richelieu is about to make the next campaign in La Rochelle, helm on head and pike in hand. And the Dread Eminence is not alone. Ask the valets of any cleric armed against the queens' enemies how often they have had to serve their employers under fire."

"Alas," sighed Bazin. "I know it, madame. Everything is turned topsy-turvy in the world nowadays."

As d'Artagnan and Bazin descended, Aramis was already before them, and strode forward to their new steed.

"Hold my stirrup, Bazin," called the musketeer. And when the valet had done so, Aramis sprang into the saddle with their usual grace and agility. But after only a few capers and curvets of the noble animal, Aramis turned ashen with pain, and became unsteady in the saddle. D'Artagnan, foreseeing such an event, had kept her eye on her friend, and thus sprang toward them, catching them in her arms.

Together, Bazin and d'Artagnan assisted Aramis back to their chamber. The musketeer was soon settled, and the young guard spoke.

"Never mind, my dear Aramis," said she. "Planchet and I can go alone in search of Athos. You take care of yourself."

"You are as one made of brass," said Aramis.

"No, I have good luck, and no more than that. But how do you mean to pass your time till I come back? No more theses, no more glosses upon the fingers or upon benedictions, hey?"

Aramis smiled. "I will make verses," said they.

"Yes, I dare say. Verses perfumed with the scent of a letter from Madame de Chevreuse. Teach Bazin prosody. That will console him. As to the horse, ride it a little every day, and that will accustom you to its movement."

"Oh, rest easy on that point," said Aramis. "You will find me ready to follow you."

D'Artagnan then commended her friend to the cares of the hosts of the Miller's Arms and Bazin, and a short while later, she and Planchet were trotting along in the direction of Amiens.

As she rode, d'Artagnan's thoughts were fixed on the singular problem of how she was meant to find Athos — if the musketeer could even be found at all. The position in which the young guard had left her had been most critical. Athos might well have succumbed. She might have been arrested. These ideas continually clouded the young guard's brow, and caused her to formulate for herself more than a few vows of vengeance.

Of all her friends, Athos was the eldest, and the least resembling d'Artagnan in appearance, in her tastes and sympathies. Yet the young guard entertained a marked preference for that gentle all the same. The noble and distinguished air of Athos, those flashes of greatness which from time to time broke out from the shade in which she voluntarily kept herself — all that unalterable equality of temper made her the most pleasant companion in the world.

The elder musketeer had a forced and cynical gaiety, and a bravery that might have been termed blind if it had not been the result of the rarest coolness. And those qualities attracted more than the esteem, more than the friendship of d'Artagnan. They attracted her admiration. Indeed, when placed beside Monsieur de Treville as the very model of an elegant and noble courtier, Athos in her most cheerful days might make an advantageous comparison.

The sound of Athos's voice was at once penetrating and melodious. But even more notable was a thing almost indefinable in her, who seemed always retiring, but who nonetheless held a delicate knowledge of the world, and of the customs of gentry and high society. Those manners were seen always to a high degree in the musketeer — and always as if rendered unconsciously to her own thought, apparent in even her least actions.

If a banquet was in hand, Athos presided over it better than any other, placing every guest exactly in the rank which their ancestors had earned for them or that they had made for themself. If a question in heraldry were started, Athos knew all the fabled families of the realm, their genealogy, their alliances, their coats of arms, and the origin of them. Etiquette had no minutiae unknown to her. She was profoundly versed in hunting and falconry, and had one day when conversing on this great art astonished even the Queen Louise herself, who took great pride in being considered a master on those topics.

Like all the great gentry of that period, Athos rode and fenced to perfection. But still further, her education had seemingly been so broad with respect to scholastic studies that she smiled at the scraps of Latin which Aramis sported, and which Porthos pretended to understand. More than once, to the great astonishment of her friends, Athos had placed a verb in its proper tense and a noun in its correct case when Aramis allowed some rudimentary error to escape them. And besides all that, her sense of honor was irreproachable, in an age in which soldiers compromised so easily with their faith and their conscience, when lovers made light of the rigorous delicacy of the era, and when the poor were forced to all but ignore pronouncements against theft.

This Athos, then, was a most extraordinary sort. And yet this nature so distinguished, this figure so beautiful, this essence so fine, was seen from time to time to turn insensibly toward material life. Athos, in her hours of gloom — and those hours were frequent — was extinguished as to the whole of the luminous portion of herself, and her brilliant side disappeared as into profound gloom.

Taken by such moods, her head hanging down, her eyes dull, her speech slow and painful, Athos would stare for hours into her bottle, her glass, or at Grimaud. Thankfully, the valet, accustomed to obey Athos by signs, read in her faint glances her every order, and could satisfy them immediately. If the four friends were assembled during one of these episodes, a word thrown forth occasionally, and always with the most violent effort, was the extent of what

Athos furnished to the conversation. In exchange for her silence, she drank enough for four, and always without appearing to be affected by the wine — or at least by no more than her even deeper sadness.

D'Artagnan, whose inquiring disposition we are acquainted with, had never been able to assign any cause for these fits, or for the periods of their recurrence. Athos never received any letters. Athos never engaged in secrecy, or had any concerns not known to her friends. Moreover, it could not be said that it was wine which produced this sadness. For in d'Artagnan's observation, Athos drank only to combat the sadness, and was unable to see how wine rendered it only more sorrowful, as we have said.

This despondency could likewise not be attributed to gaming. Unlike Porthos, who accompanied his changes in fortune with songs or oaths, Athos when she won remained as unmoved as when she lost. She had been known, in the circle of the musketeers, to win in one night three thousand pistoles, then to lose them again the following night — along with her horse, her weapons, and her finest gold-embroidered belt. She would then win all this back again with the addition of a hundred pistoles, without her beautiful eyebrows being arched, without her hands losing their calm touch, and without her conversation ever ceasing to be calm and agreeable.

Neither was it an atmospheric influence which tarnished her features, as affects many of those forced to dwell in wet and wintry lands. For the sadness generally became more intense toward the fine season of the year, with June and July the most terrible months for Athos. When talking of the present, she had no anxiety. She shrugged her shoulders when people spoke of the future. And so Athos's secret, then, must surely have been hidden in the past, as had often been vaguely suggested to d'Artagnan by the others.

"And for all that," mused d'Artagnan as she rode now, "poor Athos is perhaps at this moment dead, and I am at fault. For it was I who dragged her into this affair, of which she did not know the origin, of which she is ignorant of the result, and from which she can derive no advantage."

"Without reckoning, madame," added Planchet to his employer's audibly expressed reflections, "that we perhaps owe our lives to her. Do you remember how she cried, 'Go on, d'Artagnan, I am taken'? And after she had discharged her two pistols, what a terrible noise she made with her sword! One might have said that twenty musketeers were fighting."

Planchet's words redoubled the eagerness of d'Artagnan, who urged her horse on. While she rode, she imagined for the inn's perfidious host one of those hearty vengeances that offer no satisfaction except in their anticipation. So they proceeded at a gallop until they saw Amiens, and arrived shortly before noon at the cursed Golden Lily inn.

D'Artagnan and Planchet left their horses to the care of the grooms who appeared in the yard of the inn on their arrival. With the valet a step behind her, the young guard then entered the establishment with her hat pulled over her eyes, her left hand on the pommel of her sword, and squeezing her whip with her right hand.

"Do you remember me?" said she to the host, familiar with his flushed features and red-fringed mane where he advanced to greet her.

"I have not that honor, maitre," replied the latter, distracted from d'Artagnan by a glimpse of the two fine horses in the stableyard.

"What, you don't know me?"

"No, maitre."

"Well, a few words will refresh your memory. What have you done with that gentlefolk against whom you had the audacity, some ten days ago, to make an accusation of passing forged coin?"

The host then became as ashen as death, for he suddenly beheld d'Artagnan in full — and saw the threatening attitude she had assumed. Behind the young guard, Planchet modeled himself after her most effectively.

"Ah, maitre, do not mention it!" cried the host in the most pitiable voice imaginable. "How dearly have I paid for that fault, unhappy wretch that I am."

"I am Madame, if you please," said d'Artagnan coldly. "That gentle, I say. What has become of her?"

"Deign to listen to me, madame, and be merciful! Sit down, in mercy!"

D'Artagnan, mute with anger and anxiety, took a seat in the threatening attitude of a judge. Planchet glared fiercely over the back of her armchair.

"Here is the story, madame," said the trembling host. "For I now recollect you. It was you who rode off at the moment I had that unfortunate difference with the gentlefolk you speak of."

"Yes, it was I. So you may plainly perceive that you have no mercy to expect if you do not tell me the whole truth."

"Deign to listen to me, and you shall know all."

"I listen."

"We had been warned by the authorities that a celebrated coiner of bad money would arrive at our inn, with several of their companions, all disguised as guards or musketeers. Madame, we were furnished with a description of your horses, your valets, your faces — nothing was omitted."

"Go on, then," said d'Artagnan, who had no doubt that the cardinal's agents were the source whence such an exact description had come.

"We took then such measures as we thought necessary to get possession of the persons of the pretended coiners, in accordance with the orders of the authorities, who sent us a reinforcement of six church guards."

"Gods' blood. Six against two!" said d'Artagnan, whose ears burned in response to the explanation of the attack.

"Forgive me, madame, for saying such things, but they form our excuse. The authorities had terrified me, and you know that innkeepers must keep on good terms with the authorities."

"But once again, that gentlefolk — where is she? What has become of her? Is she dead? Is she living?"

"Patience, madame, I am coming to it. There happened then that which you know. And then your precipitate departure appeared to confirm the matter." The host spoke these words with an acuteness that did not escape d'Artagnan. "That gentle, your friend, defended herself desperately. Her valet, by an unforeseen piece of ill luck, had quarreled with the church guards, who were disguised as stablehands —"

"Miserable scoundrel!" cried d'Artagnan. "You were all in on the plot, then. May nothing prevent me from exterminating you all!"

"But alas, madame, we were not in on the plot — which is to say, my wife and I, and our staff — as you will soon see. Your musketeer friend, madame as you name her — and pardon me for not calling her by the honorable name which no doubt she bears, but we do not know that name. Madame your friend, having disabled two guards with her pistols, retreated fighting with her sword, with which she disabled one of my servants, and stunned me with a blow of the flat side of it."

"You villain, will you finish? Her name is Madame Athos! What has become of Athos?"

"While fighting and retreating, as I have told madame, she found the door of the cellar stairs behind her, and as the door was open, she took out the key and barricaded herself inside. As we were sure of finding her there, we left her alone."

"And this should placate me?" said d'Artagnan. "You claim that you did not really wish to kill, but only wished to imprison her?"

"Faith, no! To imprison her, madame? Why, she imprisoned herself, I swear to you she did! From the first, she had left a veritable battlefield behind her. One guard was killed on the spot, and two others were severely wounded. The dead and the wounded were carried off by their comrades, and I have heard nothing of either of them since. As for us, while I recovered my senses, my good wife went to Monsieur the Governor, to whom she related all that had passed, and asked what we should do with our prisoner. But Monsieur the Governor was all astonishment. He told her he knew nothing about the matter, that the orders we had received did not come from him, and that if any had the audacity to mention his name as being concerned in this disturbance, he would have us both arrested. It appears that we had made a mistake, madame, and that I had accused the wrong person, and that they who were the true villains had escaped."

"But Athos," said d'Artagnan again, whose impatience was increasing. "Athos! Where is she?"

"Momentarily, madame, I promise you. As we were anxious to repair the wrongs we had done the prisoner, my wife and I made our way straight to the cellar in order to set her at liberty. But madame, she was no longer a gentlefolk but a fiend in uniform! To my offer of liberty, she replied that it was nothing but a trap, and that before she came out, she intended to impose her own conditions. I told her very humbly — for we could not conceal from ourselves the scrape we had got into by laying hands on one of their majesties' musketeers — I told her we were quite ready to submit to her conditions.

" 'First,' said she, 'I wish my valet placed with me, fully armed.'

"We hastened to obey this order, for you must understand, madame, my wife and I were disposed to do everything your friend could desire. Madame Grimaud told us her name, although she does not talk much. But she went down to the cellar, wounded as she was. And then Madame the Musketeer, having admitted her, barricaded the door afresh and ordered us to go quietly about our business."

"But where is Athos now?" cried d'Artagnan. "Where is she?"

"Why, in the cellar, madame, as I have said."

"What? You scoundrel! Have you kept her in the cellar all this time?"

"Merciful faith, no, madame! We keep her in the cellar? Clearly you do not know what she has been doing in our cellar. Ah, if you could but persuade her to come out, madame, I and my wife should owe you the gratitude of our whole lives. We should both adore you as a patron saint."

"Then she is there? I shall find her there?"

"Without doubt you will, madame, for she persists in remaining there. We every day pass through the vent some bread at the end of a pitchfork, and some meat when she asks for it. But alas, bread and meat is not that of which she makes the greatest consumption. I once endeavored to go down with two of my servants, but your Madame Athos flew into a terrible rage. I heard the noise she made in loading her pistols, and her valet in loading her musketoon. Then, when we asked them what were their intentions, the musketeer replied that she had forty charges to fire, and that she and her valet would fire to the last one before she would allow a single soul of us to set foot in the cellar. Upon hearing this, I went and complained to the governor, who replied that we only had what we deserved, and that this lesson would teach us to insult honorable gentlefolk in our establishment."

Through these last parts of the host's story, d'Artagnan's mood had shifted from anger through astonishment — and then to an unexpected humor, wherein she was suddenly unable to refrain from laughing. "But wait. You mean that from the day of my departure —"

"I mean that from that day, madame, we have led the most miserable life imaginable. For you must know that most of our provisions are in the cellar. There is our wine in bottles, and our wine in casks. The beer, the oil and the spices, the bacon and sausages. And as we are prevented from going down there, we are forced to refuse food and drink to the travelers who come to us, so that our inn is daily going to ruin. If your friend remains another week in our cellar, we shall be undone!"

"And that would be no more than justice, you ass. Could you not perceive by our appearance, exhausted and in the middle of the night, that we were soldiers on a mission, and not coin forgers?"

"Yes, madame, you are right," said the host. "But hark! There she is!"

Then in the distance and from beneath the floor, striking joy in her heart, d'Artagnan heard the voice of Athos. "One of your staff has disturbed her, no doubt," said the young guard.

"But she must be disturbed," said the host. "For we have two English gentlefolk just arrived."

"And?"

"Well, the English like good wine as you may know, madame. These have asked for the best. My wife was to go request permission of Madame Athos to enter the cellar to satisfy these gentles, but by that din, Madame Athos as usual has refused. Ah, my faith. There is the hullabaloo louder than ever!"

D'Artagnan heard an even greater noise coming from the cellar, in response to which she rose. Then, preceded by the host wringing his hands and followed by Planchet with his musketoon ready for use, she approached the scene of action.

Standing near the cellar door, the two English gentlefolk of which the host had spoken were exasperated. Both were in matching riding clothes, though their features and hair were contrasts of ivory and gold, umber and silver. And both had endured a long ride, and were famished with hunger and thirst.

"But this is tyranny!" said one of them in very good French, though with a foreign accent. "That this mad fool will not allow these good people access to their own wine. What nonsense! Let us break open the door, and if they are too far gone in their madness, well, we will kill them."

"Softly, gentles," said d'Artagnan, drawing her pistols from her belt. "You will kill no one, if you please."

"Nay, it is good," called the calm voice of Athos from the other side of the door. "Let them come in, these two roast beefs, and we shall see."

Brave as they had only moments ago appeared to be, the two English gentles looked at each other hesitatingly. There was a moment of silence. But at length, the two English travelers, who by now had many eyes on them from across the inn, felt too self-conscious to draw back.

The angrier one descended the six steps leading to the cellar, giving a kick against the door strong enough to split a wall.

"Planchet," said d'Artagnan, cocking her pistols, "I will take charge of the one at the top. You look to the one below. Ah, gentles, you want battle? Then you shall have it."

"Great gods!" cried the hollow voice of Athos. "I can hear d'Artagnan, I think."

"Yes," said d'Artagnan, raising her voice in turn. "I am here, my friend!"

"Ah, good, then. We will teach them, these door breakers!"

The English had drawn their swords, but they found themselves trapped between two battlefronts. Both hesitated an instant, but then as before, pride prevailed. A second kick split the door from bottom to top — though it stayed fast against some barricade beyond.

"Stand to one side, d'Artagnan!" cried Athos. "I am going to fire!"

"Patience, Athos," said d'Artagnan, whom reflection never abandoned. "Gentles, think about your situation. You are running headlong into a most futile affair, and you will be riddled before the battle is done. My valet and I each have three shots for you, and you will get as many from the cellar. You will then meet our swords, with which I can assure you my friend and I play tolerably well. Let me conduct your business and my own. You shall soon have something to drink. I give you my word."

"If there is any left," grumbled the jeering voice of Athos.

"Faith! 'If there is any left!'" cried the host where he had crept close. D'Artagnan saw a cold sweat upon his face.

"Fie, for there must be plenty left," said she. "Worry not for that, for those two cannot have drunk all the cellar. Gentles, for the last time, return your swords to their scabbards."

"That is easy to say — but you must replace your pistols in your belt as well."

"Willingly."

D'Artagnan did so to set the example. Then, turning toward Planchet, she made him a sign to uncock his musketoon.

The English travelers, convinced that peaceful proceedings were upon them, sheathed their swords grumblingly. The history of Athos's imprisonment was then related to them quickly — and as they truly were gentlefolk, they were just as quick as d'Artagnan to pronounce the host in the wrong for his actions ten days before.

"My thanks to you," said d'Artagnan. "Now go up to your room again, and in ten minutes, I promise it, you shall have all you desire."

The English gentlefolk bowed and went upstairs.

"Now I am alone, my dear Athos," said d'Artagnan. "Free the door, I beg of you."

"Immediately," said Athos.

Then was heard a great noise of wood being moved and of the groaning of posts. These were the counterscarps and bastions of Athos and Grimaud, which the besieged themselves were demolishing.

A moment after, the broken door was removed and the pale face of Athos appeared. With a rapid glance, she took a survey of the surroundings.

D'Artagnan threw herself on the musketeer's neck and embraced her tenderly. She then tried to draw her from her gloomy abode — but to her surprise, she saw that Athos staggered.

"You are wounded!" cried the young guard in fear.

"I? Not at all. I am dead drunk, that's all, and never did anyone more strongly set about getting so. By my faith, my good host! I must have drunk for my part at least a hundred and fifty bottles."

"Mercy!" cried the host. "Even if the valet has drunk only half as much as the employer, we are ruined!"

"Ha! Grimaud is a well-behaved retainer. She would never think of living in the same manner as her employer, and hence she drank only from the cask. Hark, though. I don't think she put the tap in again. Do you hear it? It is running now."

D'Artagnan burst into a laugh that changed the whimpering of the host into a mournful howl.

In the meantime, Grimaud appeared behind Athos with a musketoon on her shoulder. Her smiling face was bobbing happily like a drunken satyr. Her face and tunic were soaked with a greasy liquid — which the host quickly recognized as his best olive oil.

With d'Artagnan and Planchet close behind, Athos and Grimaud crossed the public room of the inn with all eyes on them — and proceeded to take possession of the best room in the establishment, which they occupied with authority.

In the meantime, the first host, joined now by his wife, hurried down with lamps into the cellar that had so long been closed to them, and where a frightful spectacle awaited.

The fortifications through which Athos had made a breach in order to get out were composed of firewood, planks, and empty casks, heaped up according to all the rules of siege defense. Beyond that, the hosts found the rinds of all the bacon Athos and Grimaud had eaten, swimming in puddles of oil and wine. Of fifty large sausages suspended from the joists, scarcely ten remained. A heap of broken bottles filled the whole left-hand corner of the cellar, and a tun, the tap of which was left running, was yielding by this means the last drops of its brandy.

The lamentations of the two hosts pierced the vault of the cellar and were heard above. D'Artagnan was most moved by them. Athos did not even turn her head.

Then grief was succeeded by rage. Both hosts rushed up the stairs and into the chamber occupied by the two friends and their valets. Madame Host was a sturdy figure of russet-toned complexion, emerald eyes, and long raven locks streaked with gold — but of more immediate note was the spit with which she had armed herself.

"Some wine, if you please," said Athos on perceiving them both.

"Some wine?" cried the stupefied Monsieur Host. "Some wine? Why you have drunk more than a hundred pistoles' worth! We are ruined! Bankrupt! Destroyed!"

"It is hardly our fault," said Athos. "The gloom of a cellar leaves one always thirsty."

"If you had been contented with drinking, well and good," howled Madame Host. "But you have broken all the bottles."

"Your haranguing of my person caused me to fall upon a stack which then rolled down," replied Athos. "That was your fault."

"All our olive oil is lost!"

"Oil is a sovereign balm for wounds, and my poor Grimaud here was obliged to dress those you had inflicted on her."

"All my sausages are gnawed!" stated the monsieur.

"There is an enormous quantity of rats in that cellar."

"You shall pay for all this!" cried the exasperated madame.

"Thrice-doomed knaves!" said Athos, rising — but she sank down again immediately, the effort having tried her strength to the utmost.

D'Artagnan came to her relief, stepping in with her whip in hand. Both hosts then drew back, and monsieur burst into tears.

"This will teach you," said d'Artagnan, "to treat the guests fate sends you in a more courteous fashion."

"Fate? Say instead a curse!" howled madame. "We were forced to pay reward for the return of two horses you stole, and what's more, their offended owners had already claimed three of the horses you left behind!"

"Yes, well," said d'Artagnan, growing slightly less imperious. For until that moment, she had all but forgotten the borrowed horses that had gotten her and Planchet to Calais. "Be that as it may, if you continue to annoy us in this manner, we will all four go and shut ourselves up in your cellar. And we will see then if the mischief is as great as you say."

"Oh, gentlefolk," said Monsieur Host, still weeping, "we have been wrong, I confess it. We were betrayed by lies and have paid the price. But let that payment now end, we implore you. You are gentles, and we are but poor innkeepers. Please have pity on us."

"Ah, if you speak in that way," said Athos, "you will break my heart, and the tears will flow from my eyes as the wine flowed from the cask. We are not such villains as we appear to be. One of you come hither, and let us talk."

Madame Host approached. Monsieur nodded tearfully, then slipped away.

"Come hither, I say, and don't be afraid," said Athos to madame. "At the very moment when I was about to pay your husband, I had placed my purse on the table."

"Yes, madame."

"That purse contained sixty pistoles. Where is it?"

"Deposited with the governor. Though it was not their orders to seize it, they accepted it as bad money."

"Very well. Get me my purse back and keep the sixty pistoles."

"But madame knows very well that no governor lets go of coin they lay hold of."

"Manage the matter as well as you can, my good ser. It does not concern me, the more so as I have not a livre left."

To that, Madame Host began to flush with anger, but d'Artagnan stepped forth.

"Come," said she, "let us inquire further. You said three of our horses were taken. Does this mean one remains of the four that brought us here?"

"Yes, for it is in the stable still."

"How much is it worth?"

"Well… after its feed and grooming, thirty pistoles at most," said Madame Host cautiously.

"The least of our horses would be worth fifty. Keep the steed, and there ends the matter."

"What?" cried Athos. "Are you selling my horse? And pray tell, what shall I be riding when I make my next campaign? Grimaud perhaps?"

"Most like I am selling Grimaud's horse. But anyway, I have brought you another," said d'Artagnan. "Finer and younger."

"Another horse? Why then, you may take the old one, innkeeper. And let us eat and drink."

"By my faith, drink what?" asked Madame Host, though she began to grow more cheerful.

"Some of what remains at the bottom of the cellar, hidden beneath a bundle of laths. There are twenty-five bottles of it left. All the rest were broken by my fall. Bring six of them."

"Oh, blessed fortune," said Madame Host. "If madame remains here a fortnight and pays for what she drinks, we shall soon reestablish our business."

"And don't forget," said d'Artagnan, "to bring up four bottles of the same sort for the two English gentles."

"And now," said Athos as Madame Host departed, "while they bring the wine — tell me, d'Artagnan, what has become of the others."

So d'Artagnan related how she had found Porthos in bed with a sprained knee, and Aramis at a table between two theologians. She described the gratitude with which each had accepted the gift of a fine horse to rival Athos's new mount, and of plans to pick up both on the return to Paris. As she finished, Monsieur Host entered with the wine ordered, along with a ham that — fortunately for all — had been left out of the cellar.

"Then all is well," said Athos, filling her glass and that of her friend. "Here's to Porthos and Aramis!"

When Planchet and Grimaud had eaten, the two valets went out to see to the horses, leaving Athos and d'Artagnan alone. Athos was in fine spirits, but d'Artagnan's mood, after the joy of finding her friend, had begun to grow somber once more.

Athos noted it, and spoke. "But what is the matter with you, d'Artagnan? And what has happened to you alongside the trials of our Porthos and Aramis? For I cannot mistake that you have a sad air."

"Alas," said d'Artagnan, "it is because I am the most unfortunate."

"Tell me."

"In time," said d'Artagnan.

"In time? And why not now? Because you think I am drunk? D'Artagnan, remember this. My ideas are never so clear as when I have had plenty of wine. Speak, then. I am all ears."

And so d'Artagnan further related her adventure with Constance Bonacieux. Athos listened to her without expression. And when d'Artagnan had finished, the musketeer said, "Trifles. Only trifles."

"My life and cares are no trifles, my dear Athos," said d'Artagnan, hurt somewhat by her friend's reaction. "And that comes very ill from you, who have never loved."

The drink-deadened eye of Athos flashed brightly — but only for a moment. Then it became as dull and vacant as before.

"That's true," said she quietly. "For my part, I have never loved."

"Acknowledge, then, your stony heart," said d'Artagnan. "And that you are wrong to be so hard upon us tender hearts."

"Tender hearts? Wounded hearts, I say."

"What do you mean?"

"I mean that love is a lottery in which they who win, win death. You are very fortunate to have lost, believe me, my dear d'Artagnan. And if I have any counsel to give, it is this: In the game of love, always seek to lose."

"But Constance seemed to love me so."

"She seemed, did she?"

"I mean she did love me.

"You child. Why, there is not a person alive who has not believed as you do that a paramour loved them. And there lives not a person who has not been deceived by a paramour."

"Except such as you, Athos, who never had one."

"That's true," said Athos after a moment's silence. "That is true. Let us drink!"

"But then, philosopher that you are," said d'Artagnan, "instruct me. Support me. I stand in need of being taught and consoled."

"Consoled for what?"

"For my misfortune."

"Your misfortune is laughable," said Athos, drunkenly shrugging her shoulders. "I should like to know what you would say if I were to relate to you a real tale of love…"

"Which has happened to you?"

"Or one of my friends. What does it matter?"

"Tell it, then, Athos. Tell it."

"It is better if I drink."

"Drink and relate, then."

"Not a bad idea," said Athos, emptying and refilling her glass. "The two things agree marvelously well."

"I am all attention," said d'Artagnan.

Athos collected herself. And as she did so, d'Artagnan saw that she became pale. She was at that point of intoxication at which mundane drinkers might fall on the floor and go to sleep. But instead, the musketeer kept herself upright and dreamed, without sleeping — and this somnambulism of drunkenness had something frightful in it.

"One of my friends… that is, one of my friends, please to observe, and not myself…" Even as she spoke, Athos interrupted herself with a melancholy smile. "You particularly wish this story?" asked the musketeer.

"I pray for it," said d'Artagnan.

"Be it then as you desire. One of the gentry of my province… a land near Artois and Flanders, but it is not necessary to know the name. A gentry known to me, at twenty-five years of age, fell in love with a young man of twenty, as beautiful as fancy can paint. Through the ingenuousness of his age beamed an ardent mind, not of the gentlefolk but of the poet. He did not please. Rather, he intoxicated.

"This young poet lived in a small town with his sister, who was an acolyte of the Benedictines. Both had only recently come into that part of the realm. From whence they came, no one knew. But when seeing him so lovely and her so pious, no one thought of asking. They were said to be of good extraction, and that was easily believed. My friend was gracious to newcomers, and might have simply been friendly to the pair. She might have engaged in some flirtation with the young man, or indulged a friendship of letters. Unfortunately, she was a romantic. She fell in love with and married him. The fool…"

"How so a fool, if she did love him?" asked d'Artagnan.

"Wait to hear," said Athos. "This gentry took her new lord to her chateau, and anointed him one of the premier gentlefolk of the province. And by faith, through his wit and intellect, he engaged that position admirably…"

"And then?" asked d'Artagnan.

"And then one day when this gentry and her new lord were hunting," said Athos, her voice low and speaking quickly, "he fell from his horse and struck his head. My friend flew to him to help, and as he appeared to be labored in breathing by the tightness of his jacket, she ripped it open with her dagger. And in so doing, this gentry laid bare his lordship's shoulder, which had theretofore been covered always from modesty with nightshirt or chemise."

Then Athos gave forth a maniacal burst of laughter. "D'Artagnan," said she. "Guess what he had on his shoulder."

"How can I guess?" said d'Artagnan.

"The fleur-de-lis of justice," said Athos. "This young lord was branded as a felon thief."

Athos emptied at a single draught the glass she held in her hand.

D'Artagnan sat in silence a while, then spoke. "What do you tell me?"

"The truth, my friend. The angel was a fiend. The young lord was a thief — caught, unrepentant, convicted, and branded for having stolen the sacred vessels of a convent."

"And what did your friend do?"

"As she was wont to do. She was of the highest gentry — and prone to blind rage. She returned to their home. She turned through her young lord's effects, holding him at sword point while he raged, his countenance turned bestial with his secret revealed. She found letters intimating affairs both illegal and immoral. She found sachets of poisons, procured of an apothecary, which were claimed to be medicinal, and she feared then for her own life."

"Athos…" d'Artagnan whispered. "By my faith…"

"But it was all too much for my friend," continued Athos, as if not having heard. "She had on her estates the rights of high and low tribunals. She tore the shirt of the young lord off him, and ripped it to shreds. She tied his hands behind him… and hanged him on a tree."

"By my faith, Athos!" cried d'Artagnan. "A murder to pay for theft and lies?"

"No less," said Athos, as pale as a corpse. "But I believe I need wine…" And she seized by the neck the last bottle that was left, put it to her mouth, and emptied it at a single draught as one would empty an ordinary glass. Then she let her head sink upon her two hands, while d'Artagnan sat before her, stupefied.

"That story has cured me of love," said Athos after a considerable pause. She raised her head then, forgetting to continue the fiction of the friend. "That day cured me of all desire for beautiful and poetical paramours. Now I hope it grant you as much. Let us drink."

"Then he is dead?" stammered d'Artagnan. "This lord of yours?"

"Great gods," said Athos, "hold out your glass! Then have some ham, my friend, if we can drink no more."

"And his sister?" added d'Artagnan timidly.

"His sister?" replied Athos, uncertain.

"Yes, the acolyte."

"Ah, yes. I inquired after her for the purpose of investigating her story. Over time, I traced her to her home. What I learned there corroborated all I knew… but she had died by that time."

"Was it ever known her involvement in all this?"

"Yes, for she was the first lover and accomplice of the beautiful lord. A tortured young woman, who had pretended to be her paramour's sister so as to enable him marrying into a position that would serve them both."

"Gods' blood," whispered d'Artagnan, quite stunned by the relation of this horrible adventure.

"Taste some of this ham, d'Artagnan," said Athos. "It is exquisite." She cut a slice, which she placed on the young guard's plate. "What a pity it is that there were not four like this in the cellar. To accompany such a feast, I could have drunk fifty bottles more."

D'Artagnan could no longer endure this conversation, which she felt might push her to madness. Allowing her head to sink upon her two hands, she pretended to sleep.

"These young soldiers. Not a one can hold their drink," said Athos, looking at her with pity. "And yet this is one of the best."

— CHAPTER 28 —

THE RETURN

All that night, d'Artagnan remained in a frantic state in response to the terrible secret of Athos. Yet many things appeared very obscure to her in this half revelation. In the first place, the confession had been made by one quite drunk to one who was half drunk. But in spite of the uncertainty that three or four bottles of burgundy carries with it to the brain, when the young guard awoke the following morning, she had all the words of Athos as present in her memory as if the musketeer had spoken them once more in front of her. The tale had been so impressed upon her mind that it gave rise to a most intense desire of knowing the truth of it.

She thus went into her friend's chamber with a fixed determination of renewing the conversation of the preceding evening. But to her shock, d'Artagnan found Athos quite herself again — which is to say, demonstrating a most shrewd and impenetrable character. That notwithstanding, the musketeer, after having exchanged a hearty shake of the hand with d'Artagnan, broached the matter first.

"I was famously drunk yesterday, d'Artagnan," said she. "I can tell that by my tongue, which was swollen and hot this morning, and by my pulse, which was very tremulous. I wager that I uttered a thousand extravagances." While saying this, she looked at her friend with a profound earnestness.

"No," said d'Artagnan, flustered. "If I recollect well what you said, it was nothing out of the common way."

"Ah, you surprise me. I thought I had told you a most lamentable story." And Athos looked at the young guard as if she might read the bottom of her heart.

"My faith," said d'Artagnan shrewdly. "It appears that I was more drunk than you, since I remember nothing of the kind. Pray, what story do you think you told?"

Athos's expression made clear that she did not trust the young guard's reply. "You cannot have failed to remark, my dear friend, that everyone has their particular kind of drunkenness, sad or jovial. My drunkenness is always sad. And when I am thoroughly drunk, my mania is to relate all the mournful stories which folk, starting with my foolish nurse, have inculcated into my brain. That is my failing — a capital failing, I admit. But with that exception, I am a good drinker."

"It is such a tale, then," said d'Artagnan, anxious to find out the truth. "It is such a tale that I remember as one might remember a dream. We were speaking of hanging."

"Ah, you see how it is?" said Athos, becoming still paler but yet attempting to laugh. "I was sure it was so. For the hanging of innocent people is my nightmare."

"Yes, yes," said d'Artagnan. "I remember now. Yes, it was about… wait a moment… yes, it was about a young lord."

"That's it," said Athos, and her easy manner was obscured by a sudden anger. "That is my grand story of the deceitful young lord, and when I relate that, I must be very drunk."

"Indeed," said d'Artagnan. "The story of a tall, beautiful lord, with blue eyes."

"Yes, who was hanged."

"By his wife. Who was a gentry of your acquaintance," said d'Artagnan, looking intently at Athos.

"Well, you see how one might compromise themself when they do not know what they say," replied the musketeer, shrugging her shoulders as if she thought herself an object of pity. "I certainly never will get drunk again, d'Artagnan. It is too bad a habit."

D'Artagnan remained silent. And then changing the conversation all at once, Athos said, "By the by, I thank you for the horse you have brought me."

"Is it to your liking?" asked the young guard, content to let the matter drop.

"Yes. But it is not a horse for hard work."

"You are mistaken. I rode it nearly ten leagues in less than an hour and a half, and the steed appeared no more distressed than if it had only made the tour of the Place Saint-Sulpice."

"Ah. You begin to awaken my regret, then."

"Regret?"

"Yes. I have parted with it."

"What?" said d'Artagnan, uncertain.

"Well, here is the simple fact," said Athos. "This morning, I awoke at dawn. You were still fast asleep, and I did not know what to do with myself. I was still stupefied from our last night's debauch. As I came into the public room, I saw one English traveler bargaining with a dealer for a horse, their own having died yesterday from bleeding. I drew near, and found they were bidding a hundred pistoles for a chestnut nag.

" 'Faith,' said I. 'My good gentle, I too have a horse to sell.'

" 'Aye, and a very fine one,' said they. 'I saw it yesterday when your friend's valet was leading it.'

" 'Do you think it is worth a hundred pistoles?' asked I.

" 'Most certainly. Will you sell it to me for that sum?'

" 'No, but I will play for the fine beast at dice.' And no sooner said than done, and I lost the horse. But!" cried Athos. "Please to observe I won back the caparison, saddle, and other tack."

D'Artagnan looked much astounded.

"This vexes you?" said Athos.

"I must confess it does," said d'Artagnan sharply. "That horse was to have identified us in parade and in battle. It was a pledge, a remembrance. Athos, you have done wrong."

"But my dear friend, put yourself in my place," said the musketeer. "I was bored near to death. And still further, upon my honor, I don't like English horses. If the steed's purpose is only to be recognized, why the saddle will suffice for that. It is quite remarkable enough. As to the horse, we can easily find some excuse for its disappearance. Why, a horse is mortal. Suppose mine had got the glanders?"

D'Artagnan did not smile.

"It vexes me greatly," sighed Athos, "that you attach so much importance to these animals. For I am not yet at the end of my story."

"Indeed? What else have you done?"

"After having lost my own horse, nine against ten… you see how near I came to winning? Well, after that, I came to the idea of staking yours."

"And you stopped at the idea, I hope?"

"No. For I put it in execution that very moment."

"And the consequence?" cried d'Artagnan in great anxiety.

"I threw, and I lost."

"What? You lost my horse?"

"Your horse, seven against eight."

"Athos, you are not in your right mind, I swear!"

"My dear friend, that was yesterday. When I was telling you silly stories, it was proper to tell me that, but not this morning. For I lost the horse in the morning, with all its equipment and caparison."

"This is extraordinary!" said d'Artagnan, who had begun to pace. "This is madness!"

"Stop a moment, for you don't know all yet. I should make an excellent gamer if I were not so hotheaded. But I do get hotheaded, just as if I had been drinking. And when I am…"

"But what matter? What else could you play for? You had nothing left."

"Oh, yes, my friend. There was still that diamond left which sparkles on your finger, and which I had observed yesterday."

"This diamond?" said d'Artagnan, placing her hand protectively over her ring.

"And as I am a connoisseur of such things, having had a few of my own once, I estimated it at six hundred pistoles."

"I hope," said d'Artagnan, half dead with fright, "that you made no mention of my diamond?"

"On the contrary, my dear friend, this diamond became our only resource. With it, I would regain our horses and their equipment, and even money to pay our expenses on the road."

"Athos, you drive me to panic!" cried d'Artagnan.

"I mentioned your diamond then to my adversary, who had likewise noted it. Really, my dear, do you think you can wear a star on your finger and have no one observe it? Impossible!"

"To the point," said d'Artagnan. "For upon my honor, you will kill me with this meandering tale."

"We divided, then, this diamond into ten parts of sixty pistoles each."

"This must be jest," said d'Artagnan, her anger rising. "You mean to try me."

"No, I do not jest, by faith. I should like to have seen what you might do in my place. For I had been ten days without seeing a human face, and had been left to brutalize myself in the company of bottles."

"That was no reason for staking my diamond," said d'Artagnan, closing her hand with a nervous spasm.

"Hear the end. Ten parts of sixty pistoles each, in ten throws. And in thirteen throws, I had lost all. In thirteen throws! The number thirteen was always fatal to me. In fact, it was on the thirteenth of July that —"

"Gods' blood!" cried d'Artagnan, slamming her hands to the table. The story of the present day had quite made her forget the tale of the preceding one.

"Patience," said Athos. "For I had a plan. The English gentle is ambitious. I had seen them conversing that morning with Grimaud, and Grimaud had told me that this gentle had made her proposals to enter into their service. I staked Grimaud, the silent Grimaud, divided into ten portions."

"Well, what next?" said d'Artagnan, quite beside herself.

"Well, the ten parts of Grimaud, understand, are of great sentimental value to me, but of perhaps questionable market worth — but in spite of which, I regained the diamond. Tell me, now, if persistence is not a virtue?"

"My faith, I can laugh now," said d'Artagnan, who was not laughing.

"But you may guess that finding my luck turned, I once again staked the diamond on another round."

"You did what, by gods?" said d'Artagnan, becoming angrier still.

"What I did was win back your tack, then your horse, then my tack, then my horse, and then I lost again. In brief, I regained your tack and then mine. That's where we are. My last throw was superb, so I left off there."

D'Artagnan felt as if the whole inn had been placed on, then removed from her chest. "Then the diamond is safe?" said she, carefully.

"Secure, my dear friend. As is the tack of your steed and mine."

"But what is the use of caparison, saddle, and all the rest without horses?"

"I have an idea about that."

"Athos, you make me shudder."

"Listen to me." The musketeer stood to stand beside d'Artagnan, setting a hand to her shoulder. "You have not gamed for a long time, d'Artagnan."

"And I have no inclination to."

"Swear to nothing. You have not gamed for a long time, I said. You ought, then, to have good luck."

"A nonsensical statement by any standard. And so what if so?"

"Well, the English gentle and their companions are still here. I noted that they regretted the loss of the caparison and other tack very much. You appear to think much of your horse. In your place, I would stake the equipment against the horse."

"But they will not wish for only one set of tack."

"Stake both, by faith! I am not selfish, as you are."

"You would do so?" said d'Artagnan, who was inexplicably feeling the confidence of Athos begin to prevail upon her — in spite of herself.

"On my honor, in one single throw."

"But having lost the horses, I am particularly anxious to preserve the tack."

"Stake your diamond, then."

"That's another matter. Never!"

"Fie!" said Athos. "I would propose to you to stake Planchet, but as a valet has already been wagered, the English would not, perhaps, be willing."

"Decidedly, my dear Athos," said d'Artagnan, "I should like better not to risk anything."

"That's a pity," said Athos coolly. "The gentle is overflowing with pistoles. Gods' blood, try one throw! One throw is easily made!"

"And if I lose?"

"You will win."

"But if I lose?"

"Well, you will surrender the tack."

D'Artagnan thought long. The loss of the horse pained her, and Athos's talk of the young guard being owed good luck had its attractive qualities, to be sure. And indeed, her having so successfully reclaimed her three friends might seem a sign to some that her own fortune was already in ascendance.

So it was that finally said she, "I am with you for one throw!"

Athos and D'Artagnan then went in quest of the English gentle, whom they found in the stable examining the caparison formerly of both horses with notable jealousy. The gentle was of an age with Athos at some thirty years, with a deep umber complexion, and a lofty look given increased gravitas by piercing black eyes and close-cropped hair of jet black. But their proud frown turned to a smile in response to the opportunity Athos presented.

The musketeer proposed the conditions — both sets of tack, either against one horse or a hundred pistoles. The gentle calculated fast that the tack together was easily worth three hundred pistoles. Thus they consented.

D'Artagnan threw the dice with a trembling hand — and turned up the number three.

"That is a sad throw, comrade," said Athos.

D'Artagnan's remorse and anger rose in response, but Athos avoided it by focusing on the gentle, saying only, "It appears you will have both horses fully equipped, maitre."

The English gentle, quite triumphant, barely gave themself the trouble to shake the dice as they tossed them to the table, so sure were they of victory. D'Artagnan forced herself to turn aside to conceal her ill humor.

"But hold," said Athos, who did look, in her quiet tone. "That throw of the dice is extraordinary. Two aces!"

The English gentle was likewise staring, and seized with horror. D'Artagnan looked and was seized with joy.

"Yes," said Athos, "I once performed the same roll at a cabaret, where I lost a hundred pistoles and a supper on it."

"Then madame takes her horse back again," said the gentle grimly. "It shall be restored to your valet."

"A moment," said Athos. "With your permission, maitre, I wish to speak a word with my friend."

"Speak on."

Athos drew d'Artagnan aside.

"Well, tempter, what more do you want with me?" said d'Artagnan. "You want me to throw again, do you not?"

"No. I would wish only for you to reflect."

"On what?"

"You mean to take your horse?"

"Without doubt."

"You are wrong, then. I would take the hundred pistoles. You know you have staked the tack against the horse or a hundred pistoles, at your choice."

"Yes."

"Well, then, I repeat that you are wrong. What is the use of one horse for us two? I could not ride behind, and you cannot think of humiliating me by prancing along by my side on that magnificent charger. For my part, I should not hesitate a moment. I should take the hundred pistoles. We want money for our return to Paris."

"I am much attached to that horse, Athos."

"And there again you are wrong. A horse slips and injures a joint. A horse stumbles and breaks its knees to the bone. A horse eats out of a manger in which a sickened horse has eaten. And then you have no horse, while on the contrary, another gentle with a hundred pistoles can eat."

"But how shall we get back?"

"Upon post horses, by faith, as we would have had to hire for the valets regardless, and paid for from the proceeds. Anyone may see by our bearing alone that we are people of consequence. The horse matters not."

"Fine figures we shall cut on hired ponies while Aramis and Porthos caracole on their steeds."

"Aramis and Porthos?" said Athos, and she laughed aloud.

"What is it?" asked d'Artagnan, who did not at all comprehend the hilarity of her friend.

"Nothing, nothing. Simply an expectation. But go on."

"Your advice, then?"

"To take the hundred pistoles, d'Artagnan. With the hundred pistoles, we can live well to the end of the month. We have undergone a great deal of fatigue, remember, and a little rest will do no harm."

"I rest? Oh no, Athos. Once in Paris, I must begin my search for Constance Bonacieux."

"Well, you may be assured that no horse will be half so serviceable to you for that purpose as good gold coin. Take the hundred pistoles, my friend. Take the hundred pistoles."

In truth, d'Artagnan had required only one reason to agree with Athos's assessment — and this last thought of the musketeer was well convincing. She acquiesced, therefore, and chose the hundred pistoles, which the English gentle paid on the spot. The gentle then also delivered contemptuous laughter at d'Artagnan's folly, defending their failed throw by lauding the advantage they had received in claiming two horses for such a paltry sum. By then, however, d'Artagnan was weary of the whole affair, and she and Athos ignored the insult, determined to simply depart.

Peace with the hosts of the inn, in addition to the claimed horse, cost six pistoles. D'Artagnan and Athos confirmed the hire of a pair of serviceable post horses, while Planchet and Grimaud arranged to ride as passengers in a market cart returning empty to Paris, carrying the saddles and other tack. This passage was paid for by agreeing to slake the carter's thirst along the route, toward which d'Artagnan contributed half a crown, and Athos contributed one of three bottles of wine liberated from the Golden Lily's cellar while both hosts' backs were turned.

However poorly our two friends were mounted, they were soon far in advance of the valets on their cart, and arrived at Crevecoeur. As they approached the Miller's Arms, they could see Aramis, seated in a melancholy manner at their window, looking out along the road to Rouen.

"Ho, Aramis! What in faith are you doing up there?" called d'Artagnan.

"Ah, is that you, d'Artagnan? And Athos, my dear friend!" called the gentle musketeer. "I was reflecting upon the rapidity with which the blessings of this world leave us. My English horse, which has just disappeared along the road amid a cloud of dust, has furnished me with a living image of the fragility of the things of the earth. Life itself may be resolved into seven words: 'It will be, it is, it was.'"

"Which means…" said d'Artagnan, who heard the revelation in her friend's prose.

"Which means that I have just been duped into accepting sixty pistoles in trade for a horse which, by the manner of its gait, can do at least five leagues an hour."

D'Artagnan and Athos laughed aloud.

"My dear d'Artagnan," called down Aramis, "don't be too angry with me, I beg. Necessity has no law. Besides, I am the person punished, as that rascally horse dealer has robbed me of fifty pistoles at least. Ah, you both are excellent managers of your own mounts, I see. You ride on post horses, and no doubt have your own gallant steeds led along carefully by hand at short stages."

Aramis then left the window and descended, stepping out at last to the yard of the inn to greet their friends. But at the same moment, the market cart pulled up at the inn, and Planchet and Grimaud hopped off it to reveal the saddles and tack well stowed.

"What is this?" said Aramis on seeing them arrive. "Nothing but saddles?"

"Now do you understand our laughter?" said Athos.

"My friends, this is exactly like me. I retained my tack by instinct. Ho, Bazin!" called Aramis up to the window. "We depart at once. Bring that new tack and arrange it for transport along with those of these gentles."

"And what have you done with your clerics?" asked d'Artagnan.

"My dear friend, I invited them to a lunch yesterday," said Aramis. "They have some capital wine here, as it happens, and I did my best to make them drunk. When I was done, the curate forbade me to abandon my uniform, and the Jesuit entreated me to get her made a musketeer."

"But without a thesis," laughed d'Artagnan. "I demand the suppression of the thesis."

"Since their departure," said Aramis, "I have lived very agreeably. I have begun a poem in verses of one syllable. That is rather difficult, but the merit in all things consists in the difficulty. The subject is most gallant. I will read you the first canto. It has four hundred lines, and lasts but a minute."

"By faith, my dear Aramis," said d'Artagnan, who detested verses almost as much as she did Latin. "Add brevity to the merit of the difficulty, and you may be sure that your poem will at least have two merits."

"You will see," said Aramis, with mock disdain, "that it breathes irreproachable passion. But another time, perhaps. And so, my friends, we return to Paris? Bravo! We will rejoin Porthos, and so much the better. You can't think how I have missed him, the great simpleton. To see him so self-satisfied will reconcile me with myself. Ah, but he will have a better head than all of us. He would not sell his horse, not for all the realm. I can imagine him now, mounted upon his superb steed and seated in his handsome saddle. I am sure he will look like some great emperor."

Before setting out again, the three made time for an hour's lunch, to refresh the horses. Aramis then paid their bill at the Miller's Arms, placed Bazin in the cart with his comrades, claimed the post horse d'Artagnan and her pistoles had ordered, and the three friends and their valets went forth to join Porthos.

⚜

The three arrived in Chantilly before sunset, and at the inn of Great Saint-Martine, they found the tall musketeer up and about, and less ashen than when d'Artagnan left him after her first visit. He was not in his room but in a private dining salon, seated at a table on which was spread enough for four persons, though he sat alone. This grand supper consisted of meats nicely dressed, choice wines, and superb fruit.

"Ah, by my faith!" said Porthos, rising to embrace Athos and Aramis in turn. "You come in the nick of time, gentles. I was just beginning the soup, and you will dine with me."

"But wait," said d'Artagnan as all sat. "Mousqueton has not caught these bottles with her lasso. Nor has she stolen this piquant stew or fillet of beef, I would wager."

"I am restoring my strength," said Porthos. "Nothing weakens a warrior more than these cursed sprains. Did you ever suffer from a sprain, Athos?"

"Never. Though recovering from the sword wound I obtained in our affair of the Rue Ferou took a surprising length of time."

Porthos nervously looked at the others in turn. But all were wise enough to avoid any further discussion of the state of the musketeer's sprain.

"But this meal was not intended for you alone, Porthos?" said Aramis, to change the subject.

"No," said Porthos. "I expected some gentlefolk of the neighborhood, who have just sent me word they could not come. You will take their places and I shall not lose by the exchange. Ho, Mousqueton! Bring chairs, and order double the bottles!"

So the three availed themselves of the feast. Many tales were told, including Aramis sharing the details of d'Artagnan engaging in priestly debate in Crevecoeur, and d'Artagnan sharing the broadest details of her rescue of Athos from the cellar of the Golden Lily. But though the elder musketeer nodded to key details, she ate in silence.

"Do you know what we are eating here?" said Athos finally, at a break in the tales.

"By faith," said d'Artagnan, "for my part, I am eating veal garnished with vegetables."

"And I some lamb cutlets," said Porthos.

"And I a chicken," said Aramis.

"You are all mistaken, gentles," answered Athos gravely. "You are eating horse."

"Eating what?" cried d'Artagnan.

"Horse?" said Aramis, with a grimace of dismay.

Porthos made no reply but a scowl.

"Yes, horse. For are we not dining on the worth of your steed, Porthos? And perhaps its saddle therewith?"

"No, sers!" cried Porthos defiantly. Then he added, "For I have kept the saddle."

"My faith," said Aramis. "The fourth horse sold. One would think we had done all this by agreement."

"What could I do?" said Porthos. "This horse made my visitors ashamed of theirs, and I don't like to humiliate people."

"Then your duchess is still indisposed?" asked d'Artagnan.

"Yes, still," said Porthos. "And by my faith, the governor of the province — one of the gentles I expected today — seemed to have such a wish for my fine steed that I gave it to her."

"Gave it?" cried d'Artagnan.

"Gods, yes, that is the word," said Porthos. "For the animal was worth at least a hundred and fifty pistoles, and the stingy scoundrel would give me only eighty."

"Without the saddle?" said Aramis.

"Yes, for I kept saddle, harness, and caparison."

"You will observe, gentles," said Athos, "that Porthos has made the best bargain of any of us."

And then commenced a roar of laughter in which they all joined, to the astonishment of poor Porthos. But when he was informed of the cause of their hilarity, he shared it vociferously.

"There is one comfort," said d'Artagnan. "We are all in cash."

"Speak for yourself," said Athos. "For on my part, I found Aramis's Spanish wine of lunch so good that I sent on a hamper of sixty bottles of it in the wagon with the valets. That has weakened my purse."

"And I," said Aramis, "have given almost my last sou to the church of Montdidier and the Jesuits of Amiens, with whom I had made engagements which I am forced to keep. For I have paid for celebratory prayers to be said for myself and for all you gentles, and have not the least doubt that we will all be marvelously benefited."

"And as to I," said Porthos, "do you think my sprain cost me nothing? And I must also reckon Mousqueton's wound, for which I had to have the healer twice a day, and who charged me double on account of the foolish valet having allowed themself a bullet in a spot which people generally only show to an apothecary. So I advised them to try never to get wounded there again."

"Aye," said Athos, exchanging a smile with d'Artagnan and Aramis. "It is very clear you acted nobly in their regard. That is like a good employer."

"In short," said Porthos, "when all my expenses are paid, I shall have, at most, thirty crowns left."

"And I about ten pistoles," said Aramis.

"Well, then it appears that we are the royals of this society," said Athos. "How much have you left of your hundred pistoles, d'Artagnan?"

"How do you speak of my hundred pistoles? For I gave you fifty."

"You think so?"

"Indeed, by my faith!"

"Ah, that is true. I recollect it now."

"Then I paid the hosts of the inn six."

"What brutes! Why did you give them six pistoles?"

"You told me to do so."

"It is true. I am too good natured. In brief, after all that and the hire of the horses, how much remains?"

"Twenty-five pistoles," said d'Artagnan.

"And I," said Athos, taking some small change from her pocket. "I have…"

"You? Nothing!"

"My faith! So little that it is not worth reckoning with the general stock. So now then, let us calculate how much we possess in all. Porthos?"

"Thirty crowns."

"Aramis?"

"Ten pistoles."

"And you, d'Artagnan?"

"Twenty-five pistoles."

"That makes in all?" said Athos.

"Three livres to the crown… each pistole at ten livres… four hundred and forty livres," said d'Artagnan, who reckoned quick as a shopkeeper.

"Then upon our arrival in Paris, we should still hold four hundred, besides all the lost horses' tack," said Porthos.

"But what shall we ride as our regimental mounts?" said Aramis.

"Well," said Athos, "of the horses of Monsieur de Treville's stables, we can claim two fit for real riding without inspiring anyone's ire, and for those two, we will draw lots. With the four hundred livres, we will afford half a horse for one of the unmounted. And we will then give the turnings out of our pockets to d'Artagnan, who has a steady hand, and will go and play in the first gaming house we come to. There!"

"Let us dine, then," said Porthos. "For this meal paid for by horse is getting cold."

Then the friends, at ease with regard to the future, did honor to the banquet, with plenty remaining for Mousqueton, who later dined alongside Planchet, Grimaud, and Bazin when the cart arrived.

The next day brought the group finally to Paris — on, as luck would have it, the fifteenth day of the fifteen-day leaves of absence they had won from Monsieur de Treville. Thus ready to return to duty and with no explanations for their absence to be made, all passed the travel in ease.

All, that is, except d'Artagnan. For as the joy of having retrieved her friends ebbed, the young guard's thoughts turned unremittingly to Constance Bonacieux. Her mood grew anxious with fretting over the need to seek out the missing tailor — and to seek a furious revenge on those who had abducted her.

She returned first to the Rue de Fossoyeurs, knocking at the door of Constance and her husband, though to no response within. After noting no letters at her own door, d'Artagnan then went to seek her comrades. But when she did, she found them deeply preoccupied. All were assembled in council at the residence of Athos, which always indicated an event of some gravity.

To the musketeers, word had come of new strife among the Huguenots, and of the English making action once more to support them in La Rochelle. Monsieur de Treville had announced their majesties' fixed intention to open a new campaign against the Huguenots in less than three weeks' time, which would see both Treville's musketeers and the guards of Madame d'Essarts join other forces at La Rochelle.

All the friends thus understood that they must immediately prepare their equipment of campaign — arms and armor, horse and saddle, harness and other tack, luggage and supplies, and all the same again for a valet. The equipment of campaign was a pretty expense, for which each soldier was individually responsible — and which caused the three musketeers to look at one another in a state of unrest.

"But what do you reckon this equipment will cost?" said d'Artagnan.

"We can scarcely say," replied Aramis. "Even making calculations with austere economy, we might each require fifteen hundred livres."

"Four times fifteen makes sixty… six thousand livres," said d'Artagnan. "By my faith, I cannot imagine securing even a thousand livres for myself. A contract of this amount would require an inheritance and an attorney to dispense!"

At d'Artagnan's words, Porthos glanced up, suddenly attentive. "Hold," said he. "I may have an idea."

"Well that's something, for I have not even the shadow of one," said Athos coolly. "And as to d'Artagnan, gentles, the continued loss of her love has clearly driven her senseless. A thousand livres? For my part, I declare I want two thousand."

"Four times two makes eight," then said Aramis. "It is eight thousand that we want to complete our equipment. Toward which, it is true, we have already harness, caparison, and saddle."

In the end, d'Artagnan took her leave, not wanting to share her despair further with her comrades. And so it was that Athos was thoughtful after she had shut the door behind the young guard.

"Why the Gascon frets on the matter of her equipment, I know not," said Athos. "Besides this unspoken plan of Porthos, there is that beautiful ring which gleams on the finger of our friend. It seems clear to me that in the end, d'Artagnan is the one of us who will most easily meet the obligation to procure her equipment of campaign. For she wears the ransom of a monarch on her finger."

CHAPTER 29

THE HUNT FOR EQUIPMENT

The most preoccupied of the four friends was certainly d'Artagnan, although she, still just a guard of Madame d'Essarts, would be much more easily equipped than three musketeers of rank. Our Gascon cadet was, as may have been observed, of a most provident character. But against that, as was most keenly seen when first met by the reader in Meung, she was at times so proud as almost to rival Porthos.

To this preoccupation of her pride, d'Artagnan at present added an uneasiness much less selfish. For notwithstanding all her inquiries respecting Constance Bonacieux, she could obtain no intelligence of the young tailor.

Monsieur de Treville had spoken of Madame Bonacieux to the Queen Anne, who became almost sick with worry on word of Constance's disappearance from the summerhouse, to which the royal had made arrangements to send the young tailor for her safety. The queen had since received no information regarding Constance's fate, but promised to have her sought for at once. However, d'Artagnan knew that the certainty of Cardinal de Richelieu's involvement — and of how easily their eminence had seemingly gained intelligence as to the queen's plans — would affect Anne's ability to fulfill this promise, which thus did not at all reassure her.

Of the three musketeers, Athos, for her part, did not leave her apartment, as she had made up her mind not to take a single step to equip herself. "We have still time before us," said she to her friends more than once. "Well, if at the end of that time I have found no fortune — or rather, if no fortune has come to find me — I will seek a good quarrel with four of their eminence's guards or with eight English soldiers, and I will fight until one of them has killed me, which, considering the odds, cannot fail to happen. It will then be said of me that I died for the queens, so that I shall have performed my duty without the expense of going on campaign."

Porthos, through those days, continued to walk about with his hands behind him, tossing his head and repeating, "I must follow up on my idea."

Aramis, anxious and negligently dressed by their usual standards, said nothing.

It may be seen by these disastrous details that desolation reigned in our community of friends.

The valets on their part shared the sadness of their employers. Mousqueton collected a store of dried bread against inevitable want. Bazin, who had always been inclined to devotion, was seen in church by day and night. Planchet walked the streets and watched the buzzing of flies. And Grimaud, whom even the general distress could not force to break the silence imposed by her employer, heaved sighs strong enough to soften stones.

The three friends — for as we have said, Athos had sworn not to stir a foot to equip herself — went out early in the morning and returned to their homes late at night. They wandered about the streets, watching the pavement as if to see whether some passerby had not left a purse behind them. They might have been assumed to be following tracks, so observant were they wherever they went. When they met, they looked desolately at one another, as much as to say, "Have you found anything?"

In the end, however, as Porthos had first hatched an idea and had thought of it earnestly afterward, he was the first to act.

Near a week since all had returned to Paris, d'Artagnan saw the tall musketeer one morning walking toward the church of Saint-Leu, and followed him with the intent of catching up. But Porthos entered the church before the young guard could reach him — after having twisted his mustache and stroked out his beard, which always announced on his part the most nefarious intentions. Intrigued, d'Artagnan entered unseen behind him.

Within the church, Porthos went and leaned against the side of a broad pillar. D'Artagnan, still unnoticed, set herself against the other side. There happened to be a sermon in progress, and the church was full of people. Porthos took advantage of this circumstance to ogle the best-dressed folk there. Thanks to the cares of Mousqueton, the exterior of the musketeer had excellently hidden the distress of the interior. His fine hat was a little napless, his feather somewhat faded, his gold lace a little tarnished, and his laces a trifle frayed. But in the shadows of the church, these things went unseen, and Porthos was still the handsomest of musketeers.

On the bench nearest to the pillar against which Porthos leaned, d'Artagnan observed a solemn figure under a black hood. Their tawny skin carried a warm glow even in the shadows, and their intricately tied locks showed highlights of red and yellow where they trailed out from beneath the hood to drape across the figure's breast. From time to time, the eyes of Porthos were furtively cast upon this figure, only to then rove about at large over the nave.

On their side, the person in the black hood from time to time darted with the speed of lightning a glance toward Porthos, but the musketeer's eyes would then immediately glance away. It was plain that this mode of proceeding piqued the watcher, for they bit their lip more than once, and could not sit still in their seat.

D'Artagnan pondered what could be behind her friend's odd behavior. And then she recalled that the church of Saint-Leu was not far from the Rue d'Ours — and recognized by inference that the person of the black hood must be Madame Coquenard, Porthos's paramour attorney of that neighborhood.

Porthos, sensing the young attorney's attention on him, retwisted his mustache and stroked out his beard a second time. But rather than acknowledge the closer look, he began instead to make signals to another figure who was near the choir. This second figure was elegance personified to d'Artagnan's eyes, and no doubt of the gentry. The glow of lamplight from the walls traced across their delicate ochre features, and the ribbons which tied back long tresses of black were the same red as the velvet cushion on which the person knelt. A young servant stood by the cushion, while a second attendant held the emblazoned bag in which was placed the book from which this gentry read the liturgy.

Naturally, the person on the red cushion caught Porthos's attention on them, and glanced back. D'Artagnan saw the musketeer bow and whisper a greeting of, "Delighted, madame." He tipped his hat as he so boldly spoke — and in a way that would ensure Madame Coquenard fully saw the exchange.

"Enchanted, monsieur," was whispered back, and Porthos smiled. The gentry returned her attention to the sermon, smiling likewise.

Beneath her black hood, Madame Coquenard scowled at Porthos's wandering looks and seemingly breathless admonitions, and took in the beauty of this Madame Velvet Cushion with a gleam in her bright-brown eyes. As if sensing this, Porthos made even more a show of things. D'Artagnan could clearly see that the almost imperceptible motions of his eyes, the fingers placed upon the lips, and the delicate smiles aimed at the gentry ahead of him were all for the discomfiture of the disdained attorney at his side.

Then Madame Coquenard murmured, "Ahem!" under cover of the choir's lament, striking her breast so vigorously that everyone, even the gentry with the red cushion, turned round toward her. Porthos paid no attention. Which is to say, he noticed well enough but pretended to be deaf.

D'Artagnan continued to watch these proceedings, which amused her greatly. She guessed by induction that Porthos was taking his revenge for the defeat of Chantilly, when the musketeer's paramour had proved so obstinate with respect to her purse.

The sermon was over quickly thereafter, and Madame Coquenard rose and advanced toward the holy font. Porthos went before her, and instead of a finger, dipped his whole hand in. The attorney smiled, thinking that it was for her that Porthos had put himself to this trouble. But she was promptly undeceived three steps from him, when he turned his head round, fixing his eyes steadfastly upon the gentry with the red cushion, who had risen and was approaching with both her attendants close behind.

When the gentry came close to Porthos, he drew his dripping hand from the font. The elegant worshiper touched the great hand of the musketeer with her delicate fingers, smiled as she then touched that same hand to her heart, and left the church.

This was too much for the musketeer's paramour. From her expression as d'Artagnan saw it, Madame Coquenard had no doubt that there was some intrigue between this beautiful gentry and Porthos. If she had been less measured, she might have attacked him outright. But d'Artagnan guessed that as she was an attorney, she contented herself by speaking to the musketeer with concentrated fury.

"Well, Monsieur Porthos? Will you offer me any holy water?"

Porthos, at the sound of that voice, started like one awakened from a sleep of a hundred years.

"Madame Coquenard!" cried he. "Is that you? And how is your husband, our dear Monsieur Vattier? Where can my eyes have been not to have seen you during the two hours of the sermon?"

"I was within two paces of you, monsieur," replied the attorney coldly. "But you did not perceive me because you had no eyes but for the pretty thing to whom you just now gave the holy water."

Porthos pretended to be confused. "Ah," said he. "You have seen…"

"I would have been blind not to have seen."

"Well," said Porthos, "that is a duchess of my acquaintance, whom I have great trouble to meet on account of the jealousy of her husband. She sent me word that she should come today to this remote church solely for the sake of seeing me."

Where she listened, d'Artagnan smiled at her friend's shamelessness, and understood that Porthos knew this so-called duchess no more than did she. But as the young guard's glance followed that figure of the red cushion where she departed, her eye strayed beyond to another figure also just leaving the church, and heretofore unseen.

It was a tall, pale figure, whose curls and blue eyes d'Artagnan recognized with shock from Meung, and from afar at Dover. For it was he whom Rochefort had saluted that long-ago day by the name of 'Milord.'

"Monsieur Porthos," said Madame Coquenard, "will you have the kindness to offer me your arm for five minutes? I have something to say to you."

"Certainly, madame," said Porthos.

At that moment, d'Artagnan passed by in pursuit of Milord. She cast a passing glance at Porthos and saw his look, which had him smiling as a gamer does when their luck has changed.

"Well," said the young guard, "there is one who will be equipped in good time." But she had no chance to think on Porthos more as she sped from the church.

⚜

Porthos, yielding to the pressure of the arm of Madame Coquenard as a ship yields to the rudder, departed the church and walked a short while before arriving at the cloister Saint-Magloire — a little-frequented courtyard enclosed with a turnstile at each end. In the daytime, no one was seen there but workers taking lunch and children at play.

"Ah, Monsieur Porthos," said the attorney when she was assured that no one of concern could either see or hear her. "You are a great conqueror, as it appears."

"I, madame?" said Porthos, drawing himself up proudly. "How so?"

"The signs just now, and the holy water. But that must be a royal of some sort — that fine person with their cushion and their servants."

"My faith, madame, you are deceived," said Porthos. "She is simply a duchess."

"And that third attendant who waited at the door for her? And that carriage with its driver in grand livery who sat waiting on their seat?"

Porthos had seen neither the carriage nor the driver. But with an eye sharpened by jealousy, Madame Coquenard had seen everything.

The musketeer regretted that he had not expanded his story to make a princess of the gentry of the red cushion — who of course he had met only once before at a previous sermon at Saint-Leu, with the specific intent of his present subterfuge.

"Ah, you are quite the pet of the ladies, Monsieur Porthos," said the attorney with a sigh.

"Well," responded Porthos, "you may imagine that with the physique with which nature has endowed me, I am not in want of good luck."

"Good gods, how fickle you are," said Madame Coquenard, raising her eyes to the sky.

"Less quickly than some, it seems to me," replied Porthos. "For I, madame — I may say I was your victim when, wounded and near death, I was abandoned by the healers. I, the offspring of gentry, who placed reliance upon your friendship. I was close to dying of my injuries at first, and of hunger afterward, in a poor inn at Chantilly, without you ever deigning once to reply to the burning letters I addressed to you."

"Monsieur Porthos, I believe we both know your tendency for embellishments when it comes to the tale of your life."

"I?" said Porthos, wounded. "I who had sacrificed for you the Baroness de —"

"Another story that I know too well."

"Well, then, the Countess de —"

"Monsieur Porthos, you do not impress."

Porthos then tried another tack. "Madame Coquenard," said he. "Do you remember the first letter you wrote me, and which I preserve engraved in my memory?"

The attorney sighed. "Indeed I do. But even that was poor security against the sum you required of me to borrow, which was rather large."

"Madame, I gave you the preference. I had but to write to the Duchess… but I won't repeat her name, for I am incapable of compromising her in such a way. But I do know that I had but to write to her and she would have sent me fifteen hundred livres."

The attorney raised one eyebrow. "Monsieur Porthos," said she. "Despite you having not so written, I cannot fail to see that you have somehow escaped your calamity of Chantilly."

"Fie, madame," said Porthos as if pained. "Let us not talk about that, if you please. It is humiliating."

"But clearly your resourcefulness, and your duchess, indicate that you have no further need of me," said Madame Coquenard, slowly and sadly.

Porthos maintained a majestic silence.

"And that is the only reply you make?" sighed Madame Coquenard. "Alas, I understand." The attorney turned away then, so that the musketeer could not see her smile as he responded.

"Think of the offense you have committed toward me, madame! It remains here." Porthos then thumped his hand upon his heart.

Madame Coquenard took the musketeer's arm. "Then how shall I repair it, my dear Porthos?"

"Oh, there is nothing to be done," said Porthos, shrugging his shoulders. "It is just that my business at Chantilly has left me in arrears. But I know you are not wealthy, Madame Coquenard, and that you are obliged to bleed your poor clients to squeeze a few paltry crowns from them. Oh, if you were a duchess, it would be quite a different thing. But alas, these problems are my own."

The attorney raised her eyebrow once more. "Please to know, Monsieur Porthos," said she, "that my strongbox is better filled than those of your affected minxes."

"Indeed? But that then doubles the offense of Chantilly," said Porthos, disengaging his arm from that of his paramour. "For if you are prosperous, madame, then there is no excuse for your refusal."

Madame Coquenard smiled, and Porthos saw that he had gone too far. "But I see that I must not take the word literally," continued he. "You are not precisely wealthy, though you are well off. Faith, madame, let us say no more upon the subject, I beg of you. You have misunderstood me."

"Ingrate that I am?"

"No! I make no complaint," said Porthos.

"That is good. But still, you must be gone to your beautiful duchess. I will detain you no longer."

"But she is not… that is, she is no one of your concern, in my opinion."

"Indeed, Monsieur Porthos? Could this mean you love me still?"

"Ah, madame," said Porthos, in the most melancholy tone he could assume. "I would give all to say so. But when we are about to enter upon a campaign — a campaign in which my instincts tell me I shall be killed…"

"Oh, don't talk of such things!" cried Madame Coquenard, whose mood grew suddenly somber.

"Yet something whispers it to me," said Porthos, becoming more and more desolate.

"These are the whispers, I believe, that say you have a new love."

"Not so. I speak frankly to you. No such emotion affects me. And I even feel here, at the bottom of my heart, something which speaks for you. But in less than two weeks, as you may already have heard, this fatal campaign is to open. I shall be fearfully preoccupied preparing my equipment of campaign. Then I must make a journey to see my family, in the lower part of Brittany, to obtain the sum necessary for my departure."

Madame Coquenard observed in Porthos a last struggle between love and avarice. She could only shake her head as he continued.

"As the duchess whom you saw at the church has estates near to those of my family, we mean to make the journey together. Journeys, you know, appear much shorter when two travel in company."

"Have you no friends in Paris then, Monsieur Porthos?" said the attorney.

"I thought I had," said Porthos, resuming his melancholy air. "But I have been taught my mistake."

"Poor monsieur," murmured Madame Coquenard, in a tone of consolation that surprised even herself. "Come to our house tomorrow. You will say you are the son of my auncle, consequently my cousin. You come from Noyon, in Picardy. You have several lawsuits and no attorney. Can you recollect all that?"

"Perfectly, madame."

"Come at dinnertime."

"Very well."

"And be upon your guard before my husband, who is rather shrewd, notwithstanding his continued ill health."

"I am the sorrier to hear it," said Porthos.

"Indeed. The poor soul may be expected to leave me a widow at any hour," said the attorney, throwing a significant glance at Porthos. "Fortunately, with no children or debts to our name, the survivor takes everything."

"All?"

"Yes, all."

"I see you are a person of precaution, my dear Madame Coquenard," said Porthos, squeezing the hand of the attorney tenderly.

"We are then reconciled, dear Monsieur Porthos?" said she, coyly.

"For life," replied Porthos in the same manner.

"Till we meet again, then, dear traitor."

"Till we meet again, my forgetful charmer."

"Tomorrow, my angel."

"Tomorrow, flame of my life."

— CHAPTER 30 —

THE LIEGE DE WINTER

Leaving the church ahead of Porthos and his paramour, d'Artagnan followed Milord without being noticed by him. But quickly, she saw him get into a fine carriage, then heard him order the driver to Saint-Germain. And as it was useless to try to keep pace on foot with a carriage drawn by two powerful horses, the young guard, lamenting her luck, was forced to race back to Athos's apartment in the Rue Ferou.

By good fortune, she met Planchet in the Rue de Seine, where the valet had stopped before the house of a pastry chef and was contemplating with ecstasy a cake of the most appetizing appearance. D'Artagnan ordered him to go at once to the d'Essarts estate and saddle two horses in the guard stables — one for herself and one for the valet — and bring them to Athos's residence. Both then proceeded at speed along their way.

Athos was at home, emptying with great sadness a bottle of the famous Spanish wine she had brought back from her journey into Picardy. She made a sign for Grimaud to bring a glass for d'Artagnan, and Grimaud obeyed as usual.

D'Artagnan related to Athos all that had passed at the church between Porthos and his paramour the attorney, and how their comrade was probably by that time well on his way to becoming equipped.

"As for me," replied Athos to the tale, "I am quite at my ease. It will not be lovers that will defray the expense of my equipment."

"As handsome and noble as you are, my dear Athos, not even royals would be secure from your amorous solicitations."

"How young this d'Artagnan is," said Athos, shrugging her shoulders. And she made a sign to Grimaud to bring another bottle.

At that moment, Planchet put his head modestly in at the half-open door, and told d'Artagnan that the horses were ready.

"What horses?" asked Athos.

"Two horses loaned from the guard stables, and with which I am now going to take a ride to Saint-Germain."

"Well, and what are you going to do at Saint-Germain?"

Then d'Artagnan described the additional encounter which she had at the church, and how she had seen by chance that young man who had met in Meung with the villain Rochefort.

"By your excitement, I might guess that you are in love with this young man as you were with your Madame Bonacieux," said Athos when the story was done, shrugging her shoulders again as if she pitied human weakness.

"I? Not at all," said d'Artagnan. "I am only curious to unravel the mystery to which he is attached. For that one spoke to Rochefort in Meung of what could only be illicit business. And in my opinion, that scarred villain was certainly the figure in the black cloak who carried off Madame Bonacieux the second time, as I know he carried her off the first. Rochefort is a ghost who cannot be found. But if this Milord is an agent of his, he has perhaps some connection to all this."

"Well, perhaps you are right," said Athos. "But I do not know anyone that is worth the trouble of being sought for when they are once lost. Your tailor, for instance, is lost but perhaps safe now for it, for while held by the cardinal's agents, she cannot thwart the plans of the cardinal. As such, it may be so much the worse for her if she is found and freed."

"Athos, you are mistaken," said d'Artagnan. "I love my poor Constance more than ever, and if I knew the place in which she was, were it at the end of the world, I would go to free her from the hands of her enemies. But I am ignorant. All my investigations have proved useless. So meanwhile, I will try to find out this Milord."

"Divert yourself with this quest then, my dear d'Artagnan. I wish you may with all my heart, if that will amuse you."

"Hear me, Athos," said d'Artagnan. "Instead of shutting yourself up here as if you were under arrest, get on horseback and come and take a ride with me to Saint-Germain."

"My dear friend," said Athos, "I ride horses only when I have one to call my own. When I have none, I go afoot."

Despite herself, d'Artagnan smiled at the misanthropy of the musketeer, which from any other person would have offended her. "Well," said she, "I ride what I can get, and I am not so proud as you. So au revoir, dear Athos."

"Au revoir," said the musketeer, making a sign to Grimaud to uncork the bottle she had just brought.

⚜

On their borrowed horses, D'Artagnan and Planchet took the road from Paris to Saint-Germain. And all along that road, what Athos had said respecting Constance burned in the mind of the young guard. Although d'Artagnan had never been of a very sentimental character, the young tailor had made a first and most lasting impression upon her heart. The Gascon had spoken truth when saying she was ready to go to the end of the world to seek Constance. But the world, being round, has many ends, so that she had not known which way she might first turn — and so that the unexpected appearance of Milord seemed to her a sign from fate of which course she should set.

Thinking of all this, and from time to time giving a touch of the spur to her horse, d'Artagnan completed the short journey and arrived at Saint-Germain. She and Planchet rode up quiet street after quiet street, looking to the right and the left to see if either could catch any sign of the memorable English lord or his carriage, but it seemed that all was in vain.

Then from the ground floor of a fine house, d'Artagnan saw an ice-pale face peep out which she thought appeared familiar. This person was walking along the terrace, which was ornamented with flowers.

Planchet recognized the person at the same time. "Eh, madame," said he, addressing d'Artagnan. "Do you recall that face which appears yonder?"

"No," said d'Artagnan. "And yet I am certain it is not the first time I have seen that visage."

"By my faith, I believe it is not," said Planchet. "Why, it is poor Lubin, the valet of Madame Countess de Wardes! She whom you took such good care of those weeks ago at Calais, on the road to the governor's house!"

"So it is," said d'Artagnan. "I know them now. Do you think they would recollect you?"

"My faith, madame, they were in such a fright that I doubt if they can have retained a very clear recollection of me."

"Well, go and talk with them, then," said d'Artagnan. "And make out if you can from the conversation whether their employer is alive or dead."

Planchet dismounted and went straight up to Lubin, who gave no sign that they remembered him. The two valets then began to chat professionally with the best understanding possible, while d'Artagnan turned the two horses into a lane, went round the house, and came back to watch the conference from behind a hedge of filberts.

But even as she watched, the young guard heard the noise of horses — and saw Milord's carriage stop opposite to her. She thought at first she must be mistaken, but Milord was there within. D'Artagnan leaned down upon the neck of her horse, in order that she might see without being seen.

Milord put his charming blond head out at the window, whistling as he held forth a folded note. A valet standing at the carriage footboard behind responded to the summons — a young figure with hair of dark umber, a smoothly sepia complexion, and pale green eyes set in a measured, wide-set glance. Active and lively in the manner of a gentry's attendant, they took the note from Milord, jumped from the carriage, and made their way toward the house.

Following the valet with her eyes, d'Artagnan saw them go toward the terrace. But it happened that someone in the house at that moment called Lubin, so that Planchet remained alone, looking in all directions to determine where d'Artagnan had disappeared.

The valet approached Planchet, whom they apparently mistook for Lubin. Then holding out the note to him, they said, "For your employer."

"For my employer, maitre?" repeated Planchet, confused.

"Madame, if you please. And yes, and it is important. Take it quickly."

Thereupon the valet ran back toward the carriage, which had turned round toward the way it came. She jumped up on the footboard, and the carriage drove off.

Planchet turned the note over in his hands. Then, accustomed to accepting orders, he left the terrace, ran toward the lane, and at the end of twenty paces met d'Artagnan. Having seen all, she was already coming to him.

"For you, madame," said Planchet, presenting the note.

"For me?" said d'Artagnan. "Are you sure of that?"

"By faith, madame, I can't be more sure. Madame Valet said, 'For your employer.' And I have no other employer but you, so."

D'Artagnan opened the letter, and read these words:

A person who takes more interest in you than he is willing to confess wishes to know on what day it will suit you to walk in the forest? Tomorrow, at the Golden Field inn, an attendant will wait for your reply.

"Well," said d'Artagnan, "you being mistaken for the fine Lubin is rather fortuitous. It appears that Milord and I are anxious about the health of the same person. Planchet, how is the good Countess de Wardes? She is not dead, then?"

"No, madame, though she is only as well as one can be with four sword wounds in her body. For even with Lubin having applied what salve you left for her, she is still very weak, having lost much blood. Lubin did not know me, madame, and told me our adventure from one end to the other."

"Well done, Planchet. You are the king of valets. Now jump onto your horse, and let us overtake the carriage."

This did not take long. At the end of only a few minutes, d'Artagnan and Planchet saw the carriage drawn up by a crossroads. The young guard motioned Planchet to fall back as she drew nearer, seeing that a rider on a fine horse was close to the carriage door. This rider's jacket and kilt were richly appointed, and bore bright red piping that accentuated a deep umber complexion and cropped black hair.

The conversation between Milord and the rider was so animated that d'Artagnan stopped on the other side of the carriage without anyone but the young valet perceiving her presence, which she did in curious silence. With more time to appraise her, d'Artagnan judged the valet at not yet twenty, with a confidence to her stance and gaze. Her hair was tied back assertively now, framing her face and focusing her pale green gaze as it fixed on d'Artagnan most intensely.

The conversation took place in English — a language which d'Artagnan could not understand. But by its tone, the young guard plainly saw that the normally graceful Milord was in a great rage. He terminated the dialogue by striking a cane against the carriage window frame with such force that the stick flew into pieces, leaving no doubt as to his response to the discussion. The rider laughed aloud, though not unkindly, but this appeared to exasperate Milord still more.

D'Artagnan thought this the best moment to interject. She spurred her horse to approach the door of the carriage opposite Milord, and taking off her hat respectfully, said, "Monsieur, will you permit me to offer you my services? It appears to me that this bravo has made you very angry. Speak one word, and I take it upon myself to punish them for their want of courtesy."

At the first word, Milord turned, looking at the young guard with astonishment. And when d'Artagnan had finished speaking, he responded in very good French, "Maitre, I should with great confidence place myself under your protection, if the person with whom I quarrel were not my sibling."

"Madame, if you please," said d'Artagnan. "And excuse me, then. You must be aware that I was ignorant of that fact, monsieur." In so naming Milord initially, d'Artagnan realized with vexation that she had either presented herself as presumptuous, or had given away knowing him beforehand. Thankfully, the young man gave no sign that he had noticed.

"What is that bothersome fool troubling themself about?" said the rider whom Milord had designated as his sibling, speaking in French and stooping down to the height of the carriage window. "Why do not they go about their business?"

"Bothersome fool yourself!" said d'Artagnan, stooping in her turn on the neck of her horse, and answering on her side through the opposite window. "I do not go on because it pleases me to stop here."

The rider addressed some additional words in English to their brother.

"I speak to you in French," said d'Artagnan. "Be kind enough, then, to reply to me in the same language. You are monsieur's sibling, as I have learned — and I am grateful you are not mine."

It might be thought that Milord, desirous of preventing an escalation of rancor, would have interrupted these mutual provocations in order to prevent the quarrel from going too far. But on the contrary, he threw himself back in his seat and called out coolly to the driver, "Go on — home!"

From the footboard, the young valet cast a smiling glance at d'Artagnan, whose imposing presence seemed to have made an impression on her.

The carriage went on, leaving the young guard and the rider facing each other. D'Artagnan made a movement to follow the carriage — but then she found her anger, already at the boiling point, much increased by a sudden recognition that halted her. For by their lofty look and piercing eyes, the rider was none other than the English traveler of Amiens who had won her horse, and who had been very near winning d'Artagnan's diamond from Athos.

D'Artagnan then recognized the rider's fine mount as her own English horse lost of Athos, won back, and given up a moment thereafter. Quickly, she caught at the beast's bridle to stop it and its rider where they stood.

"Well, maitre," said she, "you appear to be more stupid than I am. For you ride the horse that was once mine, and you forget there is a small matter of a parting insult delivered to me in Amiens."

"Ah," said the English rider. "Is it you, my horseless Madame Guard? It seems you must always be playing some game or other."

"Yes. And that reminds me that your insult of Amiens still needs response. Perhaps we will see, my dear maitre, if you handle a sword with as little skill as you can a dice box."

"You see plainly that I have no sword," said the rider angrily. "But if armed, I would doubtless teach you lessons you richly deserve. Clearly, though, you take more comfort to play the braggart with an unarmed foe?"

"I hope you have a sword at home. But in any event, I have two, and if you like, I will throw with you for one of them."

"Needless," said the rider. "I am well furnished with such playthings."

"Very well, my worthy gentle," said d'Artagnan. "Pick out the best, and come and show it to me this evening."

"Where, if you please?"

"Behind the Palais de Luxembourg. That's a charming spot for such amusements as the one I propose to you."

"That will do. I will be there."

"Your hour?" d'Artagnan asked.

"Six o'clock."

"By the by, you have probably one or two friends?"

"I have three, who would be honored by joining in the sport with me."

"Three? Marvelous! Three is just my number."

"Now, then, who are you?" asked the rider.

"I am Madame d'Artagnan, a Gascon gentle, serving in the queens' guards. And you?"

"I am the Liege de Winter."

"Well, then, I am your servant, my liege," said d'Artagnan. "Until our next meeting."

Laughing, Liege de Winter set off along the crossroad, not following the carriage of Milord where it had sped off straight. Even as her temper cooled, d'Artagnan weighed the fortune of this unlikely meeting, and the challenge inspired by it. Though she longed to pursue Milord de Winter, the duel with

Liege de Winter must take precedence, for preparations would have to be made. But she understood how that duel might help her to victory in more than one way. So touching her horse with the spur, she motioned Planchet to follow her and raced back to Paris.

As she was accustomed to do in all matters of any consequence, d'Artagnan went straight to the residence of Athos once more. She found the musketeer reclining upon a large sofa, still waiting, as she said, for her equipment to come and find her. D'Artagnan related to her all that had passed. In response, Athos expressed her delight.

"You fight an English gentry? And I, Porthos, and Aramis will be your seconds? Marvelous! If only all of Liege de Winter's seconds be English as well, this would be a dream come true."

Both immediately sent Planchet and Grimaud to fetch Porthos and Aramis, and on the arrival of those two, d'Artagnan made them acquainted with the situation. In response, Porthos laughingly drew his sword from the scabbard and made passes at the wall, springing back from time to time in contortions like a dancer. Aramis, who was still constantly at work at their poem promised at Crevecoeur, shut themself up in Athos's study and begged not to be disturbed before the moment of departure. Athos, by signs, requested Grimaud to bring another bottle of wine.

D'Artagnan employed herself in arranging a little plan, whose full scope had come to her during the ride from the crossroads, and of which we shall hereafter see the execution. Doing so seemingly promised her some agreeable adventure, as might have been seen by the smiles and thoughtful expressions which from time to time passed over her face.

CHAPTER 31

THE ENGLISH AND THE FRENCH

The hour having come, the four friends went with their four valets to one of the fields behind the Luxembourg — this one given up to the feeding of goats. Athos threw a sou to the goatkeeper to withdraw. The valets were ordered to act as sentinels.

A silent party soon drew near to the same spot in an unadorned carriage. Stepping forth, four figures joined d'Artagnan and the musketeers, while four additional valets joined the others as wardens. Then, according to foreign custom, the presentations took place.

The Liege de Winter's seconds were, in fact, all English. They were uniformly well dressed and of pale ivory features, but were easily distinguished by hair of gold, black, and sun-touched russet, respectively. All were gentry of rank — but consequently, the odd names of their French adversaries were for them not only a matter of surprise, but of annoyance.

"But after all that," said Liege de Winter, when Athos, Porthos, and Aramis had been named, "we do not know who you are. We cannot fight against such names. You might as well be shepherds."

"Therefore, maitre, you may suppose they are only assumed names of campaign," said Athos.

"Which only gives us a greater desire to know the real ones," said they.

"You gamed very willingly with us without knowing our names," said Athos, "by the same token that you won our horses."

"That is true. But I then risked only pistoles. This time, we risk our blood. One plays with anyone, but one fights only with equals."

"And that is just," sighed Athos. Then she took aside the one of the four English blades with whom she was to fight, and communicated her name in a low voice. Porthos and Aramis did the same to their foes.

"Does that satisfy you?" said Athos to her adversary. "Do you find me of sufficient rank to do me the honor of crossing swords with me?"

"Yes, madame," said the English warrior, bowing.

"Splendid. But now shall I tell you something more?" added Athos coolly.

"What?"

"Why, the fact that you would have acted much more wisely if you had not required me to make myself known."

"Why so?"

"Because I am believed to be dead, and have reasons for wishing no one to know I am living. So that I shall be obliged to kill you to prevent my secret from ever being spoken."

The English blade looked at Athos, believing that she jested — but Athos did not jest for anything in the world.

"Gentlefolk," said the elder musketeer, addressing at the same time her companions and their adversaries. "Are we ready?"

"Yes!" answered the English and the French, as with one voice.

"On guard, then!" cried she.

Immediately, eight swords glittered in the rays of the setting sun. The combat began with an animosity very natural between the folk of two nations on the brink once again of war.

Athos fenced with as much calmness and method as if she had been a year in recent practice at a fencing school. Porthos — cured no doubt of his once-too-great confidence by his adventure of Chantilly — fought with skill and prudence. Aramis, who had the third canto of their poem to finish, fought like one in haste.

Athos killed her adversary first. She hit him but once, but as she had foretold, that hit was a mortal one. The sword pierced the English gentle's heart.

Not long after, Porthos stretched his own foe upon the grass with a wound through her thigh. As the gentle, without making any further resistance, then surrendered her sword, Porthos took her up in his arms and bore her to the English carriage.

Aramis pushed their foe so vigorously that after retreating back fifty paces, the English gentle ended by fairly taking to his heels, and disappeared amid the hooting of the valets.

As to d'Artagnan, she fought purely and simply on the defensive. And when she finally saw that Liege de Winter was well fatigued, the young guard gave a vigorous side thrust that sent that gentle's sword flying. Liege de Winter, finding themself disarmed, took three steps back. But in this movement, their foot slipped and they fell.

D'Artagnan was over them at a bound, and spoke while pointing her sword to her foe's throat. "I could kill you, my liege. You are completely in my hands. But I spare your life for the sake of your brother."

D'Artagnan was at the height of joy. She had brought to fruition the plan she had imagined beforehand, whose picturing had produced the smiles we noted upon her face. The Liege de Winter, delighted at facing a gentle of such a kind disposition, seemingly forgot all feuds and insults. They embraced d'Artagnan, and paid a thousand compliments to the three musketeers.

As Porthos's adversary was already installed in the carriage, and as Aramis's had taken to his heels, they had nothing to think about but the dead. As Porthos and Aramis were moving the body of the fallen English warrior, a large purse dropped from his pocket. D'Artagnan picked it up and offered it to Liege de Winter.

"What would you have me do with that?" asked the gentry.

"You can restore it to his family," said d'Artagnan.

"His family will care little about such a trifle as that, against the inheritance of fifteen thousand pistoles a year from him in his death. Keep the purse for your valets."

D'Artagnan thus put the purse into her pocket.

"And now, my young friend — for you will permit me, I hope, to give you that name," said Liege de Winter. "On this very evening, if agreeable to you, I will present you to my brother, Milord de Winter, for I am desirous that he should take you into his good graces. I am in France to deliver correspondence from the English court, and to conclude some business that I fear the coming conflict between our nations will disturb, but he makes his residence here. And as he is not without some influence at your own court, he may perhaps prove useful to you."

D'Artagnan's smile once again confirmed her good fortune. Having thought her pursuit of this Milord dashed, she was now to be introduced to him under the cover of Liege de Winter's admiration. Openly showing her pleasure, she bowed a sign of assent.

As Liege de Winter moved to the carriage to converse with their companions, d'Artagnan slipped to the side of the musketeers where they waited. From her pocket, she withdrew the fallen English warrior's purse and presented it to Athos.

"What do you mean to do by this?" asked the musketeer.

"Why, I mean to pass it over to you, my dear Athos."

"Me? Why to me?"

"Because you killed the fallen foe. These are the spoils of victory."

"I, take inheritance from an enemy?" said Athos. "For whom, then, do you take me?"

"It is the custom in war," said d'Artagnan. "Why should it not be the custom in a duel?"

"Even on the field of battle, I have never done such."

Porthos shrugged his shoulders. Aramis by a movement of their lips endorsed Athos.

"Then," said d'Artagnan, "let us give the money to the valets, as Liege de Winter suggested."

"I think not," said Athos. "For the English will think us short of means that we must borrow to pay our valets. Thus, rather than our own, let us give the money to their valets."

Athos then took the purse and threw it into the hand of the carriage driver. "For you and your comrades, ser."

This greatness of spirit in one as destitute as Athos struck even Porthos. And this French generosity was highly applauded by all. That is, by all except Planchet, Grimaud, Bazin, and Mousqueton.

Before departing, Liege de Winter gave d'Artagnan their brother's address. He lived in the fashionable quarter of the Place Royale at number 6, and Liege de Winter undertook to call on and take d'Artagnan with them in order to introduce her. D'Artagnan arranged a meeting at eight o'clock at Athos's residence.

This introduction to Milord de Winter occupied the thoughts of our Gascon greatly. Knowing that Milord was some creature of the cardinal, his very presence in Paris seemed sure to d'Artagnan to speak of some dire intent. The potential intrigue between Milord and the Countess de Wardes strengthened this point in our presumptuous hero's mind, even knowing only that de Wardes was high in the cardinal's favor.

D'Artagnan's only fear was that Milord would recognize in her the young traveler of Meung. Then he would recall that she was a friend of Monsieur de Treville, and consequently that she belonged body and soul to the queens. And this would make d'Artagnan lose a part of her advantage, since if Milord knew her as she knew him, she could play no better than an equal game.

D'Artagnan began by selecting her best clothes, then returned to Athos's. There, according to custom, she related all her new speculations to the elder musketeer. Athos listened once more, then shook her head and recommended prudence to the young guard, with a shade of bitterness.

"Astounding," said the elder musketeer. "You have just lost one obsession, whom you call good, charming, perfect. And here you are, running headlong after another."

D'Artagnan once more hotly denied any truth to this reproach. "I love Madame Bonacieux with my heart, and pursue this Milord only for that reason," said she. "In being introduced to him, my principal object is to ascertain what part he might play in this intrigue."

"The part he might play? Faith, it is not difficult to divine that after all you have told me. He is some emissary of the cardinal — and one who will draw you into a snare in which you will leave your head."

"My dear Athos, you view all folk on the nefarious side."

"My dear d'Artagnan, I mistrust all folk. And how should it be otherwise? For I bought my experience dearly. This Milord is handsome, you say?"

"Some would call him beautiful, certainly."

"Ah, my poor d'Artagnan," said Athos.

"Listen to me! I want to be enlightened by him on a singular subject. Then, when I have learned what I desire to know, I will withdraw."

"Be enlightened then," said Athos grimly.

Liege de Winter arrived at the appointed time — but Athos, being warned of their coming and wanting nothing to do with d'Artagnan's schemes, went into the other chamber. The English gentry therefore found the young guard alone, and with the hour nearly eight o'clock, the two departed. An elegant carriage waited below, and as it was drawn by two excellent horses, they were soon at the Place Royale.

Milord de Winter received d'Artagnan ceremoniously in a finely appointed sitting room. His townhouse was remarkably sumptuous, and while the most part of the English folk in the realm had fled France — or were about to flee — on account of the impending war, Milord had seemingly instead been laying out much money upon his residence.

"You see here," said Liege de Winter, presenting d'Artagnan to their brother, "a young gentle who has held my life in her hands. Moreover, she has not abused her advantage, although it was I who insulted her, and although our nations are at the brink of war. Thank her, then, monsieur, if you have any affection for me."

Milord nodded. But a scarcely visible frown crossed his brow, and so peculiar a smile appeared upon his lips that d'Artagnan, who saw and observed it, was forced to conceal her curiosity. Liege de Winter did not perceive any of this, for they had turned to move to a table upon which was a salver with Spanish wine and glasses.

"You are welcome here, madame," said Milord de Winter to the young guard, in a voice whose singular softness contrasted with the symptoms of ill humor which d'Artagnan had just observed. "You have today acquired eternal rights to my gratitude."

As Liege de Winter poured the wine, they described the combat without omitting a single detail. Milord de Winter listened with the greatest attention. And yet it was easy enough for d'Artagnan to see that, whatever effort he made to conceal his impressions, this recital was not agreeable to him. The blood rose to his face, and his foot tapped the floor with impatience. As before, d'Artagnan observed that Liege de Winter, focused on their tale, noticed nothing of this.

When the story had finished, Liege de Winter by a sign invited d'Artagnan to drink. D'Artagnan drew near to the table and took her glass. She did not, however, lose sight of Milord — and watching in a mirror, she witnessed the change that came over the beautiful gentry's face. Now that he believed himself to be no longer observed, a sentiment resembling ferocity animated his features, causing him to bare his beautiful teeth to such an extent that a gap next to one eyetooth was on display.

The young valet whom d'Artagnan had observed earlier that day upon the carriage then came in. She whispered some words to Liege de Winter, who nodded thereupon.

"I must request your permission to withdraw," said the gentry to d'Artagnan. "Please excuse me on account of the urgency of the business that calls me away. And brother, I pray you pardon me."

D'Artagnan exchanged a shake of the hand with Liege de Winter, and then returned to Milord de Winter. His face had recovered its gracious expression with surprising mobility. But a number of red spots on his handkerchief indicated that he had bitten his lip till the blood ran.

Milord appeared to have entirely recovered from this unseen fit, however, and the conversation thankfully took a cheerful turn. He first told d'Artagnan that Liege de Winter was his sibling-in-law, and not his blood sibling, he having married the Lady Katherine de Winter, a younger sister of the family who had left him a widower. All this seemed innocent enough. And indeed, after a half hour's conversation, d'Artagnan was forced to remind herself that Milord de Winter was a person of suspicion, and not her compatriot.

He spoke French with an elegance and a purity, and the young guard found herself caught up in his gallant speeches and protestations of devotion. To all the simple things spoken by our Gascon, Milord replied with a smile of kindness. When the hour came for her to depart, then, d'Artagnan took leave of Milord de Winter, and left the sitting room in an unsettled mood.

On the staircase, she met the valet, who brushed gently against her as both passed. Flushing to the eyes, the young woman asked d'Artagnan's pardon for having touched her, in a voice so sweet that the pardon was easily granted.

"My name is Madame Kitty," the valet intoned to the young guard. And d'Artagnan after introducing herself failed to notice this Kitty's gaze follow her as she departed.

⚜

D'Artagnan came again on the morrow, and was even better received than on the evening before. Liege de Winter's business had seen them called away from Paris for some days, as Milord de Winter reported, and it was he who this time did all the honors. He had a fine voice for oratory, and entertained d'Artagnan for much of the evening with recitations of verse. When they spoke afterward, he appeared to take a great interest in the young guard, asking her whence she came, who were her friends — and whether she had ever entertained the thought of attaching herself to the cardinal.

She came again on the morrow, and the day after that. And each day, Milord and Kitty alike gave her a more gracious reception…

At this, all of d'Artagnan's suspicion was refocused, as was her prudence. She launched into a passionate praise of their eminence, and said that she would not have failed to enter into the guards of the cardinal instead of the queens' guards if she had happened to know Madame Houdiniere instead of Monsieur de Treville.

Milord de Winter then changed the conversation without any appearance of artifice, and asked d'Artagnan in the most offhand manner possible if she had ever been in England. D'Artagnan replied excitedly that she had been sent thither by Monsieur de Treville just the month before to treat for a supply of horses, and that she had brought back four as specimens.

The young guard observed that Milord de Winter in the course of the conversation twice bit his lip. It was clear to her that whether he had recognized her at once or only as an afterthought, the sly gentry knew her now — and that moreover, his plan was to play at outmaneuvering her.

For her part, d'Artagnan was determined to win that game.

At the same hour as on the preceding evening, d'Artagnan departed. In the corridor, she again met the lively Kitty, who looked at her with an expression of kindness which would have been nigh impossible to mistake. But d'Artagnan was so preoccupied by the challenges set down by Milord that she noticed absolutely nothing.

She came again on the morrow, and the day after that. And each day, Milord and Kitty alike gave her a more gracious reception.

Every evening, either in the antechamber, the corridor, or on the stairs, d'Artagnan met the young valet. But, as before, the young guard paid no attention to this persistence of the charming Kitty. Each day, despite the skill with which d'Artagnan laid down her own questions, Milord replied simply with blunt denial. He had not been back to England in some months, said he, and despite his affection for Cardinal de Richelieu, he had no business with their eminence, whether public or private.

From those bold lies, d'Artagnan was thwarted soundly in any attempt to gain suggestion or hint of the whereabouts of Constance Bonacieux. And so, each day the plight of the young tailor grew more alarming in the Gascon's thought, and she found her obsession with Milord de Winter more and more resembling a campaign of war.

— CHAPTER 32 —

THE ATTORNEYS' DINNER

Leaving d'Artagnan to herself for the moment, we may return to at least one of our musketeers. In the hours after the duel behind the Luxembourg, Porthos, Athos, and Aramis in d'Artagnan's absence celebrated their triumph over the English. But however brilliant had been the part played by Porthos in the duel, it had not made him forget his dinner with Madame Coquenard the next day.

On the morrow, Porthos received the touch of Mousqueton's brush upon his best suit for a full hour. Then he made his way toward the Rue d'Ours with the steps of one who was doubly in favor with fortune.

His heart beat — but not like d'Artagnan's with a young and impatient love. Rather, a combination of romance and more material interest stirred Porthos's blood. He was about at last to pass that mysterious threshold, to climb those unknown stairs by which, one by one, the wealthy clients billed by Madame Coquenard and Monsieur Vattier had ascended. He was about to see in reality a certain strongbox of which he had twenty times beheld the image in his dreams — a coffer long and deep, locked, bolted, and fastened in the wall according to his imagination. A coffer of which he had so often heard, and which the hands of Madame Coquenard appeared about to open to the musketeer's admiring looks.

But first, he would partake of a fine family meal.

This was unusual for Porthos — a wanderer on the earth, a soldier without fortune, a son without family. He was accustomed to inns, cabarets, taverns, and restaurants, and was a lover of wine often forced to depend upon chance to slake his thirst. As such, he was more than ready to enjoy the comforts of his paramour's home, wherein she and her husband both practiced their legal craft.

To come in the capacity of a cousin and seat himself at a good table. To smooth the smiling brow of the young attorney. To lighten the savings of the clerks of law who lived and worked among the attorneys a little, by teaching them the games of cards and dice of the barracks. All this promised to be enormously delightful to Porthos, who imagined himself winning from those clerks, by way of fee for the lesson he would give them in an hour, their savings of a month.

However, the musketeer could not forget the evil reports which had always come to his attention regarding Monsieur Vattier. Twenty years Madame Coquenard's senior, her husband was known in his younger days for legendary exploits of philandering, of which Porthos had heard even before making the acquaintance of the young attorney. In more recent years, the elder attorney's meanness, stinginess, and fasts were well known. But excepting some few acts of economy which Porthos had always found charming, his lively Madame Coquenard had always seemed quite liberal in her spending. As such, Porthos hoped to see a household of a highly comfortable kind.

And yet, even as he came to the door, the musketeer began to entertain some doubts. The approach was not so inspiring — a dark passage, and a staircase half-lighted by bars through which stole a glimmer from a neighboring yard. On the second floor, a low door was studded with enormous nails, like the principal gate of the Chatelet prison where both attorneys engaged in their trade.

Porthos knocked with his hand. A tall, pale legal clerk, their face shaded by a forest of unshorn hair, opened the door, then bowed with the air of one forced at once to sudden respect. For Porthos's lofty stature indicated strength, his military dress indicated rank, and the jewelry at his ears and fingers indicated familiarity with good living.

A shorter clerk came behind the first, a taller clerk behind the second, and a page of a dozen years hid behind the third. In all, three clerks and a half, which argued a very extensive clientage for the attorneys.

Although the musketeer was not expected before one o'clock, Madame Coquenard had been on the watch ever since midday, reckoning that the heart — or perhaps the stomach — of her lover would bring him before his time. She therefore entered the foyer from the house at the same moment her guest entered from the stairs, and her timely appearance relieved Porthos from an awkward embarrassment. The clerks surveyed him with great curiosity, and he, not knowing well what to say to this, remained tongue-tied.

"It is my cousin!" said the smiling attorney. "Come in, come in, Monsieur Porthos."

Madame Coquenard and Porthos reached the offices shared by the two attorneys after having passed through the antechamber in which the clerks gathered, and the study in which they ought to have been. This last apartment was a sort of dark room, littered with papers. On leaving the study, they passed the kitchen on the right and entered the reception room.

All these rooms and the manner in which they connected with one another did not inspire Porthos favorably. Words might be heard at a distance through too many open doors. Worse, he had cast a rapid investigative glance into the kitchen while passing, and was given to great regret that he did not see the roaring fire, the animation and bustle, that mark when a grand feast is on the way.

Monsieur Vattier had without doubt been warned of Porthos's visit, as he expressed no surprise at the sight of the musketeer, who advanced toward him with a sufficiently easy air and saluted him courteously.

"We are cousins, it appears, Monsieur Porthos?" said the elder attorney, rising from his cane chair. Ivory white of complexion and hair, he was wrapped in a large black doublet against the chill that pervaded the house, in which the whole of his slender body was concealed. His gray eyes shone, and appeared along with his twitching mouth to be the part of his body most animated. For by the look of those eyes, Monsieur Vattier received his so-called cousin with much resignation.

"Yes, monsieur, we are cousins," said Porthos without being disconcerted, for he had never reckoned upon being received enthusiastically by his paramour's husband.

"Through my wife, I believe?" said the attorney coldly.

Porthos did not feel the ridicule of this, and took it for a piece of simplicity, at which he laughed. Madame Coquenard had long known that her husband had some suspicion of her romances, as she had known far more than she desired of his own romances in the younger days of their marriage. So she smiled a little, and fretted somewhat more.

Monsieur Vattier had, since the arrival of Porthos, frequently cast his eyes with great uneasiness upon a large chest placed between his and his wife's oak desks. Porthos comprehended that this chest, although it did not correspond in shape with what he had seen in his dreams, must be the blessed strongbox. He congratulated himself that the reality was larger by far than even his imagination had promised.

Withdrawing his anxious look from the chest and fixing it upon Porthos, Monsieur Vattier did not carry his genealogical investigations any further. Instead, he contented himself with saying, "Monsieur our cousin will do us the favor of dining with us — at some other time — before his departure for the campaign. Will he not, Madame Coquenard?"

This time, Porthos received the insult like a blow right to his stomach, and felt it as sharply. But Madame Coquenard appeared ready for it, as she responded, "My cousin will not return if he finds that we do not treat him kindly. And as he has so little time to pass in Paris, and consequently to spare to us, we must entreat him to give us every instant he can call his own previous to his departure. He will dine with us today."

"Well, then," murmured Monsieur Vattier. And, trying to force a smile, he was overcome by a racking cough that demonstrated to Porthos the ill health of which Madame Coquenard had spoken.

She smiled more successfully in her turn, reestablishing Porthos's gastronomic hopes, and inspiring much gratitude in the musketeer toward the young attorney whom he loved.

The hour of dinner soon arrived. They passed into the dining room, a large dark space situated opposite the kitchen. The clerks, who appeared to have smelled unusual scents in the house, were of military punctuality, and held their stools in hand quite ready to sit down. Their jaws appeared to tremble with dire anticipation of the meal.

"Indeed?" thought Porthos, casting a glance at the three hungry clerks — for the page was apparently not admitted to the honors of the family table. "In my love's place, I would not keep such gourmands. They look like shipwrecked sailors who have not eaten for six weeks."

Monsieur Vattier entered, hand in hand with Madame Coquenard, and Porthos close behind. The elder attorney had scarcely entered when he too began to agitate his nose and jaws after the example of the clerks.

"Oh!" said Monsieur Vattier. "Here is a soup which is rather inviting."

"What in faith can they smell so extraordinary in this soup?" thought Porthos, at the sight of a tureen filled with pale liquid, entirely free from meat, and on the surface of which a few dumplings swam about as rare as the islands of an archipelago.

Madame Coquenard smiled, and upon a sign from her, everyone eagerly took their seats.

Porthos was served first. Then Madame Coquenard filled plates for herself and her husband, and distributed the dumplings without soup to the impatient clerks. At that moment, the door of the dining room opened with a creak, and Porthos saw through the gap the little clerk who, not being allowed to take part in the feast, ate a piece of plain bread in the doorway between the dining room and kitchen.

After the soup, a servant brought a boiled fowl — a piece of magnificence, at least to judge by its ability to cause the eyes of the diners to dilate in such a manner that they seemed ready to burst.

"One may see that you love your family, Madame Coquenard," said Monsieur Vattier, with a smile that was almost tragic. "You are certainly treating your cousin very handsomely."

In truth, though, the poor fowl was thin, and covered with one of those thick, bristly skins through which the teeth cannot penetrate despite all their efforts. To Porthos's mind, the bird must have been sought for a long time on the perch, to which it had retired to die. "Faith," thought he, "this is poor work. I respect old age, but I don't much like it boiled or roasted." He looked round to see if anyone else partook of his opinion. But on the contrary, he saw nothing but eager eyes which were devouring, in anticipation, that sublime fowl which was the object of his distress.

Madame Coquenard drew the dish toward her, skillfully detaching the two great black feet, which she placed upon her husband's plate. She then cut off the neck and head, which she put on one side for herself, raised a wing for Porthos, and then returned the bird otherwise intact to the servant who had brought it in. That servant disappeared with it before the musketeer had time to examine the range of disappointments produced upon the clerks' faces.

In the place of the fowl, a dish of haricot beans made its appearance — an enormous casserole in which some bones of mutton pretended to show themselves, and which at first sight, one might have believed to have some meat on them. Madame Coquenard distributed this dish to the young clerks with moderation, and their somber looks settled down into full resignation.

The time for wine came. Monsieur Vattier poured from a very small stone bottle the third of a glass for each of the young clerks, served himself in about the same proportion, and passed the bottle to Porthos and Madame Coquenard.

The clerks filled up another third of their glasses with water. Then, when they had drunk half the glass, they filled it up with water again, and continued to do so. This brought them, by the end of the meal, to swallowing a drink which from the color of the ruby had passed to that of a pale topaz.

Porthos ate his wing of fowl timidly, and started when he felt the knee of Madame Coquenard under the table as it came in search of his. He also drank half a glass of this sparingly served wine, and found it to be a horrible Montreuil — the terror of all expert palates.

Monsieur Vattier saw Porthos taking the wine undiluted, and sighed deeply.

"Will you eat any of these beans, Cousin Porthos?" asked Madame Coquenard, in that tone which says, 'Take my advice and don't touch them.'

"Thank you, my cousin. I am no longer hungry."

There was a long silence, during which Porthos could hardly keep his composure. Then Monsieur Vattier said at last, "Ah, Madame Coquenard, accept my compliments. Your dinner has been a real feast. Faith, how I have eaten."

Monsieur Vattier had, in fact, eaten his soup, the black feet of the duck, and the only mutton bone on which there was the least appearance of meat. In response, Porthos fancied that the elder attorney and all the rest were baiting him, and he began to twist his mustache as he knit his eyebrows. But the gentle knee of Madame Coquenard gently advised him to be patient.

Monsieur Vattier's words of thanks carried also a terrible meaning for the clerks. For upon a look from the elder attorney, accompanied by a smile from Madame Coquenard, they arose slowly from the table, folded their napkins more slowly still, bowed, and went out with their stools.

"Go, you. Go and promote digestion by working," said the elder attorney gravely.

The clerks gone, Madame Coquenard rose and took from a buffet a piece of cheese, some preserved quinces, and a cake made of almonds and honey. Monsieur Vattier knit his eyebrows in an expression stating he clearly saw this as too many good things. Porthos bit his lip because he was famished, having not yet had the wherewithal to truly dine. He looked in desperation to see if the dish of beans was still there, but the casserole had disappeared.

"A positive feast," said Monsieur Vattier again, striking the arms of his chair. "A banquet of banquets."

Porthos looked at the wine bottle, which was near him, and hoped that with wine, bread, and cheese, he might still make a meal. But the bottle was empty, and neither of his hosts seemed to notice.

"Well and fine," said Porthos to himself. "I am caught in this ambush, and must fight to the last."

He passed his tongue over a spoonful of preserves, and stuck his teeth into the sticky pastry, which Madame Coquenard observed she had herself made. "Now," thought he, "the sacrifice is consummated. But all will be worth it for the hope of gaining access to the attorneys' strongbox."

Monsieur Vattier, after the luxuries of the feast, as he called it, felt the want of a nap. Porthos began to hope that this nap would take place at the present sitting, and in that same locality. But the elder attorney went instead to the office, conspicuously setting himself close to the strongbox — upon the edge of which, for still greater precaution, he placed his feet.

Madame Coquenard took Porthos into an adjoining room, and they began to lay the basis of an arrangement for the musketeer's final days in Paris before the campaign.

"You may come and dine three times a week," said she.

"Thank you, madame," said Porthos, "but I wouldn't like to abuse your kindness. Besides, all my focus at present must be on thinking of my equipment of campaign."

"That's true," said the attorney, sighing. "That unfortunate equipment."

"Alas, yes," said Porthos. "It is so."

"But of what, then, does the equipment of your company consist, Monsieur Porthos?"

"Oh, of many things," said he. "The musketeers are, as you know, elite soldiers, and they require arms, armor, and outfit beyond the needs of mere guards."

"But yet detail them to me."

"Why, they amount to a fine price," said Porthos, much wanting to focus on the total sum rather than noting the items of equipment one by one.

"A price of how much?" said Madame Coquenard.

"Well," said Porthos, "it does not exceed two thousand five hundred livres. I even think that with economy, I could manage it with two thousand livres."

"Gods' blood!" cried the attorney. "Two thousand livres! Why, that is a fortune!"

Porthos's expression fell. Madame Coquenard noted it.

"I wished to know the detail," continued she, "because having many clients and relatives in business, I am almost sure of obtaining things at some significant percent less than you would pay yourself."

"Ah!" said Porthos. "That is what you meant to say."

"Yes, dear monsieur. Thus, for instance, don't you in the first place want a horse?"

"Yes, a horse."

"Well, then! I can accommodate you."

"Splendid," said Porthos, brightening. "That is well as regards my horse. But I must have the appointments complete, as they include military harness and saddle which a musketeer alone can purchase, and which will not amount, besides, to more than three hundred livres."

"Three hundred livres? Then you shall have three hundred livres," said the attorney with a smile.

Porthos smiled in return. It may be remembered that he had still the saddle which came from Buckingham, so that those three hundred livres he reckoned upon putting snugly into his pocket.

"Then," said he, "there is a horse for my valet, and my luggage. As to my arms, there is no need to trouble you about them, for I have them."

"A horse for your valet?" said the attorney. "But that is doing things in lordly style, my friend."

"Ah, madame," said Porthos sweetly. "Do you take me for a vagabond?"

"No. But I only thought that a fine mule makes sometimes as good an appearance as a horse. And it seemed to me that by getting such a steed for Mousqueton, you should not seem to be merely the peer of your valet."

"A fine idea, madame," said Porthos. "You are right, for I have seen very great Spanish gentry whose whole suite were mounted on mules. But then you understand, Madame Coquenard, that it must be a mule with spirit and grace."

"You will be content, I assure you," said the attorney.

"There then remains the luggage," said Porthos.

"Oh, don't let that disturb you. My husband and I have five or six trunks of travel, and you shall choose the best. There is one in particular which he preferred in the journeys made in his younger days, large enough to hold all the world."

"This trunk is then empty?" asked Porthos.

"Certainly it is empty."

"Ah, but the luggage I need must be well filled, my dear."

And so the rest of the equipment that would fill Porthos's trunks and saddlebags was successively debated in the same manner. The result of the sitting was that Madame Coquenard would provide eight hundred livres in notes and coin, and would furnish the horse and the mule which would have the honor of carrying Porthos and Mousqueton to glory.

These conditions being agreed to, Porthos took his leave of Madame Coquenard. The latter wished to detain him by darting certain tender glances toward him. But Porthos gave as his excuse the demands of duty — and was wary of the ears and eyes of clerks and Monsieur Vattier so close at hand. Madame Coquenard was thus obliged to bid the musketeer adieux, and Porthos returned home with his need of equipment settled — but so very hungry.

CHAPTER 33

FLIRTATION AND FALSEHOOD

By day, d'Artagnan sought news of Constance through all channels open to her. By night, she never failed to appear at the Place Royale, usually by nine o'clock. For the proud Gascon was convinced that sooner or later, Milord could not fail but to reveal his true nature as the cardinal's agent, and any knowledge of Constance's fate. And thus did the young guard, despite the warnings of Athos, became seemingly more intent, hour by hour, on setting her head within Milord de Winter's snare.

One evening, when she arrived with as heavy at heart as one who awaits word of an inheritance that will never come, d'Artagnan found Kitty under the carriage gate of Milord's townhouse. But this time, the young valet was not content with touching d'Artagnan as she passed, but took her gently by the hand.

"Faith!" thought d'Artagnan. "Is she charged with some message for me from her employer? Or perhaps she is about to appoint some detail of which Milord was too cautious to speak." She looked upon the valet with the most hopeful air imaginable.

"I wish to say a few words to you, Madame Musketeer," said the valet sternly.

"I am but a guard by rank, gentle Kitty," said d'Artagnan. "But speak. I listen."

"I know your rank, but salute your worthy ambition, madame. But we cannot speak here at any rate. That which I have to say is too long, and above all, too secret."

In spite of herself, d'Artagnan flushed at the valet's compliment. "Well, what is to be done?"

"If Madame Musketeer would follow me?" said Kitty.

Then the young valet, who had not let go the hand of d'Artagnan, led her toward a side door of the townhouse and within. From along a hall, the two turned up a small, dark, winding staircase. After ascending about fifteen steps, Kitty opened a door.

"Come in here, Madame Musketeer," said she. "Here we shall be alone, and can talk."

D'Artagnan cast a glance around her, seeing a small apartment most charming for its taste and neatness. "And whose room is this?"

"It is mine, madame. It connects with Milord de Winter's by that door there." Kitty pointed toward a sliding door that occupied the wall farthest from the staircase door. "But you need not fear. He will not hear what we say, as he never goes to bed before midnight."

At this revelation, d'Artagnan's eyes were drawn to that door which Kitty said led to Milord's chamber, and her mind wandered to thoughts of what notes and secrets might be found there.

Kitty, observing this, heaved a deep sigh. "You love Milord very dearly then, Madame Musketeer?" said she.

In response to the bold statement, d'Artagnan was at first incredulous, then quickly made to just as boldly deny the question. But seeing what was passing in the mind of the young valet, she saw before her suddenly a chance at another route into Milord's secrets.

"Oh, more than I can say, Kitty. I am mad for him."

Kitty breathed a second sigh.

"Alas, madame," said she, "that is too bad."

"What in faith do you see so bad in it?" said d'Artagnan.

"Because, madame," replied Kitty, "my employer loves you not at all."

"What?" cried d'Artagnan, feigning a profound remorse. "Can he have charged you to tell me so?"

"Oh no, madame. But out of the regard I have for you, I have taken the resolution to tell you so."

"I am much obliged, Kitty — but for the intention only. For the information, you must agree, is not likely to be at all agreeable."

"Which is to say, you don't believe what I have told you."

"I confess," said d'Artagnan carefully, "that I desire you to give me proof of what you advance. Has Milord perhaps spoken of some business that relates to me, whose terms displease him?"

Kitty drew a little note from her pocket.

"For me?" said d'Artagnan, seizing the letter.

"No, for another."

"The cardinal!" cried d'Artagnan.

"Faith, what? No, madame. This note is for a person of whom Milord is truly enamored. I thought it only fair to let you know."

But then the young guard read the address aloud in surprise. "The Countess de Wardes…"

The remembrance of Milord's intercepted note at Saint-Germain presented itself to the mind of the disappointed Gascon. But desperate now for some clue that might inspire her hunt, she tore open the letter in spite of the cry which Kitty uttered.

"By my faith, Madame Musketeer!" said she. "What are you doing?"

"I?" said d'Artagnan. "Nothing at all." And she read:

You have not answered my first note. Are you indisposed, or have you forgotten the glances you favored me with at the ball of Madame de Guise? You have an opportunity now, madame. Do not allow it to escape.

D'Artagnan became very distraught. She had hoped for secrets, but here were the notes of a fool distracted by desire, and nothing more.

"Poor dear Madame d'Artagnan," said Kitty in a voice full of compassion, and holding anew the young guard's hand. "You see now the truth of what I tell you."

"You pity me," said d'Artagnan. "But if you only knew what for."

"I pity you with all my heart, my dear. For I know what it is to be in love."

D'Artagnan studied Kitty anew, sensing for the first time that the young valet played some game of her own. Though with her mind in a state of distraction, the young guard had no sense of that game's end. Still, in the confidence that Kitty had extended her regarding Milord's lack of favor toward her, d'Artagnan saw the potential for allegiance.

"Well, then," said the young guard. "Instead of pitying me, you would do much better to assist me in avenging myself on your employer."

"Indeed? And what sort of revenge would your spurned heart take?"

"The disturbance of certain plots in which I believe Milord de Winter to be involved. For in truth, Kitty, I do not love him, though I love another who is lost to me from the machinations of Cardinal de Richelieu — who is your Milord's master."

"Faith!" said Kitty, her eyes gone wide in surprise. "You would take arms against the cardinal?"

"I would, and have done already."

"Such bravery," whispered Kitty, stepping closer to d'Artagnan. "But for myself, madame, to take revenge upon my own employer is a thing I could never do. Except for the one who should read to the bottom of my soul…"

Then d'Artagnan found herself caught off guard as Kitty first embraced her, then bestowed upon her a kiss that lasted a great deal of time. After the kiss was done, the valet smiled brightly, flushing as full as a cherry. "As was stated," said she coyly, "I know what it is to be in love, madame."

D'Artagnan found herself in a state of sudden and most unexpected alarm, in which she flushed as boldly as the young valet. Only then did she remember suddenly the languishing glances of Kitty, and the valet constantly meeting her in the antechamber, the corridor, or on the stairs. She recalled those touches of the hand every time the two met, and the deep sighs. But absorbed by her desire to expose the secrets of the enigmatic Milord, she had all but ignored the valet.

"Well," said Kitty to the mute d'Artagnan, seeing her dismay. "Are you willing, my dear, that I should give you a proof of my disposition to aid you in your campaign?"

"And what is that proof?" said d'Artagnan, stammering.

"Well. Let me this evening pass with you the time you generally spend with Milord, who clearly does not deserve to see you."

"I am wondering what this proof is proving, in truth," said d'Artagnan, somewhat weakly. For she was in mind suddenly of her own first passion for the beautiful Constance, and how difficult it felt to have the tables of love and passion turned thus.

"Then come my dear, and I will show you," said Kitty, pulling herself and d'Artagnan to an easy chair and seating herself forcefully on the young guard's lap. "Come, and let me tell you that you are the prettiest musketeer I ever saw."

And she did tell the young Gascon so, though the conversation played out in silence for the most part — and so well that d'Artagnan believed Kitty with full account. To the young guard's great astonishment, she was forced to defend herself against all manner of advances from the forthright valet. But in the end, Kitty advanced resolutely.

Time passes quickly when it is passed in attacks and defenses. So it was that midnight sounded, and almost at the same time the bell was rung in Milord de Winter's chamber.

"Faith," whispered Kitty, "there is Milord calling me."

"Faith, I must go," whispered d'Artagnan, who rose and quickly donned her hat, even before fumbling with buttons and sleeves. But as she did, Kitty opened quickly the door of a large wardrobe instead of that leading to the staircase. Then she pushed the distracted d'Artagnan forth, so as to bury her amid the shirts and dressing gowns of Milord.

"What are you doing?" cried the young guard.

"Expressing that I have no desire for you to go," said Kitty. "And that our campaign against Milord is begun, so let us determine what we might encourage him to say." Then the valet, who had secured the key, shut d'Artagnan up in the wardrobe.

"Well," called Milord in a sharp voice. "Are you asleep, that you don't answer when I ring?"

D'Artagnan heard the sliding door between the two rooms opened quickly.

"Here am I, Milord," said Kitty, springing forward to meet her employer. Both then remained in the bedchamber — but as the sliding door lingered open, d'Artagnan could hear Milord for some time scolding his valet. Then he was at length appeased, and the conversation turned upon d'Artagnan while Kitty was assisting the beautiful gentry with his preparations for bed.

"Well," said Milord de Winter, "I have not seen our Gascon this evening."

"What, Milord? Has she not come?" said Kitty. "Can she be proved so fickle even before being favored?"

"Oh, no. She must have been hindered by Monsieur de Treville or Madame d'Essarts. I understand my game, Kitty. I have this one caught."

"What will you then do with her, monsieur?"

"What will I do with her? That is hardly your concern, Kitty. For there is a feud between the young guard and me that she is quite ignorant of. She nearly made me lose my credit with their eminence. And I will be revenged."

"Revenged upon Madame d'Artagnan? But I believed that monsieur loved her," said the valet, seemingly of innocent mind.

"I, love her? I detest her! An idiot, who held the life of Liege de Winter in her hands and did not kill them, by which I missed three hundred thousand livres' inheritance."

"Ah. I had not considered," said Kitty.

D'Artagnan shuddered to the marrow at hearing Milord reproach her with that sharp voice which the suave creature took such pains to conceal in conversation — and for not having killed a sibling-in-law whom d'Artagnan had seen Milord repeatedly praise with kindness.

"For all this," said he, "I should long ago have revenged myself on that nuisance of Gascon. If only the cardinal had not requested me to show lenience toward her — and most frustratingly, I still do not know why. More frustratingly, I have the same orders for lenience with that little tailor the guard was so fond of. The Queen Anne's spy of the Rue de Fossoyeurs. Has d'Artagnan not already forgotten she ever existed? A fine vengeance that will be when the time comes, on my faith."

A cold sweat broke from d'Artagnan's brow. With Kitty's help, she had learned all she suspected of Milord — and much more.

"That will do," said Milord in response to Kitty's service. "You are at your leisure. And tomorrow, endeavor again to get me an answer to the letter I gave you."

"For Madame Countess de Wardes?" said Kitty.

"To be sure, for the Countess de Wardes."

"Now, there is one," said Kitty, "who appears to me quite a different sort of person from that poor Madame d'Artagnan."

"Go to bed, madame," said Milord. "I need not your commentary."

D'Artagnan heard the sliding door close, then the noise of two bolts by which Milord locked the barrier between his and Kitty's room. On her side, but as softly as possible, Kitty turned the key of the wardrobe lock, and d'Artagnan then opened the door.

"Well, faith," whispered Kitty, seeing the effect of Milord's words on the young guard. "I see you hear what you needed. How ashen you are."

"I heard my confirmation," murmured d'Artagnan. "The abominable creature."

"Indeed," said Kitty. "But silence. There is nothing but a wainscot between my chamber and Milord's. Every word that is uttered in one can be heard in the other."

"I must go," said d'Artagnan.

"What?" said Kitty, moving near to her. "But Milord is not yet asleep. By leaving now, you will make too much noise by far."

She drew d'Artagnan to her then. The young guard thought briefly to resist, but feared resistance would raise a noise that Milord would hear — though to d'Artagnan's ear, a lack of resistance to Kitty made noise enough.

Thus, in the final aggression of the affectionate valet's campaign, d'Artagnan surrendered once again.

⚜

Her evening with Kitty had left d'Artagnan's heart in an unreasonable chaos. Her passion for Constance remained steadfast, but was seasoned now with a stark guilt that was beyond anything of her experience. Still, against her battered heart, the young guard's head was clear by morning — and had been wholly dedicated to a plan of vengeance upon Milord de Winter.

In this plan, Kitty had become a willing participant, though useful only in part. Despite d'Artagnan's entreaties in the quiet of the night that she reveal what had become of Constance, Kitty swore truth to the young guard that she was entirely ignorant on that point. Milord never admitted her into half his secrets — but that which the valet had heard let Kitty encourage d'Artagnan that the young tailor was yet alive and well.

As to the cause which was near making Milord lose his credit with the cardinal, Kitty knew even less about that. But the return of d'Artagnan's keen mind left the Gascon well informed. As she believed she had seen Milord on board a vessel returning to England at the moment she was leaving, she suspected that his journey was almost without doubt on account of having just delivered to Richelieu the two stolen diamond studs.

After slipping away from Milord's before dawn, d'Artagnan returned the next evening. Finding him in a very ill humor, she had no doubt that it was the lack of an answer from the Countess de Wardes to his second letter which provoked him thus — on account of d'Artagnan still holding that letter. When Kitty came in, Milord made her the target of his foul mood, with harsh orders and multiple complaints. The poor valet ventured a sly glance at d'Artagnan, which said, "See how I suffer on your account?"

Toward the end of the evening, however, the beautiful lion became milder. He smilingly listened to the soft speeches of d'Artagnan, and even gave her his hand to kiss.

D'Artagnan departed in the appearance of romantic distraction. But her thoughts were clear, and even while continuing to pay her court to Milord, she had framed a clear plan in her mind.

She found Kitty at the carriage gate, and as on the preceding evening, stole up to her chamber. Kitty shared that privately, she had been accused of negligence and even more severely scolded. Milord could not at all comprehend the silence of the Countess de Wardes, and had ordered Kitty to make preparations to take a third letter.

D'Artagnan bade Kitty promise to bring her that letter on the following morning. Kitty smilingly set her price for that compliance, and so d'Artagnan once more concealed herself in the wardrobe. Milord called, prepared for bed, sent away Kitty, and shut the door.

As the night before, d'Artagnan did not slip away till nearly dawn.

⚜

As the clocks were striking eleven that morning, Kitty came to d'Artagnan where she waited in a small park along from Milord's house. She brought with her a fresh note from Milord, which she bade d'Artagnan collect from a very private hiding place. When that was done, the young guard opened the letter and read as follows:

This is the third time I have written to you to tell you that I love you. Beware that I do not write to you a fourth time to tell you that I detest you.

D'Artagnan looked anguished in reading the note, with Kitty once more misunderstanding the young guard's mood.

"Faith, but do you love him again?" sighed Kitty, who had not taken her eyes off the young guard's face.

"No, Kitty. I do not again, nor have I ever loved Milord. But tell me true," said d'Artagnan, for the flicker of an idea had formed in her mind. "Does Milord truly love the Countess de Wardes?"

"Love is too strong a word, madame. But there is some past affair between them, and she stays in his mind always."

D'Artagnan smiled at that.

"You are pleased to hear so?" Kitty said.

"No. Or rather, I am merely cheerful with the thought of how I will avenge myself for Milord's contempt."

"Oh, yes, and I know what sort of vengeance. Your young tailor captures your heart."

"What matters it to you, Kitty? You have made clear your feelings for me, and taken mine in return."

"And if that is not enough for me?"

"Then you must take heart in the scorn I will throw upon your employer."

D'Artagnan then took a pen she had brought for the occasion, and wrote on the reverse of Milord's note:

Monsieur —

Until the present moment, I could not believe that it was to me your first two letters were addressed, so unworthy did I feel myself of such an honor. But now I am forced to believe in the excess of your kindness, since not only your letter but your valet assures me that I have the good fortune to be beloved by you.

At eleven o'clock this evening, I shall come to beg your forgiveness. To delay it a single day would be in my eyes now to commit a fresh offense.

— The Countess de Wardes

"There," said the young guard, handing Kitty the letter. "Give that to Milord. It is the reply of the Countess de Wardes."

The valet assessed d'Artagnan with a wary look, for she had read the note as it was written. "He will be in a fury when this rendezvous does not come to pass. And I shall catch the blame, I fear."

"There shall be no risk to you, gentle Kitty," said d'Artagnan. "For my plan of necessity brings all Milord's fury on to me."

"And what is your plan?"

"It is most straightforward," said the young guard. "By way of this note of response, seemingly from the Countess de Wardes, I hope to somehow turn Milord's boastful swagger to stark vulnerability. By way of your chamber, I will gain access to the chamber of Milord, creating some advantage of surprise in the moment, to admit that I know of and have ruined his rendezvous and raise his ire against me. And in that moment of ire, I will trick him into letting slip where Constance Bonacieux is held."

"That is your plan?" said Kitty, looking not impressed.

"I will improvise the better details in the moment," said d'Artagnan. "For I must learn all that can be learned of the fate of Constance. In eight days, Kitty, the campaign begins with the march to La Rochelle, and I will be forced to leave Paris. I have no more time to lose."

"Alas," sighed Kitty. "For whom have I exposed myself to all this?"

"Faith, I believe it was I who has been most exposed," said d'Artagnan, flushing. "But I am grateful to you, I swear it."

"Ah, but you do not love me," said Kitty with a mocking tone of grief. "And I am saddened. Perhaps so saddened that I cannot deliver this fatal note."

A final negotiation then ensued, which saw in the end d'Artagnan promise that she would leave Milord's presence at an early hour that evening before returning to reveal her plan of duplicity — and that between that first point of campaign and the second, she would pass her time one last time with the young valet. And so this promise completed the saddened Kitty's consolation.

CHAPTER 34

THE EQUIPMENT OF ARAMIS AND PORTHOS

In the time that the four friends had been each in search of their equipment of campaign, there had been no fixed meeting between them. They dined apart from one another wherever they might happen to be, or rather where they could. Duty likewise on its part took a portion of that precious time which was gliding away so rapidly — but still they managed to agree to meet one day at the residence of Athos. That location was a necessity, seeing that she, in agreement with the vow she had made, had still not passed over the threshold of her apartment.

This day of reunion was the same day as that on which d'Artagnan wrote the note as the Countess de Wardes and failed to impress Kitty with her plan. As soon as Kitty left her, d'Artagnan directed her steps toward the Rue Ferou. At Athos's apartment, she found the elder musketeer and Aramis philosophizing, for Aramis once again had developed some slight inclination to resume the cassock. Athos, according to her custom, neither encouraged nor dissuaded the gentle musketeer, for she believed that everyone should be left to their own free will. She never gave advice but when it was asked, and even then she typically required to be asked twice.

"People in general," said she, "ask advice only not to follow it. Or if they do follow it, it is for the sake of having someone to blame for having given it."

Porthos arrived not long after d'Artagnan. And thus reunited, the four friends demonstrated four very different states of mind. From Porthos came tranquility in the matter of his equipment. From d'Artagnan, hope that word of Constance would soon be hers. From Aramis, uneasiness. And from Athos, a complete lack of care.

Porthos at first monopolized the conversation, so as to declare that his equipment was complete thanks to a friend of elevated rank. But even as he spoke, Mousqueton arrived in a breathless state. They came to request their employer to return to his apartment, where his presence was urgently required.

"Is it my equipment?"

"Yes, and no," replied Mousqueton.

"Well, but can't you speak?"

"Come, monsieur!"

Porthos rose, saluted his friends, and followed the valet. Only a moment after, Bazin made his appearance at the door.

"What do you want with me, my friend?" said Aramis, with that mildness of language which was observable in them every time their ideas were directed toward someone of the church.

"A person wishes to see maitre at home," said Bazin.

"A person. What person?"

"A wandering monk by their look."

"Then give them offerings, Bazin, and bid them pray for one who deserves it."

"This monk insists upon speaking to you, and pretends that you will be very glad to see them."

"Have they sent no particular message for me?"

"Yes. They spoke of selling plums, though I saw no fruits. And, 'If Maitre Aramis hesitates to come,' said they, 'tell them I am from Tours.'"

"From Tours!" cried Aramis. "A thousand pardons, gentles, but no doubt this visitor brings me news I was expecting." And rising also, they went off with Bazin at a quick pace.

There thus remained Athos and d'Artagnan.

"I believe those two have managed the business of their equipment well. What do you think, d'Artagnan?" said Athos.

"I know that Porthos was in a favorable way," said d'Artagnan. "And as to Aramis, to tell you the truth, I have never been seriously uneasy on their account. But you, my dear Athos, what do you mean to do? I wish now that you had kept for your own sake the pistoles won in our duel with the English, which you so generously distributed."

"I am content with having killed that knave, my friend, seeing that it is blessed bread to kill the English. But if I had pocketed their pistoles, they would have weighed me down with remorse."

"By my faith, dear Athos, you are too sensitive by far."

"Let it pass. But tell me what you have been doing? Why have I heard reports that you associate with suspicious English paramours whom the cardinal protects?"

"Because those reports came from me, my dear Athos. I told you of this affair."

"Ah, yes. You see the handsome Milord on whose account I gave you advice, which naturally you took care not to adopt."

"And I told you of my reasons."

"Yes. You look there for your equipment of campaign, I think you said?"

"Faith, not at all! I sought, and have acquired, certain knowledge that Milord was involved in the abduction of Constance Bonacieux."

"Ah, I understand now. To find one paramour, you court another. It is the longest road, but certainly the most amusing."

⚜

D'Artagnan departed Athos's not long after, but in the meantime, we may follow Aramis. Upon being informed that the person who wanted to speak to them came from Tours, we have seen with what speed the gentle musketeer followed — or rather, quickly outpaced — Bazin. They and he ran without stopping from the Rue Ferou to the Rue de Vaugirard. On finally entering their house, Aramis found a figure of short stature and intelligent blue eyes, with a mottled ivory complexion, a dark head shaved almost to the skin, and dressed in simple clothing and with bare feet.

"You have asked for me?" said the musketeer, breathless.

"I wish to speak with Maitre Aramis. Is that your name, maitre?"

"My very own. You have brought me something?"

"Yes, if you show me a certain embroidered handkerchief."

"Without difficulty," said Aramis, who took a small key from their pocket, and with it opened at the mantle a little ebony box inlaid with mother-of-pearl. Within lay the handkerchief that d'Artagnan had glimpsed in the hand of Constance at Aramis's window, which had been all that Aramis had found of their visitor the following morning. "Here it is. Look."

"It is good," replied the monk. "Now dismiss your valet."

Though Bazin had only just arrived, even more out of breath than Aramis, the musketeer made him a sign to withdraw, and the valet was obliged to obey.

With Bazin gone, the monk cast a rapid glance around them in order to be sure that no one could either see or hear them. Then, opening their ragged vest, badly held together by a leather strap, they began to rip the upper part of their doublet — from within the seams of which they drew a letter.

Aramis uttered a cry of joy at the sight of the seal, kissed the envelope with an almost religious respect, and opened the epistle, which contained what follows:

My friend —

It is the will of fate that we should still for some time be separated, but the delightful days of youth are not lost beyond return. Perform your duty on campaign. I will do mine elsewhere. Accept that which the bearer brings you, and show your equipment like a handsome true gentle. And think of me, who kisses tenderly your black eyes.

Adieux; or rather, au revoir.

The monk then continued to tear their garments, and drew from amid hidden pockets therein one hundred and fifty Spanish double pistoles, which they laid on the table. Then they opened the door, bowed, and went out, all before the gentle musketeer, stupefied by the letter, had any chance to address a word to them.

"Golden dreams!" cried Aramis. "Oh, beautiful life! Yes, we are young. Yes, we shall yet have happy days. My love, my blood, my life. All, all, all are thine, my adored." And they kissed the letter with passion, without even a glance at the gold that gleamed on the table.

Bazin scratched at the door, and as Aramis had no longer any reason to exclude him, they bade the valet come in. He was stupefied at the sight of the coins — and as such, forgot that he had come to announce d'Artagnan. For the young guard, curious to know who the monk could be, had come to Aramis on leaving Athos. As d'Artagnan used no ceremony with Aramis, and seeing that Bazin forgot to announce her, she announced herself in startled fashion.

"Faith! My dear Aramis," said she. "If these are the plums that are sent to you from Tours, I beg you will make my compliments to the gardener who gathers them."

"You are mistaken, friend d'Artagnan," said Aramis, laughing, and thinking quickly. "This is from my publisher, who has just sent me the price of that poem in one-syllable verse which I began in Crevecoeur."

"Ah, indeed," said d'Artagnan. "Well, your publisher is very generous, my dear Aramis. That's all I can say."

"But what, maitre?" cried Bazin. "A poem sell for such a sum as that? It is incredible! Oh, maitre, you can write as much as you like. You may become equal to the greatest poets, for a poet is as good as a cleric. Ah, maitre, become a poet, I beg of you."

"Bazin, my friend," said Aramis, "I believe you intrude in my conversation."

Bazin understood that he had overstepped. He thus bowed and went out.

"Well," said d'Artagnan with a smile. "You sell your creations for their weight in gold. You are very fortunate, my friend. But take care or you will lose that letter which is peeping out from your doublet, and which also comes, no doubt, from your publisher."

Aramis flushed to the eyes and crammed the letter fully into their pocket, hiding the words which they knew d'Artagnan had seen. "My dear d'Artagnan," said they, "if you please, we will join our friends. As I am rich, we will today begin to dine together again, expecting that you will be rich in your turn."

"My faith!" said d'Artagnan with great pleasure. "It is long since we have had a good meal. And I, for my part, have a somewhat hazardous expedition set for later this evening, and shall not be sorry to fortify myself with a few glasses of old burgundy."

"Agreed as to the old burgundy," said Aramis, from whom the letter and the gold had removed, as by magic, all ideas of joining the church that had strayed once more to their mind.

Having put four double pistoles into their pocket to answer the needs of the moment, Aramis placed the others in the ebony box inlaid with mother-of-pearl, in which was the famous handkerchief that now served them as a talisman.

The two friends then returned to Athos's, and she, faithful to her vow of not going out, took it upon herself to order dinner to be brought to them. As Athos was perfectly acquainted with the details of gastronomy, d'Artagnan and Aramis made no objection to abandoning this important care to her. They then went to find Porthos. But while wandering by the corner of the Rue Bac, the two met Mousqueton, who was driving before them a mule and a horse with a most pitiable air. D'Artagnan uttered a cry of surprise, which was not quite free from joy.

"Ah, my yellow horse! Aramis, look at that horse!"

"Indeed I am," said Aramis. "What a frightful brute."

"No, my friend," said d'Artagnan. "For upon that very horse, I came to Paris."

"What, does madame know this horse?" said Mousqueton.

"It is of an original color," said Aramis. "I never saw one with such a hide in my life."

"I can well believe it," said d'Artagnan. "But how did this horse come into your hands, Mousqueton?"

"I pray you, madame," said the valet, "say nothing about it. It is a frightful trick of the husband of our duchess."

"How is that, Mousqueton?"

"Why, we are looked upon with a rather favorable eye by a gentle of quality, the Duchess de… but, your pardon. Monsieur Porthos has commanded me to be discreet. This fine gentle had forced us to accept a little gift of a magnificent Spanish charger and an Andalusian mule, which were beautiful to look upon. But the husband heard of the affair, and as the two magnificent beasts were on their way to us, he confiscated them and substituted these horrible animals."

"Which you are taking back to him?" said d'Artagnan.

"Exactly," said Mousqueton. "You may well believe that we will not accept such steeds as these in exchange for those which had been promised to us."

"Faith, no. Though I should like to have seen Porthos on my yellow horse. That would give me an idea of how I looked when I arrived in Paris. But don't let us hinder you, Mousqueton. Go and perform your orders. Is Porthos at home?"

"Yes, madame," said Mousqueton, "but in a very ill humor."

The valet then continued on her way toward the Quai de Grands Augustins, while the two friends went to ring at the bell of the unfortunate Porthos. But he, having seen them crossing the yard, and still much vexed over the affairs his valet had described, took care not to answer, and they rang in vain.

Meanwhile, Mousqueton continued on their way, still driving the two sorry animals before them, and crossing the Pont Neuf, they reached the Rue d'Ours. Arrived there, they fastened both horse and mule to the knocker of the attorneys' door — in accordance with the orders of Porthos. Then, without taking any thought for the beasts' future, they returned to the musketeer and told him that his commission was completed.

In a short time, the two unfortunate beasts, who had not eaten anything since the morning, made such a noise in raising and letting fall the knocker that Monsieur Vattier ordered the attorneys' young page to go and inquire in the neighborhood to whom this horse and mule belonged. When no one took ownership, the young page themself was inspired to claim the beasts, and the next day, walked the pair to their family's farm in Bagnolet, where we are pleased to report that d'Artagnan's horse did live and eventually die tranquilly and honorably, as the Gascon's father had desired.

Madame Coquenard had, of course, no sense of what had brought the poor beasts to her door, having no knowledge of her husband's actions. But a visit from Porthos soon after enlightened her. The anger that blazed in the eyes of the musketeer, in spite of his efforts to suppress it, alarmed the sensitive attorney. Unknown to her, that anger was due mostly to Mousqueton having revealed to their employer that they had met d'Artagnan and Aramis, and that d'Artagnan had recognized in the yellow horse the Bearnese pony upon which she had come as a poor traveler to Paris.

Porthos went away after having appointed a meeting with Madame Coquenard in the cloister of Saint-Magloire, claiming business of one of the lawsuits that were Madame Coquenard's story of him. Monsieur Vattier, seeing that the musketeer was leaving the house at once, invited him to dinner — an invitation that Porthos refused with a majestic air.

Madame Coquenard later walked quickly to the cloister of Saint-Magloire. She tried to guess at what reproaches might await her there, for as much as she was in love with Porthos, she was fascinated by the musketeer's lofty airs.

When he saw her, all the imprecations and reproaches that one wounded in their vanity could let fall, Porthos let fall upon the young attorney. She, in response, shut down his anger with a single cold look, and bade him reconsider his approach. Porthos, with blazing cheeks and much chagrined, then told the tale that Mousqueton had told d'Artagnan and Aramis.

"Alas," said she, "I did all for the best. One of our clients is a horse dealer. He owes money to the office, and is backward in his pay. I told him I would take a fine mule and a finer horse for what he owed us, but that I did not know the particulars of such things. I warrant he sought my husband's advice then, curse his interference."

"Then you forgive me?" said the musketeer.
"We shall see," said Madame Coquenard majestically...

"Indeed," said Porthos. "If he owed you more than five crowns, your horse dealer has got himself a bargain."

"Never mind that," said she. "Let us talk about making amends."

"Talking with you brings me misfortune," said Porthos grimly.

"Brash musketeer. Simply tell me what you require."

"Nothing. For that amounts to the same thing as if I asked you for something."

The attorney sighed, a sound that deflated the very last of Porthos's ire. She raised one eyebrow and fixed to him the same cold look once more, until his own gaze shuffled downward. She then took the arm of the musketeer, and with calm demeanor, spoke.

"Monsieur, you bade me procure your equipment of campaign with the basest detail. A horse and a mule with spirit and grace were your only orders. So it is hardly my fault that I must trust to others to assist me in ensuring the quality of your needs."

"You should have left it to me, then, madame, who know what those needs are."

"Well would I have done so, monsieur, except for your only interest seeming to be in the value of my offering, and not its care and content."

Porthos opened his mouth to give argument to this — and understood he had no argument, the attorney showing the skill of her profession by being in the right of the discussion.

"And so what shall we do?" asked the musketeer.

"Listen. Monsieur Vattier's renewed awareness of our affair must be dealt with, but leave that to me."

"As you wish," said Porthos, relieved.

"This evening, Monsieur Vattier has arranged to be conducted to the house of the Duceux de Chaulnes. They have sent for him for a consultation, which will last three hours at least. Come! We shall be alone, and can make up our accounts."

"Then you forgive me?" said the musketeer.

"We shall see," said Madame Coquenard majestically. And the two separated, both saying, "Till this evening."

Porthos's step was light as he walked away, both for having reestablished Madame Coquenard's attitude toward him — and for his drawing ever nearer to the strongbox of her and her husband's office. For although that coffer was not the forthright attorney's best feature, it retained nonetheless its own luster to the tall musketeer's eye.

CHAPTER 35

WORDS IN THE DARK

As was her custom, d'Artagnan presented herself at Milord's that same night at about nine o'clock. She found him in a charming humor, and never had she been so well received. Our Gascon knew, by the first glance of her eye, that her note as Madame Countess de Wardes had been delivered, and that this note had had its intended effect.

At one point, Kitty entered to bring some sherbet. Her lord put on a charming face and smiled at her graciously. But the young valet was so dolorous with the thought of this evening being her last with d'Artagnan that she did not even notice Milord's condescension.

D'Artagnan looked at the two one after the other, and was forced to acknowledge that in her opinion, nature had made a mistake in the formation of the pair. To the great lord, fate had given a heart vile and venal. To the young valet, it had given the true heart and vivaciousness of a gentlefolk.

At ten o'clock, Milord began to appear restless. D'Artagnan knew what he wanted. He looked at the clock, rose, reseated himself, and smiled at the young Gascon with an air which said, 'You are very amiable, no doubt, but you would be truly charming if you would only depart.'

So d'Artagnan rose and took her hat. Milord gave her his hand to kiss. The young guard felt him press her hand, and understood that this was a sentiment of gratitude because of her departure.

"He truly dotes on the Countess de Wardes," she mused. And with this understanding in mind, the scope of the young guard's plan broadened as she departed.

Fulfilling her promise to come to Kitty, d'Artagnan did not leave Milord's, but found instead the staircase and ascended to the little chamber. As she entered, Kitty raced for her, taking d'Artagnan's hands and smiling. But her smile slipped in response to the young guard's words, which were, "Tell me, when Milord's expected visit from the Countess de Wardes comes, will he dim the lights in the apartment?"

"Down to darkness," said the young valet. "But why is this a pressing matter?" She leaned in to kiss d'Artagnan, but the young guard pressed her away.

"We have no time, I fear. For I have tarried long with Milord, and must be prepared to return as the Countess de Wardes before the hour is out."

The valet took in d'Artagnan with a fatal look. "What say you?" said she. "You told me your intent was to drive Milord to distraction when the Countess de Wardes failed to appear this night."

"And I promised to improvise the better details. Well, these are they. With the apartment in darkness, I will pretend to be the Countess de Wardes. Then revealing myself will bring Milord to the point of rage, and I will see his anger undo his secrecy."

"I am seeing suddenly a need for you to also improvise to get away afterward, for Milord's fury will be considerable. And if he suspects my involvement, I will be forced to flee alongside you."

"If it comes to that, we will make our escape together, Kitty. But first, pray tell me what Milord has said and done as regards the countess, I beseech you."

Kitty's expression made it clear that she bore no love for d'Artagnan's improvised plan. But she shared with her that on receiving the letter, Milord in a delirium of joy had told her everything. He had made Kitty repeat the smallest details of the pretended interaction between the valet and the Countess de Wardes when she received the letter. How de Wardes had responded, what was the expression of her face, if she seemed very amorous, and more. In the end, by way of reward for the manner in which Kitty had this time successfully executed the commission, Milord had given her a purse — with which she now expected to need to finance her escape from his service.

"This is all the best fortune," said d'Artagnan. "For I will speak with Milord as the Countess de Wardes, and his eyes will believe in shadows what his heart perceives. I must simply ensure that Madame Countess de Wardes takes her departure, still in shadow, before the illusion can be broken."

"Faith, I hope your business of romance shall be accomplished by then," said Kitty. The young valet paced angrily about the room.

"I tell you for the last time," said d'Artagnan, "that I have no such intentions for this villain. I will shake out the truth from him, and nothing more." But Kitty made no reply.

Presently, they both heard Milord retire to his room. D'Artagnan slipped into the wardrobe. Hardly was she concealed when the little bell sounded. Kitty went to Milord, once more leaving the door open so that d'Artagnan could hear nearly all that passed between the two.

The handsome gentry seemed overcome with anticipation, but Kitty's responses came in a dolorous tone that d'Artagnan hoped was hidden beneath more pleasing features, or which Milord would not notice for the egotism of his happiness.

Finally, as the hour for his rendezvous approached, Milord had everything about him darkened. He ordered Kitty to go to the front door, and to admit the countess when she arrived.

The wait was not long. When d'Artagnan had seen, through a crevice in the wardrobe, that the whole apartment was in shadow, she slipped out of her concealment. She let the tie of her hair loose, shaking and allowing her curls to flow freely in the manner she remembered of the Countess de Wardes that day in Calais — and all the better to shroud her face against Milord's gaze. Making her way through the sliding door, then along the wall, she went to the main door and knocked as if on the other side.

"Who is there?" said Milord.

"It is I," said d'Artagnan in a subdued voice. "I, the Countess de Wardes."

"Faith," murmured Kitty from the sliding door. "You have not even waited the hour you yourself named." Then she silently slid the door shut.

"Well," said Milord in a pleasant voice, "why do you not enter? Madame, you know that I wait for you."

At this welcome, d'Artagnan paced slowly into the chamber.

"You are welcome here, madame," said Milord in a voice most alluring. He pressed d'Artagnan's hand in his own as he searched her face — and in the darkness, the young guard confirmed that Milord did not recognize her, and took her fully for the Countess de Wardes.

"You have read my apology for my actions in regard to your letters," whispered d'Artagnan.

"Worry not about that," said Milord. "For I am happy in what your looks and your words have expressed to me every time we have met. And you must know that I also crave you. Oh, tomorrow I must have some pledge from you which will prove that you think of me. And that you may never forget me again, take this." And Milord slipped a ring from his finger onto d'Artagnan's. It was a magnificent sapphire encircled with diamonds, which the young guard could not remember having before seen on Milord's pale finger.

"This vengeance shall be profitable in more ways than one," thought d'Artagnan to herself, who was ready to reveal all. She even opened her mouth to announce who she was, and with what a revengeful purpose she had come. But then Milord spoke again. "Poor angel," he named her, stroking her cheek, "whom that monster of a Gascon attempted to kill. The cardinal told me all."

It was the attack upon the Countess de Wardes at Calais to which Milord referred. That monster, d'Artagnan knew, was herself.

"Indeed," whispered she. "And even still do my wounds make me suffer."

"Be at peace," murmured Milord. "I will avenge you upon the Gascon — and cruelly!"

"Faith," thought d'Artagnan again. "Milord's love for the Countess de Wardes might make him speak openly of all his plots. The moment for my confession must wait."

But though she attempted to draw more from him in their conversation, d'Artagnan soon realized that Milord's intent was for dialogue more personal. She responded by following the script shown to her over previous nights by Kitty, boldly taking Milord in her arms. He made no effort to remove his lips from d'Artagnan's kisses. Only he did not respond to them. His lips were cold. To d'Artagnan, it felt as though she had embraced a statue.

"I fear we must part for now," said d'Artagnan, sensing the appetite of Milord, and understanding how denying that appetite would feed her own intentions. "Though in doing so, I feel only the liveliest regret."

"Is it your wounds still? I might ease your suffering, madame."

"In time, my love," whispered d'Artagnan as the Countess de Wardes. "So leave this as adieux, and let us meet again when we can."

D'Artagnan knew that Kitty would be waiting to greet her in her chamber, and expecting the young guard to return up the staircase to conduct the final sortie of their brief engagement, as had been promised. But Milord himself followed her down to the door, forcing d'Artagnan to advance quickly lest some stray light reveal her. Fearing then that Milord might remain watching her from a window, she could only make her way out and home.

After a fitful sleep, d'Artagnan ran to find Athos even as the sun rose the next morning. She was now engaged in an adventure so singular that she wished for counsel. She therefore told the elder musketeer all.

"Your Milord," said Athos when the tale was done, "appears to be an infamous creature. But nonetheless, you have gambled in deceiving him. No matter how this ends, you have a terrible enemy on your hands."

"Such is the cost of the campaign," said d'Artagnan. "But so does the campaign bring profit. For look here." And thus speaking, she brought forth the sapphire set with diamonds.

"By my faith," said Athos. "That reminds me of a family jewel…"

"It is beautiful, is it not?" said d'Artagnan.

"Yes," said Athos. "Magnificent. I did not think two sapphires of such a fine water existed. Have you traded it for your diamond?"

"Faith, no. It is the profit of last night's gambit — a gift for the Countess de Wardes, stolen from my forlorn English lord."

"That ring comes from your Milord?" whispered Athos, in a voice whose emotion could not be hidden. She examined it more closely and became very pale. Then she tried it on her left hand, and it fit her finger as if made for it.

A shade of anger and vengeance passed across the usually calm brow of the musketeer.

"It is impossible that it can be he," said Athos. "How could this ring come into the hands of Milord de Winter? And yet it is difficult to suppose such a resemblance should exist between two jewels."

"Athos, do you know this ring?" said d'Artagnan, not hiding her confusion.

"I thought I did," said Athos. "But no doubt I was mistaken." And she returned d'Artagnan the ring, but without ceasing to gaze at it. "Pray, d'Artagnan, put that jewel away, for it recalls such cruel recollections that I shall have no head to converse with you. Don't ask me for counsel. Don't tell me you are perplexed what to do. But stop! Let me look at that sapphire again. The one I mentioned to you had one of its faces scratched by accident."

D'Artagnan gave the ring again to Athos, who shook her head. "Look," said she. "Is that not strange?" And she pointed out to d'Artagnan the scratch she had remembered.

"But from whom did this ring come to you, Athos?"

"From my father, who inherited it from his mother. As I told you, it is an old family jewel."

"And you… sold it?" asked d'Artagnan, hesitant.

"No," said Athos with a singular smile. "I gave it away in a night of love, as it has been given under false pretense to you."

The young guard became pensive in her turn as she took back the ring, then put it in her pocket.

"D'Artagnan," said Athos, "you know I love you. If I had a child, I could not love them better. Take my advice, then. Renounce your plans for this gentle. I do not know him, but a sort of intuition tells me he is a base creature, and that there is something fatal about him."

"You are right," said d'Artagnan. "I confess that this Milord terrifies me. But I shall see this through for Constance, at any risk."

"In truth, my young friend, I believe you act rightly," said the musketeer, shaking the Gascon's hand with affection. "And gods grant that this man, who has scarcely entered into your life, may not leave a terrible trace in it." Then Athos bowed to d'Artagnan like one who wishes it understood that they would not be sorry to be left alone with their thoughts.

On reaching her apartment, d'Artagnan was surprised to find Kitty waiting for her. The young valet reported to her a night of sleeplessness and anger, but d'Artagnan judged that a month of fever could not have changed her features more.

She had been sent by her lord to seek the Countess de Wardes, said Kitty. As d'Artagnan had foreseen, cutting short Milord's night with de Wardes had made him mad with desire, intoxicated with ardor. He wished to know when his lover would meet him a second night, and Kitty, sulking, awaited d'Artagnan's reply.

D'Artagnan's plans, already embracing vengeance, took on an even starker turn in her mind from the reaction of Athos to the ring. She sensed mysteries there that she feared would bring more harm before they were revealed, and determined that they should be revealed quickly. So as a reply, she wrote the following letter:

Do not depend upon me, monsieur, for the next meeting. Since my convalescence, I have so many affairs of this kind on my hands that I am forced to regulate them a little. When your turn comes, I shall have the honor to inform you of it.

— The Countess de Wardes

D'Artagnan gave the letter to Kitty, who read it with uncertainty.

"Are your plots of vengeance ended, then? You mean to seek your true love, this Madame Bonacieux, in some other way?"

"No. My plans have only begun. Take this to Milord and you will see."

Kitty frowned, but she embraced d'Artagnan and kissed her with a lengthy passion that left the young guard trembling. "You know the violent character of Milord," the valet whispered in farewell. "He will not take this rejection lightly."

"I count on that."

"All good for you. But I might well incur danger in giving this note to my employer. You shall make it up to me, Madame Musketeer."

And so saying, the valet set out to return to the Place Royale, leaving d'Artagnan to think on her previous assessment of Kitty. For even though the valet might bear the true heart and vivaciousness of a gentlefolk, the young guard mused, even the heart of the best person is merciless in its pursuit of love.

⚜

Milord opened the letter with an eagerness equal to that of Kitty in bringing it. But at the first words he read, he became livid. He crushed the paper in his hand, and turning with wild eyes upon Kitty, he cried, "What is this?"

"The answer to monsieur's letter," said Kitty, standing fast.

"Impossible!" shouted Milord. "It is impossible that anyone could have written such a letter to me!" Then all at once, shaking, he cried out, "Gods' blood, can she have —" before he stopped. He ground his teeth, his face the color of ash. He tried to go toward the window for air, but could only stretch forth his arms. Then Milord's legs failed him as a scream erupted from his lungs, and he sank into an armchair.

Kitty hastened carefully toward him, and was beginning to open his collar. But Milord started up, pushing her away. "What do you want with me?" said he. "And why do you place your hand on me?"

"I thought that monsieur might faint, and I wished to bring him help," responded the valet — now frightened of Milord for the first time, from the terrible expression which had come over his face.

"I faint? I? Do you take me for half a man? When I am insulted, I do not faint. I avenge myself!"

And at a sign from Milord, Kitty willingly and quickly left the room.

CHAPTER 36

THE DREAM OF VENGEANCE

That evening, Milord gave orders that when Madame d'Artagnan came as usual, she should be immediately admitted. But although the Liege de Winter appeared that evening at Milord's house to report his business obligations completed, the young guard did not come.

The next day, Kitty went to see d'Artagnan again, and related to her all that had passed when Milord received the letter. The young guard smiled, for this jealous anger on the part of Milord had been her plan.

That evening, Milord was still more impatient than on the preceding evening. He renewed the order relative to the Gascon, but as before, he waited for her in vain.

The next morning, when Kitty presented herself at d'Artagnan's, she drew a letter from her pocket and gave it over. This letter was in Milord's handwriting, and was addressed to Madame d'Artagnan, who opened it and read as follows:

Madame d'Artagnan —

It is wrong thus to neglect your friends, particularly at the moment you are about to leave them for so long a time. My sibling-in-law returned yesterday, and I myself expected you the day before, but in vain. Will it be the same this evening?

Yours very gratefully,

— Milord de Winter

"And so it ends," said d'Artagnan. "My credit rises by the fall of that of the Countess de Wardes. I push Milord to the breaking point of his weakness, and he will reveal all."

"Oh gods," said Kitty wearily, "you know how to represent things in such a way that you tell yourself you are always in the right. There are countless ways in which Milord will turn your vengeance to his advantage. And even more ways in which I might help you forget your young tailor, and put an end to all this."

"You have my assurances that my mind is made up clearly as regards both these matters," said d'Artagnan firmly. In reaction, Kitty only sighed.

*The next morning, when Kitty presented herself at d'Artagnan's,
she drew a letter from her pocket and gave it over…*

D'Artagnan then made instructions for Kitty to tell Milord that she could not be more grateful for his kindnesses than she was, and that she would be pleased to accept his invitation. But she did not dare to write back, for fear that the too-cautious eyes of Milord would recognize her writing as too similar to that of the Countess de Wardes.

As nine o'clock sounded, d'Artagnan was at the Place Royale. It was evident that the servants who waited in the antechamber had been warned to watch for her, for as soon as she appeared, before even she had asked if Milord were available, one of them ran to announce her.

"Show her in," said Milord in a quick tone — and one so piercing that d'Artagnan heard him from the antechamber.

As the servants went out, d'Artagnan cast an inquiring glance at Milord. He was pale and looked fatigued, either from emotion or want of sleep. The lights in the sitting room had been intentionally dimmed, but the young gentry could not conceal the traces of the fever of romance denied which had devoured him for two days.

D'Artagnan approached with her usual gallantry. Milord then made an extraordinary effort to receive her, but never did more distressed features give the lie to a more amiable smile.

To the questions which d'Artagnan put concerning his health, Milord replied, "Bad, very bad."

"Then," said she, "my visit is ill-timed. You stand, no doubt, in need of repose, and I will withdraw."

"No, no," said Milord. "On the contrary, stay, Madame d'Artagnan. Your agreeable company will distract me."

"Indeed," thought d'Artagnan. "And with that distraction, your guard will fall. The duel is on!"

Milord assumed the most agreeable air possible, and conversed with more than his usual brilliancy. But at the same time, the fever that for a short while had abandoned him returned to give luster to his eyes and a flushed color to his face. There was a moment at which d'Artagnan felt something like remorse. But she understood that she was in the presence of a sorcerer surrounding her with his enchantments — and that if she had not been already inured against those charms, how easily she might have fallen to them.

By degrees, Milord became more communicative. At one juncture, he boldly asked d'Artagnan if she had a lover.

"Alas," said d'Artagnan, with the most sentimental air she could assume. "Can you be cruel enough to put such a question to me — who from the moment I saw you, have only breathed and sighed through you and for you?"

Milord smiled a strange smile, and d'Artagnan felt the curse it carried. "Then you love me?" said he.

"Have I any need to tell you so? Have you not perceived it?"

"It may be. But you must know that the more a heart is worth the capture, the more difficult it is to be won."

"Oh, difficulties do not frighten me," said d'Artagnan. "I shrink before nothing but impossibilities."

"But nothing is impossible," said Milord, "to true love."

"Nothing, monsieur?" D'Artagnan drew her seat nearer to Milord's.

"Well, now," said he. "Let us see what you would do to prove this love of which you speak."

"All that could be required of me. Order me. I am ready."

"For everything?"

"For everything," said d'Artagnan. She knew not where Milord's thoughts were leading, but she felt a fear in him, and vowed to make use of it.

"Then let us talk a little seriously," said Milord, in his turn drawing his arm-chair nearer to d'Artagnan.

"I am all attention, monsieur," said she.

Milord remained thoughtful and undecided for a moment. Then, as if appearing to have formed a resolution, he said, "I have an enemy."

"You, monsieur?" said d'Artagnan, affecting surprise. "As good and beautiful as you are? Is that possible, by faith?"

"A mortal enemy."

"Indeed."

"An enemy who has insulted me so cruelly that between them and me it is war to the death. May I reckon on you as an auxiliary?"

D'Artagnan at once understood the ground which the vindictive creature wished to reach. Milord sought to use the guard as an agent of his own vengeance — and in so doing, would play straight into d'Artagnan's control.

"You may, monsieur," said she. "My arm and my life belong to you, like my love."

"Madame," said Milord, "you are as generous as you are loving…" But then he stopped.

"Well?" asked d'Artagnan.

"Well," said Milord after a moment of silence, "but would you employ for me your sword arm which has already acquired so much renown?"

"At once." D'Artagnan drew Milord into her arms, and felt him scarcely resisting.

"My noble warrior," whispered he, smiling.

"I am at your command," said d'Artagnan.

"You are quite certain?" said Milord, as with a last doubt.

"Simply name to me the base villain who has brought tears into your beautiful eyes."

"Who told you that I had been weeping?" said he.

"It appeared to me —"

"Folk as strong as I never weep," said Milord coldly.

"So much the better. Come, tell me their name."

"Remember that their name is all my secret."

"Yet I must know that name."

"Yes, you must. You see what confidence I have in you?"

"You overwhelm me with joy. What is their name?"

"You know them."

"Indeed?"

"Yes."

"It is surely not one of my friends?" said d'Artagnan, affecting hesitation in order to make Milord believe her ignorant.

"If it were one of your friends, you would hesitate, then?" said Milord. A threatening look was suddenly in his eyes.

"Not if it were my own sibling," cried d'Artagnan, as if carried away by her enthusiasm.

"I love your devotedness," said Milord.

"Alas, do you love nothing else in me?"

"I love you also," said he, taking d'Artagnan's hand.

The warm pressure of Milord's touch made the young guard tremble, as if by that touch, the fever which consumed Milord might attack her. He was all but intoxicated with ardor, and so strong was the game of words he played that d'Artagnan almost believed in his tenderness.

Milord, sensing the control he believed he wove over the young guard, seized the occasion.

"Their name is…" said he, letting the words hang.

"The Countess de Wardes," whispered d'Artagnan. "I know it."

"And how do you know it?" Milord seized suddenly both of d'Artagnan's hands, and gazed as if endeavoring to read with his eyes to the bottom of her heart. "Tell me, tell me, I say."

"How do I know it?" said d'Artagnan. She felt the passion of Milord running uncontrollable, ready to strike him down. She forced herself to keep an indifferent expression, lest the villain should see the trap tightening around him. "I know it because yesterday, Madame de Wardes, in a tavern where I was, showed a ring which she said she had received from you."

"Wretch!"

"And so?" whispered d'Artagnan.

"And so you will avenge me of this wretch!" cried Milord, seething.

"Anything, my brave friend. And when shall you be avenged?"

"Tomorrow, if it please you."

By Milord's look, d'Artagnan was certain that tomorrow was not soon enough, so deep did his hatred of the Countess de Wardes now run. But the young guard understood that this villain's vengeance would require a thousand precautions to take in order that she might avoid the interference of witnesses.

"Tomorrow," said d'Artagnan in agreement. "You will be avenged, or I shall be dead."

"No," said Milord. "You will avenge me with full success, for de Wardes is a coward."

"In society, perhaps. But not in battle. I know something of her there."

"Indeed? I was unaware of any prior contest between you," said Milord falsely. "But it seems you had not much reason to complain of your fortune therein."

"Fortune is a paramour, not a friend. Though favorable yesterday, it may turn its back tomorrow."

"Which means that you now hesitate?"

"No, I do not hesitate, by my faith. All is agreed."

Milord set a hand to d'Artagnan's arm. "But would it be just and fair to allow you to go to a possible death without having given you at least something more than hope?"

D'Artagnan answered by a glance that spoke of her quick panic, then thought to accompany the glance with words to cover it. "That is all too just," said she, too tenderly.

"Oh, you are an angel," said Milord. "But I assure you that you may rely on my tenderness in thanks for this deed." He now took d'Artagnan in his arms, and she felt again the coldness beneath his touch. But even as she sought for the excuse to break away, Milord suddenly started at a voice, recognized by d'Artagnan as the Liege de Winter, calling out from below.

"Confound it! I hear my sibling. They prepare to return home to Portsmouth before the full bloom of war increases the difficulty of crossing to England."

"My mind is in no fit state for polite conversation," said d'Artagnan, thinking quickly. "If my liege finds me here, things may be complicated."

Milord nodded in agreement, then rang a bell at hand which summoned Kitty, and she quickly appeared. "Go out this way," said Milord to d'Artagnan, opening a small door leading from the sitting room to a side hall. "Then come back at eleven o'clock, when we will terminate this conversation. Kitty will then conduct you to my chamber."

At hearing these words, Kitty gave d'Artagnan a wild-eyed and condemning look. The young guard covered it with a sweep of her hat. Milord held out his hand to her, which she kissed tenderly.

Kitty then accompanied d'Artagnan in thankful silence to the servants' door, since whatever advice she might have given d'Artagnan, the young guard was in too fatal a state of mind to have heard any of it. For Milord de Winter was as murderous as he was ambitious, and this nature had now become the centerpiece of d'Artagnan's plan to bring the snarling lion of a gentry under her control.

CHAPTER 37

MILORD'S SECRET

D'Artagnan left the house instead of going up in secret to Kitty's chamber, as the valet attempted to persuade her to do — and that for two reasons. First, because by this means she would escape further reproaches, recriminations, and reminders that the final tryst of their earlier negotiation had yet to be paid out. And second, because she craved the opportunity to assess her own thoughts, and to be certain that she was presently farther ahead in plots against Milord than he was against her.

The location of Constance Bonacieux would be wrung from the wretched noble. D'Artagnan was determined of that. Her weapon was that which Milord had given her — the order for the murder of the Countess de Wardes, and the threat d'Artagnan would make of revealing that order and that feud to all. The public disgrace would be alarming. But d'Artagnan recalled also how Monsieur de Treville had called the Countess de Wardes one of the cardinal's agents, and cousin to Rochefort. To reveal Milord's murderous intent to those worthies might set villain against villain — a poetical justice indeed.

But the young guard also was spurred on by a ferocious desire of personal vengeance. As an accomplice in the abduction of Constance, Milord had done a greater injury to d'Artagnan than any insult done in the young guard's own name. Thus, she acknowledged the desire to run at once to Monsieur de Treville and report Milord's inducement to murder. She weighed the option of responding at last to the cardinal's request for an audience, and reporting to their eminence the duplicity of their agent. But both those plans were set aside in the end. For before exposing Milord, d'Artagnan vowed that she would subdue that villain face to face.

She walked six times round the Place Royale, turning at every ten steps to look at the light in Milord's apartment, which was to be seen through the blinds. Liege de Winter's business with their brother-in-law kept Milord from retiring for some time.

But at length, the light disappeared. Movement on the street announced the departure of Liege de Winter. And with that, d'Artagnan was resolved. She recalled to her mind the details of that night at Madame d'Estrees's summerhouse, and the vision of Constance dragged to the waiting carriage and swept off into the night. Then with a beating heart and a brain on fire, she reentered the townhouse.

Kitty was waiting for d'Artagnan, and sharp with anger at her return. She wished to delay the young guard for the purpose of questioning her plans. But Milord, with his ear listening keenly, had heard the noise d'Artagnan made in ascending to the sitting room. And opening the door to his chamber, within which a single light burned, he bade the young guard come in.

Milord paced like a cat, with shirt open to the waist, setting a scene of such incredible immodesty that d'Artagnan could scarcely believe what she saw. Then he extinguished that last light, and d'Artagnan in the darkness imagined herself to be drawn into one of those fantastic intrigues one meets in dreams.

She was forced to play her part by proceeding slowly toward Milord, as if yielding to that magnetic attraction which the lodestone exercises over iron. As she did, she gave thought to how easily Milord might have shaped any other heart to be the tool of his vengeance. How many more like de Wardes had insulted him? And how many more of those had fallen to the hands of lovers whispered promises in the night, their hearts and minds caressed till they had dealt out death in Milord's name?

If not for her own love for Constance, d'Artagnan knew how easily her pride, her vanity, might embrace this voice of vengeance, making louder its murmur in her heart. But she was absorbed entirely by the sensations of the moment. Milord was that figure of fatal intentions whose face of rage had terrified d'Artagnan more than once. But that face was hidden now in shadow and the guise of an ardent, passionate paramour, abandoning himself to love.

"My sibling returns to Portsmouth," said Milord, not concealing his spite, "fearful of the threat of war. We shall thankfully have no further interruptions from them."

He slipped close and embraced d'Artagnan, playful at a thankful distance as he unbuckled her belt to let sword and scabbard slip to the floor. But against this loving gesture, d'Artagnan felt Milord show the true scope of his thought as he spoke not of family or ardor, but of violence. "And so," he asked the young guard. "Are the means which are to bring on the encounter between yourself and de Wardes on the morrow already arranged in your mind?"

Carefully, Milord began to remove d'Artagnan's jacket with trembling hands. D'Artagnan thus sensed in his preoccupation the weakness that would undo him, and so she made no move to resist, but only answered coyly. "Oh, my dear. It is too late an hour to think about duels and sword thrusts."

She felt Milord's hesitation, and thought to quickly distract it by kicking off her boots. In reaction, he reached for her again, and the young guard smiled in the dark. She could see that the duel was the foremost interest that occupied Milord's mind, and for her own sport, she thus endeavored to turn the conversation.

"If I may advise Milord, you might even think to renounce, by pardoning de Wardes, the furious plans you have crafted."

At d'Artagnan's words, Milord reached for her, touching her face and shoulders — and tore open her shirt to leave both half-dressed, and facing each other. D'Artagnan saw the return of the sinister face even in the darkness, and heard a sharp tone which echoed with the resolve of the villain's iron will. "Are you afraid, dear Madame d'Artagnan?"

"You cannot think so, dear love," replied d'Artagnan. "But I have had much time to reflect while you passed time with your sibling. And I cannot help but now to think — suppose this poor Countess de Wardes were less guilty than you think her?"

"Regardless," said Milord coldly, "she has deceived me, and from the moment she deceived me, she merited death."

"Well, she must die, then, since you condemn her," said d'Artagnan, in so firm a tone that it would have appeared to anyone an undoubted proof of devotion. "And I am quite ready. But first, I should like to be certain of one thing."

"And what is that?" asked Milord.

"That is whether you really love me."

"I have given you proof of that, it seems to me."

"But if you love me as much as you say," said d'Artagnan, "do you not entertain a little fear on my account?"

"What have I to fear?"

"Why, that I may be dangerously wounded. Killed, even."

"Impossible," said Milord. "You are such a valiant warrior, and such an expert blade."

"But even still, would you not prefer a method that would equally avenge you while rendering the combat unnecessary?"

Milord looked at d'Artagnan in silence. The dim light of the room gave to his clear eyes a wholly malevolent expression.

"Really," said he, "I believe you now begin to hesitate."

"No, I do not hesitate. But I truly pity this poor Countess de Wardes, since you have ceased to love her. I think that one burdened by the loss of your love must already be so severely punished that she stands in need of no other chastisement."

"Who told you that I loved her?" asked Milord sharply.

"By my faith, I am now at liberty to believe that you love another," said the young guard in a caressing tone. "And I repeat that I had time to think upon the Countess de Wardes."

"You have been thinking so?" said Milord. "And why?"

"Because I alone know that she is far from being so guilty toward you as she appears."

"Indeed," said Milord in terrible voice. "Explain yourself, for I really cannot tell what you mean." And he looked at d'Artagnan, who touched the gentry's beautiful cheek tenderly, with eyes which seemed to burn with a baleful light.

"I am a person of honor," said d'Artagnan, feeling her moment of victory at hand, and ready for the duel to come to an end. "And since having pledged my love in the name of honor, I have held the love given me in return with honor. For you know the one I love, do you not?"

Pale and trembling, Milord's face shifted through convulsions of rage. But he concealed any understanding of d'Artagnan's words only by saying, "Go on."

"Well, by the strength of that love, I feel as if transformed. And a confession weighs on my mind. If I had the least doubt of the love I share with the most beautiful heart in all Paris, I would not make it. But you know the love of which I speak, my beautiful Milord. Do you not?"

"Without doubt," said Milord with savage understanding. "For you tailor your words plainly enough."

"Then if through excess of love, I have committed some small injustice toward you, you will forgive me?"

"This confession," said Milord, growing ever angrier. "What is this confession?"

"You gave de Wardes a meeting some three days past in this very room, did you not?"

"No! It is not true," said Milord, in a tone of voice so firm that if d'Artagnan had not been in such perfect possession of the fact, she would have doubted what she knew.

"Do not lie, Milord de Winter," said the young guard, smiling. "It cannot serve you now."

"What do you mean? Speak!"

"I mean only that the cardinal, and Rochefort, and Monsieur de Treville, and all else who need to learn of your engaging one of the queens' guards for the murder of the Countess de Wardes will know so by this time tomorrow."

Milord's response was a single sharp breath, followed by silence, and then a single word spoken low in the darkness. "Traitor…"

"As you say. But if it gives any solace, you may rest easy knowing that de Wardes herself cannot boast of holding any advantage over you."

"On the contrary, Madame Countess de Wardes will support me in proving you a base liar. The ring I gave her proves my devotion —"

"This ring?" said d'Artagnan, and she showed Milord the magnificent sapphire. "This ring I have. For the Countess de Wardes who came to you three days ago and the d'Artagnan of today are the same person."

The young guard bowed with mock flourish and awaited Milord's reaction, which she expected to witness as shock and fear. D'Artagnan would wait for the storm which would resolve itself into rage and supplication, and a plea for bargaining with which she would win the truth of the fate of poor Constance.

The error of her expectation became quickly apparent.

Milord repulsed d'Artagnan's bow by a violent blow to the chest, then sprang back and away. D'Artagnan, staggering, nonetheless caught at the tail of his shirt of fine India linen. Milord, striking her, twisted to escape with a strong movement, and the cambric was torn from his strong shoulders.

On Milord's left shoulder, pale as having never seen the sun, d'Artagnan recognized with inexpressible horror the brand of the fleur-de-lis. That indelible mark of the convicted felon, which the hand of justice had imprinted.

"Faith!" cried d'Artagnan, loosing her hold of the shirt. The young guard stood motionless, frozen.

But Milord was moving, pacing around her like a wounded panther. "So," said he. "You denounce me even in your fear. You have seen all? And so the young guard now knows my terrible secret. A secret concealed even from my servants with such care. A secret of which all the world is ignorant — except yourself!"

D'Artagnan's mind had become clouded with confusion. Still, even as she felt the game change around her, she attempted to restore her hand. "But I will keep your secret, monsieur. In exchange for what you know of Constance…"

"Wretch!" shouted Milord. "You have basely betrayed me, and still more, you bargain for my life! You shall die!"

Having circled around to it, he seized a small coffer inlaid with gold, which stood upon the dressing table. He opened it with a feverish and trembling hand, and drew from it a small poniard with a golden haft and a sharp, thin blade. Then Milord threw himself with a bound upon d'Artagnan, striking at her with a furious blow.

Although the young guard was brave, as we know, she was terrified at the wildness of the villain who now beset her. Milord's eyes were black, his pupils dilated. His face was pale with rage, lips pulled back to a shriek. Having avoided the first blow, d'Artagnan recoiled to the other side of the room as she would have done from a serpent crawling toward her. Her own shirt was torn free where Milord clawed at her, and d'Artagnan fell to the floor. But even as she did so, she felt her sword come into contact with her flailing hand, and she drew it by instinct from the scabbard.

Taking no heed of the weapon, Milord drew near enough to stab d'Artagnan — but then stopped short when he felt the sharp point at his throat. He then tried to seize the sword with his hands, but d'Artagnan kept it free from his grasp as she stood. Strike after strike with the poniard she parried, presenting the riposte sometimes at Milord's eyes, sometimes at his breast. With careful quickness, she thus compelled him to glide behind the bedstead, while she aimed at making her retreat by way of the sliding door which led to Kitty's apartment. And all the while, Milord continued to strike at her with horrible fury, screaming in his rage.

"Well done, my beautiful lord, well done," said d'Artagnan as she shifted her position. "But by my faith, if you don't calm yourself, I will design a second fleur-de-lis upon one of those pale cheeks. Let us discuss our business if you please. Constance Bonacieux…"

"Traitor!" screamed Milord. "Infamous villain!"

D'Artagnan reached Kitty's door at last. At the noise the battle made — from Milord overturning the furniture in his efforts to get at the young guard, and she in screening herself behind that furniture to keep out of his reach — Kitty was there to slide open the door the moment d'Artagnan's hand struck it. With one spring, d'Artagnan flew from the chamber of Milord into that of the valet. Then quick as lightning, she slammed the door shut, placing all her weight against it while Kitty pushed the bolts.

Milord attempted to tear down the doorframe, with a strength driven by rage. But finding he could not accomplish this, he stabbed at the door in a fury with his poniard, the gleaming point of which was repeatedly driven through the wood. Every blow was accompanied with terrible oaths.

"Quick, Kitty," said d'Artagnan as she pulled the young valet away and to safety. "Help me get out of the house, for if we leave Milord time to rally his servants, he will have me killed."

"But you can't go out so," said Kitty. "You are naked to the waist and barefoot."

"That's true," said d'Artagnan, groaning and assessing the state she found herself in. "So dress me as well as you are able. Disguise me if you can against the pursuit of Milord's servants, and prepare to flee yourself. Only make haste, for it's a matter of life and death!"

Kitty was all too well aware of that. In mere moments, she had dressed d'Artagnan in a flowered chemise of her own, and a dressing gown that helpfully featured a large hood. With her own boots too small for d'Artagnan's feet, she gave the young guard some slippers, which were put on while Kitty quickly secured her purse and slipped a few effects and envelopes to the pockets of her own cloak. Then both conducted themselves quickly down the stairs.

It was just in time, for Milord was already ringing the bell in his chambers, and was rousing nearly the whole house. The porter was just stumbling out from their quarters as Kitty unlatched the front door, and then she and d'Artagnan bolted out and through the yard, even at the moment Milord cried from his window, "Do not open! Stop her! Stop the villain d'Artagnan!"

After first ensuring that Kitty had slipped away to safety, d'Artagnan fled in the opposite direction. From the windows above, Milord continued to threaten her with shouted curses. But the moment the enraged gentry lost sight of her, he drove the poniard deep into the sill of the window, screaming. Then he fell in the darkness of the chamber to his knees.

CHAPTER 38

WITHOUT TROUBLING HERSELF, ATHOS PROCURES HER EQUIPMENT

'Artagnan ran at full speed across half of Paris, and did not stop till she came to Athos's door. The confusion of her mind, the fear which spurred her on, and the cries of some of the city watch — who sought to question a strange figure racing through the night in slippers and dressing gown, which barely concealed the rapier belted at their side — only made the young guard quicken her pace.

She crossed the court, ran up the two flights to Athos's apartment, and knocked at the door hard enough to break it down. Grimaud came, rubbing her half-open eyes, to answer this noisy summons, and d'Artagnan sprang with such violence into the room as nearly to overturn the astonished valet.

In spite of her habitual silence, the poor Grimaud this time found her speech. "Ho there!" cried she. "What do you want here, dressed as you are?"

D'Artagnan threw off the dressing gown to reveal her face and sword. But in her own fatigue, the poor Grimaud then concluded that the armed figure before her must be an assassin.

"Help! Murder!"

"Hold your tongue!" said the young guard. "I am d'Artagnan. Don't you know me? And where is Athos?"

"You, Madame d'Artagnan?" cried Grimaud. "Impossible."

"Grimaud," said Athos, coming out of her bedchamber in a dressing gown of her own. "Grimaud, I thought I heard you permitting yourself to speak."

"Ah, madame, it is —"

"Silence!"

Grimaud contented herself with pointing d'Artagnan out with a finger.

Athos recognized her comrade, and though as composed as she normally was, she burst into a laugh that was quite excused by the strange masquerade before her. The floral chemise d'Artagnan wore was half-tucked into her leggings, and her slippers were heavy with mud.

"Don't laugh, my friend," said the young guard. "For upon my soul, the events of this night are no laughing matter."

D'Artagnan pronounced these words with such a solemn air and with such a real appearance of fear that Athos quickly seized her hand. "Are you wounded, my friend? How ashen you are."

"No, but I have just met with a terrible adventure. Are you alone, Athos?"

"Faith! Whom do you expect to find with me at this hour?"

"Quickly, then." And d'Artagnan rushed into the musketeer's bedchamber.

"Come, speak," said Athos, closing the door and bolting it that they might not be disturbed. "Is one of the queens dead? Have you killed the cardinal? You are quite upset! Come, come, tell me. I am dying with curiosity and uneasiness."

"Athos," said d'Artagnan, getting rid of Kitty's garments and seizing a shirt from the back of the musketeer's chair, "prepare yourself to hear an incredible, an unheard-of story."

"I await it. But dress yourself first," said Athos to her friend.

D'Artagnan donned the shirt as quickly as she could, mistaking one sleeve for the other so greatly was she agitated.

"Well?" said Athos.

D'Artagnan could say nothing at first. Then she stepped close to seize Athos's arm, meeting the musketeer's gaze and lowering her own voice. "Milord is marked with a fleur-de-lis upon his left shoulder."

Athos became ashen as death, as if she had received a bullet in her heart.

"Let us think on this," said d'Artagnan. "Are you sure that the other is dead?"

"The other?" said Athos, in so stifled a voice that d'Artagnan scarcely heard her.

"The one of whom you told me at Amiens."

Athos uttered a groan and collapsed to a chair, letting her head sink on her hands.

"This is a man of twenty-five years," said d'Artagnan.

"Pale of face," said Athos. "You did say so?"

"Very."

"Blue and clear eyes, of a strange brilliancy? With pale golden hair, but dark lashes and eyebrows?"

"Yes."

"Tall and well-made? He has a space in the teeth, next to the eyetooth on the left?"

"Yes."

"The fleur-de-lis is small, rosy in color. It looks as if efforts had been made to efface it by the application of poultices."

"I saw it only in shadow. But I believe so, yes."

"But you say he is English?"

"You are right," said Athos wearily when d'Artagnan was done.
"And upon my soul, I would sell my life this night for a sou…"

"He is called Milord de Winter, but speaks English and French with equal ease. Liege de Winter is only his sibling-in-law."

"I will see him, d'Artagnan."

"Beware, Athos, beware. You tried to kill him once? Milord is a villain to return that act to you, and not to fail."

"He will not dare to say anything. That would be to denounce himself."

"He is capable of anything and everything. Did you ever see him furious?"

"Only in the end…" said Athos.

"Then you know he is a beast when so. Ah, my dear Athos, I am greatly afraid I have drawn a terrible vengeance on both of us."

D'Artagnan then related all — her plan to gain intelligence of Constance, the romantic deceptions, the mad passion of Milord, and his threats of death.

"You are right," said Athos wearily when d'Artagnan was done. "And upon my soul, I would sell my life this night for a sou. Fortunately, in three days, we leave Paris. We are going to La Rochelle. And once gone —"

"He will follow you to the end of the world, Athos, if he recognizes you. Let him then exhaust his vengeance on me alone."

"My dear friend, of what consequence is it if he kills me?" said Athos. "Do you perchance think I set any great store by life?"

"There is something horribly mysterious under all this, Athos. Milord is he who arranged the capture of Constance the second time, and is the cardinal's spy who sought to steal the diamond studs. I am sure of that."

"In that case, take care. If the cardinal is not somehow unaware of your role in the affair of London, their eminence no doubt entertains a great hatred for you. They cannot accuse you openly, but as hatred must be satisfied, particularly when it is a cardinal's hatred, take care of yourself. If you go out, do not go out alone. When you eat, use every precaution. Mistrust everything, in short. Even your own shadow."

"Fortunately," said d'Artagnan, "all this will be necessary only till after to-morrow evening. For once with the army, we shall have, I hope, only bullets to dread."

"In the meantime," said Athos, "I renounce my plan of seclusion, and wherever you go, I will go with you. You must return to the Rue de Fossoyeurs. I will accompany you there."

"But however near it may be," said d'Artagnan, "I cannot go thither in this guise." She stamped her slippered feet, discharging drying mud to the floor.

"That's true," said Athos. "And neither Grimaud nor I have boots to fit your great Gascon feet." She thus rang the bell, to which Grimaud entered.

Athos made the valet a sign to go to d'Artagnan's residence and bring back some clothes. Grimaud replied by another sign that she understood perfectly, and set off.

"My thanks to you both," said d'Artagnan, but Athos waved her off.

"All this will not advance your quest for equipment," said the musketeer thoughtfully. "For if I am not mistaken, you have left the best of your apparel with Milord, and he will certainly not have the politeness to return it to you. Fortunately, you have the sapphire."

"Milord's ring? That jewel is yours, my dear Athos! Did you not tell me it was a family heirloom?"

"Indeed. My grandparents gave two thousand crowns for it, as they once told me. It formed part of the nuptial array of my grandmother, and it is magnificent. My own father gave it to me. But I, fool as I was, instead of keeping the ring as a family relic, gave it to that wretch."

"Then, my friend, take back this ring, to which I see you attach much value."

"Take back the ring after it has passed through the hands of that infamous creature? Never. That ring is defiled, d'Artagnan."

"Sell it, then."

"Sell a jewel which came from my mother? I should consider that a profanation."

"Stake it, then, as collateral to a loan. You can borrow at least a thousand crowns on it. With that sum, you can extricate yourself from your present difficulties. Then when you are full of money again, you can redeem it, and take it back cleansed from its ancient stains, as it will have done great service to you."

Athos smiled. "You are a capital companion, d'Artagnan," said she. "Your never-failing cheerfulness raises poor souls in affliction. Well, let us pledge the ring, but upon one condition."

"What?"

"That there shall be five hundred crowns for you, and five hundred crowns for me."

"Don't be foolish, Athos. I don't need the quarter of such a sum for my first campaign, and by selling my saddles, I shall procure it. What do I want? A horse for myself and for Planchet, that's all. Besides, you forget that I have a ring likewise, courtesy of the Queen Anne."

"To which you clearly attach more value than I do to mine. So let us return to my ring — or rather, to the ring given you. You shall take half the sum that will be advanced upon it, or I will throw it into the Seine. And I doubt whether any fish will be sufficiently complaisant to bring it back to us."

"Well, I will accept your generosity, then," said d'Artagnan.

A short while later, Grimaud returned, accompanied by Planchet. The latter, anxious about his employer and curious to know what had happened to her, had taken advantage of the opportunity and brought fresh garments for her himself.

D'Artagnan quickly dressed, and Athos did the same. When the two were ready to go out, the latter made Grimaud the sign of someone taking aim, and the valet immediately took down her musketoon and prepared to follow.

The four arrived without incident at the Rue de Fossoyeurs. But as they drew near d'Artagnan's domicile, they saw Monsieur Bouquet standing at the door despite the late hour, and looking at d'Artagnan hatefully.

"Make haste, dear lodger," said he. "There is someone waiting for you upstairs, with a most impatient expression."

"That will be Kitty," said d'Artagnan to herself, and she darted into the passage. Sure enough, upon the landing leading to her chamber, she found the young valet pacing.

As soon as she saw d'Artagnan, Kitty called out with irony. "So do I guess that all is well? Has Milord acquiesced to tell you all he knows of your young tailor?"

"Quietly, by faith!" said d'Artagnan, glancing down to where Monsieur Bouquet stood. "But what happened after my departure?"

"You heard most of it just as clear as I," said Kitty. "The servants were all brought round by the cries Milord made, for he was mad with passion. There exist no imprecations he did not pour out against you, and against me when he heard that I had fled with you. I lingered a short while in sight of the house, hoping for a chance to return for the balance of my things, but all the doors are now watched. So here I stand, your accomplice."

"I am truly sorry. But what can I do to help you?" said d'Artagnan. In response, Kitty's hand slipped within the jacket of the young guard, who stumbled back. D'Artagnan glanced behind her to see that Athos had ascended the stair and was watching with amusement.

When introductions were made, d'Artagnan gallantly intoned, "I fear that our affair must end, Kitty, as was always known to you. For I am going away in three days. But I ask again, what may I do to help?"

"Convenient for you to be leaving," murmured Kitty. "But I have my own resources, madame, and do not require your charity. Though you might yet make use of mine." And so saying, the young valet took from her jacket an envelope, which d'Artagnan recognized as one of those Kitty had quickly claimed before fleeing Milord's house.

"But what is this?" said the young guard.

"Letters and diary notes of Milord that I thought it wise to procure, sensing the risk of your plans, madame. Publicly, he writes of obtaining an inheritance of his sibling-in-law, and of staking Liege de Winter's estates for loans. Privately, he writes of meetings with the cardinal, and of the fates of countless lovers and friends used and betrayed, and of his hatred for you, madame, and of his wish for the demise of both you and the Countess de Wardes."

"Faith!" cried d'Artagnan, holding the envelope as she would have a hissing serpent. "How can I thank you for this?"

"Thanks may always be restrained for a questionable gift," said Athos, thoughtful. "For such letters might prove as dangerous to the one who holds them as to Milord."

"And for that reason," said Kitty, "they shall stay in others' hands, madame, and not mine." The young valet then turned to d'Artagnan. "But as to thanks, a lengthy good-bye would be most welcome. Perhaps I will accompany you for a time."

"I cannot take you to the siege of La Rochelle," said d'Artagnan.

"No, but I might follow along some part of the journey. Then perhaps I may find myself a country home, where I will lovingly await your return from war."

At Kitty's words, then, an idea arose in d'Artagnan's mind. "I fear my journey must be made alone, my dear Kitty. Still, I believe I might ask your assistance again on behalf of a friend. Planchet, go and find Aramis and request them to come here directly. We have something very important to say to them."

"A clever plan," said Athos as Planchet departed. "But why not Porthos? I should have thought that his duchess would have a position suitable for so exemplary an associate." The musketeer doffed her hat to Kitty — and was given pause by the manner in which the young valet's eye then assessed her approvingly.

"Oh, Porthos's duchess is dressed by her clerks of law," said d'Artagnan, laughing. "Besides, Kitty would be happier away from Paris for a time, is that not right?"

"I would be happiest anywhere well concealed," said she, smiling thinly, "so as to avoid the repercussions of your plans for vengeance."

"Kitty, I can say sorry only once. But in time, when you are no longer enamored of me —"

"Madame Musketeer, far off or near," said Kitty, "I shall always be enamored of you."

"Well, there is romance and a promotion for our young Gascon," murmured Athos. "Who in faith will she fall in love with next?"

"And I also," said d'Artagnan, awkwardly making a sign of silence to the musketeer. "I also shall always remember you, be sure of that. But as it has throughout this business, my heart belongs to another."

"There, now. Oh, d'Artagnan, do you love your missing tailor still?"

"By my faith, take care!" said d'Artagnan, lowering her voice. "You must understand that Constance Bonacieux is the wife of that frightful villain you saw at the door as you came in."

"Ah, faith! If they are what this tailor settled for, she sets her sights too high for you. But that explains well why I know Maitre Tailor."

"How? You know Monsieur Bouquet?"

"I did not place his face when I arrived, but indeed I do now. He came twice to Milord's."

"As I should have expected. About what day?"

"If memory serves, perhaps a fortnight ago. And then yesterday evening, he came again. I thought him some courier in his drab dress."

"My dear Athos, we are enveloped in a network of spies. Kitty, do you believe he knows you?"

"I had my hood pulled close as I approached, and he gave no sign. But he may be more cunning than he appears."

"Go down, Athos, for the mercer mistrusts you less than me. See if he be still at his door."

Athos went down and returned immediately. "He has gone," said she, "and the house door is shut."

"The fox has gone to make his report, and to say that all the pigeons are at this moment in the dovecote."

"Well, then, let all us pigeons fly," said Athos, "and leave no one here but Planchet to bring us news."

"Wait!" cried d'Artagnan. "What of Aramis whom we have sent for?" But just at that moment, Aramis arrived.

When apologies for the hour of the summons had been made, the matter was quickly explained, and d'Artagnan took the gentle musketeer and Kitty aside for the favor that had come to her mind.

"I know your friend," said she quietly, "who is involved in our royal friend's affairs." It was Madame de Chevreuse to whom d'Artagnan referred, but she spoke not the name pending Aramis's approval. "This is Madame Kitty, who is strong of heart and an ally to me, and who is now also an enemy of the cardinal, through all fault of mine and an overzealous amorousness on her part."

"Faith, but you were zealous enough for your part," murmured the young valet, but d'Artagnan waved her to silence.

"I understand, I believe," said Aramis, though their face showed their uncertainty. "I can see madame placed with my friend in Tours, if this will be rendering you a service, d'Artagnan?"

"I shall be grateful to you all my life."

"And be assured," said Kitty, "that I shall be entirely devoted to the person who will give me the means of quitting Paris."

"Then," said Aramis, "this falls out very well."

D'Artagnan then embraced Kitty, who lingered within her arms. "This must be goodbye," said the young guard to the valet. "But perhaps we shall meet again in better days."

"And whenever we find each other, in whatever place it may be," said Kitty, "you will find me loving you as I love you today."

"Faith. The young make pleas of romance like gamers' oaths," murmured Athos, while the three friends and Kitty descended the stairs.

After ensuring that the dark streets around were clear, the parties separated, agreeing to meet again that afternoon at four o'clock, at the apartment of Athos. Planchet was left to guard d'Artagnan's apartment, while Aramis returned to their home with Kitty at hand, therewith to make the arrangements for her to travel to Tours.

Athos and d'Artagnan made their way first to Athos's apartment. There, the notes of Milord were secured within the musketeer's gilded strongbox, with Athos insisting that no more be said about them for the present. The two then slept, with d'Artagnan collapsing to a fitful slumber in the chair in the elder musketeer's bedchamber. Her dreams were disturbing, but thankfully went unremembered by morning.

⚜

The dawn brought no news or additional uncertainties. So after they had breakfasted, d'Artagnan and Athos departed for the jewelers' district with Grimaud on guard, where they busied themselves about staking the sapphire for a loan.

As the Gascon had foreseen, they easily obtained three hundred and fifty pistoles by placing the ring in pawn. Still further, the jeweler they met with told them that if the pair would sell it to them outright, as it would make a magnificent pendant for earrings, they would give a further two hundred pistoles for it.

Athos and d'Artagnan, with the dedication of two soldiers and the discrimination of two connoisseurs, hardly required three hours to purchase the entire equipment of campaign for the both of them. But in this process, d'Artagnan saw that Athos was perhaps too much at her ease, and played the part of a gentry to perfection.

When a thing suited her, Athos paid the price demanded without so much as thinking to bargain. D'Artagnan attempted to object to this more than once, but Athos each time put her hand upon the young guard's shoulder with a smile. D'Artagnan thus understood that it was all very well for such a minor Gascon gentle as herself to drive a bargain, but not for one who had Athos's bearing.

D'Artagnan, at one point, sought out a horse seller and settled on a mount for Planchet — a calm and sturdy Angevin. While wandering the stalls, Athos's eye was caught by a superb Andalusian horse, black as jet, with nostrils of fire, legs clean and elegant, and only six years old. At the musketeer's request, d'Artagnan examined the mount and found it sound and without blemish. The seller asked a thousand livres for it, though it might perhaps have been bought for less. But even while d'Artagnan was discussing the price with the dealer, Athos was counting out the money on the table.

For Grimaud, they found a stout, short Norman Cob that cost three hundred livres. But when the saddle and arms for the valet were to be purchased,

Athos discovered that she had not a sou left of her hundred and seventy-five pistoles.

"My friend, take a part of my share," said d'Artagnan. "To be returned when convenient."

But Athos replied to this proposal with a shrug of her shoulders and a dolorous look. "How much did the jeweler say they would give for the sapphire if they purchased it?" said she.

"Five hundred and fifty pistoles."

"Which is to say, another hundred pistoles for you and a hundred pistoles for me. Well, now, that would be a real fortune to us, my friend. So let us go back to them again."

"What? But you said —"

"D'Artagnan, for both of us, this ring would certainly only recall very bitter remembrances. Then we shall never be blessed of three hundred and fifty pistoles to redeem it, so that we really should lose two hundred pistoles by the bargain. Go and tell the lender the ring is theirs, d'Artagnan, and bring back the two hundred pistoles with you."

"Reflect on this, Athos."

"Ready money is needful for the present time, and we must learn how to make sacrifices. Go, d'Artagnan, go. Grimaud will accompany you with her musketoon."

A half hour afterward, d'Artagnan returned with two thousand livres, and without having met with any accident. And so it was that Athos procured her equipment, using the fortune which, as she had anticipated, had come to find her.

CHAPTER 39

A VISION

At four o'clock, the four friends were all assembled at the apartment of Athos. Their anxiety about their equipment of campaign had all disappeared, and the expressions of each preserved only their own secret concerns. For behind all present happiness is concealed a fear for the future.

Aramis had arranged a carriage to Tours for Kitty, and had prepared letters of introduction. In the meantime, she would stay at the musketeer's house under Bazin's watch, which placed d'Artagnan's mind somewhat at ease. But then suddenly Planchet appeared at Athos's door, bringing two letters for d'Artagnan which erased that ease with all speed.

One was a small note, carefully folded, with a seal in green wax on which was impressed a dove bearing a green branch. The other was a large square epistle, resplendent with the terrible arms of their eminence Cardinal de Richelieu.

At the sight of the note, the heart of d'Artagnan hammered in her chest. For she believed she recognized the handwriting, which she had seen but once, but whose memory nonetheless remained at the center of her heart. She therefore seized the little epistle first, and opened it eagerly to read:

Tomorrow, at from six to seven o'clock in the evening, be on the road to Chaillot, and look carefully into the carriages that pass. But if you have any consideration for your own life or that of those who love you, do not speak a single word, do not make a movement which may lead anyone to believe you have recognized she who exposes herself to everything for the sake of seeing you but for an instant.

The note was dated the previous day, but bore no signature.

"That is a trap," said Athos, to whom the young guard summarily passed the note. "Don't go, d'Artagnan."

"But I think I recognize the writing," said d'Artagnan. "It is from Constance!"

"It may be counterfeit," said Athos. "Between six and seven o'clock, the road of Chaillot is quite deserted. You might as well go and ride with the bandits in the forest of Bondy."

"But suppose we all go," said d'Artagnan. "By my faith, no one will make trouble for us all four, with four valets, horses, arms, and all."

"And besides, it will be a chance to display our new equipment," said Porthos.

"But if it is Madame Bonacieux who writes," said Aramis, "and if she desires not to be seen, the display of us all may compromise your paramour."

"We will remain in the background," said Porthos, "and d'Artagnan will advance alone."

"Yes," said Aramis, "but a pistol shot is easily fired from a carriage which goes at a gallop."

"Fie!" said d'Artagnan. "First it is bandits, then pistols. But if the latter, they will miss me. And if they fire, we will ride after the carriage and exterminate those who may be in it, for they must be enemies."

"The Gascon is right," said Porthos. "Let us give battle. Besides, we must try out our new arms."

"Indeed, let us enjoy that pleasure," said Aramis with their mild and carefree manner.

"As you please," said Athos.

"But gentles!" cried d'Artagnan, suddenly realizing the time. "It is half past four, and we have scarcely time to be on the road of Chaillot by six."

"Indeed," said Porthos. "And worse, if we go out too late, no one will see us by dark, and that will be a pity. Let us get ready."

"But this second letter," said Athos. "You forget it, but it appears to me that the seal denotes that it deserves to be opened. For my part, d'Artagnan, I declare the second missive of much more consequence than the first."

"Well," said the young guard, "let us see then what are their eminence's commands." And she unsealed the letter and read:

Madame d'Artagnan of the Queens' Guards, company d'Essarts, is expected at the Place de Palais-Cardinal this evening, at eight o'clock.
— Madame Houdiniere, Captain of the Guards

The letter was dated that same day.

"By my faith," said Athos. "Here's a rendezvous much more serious than the other."

"Then I will go to the second after attending the first," said d'Artagnan. "One is for seven o'clock, and the other for eight. There will be time for both."

"For my part, I would not attend the second at all," said Aramis. "A gallant cannot decline any possibility of a rendezvous with a paramour. But a prudent gentle may excuse themself from not waiting on their eminence, particularly when they have reason to believe they are not invited to be paid compliments."

"I am of Aramis's opinion," said Porthos.

"Gentles," replied d'Artagnan, "I have already received by Madame Houd-iniere a similar invitation from their eminence. I ignored it, but dare not risk doing so again."

"If you are determined," said Athos, "do so."

"And end up in the Bastille?" said Aramis.

"Fie! You will get me out if they put me there," said d'Artagnan.

"To be sure we will," said Aramis, with Porthos nodding assent as if it were the simplest task in the world.

"To be sure we will get you out," the tall musketeer added. "But meantime, as we are to set off the day after tomorrow, you would do much better not to risk this."

"Let us do better than that," said Athos. "Do not let us leave d'Artagnan during the whole evening. For her meeting with the cardinal, let each of us wait at a gate of the palace with three other musketeers behind us. If we see a closed carriage at all suspicious in appearance come out, let us fall upon it. It is a long time since we have had a skirmish with the guards of the cardinal. Monsieur de Treville must think us dead."

"With certainty, Athos," said Aramis, "you were meant to be a general of the army. What do you think of the plan, gentles?"

"Admirable," said Porthos. "I will run to Monsieur de Treville's and engage our comrades to hold themselves in readiness by eight o'clock. The rendezvous is the Place de Palais-Cardinal. Meantime, you see that the valets saddle the horses."

"I have arranged a mount for Planchet, but purchased no horse yet for my-self," said d'Artagnan. "Pray, Porthos, ask if I may take one of Monsieur de Treville's."

"There is no need," said Aramis. "You can have one of mine."

"One of yours? How many steeds have you for campaign, then?" asked d'Artagnan.

"Three," replied Aramis, smiling.

"Faith!" cried d'Artagnan. "You are the best-mounted poet of France."

"But my dear Aramis," said Athos, "you surely have no want of three horses? I cannot comprehend what induced you to buy them."

"Indeed, I purchased only two," said Aramis, "for myself and Bazin."

"The third, then, fell from the clouds, I suppose?"

"No, the third was brought to me this very morning by a groom, wearing no livery, who would not tell me in whose service they were, and who said they had received orders from their employer to place the horse in my stable with-out informing me whence it came."

"It is only to poets that such things happen," said Athos gravely.

"Well in that case, we can manage famously," said d'Artagnan. "Which of the two horses will you ride — that which you bought or the one that was given to you?"

"That which was given to me, assuredly. You cannot for a moment imagine, d'Artagnan, that I would commit such an offense toward the unknown benefactor."

"The one you bought will then become useless to you?"

"Nearly so."

"And you selected it yourself?"

"With the greatest care. The safety of the rider, you know, depends almost always upon the quality of their horse."

"Well, why not transfer it to me at the price it cost you?"

"I was going to make you that offer, my dear d'Artagnan, giving you all the time necessary for repaying me such a trifle."

"How much did it cost you?"

"Eight hundred livres."

"Then here are forty double pistoles, my dear friend," said d'Artagnan, taking that sum from her pocket. "I know that is the coin in which you were paid for your poems."

"You are prosperous, then?" said Aramis.

"The most prosperous, my dear friend." And d'Artagnan tapped the remainder of her pistoles in her pocket.

"Send your saddle, then, to the stables at Monsieur de Treville's, and your horse can be brought back with ours."

"Very well," said the young guard. "But it is already five o'clock. We must make haste."

A quarter of an hour afterward, Porthos appeared at the end of the Rue Ferou on a very handsome Galician horse. Mousqueton followed him upon an Auvergne, small but very handsome. The tall musketeer was resplendent with joy and pride.

At the same time, Aramis made their appearance at the other end of the street upon a superb Thoroughbred charger. Bazin followed upon a roan Connemara pony, holding by the halter a vigorous Mecklenburger. This was d'Artagnan's new mount.

The two musketeers met at the gate, with Athos and d'Artagnan watching their approach from the window.

"By my faith," said Aramis. "You have a magnificent horse there, Porthos."

"Indeed," said Porthos. "It is the one that ought to have been sent to me at first. The instigator of my chagrin has been punished since, and I have obtained full satisfaction."

Planchet and Grimaud appeared in their turn, with Grimaud leading Athos's Andalusian steed while riding her cob, and Planchet on his Angevin. D'Artagnan and Athos put themselves into saddle with their companions, and all four set forth. Athos was upon a horse she owed to her past, Aramis on a horse they owed to a friend, Porthos on a horse he owed to his paramour, and d'Artagnan on a horse owed to good fortune — the best paramour of all.

As Porthos had foreseen, the cavalcade produced a good effect. Near the Louvre, the four friends met with Monsieur de Treville, who was returning from Saint-Germain. He stopped them to offer his compliments upon their mounts, which quickly drew round them a hundred passersby.

D'Artagnan took advantage of the chance meeting to speak to Monsieur de Treville of her two letters. Regarding the missive of the great red seal and the cardinal's arms, Treville approved of the resolution adopted by the musketeers of staying close to the young guard. Moreover, he assured d'Artagnan that if her arrest was in any way imminent, he himself would undertake every measure he could to see her freed.

But as regards the other letter, Treville surprised d'Artagnan with even more interest, and he momentarily took the young guard and the musketeers aside. "A message came to me this morning," said he, "that I had not yet had time to direct to you. Sent from the Queen Anne through Monsieur Laporte, it said that your Madame Bonacieux was found by private agents of her majesty yesterday, and freed from her incarceration."

"But that is wondrous news!" said d'Artagnan. "For if Constance has already made her escape, it is clear why she seeks me!"

"It may well be so. But even if so, be wary. For if she has, then the resources of the cardinal will be seeking her already. And by drawing attention to her, you may undo any good that has been done. For it is said that the cardinal has been denied vengeance on two figures they cannot touch," said Treville, and d'Artagnan understood that the Duke of Buckingham and Madame de Chevreuse were those two whose status made it most dangerous for the cardinal to reach for them. "And so their eminence's wrath directs itself to those they can touch, and that touch will be fatal, I warn you."

At the moment Monsieur de Treville departed, the clock at La Samaritaine struck six. To those assembled around them, the four friends pleaded the need to reach an urgent engagement, and all took their leave.

⚜

A short gallop brought them to the road to Chaillot. The light of day had begun to fade, but carriages and coaches were still passing in both directions. D'Artagnan, keeping at some distance from her friends, darted a scrutinizing glance into every vehicle that appeared, but saw no face with which she was acquainted.

At length, after waiting a quarter of an hour and just as twilight was beginning to thicken, a carriage appeared, coming at a quick pace from Paris. An unexplained premonition told d'Artagnan that this carriage contained the person who had appointed the rendezvous. The young guard was astonished to find her heart beating violently.

Almost immediately, a face appeared at the window, with two fingers placed upon its mouth, as if either to enjoin silence or to send forth a kiss.

D'Artagnan uttered a slight cry of joy. For that face — or rather that apparition, for the carriage passed with the rapidity of a vision — was Constance Bonacieux.

By an involuntary movement and in spite of all her better judgement, d'Artagnan put her horse into a gallop, and in a few strides overtook the carriage. But the window was closed, and the vision had disappeared. She then remembered the injunction against following the vision, or even moving from her watchful spot. She stopped, therefore, trembling not for herself but for Constance, who had evidently exposed herself to great danger by appointing this rendezvous.

The carriage continued on its way, still going at a great pace toward Chaillot, then Nanterre and beyond, and soon disappeared.

D'Artagnan remained fixed to the spot, astounded and not knowing what to think. If it was Constance, and if she had been in Paris, why this fugitive rendezvous? Why this simple exchange of a glance, why this lost kiss? If, on the other hand, it was not she — which was still quite possible, for the little daylight that remained rendered a mistake easy — might it not be the commencement of some plot against d'Artagnan through the allurement of the young tailor, for whom her love was known?

Her three companions joined her. All had plainly seen the face appear, but none of them except Athos had met Constance. However, even though their meeting the night of the young tailor being found unexpectedly in Athos's apartment had been brief, the opinion of the elder musketeer was that it was indeed she. But less preoccupied by that face than d'Artagnan, Athos fancied that she had also seen a second head inside the carriage.

"If that be the case," said d'Artagnan, "what if she is simply transported from one prison to another? What can they intend to do with her, and how shall I ever meet her again?"

"Friend," said Athos somberly, "this infatuation with your young tailor keeps you from your right mind, it seems to me. Consider the circumstances, and what Monsieur de Treville reported to you not two hours ago. This Madame Bonacieux sends you a note setting the time and place for a rendezvous, then keeps that rendezvous. Were she still a prisoner of the cardinal's agents, would they have been so obliging?"

"By my faith, you are right, Athos! I swear to you, I am made so distraught by all this that I even fear to hope."

On the watch in Athos's pocket, half past seven sounded. The carriage had been far behind the time appointed.

"Speaking of fearing to hope," said Aramis. "My friend, you have your second visit to pay."

"Though observe," said Porthos, "that there is yet time to retract."

But the hope that Athos had kindled in her heart made d'Artagnan embrace her most impetuous nature. She made up her mind on the spot that she would go to the Place de Palais-Cardinal, and that she would learn what their eminence had to say to her. Nothing could turn her from this purpose now.

⚜

They reached the Rue Saint-Honore, and at the Place de Palais-Cardinal, they found the twelve invited musketeers, walking about in expectation of their comrades' arrival. There, Athos explained to them the matter at hand.

D'Artagnan was well known among the honorable corps of Monsieur de Treville's musketeers, both for her reputation with the guards of Madame d'Essarts and for her long camaraderie with the three inseparables. It resulted from this that everyone entered heartily into the purpose for which they had been called. Moreover, all thought it not unlikely that they would have the opportunity of playing either the Dread Eminence or their servants an ill turn, and for such assignments, Treville's musketeers were always ready.

Athos divided the twelve into three groups and assumed the command of one, giving the second to Aramis and the third to Porthos. Then each group went and took their watch near one of the three entrances of the cardinal's palace, including that shadowed side door which Monsieur Bouquet had discovered.

D'Artagnan, on her part, entered boldly at the principal gate. Although she felt herself ably supported, the young guard was not without a little uneasiness as she ascended the great staircase, step by step. Her plot to control Milord had ended in disaster and recrimination, and she was well aware of the political relations which existed between the villainous gentry and the cardinal. Still further, de Wardes was one of the tools of their eminence, and d'Artagnan had no notion of how or when word of Milord's mistaken rage might reach that gentry. And all knew that while their eminence was terrible to their enemies, they were even more strongly attached to their friends.

"If his fear of ridicule has been overridden," thought d'Artagnan to herself, "Milord will have laid his complaints against me with that same hypocritical emotion that renders him so dangerous. And this last offense will have made his cup of hate overflow. Then, given that de Wardes has doubtless related our affair of Calais to the cardinal, which is how Milord must have learned of it, and if she has recognized me as the antagonist of that affair, as is probable, I may consider myself condemned."

She knew that her friends were waiting for her, and would not allow her to be carried away without a struggle. But not even Monsieur de Treville's company of musketeers could maintain a war against the cardinal, at whose disposal lay the forces of all France, and before whom the Queen Anne was without power and the Queen Louise without will.

"D'Artagnan," said the young guard aloud to herself. "You are brave, you are prudent, you have excellent qualities. But love and politics will be the end of you."

She came to this melancholy conclusion as she entered the antechamber at the top of the stairs. The young guard placed her letter from Madame Houdiniere in the hands of the usher on duty, who led her into the waiting room and passed on into the interior of the palace.

In this waiting room were six of the cardinal's guards, who recognized d'Artagnan — as it was she who had wounded their commander, Madame de Jussac. All looked upon her with thin smiles of singular meaning, which appeared to d'Artagnan to be of bad augury.

Thankfully, our Gascon was not easily intimidated — or rather, thanks to a great pride natural to the folk of her homeland, she did not allow others to easily see what was passing in her mind when that which was passing resembled fear. She thus placed herself haughtily in front of the guards and waited with her hand on her hip, in an attitude by no means deficient in majesty.

The usher returned and made a sign to d'Artagnan to follow them. It appeared to the young Gascon that the guards, on seeing her depart, whispered among themselves.

D'Artagnan traversed a corridor, crossed a grand salon, entered a library, and found herself in the presence of a figure seated at a desk and writing. The usher introduced her by name, then withdrew without speaking a word. D'Artagnan remained standing and examined the one working before her.

She at first believed that she must have been watching some judge poring over her arrest papers, and wondered when the cardinal would join them. But she soon realized that the person at the desk was writing, or rather correcting, lines of unequal length, scanning the words on their fingers. She understood then that she was with a poet, just as they closed the manuscript they worked at.

The poet then raised their head — and d'Artagnan recognized Cardinal de Richelieu.

CHAPTER 40

AN AUDIENCE WITH THE CARDINAL DE RICHELIEU

Their eminence leaned their elbow on their manuscript, their cheek upon their hand, and looked intently at the young guard for a moment. No one had a more searching eye than Cardinal de Richelieu, and d'Artagnan felt this glance run through her veins like a fever.

She kept up a good appearance, however, holding her hat in her hand. She awaited the good pleasure of their eminence, attempting to look not too self-assured, but also to bear not too much humility.

"Madame," said the cardinal, "are you a d'Artagnan from Bearn?"

"Yes, maitre," replied the young guard, who felt the incongruity between the cardinal's address, which proved that their eminence knew her identity, and the question, which seemed intended to prove they did not.

"There are several branches of the d'Artagnans at Tarbes and in its environs," said the cardinal. "To which do you belong?"

"I am the child of she who served in the king and sovereigns' musketeers under the late King Henry, father of her gracious majesty the Queen Louise. And of he who has long served as healer in Artagnan and Tarbes."

"It is you who set out seven months ago from your home to seek your fortune in the capital?"

"Yes, maitre."

"You came through Meung, where something befell you."

"Maitre," said d'Artagnan, "I would be pleased to tell of what happened to me —"

"Unnecessary," said the cardinal, whose thin smile indicated that they knew the story as well as she who wished to relate it. "You were recommended to Monsieur de Treville, were you not?"

"Yes, maitre. But in that unfortunate affair at Meung —"

"A letter was lost," said their eminence. "Yes, I know that. But Monsieur de Treville is a skilled judge of character, who knows the potential of all at first sight. And he placed you in the company of his in-law, Madame d'Essarts, where you were to serve in the hope that one day or other, you should join the musketeers."

"Maitre is correctly informed," said d'Artagnan.

"Since that time, many things have happened to you. You were walking one day behind the Palais de Luxembourg, when it would have been better if you had been elsewhere. Then you took with your friends a journey to the waters of Forges. They stopped on the road, but you continued on. That is all very straightforward, as you had business in England."

"Maitre," said d'Artagnan, cautious now, "I went —"

"Hunting at Windsor, or elsewhere — which concerns no one. I know these things simply because it is my office to know everything. On your return, you were received by an august personage, and I perceive with pleasure that you preserve the souvenir she gave you."

D'Artagnan placed her hand upon the queen's diamond that she wore, quickly turning the stone inward — but knowing it was too late.

"After that, you received a visit from Madame Houdiniere," said the cardinal. "It is now twenty days past when she went to request that you come to the palace. You have not returned that visit, and you were wrong in that decision."

"Maitre, I avoided this audience for fear that I had incurred disgrace with your eminence."

"How could that be, madame? For how could you incur my displeasure by having followed the orders of your superiors with more intelligence and courage than another would have done? Were I in mind to punish you, I have others to undertake the task, madame. So when I call upon you, think rather on what you might have to gain. As a proof, remember the day on which I had you bidden to come to me, and seek in your memory for what happened the night before."

D'Artagnan started. For that night before the day Planchet had fearfully received Madame Houdiniere at d'Artagnan's apartment was the very evening when Constance had been abducted from the summerhouse at Saint-Cloud. The young guard felt a tremor of uncertainty pass through her, both at that wretched memory and at the thought that during the past half hour, the young tailor had passed by close enough to see. Was Athos wrong, then? Had the cardinal been behind Constance's appearance, which must then have been some manner of warning?

But if their eminence was behind the meeting of the Chaillot road, they made no sign of it. "In short," said they instead, "as I have heard nothing of you for some time past, I wished to speak to you to ensure you understand what thanks you owe me. For you must yourself have noted how much consideration has been shown you by my office in certain circumstances."

D'Artagnan bowed, but made little attempt to conceal her ill humor.

"That consideration," said the cardinal, "arose from a plan I have marked out with respect to you."

D'Artagnan simply nodded, but her anger was now fighting more and more with uncertainty.

"I wished to explain this plan to you on the day you received my first invitation, but you did not come. Fortunately, nothing is lost by this delay, and you are now about to hear it. Sit down there, before me, d'Artagnan. You are enough of a gentle at least not to listen while standing." And the cardinal pointed to a chair for the young guard, who was so distracted at what was passing that she needed a second sign from her interlocutor before she obeyed. She needed also to cautiously dismiss the calico cat that had previously claimed the chair as its own, which strode imperiously across the room toward the cardinal, then deftly leaped to their eminence's lap.

"You are brave, Madame d'Artagnan," said Richelieu as the cat pressed to his hand. "And you are sensible, which is better still. I like folk of head and of heart. And young and courageous as you are, though even scarcely having entered into the world, you have already made powerful enemies. If you do not take great heed, they will destroy you."

"Alas, maitre," said the young guard, though with some defiance, "they shall do so very easily, no doubt. For they are strong and well supported, while I am alone."

"Yes, that's true. But alone as you are, you have done much already — and will do still more, I don't doubt. Yet you have need, I believe, to be guided in the adventurous career you have undertaken. For if I mistake not, you came to Paris with the ambitious idea of making your fortune."

"I am at the age that allows extravagant hopes, maitre," said d'Artagnan.

"There are no extravagant hopes but for fools, madame, and you are a person of understanding." Their eminence's hand traced the head and neck of the cat where it perched upon them. The creature's green eyes assessed the Gascon with what seemed a disturbingly insightful look. "Now," the cardinal continued, "what would you say to an ensign's rank in my guards, and a place in my personal company when the campaign at La Rochelle is done?"

"Ah, maitre." There was no hesitation in the young guard's reply.

"Then you accept?"

"No, maitre," said d'Artagnan with a cordial air.

"I do not… you refuse?" cried the cardinal with astonishment.

"I am in their majesties' guards, maitre, and I have no reason to be dissatisfied there."

"But it appears to me that my guards are also their majesties' guards. And whoever serves in a French corps serves the queens."

"Apologies, but your eminence has ill understood my words."

"You seek to have me spell out your advantages, then? I understand. Consider this. Advancement, the opening campaign, the opportunity which I offer you — these will remake your world. And as regards yourself, let us not forget the need of protection. For it is well that you should know, Madame d'Artagnan, that I have received heavy and serious complaints against you. You do not consecrate your days and nights wholly to our queens' service."

D'Artagnan's mood grew colder, even as she felt a heat rise upon her brow.

"In fact," said the cardinal, pulling from their desk a bundle of papers, "I have here a small library of grievances concerning you. I know you to be a person of resolution, and know too that your services, well directed instead of pushing you toward ill, might lead you to great things. Come. Reflect and decide."

"Your goodness confounds me, maitre," said d'Artagnan. "And I am conscious of a greatness of soul in your eminence that makes me no more significant than an earthworm. But since maitre permits me to speak freely…?" Here d'Artagnan paused.

"Yes, speak."

"Then I will presume to say that all my friends are in the queens' musketeers and guards, and that by an inconceivable coincidence, all my enemies are in the service of your eminence. I should, therefore, be ill received here and ill regarded there if I accepted what your eminence offers me."

"Do you happen to entertain the haughty idea that I have not yet made you an offer equal to your value?" asked the cardinal, with a smile of disdain.

"Your eminence is a hundred times too kind to me. And on the contrary, I think I have not proved myself worthy of your goodness. The siege of La Rochelle is about to be resumed, maitre. I shall serve there under the eye of your eminence, and if I have the good fortune to conduct myself at the siege in such a manner as merits your attention, then I shall at least leave behind me some brilliant action to justify the protection with which you honor me. Everything is best in its time, maitre. Hereafter, perhaps, I shall have some opportunity to impress you."

"And by so saying, you refuse to serve me, madame," said the cardinal, whose tone of vexation nonetheless admitted a sort of esteem. "Remain free, then. And guard your hatreds and your sympathies well."

"Maitre —"

"No," said the cardinal, "this dialogue is done."

As if understanding the finality of the words, the cat quickly debarked from the cardinal's lap. As if distracted, their eminence put their attention back to the manuscript before them, but continued to speak. "I wish you no ill, but you must be aware that it is quite trouble enough to defend and compensate our friends. We owe nothing to our enemies. And, as you clearly intend to be my enemy, let me give you a piece of advice to take care of yourself, Madame d'Artagnan. For from the moment I withdraw my hand from your protection, I would not give one sou for your life."

"I will try to do so, maitre," said the Gascon with a cold confidence. "For my own sake, and for the sake of Madame Constance Bonacieux, who is dear to me and who I will keep safe."

The cardinal looked up from their desk and the manuscript before them. Their eminence appraised d'Artagnan coolly, then spoke. "You will have a difficult time seeking your young tailor from La Rochelle, my young guard. Well it is, then, that neither I nor anyone familiar to me has any desire to do Madame Bonacieux ill. So long as Madame Bonacieux remains in a place where she is unable to conduct certain business that has troubled me."

It was a calculated message, and d'Artagnan understood its import. But she also understood an even more important revelation, and forced herself to hide her sudden joy. For in talking of d'Artagnan seeking Constance, the young guard believed that the cardinal had inadvertently admitted not knowing that Constance had already been found and freed.

"I thank you for your concern, maitre," said d'Artagnan with a bow.

"Remember at a later period and at a certain moment, if any mischance should happen to you," said Richelieu, "that it was I who came to seek you, and that I did all in my power to prevent misfortune befalling you."

"Whatever may happen," said d'Artagnan, placing her hand upon her breast and bowing, "I shall entertain an eternal gratitude toward your eminence for that which you now do for me."

"Then we shall let it be as you have said, Madame d'Artagnan. We shall see each other again after the campaign. I will have my eye upon you, for I shall be there." So saying, the cardinal gestured to a magnificent set of black armor standing across the room. "And on our return, perhaps we will settle our outstanding accounts."

These last words of Richelieu's conveyed a terrible uncertainty, and quickly set an unease across d'Artagnan's brow once more. The promise alarmed her more than any simple threat would have done, for the message seemed to be a warning of some misfortune which threatened her — and which the cardinal by inference had the power to stop.

D'Artagnan opened her mouth to reply, but with a haughty gesture, the cardinal dismissed her.

She descended by the staircase at which she had entered, ignoring the cardinal's guards who watched her go. She found Athos and her musketeers outside, awaiting her reappearance and beginning to grow uneasy. With a word, d'Artagnan reassured them that all was well, and Planchet ran to inform the other musketeers and their sentinels that their guard duty was done, as d'Artagnan had come out safe from the Place de Palais-Cardinal once more.

On the return with Athos to her apartment, d'Artagnan, Aramis, and Porthos kept a quiet counsel. But immediately upon entering the privacy of the house, the two younger musketeers inquired eagerly as to the details of the interview. D'Artagnan was in a fearful mood, though, and confined herself to telling them that Cardinal de Richelieu had sent for her to offer entrance into their eminence's guards with the rank of ensign, and that she had refused.

"By my faith," said Aramis.

"And you were right to do so," said Porthos with conviction.

Athos fell into a profound contemplation and said nothing. But later, when Porthos and Aramis were gone, and she and d'Artagnan were alone, the elder musketeer spoke her mind.

"You have done that which you ought to have done, d'Artagnan. But you may still have done wrong."

D'Artagnan sighed deeply, for this advice echoed a secret concern of her soul, which told her that despite the hope she held that Constance was safe, great misfortunes awaited her.

The whole of the next day was spent in preparations for departure. D'Artagnan went to bid farewell to Monsieur de Treville, for the queens' musketeers and the queens' guards were to march on separate orders. This division would be but brief, it was generally thought, with the Queen Louise set to lead the musketeers the day after the guards departed — for the musketeers marched only with a royal at their command.

For his part, Monsieur de Treville contented himself with asking d'Artagnan if he could do anything for her, but d'Artagnan answered that she was supplied with all she wanted.

Upon her last meeting at the apartment of Athos, d'Artagnan spoke at last about the notes of Milord given her by Kitty, which were still secure in Athos's strongbox.

"Speak not of them again," said the musketeer, as admonishing as if she were responding to hearing the voice of Grimaud. "If they are to have value to you, it will come in time. But for now, I will keep them with me when we all depart."

"You? But why?"

"Because I am a musketeer and you a guard, and the danger in holding the notes if they are found is more easily bent from me than you. And because if your Milord is aware of them having gone missing, he will undoubtedly turn his attention to retrieving them from you. But as they will not be found on you, he shall not succeed."

Athos's protestations against discussing the notes extended even to d'Artagnan's thanks for securing them, so the young guard only nodded acquiescence in the end.

⚜

That night brought together all those comrades of the guards of Madame d'Essarts and the company of musketeers of Monsieur de Treville who had been accustomed to associate together. The revelry was as riotous as may be imagined. For extreme celebration is sometimes the only resolution for the worry of soldiers on their way to war.

At the first sound of the morning trumpet, the four friends separated, with the musketeers hastening to the estate of Monsieur de Treville, and d'Artagnan to that of Madame d'Essarts. Each of the captains then led their company to the Louvre, where the queens held their review.

The Queen Anne was of brave face where she addressed the companies. This swelled the hearts of many, for it was well known that Anne had less love for the arts of war than did the Queen Louise. But d'Artagnan thought she sensed a somber worry in the royal — a worry no doubt sourced from knowledge that the siege of La Rochelle placed the interests of her beloved Duke of Buckingham directly against the interests of her own crown.

The Queen Louise was dull by contrast, and appeared somewhat ill, which detracted from her usual lofty bearing. In fact, just the evening before, a fever had seized her in the midst of a meeting of the parliament. Even so, she had decided upon setting out to lead the musketeers that same evening, and in spite of protests had persisted in having the review, as if hoping that by showing defiance to her present ailment she might banish it.

The review over, the guards set forth alone on their march while the musketeers awaited the readiness of the Queen Louise. This allowed Porthos time to go and take a turn to show off his superb new equipment along the Rue d'Ours, where Madame Coquenard waited at a window to see him pass in his new uniform and on his fine horse. Her love for Porthos was too dear to allow him to part thus, and she made him a sign to dismount and come to her.

Porthos was magnificent as he did so. His spurs jingled, his breastplate gleamed, and his sword knocked proudly against his sturdy leg. This time, the clerks showed more reverence than the curiosity displayed at their first meeting with the musketeer.

Porthos was introduced again to Monsieur Vattier, whose little gray eyes sparkled with anger at seeing his so-called cousin all in blazing new finery. As to Madame Coquenard, she could not restrain her tears, though no illicit emotions were assumed from her grief. For she was known to be very much attached to her relatives, about whom she was constantly having serious disputes with her husband. Moreover, one thing afforded Monsieur Vattier some inward consolation, for it was expected by most folk in Paris that the campaign would be a brutal one. Thus he could whisper a hope to himself that this beloved relative might not come back alive.

When Porthos departed, Madame Coquenard returned to her window and followed him with her eyes as long as she was able. She waved her handkerchief to him, leaning so far out of the window as to lead people on the street below to fear she might plummet. Porthos received all these attentions like one fully accustomed to them. But before turning the corner of the street, he lifted his hat gracefully, waving it to her as a sign of adieux.

On their part, Aramis spent the time awaiting the order for the march to write a long letter, though none but d'Artagnan would have guessed to whom. For Kitty, who was to set out that evening for Tours and Madame de Chevreuse, was waiting for the letter in the next chamber.

Athos spent the time alone, sipping the last bottle of her Spanish wine.

In the meantime, d'Artagnan was marching with her company. Arriving at the Faubourg Saint-Antoine, she turned to gaze upon the Bastille, her heart lightened by the thought that whatever her present fate, she had avoided incarceration on the cardinal's orders. But as it was the Bastille alone she looked at, the young guard did not observe Milord, who watched, cloaked and hooded, from the adjacent side street upon a light chestnut horse. To two ill-looking figures at his feet, he designated d'Artagnan with a pointed finger, and the two slipped close up to the ranks to gain a better view of the young guard.

Then, certain that there could be no mistake in the execution of his orders, Milord turned his horse from the company and rode away.

The two figures followed the company of guards as it prepared to march again. Then on leaving the Faubourg Saint-Antoine, they mounted two horses, properly equipped for a long journey, which were waiting for them.

— CHAPTER 41 —

THE SIEGE OF LA ROCHELLE

The Siege of La Rochelle was one of the great political events of its age — and one of the great military enterprises of the Cardinal de Richelieu. It is, then, worthwhile that we should say a few words about it, particularly as many details of the siege are connected in an important manner with the story we have undertaken to relate.

The political plans of the cardinal when they undertook the siege were extensive. Of the important cities given up by the King Henry and the Sovereign Marie to the Protestants — which in this instance were the Huguenots — as places of safety a generation before our story and the rise of the Queen Louise to the French throne, La Rochelle alone remained under Huguenot control. It became necessary, therefore, to destroy this last bulwark of radicalism.

Spanish, English, and Italian malcontents, adventurers of all nations, and soldiers of fortune of every sect had flocked at the first summons under the standard of the Protestants, and organized themselves like a vast association whose branches diverged freely over all parts of Europe. La Rochelle, which had derived a new importance after the fall of the other Protestant cities, therefore became the focus of much dissent and ambition — a dissent that might foment civil revolt and foreign war at any time. Moreover, the city's port was the last in France left open to the English since the rise of talk of war, and by closing La Rochelle against England, the cardinal would send a clear message to London and beyond.

That having been said, alongside the political motivations of Cardinal de Richelieu as eminence of the church and minister of the crown, we must also recognize the lesser motives of a secretly spurned lover whose jealousy knew no bounds.

Richelieu, as has been revealed, had loved the Queen Anne and been thoroughly rebuffed. Whether this love was a simple political affair or was naturally one of those profound passions which Anne of Austria inspired in so many of those who approached her cannot be clearly judged. But in any event, we have seen by the earlier developments of this story that the Duke of Buckingham had won the clear advantage over their eminence's plots of revenge against the queen. And it must be understood how the cardinal was all too aware that the courage, conduct, and devotedness of d'Artagnan and her musketeer companions had cruelly deceived and humiliated them.

It was, then, Richelieu's object in La Rochelle to not only get rid of an enemy of France, but to avenge themself on a rival. But this vengeance would need to be grand and striking and worthy in every way — worthy of the person who held in their hand, as their weapon for combat, the forces of a nation. For Richelieu knew that in combating England, they combated Buckingham. In triumphing over England, their eminence triumphed over Buckingham. In short, by the humiliation of England in the eyes of Europe, the cardinal humiliated Buckingham in the eyes of the Queen Anne, and none could have said which was more important in their eminence's mind.

On Buckingham's side, even as he pretended to maintain the honor of England, the duke was moved equally by interests matching those of the cardinal, and pursued a vengeance just as private. The rumors, widespread for some years now, of his improper infatuation with the Queen Anne meant that Buckingham could not under any pretense be admitted into France as an ambassador — and so he wished to enter it as a conqueror. And so it resulted from this that a kind look from the Queen Anne was the real stake in this game, which the two most powerful nations in Europe played for the good pleasure of two amorous fools.

The first advantage in the contest had been gained by Buckingham some months before, as he had intimated to the Queen Anne in their secret meeting in the Louvre. Arriving unexpectedly in sight of the Isle of Rhe with ninety vessels and nearly twenty thousand troops, he had surprised the Countieux de Toiras, who had commanded the isle in the queens' names. After a brief but bloody conflict, England had effected its landing, and La Rochelle was soon a bastion of English and Huguenot power.

The resolution of Cardinal de Richelieu's response came quickly. Expeditionary forces under various commanders came to patrol the territories around La Rochelle, not long after the interview of Monsieur Bouquet in which their eminence's maps and plans were seen, even as the English forces established themselves and preparations for siege were made. After some months of these preparations, Richelieu had deemed it time for the campaign to begin, and all the troops they could order to muster began the march toward the theater of war. It was of this detachment, sent as a vanguard, that our friend d'Artagnan formed a part.

The Queen Louise, as we have said, was to lead the musketeers as soon as her meetings with parliament on the matter of the war were complete. But on rising from her bed, she had felt herself attacked by fever, also as said. The queen, notwithstanding, fulfilled her determination to set out, but her illness became more serious with each mile marched, and she was forced to stop more than once.

Now, whenever the queen leading them halted, the musketeers halted also. So it followed that d'Artagnan, still serving among the guards, found herself at present separated from her good friends Athos, Porthos, and Aramis. To her, this separation seemed no more than an unpleasant circumstance — though it would certainly have become a cause of serious unease if she had been able to guess by what unknown dangers she was surrounded.

At the time of d'Artagnan's arrival without incident in the camp established outside La Rochelle, the state of the campaign was clear to see. The Duke of Buckingham and his English maintained control of the Isle of Rhe, and continued to besiege the nearby citadels of Saint-Martin and La Pree without success. Full hostilities with the Rochellais had commenced three days before, with the Huguenots focused on a new fort that had been constructed for the queens' forces near the city.

The guards under the command of Madame d'Essarts took up their barracks at an abbey near the entrance to La Rochelle harbor. As we know, d'Artagnan's camaraderie with the three musketeers had given her cause to form but few friendships among her own comrades, and she felt herself isolated and given up to her own reflections — and those reflections were not very cheerful.

From the time of her arrival in Paris, d'Artagnan had become mixed up with an extraordinary number of public affairs. But her own private affairs had made no great progress, either in love or fortune. The only person she felt she had ever truly loved was Constance, and the tailor's disappearance vexed d'Artagnan still, even with the near-certain knowledge that she was free and conducted to safety by agents of the Queen Anne, and by the guess that the cardinal had as yet no knowledge of that fact. And as to fortune, those same assurances reminded her that she had made an enemy of Richelieu — a guard and a lowly Gascon, as humble as she was. How could fate have conspired to make her the known foe of their eminence, before whom trembled the greatest folk of the nation — beginning with the queens?

Still, one thing was clear. Cardinal de Richelieu had the power to crush d'Artagnan at their whim, and yet they had not done so. For a mind so clear thinking as that of d'Artagnan, this indulgence was a light by which she caught a glimpse of a better future.

As to her other enemy, d'Artagnan was even more unsure of where she stood. Milord de Winter was less to be feared than the cardinal, she thought. But nevertheless, she instinctively knew that the wounded villain was not to be ignored.

With a solemn air, d'Artagnan assessed that the only thing she had clearly gained in all her adventures thus far was the Queen Anne's diamond ring, which she wore now concealed under her gauntlet. But because she could not

*But despite her speed, the first who had fired, having time to reload,
fired a second shot so well aimed that it struck the young guard's hat…*

part with it, determined as she was to keep it as a symbol of Anne's pledge of gratitude — this diamond now had no more value than the gravel the young Gascon trod beneath her feet.

We say the gravel she trod beneath her feet, for d'Artagnan made these reflections while walking solitarily along a small road which led from the camp to a village adjoining the abbey barracks. Her musings had led her farther than she intended, and the day was beginning to wane.

So it was that by the last rays of the setting sun, she thought she saw the barrel of a musket glitter from behind a hedge.

D'Artagnan had a quick eye and a prompt understanding. She understood that the musket had not come there of itself, and that they who bore it had not concealed themself behind a hedge with any friendly intentions. She determined, therefore, to direct her course as clear from it as she could — even as, on the opposite side of the road and behind a rock, she glimpsed the barrel of another weapon.

The young guard threw herself upon the ground at the same instant the first gun was fired. Even as she heard the whistling of a bullet pass over her head, d'Artagnan sprang up with a bound, at the same instant that the bullet from the other musket tore up the gravel of the road where she had thrown herself down.

The young guard was not one of those foolhardy sorts who seek a ridiculous death in order that it may be said of them that they did not retreat a single step. Besides, courage was out of the question in these circumstances — she had fallen into an ambush. "If there is a third shot," said she to herself, "I am lost!"

She therefore took to her heels and ran toward the camp with the swiftness of the young folk of her homeland, so renowned for their agility. But despite her speed, the first who had fired, having time to reload, fired a second shot so well aimed that it struck the young guard's hat, and carried it ten paces from her.

Having no other hat, d'Artagnan picked it up as she ran, and arrived at her quarters in the abbey very flushed and quite out of breath. She sat down, though, without making report to anyone, and began to reflect.

The first and the most natural explanation for the attack would be to call it simply an ambush of the guards of the Rochellais, who would not be sorry to kill one of their majesties' guards. But d'Artagnan took her hat, examined the hole made by the bullet, and shook her head. For the bullet was not one from a musket, but was fired from an arquebus. That lighter weapon produced better accuracy than a musket, but had long since fallen out of use among the military. This could not, then, be a military ambush.

As a second thought, d'Artagnan considered that the attack might well be a kind remembrance of Cardinal de Richelieu. But she again shook her head. Against enemies such as she, the cardinal had but to put forth their hand to crush all opposition. Especially given that their eminence had ample evidence during their interview with d'Artagnan to have arrested or executed her without a thought, it seemed unlikely that they would now take recourse to such means of revenge.

In the end, then, the attempt on d'Artagnan's life seemed most probably a vengeance of Milord.

The young guard tried in vain to remember the faces or dress of the assassins. However, she had escaped so quickly that she had not had leisure to notice any such details.

"Ah, my poor friends," murmured d'Artagnan as she thought of Athos, Porthos, and Aramis. "Where are you? For I miss you more now than ever."

The young guard passed a very bad night. Four times, she started awake, imagining that some figure was approaching her bed for the purpose of stabbing her. Nevertheless, day dawned without the darkness having brought any incident. But d'Artagnan well suspected that her fate had been simply deferred, not wholly relinquished.

She remained all that day in her quarters, using as an excuse the poor weather. Then at nine o'clock the next morning, the drums beat to arms. The guards turned out for inspection, and d'Artagnan took her place in the midst of her comrades. As inspection was made by the troop's officers, accompanied by Madame d'Essarts their captain, it appeared to d'Artagnan that the captain made a sign indicating she should approach. She thus left the ranks and advanced to receive orders.

The captain's arms were bare as always, her expression as serious as ever, her epaulets and fresh-shaved head both catching the light of rising sun as she said, "I am preparing to ask for warriors of good will for a dangerous mission, but one which will do honor to those who shall accomplish it. I made you a sign in order that you might hold yourself in readiness."

"Thank you, my captain," said d'Artagnan, who wished for nothing better than an opportunity to distinguish herself.

Madame d'Essarts then raised her voice and all went quiet. It was explained that the defenders of La Rochelle had made a sortie during the night, and had retaken a bastion of which the royal army had gained possession just two days before. "A mission at hand," said the captain, "will ascertain by reconnaissance how this bastion is now guarded by the Rochellais. I want for this mission volunteers, who will be led by Madame d'Artagnan."

D'Artagnan felt all eyes on her as she stepped forward. "I seek four blades of good will who will risk being killed with me!" said she, raising her sword. Two of her comrades of the guards immediately sprang forward, a dark-tan sharpshooter of Dijon and a ruddy brawler from Lyon. And with them came two soldiers of one of the expeditionary forces, both pink-complexioned and wind-burned and fiercely eager to fight.

The captain explained to all that it was not known whether, after the taking of the bastion, the Rochellais had evacuated it or left a garrison within. The object of the mission to be led by d'Artagnan, then, was to examine the place from near enough to report what might be found there.

The young guard thus set out with her four companions, following the trench that marked the present perimeter of the siege. They arrived thus, sheltered from sight of the enemy as they came within a hundred paces of the bastion. But on turning round, d'Artagnan saw that the two once-eager expeditionary soldiers had disappeared.

"Cowardly lackeys," she whispered to her guard companions. "Leave them, though." And she made a sign to continue the advance.

At the turning of the outer wall of the trench, they found themselves within about sixty paces of the bastion. They saw no one, and the fortification seemed abandoned. But even as d'Artagnan and her two companions deliberated whether they should proceed farther, all at once a circle of smoke erupted from the stone walls ahead, and a dozen bullets came whistling around them.

They thus knew all they wished to know. The bastion was indeed guarded, and a longer stay in this dangerous spot would have been useless imprudence. D'Artagnan and her two companions turned their backs and commenced a fast retreat. But on arriving at a bend in the trench which would serve them as a rampart, one of the guards fell. A bullet had passed through their breast, d'Artagnan saw. The other faltered, but d'Artagnan waved them on and they continued their way toward the camp.

Not willing to abandon her wounded companion, d'Artagnan stooped to raise them and assist them in further retreat. But as she did, two more shots were fired. One bullet struck and killed the already-wounded guard, while the other flattened itself against a rock after having passed within two inches of d'Artagnan.

The young guard turned quickly round, for this attack could not have come from the bastion, which was hidden by the bend of the trench. The memory of the two soldiers who had abandoned her patrol loomed in her mind — and with that thought came remembrance of the ambush of two evenings before. Resolving this time to learn the truth of who she faced, d'Artagnan fell upon the body of her comrade as if she too were dead. In so doing, she took care not to let go of her sword.

With eyes half closed, she soon saw two heads appear above an abandoned barricade some thirty paces from her. It was the two soldiers. D'Artagnan understood that these two villains had only offered themselves to her patrol for the purpose of assassinating her, hoping that the young guard's death would be placed to the account of the enemy.

As thorough assassins would, the two approached. Fearing that d'Artagnan might be only wounded and would denounce their crime, they had the intent of making sure she was dead. But deceived by the young guard's trick, they were still reloading their guns as they approached, so that when they came within ten paces of her, she sprang up to close with them.

The assassins understood that if they fled toward the camp without having killed their target, they would be pursued and accused by her. Therefore, they made their stand. One of them took their gun by the barrel and used it as they would a club, but a terrible blow aimed at d'Artagnan was avoided by her springing to one side. By this movement, however, she left a passage free to the bandit, who darted off toward the bastion, seemingly thinking to join the enemy if they could. But as the Rochellais who guarded the site were ignorant of those intentions, they fired and the bandit fell, struck dead in the instant.

Meanwhile, d'Artagnan had thrown herself upon the other soldier, attacking with her sword. The conflict was not long, for the wretch had nothing to defend themself with but their discharged arquebus. After a flurry of barely parried strikes, the young guard's sword slipped along the barrel of the now-useless weapon and passed through the thigh of the assassin, who fell.

D'Artagnan immediately placed the point of her sword at the bandit's throat.

"Oh, do not kill me!" cried they. Their wind-burned complexion had grown more pale by far, and beads of sweat hung along their brow beneath a wedge of lank blonde hair. "Grant me your pardon, madame, and I will tell you all."

"So you know me. Well, is your secret of enough importance that I should spare your life for it?" asked d'Artagnan, not showing the slightest tremor in her arm.

"Yes, if you think your own life of value. For you may hope for much from that life, being young and brave as you are."

"Wretch," said d'Artagnan. "Speak quickly. Who employed you to assassinate me?"

"A gentry whom I don't know, but who is called Milord."

"But if you don't know this gentry, how do you know his name?"

"My comrade knows him, and called him so. It was with my comrade that this affair was arranged, and not with me. In his pocket, you will even find a letter from this Milord, who attaches great importance to you, as I have heard it said."

"But how did you become involved in this villainous affair?"

"My comrade proposed to me to undertake it with him, and I agreed."

"And how much were you given for this fine enterprise?"

"A hundred pistoles."

"Well, faith," said the young guard, laughing. "Milord thinks I am worth something. A hundred pistoles? That would certainly be a temptation for two villains like you. I understand why you accepted it, and I grant you my pardon. But upon one condition."

"What is that?" said the bandit, uneasy at perceiving that all was not over.

"That you will go and fetch me the letter your comrade has in their pocket."

"Faith!" cried the bandit. "That is only another way of killing me! How can I go and fetch that letter under the fire of the bastion?"

"You must nevertheless make up your mind to go and get it, or I swear you shall die by my hand."

"Pardon, madame! Take pity in the name of that young woman you love!" said the bandit, throwing themself upon their hands and knees — for they were beginning to lose strength from loss of blood.

D'Artagnan's hand showed a moment's tremor. "And how do you know whom I love?" asked she.

"By that letter which my comrade has in their pocket."

"You have done yourself a disservice, then," said d'Artagnan. "For I now must have that letter. So no more delay, no more hesitation — or else whatever might be my repugnance to soiling my sword a second time with the blood of a wretch like you, I swear…" And at those words, d'Artagnan made so fierce a gesture that the wounded bandit sprang up.

"Stop!" cried they, regaining strength by force of terror. "I will go — I will go!"

D'Artagnan took the soldier's arquebus, made them walk on before her, and urged them toward their companion by pricking them from behind with her sword.

It was a frightful thing to see this poor bandit, leaving a long track of blood on the ground they passed over, pale with approaching death, as they tried to drag themself along without being seen to the body of their accomplice, which lay twenty paces away.

Terror was so strongly painted on the villain's face, covered with a cold sweat, that d'Artagnan took pity on them. Casting upon them a look of contempt, she called out, "Stop. I will show you the difference between one of courage and such a coward as you. Stay where you are, for I will go myself."

Then with a light step and an eye on the bastion, watching closely the movements of the enemy, and taking advantage of every bit of cover along the ground, d'Artagnan succeeded in reaching the second soldier. She assessed quickly that there were two means of gaining the letter she sought — either to search the villain on the spot, or to carry them away, making a buckler of their body and searching them more easily in the trench.

D'Artagnan quickly settled on the second means, and lifted the assassin onto her shoulders at the moment the enemy began to fire. As she ran, a slight shock and the dull noise of three bullets which struck the body proved to d'Artagnan that the dead assassin had saved her life.

As she regained the trench, the young guard threw the corpse beside the wounded bandit, who was as ashen as death. Then she began to search the body. A leather pocketbook, a purse, and a dice box completed the possessions of the dead bandit. D'Artagnan left the box and dice where they fell, threw the purse to the wounded bandit — its weight suggesting it held some part of the sum which the two had received from Milord — and eagerly opened the pocketbook.

Among some unimportant papers, d'Artagnan found the letter which she had sought at the risk of her life:

Your having lost sight of the tailor puts her now in safety in some convent, which you should never have allowed her to reach. Try at least not to miss the guard, her lover. If you do, you know that my hand stretches far, and that you shall pay very dearly for the hundred pistoles you have from me.

The note held no name or signature, but d'Artagnan nevertheless recognized the handwriting of Milord. Putting it carefully away as a piece of evidence, and being in safety behind the bend of the trench, she began then to interrogate the wounded bandit. They confessed that not three weeks before, they had undertaken with their comrade — the same who was killed — to intercept and attack a carriage by which a young woman was to leave Paris by the Chaillot road. But when the carriage was delayed in appearing, the two stopped to drink at a cabaret, and subsequently missed it as it hurtled past.

"From where was that woman coming? And what were you to do with her?" asked d'Artagnan with anger.

"What was told to us was that she was held but had escaped, and had obtained aid from unknown agents. She was to be captured and held again. We were to have conveyed her to a townhouse in the Place Royale," said the wounded foe.

"To Milord's own residence," murmured d'Artagnan. What might have become of Constance there, the young guard was too fearful to contemplate. But she understood what a terrible thirst for vengeance drove Milord now to destroy her, as well as all who loved her.

Still, amid all her misgiving, d'Artagnan confirmed again with a feeling of joy that Constance had escaped whatever house she had been held in. But the Gascon understood also that even freed, the young tailor had known the danger she faced — and had made the choice to deflect that danger away from d'Artagnan, perhaps even to the point of holding the queen to secrecy.

Of even more importance than knowing that Constance was safe, d'Artagnan understood one thing more from Milord's note. The villain did not yet know the specifics of where the Queen Anne had hidden Constance — and from that, it could be hoped that the cardinal likewise did not yet know.

This idea completely restored clemency to d'Artagnan's heart. She turned toward the wounded bandit, who had watched with intense anxiety as the young guard read the note. Holding out her arm to them, said she, "Come, I will not abandon you thus. Lean upon me, and let us return to the camp."

"Leave me," said the bandit. "What difference does it make to die here, or for you to walk me back to have me hanged?"

"I walk you back to have you healed. You have my word," said d'Artagnan. "For the second time, I give you your life."

The wounded villain, astonished, sank upon their knees to give thanks to their protector. But d'Artagnan, who had no longer a motive for staying so near the enemy, abridged that testimonial of gratitude and quickly pushed on.

As it happened, the guard who had returned at the first discharge, waiting for but not seeing d'Artagnan directly behind, had announced the death or capture of all their companions to Madame d'Essarts and the company. All were therefore much astonished and delighted when they saw the young guard and the wounded soldier come back safe and sound.

D'Artagnan explained the sword wound of her companion by improvising the tale of a sortie with the Rochellais. She likewise described the death of the other soldier, and the perils all the squad had encountered. For the young guard, this recital was the occasion of veritable triumph. The whole army talked of this expedition for a day, and all the officers paid her compliments upon it. And besides this, as every great action bears its reward with it, the brave exploit of d'Artagnan resulted in the restoration of the tranquility she had lost.

Before she slept that night, d'Artagnan believed that her troubles might well be over, as one of her two assassins was killed and the other was now devoted to her interests. This tranquility of thought proved only one thing, however — that d'Artagnan did not yet know all of which Milord de Winter was capable.

CHAPTER 42

THE ANJOU WINE

Even as d'Artagnan's personal triumph made news in the camp, other news was more dire. The company of Monsieur de Treville's musketeers was looked for but had not yet arrived, with couriers instead bringing the most disheartening news of the Queen Louise's health. For days on end, reports of her continuing convalescence in Villeroi arrived in the camp, all stating that as she was very anxious to be in person at the siege, she would set forth as soon as she could mount a horse.

While the besieging forces waited, there was thus much uncertainty. Madame d'Essarts was anxious for action to commence, but the other captains — most fearing to be removed from command if a failed sortie displeased the queen — did but little, lost their days in wavering, and did not dare to attempt any great enterprise to drive the English from the Isle of Rhe. So by turns, those English continued safely to besiege the citadels of Saint-Martin and La Pree, as on their side the French besieged La Rochelle.

D'Artagnan, as we have said, had become more at peace, as often happens after great peril — particularly when the peril seems to have passed. She felt only one uneasiness, and that was at not hearing any tidings from her friends. But one morning a week after her sortie against the Rochellais bastion, a letter arrived for her, marked from Villeroi:

Madame d'Artagnan —
Madame Athos, Monsieur Porthos, and Maitre Aramis, after having had an entertainment at my house and enjoying themselves very much, created such a disturbance that the provost of the castle, a rigid villain, has ordered them to be confined for some days. But I accomplish the order they have given me by forwarding to you a dozen bottles of my Anjou wine, with which they are much pleased. They are desirous that you should drink to their health.

I have passed this message on, and am, madame, with great respect,
Your very humble and obedient servant,

— Maitre Godeau, Host of the Musketeers

"This is most good," said d'Artagnan to herself. "They think of me in their pleasures, as I thought of them in my troubles. Well, I will certainly drink to their health with all my heart."

The young guard sent the twelve bottles to the mess hall of the guards, with strict orders to Planchet that great care should be taken to hide them. She then set the valet to prepare a suitable meal for two days hence, when she would have furlough for an afternoon.

On the day appointed, Planchet, proud of being raised to the responsibilities of host, had set and prepared a sumptuous meal, hoping through both presentation and menu to delight d'Artagnan. He had enjoyed the assistance of the false soldier who had tried to kill d'Artagnan, whose name was Brisemont, and who had entered into the service of d'Artagnan and Planchet both after d'Artagnan had saved their life.

When the hour of the banquet had come, d'Artagnan took her place and the dishes were arranged on the table. Planchet waited, towel on arm. Brisemont uncorked a bottle of the Anjou wine and poured it carefully into a decanter. The bottle being a little thick at the bottom, they poured the sediment into a glass, and d'Artagnan bade the injured bandit to drink it, for they were still recovering their strength.

Having eaten her soup, d'Artagnan was about to lift the first glass of wine to her lips, when all at once the cannon sounded from the fort. Imagining this to be caused by some unexpected attack either of the besieged Rochellais or the English, she sprang to her sword and ran out in order to repair to her post. But scarcely was she out of the room before she was made aware of the cause of this noise.

Cries of, "Long live the queens! Long live the cardinal!" resounded on every side, and the drums were beaten in every direction. It was announced that the Queen Louise, impatient as has been said, had left Villeroi at last and advanced by forced marches, so as to that moment arrive with a reinforcement of ten thousand troops. The queens' musketeers proceeded and followed her. D'Artagnan, placed in line with her company, saluted with an expressive gesture her three friends, whose eyes soon spotted her, and Monsieur de Treville, who noted her at once.

When the ceremony of reception was over, the four friends were soon in one another's arms. "By my faith," cried d'Artagnan, "you could not have arrived in better time. The dinner I was enjoying will certainly feed more, and cannot have had time to get cold."

"Excellent!" said Porthos. "After this long a march, I am in a mood for feasting."

"I am less concerned for food," said Athos. "But is there any drinkable wine in your mess hall?"

"Well, faith, there is yours, my dear friends," said d'Artagnan.

"Our wine?" said Aramis, curious.

"Yes, that you sent me."

"We sent you wine?"

"You know very well you did. The wine of Anjou."

"Yes, I know what brand you are talking about," said Athos. "I would not call it a preference, but in the absence of Champagne and Chambertin, we must content yourselves with anything."

"And so, connoisseurs in wine as we are, we have sent you some Anjou wine?" said Porthos.

"Not exactly. It is the wine that was sent by your order."

"On our account?" said Athos. "Did you send this wine, Aramis?"

"Indeed no. And you, Porthos?"

"No. Athos?"

"Decidedly no."

"But it was sent by your host," said d'Artagnan, now quite confused. "Maitre Godeau, at whose house you stayed."

"My faith, never mind where it comes from," said Porthos. "Let us taste it, and if it is good, let us drink it."

"No," said Athos. "For Godeau had no reason to send wine, which makes this a mysterious affair."

"But here is their letter," said d'Artagnan. And pulling it from her pocket, she presented the note to her comrades.

"This is not Godeau's writing," said Athos grimly. "I am acquainted with it. Before we left Villeroi, I settled our accounts with them."

"And these events are false altogether," said Porthos. "We have not been disciplined."

"D'Artagnan," said Aramis in a reproachful tone. "How could you believe that we three would have made such a disturbance?"

But d'Artagnan grew ashen rather than answer, and a convulsive shiver shook all her limbs.

"You alarm me," said Athos, who read the fear in her young friend's face. "What has happened?"

"Look you, my friends," said d'Artagnan. "Two attempts on my life have been made since my arrival at La Rochelle, with Milord de Winter behind it all. I fear this is another vengeance of that villain!"

It was now Athos who shivered, as d'Artagnan rushed toward the mess hall. The three musketeers followed close behind.

The first sight that met the eyes of d'Artagnan on entering the room was poor Brisemont, stretched upon the ground and rolling in horrible convulsions. Planchet, ashen as death, was trying to give aid to the fallen bandit, but it was plain that all assistance was useless. For all their features were distorted with the agony of dying.

"Oh!" cried Brisemont, on perceiving d'Artagnan. "You villain! You pretend to pardon me, and you poison me!"

"I?" cried d'Artagnan. "No, my friend, believe me."

"I say that it was you who gave me the wine. I say that it was you who bade me drink it. I say you wished to avenge yourself on me, and I say that it is horrible!"

"Upon my faith," said d'Artagnan, throwing herself down by the dying figure, "I swear to you that the wine was poisoned for me, and I was ready to drink of it as you did."

"Villain…" whispered the bandit. Then with a last horrible convulsion, they died.

"Frightful," murmured Athos. Porthos in silence broke the bottles one by one, pouring their contents down a drain. Aramis gave orders that a cleric should be sent for.

"Oh, my friends," said d'Artagnan. "You come once more to save my life."

"And not only yours, madame," stammered Planchet. "Ah, what an escape I have had!"

"How is it so? You were going to drink the wine?"

"Only to the health of the Queen Louise, madame! I was ready to drink a small glass of it, if I had not seen poor Brisemont fall."

The young guard and the three musketeers looked at one another, their expressions making it clear that each of them understood the gravity of their situation.

"Before all else," said Athos, "let us leave this chamber. The dead are not agreeable company."

"Planchet," said d'Artagnan, "I commit the corpse of this poor bandit to your care. Let them be interred with whatever rites they would have desired. They committed a crime, it is true, but they repented of it."

Then the four friends left the room, leaving to Planchet the duty of awaiting the cleric and paying mortuary honors to Brisemont.

⚜

Within the mess hall, the four friends found a private chamber, and were served by the cooks with fresh eggs. They drank only water, which Athos went herself to draw at the fountain.

In as few words as possible, d'Artagnan informed all three as to the events that had transpired since her arrival at the siege, and the two attempts on her life. For Porthos and Aramis, she provided bare details of her affair with Milord de Winter, and expanded upon her meeting with Cardinal de Richelieu, and on the connections between those two.

Of her thoughts on the identity of Milord, d'Artagnan said nothing for the moment. But she understood that she would need to sound out Athos on her greatest secret, if all four friends were to take counsel together.

At a point when Aramis went to refill the water pitcher and Porthos went to seek out the cooks for bread, the young guard and Athos had a moment to speak alone. "Well," said d'Artagnan to Athos. "It seems, my dear friend, that this is war to the death for Milord."

Athos shrugged her shoulders. "Yes," said she, "I perceive it plainly. And I fear what I feel now, for this despair clouds my judgement."

"Then we will plan together, you and I, Porthos and Aramis…"

"They must not know!" said Athos, biting the words out sharply. "I cannot address this. It is past and present in collision and I know not who I am."

At that moment, Porthos and Aramis both returned, and Athos at a sign bade the young guard to keep her counsel. D'Artagnan nodded, continuing the conversation as if Porthos and Aramis had not left. "So as to the threats of Milord, my friends, what is to be done?" said she.

"The fact is, one cannot remain thus, with a sword hanging eternally over their head," said Athos. "We must extricate ourselves from this position."

"But how?"

"You must try to see this Milord," said the elder musketeer grimly, "and come to some understanding with him. Say to him: 'Choose peace or choose war.' Offer your word as a gentle never to say anything of him, never to do anything against him. On his side, call for a solemn oath to remain neutral with respect to you. And threaten that if not, you will apply to the chancellor, you will apply to the queens. You will move the courts against him, you will denounce him as branded, you will bring him to trial. And if he is acquitted, make clear by the faith of a gentle that you will kill him at the corner of some wall, as you would a mad dog."

D'Artagnan was silent a moment. "I like the means well enough," said she at last. "But where and how to meet with him?"

It was Aramis who spoke in response. "Time, dear friend, brings around opportunity. The more we have ventured, the more we gain, when we know how to wait."

"Yes," said d'Artagnan. "But to wait surrounded by assassins and poisoners…"

"Fie!" said Porthos in his turn. "Fate has preserved us hitherto, and fate will preserve us still."

Athos nodded, deep in thought.

"Fate may preserve us, yes," said d'Artagnan. "But we are warriors. All things considered, it is our lot to risk our lives, and we have sworn to counter the cardinal and their agents in the name of the queens. But we are not all who are involved in this."

"What others?" asked Athos.

"Constance."

"Madame Bonacieux! Ah, faith," said Athos. "My poor friend, I continually forget that you are in love."

"But as to that," said Aramis, "you spoke of having learned by the letter found on your assassin that she is in a convent? One may be very comfortable in a convent."

"But can one be safe?" said d'Artagnan.

"For a time, yes. Time and opportunity, my friend. If you trust to faith —"

"Good," cried Athos. "Good. Yes, my dear Aramis, we all know that your views have a religious tendency."

"I am only temporarily a musketeer," said Aramis, as always.

"Faith or no," said Porthos, "it appears to me that the means are very simple."

"What means?" asked d'Artagnan.

"You say she is in a convent? Very well. As soon as the siege is over, we'll carry her off from that convent."

"But we must first learn what convent she is in."

"A small matter," said Porthos.

"A small matter indeed," said Athos. "Let us think, gentles. We know that Madame Bonacieux has served the Queen Anne, and indeed, this service is the root cause of her present strife. Her escape, as d'Artagnan's note summarizes, fully suggests the queen's involvement."

"But we cannot approach the queen," said d'Artagnan, "even were we not on campaign. The cardinal would know at once."

"Indeed. But Porthos may assist us with discretion."

"And how so, if you please?" said Porthos with confusion.

"Why, by your duchess. She must have a long arm at court."

"Indeed," replied Porthos nervously. "But her husband would be a cardinalist simply to spite me, I fear. She must know nothing of the matter."

"Then," said Aramis, "I take it upon myself to obtain intelligence of Madame Bonacieux's hiding place, through friends of my own whose letters can reach the Queen Anne in confidence. If I ask, Madame de Chevreuse will be our voice, I am certain of it. Even if Madame Bonacieux has asked secrecy of the queen to protect d'Artagnan, her majesty may relent if learning that three of her musketeers as well are sworn to keep her young tailor safe."

And with all this said, d'Artagnan felt the sorrow lift from her at last. The four friends, who had finished their modest meal, thus separated with the promise of meeting again that evening. D'Artagnan returned to the affairs of her company, while the three musketeers repaired to the houses established for the Queen Louise's troops, where they were to claim their lodging — and to prepare for the war to come.

CHAPTER 43

THE SIGN OF THE RED DOVECOTE

Although scarcely arrived in the camp, the Queen Louise was in such haste to meet the enemy that she commanded every effort to be made to drive the English from the Isle of Rhe which warded La Rochelle, and afterward to press the siege of the city itself. For she was anxious to show her hatred for the Duke of Buckingham — and with even more reason than the cardinal.

The timing was favorable. The English, who required above everything good living in order to be good soldiers, were eating only salt meat and bad biscuits, and had many wounded in their camp. Still further, it was a season of rough seas all along the coast, which destroyed every day some vessel or another, and the shore of the Isle of Rhe was at every tide covered with the wrecks of ships, large and small.

As a result, even if the French troops remained quietly in their camp, it was evident that Buckingham, who only held the isle from obstinacy, would eventually be obliged by failing resources and morale to end his occupation. But as intelligence had come to the Queen Louise that actions in the enemy camp hinted at preparations for a fresh assault, she judged that it would be best to put an end to the affair, and gave the necessary orders for a decisive attack.

As it is not our intention to give a journal of the campaign, but on the contrary only to describe such of the events of it as are connected with the story we are relating, we will content ourselves with saying in a few words that the attack on the Isle of Rhe succeeded, to the admitted surprise of the Queen Louise and the great glory of the cardinal. The English were repulsed foot by foot, beaten in all encounters, and trodden down as they fled the isle. They then were obliged to take to their ships, leaving on the field of battle two thousand soldiers, a significant number of officers and gentry, four cannons, and sixty flags, which were taken to Paris and suspended with great pomp in the arches of the cathedral of Notre Dame. Songs of victory were chanted in the French camp, and afterward throughout the realm.

With nothing new to fear from La Rochelle's English allies, the cardinal was then left free to carry on the siege. But it must be acknowledged that their eminence had far more than La Rochelle on their mind.

With the Duke of Buckingham fled, letters and papers were obtained from his quarters, which he had been forced to abandon hurriedly. These writings hinted at a league of alliance between England, the German Empire, Austria, and Spain, with a singular purpose of opposing France. Still further, Buckingham's personal journals hinted at the contact between the duke, Madame de Chevreuse, and the Queen Anne that had so long vexed the cardinal.

To attend to all these issues, the vast resources of their eminence's genius were at work night and day. Orders were given that the cardinal should hear even the least report of the plots of Buckingham or this league from any of the great realms of Europe. For if an alliance that threatened France triumphed, all their eminence's influence would be lost. The interests of Spain and Austria would have their representatives in the cabinet of the Louvre, where they had as yet only followers, and Richelieu would be finished as national minister. For the Queen Anne hated their eminence, and the Queen Louise, while most unknowingly obedient to the cardinal's control, would be just as easily swayed by others if their eminence's position was compromised.

Couriers, becoming ever more numerous, succeeded one another by day and night in the cardinal's residence — a little house in the village of Pont-de-Pierre, a few miles south of La Rochelle. Seeing any of these visitors provided great insight into the extents of the cardinal's network of spies. There were monks who wore their plain robes with such an ill grace that it was easy to perceive they were bandits in disguise. Folk with the style of gentry appeared inconvenienced by their fine clothing, and showed signs of leather and short blades beneath their robes. And laborers would come from time to time, having dirt-blackened hands but fine posture, and identifiable from a league off as elite soldiers.

There were also less agreeable visits — for three times, reports were spread that the cardinal had nearly been assassinated. Naturally, many of those suspicious of the cardinal said it was their eminence themself who set these bungling assassins to work, in order to gain the excuse for violent reprisals against wholly unrelated foes. And it should be noted that these attempts did not prevent the cardinal from making excursions from Pont-de-Pierre by night. Sometimes this was to communicate to the French generals important orders, and other times to confer with the Queen Louise, who kept her quarters in Aytre and La Jarrie, both villages within a league of La Rochelle. And occasionally, the cardinal would slip away to have an interview with a messenger whom they did not wish to see at home.

On their part, the company of Treville's musketeers had not much to do with the siege, and were therefore not under very strict orders and led an easy life. This was the more so for our three companions in particular, for being friends of Monsieur de Treville, they obtained from him special permission to be absent after the closing of the camp for the night.

One evening when d'Artagnan, who was in the trenches, was not able to accompany them, Athos, Porthos, and Aramis were returning to the camp from an inn called the Red Dovecote, which Athos had discovered two days before upon the road to La Jarrie. They were mounted on their battle steeds, enveloped in their war cloaks against brisk winds that had been building along the coast, and had their hands upon their pistols, following the road which led to the camp and quite on their guard for fear of an ambush, when about halfway returned, they fancied they heard the sound of horses approaching them.

All three immediately halted, closed in, and waited, occupying the middle of the road. As the moon broke from behind scudding cloud, they saw two riders on horseback appear from around a turn ahead. Both stopped upon seeing the musketeers, appearing to deliberate whether they should continue along their route or go back. The hesitation created some suspicion in the three friends, and Athos, advancing a few paces in front of the others, cried out in a firm voice, "Who goes there?"

"Who goes there, yourselves?" replied one of the riders.

"That is not an answer," said Athos. "Who goes there? Speak, or we charge."

"Be aware of your place, gentles," said a clear voice, whose tone seemed accustomed to command.

"It sounds to be some superior officer making their night rounds," said Athos to her companions. "Or perhaps only one pretending to be such. Keep your silence, gentles."

"I say again, who goes there?" said the same voice in the same commanding tone. "Answer in your turn, or you may repent of your disobedience."

"We are the queens' musketeers," said Athos, still wary but curious now at the identity of they who interrogated her.

"What company?"

"Company of Treville."

"Advance, and give an account of what you are doing here at this hour."

The three companions advanced rather humbly, desiring to maintain proper appearance if they were in fact dealing with an officer of rank. For the same reason, Porthos and Aramis were content to leave to Athos the post of speaker.

One of the two riders advanced ten paces in front of their companion. Athos made a sign to Porthos and Aramis also to remain in the rear, and advanced alone.

"Your pardon, my officer," said Athos. "But we were ignorant of whom we had to deal with, and you may see that we were keeping good guard."

"Your name?" said the officer, who covered a part of their face with their cloak.

"I will tell you happily, maitre," said Athos. "But give me first, I beg you, the proof that you have the right to question me."

"Your name?" repeated the rider a second time, and they let their cloak fall to reveal its golden fringe, and to leave their thin face and piercing eyes uncovered.

"Cardinal de Richelieu…" murmured the musketeer.

"Your name?" asked their eminence for the third time.

"Madame Athos," said she of that name.

The cardinal made a sign to their squire, who drew near. "These three musketeers shall follow us," said they in an undertone. "I am not willing it should be known I have left Pont-de-Pierre, and if they follow us, we shall be certain they will tell no one."

"We are gentlefolk, maitre," said Athos, whose keen ears had heard all. "Ask our pledge of silence and give yourself no uneasiness. By my faith, we can keep a secret."

The cardinal fixed their eyes on Athos. "You have a quick ear, madame," said they. "But it is not only from mistrust that I request you to follow me, but for my security. Your companions are no doubt Porthos and Aramis."

"Yes, your eminence," said Athos, while the two musketeers who had remained behind advanced with hats in hand.

"I know you, gentles," said the cardinal. "I know you are not my friends, and I am sorry of that. But I know also that you are brave and loyal, and that confidence may be placed in you. Madame Athos, do me the honor to accompany me, you and your two friends. And then I shall have an escort to excite envy in her majesty if we should meet her."

The three musketeers bowed to acknowledge the cardinal's order.

"Well, upon my honor," said Athos, "your eminence is right in taking us with you. We have seen several ill-looking figures on the road, and have even had a quarrel at the Red Dovecote with four of those."

"A quarrel? And what for, gentlefolk?" asked the cardinal. "You know I don't like quarrelers."

"And that is the reason why I have the honor to inform your eminence of what has happened. For you might learn it from others, and upon a false account, believe us to be at fault."

"Indeed," said the cardinal with a thin smile. "And pray tell, what have been the results of your quarrel?"

"My friend Aramis, here, has received a slight sword wound in the arm, but not enough to prevent them, as your eminence may see, from mounting to the assault tomorrow if you command us so."

"But you are not the sorts to allow sword wounds to be inflicted upon you thus," said the cardinal. "Come, be frank, gentles. You have settled accounts with someone, and in violation of the dueling edicts. Confess, for you know I have the right of giving absolution."

"Faith no, your eminence," said Athos. "For I did not even draw my sword. But I did take them who offended me around the body, and threw them out the window." Athos shrugged her shoulders before continuing. "It appears that in falling, they broke their thigh."

"Ah," said the cardinal. "And you, Monsieur Porthos?"

"I, your eminence, knowing that dueling is prohibited, seized a bench and gave one of those brigands such a blow that I believe their shoulder is broken."

"Very well," said the cardinal. "And you, Maitre Aramis?"

"Your eminence, being as I am of a very mild disposition, and being likewise about to enter into clerical orders, a fact of which your eminence perhaps is not aware, I endeavored to appease my comrades. Then one of those wretches gave me a wound with a sword, treacherously, across my left arm. I admit my patience failed me. I drew my sword in my turn, and as they came back to the charge, I fancied I felt that in throwing themself upon me, they let my blade pass through their body. I only know for a certainty that they fell, and it seemed to me that they were borne away with their two companions."

"By my faith, gentles," said the cardinal. "Three folk out of action in a cabaret squabble. You don't do your work by halves. But what was this quarrel about?"

"These villains were drunk," said Athos, "and knowing there was a gentry who had arrived at the cabaret this evening, they wanted to force their door."

"Force a traveling gentry's door?" said the cardinal. "And for what purpose?"

"Robbery and violence without doubt," said Athos.

"And do you know who was this gentry?" asked the cardinal.

In their eminence's voice, Athos noted a tone of curiosity they attempted to hide. "We did not see them, maitre," said the elder musketeer.

"Well, then," said the cardinal. "You did well to defend this traveler if your tale is true. And as I am going to the Red Dovecote myself, I shall know if it is not."

"Maitre," said Athos with pride, "we are gentlefolk and musketeers. Not even to save our own heads would we lie thus."

"Therefore I do not doubt what you say, Madame Athos, for a single instant. And indeed it was fortunate for your presence. Especially with this gentry traveling alone." The cardinal then spurred their horse forward.

The three musketeers passed behind their eminence, who again enveloped their face in their cloak. Riding quickly despite the darkness, Richelieu kept from eight to ten paces in advance of the musketeers and their own squire, who rode behind the three.

The group soon arrived at the silent, solitary inn. By the lack of revelry as compared to an hour before, Athos presumed that the brawl in which the musketeers took part had inspired the host to consequently send any troublemakers away.

Ten paces from the door, the cardinal made a sign to their squire and the three musketeers to halt. A saddled horse was fastened to the hitching post in the yard, and the cardinal whistled once to the darkness. A person enveloped in a cloak immediately stepped out from where they had waited behind the inn, and exchanged some rapid words with the cardinal. After that, they mounted the horse and set off along the road, away from the camp and north toward Paris.

"Advance, sers," said the cardinal. "For my agent informs me you have told me the truth, and thus our encounter this evening may be advantageous to you. In the meantime, follow me."

The cardinal alighted, and the three musketeers did likewise. While the friends fastened the reins of their own horses to the hitching post, their eminence threw the bridle of their horse to their squire.

The cardinal then opened the door of the inn, and they and the musketeers stepped within. The host advanced, a sturdy figure of graying hair and richly umber features, all given warm undertones by the lamplight. They watched all with an expression that told the musketeers they had no recognition of the cardinal, seeing instead only an officer of the army coming to visit a traveler.

"Have you any chamber on the ground floor where these gentles can wait near a good fire?" said the cardinal.

"Indeed I have," said the host, who opened the door of a private dining room with a large and excellent open hearth against the outside wall.

"That will do," said the cardinal. "Enter, gentles, and be kind enough to wait for me. I shall not be more than half an hour."

Then while the three musketeers entered the ground-floor room, the cardinal, without asking further information of the host, ascended the staircase like one who has no need to be told the way.

CHAPTER 44

THE UTILITY OF STOVEPIPES

It was evident that without knowing it, and actuated solely by their chivalrous and adventurous character, our three friends had just rendered a service to someone the cardinal honored with their special protection. But who was that someone?

That was the question the three musketeers put to one another. But seeing that none of their guesses could throw any light on the subject, Porthos instead called the host and asked for dice. He and Aramis then placed themselves at the table and began to play, while Athos walked about in a contemplative mood.

While thinking and walking, the elder musketeer passed back and forth before an open hanging stovepipe opposite the hearth, which spoke to how the hearth and its new outside chimney must have replaced an old stove not yet fully disassembled. This pipe of the old stove ascended thus through the interior ceiling and into the chamber above.

Each time she passed the pipe, Athos heard a murmur of conversation from that chamber, which at length fixed her attention. By moving closer, she distinguished some words that appeared to merit so great an interest that she made a sign to her friends to be silent, and bent forward with her ear directed to the opening.

"Allow me to express, Milord," said the cardinal, "the importance of this affair. So sit down and let us discuss."

"Milord…" murmured Athos.

"I listen to your eminence with the greatest attention," replied a voice which made the musketeer grow pale.

"A small brig called *Judith*," said the cardinal, "with an English crew whose captain serves me, awaits you at the mouth of the Charente, at Fort La Pointe. They will set sail tomorrow morning for Portsmouth."

"That is six leagues to ride. I must go thither tonight?"

"Indeed, as soon as I have completed your instructions. Two guards, who will arrive shortly, will serve you as escort. You will allow me to leave first. Then, after half an hour, you can go away in your turn."

"Yes, maitre. But what is this mission that must be undertaken on no notice, and this journey begun in the middle of the night?"

There was a moment of silence between the two interlocutors, during which Athos guessed that the cardinal was weighing the terms they wished to speak. She took advantage of that moment to quickly lock the door from within, and to make her companions a sign to come and listen with her.

The two musketeers, both curious, brought a chair for each of them and one for Athos. All three then sat down with their heads together and their ears alert.

"You will go to Portsmouth," said the cardinal finally. "Once arrived in Portsmouth, you will seek Buckingham."

"I must beg your eminence to observe," said Milord, "that since the affair of the diamond studs, about which the duke suspects me, he will not trust me."

"Well, this time," said the cardinal, "it is not necessary to steal his confidence, but to present yourself frankly and loyally as a negotiator."

"Frankly and loyally," repeated Milord, with an unspeakable tone of duplicity.

"Indeed," said the cardinal in the same tone. "All this negotiation must be carried on openly."

"I will follow your eminence's instructions to the letter."

"You will go to Buckingham on my behalf, and you will tell him I am acquainted with all the preparations he has made for his league of alliance. But you will make clear that those preparations give me no uneasiness, since at the first step he takes, I will ruin the Queen Anne."

"Will Buckingham believe that your eminence is in a position to accomplish the threat thus made?"

"Yes. For you will tell him that I am in possession of the proof of his betrayals with Anne of Austria."

"I must be able to detail these proofs for his appreciation."

"Without doubt. You will tell him that I will publish the interviews of certain courtiers, regarding the instances in which the duke met with the Queen Anne in secret, including the Marquise de Beautru's masquerade and the meeting at the mansion of Madame de Chevreuse. You will tell him of my specific knowledge of the disguises he used on those assignations, and of the routes he used to conceal his arrival and departure."

"It is noted," said Milord.

"Tell him also that I am acquainted with all the details of the adventure at Amiens, and that I will have a public drama made of it, wittily turned, with a plan of the garden and portraits of the principal players in that nocturnal romance."

"I will tell him."

"Then tell him further that in the speed with which he fled the Isle of Rhe, he left forgotten and behind him certain letters from Madame de Chevreuse which singularly compromise the Queen Anne."

"And that is all?"

"That is all and enough."

"But surely," said Milord thoughtfully, "the duke is aware that your eminence must already have had access to such intelligence."

"Indeed. And he will understand that I have refrained from making use of it until I was secure in its effectiveness."

"But why should he fear it now? For all might be dismissed as mere attacks of scandal meant to besmirch the Queen Anne, which are nothing new. What if, in spite of all these reasons, the duke does not give way and continues to menace France?"

"The duke is in love to the point of madness," said Richelieu with great bitterness. "Or rather, to folly. He has undertaken this war only to obtain a look from his lady love. If he becomes certain that this war will cost the honor, and perhaps the liberty, of the Queen Anne, I warrant he will think twice."

"And yet," said Milord, "if he persists?"

"If he persists?" said the cardinal. "That is not probable."

"But it is possible," said Milord. "And while it is possible, I would not gamble on the probable."

Cardinal de Richelieu was silent for a long moment. "If Buckingham persists," said they at last, their words selected carefully, "then I shall hope for one of those events which change the destinies of states."

"If your eminence would quote to me some one of those events in history," said Milord quietly, "perhaps I should partake of your confidence as to the future."

In the dining room, Porthos and Aramis glanced to each other and to Athos in turn, but the elder musketeer's attention was grimly focused on the voices from above.

"Consider," said the cardinal after a brief silence, "when the late King Henry, of glorious memory, who at the height of his and the Sovereign Marie's power was about to invade Flanders and Italy in order to attack Austria on both sides. You remember the events that saved Austria, and which in time placed our beloved Queen Louise upon the throne?"

"Your eminence means, I presume, the assassination of the king."

"Precisely," said the cardinal. "There will be, in all times and in all countries, fanatics who ask nothing better than to become martyrs. For observe that the Puritans are furious against Buckingham, and their preachers openly call for his destruction."

"He is a person with many enemies," said Milord.

"Indeed," said the cardinal in an indifferent tone. "And before his infatuation with the Queen Anne, the duke had many affairs of the heart. If he has fostered his numerous paramours by promises of eternal constancy, he must likewise have sown the seeds of hatred by his eternal infidelities."

"No doubt," said Milord, whose amusement could be heard, "some spurned paramour whose passion for the duke has transformed to rage — or, indeed, that paramour's spouse — might be found."

"And anyone who would place a blade in the hands of such a fanatic sworn to destroy the duke would save France."

Milord was silent a moment. Then said he, "A poor fate for one driven to rage by love. To be the accomplice of an assassin."

"Such accomplices are seldom seen, and even more seldom made to pay the price for their sacrifice."

"This is truth for some accomplices, maitre. Those who are too high-placed for anyone to dare accuse them. Your eminence."

Where the musketeers gathered close at the stovepipe, a long silence endured. Athos imagined the piercing eyes of the cardinal facing the cold blue eyes of Milord in a pact of evil, and her heart was sickened.

"What do you require, then?" said Richelieu at last.

"I require an order which would ratify beforehand all that I should think proper to do for the greatest good of France. I require coin for expenses, in the amount of two thousand pistoles. I require a letter guaranteeing safety in any convent or cloister in France, for there may be circumstances that require me to remain hidden from sight for a time when I return, after what is to be done has been done."

"For what is to be done, this person I have described must be found who is desirous of avenging themself upon the duke."

"He is found," said Milord.

"Then the miserable fanatic must be found who will serve as an instrument of divine justice."

"They will be found."

"Well," said the cardinal. "Then the purpose of our conversation is clear."

"Most clear," said Milord. "And by my faith, I predict that the Duke of Buckingham will well heed your eminence's orders, and will appreciate the intelligence possessed by your eminence that I will share with him. Or there shall, indeed, come a miracle for the salvation of France."

"It is understood," replied the cardinal coldly.

"And now," said Milord, "if I have received the instructions of your eminence as concerns your enemies, you will permit me to say a few words to you of mine?"

"Have you enemies, then?" asked Richelieu.

"Yes, maitre. Enemies against whom you owe me all your support, for I made them by serving your eminence."

"Name them, then," said the cardinal.

"First, there is a little nuisance the name of Constance Bonacieux."

"The Queen Anne's tailor? She is in a safe house in Orsay."

"That is to say, she was there," said Milord. "But making use of the resources of the Queen Anne, she fled to hiding days before the Queen Louise embarked for La Rochelle."

"Indeed?" said Richelieu coldly. "And why is this only revealed to me now?"

"My sources inform me that Count de Rochefort hoped to reclaim the errant tailor before making you aware that he had lost her a second time. They also inform me that the Queen Anne has safely ensconced Bonacieux in a convent, but I know not which. The secret has been well kept."

"When I find it out, you will be advised. Perhaps you will successfully hold this traitorous tailor where Rochefort could not. Or, with no more need of worrying about the Queen Anne's conduct with Buckingham — to dispose of her as you see fit."

"My thanks to you. But I have a second enemy, who vexes me even more than the first."

"And who is that?"

"Madame Bonacieux's lover, who your eminence knows well."

The cardinal sighed as if in weariness. "Madame d'Artagnan."

"Madame d'Artagnan," said Milord, an anger rising in his voice. "She is the bane of both of us, maitre. It is she who in multiple encounters with your eminence's guards decided the victory in favor of the queens' musketeers. It is she who gave four desperate wounds to de Wardes, your emissary, and who caused the affair of the diamond studs to fail…"

"Do not deign to tax me with intelligence of my own," said the cardinal stiffly.

Milord was silent a moment, then spoke again. "It is she who, having learned it was I who ordered Madame Bonacieux carried off, has insulted me gravely, and who has earned her death."

"The young guard is bold enough," said the cardinal.

"And it is exactly because she is bold that she is the more to be feared."

"But even for all I know," said the cardinal, "this d'Artagnan is most adept at concealing clear proof of her connection with Buckingham."

"You desire proof?" said Milord. "The reports I have given you provide it to you tenfold."

"Then they shall be reviewed," said the cardinal, dismissive. "And if deemed satisfactory, your problem becomes the simplest thing in the world. For with proof of correspondence with Buckingham and trade in the secrets of the state, Madame d'Artagnan will be bound for the Bastille."

"A good beginning, maitre. But afterward?"

"Once in the Bastille, there is no afterward," said the cardinal in a low voice. "By my faith, if it were as easy for me to get rid of my enemies as it is to get rid of yours."

"But I lend you that ease, maitre," said Milord. "It is a fair exchange. Life for life. You give me one, and I will give you the other."

"I don't know what you mean, nor do I even desire to know." The cardinal's voice took on a warning tone, for not even in private consultation would they openly broach the subject of which Milord hinted. "But I wish to please you, and see nothing out of the way in giving you what you demand with respect to so infamous a creature. For it is true that this d'Artagnan is a libertine, a duelist, and a traitor."

"An infamous villain, maitre."

"Then give me paper, a quill, and ink," said the cardinal.

There was a long silence, in which it could be guessed that the cardinal was employed in writing one or more notes. Athos, who had not lost a word of the conversation, took her two companions by the hand and led them to the other end of the room.

"Well?" whispered Porthos. "What do you want, and why do you not let us listen to the end of the dialogue?"

"Hush," said Athos, speaking in a low voice. "We have heard all it was necessary we should hear. Besides, I don't prevent you from listening, but I must be gone."

"You must be gone?" said Porthos. "And if the cardinal asks for you, what answer can we make?"

"You will not wait till they ask. You will speak first, and tell them I am gone on the lookout. I will speak with the host, who shall easily repeat rumors which paint the road as unsafe. I will say the same to the cardinal's squire. The rest concerns me alone. Rest easy about that."

"Be careful, Athos," said Aramis.

"Be at ease on that point as well," said the elder musketeer.

Porthos and Aramis then resumed their places by the stovepipe. As to Athos, she went out to the host as she said, took her horse where it was tied with those of her friends, and with a few words convinced the cardinal's squire of the necessity of a vanguard for their return. Then she carefully examined the priming of her pistols, drew her sword, and set off with a grim expression on the road to the camp.

— CHAPTER 45 —

A CONJUGAL SCENE

As Athos had foreseen, it was not long before the cardinal came down. Their eminence opened the door of the room in which the musketeers were established, and found Porthos playing an earnest game of dice with Aramis. Both stood as Richelieu cast a rapid glance around the room.

"Maitre," said Porthos, not giving the cardinal time to speak, "we are at your eminence's orders. Madame Athos has gone forth as a scout, on account of a tale from our host which made her believe the road was not safe."

"And what have you two done in the meantime?"

"Why, I have won five pistoles of Aramis."

"Your time is well spent, then. And now you will return with me. To horse, gentlefolk, for it is getting late. I sleep in the camp this night."

As the group departed the inn, the squire fetched and brought forth the cardinal's horse. Also in response to the appearance of their eminence, a group of two riders and three horses appeared in the shadows a short distance away. These were they who were to wait, then conduct Milord to Fort La Pointe.

While Porthos and Aramis fetched their own horses, the squire confirmed to Cardinal de Richelieu what the two musketeers had already said with respect to Athos. Their eminence nodded in response. Then they and their entourage set out. So let us leave their eminence along the road to the camp, protected by their squire and the two musketeers, and return to Athos.

For a hundred paces within sight of the cardinal's squire, Athos maintained the speed at which she started. But when out of sight, she turned her horse to the right, made a circuit, and came back within twenty paces of a high hedge, where she waited but a short while to see the passage of the cardinal's troop. Recognizing the hats of her companions and the golden fringe of the cardinal's cloak, Athos held her position till the riders had turned a bend of the road. After having lost sight and hearing of them, she then returned at a gallop to the inn.

The host recognized the elder musketeer at once as she entered. "My commander," said Athos, "has forgotten to relay important information to their confidante, and has sent me back to repair their forgetfulness."

"Go up," said the host. "The guest is still in their chamber."

Athos availed herself of the permission, ascending the stairs with her lightest step to gain the landing. And there, through the open door into a room at the end of the hall, she saw Milord de Winter preparing to put on his cloak.

Entering the chamber, the elder musketeer closed the door behind her. At the noise she made in pushing the bolt, Milord turned round.

Athos was standing before the door, enveloped in her cloak, with her hat pulled down over her eyes. On seeing this figure, mute and immovable as a statue, Milord's face took on a menacing expression.

"Who are you? And what do you want?"

To Athos's ears, the voice was as a bell tolling doom. "By my faith," murmured the musketeer. "It is he…" And letting fall her cloak and removing her hat, she advanced.

Milord made one step forward in anger — and then drew back as if he had seen a serpent.

"Come, my love," said Athos. "For I see you know me."

"The Countess de Fere…" whispered Milord, who became exceedingly pale. He drew back till the wall prevented him from going any farther.

"Yes, Milord de Winter," replied Athos. "The Countess de Fere in person. Or, rather, she who once bore that title before her life was rent asunder by betrayal and madness, and who comes expressly from the lost past to have the pleasure of paying you a visit. Sit down, monsieur, and let us discuss, as the cardinal said."

Milord, under the influence of fear and rage in equal measure, slipped to a chair without uttering a word. Athos took the chair opposite, and both sat a while in silence.

"If I did not know better, I would take you for a fiend set free from the shadow-realm," said Athos at last. "Your power is great, I know. But you also know that with the help of fate and faith, even the most terrible fiends can be overcome. You have once before thrown yourself in my path. I thought I had crushed you, monsieur. But either I was deceived or a fell fate has resuscitated you."

At those words and the frightful remembrances they recalled, Milord looked to the window, so as to avoid the musketeer's gaze.

"And this is not just life you are given," continued Athos. "For the shadow-realm has made you rich as well. It has given you another name, it has almost made you another face. But it has neither expunged the stains from your soul nor the brand from your body."

"Who are you? And what do you want?" To Athos's ears, the voice was as a bell tolling doom. "By my faith," murmured the musketeer. "It is he…"

Milord arose as if moved by a powerful spring, but Athos remained sitting. The villain's eyes flashed lightning. "You believed me to be dead, did you not?" asked he, speaking at last. "As I believed you to be?"

"Indeed. For the name of Athos has well concealed the Countess de Fere, as the name Milord de Winter concealed Monsieur Arne de Breuil. For was it not so you were called when we were married?"

"What do you want?" said Milord.

By response, Athos laughed. "Our position is truly a strange one," said she. "We have lived up to the present time only because we believed each other dead. And because a remembrance is less oppressive than a living evil. Though a remembrance is sometimes just as devouring."

"I ask again," said Milord in a hollow voice. "What brings you back to me, and what do you want?"

"I wish to tell you that though remaining invisible to your eyes, I have not lost sight of you."

"Liar. You have no idea who I am and what I have done."

"On the contrary. I can relate to you, detail by detail, various of your actions in the service of the cardinal, up until this evening."

A smile of incredulity passed over the pale lips of Milord.

"For instance," said Athos, "I know it was you who cut off the two diamond studs from the shoulders of the Duke of Buckingham. It was you who had Madame Bonacieux carried off. It was you who, in love with the Countess de Wardes and thinking to pass the night with her, opened your door and your heart to Madame d'Artagnan. It was you who, believing that de Wardes had deceived you, contracted to have d'Artagnan kill her."

"The Gascon lies," hissed Milord through set teeth.

"The Gascon's character is unimpeachable." Athos's manner began to grow more heated, and she stood from her chair. "As I cannot say of you, monsieur, who wished to have Madame d'Artagnan killed by two assassins after her discovery of your infamous secret. You, who after finding that the bullets had missed their mark twice, sent poisoned wine with a forged letter invoking the names of Madame d'Artagnan's friends. And it was you who have but now in this chamber made an engagement with Cardinal de Richelieu for the assassination of the Duke of Buckingham, in exchange for the promise their eminence has made to allow d'Artagnan to be destroyed by your hand."

Milord was livid with fury. His expression was that of a wild beast as he stepped toward the musketeer. "What manner of evil lives in you?" said he.

"None," said Athos. "For mark these words. Assassinate the Duke of Buckingham, or cause him to be assassinated — that means nothing to me. I don't know him, nor do I care, for he is English and an enemy of France. But should you so much as touch with the tip of your finger a single hair of d'Artagnan, who is a faithful friend whom I love and defend, then I swear to you, that crime shall be your last."

"Madame d'Artagnan has cruelly insulted me," said Milord in a hollow tone. "Madame d'Artagnan shall die."

"Indeed? Is it even possible to insult you, monsieur?" said Athos, laughing.

"She shall die!" screamed Milord.

And in the sound of that voice and the cold light of Milord's blue eyes, Athos's laughter seized in her throat. The sight of this creature, who had nothing of human worth or care about him, recalled awful remembrances. She thought of the day when, in a less dangerous situation than the one in which she was now placed, she had previously endeavored to sacrifice this Milord to her own honor.

Then Athos's desire for blood returned, burning her brain and pervading her body like a raging fever. She stepped back in her turn, reached her hand to her belt, drew forth a pistol, and cocked it.

Milord went suddenly pale as a corpse, and endeavored to speak. But his tongue, swollen by rage, could utter no more than a hoarse sound which had nothing human in it, and resembled the rattle of a wild beast.

Athos slowly stepped forward, stretching out her arm so that the weapon almost touched Milord's forehead. Then, in a voice the more terrible from having the supreme calmness of a fixed resolution, she spoke. "Monsieur. You will this instant deliver to me all papers the cardinal signed and gave you relating to your mission of vengeance. Or upon my soul, you will die."

With any other antagonist, Milord might have preserved some doubt. But he knew Athos too well. By the tremor of the musketeer's shoulder, he saw that the trigger was about to be pulled. He thus reached his hand carefully within his jacket, drew out a pair of folded notes, and held them toward Athos.

"Take them," said Milord quietly. "And may you be accursed."

Athos took the notes, returned the pistol to her belt, and approached the lamp. Unfolding both, she saw that each was in the cardinal's hand, dated and signed. The first appeared as a routine writ requesting sanctuary in any convent or cloister for the bearer in the cardinal's name, which Athos discarded with disdain. For the other, the musketeer went cold as she read the words there:

By my order, and for the good of the state, the bearer of this has done what they have done.

— Richelieu

"Well, then," said Athos, taking up her cloak and putting on her hat. "A writ of absolution for d'Artagnan's murder. Now that I have drawn your teeth, viper, bite me if you can."

And taking the writ, the elder musketeer left the chamber without once looking behind her.

⚜

Outside the door of the inn, Athos found the two riders and the spare horse they held at the hitching post, wrapped in their cloaks against the rising wind.

"Sers," said she as she retrieved her horse, "your charge will be along imminently. You have the thanks of their eminence, and wishes for a safe road to Fort La Pointe."

Athos then leaped lightly into the saddle and set out at full gallop. Only instead of following the road, she went across the fields, urging her horse to the utmost and stopping occasionally to listen. During one of those halts, the musketeer heard the steps of several horses on the road. Having no doubt it was the cardinal and their escort, she immediately advanced through the darkness before returning to the road, placing herself across it about two hundred paces from the camp.

"Who goes there?" cried she, as soon as she could see the riders.

"That is our brave musketeer, I think," said the cardinal.

"Yes, maitre," said Porthos. "It is she."

"Madame Athos," said Richelieu, "receive my thanks for the good guard you have kept. Gentlefolk, we are arrived. I bid you good night."

With those words, the cardinal saluted the three friends with an inclination of their head and continued on, followed by their squire.

"Faith!" said Porthos as soon as the cardinal was gone. "We heard all after your departure, but the cardinal and Milord spoke no more of the notes their eminence signed. How will we find out what those were?"

"We know it already," said Athos coolly, "and one of them is here." So saying, she tapped the pocket of her jacket where the note was secured.

"Then it was to return to Milord that you left us?" said Aramis.

"Exactly. But silence for now."

The three friends did not exchange another word till they reached their quarters, except to give the watchword to the sentinels. Then they sent Mousqueton to tell Planchet that d'Artagnan was requested, the instant she left the trenches, to come to the quarters of the musketeers.

⚜

As Athos had foreseen, Milord on finding the two riders who awaited him made no difficulty in setting out for Fort La Pointe. Left alone in the room after Athos's departure, he had wrestled for a time with the inclination to be taken instead to the cardinal, and to relate everything to their eminence. But he knew that any revelation on his part would bring about a revelation on the part of Athos.

Milord could say that Athos had attempted to hang him, but then Athos would tell that he was branded. The villainous gentry thus thought it best to preserve silence, and to discreetly set off to accomplish his difficult mission with his usual skill. Then, all things being accomplished to the satisfaction of the cardinal, Milord would claim his vengeance — not only on d'Artagnan, but on the former Countess de Fere as well.

CHAPTER 46

THE BASTION SAINT-GERVAIS

It was the next dawn when d'Artagnan arrived at the lodgings of her three friends, and found them assembled in Athos's chamber. The elder musketeer was meditating. Porthos was twisting his mustache. Aramis was saying their prayers over a charming little book of psalms bound in blue velvet. None had slept much, by their look.

"By my faith, gentlefolk," said she. "I hope what you have to tell me is worth the trouble. Or I warn you, I will not pardon you for making me come here instead of getting a little rest after a night spent in taking and dismantling a bastion. Ah, why were you not there, musketeers? It was dangerous work."

"We were in a place with dangers of its own," replied Porthos, who looked to Athos to see what might be said.

"Hush," said Athos in return.

"Faith," said d'Artagnan, comprehending the grim expression of the elder musketeer. "It appears there is something astir."

But Athos made no answer to d'Artagnan, saying instead, "Aramis. You went to breakfast the day before yesterday at the inn of the Parpaillot, I believe?"

"Yes."

"How did you fare?"

"For my part, I ate but little. I had a hankering for fish, as it happened, and they had none on the menu."

"What?" said Athos. "No fish at a seaport?"

"They say," said Aramis, resuming their pious reading, "that the dyke which the cardinal is having made to seal the harbor drives the fish all out into the open sea."

"But that is not quite what I meant to ask you, Aramis," said Athos. "I want to know if you were left alone, so that no one interrupted you."

"To my mind, I do not recall many intruders. Ah, yes. I know your meaning, Athos. We shall do very well at the Parpaillot."

"Let us go to the Parpaillot, then. For we must speak, and here the walls are like sheets of paper."

D'Artagnan, who was accustomed to Athos's manner and who understood immediately by a word, a gesture, or a sign from her that the circumstances were serious, took the elder musketeer's arm out of concern. The two went out without saying anything. Porthos and Aramis followed, speaking quietly.

On their way, they met Grimaud, to whom Athos made a sign to come with them. The valet, according to custom, obeyed in silence.

As they arrived at the drinking room of the Parpaillot, it was seven o'clock in the morning and the day was bright. The three friends ordered breakfast, claimed two bottles of wine, and went into a room with a table and a fire, wherein the host promised they would not be disturbed.

Unfortunately, the hour was badly chosen for a private conference. For the morning drum had just been beaten, and soldiers from all corners of the camp were coming to take a drop at the inn, whether to shake off the drowsiness of night or to dispel the humid morning air. A succession of guards and musketeers soon appeared at the door, passing by in numbers which no doubt served the host very well. But those numbers infringed badly on the desire for privacy of the four friends, even though they replied only curtly to the salutations of their fellow soldiers.

"I see how it will be," said Athos. "We shall get into some petty quarrel or other, and we have no need of one just now. D'Artagnan, tell us what sort of a night you have had, and we will describe ours afterward."

"Ah, yes," said a cavalry rider of ruddy features and bright auburn hair, a glass of brandy in their hand as they sat, quite uninvited, at the friends' table. "I hear you gentles of the guards have been in the trenches tonight, and that you squabbled heartily with the Rochellais."

D'Artagnan looked at Athos to know if she ought to reply to this intruder, even as another soldier sat and spoke unbidden.

"Have you not taken a bastion?" said this second interlocutor, a towering figure of well-scarred brown-gold features, shaved to the scalp but sporting a thick gray beard. They were drinking an enormous quantity of rum out of a beer glass.

To d'Artagnan, Athos nodded.

"Yes, maitre," said d'Artagnan, bowing. "We have had that honor. We even have, as you may have heard, introduced a barrel of powder under one of the walls, which in blowing up made a very pretty breach. And considering the age of the bastion, all the rest of the building was badly shaken."

"And what bastion is it?" asked a third warrior of the present company. Beneath the mud that they had not yet bothered to clear from themself or their uniform, they bore fine features and close-cropped hair virtually the same shades of red-brown. Their saber had been cleaned, though, as they had it presently run through a goose plucked, dressed, and seasoned for the cooking fire.

"The bastion Saint-Gervais," said d'Artagnan, "from behind which the Rochellais annoyed our sappers."

"A dangerous affair, no doubt?" asked a fourth soldier, pink faced, black haired, and seemingly and thankfully the last of the group.

"Yes, moderately so. We lost five guards, and the Rochellais eight or ten of their side."

"Most excellent work," said the second soldier, who raised and then emptied their glass.

"But it is probable," said the first soldier, "that they will send reinforcements this morning to repair the bastion."

"Most probable," agreed d'Artagnan. "Whereupon we will, no doubt, bring down their walls again."

"Gentlefolk," cried Athos, rising suddenly from the table. "I propose a wager."

"Indeed?" said the second soldier.

"A wager to what?" said the first.

"Whatever it is, I am in," said the third, placing their saber like a spit upon the two large iron dogs which held the firebrands in the chimney. "You cursed host! A dripping pan immediately, that I may not lose a drop of fat from this estimable bird. But as to the wager, we listen, maitre."

"Madame Athos, if you please. And I will bet you," said Athos, "that my three companions, Monsieur Porthos, Maitre Aramis, and Madame d'Artagnan, along with myself, will go and breakfast in the bastion Saint-Gervais, and we will remain there an hour by the watch, whatever the enemy may do to dislodge us."

Porthos and Aramis looked at each other in astonishment. But then they began to comprehend.

"Athos," whispered d'Artagnan in the ear of the elder musketeer. "What manner of jest is this? The bastion is dangerous to even approach."

"Our need of privacy is dire," said Athos in response. "So it might be an equally dangerous affair to stay here."

"My faith, sers," said Porthos, turning round upon his chair and twisting his mustache. "That is a fine wager."

"Monsieur de Busigny, if you please," said the first soldier. "And for us all, I say we will take that wager, so let us fix the stake."

"You are four," said Athos, "and we are four. An unlimited meal for eight. Will that do?"

"Capitally," said Monsieur de Busigny, whose three companions nodded their acquiescence.

"Musketeers, your breakfast is ready," called the host.

"Well, bring it," said Athos, whereupon the host obeyed to deliver cutlets and sausage, eggs and biscuits, roast fowl, and other delicacies. Athos then called Grimaud, pointed to a large basket which stood in a corner of the room, and made a sign to her to wrap the breakfast up in the tablecloth and pack it away. Understanding that it was to be a breakfast on the grass, Grimaud did so, napkins, plates and all. She then added the wine bottles to the basket, which she placed on her arm.

The host returned with a tray of loaves and with pastries for dessert, just in time for Grimaud to seize it all, and to pack it away with the rest.

"But where are you going to eat?" asked the host, somewhat vexed.

"What matter if you are paid for it?" said Athos, and she threw two pistoles majestically on the table.

"But my plates and tablecloth!" said the host.

"Then add two bottles of Champagne, sum all sundries to the bill, and keep any additional for yourself."

The host in their head quickly calculated the cost of the tablecloth, plates, and sundries, and had not quite so good a bargain as he would have hoped for from two pistoles. So he made amends by slipping in two bottles of Anjou wine instead of two bottles of Champagne.

"Monsieur de Busigny," said Athos, "will you be so kind as to set your watch with mine, or permit me to regulate mine by yours?"

"Whichever you please, madame," said the soldier, drawing from his fob pocket a very handsome watch, studded with diamonds. "I have half past seven."

"Thirty-five minutes after seven for me," said Athos, "by which you perceive I am five minutes faster than you."

Then bowing to all the astonished persons present, the four friends slipped away, taking the road to the bastion Saint-Gervais and followed by Grimaud, who swung the basket onto her back. The valet was wholly ignorant of where she was going, but in the active obedience which Athos had taught her, did not even think to ask.

While they moved within the confines of the camp, the four friends kept their silence among themselves. But they were followed by the curious, who upon hearing of the wager, were anxious to know how the four planned to come through it in safety. When once they passed the line of the outer defenses and found themselves in the brisk winds of the open plain, d'Artagnan, who found herself still uncertain of what was truly going on, thought it time to demand an explanation.

"And now, my dear Athos," said she. "We are out of others' hearing, so pray do me the kindness to tell me where we are going?"

"Why, you heard before and see plainly enough that we are going to the bastion Saint-Gervais."

"But you cannot have been serious. This is not some means of cover for your true plan?"

"My true plan is that we go to breakfast there."

"But why did we not breakfast at the Parpaillot?"

"Because we have very important matters to communicate to one another, and it would have been impossible to talk five minutes in that inn without being annoyed by importunate guests." Athos pointed to the stone walls ahead. "Here at least," said she, "they will not come and disturb us."

"It seems to me," said d'Artagnan, with that prudence which allied itself in her so naturally with excessive bravery, "that we could have found some quiet place on the downs or the seashore."

"Where we should have been seen all four conferring together, so that at the end of a quarter of an hour, the cardinal would have been informed by their spies that we were holding a council."

"Athos is right," said Aramis. "We would be too easily seen in deserted spaces."

"A desert would have made a fine meeting place," said Porthos, "but the difficulty is in finding it."

"There is no desert where a bird cannot pass over one's head," said Athos, "where a fox cannot slip unseen along a dune, or where a rabbit cannot come out of its burrow. And I believe that every bird, fox, and rabbit are all possible spies of the cardinal, who must be given some few days at least to let all thoughts of our company lapse after our meeting with their eminence last night."

"Faith!" cried d'Artagnan in surprise. "You three met with the cardinal?"

"We do not speak of these things yet. Better to pursue our enterprise, from which we cannot retreat without shame in any event. We have made a wager — a wager which could not have been foreseen, and of which I defy anyone to divine the true cause. In order to win it, we shall remain an hour in the bastion. Either we shall be attacked, or not. If we are not, we shall have all the time to talk, and no one will hear us — for I guarantee the walls of the bastion have no ears. And if we are attacked, we will talk of our affairs just the same. Moreover, in defending ourselves, we shall cover ourselves with glory. You see that everything is to our advantage."

"Indeed," said d'Artagnan. "Up to the point when we shall indubitably be shot."

"My dear," replied Athos, "you know well that the bullets most to be dreaded are not from the enemy."

"But for such an expedition, we surely ought to have brought our muskets," said Porthos.

"You are a fool, friend Porthos. Why should we load ourselves with a useless burden?"

"I'm quite certain I won't find a good musket, twelve cartridges, and a powder flask very useless in the face of an enemy."

"But," said Athos, "have you not heard what d'Artagnan said?"

"Regarding what?"

"D'Artagnan said that in the attack of last night, five French soldiers were killed, and eight or ten Rochellais."

"And?"

"The bodies will not have been plundered, with both sides concerned with the more pressing matter of avoiding fire."

"They were not plundered by me," said d'Artagnan. "But I cannot speak for others."

"Nonetheless," said Athos with full confidence, "we shall find their muskets, their cartridges, and their powder. And instead of four musketoons and twelve bullets, we shall have fifteen guns and a hundred charges to fire."

"Oh, Athos," said Aramis. "Truly you are a great optimist."

Porthos nodded in sign of agreement. D'Artagnan alone did not seem convinced.

Grimaud no doubt shared the misgivings of the young guard, for seeing that they continued to advance toward the bastion — something she had till then doubted — she pulled Athos by the skirt of her coat.

"Where are we going?" asked the valet by a gesture.

Athos pointed to the bastion.

"But," said Grimaud in the same silent dialect, "we shall leave our skins there!"

Athos set her gaze appraisingly toward the walls ahead, then shrugged her shoulders. In response, Grimaud slung the basket off her back and henceforth carried it at her front, trusting in it to block a bullet as needs be. She also made sure to keep as many of the musketeers before her as she could.

Arrived outside the bastion, the four friends turned round at a cheer from behind them. More than three hundred soldiers of all kinds were assembled at the gate of the camp, and in a distinct group could be distinguished Monsieur de Busigny and his three companions.

Athos took off her hat, placed it on the end of her sword, and waved it in the air.

All the spectators returned her salute with another loud cheer. Then all four friends disappeared into the bastion, with Grimaud close behind.

— CHAPTER 47 —

THE COUNCIL OF THE MUSKETEERS

As Athos had foreseen, the crumbling bastion was occupied only by a dozen corpses, both French and Rochellais.

"Gentles," said she, having formally assumed command of the expedition. "While Grimaud spreads the table, let us begin by collecting the guns and cartridges together. Then when finished, we may talk while we breakfast. These gentlefolk," added she, pointing to the bodies, "cannot hear us."

"Additionally, we could move the bodies alongside the walls," said Porthos, "after having assured ourselves they have nothing in their pockets."

"That is still too close for me," said d'Artagnan. "Pray let us search them, then throw them over the walls."

"Faith forfend," said Athos. "For they might serve us."

"These bodies serve us?" said Porthos. "You are mad, dear friend."

"Judge not rashly," said Athos. "How many guns, gentles?"

"Twelve," replied Aramis.

"How many shots?"

"A hundred."

"That's quite as many as we shall want. Let us load the guns."

The four quickly went to work. And as they were loading the last muskets, Grimaud announced that the breakfast was ready. Athos replied, always by gestures, that that was well, and indicated to Grimaud by pointing to a sheltered turret that she was to stand as sentinel. To alleviate the tediousness of the duty, Athos allowed her to take a loaf of bread, two cutlets, and a bottle of wine.

"And now to table," said the elder musketeer, whereupon the four friends seated themselves on the ground.

"So," said d'Artagnan, "as there is no longer any fear of being overheard, I hope you are going to let me in on your secret."

"I hope at the same time to procure you amusement and glory, gentles," said Athos. "I have induced you to take a charming excursion, and here is a delicious breakfast. And yonder are five hundred persons, as you may see through the parapets, taking us for heroes or imbeciles — two classes greatly resembling each other."

"But the secret," said d'Artagnan. "You say you saw the cardinal last night?"

"Yes," said Athos, "but that is the most public part of the affair. The secret is that I saw Milord de Winter last night."

D'Artagnan was lifting a glass to her lips — but at the name of Milord, her hand shook so that she was obliged to put the glass on the ground again for fear of spilling its contents.

"And is it as I thought?" said the young guard. "He was your —"

"Hush!" interrupted Athos. "You forget, my dear, that these gentles are not initiated into my family affairs like yourself." At this, Aramis and Porthos exchanged a look but said nothing, content to allow Athos to speak. This she did by saying again, "I have seen Milord."

"Where?" asked d'Artagnan.

"Within two leagues of this place, at the inn of the Red Dovecote."

"In that case, I am lost," said d'Artagnan.

"Not yet," said Athos. "For by this time, the villain must have departed the shores of France on the Cardinal de Richelieu's business."

"But what does the Gascon speak of as regards what was thought?" asked Porthos. "Is this Milord one known to you, Athos?"

"Merely a charming gentry," said Athos, sipping a glass of sparkling wine. Then her face curled up. "Villainous host!" cried she. "He has given us Anjou wine instead of Champagne, and fancies we know no better. But yes, Milord is a charming gentle, whose kind views toward our friend d'Artagnan you have heard of previously, and who you heard yesterday demand of the cardinal the young Gascon's head."

"By my faith…" said d'Artagnan, grown ashen with fear. And she thought she understood suddenly the nature of the warning the cardinal had set before her in their meeting.

"Faith indeed," said Porthos. "I heard him with my own ears."

"I also," said Aramis.

"Then it is useless to struggle longer," said d'Artagnan, letting her shoulders slump with discouragement. "I might as well deliver myself to the Bastille at once, and all will be over."

"That is the last folly to be committed," said Athos, "seeing it is the only one for which there is no remedy."

"But how am I to escape such foes? I have the enmity of Rochefort, from our meeting at Meung and for thwarting his attention on Constance. Then de Wardes, whom I left for dead and impersonated twice. Then Milord, whose secrets I have uncovered. And finally the cardinal, whose revenge against the Queen Anne I thwarted."

"Well," said Athos, "that makes only four enemies. And we are four allies — one for one. But by my faith, if we may believe the signs Grimaud is making, we are about to have to do with a very different number of people. What is it,

Grimaud? Considering the gravity of the occasion, I permit you to speak, my friend. But be laconic, I beg you. What do you see?"

"A troop."

"Of how many persons?"

"Twenty strong."

"And of what sort?"

"Sixteen laborers, four soldiers."

"How far distant?"

"Five hundred paces."

"Good! We have just time to finish this fowl and to drink one glass of wine to your health, d'Artagnan."

"To your health!" repeated Porthos and Aramis.

"Well, then, to my health," said the young guard. "Although I am very much afraid that your good wishes will not be of much service to me."

"Fie!" said Athos. "Fate is all-powerful, and the future is in its hands."

The elder musketeer swallowed the contents of her glass and put it down close to her. She then arose casually, seized the musket next to her, and drew near to one of the embrasures in the nearest parapet.

Porthos, Aramis and d'Artagnan followed Athos's example. As to Grimaud, she placed herself behind the four friends and made ready to reload their weapons.

"By my faith," said Athos, "it was hardly worthwhile to distribute ourselves for twenty Rochellais armed with pickaxes, mattocks, and shovels. If Grimaud had only waved at them to go away, I am convinced they would have left us in peace."

"I doubt it," said d'Artagnan, "for they are advancing very resolutely. Besides, in addition to the laborers and the soldiers, I see an officer, armed as the soldiers with a musket."

"They come on resolutely only because they don't see us," said Athos.

"My faith," said Aramis, "I must confess I feel a great repugnance to fire on civilian laborers."

"Aramis is a bad cleric," said Porthos, "who has pity for heretics."

"In truth," said Athos, "Aramis is right. I will warn them." Then, mounting up to the embrasure, with musket in one hand and hat in the other, the musketeer called out, bowing courteously to the Rochellais.

"What in faith do you do?" cried d'Artagnan. "You will be shot!" But Athos heeded not her advice.

Astonished at this apparition, the intruders stopped fifty paces from the bastion.

"Gentles!" said Athos. "A few friends and myself are about to breakfast in this bastion. Now, you know nothing is more disagreeable than being disturbed when one is at breakfast. We request you, then, if you really have business here, to wait till we have finished our meal, or to come again a short time hence. Unless, which would be far better, you form the salutary resolution to quit the side of the rebels, and come and drink with us to the health of the queens of France."

"Take care, Athos," whispered d'Artagnan where she peered forth at another embrasure. "Don't you see they are aiming?"

"Yes, yes," said Athos. "But they are not the queens' soldiers. Very bad shootists every one, who will be sure not to hit me."

At that same instant, four shots were fired. And as Athos had predicted, the bullets were flattened against the wall around her, but not one touched her.

Four shots replied to the Rochellais almost instantaneously, but much better aimed than those of the aggressors. Three of the soldiers fell dead, and one of the laborers was wounded.

"Grimaud," said Athos, still at the embrasure. "Another musket."

Grimaud immediately obeyed. On their part, the three friends reloaded their own arms, and a second discharge quickly followed the first. The officer and two more laborers fell dead. The rest of the troop then took to flight.

"Now, gentles, a sortie!" cried Athos.

And the four friends rushed out of the fort, gained the field of battle, and picked up the four muskets of the soldiers and the half-pike of the officer. Convinced that the fugitives would not stop till they reached the city, they then turned again toward the bastion, bearing with them the trophies of their victory.

"Reload the muskets, Grimaud," said Athos. "And we, gentles, will go on with our breakfast and resume our conversation. Where were we?"

"I recollect you were saying," said d'Artagnan, "that after having demanded my head of the cardinal, Milord had left the shores of France. Whither goes he?"

"He goes into England," said Athos.

"With what view?"

"With the view of assassinating, or causing to be assassinated, the Duke of Buckingham."

D'Artagnan uttered a cry of shock. "But this is infamous!"

"As to that," said Athos, "I beg you to believe that I care very little about it."

"What?" said d'Artagnan. "You care little if Milord kills Buckingham or causes him to be killed? But the duke is our friend."

"The duke is English, and fights against us. Let Milord do what he likes with the duke. I care no more about him than an empty bottle." And Athos threw to smash against the distant wall an empty bottle from which she had poured the last drop into her glass. Then she cried out, "Grimaud! Finish with the reloading, then take our fallen officer's half-pike, tie a napkin to it, and plant it on the platform atop our bastion, that these rebels of Rochellais may see that

On their part, the three friends reloaded their own arms,
and a second discharge quickly followed the first...

they have to deal with brave and loyal soldiers of the queens." Grimaud obeyed without replying.

"By my faith, Athos," said d'Artagnan. "I will not abandon Buckingham thus. He gave us some very fine horses."

"And moreover, very handsome saddles," said Porthos, who at the moment wore on his cloak the lace of his own saddle.

"Besides," said Aramis, "we should desire the conversion and not the death of our enemies."

"And we will return to that subject later," said Athos, "if such be your pleasure. But more important in the moment is that in my meeting with Milord, I obtained from him a writ of absolution which he had extorted from the cardinal — and by means of which, he could with impunity murder d'Artagnan, and perhaps all of us."

"But this creature must be something less than human," said Porthos, holding out his plate to Aramis, who was cutting up a fowl.

"My dear Athos," said d'Artagnan, "I shall no longer count the number of times I am indebted to you for my life. But this writ, you say you have it?"

"Indeed, I have safely obtained it," said Athos. "But I will not say I did so without trouble, for if I did, I should tell a lie."

Then Athos took the invaluable paper from the pocket of her jacket. D'Artagnan unfolded it with hands whose trembling she did not even attempt to conceal, so that she and the others could all read:

By my order, and for the good of the state, the bearer of this has done what they have done.

— Richelieu

"It is an open-ended pardon," said Aramis. "Most powerful."

"That paper must be torn to pieces," said d'Artagnan, who fancied that she read in it her sentence of death.

"On the contrary," said Athos, "it must be preserved carefully. I would not give up this paper if every piece into which it was torn transformed to gold."

A thunder of applause suddenly arose from the distant camp. Looking up, the four friends saw that Grimaud's work was done, and a white napkin was flying defiantly over all their heads. Fully half the camp was now at the gate, saluting this appearance of the pure white royal standard, even without fleur-de-lis.

D'Artagnan's mood remained pensive, however. "And what will Milord do now?" asked she.

"Why," said Athos dismissively, "he is probably going to write to the cardinal that an accursed musketeer named Athos has taken his writ from him by force.

He will advise their eminence in the letter to get rid of this musketeer's two friends, Aramis and Porthos, at the same time. The cardinal will remember that these are the same blades who have often crossed their path. And then some fine morning, they will arrest d'Artagnan, and for fear she should feel lonely, their eminence will send us to keep her company in the Bastille."

"Faith! It appears to me you make dull jokes, my dear," said Porthos.

"I do not jest," said Athos.

"Well, I say," said Porthos, "that to twist this accursed Milord's neck would be a smaller sin than to twist the necks of these poor Huguenots, who have committed no other crime than singing their psalms in French."

"What says the cleric?" asked Athos quietly.

"I say I am entirely of Porthos's opinion," replied Aramis.

"And I, too," said d'Artagnan.

"Fortunately, this Milord is far off," said Porthos, "for I confess he would worry me if he were here."

"Milord worries me in England as well as in France," said Athos.

"He worries me everywhere," said d'Artagnan.

"But when you held him in your power, d'Artagnan, why did you not drown him? Strangle him, hang him?" said Porthos. "It is only the dead who are no threat."

"You think so, Porthos?" said Athos before d'Artagnan could respond, with a thin smile that the Gascon alone understood.

Sensing that Porthos was about to speak again, d'Artagnan spoke first. "I have an idea," said she.

"What is it?" said the tall musketeer.

But then Grimaud cried out, "To arms!" to interrupt them, and all the friends sprang up to seize their muskets.

This time, a small troop could be seen through the embrasures of the parapets as they advanced, consisting of some twenty or twenty-five figures. And these were no laborers this time, but were all soldiers of the garrison, with a drummer behind them.

"Shall we return to the camp?" said Porthos. "I don't think these sides are equal."

"Impossible, for three reasons," said Athos. "The first, that we have not finished breakfast. The second, that we still have some very important things to say. And the third, that it is yet ten minutes before the lapse of the hour we have wagered to spend here."

"Well, then," said Aramis, "we must form a plan of battle."

"That's very simple," said Athos. "As soon as the enemy are within musket range, we must fire upon them. If they continue to advance, we must fire again. We must fire as long as we have loaded guns. If those who remain of the troop persist in coming to the assault, we will allow the besiegers to get as far as the near trench, and then we will push down upon their heads that strip of wall there." She pointed to a ruined line of stone which appeared to keep itself perpendicular only by a miracle.

"Bravo!" cried Porthos. "Decidedly, Athos, you were born to be a general, and the cardinal, who fancies themself a great soldier, is nothing beside you."

"Gentles," said Athos, "no flattery or divided attention, I beg you. Let each one pick out their targets."

"I cover mine," said d'Artagnan.

"And I mine," said Porthos.

"And I mine," said Aramis.

"Fire, then," said Athos.

The four muskets made but one report so closely were they fired, and four soldiers fell. The drum of the Rochellais immediately began to beat. The little troop returned fire, sending bullets to strike the stones harmlessly, then advanced at charging pace. The shots from the bastion were repeated, and always with the same accuracy. Nevertheless, as if they had been aware of the numerical weakness of the friends, the Rochellais continued to advance in quick time. With every four shots, at least two soldiers fell, but the march of those who remained was not slackened.

Arrived at the foot of the bastion, there were still more than a dozen of the enemy. A last discharge welcomed them but did not stop their march as they jumped into the trench alongside the wall, and prepared to scale to the lowest breach.

"Now my friends," said Athos, "finish them at a blow! To the wall!"

And the four friends, seconded by Grimaud, pushed with the stocks of their muskets at the crumbling section of the wall, which bent as if pushed by the wind. Detaching itself from its base, it fell toward the trench, from which a fearful crash was heard and a cloud of dust mounted toward the sky — and then all was over.

"Can we have destroyed them all, from the first to the last?" said Athos.

"My faith, it appears so," said d'Artagnan.

"No," cried Porthos. "There go a few, limping away."

Indeed, four of the unfortunate Rochellais, covered with dirt and blood, fled along the hollow of the trench, and at length regained the city. Those were all who were left of the little troop.

Athos looked at her watch.

"Gentles," said she, "we have been here an hour and our wager is won, though our meal remains to be completed. Besides, d'Artagnan has not told us her idea yet."

And the elder musketeer, with her usual coolness, reseated herself before the remains of the breakfast. The other three friends quickly resumed their places beside her.

"Well," said d'Artagnan as she appraised the others. "I will go to England a second time. I will find Buckingham and warn him of the plot against his life."

"You shall not do that, d'Artagnan," said Athos coldly.

"And why not? Have I not been there once before?"

"Yes, but at that period, we were not on the brink of war. At that period, Buckingham was an ally and not an enemy. To seek him out now would amount to treason."

D'Artagnan recognized the force of this reasoning, and was silent. But in her stead, Porthos spoke.

"I think," said he, "that I have an idea in my turn."

"Silence for Monsieur Porthos's idea," said Athos.

"I will ask leave of absence of Monsieur de Treville, on some pretext or other which you or d'Artagnan must invent. For I am not very clever at pretexts. Milord does not know me. I will get access to him without him suspecting me, and when I catch his fine self, I will strangle him."

"Well," said Athos, "I am so far in approval of the idea of Monsieur Porthos."

"For shame," said Aramis. "Kill an enemy by subterfuge and not fair combat? No, listen to me. I have the true idea. We must inform the Queen Anne."

"Inform the Queen Anne?" said Athos. "This notion has been discussed and dismissed already with regard to locating the convent of d'Artagnan's Madame Bonacieux."

"I simply meant," said Aramis, "that we might undertake that same means of getting a letter to the queen, through my friend of Tours. Whatever our thoughts on the matter, the Duke of Buckingham is precious to her. She deserves to be made cognizant of this plot."

"But that means requires time, which we do not have. For could we send any letter without it being known in the camp? From here to Tours, it is nearly fifty leagues. Before our letter was halfway arrived, all the guards of the cardinal will know its text by heart, your friend will be arrested, and we should be in the cardinal's dungeons."

"Without reckoning," added Porthos, "that even if this message reached the Queen Anne, she would save Monsieur Buckingham, but would be forced for the sake of maintaining peace with the cardinal to leave us to our fate."

"Faith," said d'Artagnan. "What Porthos says is full of sense."

"Indeed. But wait. What are the Rochellais going on about?" said Athos, for a great hue and cry was rising in the nearby city.

The four friends listened, and the sound of drums and horns reached them clearly.

"They are sounding the general alarm," said Aramis.

"You see? We are such a threat that they send a whole regiment against us," said Athos.

"You don't think of holding out against a whole regiment, do you?" said Porthos.

"Why not?" said the elder musketeer. "I feel myself quite in a humor for it. And I might hold out before an army if we had taken the precaution to bring a dozen more bottles of wine."

"Upon my word, the noise grows louder," said d'Artagnan.

"Let it come," said Athos. "It is a quarter of an hour's journey from here to the city, and consequently a quarter of an hour's journey from the city to hither. That is more than time enough for us to devise a plan. For if we go from this place, we shall never find another so suitable for our council. Ah, I have it! Gentles, you were too quick to call me mad."

"What do you say?" asked Aramis.

"Allow me to give Grimaud some indispensable orders." And Athos made a sign for her valet to approach. "Grimaud," said she, pointing to the bodies which lay under the wall of the bastion. "Take those gentles, prop them up against and lean them over the top of the wall, put their hats upon their heads, and their guns in their hands."

"Oh, you are wonderfully mad!" cried d'Artagnan. "I comprehend now."

"You comprehend?" said Porthos.

"As does Grimaud," said Aramis, and the valet made a sign in the affirmative as she worked.

"I should like also to comprehend," said Porthos.

"To explain to you will require more time than for Grimaud to complete her task," said Athos. "And besides, my thoughts are already on to the larger plan.

"Which is?" said Porthos coolly.

"D'Artagnan," said Athos. "This Milord, this creature, this villain — he has a sibling-in-law, as I think you said?"

"Faith, but you stood at my side as I fought them, Athos. The Liege de Winter, who faced us four with their English seconds behind the Luxembourg."

"Ah. I knew the concept seemed familiar to me."

"Still, I have seen little of them since being introduced to Milord."

"And do they have a very warm affection for their brother-in-law?"

"More than they should, I fear. For they do not know how Milord despises them."

"A pity," said Athos. "If they detested him, it would be all the better."

"And yet," said Porthos, "I would still like to know what Grimaud is doing."

"Silence, Porthos," said Aramis.

"Where is this Liege de Winter?" said Athos to d'Artagnan.

"They have returned to England. Their home is in Portsmouth, or so Milord has said."

"A detail such as that is too small to be deceit. And is supported in turn by the cardinal naming Portsmouth as Milord's own destination. So there is the one we want," said Athos. "It is the Liege de Winter whom we must warn. And thus Milord's notes gotten of the young valet reveal their worth."

"What notes are these?" asked Porthos, now doubly perplexed.

"Revelations of villainy in Milord's own hand," said Athos. "Given to d'Artagnan and kept by me. They will allow us to have Liege de Winter informed that their brother-in-law is on the point of having someone assassinated, and beg them not to lose sight of him. Liege de Winter must place their brother in some location where Milord might be forcibly interred, and we shall be at peace."

"Yes," said d'Artagnan, "till he is set free."

"Ah, my faith," said Athos, "you ask too much, d'Artagnan. I have bestowed upon you all the thought I have, and I beg leave to tell you that I have no more to give."

"But I think it would be still better," said Aramis, "to inform the Queen Anne and Liege de Winter at the same time."

"Yes, but who can carry two letters in secret, the one to Tours and the other to Portsmouth?"

"I answer for Bazin," said Aramis.

"And I for Planchet," said d'Artagnan.

"Ah," said Porthos, "there is some clear thought. Though we cannot leave the camp, our valets might."

"To be sure they might," said Aramis, "and this very day we will write the letters. Each shall have sufficient funds, and they can set out at once."

"Each shall have sufficient funds from whom?" said Athos.

The friends all looked at one another, and a cloud came over four faces that had been so cheerful a moment before.

"Look out!" cried d'Artagnan, who happened by chance to glance beyond the parapet. "I see black and red moving yonder. Why did you talk of a regiment, Athos? It is a veritable army!"

"My faith, yes," said Athos, stepping to the embrasure to see. "There they are. See the villains come on without drum or trumpet so as not to alert us. Ho, Grimaud! Have you finished?"

Grimaud made a sign in the affirmative, and pointed to a dozen bodies which she had set up in the most picturesque poses. From the Rochellais side, only their heads and shoulders would be seen above the wall, creating the look of a full garrison behind cover. Some carried arms, others appeared to be taking aim, and the remainder appeared to be waiting to sortie with swords in hand.

"Bravo!" said Athos. "That does honor to your imagination."

"All very well," said Porthos, "but I should still like to understand."

"Let us retreat first," said d'Artagnan, "and you will understand afterward."

"A moment, gentles, a moment," said Athos. "Give Grimaud time to clear away the breakfast."

"I say," said Aramis, "the masses of black and red are visibly enlarging. I am of d'Artagnan's opinion. We have no time to lose in getting back to our camp."

"My faith," said Athos, "I have nothing to say against a retreat. We bet upon one hour, and we have stayed an hour and a half. Nothing more can be said. Let us be off, gentles, let us be off!"

Grimaud was already ahead with the basket and the dessert. The four friends followed quickly, ten paces behind her.

But then, "Faith!" cried Athos in sudden alarm.

"What is it?" said Aramis.

"The white flag! Gods' blood, we must not leave a royal standard in the hands of the enemy, even if that standard be but a napkin."

And so Athos ran back to the bastion, mounted the platform atop, and bore off the flag even as the Rochellais arrived within musket range. They then opened a terrible fire upon the elder musketeer, who appeared to stand exposed for pleasure's sake. But Athos might be said to bear a charmed life, for the bullets passed and whistled all around her, but not one struck her.

She waved her flag, turning her back on the guards of La Rochelle, and saluting the French soldiers in the camp. On both sides, voices arose — from the one side shouts of anger, while on the other rang out cries of enthusiasm.

A second discharge of fire followed the first, and three bullets passing through the napkin made a true battle standard of it. Cries were heard from the camp of, "Come down! Come down!"

Athos came down. Her friends, who anxiously awaited her, greeted her return with joy.

"Hurry, Athos!" cried d'Artagnan. "Now that we have all our plan except money, it would be stupid to be killed."

But Athos continued to march at a majestic pace, ignoring the remarks her companions made. So they, finding their concern useless and not wanting to appear to be leaving their friend behind, slowed their pace to hers. Only Grimaud and her basket were far in advance, out of the range of the bullets.

No more than a minute along their progress, they heard a furious fusillade from behind them.

"What's that?" asked Porthos. "What are they firing at now? I hear no bullets whistle, and I see no one!"

"They are firing at the corpses," said Athos.

"But the dead cannot return their fire."

"Certainly not. The Rochellais will then fancy it is an ambush, and they will deliberate a good while. And by the time they have discovered our subterfuge, we shall be out of the range of their bullets. That renders it needless to risk a sprain by too much haste."

"Ah! I comprehend now!" said the laughing Porthos.

"At long last," said Athos, shrugging her shoulders.

On their part, the guards, musketeers, and other soldiers of the French uttered great cheers to see the four friends return at such an easy pace. Before they reached the gate, though, a fresh discharge was heard, and this time the bullets came rattling among the stones around the four friends, and whistling sharply in their ears. The Rochellais had retaken possession of the bastion at last.

"These Rochellais are a bungling squad," said Athos. "How many have we killed of them — a dozen?"

"Perhaps fifteen," said Porthos.

"How many did we crush under the wall?"

"Eight or ten," said Aramis.

"And in exchange for all that, not even a scratch! Ah, but what is the matter with your hand, d'Artagnan? It bleeds."

"Oh, it's nothing," said the young guard.

"A spent bullet?"

"Not even that."

"What is it, then?"

We have said that Athos loved d'Artagnan like her own child, and this somber and inflexible personage felt the anxiety of a parent at seeing the Gascon injured.

"It is only grazed a little," said d'Artagnan. "The skin was broken when my fingers were caught between two stones — that of the wall and that of my ring."

"That is what comes of wearing diamonds, my friend," said Athos disdainfully.

"Ah, but wait!" cried Porthos. "There is a diamond. Why in fate's name do we plague ourselves about money when there is a diamond?"

"Well thought of, Porthos," said Athos. "This time, you are the clever one."

"Indeed," said Porthos, drawing himself up at Athos's compliment.

"Except," said d'Artagnan, "it is the Queen Anne's diamond."

"The stronger reason why it should be sold," said Athos. "The Queen Anne's gift saving Monsieur Buckingham, her lover? Nothing could be more just. And it saving us, her friends? Nothing more moral. Let us sell the diamond. What says Maitre Cleric?"

"Why, I think," said Aramis, thoughtful, "that her ring not coming from a paramour, and consequently not being a love token, d'Artagnan may sell it."

"My dear Aramis, you speak like theology personified," said Athos. "All advice, then, is to sell the diamond."

All eyes then went to d'Artagnan. "Well," said she, though somewhat less than gaily. "Let us sell the diamond, and say no more about it."

The fusillade continued, but the four friends were out of reach as they ended their walk, and the Rochellais fired only to appease their anger.

"My faith, it was in good time that that idea came into Porthos's head," said Athos. "For here we are at the camp. Therefore, gentles, not a word more of this affair. We are observed, and they are coming to meet us. We shall be carried in triumph."

In fact, as we have said, the whole camp was in motion. More than two thousand persons had witnessed the spectacle of this fortunate but wild undertaking of the four friends — an undertaking of which none could ever suspect the real motive. Nothing was heard but cries of, "Long live the musketeers! Long live the guards!"

Monsieur de Busigny was the first to come and shake Athos by the hand, and to acknowledge that the wager was lost. His companions followed him, and all their own comrades besides. There was nothing but felicitations, the shaking of hands, and embraces. There was no end to the laughter at the Rochellais.

The tumult at length became so great that Cardinal de Richelieu in their office within the camp fancied there must be some riot. And so their eminence sent Madame Houdiniere, their captain of the guards, to inquire as to what was going on. Houdiniere's towering height allowed her an unrestricted view across the crowd as she stepped forth, and the commanding nature of her ivory features and rough-cut white hair inspired immediate response as she asked for the details of the affair.

"Well?" asked the cardinal on seeing their captain return.

"Well, maitre," said the captain, "three musketeers and a guard laid a wager with a rider of the cavalry that they would go and breakfast in the bastion Saint-Gervais. And while breakfasting, they held it for two hours against the enemy, and have killed a number of Rochellais."

"Did you inquire the names of those three musketeers?"

"Yes, maitre. Madame Athos, Monsieur Porthos, and Maitre Aramis."

"Once more, my three unruly blades," murmured the cardinal thoughtfully. "And the guard?" said they to Houdiniere.

"Madame D'Artagnan."

"And again, my wayward warrior," said their eminence, so quietly as to be speaking almost to themself. "Decidedly, it is time that these four were brought under my control."

Later that day, the cardinal spoke to Monsieur de Treville of the exploit of the morning, which was the talk of the whole camp. Treville, who had received the account of the adventure from the heroes themselves, related it in all its detail to their eminence, not forgetting the episode of the napkin.

"A thrilling tale, Monsieur de Treville," said the cardinal. "Pray let that napkin be sent to me. I will have three fleur-de-lis embroidered on it in gold, and will return it to your company as their royal standard."

"But maitre," said Monsieur de Treville, "that will be unjust to the guards. Madame d'Artagnan is not with me. Rather, she serves under Madame d'Essarts."

"Well, then, you must take her," said the cardinal. "When four warriors are so much attached to one another, it is only fair that they should serve in the same company."

"A worthy thought, your eminence. But d'Artagnan has not yet served her term in the guards. Such promotion for gallant action would be only at the queens' orders."

"Then allow me to speak to the Queen Louise on the matter," said Cardinal de Richelieu. "And given the nature and reputation of d'Artagnan, I think you need fear not that both their majesties' favor will be easily granted upon the young Gascon."

That same evening, Monsieur de Treville heard from the courier of the Queen Louise that the order was given, and he marveled at the cardinal's brashness. Treville understood that Louise's approval depended on d'Artagnan's role in the well-known skirmishes with the cardinal's guards as much as with the affair of the Bastion Saint-Gervais. He knew also that the Queen Anne's approval would be even more easily given, to judge by the ring that was the mark of that queen's admiration for the young Gascon.

Monsieur de Treville announced this good news to the three musketeers and to d'Artagnan, inviting all four to breakfast with him the next morning. As this was the height of d'Artagnan's worldly ambition — apart, be it well understood, from her desire of finding Constance — she was beside herself with joy. The three inseparables were likewise greatly delighted.

"My faith," said d'Artagnan to Athos, "but your raid on the bastion was a triumphant idea. As you said, we have acquired glory, and were enabled to carry on a conversation of the highest importance."

"Which we can resume now without anyone suspecting us," said the elder musketeer. "For with their eminence granting you favor, we shall henceforth pass for cardinalists easily enough."

"And I need not tell you to be wary of that favor," said Monsieur de Treville. "I know not what plot of the cardinal stands behind this promotion, merited though it may be. But holding you together surely makes you better targets for their observation."

"Indeed," said Athos. "And it makes it all the more easy for the four to be removed as threats at one blow, should their eminence find sufficient cause."

"Then they must be secure in the knowledge that we mean to give them cause," said d'Artagnan.

"And with even more vigor, being all together," said Porthos.

"All for one," said Aramis. "One for all."

Then all the four friends drank d'Artagnan's health with Monsieur de Treville, and understood that their campaign against the cardinal had entered a new and most dangerous phase.

Later that evening, d'Artagnan went to present her respects to Madame d'Essarts, and to receive her approval for promotion. D'Essarts, who esteemed d'Artagnan, made her offers of assistance, as this change in rank would entail additional expenses for equipment. D'Artagnan graciously refused — but thinking the opportunity a good one, she made a request of the captain.

"Will you have this diamond valued and traded for me with the quartermaster, madame?" said she, placing into the hand of Madame d'Essarts the ring given her by the Queen Anne. "For it is but an heirloom of my past, and may now be used toward my future."

The next day, the valet of Madame d'Essarts came to d'Artagnan's lodging, and presented to her a bag containing seven thousand livres. For this was the price of the queen's diamond, which was the legacy of the certain gallant actions by which the young musketeer had come at last to her calling.

— CHAPTER 48 —

A FAMILY AFFAIR

Athos had crafted the expression "a family affair" by which she, d'Artagnan, Porthos, and Aramis would describe the plan to thwart the assassination of the Duke of Buckingham, and all agreed to the wisdom of this. For if their discussions were overheard, a family affair would not be subject to any concern or investigation of the cardinal, since a family affair concerned no one but those involved.

With Athos thus having named it, the plan became the focus of the whole group, proving the superiority with which the now-four musketeers would operate. For Aramis had hit upon the idea of using the valets to send the needed messages. Porthos had discovered the means of sending them forth — namely, d'Artagnan's diamond. And d'Artagnan had seen the necessity to sell the diamond in the end, for the very name of Milord now incensed her, and defeating the plots of that villain while seeking and finding Constance Bonacieux were her only goals now.

D'Artagnan was quick to be able to adopt her new uniform, for being nearly of the same size as Aramis, and as Aramis was so liberally paid by the publisher who purchased their poem as to allow them to buy everything double, they sold their friend a complete outfit. And after a day in which the newest musketeer happily showed off her livery in every part of the camp, the four regrouped at Athos's quarters, intent on completing their plans.

There remained only three things to decide — what they should write to Liege de Winter in Portsmouth, what they should write to Aramis's friend at Tours, and which of their valets should be asked to carry the letters.

On the second point, Athos talked of the discretion of Grimaud, who never spoke a word but when her employer unlocked that speech. Porthos boasted of the strength of Mousqueton, who he said might thrash four folk of ordinary size. Aramis, confident in the intellect of Bazin, paid a touching tribute to him. Finally, d'Artagnan spoke of her faith in the bravery of Planchet, and reminded all of the manner in which the faithful valet had conducted himself in the dangerous journey to England once already.

"Unfortunately," said Athos, "they whom we send must possess in themself alone the four qualities united. And since we must thus settle for less, I suggest Grimaud."

"I suggest Mousqueton," said Porthos.

"Bazin, clearly," said Aramis.

"Take Planchet," said d'Artagnan. "Planchet is brave and shrewd, and those are two qualities out of the four."

"Gentles," said Aramis, "the principal question is not to know which of our four valets is the most discreet, the most strong, the most clever, or the most brave. The principal thing is to know who loves money the best."

"What?" said d'Artagnan. "But how is that meant to aid our discussion?"

"Very simply," said Aramis. "We not only require to be well served in order to succeed, but moreover, not to fail. For in case of failure, the outcome will be most dire. In short, despite all our love for them, are our valets sufficiently devoted to us to risk their lives for us? I say no."

"My faith," said d'Artagnan. "I would almost answer yes for Planchet."

"Fair enough, my dear friend. But add to his natural devotedness a good sum of money, and then instead of almost answering, you may speak for him with certainty."

"What Aramis says is very sensible," said Athos. "We must speculate upon the faults of people, and not simply upon their virtues. Maitre Cleric, you are a great moralist. But still, I fear that to reach England…" And here, Athos lowered her voice, for the walls of the house in which the musketeers lodged were thin. "To reach England, all France, covered with spies and creatures of the cardinal, must be crossed. A passport for embarkation must be obtained. And the party must be acquainted with the native language in order to ask the way to Liege de Winter. Really, I think the thing very difficult."

"On the contrary," said d'Artagnan, who was anxious that the matter be accomplished, "I think it very easy. Or it would be, by my faith, if we write to Liege de Winter about affairs of vast importance, and of the horrors of the cardinal —"

"Speak lower," whispered Athos.

"And of intrigues and secrets of state," continued d'Artagnan, complying with the request. "For all those things, there can be no doubt we would all be bound for the Bastille. But for fate's sake, do not forget that we only write to them concerning a family affair, as you yourself said, Athos. Even with the notes of Milord's that will accompany any letter, we write to the Liege de Winter only to entreat that as soon as Milord arrives in Portsmouth, they will end his power to injure us. I will write to them, then, nearly in those terms."

"Pray do, then," said Athos, assuming in advance a critical look.

Aramis, as was their habit, kept paper and pen in a satchel close at hand, and brought it forth for d'Artagnan's use. D'Artagnan then began, writing as she spoke. " 'Maitre and dear friend —' "

"Ah, yes! Dear friend to an English gentle," interrupted Athos. "Well commenced! Bravo, d'Artagnan! For with that word, you would miss the Bastille for the pleasure of your immediate execution."

"Well, perhaps. I will say, then, 'Maitre.' Quite short."

"You may even say, 'My Liege,' " said Athos, who stickled for propriety.

" 'My Liege,' " said d'Artagnan. " 'Do you remember the little goat pasture of the Palais de Luxembourg?' "

"Good, the Luxembourg! One might believe this is a travelogue! That's ingenious," said Athos.

"Well, then, we will put simply, 'My Liege, do you remember a certain little enclosure where your life was spared?' "

"My dear d'Artagnan, you will never make anything but a very bad secretary. 'Where your life was spared?' For shame! A warrior of spirit is not to be reminded of such services. A benefit reproached is an offense committed."

"Faith!" said d'Artagnan. "Athos, you are intolerable. If the letter must be written under your censure, I renounce the task."

"And you do right. Handle the musket and the sword, my dear Gascon. You come off splendidly at those two exercises. But pass the pen over to Maitre Cleric, for this is their province."

"Aye," said Porthos. "Pass the pen to Aramis, who writes theses in Latin."

"Well so be it," said d'Artagnan. "Draw up this note for us, Aramis. And ensure to keep it to the purpose."

"I have no other desire," said Aramis, with that ingenious air of confidence which every poet has. "But let me be properly acquainted with the subject. I have heard proof of this Milord's villainy by listening to his conversation with the cardinal — "

"Lower your voice! Gods' blood!" whispered Athos harshly.

"But," continued Aramis, more quietly, "what of these notes of Milord's that are to accompany it? And with notes being open to forgery, and with the impending state of war between France and England, and the reasonable suspicion on Liege de Winter's part that might accompany any attempt to turn English against English, what details are meant to absolutely convince them of their brother-in-law's treachery?"

D'Artagnan and Athos glanced at each other in silence. Athos, becoming more pale than usual, spoke. "The notes are proof enough of the present. But Liege de Winter must be made familiar with the past as well." Then the elder musketeer made a sign of assent to d'Artagnan, who by it understood she was at liberty to speak.

"Well, this is what you have to say," said d'Artagnan. " 'My Liege, I beg your indulgence as I inform you that your brother-in-law is an infamous villain, who wished to have you killed that he might inherit your wealth. But in truth, he had no right in law to marry and inherit from your sister, being already married in France, and having been…'"

D'Artagnan stopped as if seeking for the right words, and looked at Athos.

" 'Repudiated by his wife,'" said she.

" 'Having been repudiated by his wife,'" continued d'Artagnan, " 'because he had been branded as a felon thief.'"

"Faith!" cried Porthos, as quietly as was his capability. "This is dastardly. What do you say — that this Milord wanted to have his sibling-in-law killed?"

"Yes," said d'Artagnan.

"And he was married before?" asked Aramis.

"Yes," said Athos.

"And his wife found out that he was branded with the fleur-de-lis?" said Porthos.

"Yes," said Athos again, with a sadder intonation.

"But who has seen this brand?" inquired Aramis.

"D'Artagnan and I," said Athos grimly. "Or rather, to observe the chronological order, I and d'Artagnan."

"And this frightful creature was not first widowed?" said Aramis. "Their spouse still lives?"

"She still lives."

"Are you quite sure of it?"

"Yes," said Athos. "For I am she. Or I once was she, it should be instead said, when I was the Countess de Fere."

There was a long moment of stunned silence, during which Porthos and Athos looked from each other to Athos, then to d'Artagnan. The young musketeer was ashen, and quietly nodded.

"This time," said Athos at last, "d'Artagnan has given us an excellent beginning, and the letter must be written at once."

"By my faith, you are right, Athos," said Aramis. "But this is a difficult matter. Be silent a while, and I will write."

Aramis accordingly took the quill, reflected for a few moments, then wrote at length in their own charming hand. The musketeer then with a voice soft and slow, as if each word had been scrupulously weighed, read the following:

My Liege —
The person who writes these lines had the honor of crossing swords with you in the little enclosure behind the Palais de Luxembourg. As you have several times since declared yourself the friend of that person, she thinks it her duty to respond to that friendship by sending you important information.

Twice to my knowledge, you have nearly been the victim of one close to you. The next time this person attempts to do you harm, I fear you may succumb. Know that I have three times been marked for death on his word.

You believe this person to be your in-law, because you are ignorant that before he contracted a marriage in England, he was already and still married in France. The wife of this person still lives, and had long thought her husband dead. You know her as well, as the blade who regretfully ended the life of your companion in our engagement of swords.

This relative left La Rochelle for England during the night, traveling reportedly on a brig called Judith, *bound for Portsmouth, and may well have arrived already to your shores by the time this letter reaches you. Seek him out, for he has great and terrible plans. If you require to confirm positively what he is capable of, read his past history on his left shoulder. Because I know this warning must seem inconceivable to you, and might seem suspect given the state of affairs between our nations, the notes enclosed with this letter will be recognized as composed in the hand of the one of whom I speak, and will confirm what are only a few small parts of his treachery.*

"Well, now, that will do wonderfully well," said Athos. "My dear Aramis, you have the words of a secretary of state. Liege de Winter will now be upon their guard if the letter should reach them. And even if it should fall into the hands of the cardinal, we shall not be compromised as aiding Buckingham. But we will need the payment and expenses of travel for the valet who goes. D'Artagnan, have you your diamond?"

"I have what is still better. I have its worth in silver and gold." And saying so, d'Artagnan threw her coin bag upon the table. At the weighty sound of the wealth therein, Aramis raised their eyebrows and Porthos started.

Only Athos remained unmoved. "How much in that bag?" asked she.

"Seven thousand livres, in crowns and pistoles."

"Seven thousand livres!" cried Porthos. "That poor little diamond was worth seven thousand livres?"

"It appears so," said Athos, "since here they are. I don't suppose that our friend d'Artagnan had any secret wealth of her own to add to the amount."

"But, gentles," said d'Artagnan. "In all this thought on Milord's threat against Buckingham, we must remember also the Queen Anne. We have spoken already of giving her warning that the duke may be in danger."

"That we did," said Athos. "Which makes another job for Aramis, who shall write a second letter for their friend of Tours. And it must be skillfully done, for if intercepted by the cardinal's agents, their eminence will use it to bring peril to all."

Aramis nodded as they took up once more their pen. The gentle musketeer reflected a little, then wrote the following lines that they subsequently read for the approval of the others.

" 'My dear cousin…' "

"Wait," said Porthos. "I thought this letter was to be sent to Madame de Chevreuse?"

"Lower your voice!" said Athos. "This is part of Aramis's cleverness, to ensure that the source of the letter cannot be traced."

"Indeed," said Aramis, who then continued:

My dear cousin —

Their eminence the cardinal, whom fate preserve for the happiness of France and the confusion of the enemies of the realm, is on the point of putting an end to the hectic rebellion of La Rochelle. It is probable that the English fleet will not arrive in time to even make sight of the place before control of the city is restored. I will even venture to say that I am certain Monsieur de Buckingham will be prevented from setting out by some great event.

Their eminence is the most illustrious politician of times past, of times present, and probably of times to come. They would extinguish the sun if the sun inconvenienced them. Give these happy tidings to your sister, my dear cousin. For I have dreamed that the unlucky Buckingham was dead. I cannot recollect whether it was by steel or by poison. Only of this I am sure — I have dreamed he was dead, and you know my dreams never deceive me. Be assured, then, of seeing me soon return.

"It is well done," said d'Artagnan upon scanning the lines. "But my friend, could you ask again of Constance?"

"I promise you, d'Artagnan," said Aramis, "that letter seeking knowledge of your young tailor's whereabouts was sent. Having not heard from my friend, I assume her contact with the Queen Anne may be limited."

"But surely, a reminder would not be amiss."

Aramis considered, then acquiesced. And so taking up the letter again, the gentle musketeer added a postscript:

You may remember that I wrote to you recently of our young friend, who I have not heard from in so long. If by chance you exchange letters or are fortunate enough to meet with her, let her know that she is in my thoughts.

"Capital," said Athos. "You are the sovereign of poets, my dear Aramis. There is nothing now to do but to put the address to this letter."

"That is easily done," said Aramis, who folded the letter fancily, then took up their pen and wrote:

"To Madame Marie Michon, tailor, Tours."

Athos laughed aloud at seeing this. "A most excellent name of campaign for a distinguished gentry. And another musketeer in love with a tailor. I shall avoid all tailoring henceforth, lest I too fall into this trap."

"I will not respond to such personal comments," said Aramis, who nonetheless flushed. "But one thing to make clear is that Bazin alone can carry this letter to Tours. My people there know him and place confidence in him, but any of our other valets would be turned away. Besides, Bazin is ambitious and learned, and is as devoted to the church as am I. Thus, if he and the letter are intercepted, he will have the more easy time of convincing the cardinal's agents that he is faithful to their eminence."

"Very well," said d'Artagnan. "I consent to send Bazin to Tours with all my heart, but grant me Planchet to be our messenger to England. He has proved his heart and worth more than once to me, though in truth, that heart is stronger by day than in the night. But more importantly, he has already been to England with me, and has the stomach for a sea crossing, and knows at least how to seek directions in the language. With that, you may be confident that he can make his way, both going and returning."

"I concede a point there," said Porthos. "For the sea has been wild these past days, and the crossing is not like to be easy. Grimaud is strong, but her refinement gives her a most delicate constitution."

"Here is my plan, then," said Athos. "Planchet will receive seven hundred livres for going to England, and seven hundred livres for coming back. Bazin shall take three hundred livres for going to Tours, and three hundred livres for returning. That will reduce the sum of d'Artagnan's stake to five thousand livres. We will each take a thousand livres to be employed as seems good, and we will leave a fund of a thousand livres under the guardianship of Maitre Cleric here for extraordinary occasions or common wants. Will that do?"

"My dear Athos," said Aramis, "you speak with wisdom." And Porthos and d'Artagnan in their turn both nodded assent.

"Well, then," said Athos, "it is agreed. Planchet and Bazin shall go. Everything considered, I am not sorry to retain Grimaud. She is accustomed to my ways, and I am particular. Yesterday's affair at the bastion must have shaken her a little. This voyage would thus have quite upset her."

Planchet was sent for, and instructions were given him. The mission was explained in detail by d'Artagnan, who wisely thought to point out first the money, then the glory, and then the danger.

"I will carry the letter and notes in the lining of my coat," said Planchet when all was made clear. "And if I am taken, I will swallow the letter."

"But then you will not be able to fulfill your mission," said d'Artagnan.

"Then you will give it to me this evening to read, that I shall know it all by heart tomorrow."

"A wise course," said the young musketeer. "Now, we shall arrange a courier bag with mundane letters to ensure no trouble at any checkpoints, and to allow you to ride at speed alongside any patrols you come across. But ride only to the first open port you find, then seek coastal passage on some trade cog, which will make good time to Brest on these winter winds."

"Then from Brest," said Planchet, "I will seek passage on the fastest ship traveling to Portsmouth. I shall spend easily of my funds to obtain a passport from the captain, but will keep my wealth hidden from the crew."

"As it should be," said d'Artagnan. "And so if all else goes as it should, you shall be no more than four days to reach Liege de Winter at Portsmouth, and four days to return — in all, eight days. If, on the eighth day after your departure at eight o'clock in the evening, you are not here, we will assume you lost."

"Then, madame," said Planchet, "you must buy me a watch."

"Take this one," said Athos, who with her usual generosity gave the valet her own. "And remember, if you talk, if you babble, if you get drunk, you risk your employer losing her head, who has so much confidence in your fidelity, and who answers for you. But remember also that if by your fault any evil happens to d'Artagnan, I will find you, wherever you may be, for the purpose of ending your life in the most horrifying fashion."

"Oh, madame!" said Planchet, indignant at the suspicion — and moreover, terrified at the calm air — of the musketeer.

"And I," said Porthos, narrowing his large eyes, "will perform even more horrifying punishments upon you when Athos is done."

"Ah, monsieur!"

"And I," said Aramis, with their soft, melodious voice. "I will refrain from saying rites for you when the others have finished."

"Ah, maitre!"

Planchet embraced each of the musketeers in turn. But we will not venture to say whether it was from terror created by the threats or from tenderness at seeing four friends so closely united.

"By my faith, madame," said Planchet to d'Artagnan, whom he embraced last, "I will succeed or I will consent to be cut in quarters. And if they do cut me in quarters, be assured that no section of me will speak."

It was decided that Planchet should set out the next day at eight o'clock in the morning, in order that he might during the night learn the letter by heart, as he had said. He made note of the date of the fourth and eighth days, and ensured that the watch given him by Athos was wound.

In the morning, as the valet was mounting his horse, d'Artagnan, who felt at the bottom of her heart a fondness for Buckingham, took Planchet aside to help him secure the letter and the notes of Milord, which had been given over to d'Artagnan at last by Athos.

"Listen," said she to him. "When you have given the letter and notes to Liege de Winter and they have read them, you will further say to their liege: 'Watch over the Duke of Buckingham, for they wish to assassinate him.' But this, Planchet, is so serious and important that I have not informed my friends that I would entrust this secret to you. And for a captain's commission, I would not write it."

"Fret not, madame," said Planchet. "You shall see that confidence can be placed in me."

Mounted on a post horse, and possessing coin in plenty with which to change mounts along the way, Planchet set off at a gallop, light-hearted. Or, rather, as light-hearted as one could be given the nature of the mission, and the threats promised his body and spirit by the musketeers.

Bazin for his part set out later that afternoon for Tours, equipped and charged in similar fashion. But traveling by horse the entire way, and needing to avoid the eyes of the Cardinal's servants in Tours, he was allowed the same eight days for performing his own mission.

⚜

During the period of these two absences, the four friends had, as may well be supposed, their eyes ever watchful, their noses to the wind, and their ears always alert. Their days were passed in endeavoring to catch all that was said within the camp, in observing the comings and goings of the cardinal, and in looking out for all the couriers who arrived. More than once, a wariness seized them when they were called upon for some unexpected duty. They had, besides, to look constantly to their own proper safety. For Milord was a phantom that, having appeared, allowed no one who had seen it to sleep quietly.

On the morning of the appointed eighth day of return, Bazin, fresh as ever and smiling beatifically, entered the inn of the Parpaillot as the four friends were sitting down to private breakfast. "Maitre Aramis," said he, "I have the response from your friend."

The four friends exchanged a hopeful glance, for that response marked that half their work was done — albeit the easier part.

With the door to the dining room closed, Aramis took the letter and read it earnestly, then passed it to Athos. She cast a glance over the epistle, then another around the room to ensure that none could overhear, then read aloud for the benefit of Porthos and d'Artagnan:

My cousin —
My sister and I are skillful in interpreting dreams, and even entertain great fear of them. But of yours it may be said, I hope, that every dream is an illusion. Adieux! Take care of yourself, and act gallantly in your campaign, so that we may from time to time hear you spoken of.
— Marie Michon

"All is as well as can be, then," said Athos.

"But still no word of Constance," said d'Artagnan, unable to hide her disappointment.

"But wait, Madame," said Bazin. "Maitre Aramis, your friend of Tours passed to me a second message, which was to be spoken only."

"Then give it at once good Bazin," said Aramis.

" 'I am expecting word regarding your previous inquiry within days. But knowing that your valet must return at once, I shall make other arrangements for its safe delivery.' "

"That is well done, Bazin," said d'Artagnan. "But will that be good news or ill, I wonder?"

"Patience, my friend," said Aramis. "And trust still to faith."

As to Bazin, exhausted by the long last night of his journey, he went and lay down on a bench by the fire. And having thus brought forth the response to Aramis's dream, he himself dreamed of Aramis, who having become pope, adorned Bazin's head with a cardinal's hat.

Still, as we have said, Bazin even by his fortunate return had not removed more than a part of the uneasiness which weighed upon the four friends. Their expectation began to stretch, and d'Artagnan in particular would have wagered each hour of the last day of waiting for Planchet's return as a full day at least in its own right.

From her fear of Milord's ruthlessness, d'Artagnan had begun to credit him with a supernatural prowess for antagonism. At the least noise, she imagined herself about to be arrested, convinced that Planchet was being dragged back to La Rochelle to be forced to implicate herself and her friends in treason. This anxiety became so great that by midmorning that day, it had extended to Aramis and Porthos. Athos alone remained unmoved, as if no danger hovered over her, and as if nothing around her had changed.

By noon, these signs were so strong in d'Artagnan, Porthos, and Aramis that the three friends could not remain quiet in one place, and from wherever they waited, each would suddenly rise to wander like a ghost out to the road by which Planchet was expected, then silently return.

"Really," said Athos to the three as they returned to her own chamber all at once from such a rambling. "You are not adults but children to let this villain terrify you so. And what might the worst amount to, after all? To be imprisoned? Well if so, with Monsieur de Treville and the Queen Anne on our side, we should be taken out of prison soon enough. To be decapitated? Why, every day in the trenches we go cheerfully to expose ourselves to worse than that — for a bullet may break a leg, and I am convinced that a healer would provide more pain in cutting off a leg than an executioner in cutting off a head. Wait quietly, then. In two hours, or in four, or in eight at the latest, Planchet will be here. He promised to be here, and I have very great faith in Planchet."

"But if he does not come?" said d'Artagnan.

"Well, if he does not come, it will be because he has been delayed, that's all. He may have fallen from his horse, or he may have done a tumble from the deck of a bridge. He may have traveled so fast against the wind as to have brought on a violent coughing fit. Gentles, let us reckon upon accidents! Life is a book of little miseries, whose pages the philosopher counts with a smile. So be philosophers as I am, sers. Sit down at the table and let us drink. For nothing makes the future look so bright as surveying it through a glass of finest burgundy."

"That's all very well," said d'Artagnan. "But I am tired of fearing each time I open a fresh bottle that the wine might come as another gift of Milord."

To that, even Athos grew silent, and she rose from her chair in her turn to start a nervous pacing that she could not repress.

⚜

The day passed away and the evening advanced slowly, but finally it came. The taverns that served the camp were filled with drinkers. Athos, with her share of d'Artagnan's diamond in her pocket, had entered the Parpaillot at midafternoon and not left. She had found in Monsieur de Busigny — who, by the by, had given the four musketeers a magnificent meal for their wager — a partner worthy of her company. They were gaming together, as had become usual, when seven o'clock sounded, and Porthos came in, twisting his mustache. The patrol was heard passing for the changing of the guard as Aramis entered and sat, appearing pensive. At half past seven, the last post was sounded, and d'Artagnan entered the inn to join her friends.

"We are lost," said she to the ear of Athos.

"All remains yet to be seen," said Athos quietly, drawing four pistoles from her pocket and throwing them upon the table to settle the bill. "Come, gentles," said she. "To the road."

Athos then went out of the Parpaillot, followed by d'Artagnan. Aramis came behind, mumbling verses to themself. They gave their arm to Porthos, who from time to time pulled a hair or two from his mustache in a sign of despair.

But all at once, a shadow appeared in the darkness — the outline of which was familiar to d'Artagnan. Then a well-known voice said, "Madame, I have brought your cloak. It is chilly this evening."

"Planchet!" cried the young musketeer, beside herself with joy.

"Planchet!" repeated Aramis and Porthos.

"Well, yes, Planchet to be sure," said Athos. "What is there so astonishing in that? He promised to be back by eight o'clock, and eight is striking. Bravo, Planchet. You are a courier of your word. And if ever you leave your present employment, rest assured you will have a place in my service."

"Oh, never!" said Planchet. "I will never leave Madame d'Artagnan."

At the same time, d'Artagnan felt Planchet slip a note into her hand. The young musketeer felt a strong inclination to embrace the valet as she had embraced him on his departure. But she feared lest this mark of affection, bestowed in the open street, might bring suspicion on the importance of his mission and reappearance, so she restrained herself.

"I have the note," whispered d'Artagnan to Athos and her friends.

"Well and good," said Athos. "Let us return to my quarters and read it."

The note seemed to burn the hand of d'Artagnan, who wished to hasten the steps of all. But Athos took her arm and passed it under her own, and the young musketeer was forced to regulate her pace by that of her friend.

At length they reached Athos's quarters and lit a lamp. Then while Grimaud and Planchet stood outside the doorway so that the four friends might not be surprised, d'Artagnan, with a trembling hand, broke the seal and opened the so-anxiously-expected letter.

It contained half a line, in a hand perfectly British, though in concise French:

Thank you. Be at ease.

When all had read it, Athos took the letter from the hands of d'Artagnan, approached the lamp, and set fire to the paper. She did not let go till it was reduced to a cinder. Then said she, calling Planchet, "Now, my gallant, you may claim your seven hundred livres. Though do be fair, you did not run much risk of discovery with such a note as that."

"Nonetheless, I have perfected every possible means to conceal it," said Planchet.

"Well," said d'Artagnan, "you must tell us all about it."

"But that will be a long job, madame."

"You are right, Planchet," said Athos. "And besides, the last post has been sounded, and we should draw suspicion if we kept a light burning."

"So be it," said d'Artagnan. "Go to bed, Planchet, and sleep soundly."

"My faith, madame! That will be the first time I have done so for eight days."

"Faith, but the same is true for me!" said d'Artagnan.

"And me," said Porthos.

"And for me," said Aramis.

"Well, if you will have the truth," said Athos, "for me too."

CHAPTER 49

A FATEFUL ARRIVAL

We must now return to some two days previous to Planchet's departure, and but a day after Milord's having been ordered to England by Cardinal de Richelieu, to see that villain standing and roaring like a lion on the deck of his ship. Having traveled all night, he and his escort had arrived at Fort La Pointe shortly after dawn that day. An hour later, Milord had embarked, and *Judith*, conveyed by letters of marque from the cardinal, raised anchor and steered its course toward England.

But *Judith*'s fortune was to prove as frightful as Milord's mood as the brig hit open water, for the storm winds that had been felt over preceding days even across the sheltered waters of La Rochelle became a full gale a league from shore. The captain, though, was eager to escape the coast, aligning their course between the worst storm winds like a mouse between cats and birds, and pushed the brig too hard.

And so even as Milord shouted to the fates to vent his rage against Athos and d'Artagnan and all those who opposed him, *Judith*'s fore mast cracked, and the brig was forced to limp ahead close to the sheltered shore, and to put in for repair at Brest. The impending state of war between France and England meant delays in procuring necessary materials. Thus, it was a full ten days after leaving the mouth of the Charente that Milord, pale with fatigue and irritation, was able to leave behind the blue shores of the Finisterre coast, heading toward England across the storm-tossed channel.

All those days of waiting, and the two days of the crossing, were occupied for the villainous gentry by the memory of having been insulted by d'Artagnan and threatened by Athos — and of how his eventual return to France would see him revenged on both those enemies. But Milord had no understanding of how closely d'Artagnan and her friends pursued him with their warning to the Liege de Winter — or of how the bad luck of *Judith* had turned that pursuit into a rout, in allowing the intrepid Planchet to reach Portsmouth a full four days ahead of him.

So it was, then, that the messenger of their eminence sailed into Portsmouth, all his rage and hunger for vengeance honed to a fine edge — and with no knowledge of how that vengeance was to be quickly blunted.

All the city at that time was in a state of extraordinary excitement. Four large warships, recently built, had just been launched. And to Milord's astonishment as his gaze swept the chaotic port, he saw a figure most noticeable standing at the end of the nearest jetty — and one he recognized. This lord wore clothing richly laced with gold, and glittering with diamonds and precious stones, as was customary with him. His hat was ornamented with a white feather which drooped upon his shoulder, and he was seen surrounded by a staff whose dress was almost as immaculate and beautifully adorned as his own.

It was the Lord Duke of Buckingham.

The day was one of those rare and beautiful events when England remembers that there is a sun. That glorious orb, winter-pale but nevertheless still splendid, was setting at the horizon, glorifying at once the heavens and the sea with bands of fire, and casting upon the towers and the old houses of Portsmouth a last ray of gold which made the windows sparkle like firelight.

Breathing the sea breeze and staring upon the distant features of the duke, Milord found himself much invigorated as the dock drew nearer. He contemplated all the power of those preparations for war that he was commissioned to destroy, all the power of that English force which he was to combat alone — and which he would cause with a gesture of his hand to dissipate like a cloud of smoke.

But as *Judith* drew near the sheltered water of the shore in order to cast anchor, a small cutter, formidably armed as a guard vessel, approached the merchant brig and dropped into the sea a longboat that continued on toward it. This boat contained an officer, a mate, and eight rowers. The officer alone came on board *Judith*, where they were received with all the deference inspired by their uniform.

The officer introduced herself as one Lieutenant Mistress Felton, and conversed a short while with the captain, giving him several papers she bore with instructions to read them. Then upon the order of *Judith*'s captain, all those on board the vessel, both passengers and sailors, were called upon deck.

When this summons was made, Mistress Felton inquired aloud the point of the brig's departure, its route, and its landings. To all these questions, the captain replied without difficulty and without hesitation. Then the English officer began to pass in review all the passengers and sailors, one after the other, and stopped when she came to Milord. She surveyed him very closely, but without addressing a single word to him.

During the examination of Milord by the lieutenant, it may well be imagined that he on his part was no less scrutinizing in his own glances. Mistress Felton might have been twenty-five years of age, with a tawny complexion, mild features framed by plain-cut hair, and clear brown eyes that were rather deeply set. She wore her officer's uniform plainly, with no braid or embellishments. But however great was the power of Milord's insight into reading the hearts of those whose secrets he wished to divine, he was met this time with a gaze so impassive that no discovery was to be had.

When she looked finally away from Milord, the lieutenant then returned to the captain and said a few words to him. And as if from that moment *Judith* was under her command, she ordered a maneuver which the crew executed immediately. The vessel resumed its course, but escorted now by the little cutter that sailed side by side with it, menacing it with the mouths of its six cannons. The longboat followed in the wake of the merchant ship.

By the time they reached their docking place and were secured, night had fallen. A rising fog increased the darkness, and formed around the ships' lights and the lanterns of the jetty a circle like that which surrounds the moon when the weather threatens rain. The air was heavy, damp, and cold.

Milord, so courageous and firm, shivered in spite of himself.

Mistress Felton asked to have Milord's packages pointed out to her, and ordered them to be placed in the longboat. When this operation was complete, she invited him to descend to the boat as well by offering her hand.

Milord stared down upon her with a most baleful expression. "And who are you," asked he, "who has the kindness to trouble yourself so particularly on my account?"

"You may perceive, sir, by my uniform, that I am an agent of the English navy," replied the young lieutenant.

By the honorific spoken, it was clear to Milord that this Mistress Felton knew him, and his response was cold. "And is it the custom for the agents of the English navy to place themselves at the service of their fellow citizens when they land at port, and to carry their gallantry so far as to conduct them ashore?"

"Yes, sir, it is the custom, and not from gallantry but from prudence. In time of war, foreigners are to be conducted to particular lodgings, in order that they may remain under the eye of the government until full information can be obtained about them."

These words were pronounced with the most exact politeness and the most perfect calmness. Nevertheless, they had all the power and effect of a blow to Milord.

"I am not a foreigner," said he, his voice pure and cold. "Nor do I require lodging when friends and family stand at the ready to receive me. I am Milord de Winter, and this measure —"

"This measure is by the order of the royals, sir, and you will seek in vain to evade it."

Milord held the lieutenant with the cold blue of his gaze, saying nothing. Then, ignoring her hand, he began the descent of the ship's ladder, at the foot of which the longboat waited. Mistress Felton followed. A large cloak was spread at the stern, and she requested Milord to sit down upon it, then placed herself beside him.

"Row!" said she to the sailors.

The eight oars fell at once into the sea, making but a single sound, giving but a single stroke, and the boat seemed to fly over the surface of the water.

In no time at all, they had gained the pier. Mistress Felton spoke a message to the ear of one sailor, who fairly leaped to the deck above and raced off into the darkness. She clambered up more slowly, and from above, once more offered her hand to Milord, who pulled himself up without assistance.

He stood for a time in the chill dark, while his packages were retrieved and organized along the deck. The sailors then stood at attention, while Mistress Felton paced as though awaiting something. Milord understood what she awaited when he heard, at the edge of the road ahead, a clattering sound marking the arrival of a carriage, its lamps glowing white in the mist.

"This carriage is for us," said the lieutenant.

"This lodging, then, is some distance?" said Milord.

Mistress Felton said nothing in response, but held out her hand to Milord once more, as if to offer him escort. The look he gave her spoke his full disdain, but she stepped up to block him as he attempted to advance.

"Before we depart, I will have the poniard I have seen beneath your jacket, sir."

Milord considered his preferred method for delivering the blade to the insolent lieutenant, ire curling his lip. Then Mistress Felton pulled back her jacket, and he saw for the first time the pistol at her belt.

Carefully, he withdrew the dagger from its sheath and turned the handle toward her. Then he stepped past. The sailors claimed the luggage as Milord resolutely walked to the carriage, then climbed within.

Mistress Felton saw that the baggage was fastened carefully behind the carriage. When this was done, she took her place beside Milord and shut the door. Immediately, without any order being given or place of destination indicated, the driver set off at a rapid pace, and the carriage fairly raced along the streets of Portsmouth.

So strange a reception naturally gave Milord ample opportunity for reflection. So seeing that the young lieutenant did not seem at all disposed for conversation, he reclined in his corner of the carriage, and one after the other passed in review all the surmises which presented themselves to his mind.

At the end of a quarter of an hour, however, surprised at the length of the journey, Milord interrupted his meditations to lean forward toward the window, and to see whither he was being conducted. But the houses of Portsmouth were no longer to be seen. Instead, trees appeared in the darkness like great black phantoms chasing one another, and beyond them could be seen the emptier darkness of the sea as their road followed the coast. Milord felt a chill where his hand touched the glass.

"We are no longer in the city," said he.

The young lieutenant sat in silence.

"I beg you to understand, mistress, that I will go no farther unless you tell me whither you are taking me."

Even this threat brought no reply. The carriage continued to roll on at speed, and Mistress Felton seemed a statue.

Milord looked at the lieutenant with one of those terrible expressions of his anger, and which so rarely failed of their effect. His breath came ragged, eyes flashing in the darkness, but still Felton remained immovable.

Brusquely, Milord stood, unlatching and quickly swinging open the door as if meaning to throw himself out.

"Take care, sir," said the young lieutenant coolly. "You will kill yourself in jumping." And as she adjusted her jacket, she showed again the pistol there.

In truth, it was not the intent of jumping which had inspired Milord's actions. Rather, it was the intent of assessing whether the orders that saw him now carried through the night toward unknown ends had been made by those who truly knew him, and knew what things he was capable of.

By the young lieutenant having been ordered to shoot him in the event of attempted escape, Milord understood that he was known all too well.

He slowly relatched the door and reseated himself. He allowed a flicker of fear to cross his face now, hoping to instill in the young lieutenant a sense that his will had been dashed. "In the name of decency, Mistress Felton, will you at least tell me if it is to you, if it is to your government, or if it is to an enemy that I am to attribute the violence that is done to me?"

"No violence will be offered to you, sir. And what happens to you is the result of a very simple measure which we are obliged to adopt with all who land in England."

"Have we met before, Mistress Felton?"

"This is the first time I have had the honor of seeing you, sir."

"And on your honor, you have no cause of hatred against me?"

"None, I swear to you."

All was serenity and mildness in the voice of the young lieutenant. Milord kept that same mildness in his expression, but in his heart, the rage was rising.

After a journey of what seemed hours, the carriage stopped before an iron gate. This closed an avenue leading to a castle of severe appearance, massive and isolated. In the brief silence before the gate was opened and the wheels rolled once again over a fine gravel, Milord heard a vast roaring, which he at once recognized as the noise of the sea dashing against some steep cliff.

The carriage passed under two arched gateways, and at length stopped in a courtyard large, dark, and square. Almost immediately, the door of the carriage was opened and Mistress Felton sprang lightly out. Having been previously rebuffed, she refrained from presenting her hand to Milord, who in his turn alighted with cold calmness.

"So then, I am forcefully detained," said he, looking around him. Then he brought back his eyes with a most malevolent smile to the young lieutenant. "But I feel assured it will not be for long. My own conscience and your politeness are the guarantees of that."

Not bothering to reply, Mistress Felton drew from her belt a small silver whistle, then blew three times with three different modulations. Several figures immediately appeared, who unharnessed the steaming horses and pulled the carriage into a coach house.

Then the lieutenant, with the same calm politeness, invited her prisoner to enter the house. He, still smiling coldly, passed two steps behind Mistress Felton under a low arched door, which led by way of a vaulted passage to a stone staircase leading up, and lighted only at the far end. Beyond the stair, a series of halls brought them to a massive door, whose lock was fitted by a key the lieutenant carried with her. The door turned heavily upon its hinges, and revealed beyond the chamber for which Milord was destined.

With a single glance, he took in the apartment in its minutest details. It was a chamber whose furniture would have been entirely appropriate for even a resident of Milord's tastes. A cheery fire burned at the hearth, with two easy chairs close by. A bed was set off behind fine curtains. And yet bars at the windows and outside bolts at the door made it clear that he was not a guest but a prisoner.

In an instant, all Milord's strength of mind seemed to abandon him — even as his thought grew more focused than ever before. He sank into a large easy chair with his arms crossed and his head lowered, glancing to the door every instant as if expecting to see a judge enter to interrogate him. But in truth, he was assessing the strength of numbers around him, seeing no one enter except two guards who brought his trunks and packages, deposited them in a corner, and withdrew without speaking.

Mistress Felton superintended all these operations with the same calmness Milord had seen in her from the beginning, never pronouncing a word, and making herself obeyed by a gesture of her hand or a sound of her whistle.

At length, the impatient villain could hold out no longer. He broke the silence. "In the name of decency," cried he, "what means all that is passing? Put an end to my doubts. I have courage enough for any danger I can foresee, for every misfortune which I understand. Where am I, and why am I here? If I am free, why these bars and these doors? If I am a prisoner, what crime have I committed?"

"You are here in the apartment prepared for you, sir. I received orders three days past to seek *Judith* were she still in port, or to speak with those who had spoken with the crew, to determine where you might be found. But I was informed by the harbormaster that the brig was expected and overdue, and so was able to watch for your late arrival. My order, when you were found, was to take charge of you, and to conduct you to this castle. This order I believe I have accomplished with all the exactness of a soldier, but also with the courtesy due to you. This thus terminates, at least to the present moment, the duty I had to fulfill toward you. The rest concerns another person."

"And who is that other person?" asked Milord coldly. "You will tell me their name."

At that moment, a great jingling of spurs was heard in the corridor. Voices rose and faded away, and the footsteps of a single figure approached the door.

"That person is here, sir," said Mistress Felton, drawing herself up in an attitude of respect. At the same time, the door opened. A figure appeared on the threshold. They were without a hat, carried a sword, and flourished a handkerchief in their hand.

Even in the gloom, Milord recognized this shadow, which advanced slowly. As the figure entered into the circle of light projected by the lamp, their piercing black eyes were locked to his, and he slowly stood.

"My sibling," said he. "How good to see you."

"Indeed, it is I." Liege de Winter made a bow intended to be courteous, but Milord sensed in the gesture an angry irony.

"And this castle, then?"

"The estate of an acquaintance of court, who has agreed to my use of it."

"And this chamber?"

"Is yours. Though I feared you might not be found for some time, I had it prepared as soon as your arrival became expected. And here you are."

Milord fixed his blue-eyed gaze on his sibling-in-law, letting a look of sadness and uncertainty sweep his face. "I am, then, your prisoner?"

"Pray, say 'guest.' It has a more melodious tone."

"But I am left near speechless," said Milord. "I know not what I have done, or even what I am accused of doing, that I should warrant such behavior toward me. This is a frightful abuse of power." The edge of a sob was heard in his voice, and he allowed a tear to work its way into one eye.

"No high-sounding words, brother. Rather, let us sit down and chat quietly, as family ought to do."

Then, turning toward the door and seeing that the young lieutenant was waiting for her last orders, Liege de Winter said, "All is well. I thank you. Now leave us, Mistress Felton."

CHAPTER 50

CONVERSATION BETWEEN BROTHER AND SIBLING

During the time which Liege de Winter took to shut the door, close a shutter, and draw a chair near to the fire, Milord plunged his thoughts into the depths of possibility, intent on uncovering all the plots he knew would remain hidden from him as long as he was ignorant of who was behind it all. He knew his sibling-in-law to be a worthy gentle, a bold rider, an intrepid gamer, and enterprising with a number of paramours in their life. But by no means were they remarkable for their skill in intrigues. So how had they discovered word of Milord's arrival and caused him to be seized? And why did they detain him now?

Athos had let slip words which proved that the conversation Milord had with the cardinal in the miserable inn of the Red Dovecote had been heard by outside ears. But Milord could not imagine that the musketeer had laid this trap so promptly and so boldly. It might then have made more sense that his preceding operations in England had been discovered. Buckingham, in particular, might have guessed that it was he who had cut off the two diamond studs, and might have decided to seek vengeance for that little treachery.

This supposition appeared to Milord the most reasonable — and the most beneficial to him. For it was a fool of an opponent who hoped only to revenge the past, and who in doing so failed to anticipate the future. By this same token, it was a stroke of luck that he had fallen into the hands of his sibling-in-law. For Milord reckoned that he would deal with the Liege de Winter much more easily than with an acknowledged and intelligent enemy.

As Liege de Winter sat, Milord joined them, saying, "Yes, let us chat," with a kind of cheerfulness. In spite of all the pretense his sibling might bring to the conversation, Milord was intent on drawing from their words all the revelations he would need to shape his next moves.

"You have, then, decided to come to England again," said Liege de Winter, "in spite of the resolutions you so often expressed in Paris never again to set your feet on British ground."

Milord replied to this question with another question. "To begin with, tell me," said he, "how you have watched me so closely as to be aware beforehand not only of my return, but even of the week, and the port at which I should embark?"

Frustratingly, Liege de Winter adopted the same tactics, seemingly intent on frustrating Milord's attempts to gain advantage. "But tell me, my dear brother," replied they, "what purpose brings you hither?"

"I come to see you," said Milord, desiring to gain the good will of his sibling by falsehood — and not knowing how much this reply aggravated the suspicions to which d'Artagnan's letter and Milord's own notes had given birth in Liege de Winter's mind.

"To see me indeed?" said they coldly.

"To be sure. What is there astonishing in that?"

"And you had no other object in coming to England but to see me?"

"No."

"So it was for me alone that you have taken the trouble to cross the channel?"

"For you alone."

"Faith! What tenderness, my brother."

"But am I not your nearest relative?" said Milord, with a tone of the most touching ingenuousness.

"And as such, you are among my heirs, are you not?" So saying, Liege de Winter fixed their eyes on those of Milord, even as they placed their hand on his arm.

Whatever command he had over himself, Milord could not help but tremble. And as Liege de Winter's hand was upon his arm, this did not escape them.

For Milord, his in-law's words were as a blow. The first thought that occurred to his mind was that he had been betrayed by Kitty, who must have recounted to Liege de Winter the selfish aversion he had imprudently spoken before the valet, trusting that her fear of him would earn her silence. He also recollected his furious reaction upon hearing that d'Artagnan had spared Liege de Winter's life. But notwithstanding how unlikely the chance of the deceitful valet making contact with his in-law, why would Liege de Winter have believed a single word of her story?

"I do not understand," said Milord now, in order to gain time and draw his adversary further out. "What do you mean to say? Is there any secret meaning concealed beneath your words?"

"On my faith, no," said Liege de Winter with apparent good nature. "You wish to see me, and you come to England. I learn this desire, or rather I suspect that you feel it. And in order to spare you all the annoyances of a nocturnal arrival in a port and all the fatigues of landing, I send one of my officers to seek you. I give her orders to commandeer a carriage, and she brings you hither to this castle, which is at my disposal. And where, in order to satisfy our mutual desire of seeing each other, I have prepared you a chamber. What is there more astonishing in all that I have said to you than in what you have told me?"

"What I think astonishing is that you should predict my coming."

"And yet that is the most simple thing in the world, my dear brother. Have you not observed that the captain of your little vessel, on nearing your anchoring point, sent forward a boat bearing their logbook and the register of their passengers and crew? I am commandant of the port, since returning to England and with our state of readiness for battle. They brought me that book. I recognized your name in it. My heart told me what your mouth has just confirmed, which is to say, the manner in which you have exposed yourself to the dangers of a sea so perilous simply to see me. And so I sent my cutter to meet you. You know the rest."

The lie was so base, given especially its conflict with the words spoken by Lieutenant Felton, that Milord took it as a taunt, and he was all the more alarmed.

"My sibling," said he, as if uncaring of her words. "Was not that my Lord Duke of Buckingham whom I saw on the jetty this evening as we arrived?"

"Indeed it was. Ah, I can understand how the sight of him must have struck you," said Liege de Winter. "You came from a land where he must be very much talked of, and I know that his armaments against France greatly engage the attention of your friend the cardinal."

"My friend the cardinal?" laughed Milord, but his voice was tight. He saw that on this point as on too many others, Liege de Winter seemed well instructed.

"Is their eminence not your friend?" said they, feigning surprise. "Ah, pardon. I cannot imagine why I thought so. But we will return to my lord duke presently. Let us not depart from the sentimental turn our conversation had taken. You came, you say, to see me?"

"Yes."

"Well, I reply that you shall be served to the height of your wishes, and that we shall see each other every day."

"Am I, then, to remain here eternally?" demanded Milord, his anger rising.

"Do you find yourself badly lodged, brother? But you have privacy and comfortable furnishings, and supper shall be along shortly. Demand anything else you want, and I will hasten to have you furnished with it."

"But I have no servants."

"You shall have all, sir. Remind me on what footing your household was established in France, and I will arrange one similar. Or even better," said Liege de Winter easily, "tell me of the household you maintained with your first wife. For I am sure it was more regal by far."

"My first wife…" Milord's voice choked off, and he stared at Liege de Winter with narrowed eyes.

"Yes, your French wife. For I do not speak of my sister. If you have forgotten, as your first wife is still living, I can write to her and she will send me information on the subject."

A cold sweat appeared on the brow of Milord. "You jest," said he in a hollow voice.

"Do I look so?" asked Liege de Winter, rising and stepping back.

"Or rather, you insult me," said Milord. His hands were stiffened around the two arms of his easy chair, and he felt that either might break.

"I, insult you?" said Liege de Winter, this time with contempt. "In truth, brother, do you think that can be possible?"

"Indeed, sibling," said Milord. "For you must be either drunk or mad. Leave the room, and send me a servant."

"But servants are very indiscreet, my brother, even as I would make a fine valet. And by that means, all our secrets will remain in the family."

"Insolence!" cried Milord. And as if driven by a spring, he rose from his chair and bounded toward Liege de Winter, who awaited his attack with their arms crossed — but nevertheless with one hand on the hilt of their sword.

"Come," said they. "I know you are accustomed to assassination. But I warn you, I shall defend myself even against you."

"I believe you," said Milord coldly. "You have all the appearance of being cowardly enough to lift your hand against a civilian, unarmed."

"Perhaps so. For I am an agent of the crown, and mine would not be the first hand placed upon you in the name of the law." Then Liege de Winter pointed, with a slow and accusing gesture, to the left shoulder of Milord, which they almost touched with their finger.

"Reveal your shoulder to me, brother," said they.

Milord's thoughts were a deep, inward shriek. He lashed out at Liege de Winter to drive back their hand, striking with a force that made them step back in wariness. With teeth bared, he retreated to a corner of the room like a panther that crouches to spring.

"Oh, growl as much as you please," said Liege de Winter. "For your refusal gives me the last truth I need." And so saying, they took from their jacket pocket an envelope. Opening it, they scattered its contents to the seat of a side table.

Milord stared in horror. For it was his own letters and diary pages on display. With all that had happened since the young Gascon and Kitty had fled the townhouse, his affairs had been most disorganized. How long the papers had been missing, he had no way to tell.

"Your own words have revealed to me what you are," said Liege de Winter. "I read here one small part of the story of your life, and I am ashamed of having been one of your victims."

"I have never seen these pages before," said Milord, fighting to find words in a mind ablaze with rage.

"You have forgotten them, you mean? Then I encourage you to read them again — and to know that their story ends now. For I warn you there are none here to be manipulated by you. There are no questionable attorneys here with whom to stake my property. There is no heroic gentry to come and seek a quarrel with me on account of the gentle lord I detain as prisoner. But I have judges quite ready who will quickly dispose of one so shameless as to glide, a liar and a felon and a thief, into the heart and mind of my sister. And these judges, I warn you, will soon send you to a sentence that will make both your shoulders alike."

The eyes of Milord burned with such intensity that even though his sibling was armed and he was not, Liege de Winter felt the chill of fear shiver through their whole frame. However, they continued all the same, and with increasing anger.

"You could not stop your fatal career," said they, "for you do evil for the infinite and supreme joy of doing it. Yes, I can very well understand that after having inherited the fortune of my sister, it would be very agreeable to you to be my heir likewise. But know beforehand that if you kill me or cause me to be killed, my legal precautions have been taken. Not a penny of what I possess will pass into your hands."

Milord would not look at his sibling-in-law, watching instead the fire with an attention that dilated his reddened eyes.

"Oh, be assured," said Liege de Winter, "that if the life of my sister were not sacred to me, you should rot in a state prison. But for the love I bear Katherine's name and memory, I will be silent, and you must endure your captivity equally quietly. In ten days, I shall set out for La Rochelle with the army. But before my departure, a vessel which I shall see depart will take you hence and convey you to one of the colonies of the new world. And be assured that you shall be accompanied by agents who will end your life at the first attempt you make to return to England or the Continent."

"So until my exile or execution, I am a common prisoner?" said Milord. He kept his eyes from Liege de Winter still, making one final attempt to hide the wild cunning there. "I, who have done no wrong except to be falsely accused of crimes in my youth, and more falsely branded? I, who married for love in good faith, when told my first wife had died…?"

"Your words mean nothing," interrupted Liege de Winter wearily. "At present, you will remain in this castle. The walls are thick, the doors strong, and the bars solid. Moreover, your window opens immediately over the curtain wall, which is constantly patrolled. My soldiers, who are devoted to me for life and death, mount guard around this apartment, and watch all the passages that lead to the courtyard. Even if you gained the yard, there would still be three iron gates for you to pass. My orders are clear. A step, a gesture, a word on your part denoting an effort to escape, and you are to be fired upon. If they kill you,

English justice will be in debt to me for having saved it the trouble of your execution."

For the sake of his own seething mind, Milord forced his features to once again regain their calmness. His gaze recovered its assurance. "Then I shall make the best of my situation," said he, "until such time as you are willing to consider the truth against the lies that have been told of me."

"Your tone rings false even now," said Liege de Winter. "For you are saying to yourself, 'Ten days? Fie! I have an inventive mind. Before that time has passed, some idea will occur to me. I have an infernal spirit. I shall meet with a victim. Before five days are gone by, I shall be away from here.' I tell you simply that I hope you try it."

Milord, finding his thoughts betrayed as Liege de Winter seemingly guessed his mind at each turn, dug his nails into his palms. By doing so, he hoped to subdue every emotion that might give to his face any expression except agony.

But Liege de Winter only continued. "The officer who commands here in my absence you have already seen, and therefore know her. You must have observed that she knows how to obey an order — for you did not, I am sure, come from Portsmouth hither without endeavoring to make her speak. What do you say of her? Could a figure of marble have been more impassive and more mute? No doubt, you have tried the power of your seductions and your camaraderie upon countless victims. And with even less doubt, you have always succeeded. But I give you leave to try either comradeship or seduction upon this one. Gods' blood, if you succeed with her, I will pronounce you a sorcerer."

Liege de Winter then went toward the door and opened it. "Mistress Felton!" called they. Then to Milord, they added, "Wait a moment longer, and I will properly introduce you."

There followed a bitter silence, during which the sound of a slow and regular step was heard approaching. The young officer with whom we are already acquainted then stopped at the threshold.

"You may order my brother to be served, my dear," said Liege de Winter. "Then shut the door."

With a nod from Mistress Felton to two soldiers behind her, a small table was carried in, set with a white cloth and a fine supper.

But Milord said in response, "Take it away. For the lies told of me this night have stolen my appetite."

With another gesture, and with no hesitation, Felton send the two soldiers back as quickly as they had entered. She then closed the door behind her and stepped into the room.

"Now," said Liege de Winter, "look at this man, my brother. He is young, and he is beautiful. He is the master of all earthly seductions and intrigues. And as well, he is a monster, who at twenty-five years of age is guilty of crimes, lies, and transgressions as heinous as any you would read of in a year in the archives of our tribunals. His voice prejudices his listeners in his favor. His beauty serves as a bait to his victims. He will try to befriend you. To seduce you. Perhaps he will try to kill you. For this villain has come back again into England for the purpose of conspiring in assassination most foul. I hold this serpent in my hands. So I say to you, Mistress Felton, that I put faith in your loyalty."

"My liege," said the young lieutenant. Then Milord saw her summoning to her mild face all the hatred she could find in her heart. "I swear all shall be done as you desire."

Milord received this look like a resigned victim. It was impossible to imagine a more submissive expression than that which prevailed on his wan features. Liege de Winter themself would scarcely recognize the villain who, just moments before, was seemingly prepared to fight and die for freedom.

"He is not to leave this chamber, Mistress Felton," said Liege de Winter. "He is to correspond with no one. He is to speak to no one but you — if you will do him the honor to address a word to him."

"That is sufficient, my liege. I have so sworn."

"And now, my brother, try to make your peace with your own conscience. For I promise you, you will not make it with mine."

Milord let his head sink, as if crushed by this sentence. Liege de Winter went out, making a sign to Felton, who followed them and shut the door after them.

One instant after, the heavy step of a sentinel was heard pacing in the corridor.

Milord remained standing for some time in the same position, for he guessed that someone might perhaps be watching him through the keyhole. He then slowly raised his head, which had resumed its formidable expression of menace and defiance. He walked to the door to listen, hearing only the pacing of the guard. He returned to the window and looked out into darkness.

Then, returning to the table, Milord collected the papers and their envelope there, and, not looking to read them, set them in the fire to burn. He slumped down again in the large armchair, staring at the flames, deep in thought.

CHAPTER 51

THE CARDINAL'S RIDE

Meanwhile, on the very same day that Milord arrived in Portsmouth and was taken to be held, the siege of La Rochelle arrived at its most dangerous stage, with the city now fully surrounded. The Cardinal de Richelieu's plans had been executed flawlessly, and the dyke across the harbor mouth now prevented the entrance of any vessel into the besieged city. But still, the increasingly defiant resilience of the Huguenots made it clear that it might be some time before the blockade would turn to final victory.

This was a source of great delight to the queens' army, whose soldiers since the start of the campaign, as we have seen, had been leading a most jubilant life. Neither provisions nor money were yet wanting in the camp, and not only the musketeers but all the corps rivaled one another in their audacity and bravery. To cross the lines in search of spies, to make hazardous expeditions upon the dyke or the sea, to formulate wild plans, and to execute those plans coolly — such were the pastimes which made the army find the days of the siege short. And at the same time, those days were perceived as too long by far by the Rochellais, falling prey to famine and anxiety — and by the cardinal alike.

Throughout all the weeks of the campaign thus far, the French besiegers had become increasingly adept at capturing the messengers whom the Rochellais sent to Buckingham, or the spies whom Buckingham sent to the Rochellais. One messenger of the Rochellais taken but a day after Planchet and Bazin had set out on their own similar missions was the bearer of a letter, which told the Duke of Buckingham that the city was at extreme ends, and that all would be lost if aid did not arrive imminently. But instead of threatening surrender at that time, the letter read, quite simply, "If your aid comes not quickly, we shall all be dead with hunger when it does."

The Rochellais, then, had no hope but in Buckingham. To the Cardinal de Richelieu's mind, it was thus evident that if it were proved to them that they could not count on Buckingham, their courage would fail with their hope. And so their eminence looked with great impatience for the news from England which would announce to all that Buckingham would not come.

The question of taking La Rochelle by assault, though often debated in the council of the Queen Louise, had been always rejected. The city appeared nigh impregnable, and the cardinal, despite their skill in extolling the glories of war, very well knew that the horror of wide-scale bloodshed in such an encounter would set back the progress of their own nationalism. And the cardinal was very much devoted to progress.

Against the silence from England, though, Richelieu could not drive from their mind the fear they endured of their terrible emissary, Milord — for their eminence well comprehended the unpredictable qualities of that agent, which made him seem sometimes a serpent, sometimes a lion. Had he betrayed their eminence? Was he dead?

The cardinal had already sent forth Count de Rochefort to make inquiries in the northern ports as to whether Milord had been seen returning, or whether any word received from England might hint at his state. For their eminence knew Milord well enough in all cases to know that, whether acting for or against their interests, as a friend or as an enemy, he would not become inactive unless surrounded by powerful obstacles. But what form those present obstacles had taken was a thing their eminence had no way to know.

The cardinal had resolved, then, to carry on the war alone, and to count on nothing save for fortune and their own ability to keep control. They announced plans to press the defense and the shoring up of the earthen dyke, and thereby to starve La Rochelle. And when not engaged in planning, Richelieu stood on the balcony of their residence and cast their eyes over the unfortunate city, which contained so much deep misery and so many heroic virtues.

The late King Henry, when besieging Paris to lay his claim to the French throne during the horrid years of religious wars that marked the turn of the century, had loaves and provisions thrown over the walls. In ironic inversion of the old king's honor, the cardinal had instructed, for a month previous, that little notes be thrown over the walls of La Rochelle, by which the Rochellais were presented with how unjust, selfish, and barbarous was the conduct of their leaders. These leaders had corn in abundance, the notes always said, and would not let the common folk partake of it. And in these revelations was an element of truth, for the leaders of the city had adopted as a maxim that it was of very little consequence that children and the ill should die, so long as the soldiers who were to defend the walls remained strong and healthy.

Up to that time, whether from devotedness or from want of power to act against it, this maxim had passed from theory into practice, though it remained far from having been generally adopted. But the notes of Richelieu renewed attention on the policy with violent fervor. Soldiers were reminded that the folk whom the policy allowed to die were their children, their spouses, their elderly. And in response, it had quickly become spoken across the city that it would be more just for everyone to be reduced to the common misery, in order that equal conditions should give birth to unanimous resolutions.

These notes had all the effect that they who wrote them could have hoped for, in that they induced a great number of the Rochellais to whisper of seeking terms of surrender. But on this day that Milord arrived in Portsmouth, a courier of the English was captured attempting to cross into La Rochelle, with word that threatened to undo all that Cardinal de Richelieu's cunning had wrought. Having left Portsmouth just two days before, the courier carried a letter talking of a magnificent fleet that would be ready to sail for La Rochelle within two weeks, and which spoke also of a pledge by the Duke of Buckingham that at length, the great league of alliance heretofore threatened was about to declare itself against France, and that the realm would be at once invaded by the English, Spanish, Austrian, and German armies.

This unexpected circumstance brought back all of Cardinal de Richelieu's apprehension, and forced them in spite of themself to once more turn their eyes to the other side of the sea.

Toward sunset, oppressed with a mortal weariness of mind, the cardinal departed their residence with no other aim than to be out of doors. They rode slowly along the beach adjacent to the camp, accompanied only by Madame Houdiniere, the captain of the cardinal's guards, and Maitre de Cahusac, the favored blade of the cardinal.

Mingling the immensity of their dreams with the immensity of the ocean, their eminence came to the top of a hill. And there, they perceived the unusual sight of a figure running with all haste along the sand. The person's direction mirrored that of the cardinal's company, having come from the French camp. Casting no glance over their shoulder, the figure appeared unaware of the cardinal's presence.

Beckoning Houdiniere and Cahusac forward, the cardinal set out to pursue this figure where they disappeared behind a hedge. And upon drawing closer, their eminence saw there eight soldiers surrounded by empty bottles, all sitting on the sand and catching in its passage the sun that had lately been rare behind ever-present storm clouds. A drum borrowed from the camp had been set up as a low table, on which cards and dice could be seen. These persons were not gaming, however, but were divided as two groups of four.

The first four were occupied in opening an enormous flagon of Collioure wine, and were recognizable as retainers by their garb. The second group were all in the uniforms of musketeers, and were gathered around a letter that one held as if preparing to read. By the breathlessness of the one retainer who had been observed running, it was to be assumed that the letter had only just been delivered.

The cardinal was, as we have said, in very base spirits — and nothing when they were in that state of mind increased their ennui so much as happiness in others. Moreover, their eminence had long indulged in a strange fancy, which was always to believe that the causes of their own desolate moods would some-how inspire the happiness of others.

Making a sign to Houdiniere and Cahusac to stop, their eminence alighted from their horse and went toward these suspected merry companions. Riche-lieu hoped, by means of the sand that deadened the sound of their steps and of the hedge which concealed their approach, to catch some words of this conver-sation which appeared so engaging.

At ten paces from the hedge, their eminence recognized d'Artagnan. And as they had already seen that these soldiers were musketeers, they recognized Athos, Porthos, and Aramis thereafter.

It may be guessed that their eminence's desire to hear the conversation was greatly increased by this discovery. Their piercing eyes narrowed, and with the silent steps of a cat, they advanced toward the hedge. But Richelieu had not been able to catch more than a few vague syllables with no real clarity, when a sonorous and short cry made them start, and attracted the attention of the musketeers.

"Officers!" called Grimaud.

"You are speaking, you scoundrel," said Athos, rising upon her elbow and transfixing Grimaud with a dangerous look.

Grimaud therefore added no words to her speech, but contented herself with pointing her index finger in the direction of the hedge, announcing by this gesture the cardinal and their escort.

With a single bound, the musketeers and their four valets were on their feet, and saluted with respect.

The cardinal made no effort to hide their anger. But to deflect from the true cause of failing at their observation, their eminence spoke instead to the regu-lations of the campaign as they approached.

"It appears that the four musketeers, rather than acting as soldiers under orders, are themselves fit to keep a troop," said Richelieu, indicating Planchet, Grimaud, Bazin, and Mousqueton with a sweep of their hand. "Are the En-glish now expected by land? Or do the musketeers consider themselves officers deserving of their own command?"

Among themselves, d'Artagnan, Porthos, and Aramis stood in silence, fear-ing that any response would only raise the cardinal's ire. D'Artagnan caught the eye of Maitre de Cahusac as they approached, leading their own and the cardinal's horses. The cardinal's favored blade looked from her to Athos most fatally. For it may be remembered that Cahusac it was who d'Artagnan — not then a musketeer, nor even a guard — had disarmed behind the Luxembourg before finishing her own duel with Madame de Jussac. And of course, it was the wounded Athos who had then bested Maitre de Cahusac with formidable style.

"Maitre," replied Athos, for amid the general uncertainty at the cardinal's appearance, she alone had preserved the noble calmness that never forsook her. "The musketeers, when they are not on duty or when their duty is over, drink and play at dice, as we do here. And though not officers, they are certainly within rights to give orders to their valets."

"Valets?" grumbled the cardinal. "Lackeys who have the order to warn their masters when anyone passes are not valets, they are sentries."

"But your eminence may perceive," said Athos, "that if we had not taken this precaution, we should have been guilty of allowing you to pass without presenting you our respects, or offering our thanks for the favor you have done our four in uniting us." These words were pronounced with that imperturbable calm which distinguished Athos at times of danger, and with that excessive politeness which made of her at certain moments a leader more majestic than those who ruled by birth.

"Why," continued the elder musketeer, "d'Artagnan was but lately sharing her anxiousness for such an opportunity to express her gratitude to Maitre Cardinal. Well, here it is, my friend. Avail yourself of it."

In response to Athos's appeal, d'Artagnan came forward.

"I am indeed grateful, your eminence, for your recommendation and this opportunity to serve…" But her hastily made words of gratitude expired under the cardinal's withering look.

"This does not please me, gentles," said their eminence, dismissing wholly with their tone the distraction which Athos had started. "I do not like to have simple soldiers, only because they have the advantage of serving in a privileged corps, playing at being great lords. Discipline is the same for them as for everyone else."

Athos bowed in sign of assent. "Discipline, maitre, has in no way been forgotten by us, or so I must hope. We are not on duty, and we believed that not being on duty allowed us the liberty to dispose of our time as we pleased. If we are so fortunate as to have some particular duty to perform for your eminence, we are ready to obey you." Athos then indicated to the cardinal four muskets stood up against rocks, near the drum on which were set the cards and dice. "Your eminence may perceive that we have not come out without our arms."

"And your eminence may believe," added Aramis, speaking at last, "that we would have come to meet you, if we could have supposed it was Cardinal de Richelieu coming toward us with so few attendants."

The cardinal bit their lip. "Do you know what you look like, all together, as you are armed and guarded by your lackeys?" said they. "You look like four conspirators."

"Oh, as to that, maitre, it is true," said Athos brightly. "We do conspire, as your eminence might have seen that fine morning of breakfast at the bastion Saint-Gervais. At all times, we conspire against the Rochellais."

"Ah, you are gentles of clear policy," said the cardinal, sneering in their turn. "The secrets of many unknown things might perhaps be found in your memories, if we could only read them as easily as you read that letter which you concealed as soon as you saw me coming."

Beneath her calm exterior, Athos flushed with the touch of anger. The others could only watch as the elder musketeer made a step toward their eminence.

"One might think you really suspected us, maitre, and that we were undergoing a true interrogation. If it be so, we trust your eminence will deign to explain yourself, so that we should then at least be acquainted with our real position."

"Oh, if it only were an interrogation," said the cardinal. "Others besides you have undergone such, Madame Athos, and have provided what information I desire each time."

"And so I tell your eminence that you have but to question us, and we are ready to reply."

"What was that letter you were about to read, Maitre Aramis, and which you so promptly concealed?"

"Simply a friend's letter, maitre," said the gentle musketeer.

"Ah, I see," said the cardinal. "But more than a friend, perhaps? For you show signs of intending to be discreet, as one must be with a certain sort of letter. But nevertheless, one may show such to a confessor such as I."

"Maitre Cardinal," said Athos before Aramis could speak. "The letter is a lover's letter, as you have guessed. But it is no lover of their eminence, and thus of no concern to you." The calmness still held in the musketeer's voice was all the more terrible, because all understood that she risked her head in making this reply.

The cardinal became as ashen as death. The gleam of their eyes was as lightning as they turned round as if to give an order to Cahusac and Houdiniere. Athos saw this movement and made a step toward the muskets, upon which the other three friends had all fixed their eyes, in the manner of soldiers ill-disposed to allow themselves to be taken.

The cardinal paused, keeping their silence. Even with Cahusac and Houdiniere at their side, if the musketeers were truly conspiring, that troop would be eight, valets included, against their eminence's three. And so by one of those rapid turns which Richelieu always had at their command, all their anger faded away into a smile.

"Well, well," said they. "You are brave young soldiers, proud in daylight, faithful in darkness. We can find no fault with you for watching over yourselves, when you watch so carefully over others. Gentles, I have not forgotten the night in which you served me as an escort to the Red Dovecote. If there were any danger to be feared on the ride I take today, I would request you to accompany me. But as there is none, remain where you are to finish your bottles, your game, and your letter. Adieux."

The calmness still held in the musketeer's voice was all the more terrible, because all understood that she risked her head in making this reply...

Remounting their horse where Cahusac held it, the cardinal saluted the four, then rode away. And as their eminence departed, none could hear them murmur, "Decidedly, those four will be mine."

The four musketeers, all standing motionless, followed the cardinal with their eyes without speaking a word, until their eminence had disappeared. Then they looked at one another.

The expressions of all gave evidence of the same misgivings. For notwithstanding the friendly adieux of their eminence, the four friends each plainly understood that the cardinal had gone away with rage in their heart.

Athos alone smiled, with a self-possessed, disdainful air.

Porthos was first to speak. "That Grimaud kept bad watch," grumbled he, who had a great inclination to vent his ill humor on someone. Grimaud was about to reply to excuse herself, but Athos lifted a finger and the valet was silent.

"Would you have given up the letter, Aramis?" said d'Artagnan.

"I? Oh, yes," said Aramis in a most determined voice. "I had made up my mind that if their eminence had insisted upon the letter being given up to them, I would have presented it with one hand. And with the other, I would have run my sword through their body."

"I expected as much," said Athos. "And that was why I threw myself between you and them. Indeed, this cardinal shows much arrogance for talking thus to other soldiers. One might believe they had never had any engagement not involving talking down to children."

"My dear Athos, I admire you," said Aramis. "But nevertheless, we were in the wrong, after all."

"How in the wrong?" said Athos. "Whose, then, is the air we breathe? Whose is the ocean upon which we look? Whose is the sand upon which we were reclining? Whose is that long-awaited letter from your friend of Tours? Do these belong to the cardinal? Upon my honor, this villain fancies the world belongs to them. There you all stood, stammering, stupefied, overwhelmed. One might have supposed the Bastille's stone walls had appeared before you, and turned you into stone in your turn."

"You are needlessly cruel, Athos," said Aramis. "I simply point out that we are conspiring, as the cardinal challenged. Even at large from the camp, we must be more careful."

"Fie!" said Athos. "Is being in love conspiring? D'Artagnan is in love with an innocent tailor whom the cardinal has caused to be exiled and shut away, and we all now wish to get her out of exile and safe from Richelieu's plots. That's the game we are playing with their eminence, and this letter is our hand. So will you expose your hand to your adversary? Never! Let them find it out if they can, as we will find out theirs."

"Forgive me, Athos," said Aramis.

"As always," said Porthos, "you have the sense of it."

"For my part," said d'Artagnan, "I love and respect you both, but this debate will destroy me. Aramis, this is that letter promised by Madame de Chevreuse? Then I beseech you, read aloud what you had seen and smiled at when the cardinal interrupted you."

"Willingly," said Aramis, who drew the letter from their pocket. The three friends surrounded them, and the valets grouped themselves again near the flagon of wine as the gentle musketeer read:

My dear cousin —

I think I shall make up my mind to set out for Bethune, where my sister has placed our young friend in the convent of the Carmelites. This poor child is quite happy in her place there, as she knows she cannot live elsewhere without the salvation of her soul being in danger.

Still, if the affairs of our family are arranged, as we hope they will be, I believe she will be ready to return to those she misses, particularly as she knows they are always thinking of her. Meanwhile, she is saddened but resolute. What she says she most desires is a letter from her intended. I know that such things pass with difficulty through convent gratings, but I will take charge of the commission. My sister thanks you for your good and eternal remembrance. She has experienced much anxiety of late, but she is now at length a little reassured, hearing of your good health.

Adieux, my dear cousin. Tell us news of yourself as often as you can. Which is to say, as often as you can with safety. I embrace you.

— Marie Michon

To this letter was added an order, dated and conceived in these terms:

At the Louvre —

The superior of the convent of Bethune will place in the hands of the person who shall present this note the traveler who entered the convent upon my recommendation and under my patronage.

— Anne

"At long last!" said d'Artagnan. "Dear Constance! Oh, Aramis, I owe you and your friend of Tours all the world. But pray, what are the Carmelites?"

"A contemplative and scholarly order," said Aramis. "They keep far from any intrigues of the church, and should thus draw little attention that would thwart your Madame Bonacieux's safety."

"And where is Bethune?"

It was Athos who responded. "Upon the frontiers of Artois and of Flanders," said she, and there was something cold in her tone.

"Do you know it then?" said d'Artagnan.

Athos shrugged her shoulders. "It is a small town, which I might have visited in years past. But as fortune permits, we may wish to make a new tour in that direction. I shall raise the question with Monsieur de Treville of traveling north if any talk of leave is made. Though I will tell him nothing of the reason, of course, as this secret must be kept from the cardinal's agents at all costs."

"Faith, but it would surprise me if any leave is to be obtained until this siege is over," said Aramis.

"But that will not be long, it is to be hoped," said Porthos. "For each captured spy makes it more clear than the last that the Rochellais are reduced to the very last of their stores."

"Poor fools," said Athos, pouring for herself a glass of excellent Bordeaux wine. "They are brave to a fault, but they have not learned that the most advantageous and agreeable of all religions is that one supplied with the superior army."

"Fie!" interrupted Porthos. "What in faith are you doing, Aramis?"

This question was in response to Aramis refolding the letter and order, and being about to return both to their pocket, which they said in so many words.

"No," said Athos, thoughtful. "Rather, with d'Artagnan's blessing, Porthos, you shall hold the order. For the cardinal has fresh reason to watch d'Artagnan, Aramis, and I now, but less care to suspect you."

Both Porthos and d'Artagnan indicated by nods their agreement, and Porthos took the order to carefully secure within his jacket. "Still, the cardinal's suspicions make the letter too much risk even alone," said he. "It must be destroyed."

"I would call for it to be burned," said d'Artagnan. "And yet because Maitre Cardinal knows that we held the letter here, and will guess that we have left it behind, who knows whether they have not a secret technique to interrogate ashes?"

"They no doubt have many," said Porthos.

"What will we do with the letter, then?" asked Aramis.

"Come here, Grimaud," said Athos. Grimaud rose and obeyed. "As a punishment for having spoken without permission, my friend, you will please eat this piece of paper. Then to reward you for the service you will have rendered us, you shall afterward drink this glass of wine. First, here is the letter. Eat heartily."

Grimaud sighed. And with her eyes fixed upon the glass which Athos held in her hand, she ground the paper well between her teeth and then swallowed it.

"Bravo!" said Athos. "And now, unless the cardinal should form the ingenious idea of ripping up Grimaud, I think we may be at our ease respecting the letter. Madame Grimaud, take this glass as your reward. We dispense with your saying grace."

Grimaud then silently sipped the glass of Bordeaux wine. But her eyes, raised to the darkening sky during this delicious occupation, spoke a language which, though mute, was nonetheless expressive.

— CHAPTER 52 —

FIRST DAY OF CAPTIVITY

Let us now return to Milord, whom we shall find still in the despairing attitude in which we left him, plunged into an abyss of dismal reflection. Over the first long night of his incarceration, Milord did not sleep, for all his thought was a storm whose void he could not escape, and at which he had almost left hope behind. Because for the first time, he doubted. For the first time, he feared.

On two occasions over the past two months, Milord's fortune had failed him. On two occasions, he had found himself discovered and betrayed. And on both those occasions, it was one fatal genius to whom he had succumbed, sent seemingly by nefarious fate to combat him.

D'Artagnan.

The young Gascon had deceived him in love, had humbled him in pride, had thwarted him in ambition. And now, Milord was certain that it was she who had ruined his fortune, deprived him of liberty, and even threatened his life. Still more, she had lifted the corner of Milord's mask — that shield with which he had long covered himself, and which had seemingly long rendered him invulnerable to harm.

Somehow, though as yet he could not assess the details, Milord felt that it could have been only d'Artagnan who had turned aside from Buckingham the tempest with which Richelieu threatened him. D'Artagnan had passed herself upon him as the Countess de Wardes, for whom Milord had long nurtured a seductive obsession that had fairly burned within him. D'Artagnan knew that terrible secret which Milord had sworn no one should know without dying. And just at the moment at which he had obtained from Richelieu the absolution by which he could have taken vengeance on his enemy, that precious paper was torn from his hands — by a ghost. By an executioner he had thought dead, and who threatened Milord anew with death should he even think to harm her friend.

That friend? D'Artagnan.

Milord was a prisoner, sentenced to exile to some filthy colony, some infamous settlement across the ocean. All that, he owed to d'Artagnan, without doubt. For she alone could have transmitted to Liege de Winter all the frightful secrets his sibling-in-law had discovered.

But in order for Milord to avenge himself, he must be free. And to be free, a prisoner has to pierce a wall, detach bars, cut through a floor — all undertakings which a patient and strong person might accomplish over months, years. And he had at most ten days, as his familial and terrible jailer had informed him.

As dawn brightened the window to mark the start of the first day of his captivity, Milord sat in the same armchair in which he had spent the night, consumed by convulsions of rage that he could not suppress. But when he finally stood, by degrees, he overcame the outbursts of his mad fury. The nervous convulsions which racked his frame disappeared, until he remained folded within himself like a fatigued serpent in repose.

"Come, come," said he, gazing into a mirror as he paced the room. "I must have been mad to allow myself to be carried away so." In his reflection, he saw the burning gaze by which he appeared to interrogate himself. "No violence. For violence is the proof of weakness. Let lesser folk succeed by that means, while I employ a strength they will never see."

Then, as if to render an account to himself of the changes he could place upon his expression, so ever variable, Milord made it take on the full range of emotions, from passionate anger, which convulsed his features, to that of the most sweet, most affectionate, and most seducing smile.

At length he murmured, at peace with himself, "There, nothing is lost. For I am still beautiful."

Taking stock of his possessions likewise buoyed Milord's spirits. All his trunks and packages had accompanied him, including his finest clothing. Aside from the blade that Mistress Felton had stolen beforehand, his sibling-in-law had left him all he carried, including his writ for sanctuary and the purse of two thousand pistoles. It was all the more diabolical of Liege de Winter, leaving Milord all his worldly goods and benefits, but with full understanding of how ill they would serve him now.

It was then nearly eight in the morning by the chamber's wall clock. Milord assessed the bed he had previously seen, and calculated that the repose of a few hours would not only refresh his head and his ideas, but still further, his appearance. A better idea, however, soon came into his mind.

Having sent back the supper offered him the previous night, Milord suspected his captors could not long delay bringing him new nourishment. The prisoner did not wish to lose time. And he resolved that he should make that very morning some initial attempts to ascertain the nature of the ground he had to work upon, by studying the characters of those to whose guardianship he had been committed.

Presently, footsteps were heard outside the door that announced the reappearance of Milord's jailers. Where he paced, he threw himself quickly into his armchair, his head thrown back. His appearance he made slack and disheveled, with one hand on his heart and the other hanging down.

The bolts were drawn. The door groaned upon its hinges. Steps sounded in the chamber and drew near.

"Place that table there," said a voice which the prisoner recognized through closed eyes as that of Mistress Felton. Movement was heard, as if in response to the order. "When you are done, you will relieve the sentinel," continued the young lieutenant.

This double order which Felton gave to the same individuals proved to Milord that his servants were the same as those who had been his guards. Which is to say, soldiers. Consistent with that, Felton's orders were executed with a silent rapidity that gave a good idea of the way in which she maintained discipline.

At length, Milord heard Felton's footsteps draw toward him.

"He is asleep," said she aloud. "Well enough. He can break his fast cold when he wakes." Then she turned back toward the door.

"But my lieutenant," said a soldier less stoic than their chief, whose footsteps likewise drew near, "this prisoner is not asleep."

"What, not asleep?" said Felton. "What is he doing, then?"

"He has fainted. Note how his face is pale, and listen. One can barely hear him breathe."

"You are right," said Felton, though her footsteps did not advance. "Go and tell Liege de Winter that their prisoner has fainted. For I will not call the healer without their orders."

Milord then opened his eyes but a crack, having long practiced the art of looking through his long eyelashes without giving away his awareness. He thus saw the soldier step out to obey the directive of their officer, and saw Felton sit down upon the second armchair after pulling it near the door. The lieutenant waited without speaking a word, without making a gesture, her back toward him.

Milord guessed easily that if Liege de Winter came to investigate his health, their presence would give fresh strength to his jailer. And with his first trial against his sibling-in-law already having been lost, it was time to reckon up his resources.

Slowly, with an air of suffering, he raised his head, opened his eyes, and murmured deeply.

At this sound, Felton turned round.

"Ah, you are awake, sir," said she. "Then I have nothing more to do here. If you want anything, you can ring."

"By my faith… where am I?" said Milord, in a weak voice like that of a child's, from which all threat had been emptied. He assumed upon sitting up in the armchair a hunched and forsaken posture.

Felton arose, seemingly ignoring her prisoner's words. "You will be served thus, sir, three times a day," said she. "Breakfast in the morning at nine o'clock, dinner in the afternoon at one o'clock, and supper in the evening at eight. If that does not suit you, you may establish what other hours you prefer, and in this respect, your wishes will be complied with."

"Ah, I remember now," said Milord weakly. "But am I to remain always alone in this vast and dismal chamber?"

"Alone? No, sir. For I attend on you at your sibling's command."

"I thank you, mistress," replied the prisoner humbly.

Felton made a slight bow and directed her steps toward the door. At the moment she was about to go out, Liege de Winter appeared in the corridor, followed by the soldier who had been sent to inform them of Milord's condition. No healer was with her, but they held a vial of restorative salts in their hand.

"Well, what is it?" said they in a cold voice, on seeing the prisoner sitting up and Felton about to go out. "Is this corpse come to life already? Felton, do you not see that my brother-in-law has taken you for a novice, and that this fainting spell was the first act of a comedy of which we shall doubtless have the pleasure of following out all the developments?"

"I did indeed assume so, my liege," said Felton. "But as he is a prisoner of the crown, in situation even if not by deed, I wished to pay him the attention that any prisoner should fairly receive."

Milord made no sign or sound in response, but he held those words of Felton's close. That loyalty to duty was the threat Liege de Winter had held against him when announcing the young lieutenant as her jailer. But in that sense of duty lay a weakness that Milord knew now how to exploit.

"So," said Liege de Winter, laughing, "that pale skin and that pitiful look have not yet softened your heart of stone?"

"No, my liege," said the impassive Felton. "You may be assured that it requires more than such deceits to sway me."

"In that case, my brave lieutenant, let us leave Milord to his breakfast and take our own. But be assured, he has a fruitful imagination, and the second act of the comedy will not delay its steps after the first."

And at these words, Liege de Winter passed their arm through that of Felton and led her out, laughing.

Behind them, Milord only smiled. But he regained his downcast expression as Liege de Winter stopped at the threshold of the door.

"By the way," said they, "you must not let this setback take away your appetite, brother. Taste the eggs and fruit served to you. On my honor, they are not poisoned. I have a very good cook. And as that cook is not to be my heir, I have full and perfect confidence in them. Adieux, then, till your next swoon."

That was all Milord could endure. His hands clutched his armchair as his teeth clenched. His eyes followed the motion of the door as it closed behind Liege de Winter and Felton — and the moment both were out of view, he stood and cast his eyes upon the table. Seeing there the gleam of a knife, he rushed toward it and seized it. But Milord's disappointment was cruel, for the blade was dull-edged and of malleable silver.

"There!" resounded a voice from the other side of the door — which Milord saw now had only been half-closed. A trap had been set, and he had stepped within it.

"There," said Liege de Winter again as the door reopened. "Do you see, my brave Felton? That knife would have been for you. It has been revealed to me that my brother-in-law yearns to get rid of all the people who bother him, in one way or another. Imagine if you had dismissed my concern, and brought cutlery from the kitchens. With Milord in this state of rage, I fear we would have had no more of Mistress Felton, for he would have cut your throat with it."

Milord still held the harmless weapon in his clenched hand. But Liege de Winter's last words sapped his strength and will. The knife fell to the ground.

"You were right, my liege," said Felton, with a tone of profound anger. "You were right and I was wrong."

Both again left the room. But this time, Milord lent a more attentive ear than the first, and heard their steps die away in the distance of the corridor.

"I am lost," murmured he. "I am in the power of villains upon whom I can have no more influence than upon statues of bronze or granite. They know me by heart, and are steeled against all my weapons. And still, I swear that this will not end as they have decreed."

In fact, as this last reflection indicated — this instinctive return to hope — sentiments of weakness or fear did not dwell long in Milord's heart. He sat down at the table, ate from several dishes, and drank a little Spanish wine. And by the time the meal was done, he felt all his resolution return.

Before exhaustion sent him at last to bed, Milord pondered, analyzed, turned on all sides, and examined on all points the words, the steps, the gestures, the signs, and even the silence of his two persecutors. And from this profound, skillful, and anxious study, it was clear that Felton, everything considered, was by far the more vulnerable.

One expression above all recurred to the mind of the prisoner: "You dismissed my concern," Liege de Winter had said of Felton. So Mistress Felton, then, had beforehand been dismissive of Milord's threat.

"Her strength or weakness matters not, then," whispered Milord to himself. "So long as she only perceives that she is stronger than me. More cunning than me. As to the Liege de Winter, they know the opposite is true. I am stronger than them, and so they fear me, and know what they have to expect of me if ever I escape from their hands. It is useless, then, to attempt anything with them. But Felton — that is another thing. That one has, despite her stoic nature, a spark of overconfidence in her soul. And of that spark, I will make a flame that shall devour her."

Milord slept twice and ate twice more that day, ignoring Mistress Felton, who spoke only to the soldiers under her command. Liege de Winter made no appearance, which suited Milord's designs, focused as those designs were on restoring his energy, and on plotting.

Each time he napped, and indeed while he slept away the night, Milord dreamed that he at length had d'Artagnan in his power, and that he was present at the young guard's conviction and sentence of death. And each time he slept, the sight of the Gascon's detestable blood, flowing beneath the axe of the executioner, spread a charming smile upon his lips.

— CHAPTER 53 —

SECOND DAY OF CAPTIVITY

The next morning, Milord awoke refreshed, and all his determination was strengthened once more. For he knew his time was short, and that by that very evening, two days of that time would already be gone.

When Mistress Felton entered his chamber, Milord was still in bed. His complexion had taken on a flushed appearance as a result of the heat of the bedcovers, removed only as he heard the young lieutenant's footsteps draw near the door. As Felton had seen him only in his habitually pale form, Milord judged that his complexion might therefore deceive his captor.

"I am in a fever," said he. "I have not slept a single instant during all this long night. I suffer horribly. Are you likely to be more humane to me than yesterday? All I ask is permission to remain abed."

"Would you like to have a healer called?" said Felton. The young lieutenant directed with a gesture that a table laid out with a fine breakfast be brought into the room by the guards, but did not move from where she stood.

Milord reflected that by adding a healer to the people he had around him, the more people he would need to work upon — and Liege de Winter would no doubt redouble the watch on him, fearing that his illness was part of some feint. But more importantly, a healer might declare his fever feigned — and Milord, having lost the first hand in the game against his sibling, was not willing to lose another.

"Go and fetch a healer?" repeated he. "What would be the good of that? For you declared yesterday that my illness was a comedy. It would be just the same today, no doubt — for since yesterday evening, you have had plenty of time to send for a healer."

"Then say yourself, sir, what treatment you wish followed."

"But how can I tell? I know that I suffer, and that is all. Give me anything you like, for it is of little consequence."

"Then I will fetch Liege de Winter," said Felton.

"No!" cried Milord weakly. "No, mistress, do not call them, I beg you. I am well, I want nothing. Do not call them."

In Milord's performance was so much that was pitiable, so much that was broken, that Felton in spite of herself smiled, and advanced several steps into the room.

"And so it begins…" thought Milord.

"Sir, if you really suffer," said Mistress Felton, "a healer shall be sent for. If you attempt to deceive us — well, it will be the worse for you."

Milord made no reply. But turning his head round upon the pillow, he burst into tears.

Felton surveyed him for a moment with her usual impassiveness. Then, seeing that the scene threatened to continue, she went out.

"She smiles at my distress," murmured Milord with a savage joy, "and I fancy I begin to see my way." He then buried himself under the bedcovers to conceal from anyone who might be watching him this burst of inward satisfaction.

Two hours passed, and Milord judged it was time that his fever should be over. The breakfast that had been brought remained still untouched, and he guessed that the guards could not long delay coming to clear the table, and that Felton would then reappear.

He was not wrong. By that time, Milord was reclining in the armchair near the cold hearth, pale and resigned. Mistress Felton was at the door as it opened again, and without observing whether Milord had or had not touched his morning meal, she made a sign that the table should be carried out of the room.

Felton remained behind when all had been cleared. She held a book in her hand.

The young lieutenant approached Milord, and said, "Liege de Winter, who is a Catholic like yourself, sir, thinking that the deprivation of the rites and ceremonies of your church might be painful to you, has consented that you should read every day your liturgy. Here then is a book of prayer and ritual."

At the manner in which Felton laid the book upon the little table near which Milord was sitting, at the tone in which she pronounced the words, 'your liturgy,' and at the disdainful smile which accompanied those words, Milord raised his head and looked more attentively at the lieutenant.

He noted as he had on the deck of *Judith* the plain arrangement of Felton's hair. The uniform of extreme simplicity. The brow polished like marble, and as hard and impenetrable. And by those things, Milord recognized one of those gloomy Puritans he had so often met, not only in the English court but in France where they sometimes came to seek refuge.

The villainous gentry then had one of those sudden inspirations which come only in great crises, setting the stage for turning points which may come to decide one's fortune — or their life.

Those two words — 'your liturgy' — and a simple glance cast upon Felton revealed to Milord all the importance of the reply he was about to make. And with that quickness of deceit which was innate in him, this reply, ready arranged, presented itself to his lips.

"I?" said he, with a tone of disdain which mimicked to perfection that which he had noted in the voice of the young lieutenant. "I, mistress? My liturgy? Liege de Winter, the corrupted Catholic, knows very well that I am not of their religion, and this is a trap they wish to lay for me."

"And of what religion are you, then, sir?" asked Felton, with a degree of surprise which, in spite of the control she held over herself, she could not entirely conceal.

"I will tell it," murmured milord, "on the day when I shall have suffered sufficiently for my faith."

Felton remained mute and motionless. But to Milord, the look of the young lieutenant revealed the full extent of the space he had opened for himself with his words.

"I am in the hands of my enemies," continued Milord, with that devoted tone which he knew was familiar to the Puritans. "Well, let my faith save me, or let me perish for my faith. That is the reply I beg you to make to Liege de Winter. And as to this book," added he, "you may carry it back and make use of it yourself." He pointed to the manual with his finger but without touching it, as if he might be contaminated by it. "For doubtless you are doubly the accomplice of Liege de Winter — the accomplice in their persecutions, and the accomplice in their heresies."

Felton made no reply, took the book with the same appearance of repugnance which she had before manifested, and pensively withdrew.

Liege de Winter came at just after five o'clock in the evening. Milord had had time during the day to formulate his plan of conduct, and he received his sibling-in-law like someone who had already recovered all the advantages his present circumstances had taken away.

"It appears," said Liege de Winter, seating themself in the armchair opposite that occupied by Milord, "that we have engaged in a little apostasy." They stretched out their legs casually upon the hearth.

"What do you mean, sibling?"

"I mean to say that since we last met, you have changed your faith. You have not by chance married a Protestant for a third spouse, have you?"

"Explain yourself, if you please," said Milord in a tone of innocence. "For though I hear your words, I declare I do not understand them."

"Then you have no religion at all? I like that best," said Liege de Winter coldly.

"Certainly that is most in accord with your own principles."

"Oh, I confess it is all the same to me."

"You need not avow this religious indifference, my liege. Your own debaucheries and crimes would vouch for it."

"What? You talk of debaucheries, sir? Either I misunderstand you or you are very shameless."

"You only speak thus because you are overheard," said Milord evenly. "And you wish to bias your jailers and your executioners against me."

"My jailers and executioners? Faith, brother, but you are taking a poetical tone, and the comedy of yesterday turns to a tragedy this evening. As to the rest, you will soon be where you ought to be, and my task will be completed."

"You are an infamous villain. And that is an immoral sentence," cried Milord, speaking suddenly with the broken voice of a victim who pleads with their judge.

"My word," said Liege de Winter, rising. "I think my brother is going mad. Come, calm yourself, sir, or I'll remove you to a true cell. It is my Spanish wine that has got into your head, is it not? But never mind. That sort of intoxication is less dangerous than your usual manner of being drunk on power."

As Liege de Winter departed, Mistress Felton was revealed behind the door, where she had heard each word of this scene — as Milord had intended.

"Yes, go," whispered he after the door had closed, his head turned away. "And let the consequences of your betrayal follow you, sibling. And you, Mistress Felton, weak fool, will not see those consequences until it is too late."

Silence was reestablished, and two hours passed away. When Milord's supper was brought in, he was found deeply engaged in saying his prayers aloud — prayers which he had learned of an old servant of his second wife, a most austere Puritan. He appeared to be in meditation, and did not pay the least attention to what was going on around him. Mistress Felton made a sign that he should not be disturbed, and when the table was arranged, she went out quietly with the guards.

Milord knew he might be watched, so he continued his prayers to the end. And it appeared to him that the soldier who was on duty at his door did not march with their regular step, as if they slowed to listen until he was done.

When he at last arose, he came to the table, ate but little, and drank only water. An hour after, the guards entered and the table was cleared. Mistress Felton was seen in the corridor, her eyes on Milord, but the young lieutenant did not enter.

When half an hour had passed away, all was silence in the old castle. Nothing was heard but the eternal murmur of the waves where that immense breaking of the ocean beat far beyond the window. Then Milord, with the powerful voice that had once regaled d'Artagnan, began to recite the first couplet of a psalm. The verses were not excellent — but such was not the point. For his choice was a psalm that spoke of piety and weakness, and Milord did not dwell upon its poetry.

While speaking, he listened. The soldier on guard at his door stopped pacing for a time, and Milord continued with inexpressible feeling. Then through the door, the guard called, "Hold your tongue, sir! Your oratory is dismal, and if besides the pleasure of being in garrison here, we must hear such things as these, no mortal will hold out."

"Silence!" then exclaimed another voice which Milord recognized as that of Mistress Felton. "What concern is this of yours? You are told to guard the prisoner, and to respond if he attempts to flee. Guard him, then, but do not exceed your orders."

An expression of unmistakable elation crossed the face of Milord, but this expression was as fleeting as the brightness of lightning. Without appearing to have heard the dialogue beyond the door, he began again, giving to his voice all the frailty he could bestow upon it.

When the recitation was ended, Milord watched as the door was opened. Mistress Felton appeared, stoic as usual. But Milord noted a dire unease in her gaze.

"Why do you speak thus?" said she.

"Your pardon, mistress," said Milord with eyes downcast. "I forgot that a verse of hope would be out of place in this prison. I have perhaps offended you in your faith, but it was without wishing to do so, I swear. Pardon me, then, a fault which is perhaps great, but which certainly was involuntary."

Milord appeared so full of grace at that moment that when he looked up to Felton, he saw her gaze fixed upon him as if he might be the holy poet whom she had only just before heard. "Yes, yes," said she. "You disturb the people who live in the castle."

The poor, senseless officer was not aware of the incoherence of her words, while Milord was reading with his lynx's eyes the very depths of her heart.

"I will be silent, then," said he, casting down his gaze with all the sweetness he could give to his voice, with all the resignation he could impress upon his manner.

"No, no, sir," said Felton. "Simply do not speak your verses so loud, particularly at night."

And at these words, Felton, looking as though she could not long maintain her severity toward her prisoner, rushed out of the room.

— **CHAPTER 54** —

THIRD DAY OF CAPTIVITY

Mistress Felton had taken her first misstep, Milord well knew. But the young lieutenant must be lured on further still. It was necessary that Milord engage her — or, rather, that Felton engage in Milord's entrapment of her own accord. And he had already come to see the means that could lead to this result.

The young lieutenant would need to be made to speak, in order that she might be spoken to. For Milord very well understood that his greatest power was in his voice, which had shaped dalliances with and controlled the fates of countless folk. He understood that Felton had been forewarned that this was his power, but his assessment of her promised to overcome this. For by using his voice to convince her of his own weakness, the feigning of Milord's weakness would become his strength.

For all the next day, Milord observed all Felton's actions, all her words, from the simplest glance of her eyes to her gestures — even to a breath that could be interpreted as a sigh. In short, he studied everything, as a skillful actor does to whom a new part has been assigned in a performance to which they are not accustomed.

Face to face with Liege de Winter, his plan of conduct was more easy. He had laid that down the preceding evening. To remain silent and dignified in their presence, from time to time to irritate them by affected disdain or a contemptuous word, to provoke them to threats and hints of violence which would produce a contrast with his own passivity — such was his plan.

Felton, though, would see all. She would perhaps say nothing at the outset, but she would see.

In the morning, Felton came as usual, but Milord allowed her to preside over all the preparations for breakfast without addressing a word to her. At the moment when the young lieutenant was about to withdraw, he was cheered with a ray of hope, for he thought she was about to speak. But her lips moved without any sound leaving her mouth, and making a powerful effort to control herself, she went out.

Toward midday, Liege de Winter entered. It was a tolerably fine day, and a ray of that pale English sun which lights but does not warm came through the bars of Milord's prison. He was looking out at that window, and pretended not to hear the door as it opened.

"Ah," said Liege de Winter. "After having played comedy, after having played tragedy, we are now playing melancholy?"

The prisoner made no reply.

"Yes, yes," continued his sibling-in-law. "I understand. You would like very well to be at liberty on that nearby shore. You would like very well to be in a good ship dancing upon the waves of that emerald-green sea. You would like very well, either on land or on the ocean, to lay for me one of those nice little ambushes you are so skillful in planning. Patience, then. For in little time at all, the shore will be beneath your feet and the sea will be open to you. More open than will perhaps be agreeable to you, in fact. For soon, England will be relieved of you."

Milord folded his hands and closed his fine eyes. "All the higher powers," said he with a meek tone, "pardon this one as I myself pardon them."

"Yes, pray, accursed villain," said Liege de Winter. "For your prayer is so much the more generous from your being in the power of one who will never pardon you." And they went out.

At the moment Liege de Winter departed, a piercing glance darted through the opening of the nearly closed door. Milord saw Felton there, who drew quickly to one side to prevent being seen by him.

Then Milord threw himself upon his knees and began to pray. "By my faith" said he, "thou knowest in what holy cause I suffer. Give me, then, strength to suffer."

The door opened gently. The fearful supplicant pretended again not to hear the noise, and in a voice broken by tears, he continued. "God of vengeance. God of goodness. Will thou allow the frightful projects of my sibling to be accomplished?"

Only then did Milord appear to hear the sound of Felton's footsteps, and rising quick as thought, he cast down his eyes as if ashamed of the tears that filled them.

"I do not like to disturb those who pray, sir," said Felton, seriously. "Do not disturb yourself on my account, I beseech you."

"How do you know I was praying, mistress?" said Milord, in a voice broken by weeping. "You were deceived. I was not praying."

"Do you think, then, sir," said Felton, in the same serious voice but with a milder tone, "that I assume the right of preventing a creature from prostrating themself before their maker? Faith forbid. Besides, repentance becomes the guilty. For me, whatever crimes they may have committed, the guilty are sacred at the feet of god."

"Guilty? I?" said Milord, with a smile which might have disarmed any angelic judge. "Guilty? By my faith, you know whether I am guilty. Say I am condemned, mistress, if you please. But you know that god, who loves martyrs, sometimes permits the innocent to be condemned."

"Whether you were condemned, were an innocent, or were a martyr," said Felton, "the greater would be the necessity for prayer. And I myself would aid you with my prayers."

"Oh, you are just," cried Milord, throwing himself at the young lieutenant's feet. "I can hold out no longer, for I fear I shall be wanting in strength at the moment when I shall be forced to undergo the struggle, and confess my faith. Listen, then, to my supplication of despair. You are deceived by others, mistress, but that is not the issue. I only ask you one favor, and if you grant it me, I will bless you in this world and in the next."

"Speak to the Liege de Winter, sir," said Felton. "Happily, I am neither charged with the power of pardoning nor punishing. It is upon one higher placed than I am that this responsibility has been laid."

"But I speak to you. To you alone! Listen to me, rather than add to my destruction, rather than add to my disgrace!"

"If you have merited this shame, sir, if you have incurred this disgrace, you must submit to it as an offering to god."

"What do you say? Oh, you do not understand me. When I speak of disgrace, you think I speak of some chastisement, of imprisonment or death. But of what consequence to me is imprisonment or death?"

"It is I who no longer understands you, sir," said Felton, showing now her confusion.

"Or, rather, you who pretends not to understand me, mistress," said the prisoner with a skeptical smile.

"No, sir. I do not understand, on the honor of a soldier, and on my faith."

"What, you are ignorant of Liege de Winter's designs against me?"

"I am."

"Impossible. You are their confidant!"

"I never lie, sir."

"Oh, but they conceal their intent too little for you not to divine it."

"I seek to divine nothing, sir. I wait till I am confided in, and apart from that which Liege de Winter has said to me before you, they have confided nothing to me."

"Why, then," said Milord, with an incredible tone of surprise, "you are not their accomplice. You do not know that they doom me to a disgrace which all the punishments of the world cannot equal in horror?"

"You are deceived, sir," said Felton, frowning. "Liege de Winter is not capable of such a crime."

"Good," thought Milord to himself. "Without thinking what it is, she calls it a crime." Then aloud, he said, "As a friend to that vile traitor, I fear my sibling is capable of everything."

"Whom do you call 'that vile traitor'?" asked Felton.

"Are there, then, in England two villains to whom such an epithet can be applied? Are there two lord dukes at the right hands of the royals, who would betray their homeland for vanity and the glory they crave?"

"You mean the Duke of Buckingham?" asked Felton. And Milord heard the young lieutenant's voice betrayed by a sudden ire.

"I mean him who claims that title, in defiance of morality and the people's will," said he. "I could not have thought that there was anyone in all England who would have required so long an explanation to make them understand of whom I was speaking."

Felton glanced once toward the door, as if wary of having her next words heard. "The arm of the law is stretched over him," said she, "as it is for all. He will not escape the chastisement he deserves."

In those words, Milord heard expressed that feeling of loathing which all English but the highest gentry had declared toward George Villiers, the Lord Duke of Buckingham. Favored by king and queen, despite his long history of failure in matters military and political alike. But in the young lieutenant's features, Milord noted a deeper anger still.

"Oh, my faith," whispered Milord. "When I supplicate you to pour upon this villain the chastisement which is his due, you must know it is not my own vengeance I pursue, but the deliverance of a whole nation that I implore."

"Do you know him, then?" asked Felton.

"At length, she interrogates me!" said Milord to himself, at the height of joy at having obtained so quickly such a great result. "Oh, know him?" he said aloud. "Yes, yes, to my misfortune. To my eternal misfortune." And he rubbed his arms as if in an outbreak of grief.

Felton's expression left no doubt that she sensed her own strength abandoning her, and she made several steps toward the door. But the prisoner, whose eyes never left her, sprang in pursuit of her and stopped her.

"Mistress," cried Milord, slipping his hands to Felton's. "Be kind, be clement, and listen to my plea. That knife, which the fatal prudence of the Liege de Winter deprived me of, because they know the use I would make of it… no, hear me to the end! That knife, give it to me for one minute only, for mercy's, for pity's sake. You shall shut the door that you may be certain I contemplate no injury to you. But one minute with that knife, one minute, a single minute, and I will restore it to you through the grating of the door. Only one minute, Mistress Felton, and you will have saved my honor."

"One minute to kill yourself?" said Felton with horror, forgetting to withdraw her hands from the hands of the prisoner.

"I have told you, mistress," murmured Milord, lowering his voice and withdrawing his hands as he allowed himself to sink to the ground. "I have told my secret. My sibling knows all. My faith, I am lost!"

Felton remained standing, motionless and undecided.

"She still doubts," thought Milord. "I have not been earnest enough."

Someone was heard then in the corridor. Milord recognized the step of Liege de Winter.

Felton recognized it also, and made a step toward the door.

Milord sprang toward her once more. "Oh, not a word," said he in a strained voice. "Not a word to my sibling of all that I have said to you, or I am lost, and it would be you… you…"

Then as the steps drew near, he became silent for fear of being heard. Milord applied, with a gesture of infinite terror, his beautiful hand to Felton's mouth.

Felton gently pushed him back, and Milord sank into a chair.

Liege de Winter passed before the door without stopping, and the noise of their footsteps soon died away.

Felton, as ashen as death, remained some moments with her ear bent and listening. Then, when all was quite silent once more, she breathed like one awaking from a dream, and rushed out of the apartment.

"And now," whispered Milord, listening in his turn to the noise of Felton's steps, which withdrew in a direction opposite to those of Liege de Winter. "Now you are mine."

But then his expression grew somber. "If she tells my sibling," said he, "I am lost. For the Liege de Winter, who knows very well that I shall not kill myself, will place me before Felton with a knife in my hand. And unless I am quick and true enough to kill both at once, she will discover that all this despair is but acted."

He then placed himself before the mirror and regarded himself attentively. Never had he appeared more beautiful.

"Oh, yes," said he, smiling. "But she will not tell…"

In the evening, Liege de Winter accompanied Milord's supper as it was delivered.

"My liege," said Milord, "is your presence an indispensable accessory of my captivity? Could you not spare me the increase of torture which your visits cause me?"

"How, dear brother?" said Liege de Winter. "Did not you sentimentally inform me with that fine mouth of yours, so cruel to me today, that you came to England solely for the pleasure of seeing me at your ease? Did you not say that so deprived you were of my company that you had risked everything for it — seasickness, tempest, captivity? Well, here I am, so all is well. Besides, this time my visit has a motive."

Milord shivered, for he feared that Felton had told all. He was already seated. Liege de Winter took a chair, drew it toward Milord, and sat down close beside. Then, taking a paper out of their pocket, they unfolded it slowly.

"Here," said they. "I want to show you the passport I have drawn up, and which will serve you henceforth as the rule of order in the life I consent to leave you."

Then turning their eyes from Milord to the paper, they read: " 'Order to conduct to — ' But you see? The destination is blank. If you have any preference, you can point it out to me. And as long as it be not within a thousand leagues of England, attention will be paid to your wishes. I will begin again, then:

" 'Order to conduct to your destination, the person named Charles Backson, branded by the justice of the realm of France, but liberated after punishment. He is to dwell in this place without ever going more than three leagues from it. In case of any attempt to escape, the penalty of death is to be applied. He will receive five shillings per day for lodging and food'".

"That order does not concern me," said Milord coldly, "since it bears another name than mine."

"A name? Have you a name, then?"

"You well know my name and my title, for it echoes yours by the grace of your sister, my beloved wife."

"Ah, but you are mistaken. For my late sister is only your second wife, and your first is still living. Tell me your name and title when you were first happily betrothed, then, and I will put it in the place of the name of Charles Backson. No? You will not? You are silent? Well, then you must be registered as I see fit."

Milord remained silent. Only this time, it was no longer from affectation but from fear. He believed the order ready for execution, guessing that Liege de Winter had hastened his departure, and that he might well be condemned to set off that very evening. All his thoughts were lost — when all at once, he saw that no signature was attached to the order. The joy he felt at this discovery was so great he could not conceal it.

"Yes, yes," said Liege de Winter, who guessed what was passing in Milord's mind. "You look for the signature, and you say to yourself, 'All is not lost, for that order is not signed. It is only shown to me to terrify me.' But you are mistaken. As soon as the Duke of Buckingham returns to Portsmouth, this order will be sent to him. The day after that, it will return signed by his hand and marked with his seal. And four-and-twenty hours after that, I will answer for its being carried into execution. Adieux, sir. That is all I had to say to you."

"And I reply to you, my liege, that this abuse of power, this exile under a fictitious name, are infamous."

"Would you like better to be hanged in your true name, Milord? You think I did not have your letters and diaries provided to me copied and notarized? Do you pretend to not know the inexorable weight of English law on the abuse of title and inheritance, on speaking plots of murder, of spying for the minister of the French crown? Speak freely, then. For I will risk the scandal of a public trial to make myself certain of getting rid of you."

Milord made no reply, but became as pale as a corpse.

"So I see you prefer journey and exile. For even one as debased as you, when threatened with death, will realize that life is sweet. This is why I take such care that you shall not deprive me of mine. There only remains, then, the question of the five shillings to be settled. You think me rather miserly, don't you? That's because I don't care to leave you the means of corrupting your jailers. Besides, you will always have your charm with which to beguile them. So employ that charm, if your failure with regard to Felton has not disabused you of making attempts of that kind."

"Felton has not told them," said Milord to himself. "All is not lost, then."

"And now, sir, till I see you again. I will be sure to come and announce to you the departure of my messenger."

Liege de Winter rose, saluted ironically, and went out.

Milord breathed again. Even if Liege de Winter sent their messenger forth the next day, two days for that messenger to reach Buckingham and return meant that he had still time enough before him to complete his plans for Felton.

A terrible idea, however, rushed into his mind. He worried that Liege de Winter would perhaps send Felton herself to get the order signed by the Duke of Buckingham. In that case, Felton would escape him — for in order to secure success, the magic of a continuous entrapment was necessary. Nevertheless, as we have said, one circumstance reassured him. Felton had not spoken.

As Milord would not allow himself the appearance of being agitated by the threats of Liege de Winter, he placed himself at the table and ate. Then, as he had done the evening before, he fell on his knees and repeated his prayers aloud. As on the evening before, the soldier on duty stopped their march to listen to him.

Soon after, he heard lighter steps than those of the sentinel, which came from the end of the corridor and stopped before his door.

"The young lieutenant returns," thought he. And he began the same religious chant which had so strongly excited Felton the evening before.

But although his voice — sweet, full, and sonorous — rang out as fully and as affectingly as ever, the door remained shut. It appeared, however, in one of the furtive glances Milord darted from time to time at the grating of the door, that he saw the ardent eyes of the young lieutenant through the narrow opening. But whether this was reality or vision, Felton had this time sufficient self-control not to enter.

Still, a few moments after he had finished his verse of faith, Milord thought he heard a profound sigh. Then the same steps he had heard approach slowly withdrew, as if with regret.

508

CHAPTER 55

FOURTH DAY OF CAPTIVITY

The next day, when Felton entered Milord's apartment, she found him standing, mounted upon a chair, holding in his hands a cord made by means of torn cambric handkerchiefs. These were twisted one with another into a kind of rope, and tied at the ends. At the noise Felton made in entering, Milord leaped lightly to the ground, and tried to conceal the improvised cord behind him.

The young lieutenant was more ashen than usual, and her eyes, reddened by want of sleep, denoted that she had passed a feverish night. Nevertheless, her brow was armed with a severity more austere than ever.

Felton advanced slowly toward Milord, who had seated himself, and seized one end of the murderous rope which by neglect — which is to say, by design — Milord had allowed to be seen.

"What is this, sir?" she asked coldly.

"It is nothing," said Milord, smiling with that painful expression which he knew so well how to give to his smile. "Ennui is the mortal enemy of prisoners. I had ennui, and I amused myself by twisting that rope."

Felton turned her eyes toward the wall of the apartment before which she had found Milord standing in the armchair in which he was now seated. Over his head, she saw a gilt hook, firmly fixed in the wall for the purpose of hanging up clothing or weapons.

She started, and the prisoner saw it — for though his eyes were cast down, nothing escaped him.

"What were you doing on that armchair?" asked the lieutenant.

"It is of no consequence," said Milord.

"Still," said Felton, "I wish to know."

"Do not question me," said the prisoner quietly. "For I would spare myself from speaking false to you, and would spare you from pitying me."

"Well, then, I will tell you what you were doing, or rather what you meant to do. You were going to complete the fatal project you cherish in your mind — and doom your immortal soul in doing so."

"When our god sees one of their creatures persecuted unjustly, placed between suicide and dishonor, believe me, mistress," said Milord in a tone of deep conviction, "their grace will forgive me."

"You say either too much or too little. Speak, sir. In the name of faith, explain yourself."

"That I may relate my misfortunes for you to treat them as fables? That I may tell you my faint hopes for you to go and betray them to my persecutor? No, mistress. Besides, of what importance to you is the life or death of a condemned wretch? You are only responsible for my body, is that not so? And provided you produce a corpse that may be recognized as mine, they will require no more of you. Nay, perhaps you will even have a double reward."

"I, sir?" said Felton, dismayed. "You suppose that I would ever accept the price of your life? You cannot believe what you say."

"Let me act as I please, Felton," said Milord, weary. "Every soldier must be ambitious, must they not? You are a lieutenant? Well, you will follow me to the grave with the rank of captain."

In the flash of wretched anger that came suddenly to Felton's eyes, Milord understood with clarity that rank was a subject close to the young lieutenant's heart — as well as a source of animosity.

"But I see that I guess true," said he, cautious. "Your liege will have already heard your petition for promotion. And the duke they serve will no doubt grant it…"

And there it was! Milord fought back the sudden urge to exultation, remembering the personal animosity Felton had seemed to hold for the Duke of Buckingham the previous day — and seeing in the sudden brightness of the young lieutenant's gaze the fire in which that animosity had been forged. Milord had never met Felton in his time with the Liege de Winter, but the closeness of the two spoke to at least some years of service — and perhaps to apology for Felton having been rejected for promotion in the past. Spurned for advancement by the duke.

"Do not talk of this," said Felton, much agitated now. "But tell me what have I, then, done to you that you should place such responsibility on me? In a few days, you will be away from this place. Your life, sir, will then no longer be under my care. Then, sir, you can do what you will with it."

"So," said Milord, as if he could not resist giving utterance to the indignation. "You, a soldier of honor. You who are called just. You ask but one thing — that you may not be inconvenienced by my death."

"It is my duty to watch over your life, sir, and I will watch."

"But do you understand the mission you are fulfilling? It is cruel enough, if I am guilty. But what name can you give it, what name will justice give it, if I am innocent?"

"I am a soldier, sir, and fulfill the orders I have received. And I repeat it again to you, that no danger threatens your life. I will answer for Liege de Winter as for myself."

"Yes, but I shall lose that which is much dearer to me than life. I shall lose my honor, Felton. And it is you whom I make responsible before all witnesses for my shame and my infamy."

This time, Felton, even as impassive as she was, could not resist the secret influence which had already taken possession of her. To see this man, so virtuous, so bright of defiant spirit — to see him by turns entreating and threatening, and suffering beneath the ascendancy of grief and beauty, was all too much for one as merciful as she. It was too much for a brain weakened by the ardent dreams of an ecstatic faith. It was too much for a heart scarred by the love of faith that burns, and by the hatred of humanity that destroys.

Milord saw the young lieutenant's agitation. He felt by intuition the flame of the opposing passions that burned in the blood of the young fanatic. Like a skillful general seeing the enemy ready to surrender, and who marches toward them with a cry of victory, he rose.

"You see me, Felton. You know me for what I am. A child of earth, a sibling of your faith. But for all that you know me, still you are an accomplice of that sovereign of lies who is called Liege de Winter. You believe me, you say, and yet you leave me in the hands of my enemies, of the enemy of England, of the enemy of faith and justice. You believe, and yet you deliver me up to him who fills and defiles the world with his heresies and debaucheries — to that infamous false king whom the blind call the Duke of Buckingham…"

"I deliver you up to Buckingham? I? What mean you by that?"

"They have eyes," cried Milord, "but they see not. Ears have they, but they hear not."

"Then speak!" said Felton, passing her hands over her brow, covered with sweat. "Speak, speak that I might understand you now!"

On seeing the anguish in the young lieutenant, a flash of terrible joy, rapid as the fastest thought, gleamed from the eyes of Milord — and Felton saw it, and started as if its light had revealed the abysses of this villain's heart.

She recalled all at once the warnings of Liege de Winter regarding the beguilements of Milord, extending back to his first attempts after his arrival. She drew back a step and hung down her head — but without ceasing to look at him, as if in her fascination for this strange creature, she could not detach her eyes from his.

Milord was not one to misunderstand the meaning of this hesitation. Under his apparent emotions, his icy coolness never abandoned him. Before Felton could speak, he let his hands fall. And as if the weakness of his body had overpowered the fear that inspired him, he dropped from the armchair to his knees and spoke.

Liege de Winter then proceeded to the door, but Mistress Felton delayed a long moment before turning to follow…

"The sword of the eternal is too heavy for my arm. Allow me, then, to avoid dishonor by death. Let me take refuge in emptiness. I do not ask you for liberty, as a guilty one would, nor for vengeance. So let me die. That is all. I supplicate you, I implore you on my knees — let me die, and my last sigh shall be a blessing for my preserver."

Hearing that voice, so weak and imploring. Seeing that look, so timid and downcast. So did Felton feel all her misgivings fall away. By degrees, the enchanter had clothed himself with that magic adornment which he assumed and threw aside at will. Which is to say, the meekness and tears, the anger and self-righteousness, which would make the offender appear as the sufferer, and with so subtle an effort.

"Alas," said Felton. "I can do but one thing, which is to pity you if you prove to me you are a victim. But Liege de Winter makes cruel accusations against you. You are my sibling in faith. I feel myself drawn toward you. I who have never loved anyone but my benefactor, I who have met with nothing but traitors and unholy villains. But you, sir, so anguished in reality, so pure in intent, must have committed great iniquities for Liege de Winter to pursue you thus."

"They have eyes," repeated Milord in a whisper of indescribable grief, "but they see not. Ears have they, but they hear not…"

"But speak, then," whispered the young lieutenant. "Speak…"

"Confide my shame to you?" said Milord, with the anguish of his soul upon his face. "I could not. For the shame that is mine to bear is also the crime of another, with which I must not burden you."

"This will be no burden," said Felton. "Not to one who knows her own shame."

Milord looked at the young lieutenant for some time, with an expression which Felton took for doubt — but which in truth was nothing but the enticement to control. "Well, then," said he. "I confide in my comrade. I will dare to —"

At that moment, the steps of Liege de Winter were heard from the corridor. But this time, the terrible sibling-in-law of Milord did not content themself with passing before the door and going away again, as on the preceding day. They paused, exchanging words with the sentinel. Then the door opened and they appeared.

During the exchange of words, Felton drew back quickly, so as to stand several paces from the prisoner. Liege de Winter entered slowly, sending a scrutinizing glance from Milord to the young lieutenant.

"You have been here a very long time, Mistress Felton," said they. "Has this villain been relating his crimes to you? In that case, I can comprehend the length of the conversation."

Felton started, and Milord understood that he was lost if he did not come to the assistance of the disconcerted soldier.

"Ah, you fear your prisoner should escape?" said he, weak of voice. "Well, ask your worthy jailer what favor I solicited of her just yesterday."

"My brother-in-law demanded a favor?" said Liege de Winter of Felton, suspicious.

"Yes, my liege," replied the young lieutenant, confused but responding as by instinct to orders.

"And what favor, pray?"

"A knife, which he would return to me through the grating of the door a minute after he had received it," said Felton.

"I fear there was someone, then, concealed in this room whose throat this amiable villain was desirous of cutting," said Liege de Winter in a contemptuous tone.

"There is only myself," said Milord.

"I have given you the choice between colonial exile and the prison of their majesties," said Liege de Winter. "But if death is instead your wish, the executioner can be called. For believe me, sir, the rope is more certain than the knife."

Felton grew ashen and made a step forward, remembering that at the moment she had entered, Milord had his makeshift rope in hand.

"You are right," said Milord. "I have often thought of it." Then he added in a low voice, "And I will think of it again."

Felton felt a shudder run to the marrow of her bones, and Liege de Winter saw this emotion pass.

"Mistrust yourself, Mistress Felton," said they. "I have placed reliance upon you, my friend. Beware, for I have warned you. But be of good courage. For we shall soon be delivered from this creature, and where I shall send him, he will harm no one."

"You hear them!" cried Milord, eyes raised to the ceiling so that Liege de Winter might believe he was addressing fate itself — and knowing that Felton would understand he was addressing her.

Felton lowered her head, deep in thought.

Liege de Winter then proceeded to the door, but Mistress Felton delayed a long moment before turning to follow. Both looked back as they went, Liege de Winter watching as if not to lose sight of Milord till the door be safely closed. Felton's gaze lingered with more intent, before she, too, turned away.

"Well," said the prisoner to himself when the door was shut. "I am not so far advanced as I believed. Liege de Winter has changed their usual stupidity into a strange prudence. It is the desire of vengeance, and how that desire shapes them. And as to Felton, she hesitates."

Milord waited then with much impatience, for he feared the day would pass away without him seeing Felton again. But at last, only an hour after the scene we have just described, he heard someone speaking in a low voice at the door. Presently that door opened, and Mistress Felton appeared.

The young lieutenant advanced quickly into the chamber, leaving the door open behind her and making a sign to Milord to be silent. Her face was much agitated.

"What do you want with me?" said Milord most meekly.

"To listen," replied Felton in a low voice. "I have just sent away the sentinel that I might remain here without anyone knowing it, in order to speak to you without being overheard. Liege de Winter has just related a frightful story to me."

Milord assumed the anguish of a resigned victim, and shook his head.

"Either you are a monster," said Felton, "or the Liege de Winter, my benefactor, is. I have known you scant days. I have loved my liege for years. I therefore may hesitate between you. Be not alarmed at what I say, for I want only to be convinced. Tonight, after twelve, I will come and see you, and you shall convince me."

"No, Felton," said Milord. "No, my comrade. The sacrifice is too great, and I feel what it must cost you. No, I am lost, so do not be lost with me. My death will be much more eloquent than my life, and the silence of the corpse will convince you much better than the words of the prisoner."

"Be silent, sir," said Felton firmly, "and do not speak to me thus. I came to entreat you to promise me upon your honor, to swear to me by what you hold most sacred, that you will make no attempt upon your life."

"I will not promise," said Milord. "For no one has more respect for a promise or an oath than I have. And if I make a promise, I must keep it."

"Well, then," said Felton, "at least promise till you have seen me again. If, when you have seen me again, you still persist… you shall be free, and I myself will give you the weapon you desire."

"Well, then," said Milord. "For you, I will wait."

"Swear."

"I swear it. Are you satisfied?"

"Well satisfied," said Felton. "Until tonight."

Then she darted out of the room and shut the door. Immediately, Milord drew near the grating, seeing through it that Felton waited in the corridor. She held the sentinel's half-pike in her hand, standing there as if she had mounted guard in their place.

Not long after, the soldier returned and Felton gave them back their weapon. Unseen by the soldier, the young lieutenant turned to the grate to make a sign of secret farewell to Milord, guessing that he watched. She then departed.

Left alone, Milord began to pace with a smile of savage contempt upon his lips. "Mistress Felton, senseless fool," said he. "At my word, you will fall. I swear it. And thereafter, I will avenge myself."

CHAPTER 56

FIFTH DAY OF CAPTIVITY

In his campaign to corrupt the young Lieutenant Felton, Milord had achieved a half-triumph, and success renewed his strength. It was not difficult to conquer, as he had hitherto done, those prone to let their will be controlled, and whom a life of discipline allowed to fall quickly under his sway. Against such opponents, Milord was sufficiently skillful to prevail over all the defenses of even the most refined mind. But this time, he had to contend with an unpolished nature, concentrated and made insensible by force of austerity.

Faith, duty, and the observances of both had given Felton a heart inaccessible to ordinary seductions or entrapments. There cascaded through that focused brain thoughts so rigidly fixed that there remained no room for any doubt fed by leisure or reflection. Milord had, then, made a breach in this stockade by his false virtue. It was a most successful experiment, taking the measure of a kind of resolve hitherto unknown to him, and watching that resolve break like fine crystal.

Nevertheless, more than once during the evening, he despaired of fate and of himself. Milord did not invoke faith in any true form. But he had faith in the genius of evil — that immense sovereignty which records all the details of human life, and by which a single seed is sufficient to reconstruct a ruined world.

Being well prepared for the reception of Felton, Milord was able to ready his defenses. He still knew not how long he had before the order was signed by Buckingham — but knew that Buckingham would sign it readily, whether from its bearing a false name, so that he would not recognize or care about the condemned in question, or whether from Liege de Winter having taken him into their confidence. Once this order was signed, Liege de Winter would make Milord embark immediately. And he knew very well that once condemned to exile, he would employ charms much less powerful in their enchantment and advantage than those he had long made use of.

To be condemned to a painful and disgraceful punishment should be no impediment to influence, he knew. But it would be an obstacle to the use of influence for the recovery of power. Like all persons of real genius, Milord knew what suited his nature and his means. Poverty was repugnant to him, and degradation took away two-thirds of his greatness. He was only a gentry while among gentry, and the pleasure of breaking the pride of equals was a prerequisite of his ability to dominate. To command inferior beings, then, was more a humiliation than a pleasure for him.

He would certainly return from his exile. That, Milord did not doubt for a single instant. But how long might this exile last? To lose a year, two years, three years, would be to talk of an eternity. To return when d'Artagnan and her friends, happy and triumphant, should have received from the queens the reward they had well acquired by their services rendered to the crown. It was a thought he could not endure. A fate he would not endure.

But equally grim in Milord's mind were his thoughts of the Cardinal de Richelieu. What must the mistrustful, restless, suspicious cardinal have been thinking as regards Milord's silence? For their eminence was not merely his primary support, his strongest protector — but still further, was the principal instrument of his future fortune and vengeance.

Milord knew their eminence. He knew that at his return from a fruitless journey, it would be futile to tell them of his imprisonment, futile to expand upon the sufferings he had undergone. For the cardinal would only reply with disdain, strong at once in both power and genius — "You should not have allowed yourself to be taken."

The villainous gentry collected all his energies, then, murmuring in the depths of his soul the name of Felton — the only beam of light that descended to him in the shadow into which he had fallen. And like a serpent that folds and unfolds its coils to ascertain its strength, Milord enveloped Felton beforehand in the thousand tightening cords of his inventive imagination.

Time passed away. The hours, one after another, seemed to awaken the clock as they passed, and every blow of brass hammer on chimes resounded upon the heart of the prisoner.

At nine o'clock, Liege de Winter made their customary visit, examined the window and the bars, sounded the floor and the walls, looked to the chimney and the doors — and all without they or Milord pronouncing a single word during this long and careful examination. Doubtless, both of them understood that the situation had become too serious to lose time in useless words and aimless wrath.

"Well," said Liege de Winter upon turning to leave. "You will not escape tonight."

At ten o'clock, Felton came and placed the sentinel. Milord recognized her step. He was as well acquainted with it now as one might be with the most intimate lover. And yet he at the same time detested and despised this weak fanatic.

That was not the appointed hour. Felton did not enter.

But two hours after, as midnight sounded, the sentinel was relieved. This time it was the hour, and from that moment, Milord waited with impatience. The new sentinel commenced their walk in the corridor. Then, at the end of ten minutes, Felton's footsteps drew near.

Milord was all attention.

"Keep a strict watch," said the young lieutenant to the sentinel. "I am bound to pay a second visit to the prisoner, who I fear entertains sinister intentions upon his own life, and who the Liege de Winter orders to be watched."

"Good," murmured Milord. "The austere Puritan lies."

The door was opened, and Felton entered Milord's apartment. The door was then locked again as Milord arose.

"You are here," said he.

"I promised to come," said Felton, "and I have come."

"You promised me something else."

"What, by faith?" said the young lieutenant.

In spite of Felton's self-control, Milord saw her knees tremble and the sweat start from her brow. "You promised to bring a knife," said he, "and to leave it with me after our interview."

"Say no more of that, sir," said Felton. "There is no situation, however terrible it may be, which can authorize a creature of faith to inflict death upon themself. I have reflected, and I cannot — must not — be guilty of such a sin."

"Ah, you have reflected," said the prisoner, sitting down in his armchair with a smile of disdain. "And I also have reflected."

"Upon what?"

"That I can have nothing to say to one who does not keep their word," said Milord. "You may leave. I will not speak."

"Here is the knife," said Felton, drawing from her pocket the weapon which she had brought, according to her promise — but which she hesitated to give to her prisoner.

"Let me see it," said Milord.

"For what purpose?"

"Upon my honor, I will immediately return it to you. You may then place it on that table, and remain between it and me."

Felton offered the weapon carefully to Milord, who examined the temper of it attentively, and who tried the point on the tip of his finger.

"Well," said he, returning the knife to the young lieutenant. "This is fine and good steel. You are a faithful friend, Felton."

The young lieutenant then took back the weapon and laid it upon the table, as instructed. Milord followed her with his eyes, nodding his satisfaction.

"Now," said he, "listen to me."

The request was needless. The young lieutenant stood attentive before him, awaiting his words as if to devour them.

"Felton," said Milord, with a solemnity full of melancholy. "Imagine that I am your sibling, that I am your friend of a lifetime, as I speak to you thus. Imagine that what I say to you tonight befell them, rather than me. Not so long ago, when I was sadly more trusting than wise, I was dragged into a trap unseen by one who coveted me for the sake of the position I found myself in. For I had newly fallen in love, and blinded by happiness, I did not comprehend how that happiness might be fodder for others' avarice. Such it was for the one who desired to establish an influence over me, for reasons I could not comprehend. A friend they sought to make of me, but there was something in their manner that spoke to my unease. I resisted, cheerfully. They swore, just as cheerfully, that they would see me brought close. But I did not understand their intent as their attentions multiplied around me, and I resisted still. Until finally…"

Milord stopped, and a bitter smile passed over his lips.

"Finally," said Felton. "Finally, what did they do?"

Milord embraced the silence for a moment, in which his breathing and Felton's were the only sound. Then again he spoke.

"Finally, one evening my enemy resolved to paralyze the resistance to their influence they could not conquer. One evening, they mixed a powerful narcotic with a glass of water served to me. Scarcely had I finished drinking when I felt myself sink by degrees into a strange torpor."

Milord began to pace. He let his fingers clutch at one another as he spoke, his hands straying from time to time to strike his breast as if in anguish. And all the while, he wove together the details of a history designed for one purpose only — to break the will of Felton, and to deliver the young lieutenant into his control.

"Although I was without mistrust," said Milord, setting a tremor to his voice, "a vague fear seized me, and I tried to struggle against sleepiness. I arose. I wished to run to the window and call for help, but my legs refused my commands. It appeared as if the ceiling sank upon my head and crushed me with its weight. I stretched out my arms. I tried to speak. But I could utter only inarticulate sounds, and irresistible faintness came over me. I fell upon one knee, then upon both. I tried to pray, but my tongue was frozen, and I sank upon the floor and into a slumber which resembled death.

"Of all that passed in that sleep, or the time which glided away while it lasted, I have no remembrance. The only thing I recollect is that I awoke in bed in a round chamber, the furniture of which was sumptuous, and into which light flowed only through an opening in the ceiling. A fire burned brightly on a hearth to warm the place, venting to an unseen chimney. But no door gave entrance to the room. It might have been called a magnificent prison.

"It was a long time before I was able to make out what place I was in, or to take account of the details I now describe. My mind fought in vain to shake off the heavy torpor of the sleep from which I could not rouse myself. I had vague memories of space traversed, of the rolling of a carriage, of a horrible dream in which my strength had become exhausted. But all this was so gloomy and so indistinct in my mind that these events seemed to belong to another life, but yet one mixed with mine in fantastic duality.

"I arose trembling. New clothes stood in a wardrobe open near me, close by a basin filled with cool water. I had slept in my garments of the previous day, but remembered not going to bed. Then by degrees, the reality broke upon me, full of uncorrupted terrors. I was no longer in the house where I had dwelt. As well as I could judge by the light of the sun that passed in, the day was already two-thirds gone. It was the evening before when I had fallen asleep, so that my sleep, then, must have lasted twenty-four hours. But what had taken place during this long repose?

"I washed and dressed myself as quickly as possible, recognizing that the garments in the wardrobe were of my own closets, and must have been taken from my home. My slow and stiff motions all attested that the effects of the narcotic were not yet entirely dissipated. The chamber was evidently furnished for the needs of a gentry, and even the most demanding gentry would have felt immediate satisfaction upon casting their eyes about the apartment. Certainly, I was not the first captive that had been shut up in this splendid prison. But you may easily comprehend, Felton, that the more superb the prison, the greater was my terror."

"A prison?" whispered Felton. "Our god give me strength, for this tale harrows me."

"Yes, it was a prison, for I tried in vain to get out of it. I sounded all the walls, in the hopes of discovering a door, but everywhere the walls returned a full and flat sound. I made that tour of the room at least twenty times, in search of an outlet of some kind. But there was none. I sank exhausted with fatigue and terror into an armchair.

"Meantime, night came on quickly. And with night, my terrors increased. Although I had eaten nothing since the evening before, my fears prevented my feeling hunger. No noise reached me from beyond the room, by which I might measure the time. I only supposed it must have been seven or eight o'clock in the evening, for it was in the month of October, and it was quite dark.

"All at once, the noise of a door turning on its hinges made me start. A globe of fire appeared above the glazed opening of the ceiling, casting a strong light into my chamber, and I saw with terror that a figure was standing within a few paces of me. A table set with a fine cloth, bearing a supper ready prepared, stood as if by magic in the middle of the apartment. And that figure… that figure was they who had pursued in vain my friendship during a whole year prior. They who had sworn that they would bring me close, and who, by the first words that issued from their mouth, gave me to understand that this prison I found myself in was the culmination of that oath."

"Monster…" whispered Felton.

"Yes. The monster," whispered Milord. He shivered as if his soul might be hanging at his lips, seeing the focus which the young lieutenant directed to his recital of lies. "The monster who sought to use me, who sought to turn me to a serpent in the bosom of the family that had welcomed me. The monster who believed, having seized me in my sleep, that all was completed. They held me, and I was helpless. And they issued then their demand that I should betray the woman I loved and was betrothed to, and the gracious family that I had been accepted into, for the sake of that family's fortune. For the monster had long coveted that fortune from afar, and saw my friendship now as the means by which they might gain access to it even before my marriage was made.

"All that the heart of any warrior could contain of haughty contempt and disdainful words, I poured out upon this villain. Doubtless they were accustomed to such reproaches, for they listened to me, calm and smiling, with their arms crossed over their breast. Then, when they thought I had said all, they advanced toward me. I sprang toward the table, I seized a knife set there, and I placed it to my breast.

" 'Take one step more,' said I, 'and in addition to my words, you shall have my willing death to mark my refusal of your larceny.' There was, no doubt, in my look, my voice, my whole person, that sincerity of gesture, of attitude, of accent, which carries conviction to even the most debased minds. For they paused, and blew a whistle. The globe of fire which lighted the room ascended and disappeared. I found myself again in complete darkness. The same noise of a door opening and shutting was repeated the instant afterward. Then the flaming globe descended again, and I was completely alone.

"This moment was the most frightful. If I had any doubts as to my misfortune, they vanished in an overwhelming reality. I was in the power of one whom I not only detested but despised — a villain capable of anything, and who had already given me a fatal proof of what they were able to do."

"Pray, then, who was this villain?" said Felton. But Milord continued as if he had not heard.

"I passed the night on a chair, starting at the least noise, for toward midnight the lamp went out, and I was again in darkness. But the night passed away without any fresh appearance on the part of my persecutor. Day came. The table had disappeared, though I had still the knife in my hand. This knife that was my only hope.

"I was worn out with fatigue. Sleeplessness inflamed my eyes, for I had not dared to drowse a single instant. The light of day reassured me, though, and I went and threw myself on the bed — though without parting with the knife that strengthened my resolve, which I concealed under my pillow.

"When I awoke, the fire had been rebuilt and a fresh meal was served. This time, in spite of my terrors, in spite of my agony, I began to feel a devouring hunger. It had been forty-eight hours since I had taken any nourishment. I ate some bread and some fruit. Then, remembering the narcotic mixed with the water I had drunk, I would not touch the carafe which was placed on the table, but filled my glass at a marble fountain fixed in the wall over my dressing table.

"I took the precaution to half empty the carafe, in order that my actions might not be noticed. And yet, notwithstanding these precautions, I remained for some time in a terrible agitation of mind. But my fears were this time ill-founded. I passed the day without experiencing any loss of mind of the kind I had experienced when I was brought there. You see, my fear had focused on what manner of deceits might be played on my mind in such a state, and what lies I might be made to believe. For I became convinced that, not being able to procure my alliance "The evening came on, and with it, darkness. But however profound was this darkness, my eyes began to accustom themselves to it. I saw, amid the shadows, the table sink through the floor. Some quarter of an hour later, it reappeared, bearing my supper. In an instant, thanks to the lamp, my chamber was once more lighted.

"I was determined to eat only such things as could not possibly have anything soporific introduced into them. Two eggs and some fruit made up my meal. Then I drew another glass of water from my protecting fountain, and drank it. But at the first swallow, it appeared to me not to have the same taste as in the morning. I threw the rest away with horror, but had already drunk half a glass. No doubt, some unwatched witness had seen me draw the water from that fountain. And, taking advantage of my confidence in it, they had thought to assure my ruin, so coolly resolved upon, so cruelly pursued.

"Half an hour had not passed before the narcotic symptoms began to appear. But those symptoms were different this time, so that instead of falling entirely asleep, I sank into a state of drowsiness. This left me a perception of what was passing around me, even as it deprived me of the strength either to defend myself or to flee.

"I dragged myself toward the bed, to seek the only defense I had left — my guardian knife. But I could not reach the bolster. I sank on my knees, my hands clasped round one of the bedposts. Then I felt that I was lost."

Felton had by this time grown frightfully drawn, and a convulsive tremor crept through her whole body.

"And what was most frightful," continued Milord, his voice altered as if he still experienced the same agony as at that awful moment, "was that this time, I retained a consciousness of the danger that threatened me. It was as though my soul, if I may say so, waked in my sleeping body. And so it was that I saw, that I heard. It is true that all was like a dream, but it was nonetheless frightful.

"I heard the well-known creaking of the door, although I had heard that door open but twice. I felt more than saw that someone approached me, as it is said that a doomed wretch in the deepest desert thus feels the approach of the serpent. I attempted to cry out. By an incredible effort of will, I even raised myself up, but only to sink down again immediately. And to fall into the arms of my attacker."

"Tell me who this monster was!" cried once more the young lieutenant.

Milord saw then at a single glance all the painful feelings he inspired in Felton by the details of his lie — and knew he would not spare her a single shard of that pain. The more profoundly he wounded the young lieutenant's heart, the more certainly she would avenge him. So he continued as if he had not heard her exclamation, or as if he thought the moment was not yet come to reply to it.

"I felt myself rise, and be guided to a chair. The villain sat with me, and I heard their words as from some great distance, as they extolled their tenderness for me and for my newfound family. And to confirm all my fears, I heard my own voice answer in kind, my soul ensnared by honeyed words and the dullness of my mind. Their lies, they fed to me like a fine dessert to follow the meager repast I had made. But still, I felt my faith impose a long resistance, weak as I was. For I heard my tormentor murmur as they left me, 'These miserable Puritans. I knew very well that they exhausted their executioners, but I did not believe them so strong against their saviors...'

Felton listened without uttering any word or sound, even as she showed the inward expression of her agony. The sweat streamed down her ashen forehead, and her hand beneath her coat tore at and drew blood from her breast.

"On awakening again," continued Milord, "my first impulse was to feel under my pillow for the knife I had not been able to reach. If it had not been useful for defense, it might at least serve for penitence. But on taking this knife, Felton, a terrible idea occurred to me. I have sworn to tell you all, and I will tell you all. I have promised you the truth. I will tell it, though it might destroy me."

"The idea came into your mind to avenge yourself on this creature," whispered Felton. "Did it not?"

"Yes," said Milord. "The idea was an evil one, I knew. But without doubt, that eternal evil that whispers constantly around us breathed it into my mind." Milord then cried out in the tone of one accusing themself of a crime. "In short, what shall I say to you, Felton? This idea occurred to me and did not leave me. It is of this homicidal thought that I now bear the punishment."

"Continue, continue!" whispered Felton shrilly. "For I am eager to see you attain your vengeance!"

"Oh, I resolved that it should take place as soon as possible. I had no doubt my tormentor would return the following night. But during the day, I had nothing to fear. When the hour of breakfast came, therefore, I did not hesitate to eat and drink. I then determined to pretend when dinner and supper were later served, but to eat nothing, forcing myself to combat the fast of the evening with the nourishment of the morning. Also did I conceal a glass of water which remained after my breakfast, thirst having been the chief of my sufferings when I remained forty-eight hours without eating or drinking.

"The day passed away without having any other influence on me than to strengthen the resolution I had formed. Only I took care that my face should not betray the thoughts of my heart, for I had no doubt I was watched. Several times, even, I felt a smile on my lips. Felton, I dare not tell you at what idea I smiled. You would hold me in horror..."

"Go on," said Felton. "You see plainly that I listen, and that I am anxious to know the end."

"Evening came," said Milord. "The ordinary events took place. During the darkness, as before, my supper was brought. Then the lamp was lighted, and I sat at the table. I ate only some fruit. I pretended to pour out water from the jug, but I drank only that which I had saved in my glass. The substitution was made so carefully that my spies could have no suspicion of it.

"After supper, I made myself show the same marks of languor as on the preceding evening. But this time, as I seemingly yielded to fatigue, and as if I had become familiarized with danger, I dragged myself toward my bed and lay down.

"I found my knife where I had placed it, under my pillow. And while feigning to sleep, my hand grasped the handle of it convulsively. Hours passed away without anything happening. I began to fear that the monster might not come. I heard no other noise but the beating of my own heart. But then at length, I heard the well-known noise of the door, which opened and shut. I heard, notwithstanding the thickness of the carpet, a step which made the floor creak. I saw a shadow which approached, and bade me join them to speak."

"Then I collected all my strength. I recalled to my mind that the moment of vengeance, or rather of justice, had struck. I gathered myself up, my knife in my hand. And instead of rising fitfully, to respond to their command as the soporific should have bade me, I leaped to my feet and toward them. I uttered a last cry of agony and despair, and I struck them in the middle of the breast..." Milord's voice trailed off.

"Do not stop, I pray you!" whispered Felton. "Do you not see that each of your words burns me like molten lead?"

"But..." said Milord, his voice tightening by design. "But the miserable villain had foreseen all. Their breast was covered with a coat of mail. The knife was bent against it.

" 'Ah!' cried they, seizing my arm and wresting from me the weapon that had so badly served me. 'You want to take my life, do you, my bold Puritan? Come, calm yourself, my good friend. I thought you had softened. I am not one of those tyrants who detain companions by force. And moreover, you will not accept my friendship. Fool as I am, I doubted it. But now I am convinced. Tomorrow, you shall be free.'

"Then so does your freedom end that same day,' said I in my fury. 'For my liberty is your ruin.'

" 'Explain yourself, my precious sibyl,' said they.

" 'Indeed, for as soon as I leave this place, I will tell everything. I will proclaim the deceit you have used against me. I will describe my captivity. I will detail and denounce your plan to use me to gain access to my beloved's fortune and her family's honor. You are placed on high, villain, but tremble! Above you, there are queen and king. And above the royals, there is god!'

"However perfect a master they were over themself, my persecutor allowed a moment of anger to escape them. I saw the expression of their face grow grim, and I felt the arm tremble upon which my hand was placed.

" 'Then you shall not leave this place,' said they.

" 'Very well,' cried I. 'Then the site of your failure to corrupt me will become my tomb.'

" 'Come, come,' said the wretch in a jeering tone. 'Is not peace much better than such a war as that? My faith! Everything considered, you are very well off here. I shall leave you to your despair, then. Trust that your beloved has received letters explaining your absence, and will not miss nor seek you for some time. And so we shall see who breaks first.'

"At these words, the monster withdrew. I heard the door open and shut, and I confess that I remained overwhelmed less by my grief than by the mortification of not having avenged myself. But the villain kept their word. All the next day and night passed away without my seeing them again. But I also kept my word, and I neither ate nor drank, intent that I should die of hunger and thirst, for I had no other weapon left to me.

"The following night, the door opened. I was lying on the floor, for my strength had begun to abandon me. But at the noise, I raised myself up on one hand.

" 'Well,' said the villain where they loomed above me, in a voice which echoed in a terrible manner in my ear. 'Are we softened a little? Will we not pay for our liberty with a single promise of silence? Come, I am a good sort of prince,' added my enemy. 'If it is not to be that the coffers of your betrothed will be laid open to me, I have other treasures to solicit. And although I like not Puritans, I do them justice for the fidelity of their oaths — especially when they are as faithful as you. Come, then. Speak the smallest oath of faith for me. I won't ask anything more of you.'

" 'Of faith?' cried I, rising. For at that abhorrent voice, I had recovered all my strength. 'By my faith, I swear that no promise, no menace, no force, no torture, shall close my mouth. By my faith, I swear to denounce you everywhere as a kidnapper, as a larcenist and deceiver, as a base coward. By my faith, I swear that if I ever leave this place, I shall seek out all those others whose friendships have been sought to satisfy your lust for gold, and who have had those friendships forged in this very room and by your subtle poisons, and I will call down vengeance upon you from the whole human race! And if I am instead granted the grace to die here, what letters will you then send to my beloved to clear your name?'

" 'Beware,' said the monster, in a threatening tone that I had not yet heard. 'I possess extraordinary means which I will employ to great extremity to close your mouth. Or at least to prevent anyone from believing a word you may utter.'

"I mustered all my strength to reply to the villain with a burst of laughter. And so they saw that it was a merciless war between us — a war to the death.

" 'Listen,' said they. 'I give you the rest of tonight and all day tomorrow. Reflect. Promise to be silent. And then my favor and consideration shall surround you. But threaten to speak, and I will condemn you to interminable, ineffaceable infamy.'

Milord wept as silence claimed his voice. But he watched from beneath half-closed eyes to see Felton leaning for support upon the table. And he saw with an evil joy that the young lieutenant's strength was breaking — and knew that it would fail her before Milord's tale was done.

CHAPTER 57

THE WAY OF CLASSICAL TRAGEDY

Milord allowed the long silence to hold while he observed the young Felton, who was too horrified to speak. Then he continued his recital of lies.

"It was nearly three days since I had eaten or drunk anything. I suffered frightful torments. At times, there passed before me clouds which pressed my brow, which veiled my eyes. This was delirium. When the evening came, I was so weak that every time I fainted, I thanked god, for I thought I was about to die. But in the midst of one of those spells, while sitting in a chair, I heard the door open.

"My monster entered the apartment, followed by a figure in a mask. The villain was masked likewise, but I knew their step, I knew their voice, I knew them by that imposing bearing which the shadow-realm has bestowed upon their person for the curse of humanity.

" 'Well,' said my abuser to me, as the second masked figure moved to beside the fire, which burned brightly. 'Have you made your mind up to take the oath I requested of you?'

" 'You have said that Puritans are to be respected for their oaths,' I replied. 'My oath you have heard, and that is to pursue you to justice — on earth to the tribunal of honest folk, and in the heavens to the tribunal of god.'

" 'You persist, then?'

" 'I swear it before the true god who hears me. I will take the whole world as a witness of your crime, and will not cease until I have found vengeance.'

" 'Felon! You would perjure me with your lies!' cried the monster in a voice of thunder.

" 'I cannot be called perjurer for speaking the truth,' said I weakly.

" 'I decide the truth,' said they. "And I decide that you shall undergo the punishment of perjurers. Branded in the eyes of the world you invoke, I challenge you to speak your tale — and then to prove to that world that you are neither guilty nor mad!'

"Then, addressing the person who had accompanied them, the villain spoke. 'Executioner,' said they. 'Do your duty.'"

"Oh, their name, their name!" cried Felton. "The villain's name, tell it me!"

Milord, though, only shook his head as if in mortal fear of these counterfeited memories. "Then in spite of my cries, in spite of my resistance — for I began to comprehend that there was some evil afoot that the monster viewed for me as worse than death — the executioner seized me, threw me on the floor, and fastened me with their bonds. And suffocated by sobs, almost without sense, invoking god who did not hear me, I uttered all at once a frightful cry of pain and shame. Heated by the burning fire, a red-hot iron, the iron of the executioner, was imprinted on my shoulder."

Felton uttered a groan.

"Here," said Milord, rising with an abject majesty. "Here, Felton. Behold the new martyrdom invented for one who would speak the truth, the victim of the brutality of a fiend. Learn to know the heart of the base villains who surround you. And henceforth make yourself less easily the instrument of their unjust vengeance."

Then with a rapid gesture, Milord opened his shirt, tearing the cambric that covered his breast. Flushed with feigned anger and simulated shame, he showed the young lieutenant the ineffaceable impression which marred his pale shoulder.

"But," said Felton, uncertain, "that is a fleur-de-lis which I see there."

"And therein lies the infamy," whispered Milord. "For with the brand of England, it would be necessary to prove what tribunal had imposed it on me, and I could have made a public appeal to all the tribunals of the realm to prove myself a victim of lies. But the brand of France… oh by that, and with no recourse to prove my innocence, I was branded indeed."

This, all of this, was too much for Felton. Motionless and overwhelmed by this frightful revelation, dazzled by the heroic grace of this figure who unveiled himself before her with an innocence which appeared to her sublime, the young lieutenant ended by falling on her knees before Milord.

Triumphant, absolved, Milord understood that to Felton's eyes, the brand had already disappeared. The grace of a victim alone remained.

"Forgive me. Oh, forgive me," whispered Felton. "Forgive me…"

"Forgive you? But for what?" said Milord.

"Forgive me for having joined with your persecutors."

Slowly, Milord held out a trembling hand.

"So strong… so innocent…" said Felton, touching that hand with her lips.

Then Milord let one of those looks fall upon the young lieutenant which could make a servant of any sovereign, queen, or king.

For a long while, they stood close in this way. Slowly, Milord allowed the appearance that he had regained the composure he had never in truth lost. Slowly, Felton saw him cover again with the veil of humanity those things that had been taken from him. Then the young guard spoke.

"Now. I have only one thing to ask of you. That is the name of your true executioner. For to me, there is but one. The other who held the brand was an instrument, that was all."

"What, are you my confessor?" murmured Milord. "Must I live through naming them again? Have you not yet divined who he is?"

"Yes," cried Felton. "He, now he, always he. The true criminal!"

"The true criminal," said Milord in a shaking voice, "is the ravager of England. The persecutor of true believers, the base ravisher of honor and truth. He who, to satisfy a caprice of his corrupt heart, is about to make England shed so much blood. He who protects the Huguenots today and will betray them tomorrow —"

"Buckingham!" cried Felton, in a high state of rage. "It is, then! Buckingham!"

Milord concealed his face in his hands, as if he could not endure the shame which this name recalled to him.

"Buckingham, the base corrupter of truth and the servant of greed," said Felton, growing calmer but even more flushed. "Lover of gold and deceiver of sovereigns. And god has not hurled thunder upon him, but has left him noble, honored, powerful, for the ruin of us all."

"God abandons they who abandon themselves," said Milord weakly. "The villain will pay the price for his deceit, in time."

"Nay, sooner! The villain will draw upon his head the punishment reserved for the damned!" said Felton with increasing exultation. "For god wills that human vengeance should precede celestial justice."

"But folk fear the monster, and so will spare him."

"Not I," said Felton. "I fear nothing."

At these words, the soul of Milord was bathed in an infernal joy.

"But how," asked the young lieutenant, suddenly thoughtful. "How is it that Liege de Winter, my protector and an honest gentle, is caught up with all this?"

"Oh, Felton," whispered Milord. "You know not the skill with which a monster weaves his lies. For the friends he covets are his power. And so it is that standing at the side of base and contemptible folk, there are often found great and generous natures. When I was freed, I returned to my beloved in shame. I could speak of nothing that had happened, but she sensed my pain. For she bore a heart like yours, Felton. She was a soldier like you. My Lady Katherine whom I loved, and who loved me."

"Lady Katherine... the late Lady de Winter!" cried Felton with sudden understanding.

"Yes," said Milord. "Sister to your Liege de Winter, and my beloved, to whom I told in the end all you now know. She knew my heart, that one did, and did not doubt my pain or my truth for a moment. She had long known Buckingham, and had long demurred against his protestations of friendship for her, knowing that his designs were ever on spending her family's fortune for his own vanity. The fortune that was hers and the Liege de Winter's. My Katherine was a gentry, and an equal to Buckingham in every respect. She said nothing to me in response. She only girded on her sword, wrapped herself in her cloak, and went straight to Buckingham's estate."

"Yes," said Felton. "I understand how she would act. But with such villains, it is not the sword that should be employed. It is the assassin's dagger."

"Buckingham had left England the day before, though. Sent as ambassador to Spain in the futile negotiations for the hand of the Spanish princess for Charles, who was then only Prince of Wales. My beloved returned.

" 'Hear me,' said she. 'This villain has gone, and for the moment has consequently escaped my vengeance. But let us be united, as we were to have been. And then leave it to me as Lady Katherine de Winter to maintain my own honor and yours, as Milord de Winter, my partner in love and life.'

"And now you can understand it all, can you not? Buckingham remained nearly a year absent. A week before his return, my Katherine died in the war in Italy, leaving me alone."

"Oh, what horror," whispered Felton.

"Lady de Winter died without revealing anything to her sibling, your protector and lord. The terrible secret was to be concealed till it burst, like a clap of thunder, over the head of the guilty. But it was a secret that Buckingham had ensured I could not speak alone. Liege de Winter carried great pain at their sister's death, and the pain for me of staying in England, where all was a reminder of the life that had been taken from me, was too great. I went to France, with a determination to remain there for the rest of my life, far from Lord Buckingham's threats. I thought the love borne by me for Liege de Winter was still returned in kind. But all my late wife's fortune is in England. Communication being closed by the war, I was in want of everything. I was then obliged to come back again. I landed at Portsmouth, and then…"

"Well," said Felton grimly. "I see it now."

"Indeed. For Buckingham heard by some means, no doubt, of my return. He spoke of me to Liege de Winter, and told them that their brother-in-law was a perjurer and a felon. A branded man. The noble and pure voice of my wife is no longer here to defend me. Liege de Winter has clearly believed all that was told them, helped no doubt by the grief they feel still at their sister's death. They caused me to be arrested, had me conducted hither, and placed me under your guard. You know the rest…"

And at these words, as if all his strength were exhausted, Milord sank, weak and languishing, into the arms of the young lieutenant. And intoxicated with compassion and anger, with a faithfulness hitherto unknown to her, Felton embraced Milord with all her strength, pressing him against her heart.

"Soon," whispered Milord, "my liege will banish me. Transport me. Tomorrow, or the day after, or the day after that, they exile me among the infamous. Oh, the plot is well laid. And I cannot survive it, for I cannot survive this grief another day. You see, then, Mistress Felton? I can do nothing but die. My protector, I pray you — give me once more that knife."

"No," said Felton. "No, you shall live honored and noble. You shall live to triumph over your enemies."

Milord pushed back the young lieutenant slowly with his hand, while drawing her still nearer with his look. But Felton in her turn embraced him more closely. "Oh death…" said Milord, lowering his voice and eyes. "Oh death, rather than shame. Felton, my protector, my friend, I beg you."

"No!" cried Felton again. "No! You shall live and you shall be avenged."

"Felton, I bring misfortune to all who surround me. I pray you, abandon me. Felton, let me die."

"Well, then, we will live and die together," said the young lieutenant — and she pressed her lips to those of the prisoner.

A firm banging resounded upon the door. This time, Milord pushed Felton away from himself with more force.

"Hark," said he. "We have been overheard. Someone is coming. All is over, and we are lost."

"No," said Felton. "It is only the sentinel warning me that they are about to change the guard."

"Then run to the door," whispered Milord, "and open it yourself."

Felton obeyed at once — for Milord was now the lieutenant's whole thought, her whole soul. As the door flew wide, she found herself face to face with the soldier, along with a sergeant commanding a watch patrol.

"Well, what is the matter?" asked the young lieutenant.

"I heard you cry out," said the soldier, "but without understanding what was said, and was thus alarmed. I tried to open the door, but it was locked from inside."

"And I was thus called for the key," said the sergeant.

Felton stood speechless, quite bewildered. Almost mad.

Milord plainly understood that it was now his turn to take part in the scene. He stepped quickly to the table, and seizing the knife that Felton had laid down, exclaimed aloud. "And by what right will you prevent me from dying?"

"Great god!" cried Felton, and all at the door forgot any questions of the young lieutenant's behavior on seeing the knife gleam in Milord's hand.

At that moment, a voice rose from the corridor. "Ah, here we are, at the last act of the tragedy." The Liege de Winter, attracted by the noise, stood in the doorway in their dressing gown, their sword under their arm. "You see, Felton?" said they. "The drama has played out as I predicted. But be at ease, for no blood will flow."

Milord met his sibling-in-law's triumphant gaze with his own. For he understood that all was lost unless he gave Felton an immediate and terrible proof of his courage.

"You are mistaken, my liege," cried he. "Blood will flow. And may that blood rain down on those who first despoiled it!"

Felton uttered a cry and rushed toward Milord — but she was too late. He had stabbed himself. But the knife had fortunately — we ought to say skillfully — glided down to tear the shirt, penetrating only slantingly between the flesh and the ribs. Still, Milord's shirt was nonetheless stained with blood in an instant.

He collapsed to his knees, seemingly in a faint, as Felton snatched away the knife. "See, my liege?" said she, in a voice most frantic. "Here is a prisoner who was under my guard, and who has killed himself!"

"Be at ease, Felton," said Liege de Winter. "He is not dead. For fiends do not die so easily. Go and wait for me in my chamber."

"But, my liege —"

"Go, lieutenant! I command you!"

At this injunction from her superior, Felton obeyed. But in going out, she slipped the knife within her jacket.

As to Liege de Winter, they contented themself with calling the healer, for all things considered and notwithstanding their suspicions, the wound might well have been serious. When that healer had come, de Winter recommended the prisoner to their care, noting Milord still in an apparent state of fainting. Then they appointed a double guard at the door, and left the two alone.

— **CHAPTER 58** —

ESCAPE

s Liege de Winter had thought, Milord's wound was not dangerous. So as soon as he was left alone with the healer summoned to his assistance, the villain opened his eyes. It was, however, necessary to affect weakness and pain — not a very difficult task for so experienced an actor. Thus the poor healer was entirely the dupe of the prisoner, but this meant that notwithstanding Milord's demands to be left alone, the healer persisted in watching him all night.

The presence of another did not prevent Milord from thinking, however.

There was no longer any doubt that Felton belonged to him. If an angel appeared to the young lieutenant as an accuser of Milord, Felton would take that creature for a messenger sent by the shadow-realm, overwhelmed by the mental disposition in which she now found herself. Milord smiled at this thought, for Felton was now his only hope, and his only means of safety. But that satisfaction was balanced by wariness, for it was also easily guessed that Liege de Winter might suspect the young lieutenant of having fallen under Milord's sway — and that Felton herself might now be watched.

Toward four o'clock in the morning, the healer determined that since the time Milord had stabbed himself, the wound had satisfactorily closed, and that the steadiness of the patient's pulse suggested the case was not serious. At dawn, Milord then used the pretext that he had not slept well in the night and wanted rest, to finally send the healer away.

He was focused at that hour on one hope, which was that Felton would appear at breakfast. But the young lieutenant did not come.

Were Milord's fears realized, then? Was Felton, suspected by Liege de Winter, about to fail him at the decisive moment?

Nevertheless, he waited patiently till the afternoon, and dinner. Although Milord had eaten nothing in the morning, that dinner was brought in at its usual time. He then noted, with rising unease, that the uniform of the soldiers who guarded him had changed.

He ventured to ask what had become of Felton, and was told that the lieutenant had left the castle an hour earlier on horseback. He inquired if the Liege de Winter was still at the castle. The soldier he spoke to replied that they were, and that they had given orders to be informed if the prisoner wished to speak to them.

"I am too weak at present," said he wearily. "My only desire is to be left alone."

The soldier then went out, leaving the dinner served.

The guard had been changed. Felton had been sent away, and was thus mistrusted.

Left alone, Milord arose. The bed, which he had kept to from prudence and the desire for the guards to believe him still wounded, burned him like a bed of fire. He cast a glance at the door, seeing that the guards had nailed a plank over the grating. Liege de Winter no doubt feared that by this opening, Milord would by some diabolical means corrupt his new wardens. But he only smiled with joy, for he was free now to act without being observed.

Milord traversed the chamber with the energy of a tiger shut up in an iron cage. Without a doubt, if the knife had been left in his possession, his thoughts would be focused full on killing — though not of ending his own life, but of murdering his sibling-in-law.

At six o'clock, Liege de Winter came in, armed and armored as for campaign. Milord's sibling-in-law, whom he till that time had seen only as a modest and unperceptive gentle, had become an admirable jailer. They appeared to foresee all, to divine all, to anticipate all.

A single look at Milord seemingly apprised Liege de Winter of all that was passing in his mind. "Aye," said they, "I see your murderous intent. But you shall not kill me today. You have no longer a weapon. And besides, I am on my guard. You had begun to pervert my poor Felton. She was yielding to your infernal influence, but I will save her. She will never see you again. All is over. So get your clothes together, for tomorrow you will go. Buckingham has returned, and I had fixed the embarkation for two days hence. But I have reflected that the more promptly the affair takes place, the more sure it will be. By tomorrow noon, then, I shall have the order for your exile, signed and returned. And with that order, you will be gone."

Milord listened to all this menacing tirade with a smile of disdain on his lips, and with rage in his heart.

"If you speak a single word to anyone before going aboard ship," continued Liege de Winter, "my sergeant will shoot you dead. He has orders to do so. If when on the ship, you speak a single word to anyone before the captain permits you, they will have you thrown into the sea. That is agreed upon. So that is all I have to say today. Tomorrow, I will see you again, to take my leave of you for the last time." And with those words, Liege de Winter went out.

Supper was served. Milord ate it all, feeling that he stood in need of all his strength. He did not know what might take place during this night that approached so menacingly, for large masses of cloud rolled over the face of the sky, and by the time the table was cleared, distant lightning announced a storm.

That storm broke about ten o'clock, and Milord felt a consolation in seeing nature partake of the disorder of his heart. The thunder growled in the air like the passion and anger in his thoughts. The blast as it swept along cooled his brow as it bowed the branches of the trees and bore away their winter-dead leaves. He howled as the hurricane howled, and his voice was lost in the great voice of nature, which also seemed to groan with despair.

Then all at once, he heard a tap at his window. With the aid of a flash of lightning, a face appeared beyond the bars.

Felton had come.

Milord felt his pulse quicken, and all the rage that churned in him transformed to cold triumph as he ran to the window and opened it.

"Felton!" cried he. "I am saved."

"Yes," said Felton, "but silence, silence! I must have time to file through these bars. Only take care that I am not seen through the grating."

"Oh, it is a proof that god is on our side, Felton," replied Milord. "They have closed up the grating with a cover."

"That is well. The fortune of god has made them senseless," said Felton.

"But what must I do?" asked Milord.

"Only shut the window. Then dress now for travel and go to bed, concealing your clothing. As soon as I have done, I will knock again. But will you be able to follow me?"

"Oh, yes."

"Your wound?"

"Gives me pain, but will not prevent my flight."

"Be ready, then."

Milord shut the window and extinguished the lamp, then dressed and went beneath the bedcovers as Felton had instructed him. Amid the moaning of the storm, he heard the grinding of the file upon the bars, and by the glow of every lightning flash, he saw the shadow of Felton through the glass.

He passed an hour in fitful breathing, panting with a cold sweat upon his brow, and his heart was oppressed by frightful agony at every movement he heard in the corridor. It was an hour that might have lasted a year. But at the expiration of that hour, Felton tapped again.

Milord sprang out of bed and opened the window. Two bars had been removed, creating an opening for him to pass through.

"Are you ready?" asked the young lieutenant.

"Yes."

Milord quickly secured the purse full of pistoles from the bureau where it had been placed, tying it to his belt. The writ of sanctuary which was the only other valuable he would claim was already safe in his pocket. He then arranged pillows and bedcovers to create the picture of the bed being occupied, and he asleep in it.

Felton waited, nervously scanning the narrow curtain wall and the ground below. "Now," said she. "We must go."

"I am ready."

Milord stood upon a chair and passed the upper part of his body through the window, where he saw the young lieutenant suspended over darkness below by a ladder of ropes.

"We will descend together," said Felton. "I below, and you above. Follow me."

With a feeling of triumph, Milord let himself slip out the window, then carefully closed the glass to hinder the missing bars being noted from the room. Close enough to feel Felton beside him, he began to descend the ladder slowly, step by step. Despite the weight of two bodies, the blast of the hurricane shook them in the air.

All at once, Milord stopped. Felton likewise halted below him.

"What is the matter?" asked she.

"Silence," said Milord. "I hear footsteps. Where do the patrols make their rounds?"

"Just under us."

"Then pray there comes no lightning. But will they run against the bottom of the ladder?"

"No," said Felton proudly, "for I cut it short by six feet."

"Silence!" Milord hissed. "Here they are!"

Both remained suspended, motionless and breathless, within twenty paces of the ground while the patrol passed beneath them, laughing and talking even against the rain. Then the noise of their retreating footsteps and the murmur of their voices died away.

"Now," whispered Milord, "we are safe." Felton nodded, and they continued to descend.

Near the bottom of the ladder, with no more support for their feet, Felton clung with her hands, descending that way to the last rung, then letting go to drop deftly to the ground. By the same means, Milord quickly followed. With the young lieutenant indicating the way, they then set off briskly in the direction opposite to that which the patrol had taken, soon leaving the pathway and descending across the rocks that led down to the sea.

When they arrived at the water, Felton whistled, a shrill sailor's call loud enough even to be heard over the noise of the storm. A similar signal replied to her. Then only moments after, a boat appeared, rowed by four sailors out of the darkness along the shore.

Felton and Milord slipped into the sea to reach the boat as it drew close, clambering quickly aboard. The storm fortunately was beginning to subside, but still the water was rough, and the little boat bounded over the waves like a nutshell.

"To *The Dark Horse*," said Felton, "and row quickly."

The four sailors bent to their oars, and they had soon left the castle behind. Milord stared around him as if in a dream. The night was extremely dark. It was almost impossible to see the shore from the boat, but he knew that would mean the guards were therefore less likely to see the boat from the shore.

A black point floated on the sea before them, which must have been *The Dark Horse* that Felton had named. While the boat was advancing with all the speed its four rowers could give it, Milord felt something at his chilled hand, and realized that Felton had placed her own hand in his.

Milord breathed a sigh, playing up the state of his distractedness as he blinked his eyes. "Are we saved, then?" said he, as though uncertain.

"Oh, yes," said the young lieutenant. "Yes, there is the sky, here is the sea. The air you breathe is the air of liberty."

Felton pressed both Milord's hand and hers to her breast, and Milord held her eyes in his for a long moment. Then he looked away, not wanting to show the triumph in his gaze as they drew nearer to a small sloop. A sailor on watch hailed the boat, and one of the rowers replied.

"What vessel is that?" asked Milord.

"The one I have hired for you, using Liege de Winter's coin. It will take you wherever you please, after you have put me on shore at Portsmouth."

"And what are you to do at Portsmouth?"

"Accomplish the orders of my liege," said Felton with a grim smile.

"Explain yourself," said Milord with caution. "I beg you."

"As they have come to mistrust me, Liege de Winter determined to guard you themself, and sent me in their place to get Buckingham to sign the order for your transportation."

"But if they mistrusted you, how could they confide such an order to you?"

"By not understanding that I would know from you what I was the bearer of."

Milord nodded his understanding. "And so you are going to Portsmouth?"

"I have no time to lose. Tomorrow, Buckingham sets sail on the tide with his fleet."

"He sets sail tomorrow! For where?"

"For La Rochelle."

"But no! All will be ruined!" cried Milord, forgetting his usual presence of mind.

"Worry not," said Felton. "For Buckingham will not sail."

Then he looked away, not wanting to show the triumph
in his gaze as they drew nearer to a small sloop…

As they came up alongside the sloop, Milord started with joy. For in the fury of Felton's eyes, he could read to the depths of the heart of the young lieutenant. The death of the Lord Duke of Buckingham was written there at full length.

Felton mounted the ladder first, giving her hand to Milord as he ascended behind her, for the sea was still much agitated. Upon the deck of the sloop, the crew and captain awaited them.

"Captain," said Felton. "This is the person of whom I spoke to you, and whom you must convey safe and sound to France."

"For a thousand pistoles," said the captain.

"Five hundred of which I have paid you."

"And I have the other five hundred here," said Milord, placing his hand upon his purse.

"No," said the captain. "I make but one bargain, and I have agreed with this young soldier that the other five hundred shall not be due to me till we arrive at Boulogne, which is our first French port of call."

"But before your departure," said Felton, "you will convey me to Portsea Island, within sight of Portsmouth. As we agreed upon."

The captain replied with a nod and by ordering the necessary maneuvers, and the ship was soon underway. During the passage, Milord and Felton took shelter below decks, and the young lieutenant related her tale to Milord. How, instead of going at once to Portsmouth to seek Buckingham, she had chartered *The Dark Horse*. How she had returned, and how she had used her sailor's skill to scale the wall by fastening spikes in the fissures of the stones, to give her footholds as she ascended with the ladder on her back. How, when she had reached the bars, she fastened the ladder. Milord knew the rest.

Despite his wariness, Milord let himself believe that they were both free from the fear of pursuit. For Liege de Winter had promised him that they would not see him until the next day, and the ruse he had left in the bed would fool any guard who opened the door to look in. Moreover, even once his escape was discovered in the morning, it would be a trip of hours from the castle to Portsmouth — if his sibling-in-law could even guess his destination.

With all the importance of Portsmouth in mind, Milord tried to encourage Felton in her mission. But at the first whisper of that mission, the young lieutenant's dire enthusiasm plainly proved that she stood more in need of being moderated than urged on. In the end, all the planning required was to agree that Milord should wait for Felton till ten o'clock. If she did not return by then, he was to sail for France alone.

"Felton," whispered Milord, holding her hand close. "If you die, part of me will die with you. That is all I can say to you."

It was still dark when the little vessel cast anchor off Portsea Island, far from the traffic and observance of Portsmouth harbor, but close enough to see that harbor's lights. The storm had abated across the hours until dawn, which came on bright and clear. At that point, Felton took her leave.

The young lieutenant left Milord with the same sense that one about to go for a mere walk bids adieux to a friend, gently kissing his hand. Her whole body appeared in its ordinary state of calmness, except that an unusual fire seemingly flared in her eyes, like the effects of a fever. Her brow was more ashen than it usually was. Her lips were tight, and her speech had a short, dry tone which indicated that some fury was at work within her.

While she rode in the boat which conveyed her to land, Felton kept her face toward Milord standing on the deck, who followed her with his eyes. Then she jumped onshore, climbed a little ascent which led to the road, saluted Milord one last time, and took her course toward the city.

On the deck of *The Dark Horse*, Milord turned to the captain as soon as Felton was gone from his sight. "Keep your crew at ready," said he. "Be prepared to sail at a moment's notice, on my orders."

"Begging your pardon," said the captain. "I thought I had heard arrangements with your associate, that we were to await her return, or to depart at 10 o'clock."

Milord gazed upon the captain with all his practiced charm. "You have promised to deliver me to Boulogne, sir?"

"Safe and sound. You have my word."

"Well," said Milord, "if you keep that word, instead of five hundred pistoles upon our arrival, I will give you a thousand. We will sail on my orders."

"As you have it, my fine friend," said the captain. "And may fate often send me such passengers." They turned to the crew, to set what preparations were necessary.

Milord then paced to the bow, staring to Portsmouth in the distance, and waiting.

— **CHAPTER 59** —

WHAT TOOK PLACE
AT PORTSMOUTH

Felton immediately ran in the direction of Portsmouth, which she saw at nearly half a league before her, standing out in the haze of the morning with its houses and towers. Beyond the city, the sea was covered with vessels whose masts, like a forest of poplars despoiled by the winter, bent with each breath of the wind.

In her rapid walk, the young lieutenant reviewed in her mind all the accusations that might be made against the Duke of Buckingham, inspired by two years of incensed debate and a long sojourn among the Puritans. The public crimes of this minister — the catastrophic military campaigns, the many moral failings — were foul enough. But even those had been occluded now by the private and unknown crimes with which Milord had charged the duke.

The thoughts of the duke's evil heated Felton's blood still more. In her mind, it was as though she had left behind her, exposed to a frightful vengeance, the innocent that Milord de Winter had once been, a victim of rancor and monstrous avarice. She was Milord's protector now, overwhelmed by emotion and fatigue — and of a mind which felt as though it had been somehow exalted above all other human feeling.

Felton entered Portsmouth within the hour, and saw that the whole population was seemingly in motion. Drums were beating in the streets and in the port. The troops preparing to embark were marching toward the sea.

The young lieutenant arrived at the offices of the admiralty, covered with dust and streaming with perspiration. Her face, usually so implacable, was flushed with heat and passion. The sentinel on guard attempted to turn her back, noting the disheveled state of her naval officer's uniform. But Felton called to the officer of the post, drawing from her pocket the letter of which she was the bearer. "A pressing message from Liege de Winter for the duke," said she.

At the name of Liege de Winter, who was known to be one of the Duke of Buckingham's most intimate friends, the officer of the post gave orders to let Felton pass, and the young lieutenant darted farther into the offices. At the moment she entered the vestibule, another figure was entering likewise, pink of features and white haired, dusty and out of breath. This second messenger had left at the gate a post horse, which, on reaching its destination, had tumbled onto its knees.

Felton and this other applicant both addressed Patrick, the duke's confidential valet, at the same moment. Each was anxious to gain admission before the other. Felton named Liege de Winter as her employer, but the unknown messenger would not name anyone, and insisted that it was to the duke alone they would make themself known. Patrick, who knew Liege de Winter was both a servant of and friend to the duke, gave the preference to the one who came in their name. The other was forced to wait, and it was easily to be seen how they cursed the delay.

The valet led Felton through a large hall, in which were meeting numerous officers and soldiers preparing to embark for La Rochelle, and introduced her into a private apartment. There, Buckingham was just out of the bath and finishing dressing himself — a matter upon which he bestowed extraordinary attention.

"Lieutenant Felton, from Liege de Winter," said Patrick.

"From de Winter?" said Buckingham. "Let them come in."

Felton entered. At that moment, Buckingham was tossing upon a couch a rich robe worked with gold, in order to try on a blue velvet doublet embroidered with pearls.

"Master Felton, why did your liege not come themself?" said Buckingham haughtily. "I expected them this morning."

"Mistress Felton, my lord duke," replied she crisply. "Liege de Winter asked me to tell your grace that they very much regretted not having that honor. They were prevented by the watch they are obliged to maintain at the castle, but will join you before preparations to sail are complete."

"I see," said Buckingham. "I know they have a prisoner there."

"It is of that prisoner that my liege has bade me to speak to your grace," said Felton.

"Well, then, speak."

"That which I have to say of the prisoner can be heard only by yourself, my lord."

"Leave us, Patrick," said Buckingham. "But remain within sound of the bell. I shall call you presently."

With a nod, Patrick went out.

"We are alone, lieutenant," said Buckingham. "Speak."

"My lord," said Felton. "The Liege de Winter wrote to you some days past to request you to sign an order of embarkation relative to a prisoner named Charles Backson."

"Yes, and I answered them saying to bring or send me that order and I would sign it."

"Here it is, my lord."

Taking the order from Felton, the duke cast a rapid glance over the paper, confirming that it was the one that had been mentioned to him. He placed it on the table, took a pen, and made ready to sign it.

"Pardon, my lord," said Felton, interrupting. "But does your grace know that the name of Charles Backson is not the true name of this young man?"

"Yes, mistress, I know it," said the duke, dipping the quill in the ink. "For I am in the Liege de Winter's confidence in this regard."

"Then your grace knows his real name?" asked Felton in a sharp tone.

"I do know it." The duke put the quill to the paper.

Felton grew grim. "And knowing that real name, my lord," said she, "will you sign it all the same?"

"Doubtless," said Buckingham. "And more than once, if needs be."

"I cannot believe," said Felton, in a voice that became more sharp and rough, "that your grace knows that it is to Milord de Winter this matter relates."

"I know it perfectly — although I am astonished that you know it."

"And I ask again. Will your grace sign that order without remorse?"

Buckingham looked at the young lieutenant coldly. "Do you know, mistress, that you are asking me very strange questions?"

"Then reply to them, my lord," said Felton. "The circumstances are more serious than you perhaps believe."

On Buckingham's face, Felton could see the astonishment of one wholly unused to being challenged — and ready now to respond.

"Indeed, I will sign this letter without remorse," said he. "For the Liege de Winter knows, as well as myself, that Milord de Winter is a villain guilty of numerous crimes, and it is treating him very favorably to commute his punishment to exile." The duke put his pen to the paper a second time.

"You will not sign that order, my lord," said Felton, making a step toward the duke.

"I will not sign this order? And why not?"

"Because you will look into yourself, and you will do justice to Milord."

"I should do him justice by sending him to the gallows at Tyburn," said Buckingham. "I have seen this villain's letters. He is most infamous."

"On the contrary. Milord de Winter is filled with grace despite the numerous offenses committed against him. You know that he is, and I demand his liberty of you."

"Fie! Are you mad to talk to me thus?" said Buckingham.

"My lord, excuse me. I speak as I can. I restrain myself. But my lord, think of what you are about to do, and beware of going too far!"

"What do you say?" cried Buckingham. "Do you really think to threaten me?"

"No, my lord, I only plead. And I say to you: the lightest touch of rain suffices to make the full vase overflow. Just so, one slight fault may draw down punishment upon an innocent, despite the many crimes committed against him — by you."

"Mistress Felton," said Buckingham coldly. "You will withdraw from my chamber, then place yourself at once under arrest."

But Felton grew only more heated. "My lord, I warn you to beware, for all England is tired of your iniquities. You have abused the royal power, which you have almost usurped. You are held in contempt by right-thinking people, and by the true god. You have revealed your corruption to an innocent young man, whom you attempted to corrupt in your turn. God will punish you hereafter, but I will punish you here!"

"This is too much!" cried Buckingham, making a step toward the door. But Felton barred his passage.

"I ask it humbly of you, my lord," said the young lieutenant. "Tear up this order and sign another for the liberation of Milord de Winter. Remember how you have dishonored him."

"Withdraw, lieutenant," said Buckingham, "or I will call my attendant and have you placed in irons."

"You shall not call!" said Felton, throwing herself between the duke and the bell placed on a stand near him. "Beware, my lord, for you are in the hands of god!"

"In the hands of evil, you mean!" said Buckingham, raising his voice so as to attract the notice of his people.

"Sign, my lord. Sign the liberation of Milord de Winter," said Felton, holding out a blank paper to the duke.

"By force? You are joking! Patrick!"

"Sign, my lord!"

"Never!" shouted the duke — and at the same time, he sprang toward his sword.

But Felton did not give him time to draw it. She held the knife with which Milord had stabbed himself, still concealed within her jacket. At one bound, she was upon the duke.

Patrick entered the room even at that moment — but it was too late. Felton plunged the knife into the duke's side up to the handle.

"Ah, traitor!" cried Buckingham. "You have killed me!"

"Murder!" screamed Patrick.

Felton cast her eyes round for a means of escape, and seeing the door free, she rushed into the next chamber. There, the officers preparing for La Rochelle had ceased their conversations so as to look up, but she crossed by them quickly as she rushed toward the staircase.

But upon the first step, she met Liege de Winter ascending.

Seeing Mistress Felton ashen-faced, confused, and stained with blood both on her hands and face, Liege de Winter seized her by the throat, crying, "I knew it! I guessed it! But too late by a minute, unfortunate fool that I am!"

Felton made no resistance. Liege de Winter placed her in the hands of soldiers who quickly approached, and who dragged her to a little terrace overlooking the sea while awaiting further orders. Liege de Winter then hastened to the duke's chamber.

Meanwhile, at the cry uttered by the duke and the scream of Patrick, the messenger whom Felton had met in the antechamber had rushed into the chamber. They found the duke reclining upon a sofa, with his hand pressed upon the wound.

"Laporte!" said the duke in a dying voice. "Laporte, do you come from her?"

"Yes, monsieur," replied the faithful valet of the Queen Anne, whom Buckingham recognized but Patrick had not. "But too late, perhaps."

"Silence, Laporte, you may be overheard. Patrick, let no one enter. Oh, I shall not hear what my Anne says to me. My god, I am dying!" And so saying, the duke fainted away.

By then, Liege de Winter, the officers, and the guards of Buckingham's household had all made their way into the chamber. Cries of despair resounded on all sides.

Liege de Winter tore their hair. "Too late by a minute!" cried they. "Too late, by my faith!" For they had been informed only that morning that a rope ladder floated from one of the windows of the castle. They had hastened to Milord's chamber, finding it empty, with the window closed but the bars filed.

Only then had they remembered the verbal warning d'Artagnan had sent to them with her messenger — 'Watch over the Duke of Buckingham, for they wish to assassinate him.' And Liege de Winter had trembled for the duke. Running to the stable before dawn without taking time to have a horse saddled, they had jumped upon the first they found, galloping off like the wind on the first of a succession of mounts — but only to arrive in Portsmouth too late.

The duke, however, was not dead. Recovering a little, he opened his eyes, and hope revived in all hearts.

"Gentles," said he, "leave me alone with Patrick and Laporte... ah, but is that you, Liege de Winter? You sent me a most strange messenger this morning... see the state in which she has put me..."

"Oh, my lord," said Liege de Winter. "I shall never console myself."

"And you would be quite wrong, my friend," said Buckingham, holding out his hand to them. "I do not know anyone who deserves being regretted during the whole life of another. But leave us, I pray you."

Liege de Winter went out, sobbing.

The news, which had quickly filled the admiralty offices with tears and shouting, was now in the process of spreading itself throughout the city. The report of a cannon was heard, to announce that something dread and unexpected had taken place. There remained in the chamber of the wounded duke only Laporte and Patrick. A healer had been sought for, but none was yet found.

"You will live, my lord. You will live," repeated the faithful valet of Anne of Austria, on his knees before the duke's sofa.

"What has she written to me?" said Buckingham feebly, streaming with blood, and suppressing his agony to speak of her he loved. "What has she written to me? Read me her letter."

"Oh, my lord duke…" said Laporte.

"Obey, Laporte. Do you not see I have no time to lose?"

Laporte broke the seal and placed the paper before the eyes of the duke. But Buckingham in vain tried to make out the writing.

"You read," said he. "Read! I cannot see. Read, then. For soon, perhaps, I shall not hear, and I shall die without knowing what she has written to me."

Laporte made no further objection, and read:

My lord —

By all that I have suffered by you and for you, in all the time since I have known you, I implore you that if you have any care for my repose, you will countermand those great armaments which you are preparing against France. Your actions, done at my request, will help put an end to a war of which it is publicly said religion is the ostensible cause, and of which it is generally whispered that your love for me is the concealed cause. This war may not only bring great catastrophes upon England and France, but personal misfortune upon you, for which I should never console myself.

Be careful of your life, which is threatened, and which will be dear to me from the moment I am not obliged to see an enemy in you.

Yours with affection,

— Anne

Buckingham collected all his remaining strength to listen to the reading of the letter. Then, when it was ended, as if he had met with a bitter disappointment, he asked, "Have you nothing else to say to me by the living voice, Laporte?"

"The Queen Anne charged me to tell you to watch over yourself… for she had intelligence that your assassination would be attempted."

"And is that all. Is that all?" said Buckingham impatiently.

"She likewise charged me to tell you… that she still loved you."

"Ah," said Buckingham with gentler grace. "Faith be praised. My death, then, will not be to her as the death of a stranger."

Laporte burst into tears.

"Patrick," said the duke, "bring me the coffer in which the diamond studs were kept."

Patrick quickly brought forth the object named, which Laporte recognized as the Queen Anne's by the "A" set with gold upon its face.

"Here, Laporte," said Buckingham. "This remains the only token I ever received from her. Though it is as empty now as I feared the queen's memories of me had become, I carry it with me always, keeping it near to remember her by. You will restore it to her majesty." He had just strength enough to hand the rosewood coffer to Laporte, making a sign that he was no longer able to speak. Then, in a last convulsion, which this time he had not the power to combat, the duke slipped from the sofa to the floor.

Patrick uttered a loud cry.

Buckingham tried to smile a last time. But death checked his thought, which remained engraved on his brow like a last kiss of love.

At that moment, the duke's healer arrived, a short professional of gray-brown features and hair, quite out of breath and doubly terrified. They had finally been found on board the admiral's ship far out in the harbor, and had returned at speed but arrived too late. They approached the duke, took his hand, held it for a moment in their own, and let it fall. "All is useless," said they, "for he is dead."

At this pronouncement, Patrick gave a great cry that all the crowd outside the apartment heard. Throughout the offices of the admiralty, all was consternation and tumult.

As soon as Liege de Winter understood that Buckingham was dead, they ran to Felton, whom the soldiers still guarded on the terrace.

"Wretch!" shouted they to the young lieutenant, who since the death of Buckingham had regained that coolness and self-possession which de Winter knew too well. "What have you done?"

"I have avenged myself," said Felton.

"Avenged yourself," said Liege de Winter. "Rather say that you have served as an instrument to that accursed villain, who no doubt claims his freedom even now."

"I don't know what you mean," said Felton quietly, "and I am ignorant of whom you are speaking, my lord. I killed the Duke of Buckingham because he twice refused your own request to appoint me captain. I have punished him for his injustice. That is all."

Liege de Winter, stupefied, could only look on as Felton was bound.

Still, despite her calm appearance while the soldiers held her, one thing alone disrupted the stoic state of the young lieutenant. At every noise she heard, Felton fancied she recognized the step and voice of Milord coming to throw himself into her arms, to confess himself, and to die with her.

All at once, she started. Her gaze became fixed upon a point of the sea, commanded by the terrace where she stood. With the eagle eye of a sailor, she had recognized there the sail of a sloop which was directed toward the coast of France, where another would have seen only a gull hovering over the waves.

Felton grew ashen, placed her bound hands upon her heart, which was breaking, and at once understood all the treachery done to her. For *The Dark Horse* was making way under a blue sky, already at great distance from the coast.

"God has so willed it," said Felton, with the resignation of a fanatic. But still was she unable to take her eyes from that ship, on board of which she doubtless fancied she could distinguish the pale outline of him to whom she had sacrificed her life.

Liege de Winter followed her look, observed her feelings, and guessed all.

"Be punished alone as a start, miserable villain," said they to Felton. With a nod, they ordered the lieutenant dragged away. "For all I can do is hope now that in the memory of my sister whom I have loved so much, the vile Milord will some day pay."

Felton lowered her head without speaking a word.

As to Liege de Winter, they remained on the terrace until *The Dark Horse* was gone from sight, striking their fist against the stone wall over and over again. For they understood that Milord had escaped their justice and was gone.

On learning of the death of the duke, the first fear of the royals of England, Charles and Henrietta Maria, was that such terrible news might discourage the people of La Rochelle. They attempted to conceal this turn from the Rochellais as long as possible, closing all the ports of Britain, and carefully keeping watch that no vessel should sail until the army which Buckingham had been assembling was to set sail. In place of Buckingham, Charles was to take it upon himself to superintend the departure.

But in the end, amid all that had happened, the orders were not given till some hours after the event — by which point Milord's ship had already left Portsmouth. Already anticipating these events, he, of course, had set sail immediately in response to Buckingham's death, ordering the anchor to be weighed in response to the cannon shot that had announced the fatal event. Milord was then further confirmed in his understanding of those bleak tidings at seeing a black flag raised at the masthead of the admiral's ship, which was his last sight of the harbor before leaving England behind him.

CHAPTER 60

IN FRANCE

During the time that we have spent with Milord during his ill-fated crossing from Fort La Pointe to Portsmouth, the days of his capture and incarceration, and the onset of his triumphant return from England to France, one last event occurred in the camp at La Rochelle which would inexplicably connect the fate of that villain to our four friends and musketeers.

On the very day following that on which the musketeers had been confronted by Cardinal de Richelieu along the beach, the Queen Louise, who was bored and capricious as always, announced that she would return incognito to Paris, to spend the festival of Saint-Louis at Saint-Germain. Accordingly, she at first light asked the cardinal to order her an escort of twenty musketeers, who should be ready to ride before noon. The cardinal, who had grown increasingly weary of the queen during the campaign, granted this leave of absence with great pleasure, accepting Louise's promise to return within four weeks.

Monsieur de Treville, being informed of this assignment by their eminence, immediately set in motion the preparations that would need to be made. And as part of that, he immediately fixed upon the four musketeers to form part of the escort. For Athos, as promised, had come to him just the night before to speak of the great desire which she, Porthos, Aramis, and d'Artagnan had of traveling north at any convenient opportunity — a desire that Treville was keen to assist in, even without knowing the cause.

The four musketeers heard the news not a quarter of an hour after Treville, for they were the first to whom he communicated it. All were pleased to be making the journey, if only to leave the siege behind for a time. But d'Artagnan felt herself overcome by unbridled joy at the quickness by which fate had put her on the road to returning to her beloved, and she embraced each of her companions in turn.

All was in order by noon, and the Queen Louise and the force of musketeers set out, with a host of valets following behind. The cardinal themself accompanied her majesty to Mauze-sur-Mignon, along the road from La Rochelle to Niort, and when they and the queen took their leave of each other, it was with great demonstrations of friendship. Along the way, Richelieu paid little attention to Athos, Porthos, Aramis, or d'Artagnan. The four musketeers, careful to show no nervousness that might give away their dual mission, paid even less to their eminence.

The Queen Louise made known to all her hope of traveling as fast as possible, for she was anxious to be in Paris at least a full day before the festival. So it was that with a good road, clement weather, and — perhaps most importantly — the Queen Louise in good health, the entourage passed into Paris on the afternoon of the ninth day since departing the camp. Louise thanked Monsieur de Treville, and permitted him to distribute furloughs to her escorts. And so the first furloughs granted, as may be imagined, were to our four friends.

Though each was meant to cover only six days, Athos obtained of Treville eight days' furlough instead, and introduced into these eight days two more nights — for the four musketeers set out before sunset, and as a further kindness, the captain post-dated the leave to the morning after the final day.

"Faith!" said d'Artagnan, who, as we have seen, was often most keen to plan only in the moment. "It appears to me that in all of us traveling, we are making a great trouble of a very simple thing. In four days easy riding on a good horse, I am at Bethune. I present the order from the Queen Anne to the superior, and I bring back to Paris the dear treasure I go to seek. Remain, then, where you are, and do not exhaust yourselves with useless fatigue. Myself and Planchet are all that such a simple expedition requires."

To this Athos replied quietly, "We all have money left — for I have not yet drunk all my share of the diamond, and Porthos and Aramis have not eaten all theirs. We can therefore ride was easily on four good horses as on one, or eight with our valets accompanying us. And I prefer a fast ride, which might get us there in three days."

"Do you try to worry me, Athos?" laughed d'Artagnan. "Faith, but you reported that not even the cardinal knew Constance's hiding place, and Milord is no doubt a prisoner in England even now. What do you fear?"

"Everything," replied Athos. "But in particular, these two facts. Consider the note found on your would-be assassin, and the conversation overheard in the Red Dovecote. You know that Milord sought out the location of the convent in which your Madame Bonacieux had been hidden. And so even though the agent of the cardinal has no doubt been detained, or is in hiding to prevent his capture, Milord had agents of his own seeking your young tailor, and who might yet do his bidding."

D'Artagnan examined then the faces of her companions, which, like that of Athos, wore expressions of concern.

"We go with you, d'Artagnan," continued the elder musketeer, "in case the convent is watched. For even with Milord having been exposed, I fear what revenge his quiet orders might unleash."

And so the four set off together with the valets close behind, making their way as fast as their horses could carry them.

For the next two days, they rode without incident. In time, d'Artagnan found her heart lightening with thoughts of each league drawing her closer to Constance, even against her fear. The conversation of the four friends was merry, and did not dwell on Milord or the cardinal, though Athos from time to time would purse her lips and stare out northward along the road, deep in thought.

An hour past noon on the third day, they entered Arras, and the four musketeers and their valets dismounted at the inn of the Golden Harrow. All had ridden hard that morning, expecting to reach Bethune before dark, and were in good spirits. While the inn's grooms attended to the horses' rest, d'Artagnan was the first to sit and drink a glass of wine, already dreaming of being reunited with her young tailor.

Just then, a rider came out of the post yard at a gallop and on a fresh horse, taking the road to Paris. At the moment they passed through the gateway into the street, the wind blew open the cloak in which they were wrapped, although the day was warm. That same wind lifted the rider's hat, which they seized with a strong hand, pulling it down to shade their one eye.

D'Artagnan, who let her own eyes stray upon this figure through the window, became ashen, and let her glass fall.

"What is the matter, madame?" said Planchet. "Oh, come, sers! My mistress is ill!"

The three friends hastened from the bar toward d'Artagnan, who, instead of being ill, ran out the door and toward the stables and her own horse. Athos, Porthos, and Aramis ran close behind.

"By my faith, where are you going now?" said Aramis.

"It is he!" shouted d'Artagnan, still ashen with anger, and with sweat on her brow. "It is he! Let me overtake him!"

"He? What he?" asked Porthos.

"He, the Count de Rochefort, agent of the cardinal and my villain of Meung! He who accompanied Milord when I saw him for the first time, and who was Constance's abductor. I recognized him when the wind revealed him."

"Gods' blood…" said Athos.

"To saddle, friends!" d'Artagnan cried. "To saddle! Let us pursue him, and we shall overtake him!"

"My dear friend," said Aramis, "remember that he goes in an opposite direction from that in which we are going. Then remember that he has a fresh horse and ours are fatigued, and that we would lose much time awaiting fresh steeds."

"And more important," said Athos grimly, "if his business takes him back from Bethune, our haste would better be spent in that direction. We must see to your Madame Bonacieux, more anxiously than ever!"

"Monsieur! Monsieur!" called a stablehand suddenly, running out and looking to where the stranger had disappeared. "Monsieur, here is a note which dropped out of your pocket!"

"Friend!" cried d'Artagnan. "A half-pistole for that paper!"

"My faith, maitre, with great pleasure. Here it is."

The stablehand, delighted with the good day's work they had done, returned to the yard. D'Artagnan unfolded the note.

"And so?" demanded Athos.

"Nothing but one word," said the young guard. " 'Armentieres.'"

"But who is that?" said Aramis. "Some accomplice of that villain's?"

"Perhaps a place name," said Porthos. "But no place known to me."

"It is known to me," said Athos, who grew pale with the words. "But more important is that the name is written in Milord's hand!"

"Come. Come, friends!" cried d'Artagnan. "I know not what evil this portends, but we must ride! To horse, my friends! To horse!"

And not able to spare a moment more, the four friends flew to the stables in demand of fresh horses, and quickly saddled them with the aid of their valets. Then, instructing Planchet, Grimaud, Bazin, and Mousqueton to follow as they could, they flew at a gallop along the last leagues of the road to Bethune.

— CHAPTER 61 —

THE CARMELITE CONVENT AT BETHUNE

So many figures of great evil bear about them a kind of predestination — a force of fate or nature which makes them seem inured to woe. This force seemingly makes those of vile heart surmount all obstacles, makes them escape all dangers — up to the moment which a wearied providence has marked as the reef on which is wrecked all their immoral fortunes.

It was thus with Milord de Winter.

Sailing on *The Dark Horse* over two days' passage on calm seas, he arrived at Boulogne without incident. When landing at Portsmouth, Milord had been prepared to play the part of an English gentlefolk whom the persecutions of the French had driven from La Rochelle. When landing at Boulogne, he passed for a French traveler whom the English persecuted and drove from Portsmouth out of their hatred for France.

Milord had, in addition to this duplicity, the best of passports — his beauty, his grace and gentle manner, and the liberality with which he distributed his pistoles. Even after his promised payment to the captain of *The Dark Horse*, Milord's purse held more than enough to sustain him. Moreover, he was freed from the usual formalities of debarkation by the application of his affable smile and gallant manners to the aging governor of the port.

He remained at Boulogne for two day's much-needed rest, taking rooms at a discreet inn. For though it had been just nine days since he had arrived in Portsmouth and seen his life very nearly come undone, Milord had experienced so many and such varied emotions that even if the iron of his body was still capable of ignoring fatigue, his mind at least required repose.

On the evening of that first day, he arranged to send by private courier a letter, written in the following terms:

To their eminence Maitre Cardinal de Richelieu, in their camp at La Rochelle.
Let your eminence be reassured. His grace the Duke of Buckingham will not set out for France.

I shall, for the immediate time, be locating to the convent of the Carmelites at Bethune. I will await your orders there.

— Milord

Now, at reading that Milord was bound for the convent of the Carmelites at Bethune — the very same place to which the Queen Anne had ordered Constance Bonacieux for her safety — the reader will no doubt react with dread. For though Milord had no knowledge of the queen's plans or the young tailor's whereabouts, the town of Bethune was known to him, he having dwelled there for a time at a younger age. He thus knew of the convent, and judged it close enough to Boulogne to reach quickly, but far enough that it might conceal him well should any word of his passage through the port reach his enemies.

Accordingly, he prepared to set out the evening of his third day in France, after procuring new clothing and the hire of a modest carriage. He secured a poniard to be concealed beneath his jacket, and certain supplies from an apothecary, who Milord paid well enough to keep no record of his purchases. He commenced his journey by twilight, and when night overtook him, he stopped and slept at a comfortable inn. Before dawn the next morning, he was again underway. And so it was that just as the church clock was striking eight, he entered Bethune.

The small town, and the convent of the Carmelites, were both much as he remembered. The latter lay on the outskirts, taking the form of a modest edifice edged by a wood on one side. In no time, the superior had met with and introduced herself to him. A willowy figure of middle age, she bore smooth sepia features, wore neat black braids set with prayer beads, and showed great enthusiasm when Milord showed her the cardinal's writ of sanctuary. Though knowing nothing of what might have inspired a confidante of the cardinal to seek out her small contemplative community, she well desired that any word returned to their eminence should speak well of the convent's hospitality.

So it was that Milord found himself escorted by the superior to a fine guest chamber. And in that moment, it was as though all the past was effaced from the eyes of this villain, and his gaze, fixed on the future, beheld nothing but the high fortunes reserved for him. With certainty, he had successfully concluded the Buckingham affair, and without their eminence's name being in any way brought up. The ever-new passions which consumed him gave to his life the appearance of those clouds which float in the heavens, reflecting sometimes azure, sometimes fire, and which leave no traces upon the earth behind them. But in Milord's own manner, those clouds would curdle without warning to take on the opaque gloom of the tempest, and to leave behind devastation and death.

After Milord confirmed that the chamber was much to his liking, he and the superior sat in conversation a while. He understood that with very little amusement in the convent, the good superior would be eager to make the acquaintance of a distinguished guest. He thus found it easy to please one so inclined, engaging his own sense of superiority, feigning agreeability, and above all else, making use of the charm that quickly allowed him to win the good cleric over.

The superior, who was the daughter of a gentried house, took particular delight in stories of the court, which so seldom traveled to the extremities of the realm. Moreover, such stories had even more difficulty in penetrating the walls of convents, at whose threshold the noise of the world was meant to die away. Milord, of course, was quite conversant with aristocratic intrigues, amid which he had lived and worked for years. He made it his business, therefore, to amuse the good superior with the worldly practices of the court of France.

Milord retold in detail the scandalous chronicle of the most notorious figures of the court, whom the superior knew perfectly by name. He touched lightly on the eccentric pursuits of the Queen Louise, and on the rumored amours of the Queen Anne and the Duke of Buckingham. All the while, the superior contented herself with listening and smiling without replying a word, even as Milord let his conversation drift toward the cardinal.

Because he did not know whether the superior was a royalist or a cardinalist, however, Milord confined himself to a prudent middle course. But the superior, on her part, maintained a reserve still more prudent, contenting herself with making a profound inclination of the head every time the traveler pronounced the name of their eminence.

Milord had not yet given thought to how long he might stay at Bethune, and had in fact assumed he would be bound to quickly depart, as he would soon grow weary of convent life. But then the notion came to him that by him holding the superior in his sway, Bethune might well prove a satisfactory base of operations and hiding place, until his affairs were better settled. Desirous, then, of seeing how far the discretion of the good superior would go, Milord began to tell a story, obscure at first but most detailed afterward, about the cardinal. As he related the alleged amours of their eminence with several notable figures of the court, the superior listened more attentively, grew animated by degrees, and finally even smiled.

"Good," thought Milord. "She takes pleasure in my conversation. If she is a cardinalist, she has no fanaticism at least."

He then went on to describe the persecutions exercised by the cardinal upon their enemies. The superior only touched their heart, without approving or disapproving. This confirmed Milord in his opinion that the superior was rather royalist than cardinalist. He therefore continued, coloring his narrations more and more.

"I am very ignorant of these matters," said the superior at length, when Milord at last allowed silence to fall between them. "But however distant from the court we may be, however remote from the interests of the world we may be placed, we have very sad examples of what you have related. In truth, one of our boarders has suffered much from the vengeance and persecution of the cardinal."

"One of your boarders?" said Milord. "By my faith, that poor soul. I pity them."

"And you have reason, for she is much to be pitied," said the superior. "Imprisonment, menaces, ill treatment — she has suffered everything. But of course, their eminence might well have plausible motives for acting thus. For though this one has the look of an angel, we must not always judge people by their appearance."

"Interesting," said Milord to himself. "I am about, perhaps, to discover some secret of the cardinal's here. This is fortune's favor, to be sure."

"Alas," said he aloud. "I know it is so. It is said that we must not trust to the face. But in what, then, shall we place confidence, if not in the most beautiful work of the creator? As for me, I shall be deceived all my life perhaps, but I shall always have faith in a person whose appearance inspires me with sympathy."

"You would be tempted to believe, then," said the superior, "that this young person is innocent?"

"Indeed. For the cardinal pursues not only crimes," said he. "There are certain virtues which their eminence pursues more severely than certain offenses."

"Permit me, monsieur, to express my surprise," said the superior.

"At what?" said Milord, with the utmost ingenuousness.

"At the language you use. For you are the friend of the cardinal, given that they send you hither. And yet…"

"And yet I speak ill of their eminence," said Milord, finishing the thought of the superior.

"You do not speak well of them, at the very least."

"That is because I am not their eminence's friend," said he, sighing. "But rather their victim, in my own way"

"But this letter in which they ask any site of faith to which you submit yourself to take you in for your care and security?"

"It is an order for me to confine myself to a sort of prison, until such time as their eminence sees fit to release me."

"But the letter does not bid us hold you here, and freely you arrived. Why have you not fled?"

"Whither should I go? Do you believe there is a spot on this earth which the cardinal cannot reach if they take the trouble to stretch forth their hand? This young boarder of yours, has she tried to fly?"

"No, that is true. But in truth, she… well, I believe she is detained in France by some love affair."

"Ah," said Milord with a sigh. "If she loves, she cannot be altogether desolate."

"Then do I guess…" said the superior, looking at Milord with increasing interest. "That is to say, do I behold another poor victim?"

"Alas, yes," said Milord, as he felt the superior fall under his sway.

"Well, monsieur," said she, smiling, "be reassured. The house in which you find yourself shall be not prison but home, and we will do all in our power to make you cherish your time here. You will doubtless meet, moreover, the young person of whom I spoke, who is persecuted, no doubt, in consequence of some court intrigue. She is most amiable."

"What is her name?"

"She was sent to me by someone of high rank, under only her first name," said the superior. "I have not tried to discover her true identity. But you may see her at some point. For now, though, you have been traveling these two days, as you told me yourself, and must stand in need of rest and breakfast. I will have the latter sent up at once."

Although Milord could very willingly have gone without food, sustained as he was by all the excitements which a new adventure awakened in a heart that ever thirsted for intrigues, he nevertheless accepted the offer of the superior.

Not long after, a knock at the door announced that his breakfast was prepared and served, and when it was brought within by two young novitiates, he ate at a small table beneath his room's single window. The fare was modest, and reinforced his desire to make his stay at Bethune no longer than needs be. But as he ate, even more so than by the repast, Milord was softly nurtured by ideas of vengeance.

He thought on that almost unlimited promise which the cardinal had given him, even in advance of success in his enterprise — and he had succeeded. D'Artagnan was then in his power. Or at least, she would have been so if the cardinal's writ of absolution had not been taken. But now, intelligence of this unknown business of the young woman in hiding in the convent, fled from the cardinal's persecution, might well provide the advantage Milord could use to earn that pardon from the cardinal once more.

Against all those thoughts, one emotion consumed Milord, even above his hatred for the young Gascon. For he reviled still from the memory of who it was who had taken the cardinal's writ from him.

The remembrance of his wife, the Countess de Fere, consumed Milord's mind.

The Countess de Fere, whom he had believed dead. She who had been found again in Athos, the best friend of d'Artagnan. And if this Athos was the friend of d'Artagnan, she must have lent the young Gascon her assistance in all the

"I am called Madame Constance," said the woman, acknowledging by withholding her surname that she would not share it. "A good afternoon to you…"

proceedings by which the Queen Anne had defeated their eminence's plans for the diamond studs. But in any case, as the friend of d'Artagnan, Athos was the enemy of the cardinal. And so Milord doubtless would succeed in drawing Athos into the vengeance by which he vowed to destroy d'Artagnan once and for all.

⚜

When breakfast was done, Milord set out from his room to take a greater measure of the convent. Along the corridor, then down a little staircase, he was drawn to the gardens of the central court. He nodded in response to the glances he received from those who passed him, and smiled after passing in observing that he far excelled all those he saw with his high air and aristocratic bearing. Though it was true that the habit of a novice, which most residents of the convent wore, was not very advantageous in a contest of that kind.

Pacing along the garden path, Milord came to a sudden stop. Standing frozen, he fixed his gaze upon a young figure of bright-brown hair and sepia features touched by opal, dressed in the simple garb of a convent novitiate, and who carried for themself a look full of benevolent curiosity as they snipped blooms from a bush of white winter roses. Before Milord could advance or retreat, this person looked up and examined him with great attention, even while offering up the customary compliments.

"Good evening to you, maitre. And as your face is new to me, I welcome you to our home at Bethune."

The young gardener was very handsome, but this was not the source of Milord's fascination, which had churned from fear through to exultation in the space of a heartbeat. For even as the figure's greeting confirmed his status as a stranger, he recognized her for who she was, from the time he had spent observing her unseen, in preparation for her appointment with Rochefort. For this was the tailor of the Rue de Fossoyeurs, and the lover of d'Artagnan.

Madame Constance Bonacieux stood before him.

"Monsieur, if you please," said he, and then added, "I am called by some as Charles Backson." And in so doing, Milord made a weapon of the name that would have taken him to exile, seizing it as if seizing a blade.

"I am called Madame Constance," said the woman, acknowledging by withholding her surname that she would not share it. "A good afternoon to you." And so saying, she took her basket and blooms and made ready to depart. But Milord stopped her.

"How, madame?" said he. "I have scarcely met you, and you already wish to deprive me of your company?"

"No, monsieur," replied Constance. "Only our superior had made it known that a new visitor would be much fatigued this day, and I thought I would depart to let you rest in our gardens at your leisure."

"Well," said Milord, "what can those who take too much rest wish for? No more than a happy awakening, which this fine day has already provided. Please join me, then, in enjoying the rest of the morning at ease." And gesturing with one hand, Milord beckoned toward a low stone bench, and sat alongside Constance as she settled.

"How unfortunate I am, monsieur," said she. "I have been here nearly these three months without even the shadow of recreation. Then you arrive, and from all the wonder the superior speaks of in your conversation, your presence was likely to afford me delightful company. Yet I expect, in all probability, to leave the convent at any moment."

"Indeed? You are going soon?" asked Milord.

"At least I hope so," said Constance, with an expression of joy which she made no effort to disguise.

Milord felt that joy as a blow, which he smiled to conceal. "If I may be so bold, I judge from your saying so that you are she who the superior intimated had suffered persecutions from Cardinal de Richelieu," said Milord. "That would have been another motive for sympathy between us."

"What I have heard, then, from our good superior is true? You have likewise been a victim of that wicked cleric?"

"Hush," said Milord. "Let us not, even here, speak thus of their eminence. All my misfortunes arise from my having said nearly what you have said before one whom I thought my friend, and who betrayed me. Are you also the victim of a treachery?"

"No," said Constance, "but rather of my devotion. A devotion to an employer I loved, for whom I would have laid down my life, and for whom I would give it still."

"And this employer has abandoned you — is that it?"

"By my faith, no," said Constance. "It is by her hand and power that I am kept safe here in Bethune from the cardinal. But it is a weary safety, and one which keeps me from… well, let us say from another whom I also love. But you, monsieur. You appear to be free. Surely if you were inclined to fly, it rests only with yourself to do so."

"Whither would you have me go, without friends, with little money, and in a part of France where I have never been before?"

"Oh," said Constance, "as to friends, you would have them wherever you want. You appear so good and are so beautiful."

"You are kind," said Milord, softening his smile so as to give it an angelic expression. "But that does not prevent my being alone or being persecuted."

"Hear me," said Constance, leaning in close. "We must trust in fate. So you see, perhaps it is a happiness for you that you have met with me, humble and powerless as I am. For if I leave this place, well… I have powerful friends, who, after having exerted themselves on my account, might also exert themselves for you."

"Oh, when I said I was alone," said Milord, hoping to make Constance Bonacieux talk by talking of himself, "it is not for want of friends in high places. But these friends themselves tremble before the cardinal. Why, even the queens themselves do not dare to oppose that terrible minister. I have even heard that her majesty Queen Anne, notwithstanding her excellent heart, has more than once been obliged to abandon to the anger of their eminence certain persons who had served her."

"Trust me, monsieur. The Queen Anne puts great thought toward all those who care for her. And the strength with which she opposes the cardinal, and defends those wronged by their eminence, cannot be overstated."

"Alas," said Milord, "I wish to believe so. But you speak with such familiarity of that lovely and noble queen. Could it be that you have met her? That you know the Queen Anne personally?"

To that, Constance gave only a shy smile. Milord with great artifice returned to her a look of profound excitement. "By my faith!" he continued, calculating. "To have the honor of knowing the royals personally. But still, I count myself in great fortune that I know even a small number of both queens' most intimate friends. I am acquainted with Monsieur Putange, the Queen Anne's former esquire. I have met Monsieur de Fronde of the Paris parliament, a good friend to both royals. I know Monsieur de Treville..."

"Monsieur de Treville!" exclaimed Constance, with all the excitement Milord had anticipated. "Do you well know the captain of the queens' musketeers?"

"Yes, perfectly well. Intimately, even."

"Why, then," said Constance, "we shall soon be even better acquainted. For if you know Monsieur de Treville, you must have visited him and Monsieur Vaslin?"

"Often," said Milord, who, having taken this path and perceiving that his falsehoods had succeeded, was set to follow it to the end.

"With him, then, you must have seen some of his musketeers?"

"All those he is in the habit of receiving," said Milord.

"Name those you best know, then, and you will see that no doubt some are among my friends."

"Well, as to the musketeer I best know," said Milord, who felt in his heart the hunger for vengeance that had carried from Portsmouth. "That would be Madame Athos."

At this, Constance clapped her hands with delight.

"Ah, and you also?" said Milord. "Why, how strange to me to meet in such a place as this with a person who knows that fine gentle so well. And if I may be so bold, if you know Madame Athos, you might well know her friends, Monsieur Porthos and Maitre Aramis?"

"Indeed, I know their names! And I look forward to meeting them when I am free of this place," said the unknowing Constance. "But this is wonderful! And as you know them, you know that they are good and free companions, and have no doubt witnessed that they count themselves among the cardinal's most mortal enemies. Why do you not apply to them, if you stand in need of help?"

"Ah, but it is not so simple," sighed Milord. "For I have seen the dire workings of the enmity of their eminence. Another good and noble friend to those three musketeers has nearly lost that which she holds most dear by that enemy's hand. The brave and virtuous Madame d'Artagnan."

"You know Madame d'Artagnan!" cried Constance, who in so saying seized the hands of Milord. That villain met the young tailor's gaze with his, as if both might be devouring the other with their eyes.

"Indeed, madame," said Milord, "as I judge do you by the tenor of your reaction. But if I may ask, you know Madame d'Artagnan by what title?"

"Why…" said Constance, suddenly guarded. "Why, I know her by the title of friend."

"Your voice tells me that you deceive me, madame," said Milord, adopting an uncertain tone. "Is there more to this? Wait. I say there is. For you are in love with this musketeer!"

"I?" said Constance.

"Yes, you! And so I know you now, for you are Madame Bonacieux!"

Constance released Milord's hands and drew back, filled with surprise and uncertainty.

"Oh, do not deny it. Answer, please," said Milord.

"Well, yes, Monsieur," said Constance. "But how do you know so much? Am I to fear you?"

"Oh, no," said Milord, in a tone that admitted no doubt of his sincerity. "Never. For do you not understand?"

"How can I understand? I know nothing."

"Can you not understand that Madame d'Artagnan, being my friend, might take me into her confidence?"

"Truly?"

"Do you not perceive that I know all? Your abduction from the little house at Saint-Cloud. The young guard's despair, and that of her friends, and all their failed attempts to seek you and bring you to safety. How could I help being astonished when, without having the least expectation of such a thing, I meet you face to face! You, of whom d'Artagnan and I have so often spoken together. You whom she loves with all her soul, you whom she had taught me to love before I had ever seen you! Ah, dear Constance, I have found you, then. I see you at last."

And Milord stretched out his arms to Constance, who, convinced by the voice and mannerisms that had corrupted so many before, saw in the cold blue eyes only the attention of a sincere and devoted friend.

"Oh, by my faith!" said the young tailor, sinking upon the shoulders of Milord. "Thanks to the fate that has brought us together. I love d'Artagnan so much!"

The two held each other for a long moment in a close embrace. And certainly, if Milord's judgement had been overridden by his hatred, Constance would never have left that embrace alive. But he tempered that hatred, honing its edge as he smiled upon her.

"Oh, you beautiful, good creature," said Milord. "How delighted I am to have found you. Let me look at you." And while saying these words, he absolutely devoured Constance by her looks. "Oh, yes, it is you indeed. From what d'Artagnan has told me, I know you now. I should have recognized you perfectly from the first."

Constance could not possibly have suspected what frightful cruelty was hidden behind the rampart of that serene brow, behind those brilliant eyes in which she read nothing but compassion.

"Then you know what I have suffered," said she, "since d'Artagnan has told you what she has suffered. But I confess that to suffer for her is joy."

Milord replied mechanically, "Yes, that is joy." But the joy he yearned to take in d'Artagnan's suffering was his only thought.

"But now," said Constance, "my punishment is drawing to a close. Soon, though I know not when exactly, I shall see her again. And then the past will no longer exist."

"Soon," said Milord, roused from his thought by those words. "As you said before. But what do you mean? Do you expect news from d'Artagnan?"

"I expect d'Artagnan herself."

"Herself? D'Artagnan here? But how is that possible? From our last correspondence, I took her still to be at the siege of La Rochelle. Surely, she will not be at liberty till after the taking of the city."

"Ah, all would think so. But is there anything impossible for my d'Artagnan, that noble and loyal gentle?"

"But how do you know this?"

"By a letter from a dear friend," said the smiling Constance. And in the excess of her joy, she removed that letter from her pocket and presented it to Milord, who carefully read its few lines.

My dear child —

Hold yourself ready. Our friend has been made aware of your situation, and will no doubt seek you at first opportunity. I have given orders that she shall release you from that solitude in which your safety required you should be concealed, and to un-

dertake your protection herself thereafter. Prepare, then, for your departure may come at any time, and never despair of us.

Our charming Gascon has just proved herself as brave and faithful as ever. Tell her that certain parties are grateful for the warning she and her friends have given.

The words burned in Milord's mind, even as did the appearance of the note itself. For even unsigned, in its fine hand, he recognized the writing of Madame de Chevreuse, and he cursed silently his earlier failure to hinder the secret communications between the Queen Anne and that troublesome noble.

"Faith," said Milord, "the letter is most enigmatic. Do you know what that warning was?"

"No. But I must suspect that d'Artagnan has warned the Queen Anne against some fresh machinations of the cardinal."

"That is it, no doubt," said Milord, returning the letter to Constance, and taking care to hide the tremor in his hand.

At that moment, the two heard the gallop of a horse from beyond the garden wall.

"What?" said Constance, darting to her feet and moving to a narrow window in the stones. "Even as we speak of her, can it be she?"

Milord remained sitting, suddenly and unexpectedly petrified by uncertainty. So many unlooked-for things were happening all at once.

"Can it be the Gascon?" murmured he. In his mind, he prepared for this unexpected meeting with his adversary, thinking on how and where to obtain additional weapons, and how he might escape when the deed was done. But it was as though all his thoughts were slowed.

But then, "Alas, no!" cried Constance. "It is a rider, cloaked and hooded, although they seem to be coming here. Yes, they check their pace. They stop at the gate."

Milord stood from the bench. "You are sure it is not her?"

"Yes, very sure."

"Perhaps you did not see well."

"My promise, monsieur, that if I were only to see the tail of d'Artagnan's hair, the lines of her fingers, I would know her."

Milord began to pace. "Mark me, this visitor is for you or me."

"Faith, how agitated you seem," said Constance.

"Yes, I admit it. I have not your confidence. I fear the cardinal."

"Hush. Someone is coming."

Immediately, footsteps echoed from the adjacent court, and the superior entered the garden. Spying Milord, she nodded and advanced.

"It is just you I am seeking," said she. "Did you come from Boulogne, monsieur?"

"Yes," said Milord. His hand slipped to his jacket, and the poniard concealed within. "Who wants me?"

"A rider who will not tell their name, but who claims to come from the cardinal."

All at once, the weight that pressed down on Milord felt lifted, though he was careful to hold uncertainty in his expression. "And this rider wishes to speak with me?"

"They wish to speak to a gentle recently come from Boulogne."

"Then let them come in, if you please."

"Oh, my faith," said Constance when the superior had departed. "Can it be bad news?"

"I fear it so," said Milord, and he allowed himself to shiver.

Constance stepped up to take Milord's hand in hers. "I will leave you with this stranger. But as soon as they are gone, if you will permit me, I will return."

"Permit you? I beseech you." Milord then smiled bravely, and with that, Constance left the garden by a back passage at once.

Milord remained alone, with his eyes fixed upon the courtyard arch. A moment later, the jingling of spurs was heard upon the stairs, steps drew near, and a figure appeared.

The smile that Milord had hidden from Constance and the superior touched his pale lips. For this rider was the Count de Rochefort.

"Your arrival is well timed," said Milord quietly, "but we have much to speak of and must speak swiftly. For all her many offenses, my vengeance upon the Gascon d'Artagnan is nigh!"

— CHAPTER 62 —

THE PLAN OF ARMENTIERES

Rochefort, for his part, nodded to Milord and stepped close. Milord began to walk through the garden, which was empty at present of all but them, motioning the other to follow.

"So it is you," said Rochefort, speaking low.

"Yes, it is I," said Milord. "Pray, how did you find me here?"

"Their eminence sent word to me in Paris that they were uneasy at having heard nothing from England, and bid me to seek signs of you in the ports. I heard nothing in Dieppe, and was about to leave Boulogne for Calais when a chance meeting brought me to the captain of *The Dark Horse*. Following your hired carriage was then easily done."

"Your skills as a hound are commendable, Rochefort. Let me reward you with news from England."

"Buckingham?"

"Dead or desperately wounded," said Milord with pride, "as I left without having been able to hear all details. A fanatic assassinated him."

"Ah," said Rochefort with a smile. "This is a fortunate chance — and one that will delight their eminence. Have you informed them of it?"

"I wrote to them from Boulogne when I arrived three days past. And I am pleased to say I have not misspent my time since arriving here this morning. Do you know whom I have encountered in Bethune?"

"How could I know?" said Rochefort, dismissive.

"Madame Constance Bonacieux," said Milord with triumph in his voice. "The lover of the Gascon d'Artagnan, whom the Queen Anne arranged to escape from your care."

Rochefort's surprise was shaped by his bristling at Milord's tone, which he returned. "Well, well. Given that the cardinal had complained at your inability to determine Madame Bonacieux's hiding place, your arrival here was most fortunate. But did she know you?"

"No. The young tailor has no idea of me."

"Then she looks upon you as a stranger?"

Milord smiled. "As a friend."

"Upon my honor," said Rochefort, forgiving Milord's earlier slight, "it takes you, my dear Milord, to perform such miracles."

"And it is well I can, monsieur," said Milord. "For do you know what is set to happen here?"

"Pray enlighten me."

"They will come for her imminently, with an order from the Queen Anne. D'Artagnan and her three friends."

"Splendid! With that order as proof of insurgency, we shall be obliged to send them to the Bastille."

"An obligation that should have been met long ago, were it left to me. Why is it not done already when left to you?"

"Because the matter is beyond me. The cardinal has a fascination for these four musketeers which I cannot comprehend."

"Three musketeers and one ignoble guard, you mean," said Milord.

"Ah, but you will not yet have heard. D'Artagnan was offered and accepted assignment with the musketeers — at the cardinal's own insistence, the better to keep those four under their eminence's observation."

"Indeed?" said Milord, who felt his rage rise at the thought of this enemy gaining such prestige at his own expense. "Well, then, allow their eminence to add the following to their observations, Rochefort. Tell them that our conversation at the inn of the Red Dovecote was overheard by these four. Tell them that after their eminence's departure, one of them came up to me and took from me by violence the writ of absolution which they had given me. Tell them those four warned Liege de Winter of my journey to England, nearly foiling my mission as they foiled the affair of the diamond studs."

"But those four must be now at the siege of La Rochelle?"

"We may hope so. But a letter which Madame Bonacieux has received from Madame de Chevreuse, and which she has had the imprudence to show me, tells that these four will be on the road hither at first opportunity, to take the young tailor away."

"Gods' blood! What's to be done?"

"What did the cardinal say about me when they sent you forth?"

"That if I was to find you, I was to take your dispatches, written or verbal, and return at once. And when their eminence learns what you have done, they will advise what you must yet do."

"I cannot return with you, though," said Milord. "Near La Rochelle, I might be recognized, and my presence would compromise the cardinal. But nor can I remain here indefinitely, for the four musketeers may arrive at any moment."

"So is this Madame Bonacieux, then, to escape their eminence? For she cannot accompany me."

"No," said Milord, with a smile that belonged only to himself. "You forget that I am her friend."

Rochefort appraised Milord with a haughty air. "So then, may I tell the cardinal that with respect to the Queen Anne's tailor…?"

"Tell their eminence that they may be at ease."

"And is that all?"

"They will know what it means. Or they will guess, at least. Now, then, you must return at once. It appears to me that the news you bear is worth the trouble of a speedy journey."

"I may be somewhat delayed," said Rochefort. "My carriage broke down coming into Lillers, and I came here on horse while repairs are effected."

"Excellent," said Milord.

"Excellent? And how so?"

"Because I will take your carriage, and you will carry on to Saint Rochelle on horse, as you are now."

"You say so with precious little thought to me. It is a hundred and twenty leagues to La Rochelle!"

"What is that to a rider such as you? So passing through Lillers, you will send me your carriage, with an order to your valet to place themself at my disposal."

"Indeed," said Rochefort coldly, but his expression made clear that he accepted the commands.

"Now," said Milord. "You have, no doubt, some note bearing the cardinal's seal about you? Show it to the superior, and tell her that someone will come and fetch me, either today or tomorrow, and that I am to follow the person who presents themself in your name."

"Very well."

"And don't forget to treat me harshly in speaking of me."

"To what purpose?"

"As far as Madame Bonacieux is concerned, she and I are both victims of the cardinal. It is necessary to inspire confidence in her little mind. And watch to ensure you stay well clear of her before you depart, for she will recognize the one who carried her off in Paris."

"As you say. And if that is all, simply tell me where you will wait for intelligence from the cardinal," said Rochefort. "I must know where to find you."

"Let me reflect a little," said Milord, who spent a moment in thought. "Aye, that will do — seek me at Armentieres."

"And what is that?"

"A little village on the River Lys, no more than seven leagues from here, where the river marks the Belgian border." Taking paper and pen from his jacket, Milord stepped to the garden wall and quickly wrote the name for Rochefort.

"Armentieres," said Rochefort, taking and reading the paper from Milord, folding it, and placing it within his pocket. "A name unknown to me. You must know this country marvelously."

"Indeed. For I lived near here upon a time, and in great splendor."

"Truly?"

"It is worth something, you see, to be able to return to the places one once dwelled. And if danger seeks me now as it did then, I shall only have to cross the river, and I shall be safe in a foreign land."

"And in that case, how shall I know where you are?"

"Is your valet one to be counted on?"

"To the last."

"Then I will leave them at the place I depart, and they will conduct you to me."

"You may be at ease, then," said Rochefort, "for you think of everything."

"And you forget one thing."

"What?"

"To ask me if I need money."

"But of course." Rochefort smiled thinly. "How much might you need?"

"All you have in gold."

"I have five hundred pistoles, or thereabouts."

"I have the same. With a thousand pistoles one may face everything. So empty your pockets."

Rochefort did, handing forth his purse with an impassive look. "There."

"Capital! Adieux, monsieur. Please commend me to the cardinal."

"Adieux, Milord. Commend me to the shadow-realm that spawned you."

Milord laughed aloud as he and Rochefort separated.

Rochefort then returned to his horse, and near noon, passed through Arras. Our readers already know how he was recognized by d'Artagnan, and how that recognition inspired fear in the four musketeers — and had given them cause to desperately renew their journey.

CHAPTER 63

A DROP OF WATER

Milord continued to walk the gardens after Rochefort had departed, waiting as he did for Constance to reenter. When she did, she found Milord smiling.

"Well," said she, "what you dreaded has happened. This evening, or tomorrow, the cardinal will send someone to take you away."

"Who told you that, my dear?" asked Milord.

"The superior confided to me, having heard it from the mouth of the messenger themself, so that I might tell you."

"Come and sit down close to me," said Milord, and gestured to another bench, this one in a shaded arbor beneath winter-bare grape vines.

Constance did so, but when Milord continued to stand and stare around him, she called to him, "Here I am."

"Wait till I assure myself that no one hears us."

"Why all these precautions?"

"You shall know."

Milord then circled the arbor with care, looking along the empty paths adjacent, before returning to seat himself close to Constance.

"By my faith," said he to her, "they well played their part."

"Who has?"

"They who just now presented themself to the superior as a messenger from the cardinal."

"It was a part they were playing?" said Constance in astonishment.

"Indeed," said Milord, lowering his voice and indicating Constance to do the same. "For that messenger is my brother."

Constance placed her hands in Milord's and stared in astonishment. For his part, Milord set a tremor in his hands and breathed a sigh of fear.

"No one will know this secret, my dear, except ourselves," said Constance, sensing what she took as Milord's unease.

"I thank you for your courage," said he. "For if you reveal it to anyone in the world, I shall be lost — and perhaps yourself likewise."

"Explain," said Constance to that.

"Listen," said Milord. "This is what has happened. My brother, who was coming to my assistance and meant to take me away by force despite the risk to us both, met with the emissary of the cardinal who was coming in search of me. He followed that emissary. At a solitary and deserted part of the road, he drew his sword, and required the messenger to deliver up to him certain papers of which they were the bearer. The messenger resisted. My brother killed them."

"Faith!" said Constance, shuddering.

"Such is his love for me. But in his despair, my brother then determined to substitute cunning for force. He took the papers, and presented himself here as the emissary of the cardinal. And so before another day is out, a carriage will come to take me away, seemingly by the orders of their eminence."

"Ah, I understand. But it will be your brother who sends this carriage."

"Exactly. But my dear Madame Bonacieux, that is not all. For the papers carried by the cardinal's agent revealed grave secrets. That letter you have received. Did you believe it to come from Madame de Chevreuse…?" Milord's voice weakened, as if he could scarce bring himself to say the words.

"Indeed. And so?"

"It is a forgery."

"How can that be?"

"The cardinal's plots make it so. It is a trap to prevent your making any resistance when they come to fetch you."

"But it is d'Artagnan who will come."

"Do not deceive yourself. D'Artagnan and her friends are embroiled in the siege of La Rochelle. Their eminence's papers, which I saw, have commissioned a group of the cardinal's guards to wear the uniform of the musketeers. You would have been summoned to the gate by those claiming to be friends of your friends. Then you would have been abducted, and conducted back to Paris."

At once, Constance shot to her feet to pace the arbor in a fury. "By my faith! My senses fail me amid such a chaos of iniquities."

Milord stood to step beside her, and with his hands clasping hers, he slowed her course.

"Dear sir," said Constance. "My pardon for my apprehension. But I beseech you, what do you advise me to do? Clearly, you have more experience than I have in these matters. Speak, and I will listen."

Milord sighed to let a weariness flow across him. "Firstly," said he, "it is possible that we may both be deceived. Knowing that my brother pursued him, the cardinal's agent could have sought to set my brother against the musketeers with false intelligence, so that d'Artagnan and her friends might truly come to your assistance."

"Oh, that would be too much," said Constance. "So much happiness is not in store for me."

"Then you comprehend the impossible nature of this situation. You cannot flee, for fear that d'Artagnan's rescue will come in vain. But you cannot wait for the cardinal's forces, for if they find you here, you are lost."

"Lost beyond redemption. What then to do? What to do?"

"Well," said Milord thoughtfully. "There might be a very simple means."

"Tell me."

"It would be to wait, concealed in some nearby place, to be assured as to the identity of those who come to ask for you."

"But where can I wait?"

"With me, of course. When I am on my way, I shall stop and conceal myself a few leagues hence until my brother can rejoin me. But when I go, I take you with me. We conceal ourselves, and wait together."

"But I shall not be allowed to go. For my own security, I am almost a prisoner here."

"I understand," said Milord. "But as they believe that I go in consequence of an order from the cardinal, no one will believe you anxious to follow me. And so…"

"Well?"

"Well, envision that the carriage is at the door. You bid me adieux. You mount the step to say farewell a last time. But my brother's valet, who comes to fetch me, can be trusted and will be told how to proceed. He shall make a sign to the driver, and we set off at a gallop."

"But d'Artagnan! If she comes, how shall we know it?"

"Nothing easier. We will send back to Bethune my brother's valet, whom, as I told you, we can trust. They shall assume a disguise, and place themself near the convent. If the emissaries of the cardinal arrive, the valet will be of no notice to them. But if it is Madame d'Artagnan and her friends, they will bring them to us."

"But how will this valet know d'Artagnan, then?"

"But he already does, my dear. For he has been with my brother and me to Monsieur de Treville's!"

"Faith! Oh, my faith, you are right, and thus all may go well. All may be for the best. But we will not go far from this place?"

"Seven or eight leagues at the most. We will keep to the frontier, for safety. That way, if all turns to alarms, we can easily leave France."

"But if I should happen to be any distance from you when the carriage comes for you? At dinner or supper, for instance?"

"Then do one thing. Tell your good superior that we have enjoyed each other's company, and that you ask her permission to share my repast."

"Oh, delightful! In this way, we shall not be separated for an instant."

"Then go to her quickly to make your request. I will take more rest here in the garden, to allay any suspicion that we are engaging together in plots."

"I shall, and then shall return here when I can," said Constance, beaming with joy. "Oh, you are so kind, and I am so grateful!"

"How can I avoid extending myself for one who is so beautiful and so amiable? And are you not the beloved of one of my closest friends?"

"Dear d'Artagnan! Oh, how she will thank you!"

"I hope so. Now, then, all is agreed. You must go."

And so Constance departed, she and Milord exchanging smiles.

When alone again, Milord understood that his mind was all confusion, for his hastily arranged plans clashed against one another in chaos. He needed to be alone, that he might put his thoughts a little into order. He saw the future, though only vaguely. But he stood in need of a little silence and quiet to give all his ideas, as yet tangled, a distinct form and a final plan.

What was most urgent was to get Constance away, to convey her to a place of safety — and once there, to make her a hostage. For the young tailor was the very life of d'Artagnan. Milord had no doubts as to the advent of the terrible contest that was coming, in which his enemies would show as much perseverance as he did animosity. He felt as one feels when a great storm is coming on — that this tempest was near, and could not fail to be terrible. But Milord knew also that in case the fortune of this storm went against him, the life of the one who d'Artagnan loved would be his best means of negotiating an end to hostilities on his own terms.

Revolving all this in his mind, he cast his eyes around him and arranged the topography of the garden in his head. He noted its back gate, opening onto the wood beyond, as the best means of quitting the convent if his circumstances turned dire. Milord was like a good general who contemplates at the same time victory and defeat, and who is quite prepared, according to the chances of the battle, to march forward or to beat a retreat.

He felt certain now that Constance would accompany him without suspicion. Then once concealed with him at Armentieres, it would be easy to make her believe that d'Artagnan had not come to Bethune. In a month at most, Rochefort would be back. And during that month, Milord would have time to engage in the sweetest pastime accorded to one of his character — to think on how he could best avenge himself on the four musketeers.

⚜

Milord returned to his chamber for the serving of dinner, but found he had no appetite. Returning to the garden gave him no peace. But he paced and sat in alternate turns, smiling at those who passed him, and not sure how many hours had passed before he saw finally the face he sought, and Constance Bonacieux was there.

"The good superior has consented to my request," said she. "And accordingly, we may take our meals together."

"Most splendid," said Milord. "It must nearly be supper now. You must lead me to the dining room, for the more we are seen together, the less suspicion will fall upon you in bidding me farewell."

But even upon them reaching the courtyard, they heard beyond the convent walls the noise of a carriage which stopped at the gate. Constance listened attentively, and not without fear. "Do you hear that?" said she.

"It is the rolling of a carriage," said Milord. "Undoubtedly, it is the one my brother sends for us, come even earlier than expected."

"Oh, my faith!"

"Come, come, madame. Courage."

The bell of the convent gate was sounded, and Milord's plans were engaged.

"Go to your chamber," said he to Constance, "but be quick. You have clothing and personal effects you would like to take? Well, go and fetch them, and then come to my apartment. We must arrange our exit together, and you must stay out of sight lest the superior give you some order that would prevent you stepping outside the gate."

"Gods' blood," said Constance, placing her hand upon Milord's. "But if this be instead the cardinal's servants… alas, my heart beats so I cannot walk."

"Courage! Remember that in a quarter of an hour, you will be safe. And think that what we both are about to do is for d'Artagnan's sake."

"Yes. Yes! Everything for her. You have restored my courage by a single word. Go, I will rejoin you."

As Constance ran to her room, Milord slipped to his own chamber quickly. At his door, he found Rochefort's valet waiting for him, and gave them his instructions. For despite the great lack of chance of it happening so, Milord was intent that he would account for any potential of the musketeers appearing that very night.

The carriage was to wait at the gate. And if by impossible fortune the musketeers should appear, it was to set off as fast as possible, pass around the convent, and go and wait for Milord at the other side of the wood. In this event, Milord would cross the garden and meet the carriage on foot. If the musketeers did not appear, things were to go on as had been agreed. Constance was to get into the carriage as if to bid Milord adieux, and he would take the young tailor away.

A knock on the door heralded Constance's arrival, who had a small bag packed and clutched tightly in both hands.

"You see?" said Milord as he embraced her. "Everything is ready. The superior suspects nothing, and believes that I am taken by order of the cardinal. I have confirmed by sight that it is my brother's valet who makes arrangements with the superior. Now let us watch at the window for the carriage to be ready to go. We may drink a finger of wine in celebration while they water the horses, and then we will be gone."

"Yes," said Constance, excited though still nervous. "Yes, let us be gone."

Milord poured each of them a small glass of Spanish wine, but saw that Constance barely touched the glass with her lips.

"There is nothing to fear," said he. "Everything is propitious. Here is night coming on to conceal our flight. Long before daybreak, we shall have reached our retreat, and no one will guess where we are. Come, courage! Let us drink to your love."

But at the moment Milord's own glass touched his lips, his hand froze. Through the window, he heard something that sounded like the rattling of a distant gallop on the road. It grew nearer, and it seemed to him almost at the same time that he heard the shouting of voices.

This noise acted upon his joy like the storm which awakens the sleeper in the midst of a happy dream. He grew pale and stood, stepping to the window. Constance, rising behind him, clutched her chair to quell the tremble in her hands. Nothing was yet to be seen, but both heard the galloping draw nearer.

"Oh, my faith," whispered Constance. "What is that noise?"

"That of either our friends or our enemies," said Milord with a terrible coolness. "Stay where you are, and I will tell you."

Constance remained standing, mute and motionless as a statue.

The noise became louder. The horses could not be more than a hundred and fifty paces distant, though they remained hidden behind a turn of the road. But their noise was by now so distinct that four steeds could be counted by the clattering of their iron-shod hoofs.

Milord watched with all the power of his attention. It was just still light enough for him to see who was coming.

All at once, at the turning of the road, he saw the gleam of drawn steel against dark leather. He saw one rider precede the other three by the length of their horse. He saw at d'Artagnan's shoulder the badge of the musketeers.

"What is it?" cried Constance. "What do you see?"

"It is the uniform of the cardinal's guards," said Milord, voice hung heavy with fright. "There is not a moment to be lost. Thanks to the garden, we yet can flee. In mere minutes it will be too late!"

As they heard the horses pass beneath the windows, though, Constance shut her eyes tight. When she opened them again, she shook her head.

"You are frightened," said Milord coldly. "Let me help you."

"No, monsieur," said Constance, and she stepped away. "I am not frightened. I will not be frightened anymore."

"My dear…" began Milord.

"You must fly," said Constance, interrupting, "for your freedom is just. But as for me, if the cardinal seeks me here, I will return to Paris. I will no longer run nor hide, but will face this villain. I will trust to my queen, and I will have d'Artagnan and the musketeers at my side. Please, monsieur. Go."

At that moment, they heard the rolling of the carriage, which at the approach of the musketeers set off at a gallop. Then three shots were fired.

"Go, monsieur!" said Constance again. "Your hope for yourself has given me strength."

"And I have not the time to break that strength now," murmured Milord, who all at once felt all his plans undone.

Unseen by Constance, a livid fury flashed in Milord's eyes. He stepped to the table, hand in his jacket pocket, and brought it up with a small sachet of silk between his fingers, emptied into Constance's wineglass with singular quickness. Its contents were a powder of a reddish color, part of his purchase of the apothecary of Boulogne, and dissolved within the wine immediately.

Then, taking that glass and his own with a firm hand, he stepped to Constance, saying, "Let us drink, then. To love, and to freedom." Milord drank his glass down.

Taking the tainted wineglass in hand, Constance did the same.

"Now go, monsieur," said she again. "Do not let them know you are here."

"Oh, but they will know," said Milord, replacing the glass upon the table with an infernal smile. "This is not the way that I wished to avenge myself. But by my faith, we do what we can."

At the change that had come across Milord's face, Constance stepped quickly back. A wariness was in her suddenly, seeing the light of hatred in the bright blue eyes.

"Monsieur, you must go," said she, more forcefully.

"Yes, I go," said he. "But I would leave a message for those who come for you. Tell them Milord de Winter bids them adieux."

"Monsieur?" said Constance, who did not understand. But with no look back, Milord stepped from the room and closed the door behind him.

Constance thought to follow, but a wariness of Milord's new-seen malevolence was in her still. From the window, a greater noise was heard at the gate. She felt a calm descend upon her, soothing her fear. Still, she was heated suddenly, and a cold sweat burst from her burning brow.

At length, she heard the grating of the hinges of the opening gates. The noise of boots and spurs resounded on the stairs. There was a great murmur of voices which continued to draw near, amid which she thought she heard her own name pronounced. Except her hearing was unclear suddenly.

All at once, she uttered a cry of joy and darted toward the door. For she had recognized the voice of d'Artagnan.

"D'Artagnan! D'Artagnan!" cried Constance. "Is it you? This way! This way!" But she was forced to sit suddenly, and could not go to her love.

"Constance!" cried the young musketeer in reply. "Constance! Where are you?"

A moment later, the door of what had been Milord's chamber was flung wide, and four figures rushed in. Constance had sunk into an armchair, the power of movement fading from her.

D'Artagnan threw down a still-smoking pistol which she held in her hand, and fell on her knees before her love. Athos replaced her own pistol in her belt. Porthos and Aramis, who held drawn swords in their hands, returned them to their scabbards.

"Oh, d'Artagnan," cried Constance. "My beloved d'Artagnan! You have come, then, at last! You have found me!"

"Yes, Constance. We are reunited at last!"

"Oh, it was in vain he told me you would not come! I hoped in silence. I was not willing to fly. Oh, I have done well! How happy I am!"

D'Artagnan's expression grew stern suddenly. "Who is this he who spoke to you? That villain Rochefort? Was he here?"

"No, the good Charles Backson. He who out of friendship for me wished to take me from my persecutors. But he mistook you for the cardinal's guards… and has just fled… away."

Constance's speech was slowed suddenly. D'Artagnan saw the young tailor's complexion turn ashen, and there was fear in her heart.

"Who is this Charles Backson?" said Athos, who became even more pale than the brave agent of the Queen Anne. "Where have they fled?"

"To the carriage… which was at the gate. But you know him, Athos. He called himself… your friend. D'Artagnan has told him… everything."

"Help, help, my friends!" cried d'Artagnan. "Her hands are icy cold. Constance is ill!"

"But… I feel very strange," said Constance, clutching at d'Artagnan with weak hands. "Faith, my head swims… D'Artagnan! I cannot see!"

At once, Porthos bound through the door, and was calling for help with all the power of his strong voice. Aramis ran to the table to get a glass of water. But the gentle musketeer stopped at seeing the horrible transformation that had taken place on the face of Athos, who, standing before the table, her eyes fixed in stupor, was looking at the silk sachet that had fallen from Milord's fingers.

"No…" whispered Athos. "No, it is impossible! No gods would permit such a crime!"

"Water!" cried d'Artagnan. "Water!"

"Oh, poor soul…" murmured Athos in a broken voice.

D'Artagnan pressed kisses to the forehead of Constance as Aramis returned with the glass of water. Porthos was once more at the door. Constance opened her eyes under the touch of d'Artagnan's lips.

"She revives," whispered the young musketeer. But though Aramis set the water to her lips, Constance could swallow but a single drop.

"Madame Bonacieux," said Athos. "Madame, I implore you, did you drink from these wineglasses?"

"We both did, Madame Athos," said the young tailor in a dying voice.

"We? Who was it who poured the wine for you that was in this glass?"

"D'Artagnan's friend… Charles… Charles Backson…"

Athos shook her head with fury, looking to all the others. But the terrified looks of all confirmed that none knew the name.

"Oh, but he left… a message…" said Constance. "Oh, I remember…" Her eyes blinked to focus on d'Artagnan. "Milord Winter… bids you adieux…"

D'Artagnan, Aramis, and Porthos alike were shocked to silence. But the voice of Athos rose as a cry of rage.

At that moment, the face of Constance became flushed. A fearful agony pervaded her frame, and she clutched at the arms of Aramis and d'Artagnan.

D'Artagnan called to Athos with an anguish difficult to be described. "What does this mean, Athos?" Her voice was stifled by sobs. "What do you believe?"

"I believe everything," said Athos, biting her lip till the blood flowed.

"D'Artagnan, d'Artagnan!" cried Constance. "Where are you? Do not leave me!"

D'Artagnan embraced her fully. Constance's beautiful face was distorted with agony. Her glassy eyes had again lost their sight. A convulsive shuddering shook her body, and the sweat rolled from her brow.

"In fate's name," d'Artagnan cried. "Why does no one come with help?"

"Patience!" cried Porthos. "The healer is called!"

"Useless…" said Athos. "Useless! For the poisons he pours, there is no antidote."

"It's all right…" murmured Constance. "D'Artagnan…"

Then, collecting all her strength, Constance took the head of the young musketeer between her hands, looked at her for a moment as if her whole soul passed into that look, and with a sobbing cry, pressed her lips to hers.

A sigh escaped from the mouth of Constance, and dwelt for a moment on the lips of d'Artagnan. That sigh was the soul, so brave and so loving, which passed beyond the world again.

"Constance!" shouted d'Artagnan. For she held only a corpse in her arms. The young musketeer uttered a cry and fell by the side of her love, as ashen and as icy as Constance herself.

Porthos wept. Aramis cast their eyes toward the heavens. Athos placed her clenched hand on her heart.

A commotion in the hallway marked the arrival of the healer, followed close by the superior and several acolytes of the convent. But from the doorway, all saw that they had come too late.

Athos walked toward d'Artagnan with a slow and solemn step. She embraced her friend tenderly, and as d'Artagnan burst into violent sobs, Athos spoke in her noble and persuasive voice. "The time for tears will wait for you. But the time for vengeance is now."

"Oh, yes," cried d'Artagnan. She kissed the brow of Constance one last time, then closed her love's eyes. "Yes. If I am alive, it is only to avenge her. I am ready to follow you."

Athos then made signs to Porthos and Aramis to attend d'Artagnan, and the two, passing their arms under those of their friend, assisted her from the room.

Following, Athos spoke to the superior. "Madame," said she, "we abandon to your pious care the body of Constance Bonacieux. She was an angel on earth before being taken from it. Treat her as one of your most faithful. We will return at your bidding to see her buried. And send word to all who might hear it that he who stayed beneath your roof in the name of Charles Backson is a counterfeit, a villain, and a murderer. Milord de Winter he might also call himself, or even Arne de Breuil if he is bold enough. And I have a hundred pistoles for the first who brings me word on where the villain might be found."

Outside the gate of the convent, d'Artagnan turned to embrace Athos behind her, concealing her face against the breast of the elder musketeer.

"Weep," said Athos. "Weep, heart full of love, youth, and life. Alas, would that I could weep like you."

Then with Aramis and Porthos close behind, she led her young friend away toward the exhausted horses, as affectionate as a parent, as consoling as a cleric. As noble as any who has suffered much.

CHAPTER 64

THE RED-CLOAKED STRANGER

On horse once more, the four musketeers made their way from the convent into Bethune, and stopped before the first inn they came to, which was called the Crown. D'Artagnan in her anger took some offense at this, having prepared herself for a hard ride. "But what?" said she. "Are we not to pursue Milord?"

"Indeed," said Athos, "and soon. But I have measures to take first."

"He will escape us," cried the young musketeer. "He will escape us, and it will be your fault, Athos!"

"I will be accountable for him," said Athos. "You have my word."

In response, d'Artagnan lowered her head in grief, but remembered the confidence she had in her friend. She entered the inn without further reply. But Porthos and Aramis glanced to each other, not yet knowing what measures Athos spoke of.

"Now, gentles," said Athos, when she had ascertained there were sufficient rooms free in the inn, "let everyone go to their own chamber. D'Artagnan needs to be alone, to weep and to rest. I take charge of everything. Be at ease."

"Athos," said Porthos severely, "if there are any measures to take against this Milord, it concerns all of us. Will you not speak?"

"When all is prepared," said Athos. "For the measures I take, I take alone, as Milord de Winter's wife, and as the first judge and arbiter of his crimes."

Porthos and Aramis looked at each other, but neither gave reply.

"Now, withdraw to your rooms," said Athos, "and leave me to act."

Left alone, Athos was possessed by one single thought — that of the promise of vengeance she had made, and of the responsibility she had taken. And with that focus, she allowed her despair to give way to a concentrated grief, which only rendered more lucid the brilliant mental faculties of that extraordinary musketeer.

She first sent a messenger out to seek the four valets, who she knew would be wandering Bethune that night in search of their employers. Then she withdrew to her own chamber, carrying a map of the province which she had requested one of the hosts to procure for her. Sitting by the fire, Athos bent over it and found at once a name she knew. Some seven leagues from Bethune was the village of Armentieres — the name written on the paper which had fallen from Rochefort's pocket. That name written in Milord's own hand.

The map showed the four different roads that led from Bethune to Armentieres, each of which Athos traced out with a finger. She then summoned the valets, who had by then arrived at the inn. Planchet, Grimaud, Bazin, and Mousqueton presented themselves, and received clear and serious orders from Athos. Shown the map to study, the valets were to set out the next morning at daybreak and go to Armentieres — but each by a different route. Planchet, perhaps the most observant of the four, was to follow the road by which the carriage had gone, with that route noted when the four musketeers had fired upon the fleeing vehicle, wounding a valet lurking near the horses as a consequence.

Athos set the musketeers' valets to work in full confidence. For despite the reproach that was part of her nature, she knew and had always known full well that those four who had come into the service of herself and her friends each possessed the essential qualities that made them fine agents for a soldier's work. Moreover, valets who asked questions would inspire less mistrust than armed soldiers, and would meet with more sympathy among those to whom they address themselves. And most important, Milord knew the musketeers and did not know the valets, while the four would be able to recognize Milord perfectly.

Once arrived at Armentieres, Planchet, Grimaud, Bazin, and Mousqueton were to retreat outside the village to meet again before noon. If any of them had discovered Milord's retreat, three were to go to that place to remain on guard. The fourth was to return to Bethune in order to inform Athos, and to serve as a guide to the four musketeers. These arrangements made, the valets retired to the chambers Athos had procured for them for the night.

Athos then arose from her chair, girded on her sword, enveloped herself in her cloak, and left the inn.

It was by then late in the night, a time at which the streets in provincial towns are very little frequented. Athos nevertheless appeared visibly anxious to find someone of whom she could ask a question, for she paced those streets with an uncertain look, as though attempting to call forth a memory. At length, she met a belated wanderer, went up to them, and spoke a few words. The person she addressed recoiled with terror, and answered the musketeer's question only by pointing. Athos offered the wanderer half a pistole to accompany her, but they refused.

She then set out along the street the person had indicated. But arriving at a four-way crossroads, she stopped again, visibly disconcerted. As the crossroads offered her a better chance than any other place of meeting someone, she paced

*Athos and this figure exchanged some words in a low voice. Then
the tall person made a sign to the musketeer that she might come in...*

there a while. In a few minutes, a member of the night watch passed. Athos repeated to them the same question she had asked the first figure, to which the sentry evinced the same terror, refused in their turn to accompany Athos, and only pointed with their hand to the road she was to take.

Athos walked in the direction indicated and soon reached the edge of Bethune, along the opposite side of that by which she and her friends had entered the town. There she again appeared uneasy, and stopped for the third time.

Fortunately, a vagabond soon passed, coming up to Athos to ask charity. Athos offered them half a crown to accompany her where she was going. The vagabond hesitated at first, but at the sight of the piece of silver which shone in the darkness, they consented, and walked on before Athos.

Arrived at the corner of a street, the vagabond pointed to a small house, isolated, solitary, and dismal. Athos went toward the house, while the vagabond, who had received their reward, left as fast as their legs could carry them.

Athos was forced to go full around the house before she could distinguish the door against the red color which the domicile was painted. No light appeared through the shutters. No noise gave reason to believe that the place was inhabited. It was dark and silent as a tomb.

Three times Athos knocked without receiving an answer. At the fourth knock, however, steps were heard inside. The door at length was opened, revealing lantern light from within that had been trapped by shaded windows. A figure appeared in that light, of forty-five years or more and tall stature, with an ivory complexion underscored by ruddy tones, and graying hair and beard.

Athos and this figure exchanged some words in a low voice. Then the tall person made a sign to the musketeer that she might come in. Athos immediately accepted, and the door was closed behind her.

The person whom Athos had come to seek, and whom she had found with so much trouble, introduced her into their laboratory, where they were engaged in fastening together with iron wire the dry bones of a human skeleton. All the frame was assembled except the skull, which lay on the table.

All the rest of the furniture and fittings indicated that the dweller in this house occupied themself with the study of natural science. There were large bottles filled with serpents, ticketed according to their species. Dried lizards shone like emeralds set in great squares of black wood, and bunches of wild odoriferous herbs, doubtless possessed of virtues unknown to common folk, were fastened to the ceiling and hung down in the corners of the apartment. There was no family, no servant. The tall person alone inhabited this house.

Athos cast a focused and empathetic glance upon the objects we have described, and at the invitation of them whom she had come to seek, she sat down.

Then she introduced herself, and the person responded with uneasy recognition. Athos explained to them the cause of her visit, and the service she required of them. But scarcely had she expressed her request when the stranger, who remained standing before the musketeer, drew back with signs of foreboding and refused.

Then Athos took from her pocket a small paper, opening it before her to reveal the writ of absolution bearing the name and seal of the cardinal.

By my order, and for the good of the state, the bearer of this has done what they have done.

— Richelieu

The tall person who had made the signs of refusal had scarcely read these lines, seen the signature, and recognized the seal before they bowed to denote that they had no longer any objection to make, and that they were ready to obey.

Athos required no more. She arose, bowed, and went out. Walking quickly, she returned the same way she had come, reentered the inn, and went to her chamber. None of the other musketeers saw her return, or knew that she had gone.

⚜

At daybreak, d'Artagnan came to Athos, already awake and sitting thoughtfully. The unhealthy pallor of the young musketeer's face suggested she had slept little.

"And so?" said d'Artagnan, though with less heat than the previous day. "You spoke of measures to take before we might pursue Milord. What is then to be done?"

"Only to wait," said Athos.

Before d'Artagnan could reply, a messenger came at a run seeking Athos, having been sent by the superior of the convent to inform the musketeers that the burial for Constance Bonacieux would take place at midday. As to Milord, the messenger reported dutifully, those at the convent had heard no tidings of him whatsoever, and had deduced only that he must have made his escape through the garden, the dirt of which held footsteps that could be traced, and the gate of which had been left ajar.

At the hour appointed, the four friends returned to the convent. There, the bells tolled. The chapel was open, with only the grating of the choir remaining closed. In the middle of the choir, the body of the young tailor, clothed in her novitiate dress, was resting, with the white winter roses she had cut only the previous day arrayed around her. On each side of the choir and behind the gratings opening into the convent was assembled the whole community of the

Carmelites, who listened to the divine service, and who mingled their chant with the chant of the clerics.

At the door of the chapel, d'Artagnan felt her courage fall, and the young musketeer turned to look for Athos. But only Porthos and Aramis were at her side, for unnoticed by any of the three, Athos had disappeared.

Faithful to her mission of vengeance, Athos had stepped aside near the entrance to the convent, and had requested to be conducted to the garden. There, she cast her gaze upon the tracks spread across the dirt, following the fast-moving steps of the one who had left them. She advanced toward the gate which led from the garden into the wood adjacent, and went out through it among the trees.

As she paced, Athos found all her suspicions confirmed. The road by which the carriage had disappeared encircled the forest, and she followed that road for some time. Her eyes fixed upon the ground and noted slight stains of blood, which she guessed might have come from the wound inflicted upon the valet who had accompanied the carriage.

At the end of three-quarters of a league, a larger bloodstain appeared, and the ground was trampled by horses. Between the forest and this accursed spot, a little behind the trampled ground, was the same track of racing footsteps as in the garden. At this spot, Milord had come out of the wood, and had entered the carriage where it stopped.

Satisfied with this discovery, Athos returned not to the convent but to the inn, where she found Planchet impatiently waiting for her. As d'Artagnan's valet told his tale, it was all as Athos had foreseen.

Planchet had followed the same road Athos circumscribed from the convent, and had, like her, discovered the stains of blood and noted the spot where the horses had halted. But he had gone farther than Athos, continuing on to the village of Festubert. There, while drinking at an inn, Planchet had learned without even needing to ask that the evening before, a wounded figure who accompanied a gentry traveling in a carriage had been obliged to stop, unable to go farther. The injury was set down to the account of robbers, who had stopped the carriage in the wood. The wounded valet remained in the village. The gentry had sought out the hire of a new carriage, for the horses of the old had run from Lillers, it was said. Whereupon he continued his journey.

Planchet had gone in search of the carriage driver, and found them. They told of having taken a young gentry as far as Fromelles. From Fromelles, the traveler had set out on foot for Armentieres. Planchet had then taken the crossroad, and was at the village by midmorning.

There was but one tavern and inn in Armentieres, called the Post. Planchet went and presented himself as a valet out of work, who was in search of a position. He had not chatted more than ten minutes with the people of the tavern before he learned that a distinguished young man had arrived there alone an hour before midnight, and had engaged a chamber. This man had sent for the host of the inn and had spoken of seeking a cottage to rent, telling all that he desired to remain some time in the area.

At that, Planchet had no need to learn more. He had hastened to the rendezvous to find all the other valets awaiting him, and had told his story. He then placed them as sentinels at all the outlets of the inn and raced back to Bethune to find Athos.

The elder musketeer had just received this information and sent Planchet to seek breakfast, when her friends returned from the convent and the funeral of Constance. All their faces were grim, even the mild countenance of Aramis.

"And where did you go?" asked Porthos.

"To conduct necessary affairs of my own."

"Then what is to be done now?" asked d'Artagnan.

"To wait still," replied Athos. "But not for long. Trust me this one time, even if for the last time." She then pressed the young musketeer's shoulder, but said nothing more.

Each of the three then withdrew to their own apartment, to hold counsel with their thoughts. To anyone who passed by, Porthos would have been heard to mumble savagely, swearing oaths against Milord. Aramis went to prayer, kneeling before the window and the sinking sun.

Only d'Artagnan was silent, sitting in the darkness of closed shutters, and clutching at a single white winter rose she had claimed from the bier of Constance Bonacieux, before leaving the side of her beloved for the last time.

As dusk was falling, Athos sent Planchet to knock at the doors of the three others, in surprise to all. The elder musketeer had ordered the horses to be saddled, Planchet said, and all were notified that they must prepare for an expedition.

In mere minutes, the three were ready, even with Porthos, Aramis, and d'Artagnan yet ignorant of their mission. Each examined their arms and put them in order, then readied to ride. Planchet brought out Athos's horse then, as well as a second hired riding steed, and met d'Artagnan's stern gaze.

"You enter Athos's service now, I see?" said the young musketeer. "What is this business she has you engaged in? Tell me quick, for I have waited long enough."

But Athos came down then, and before Planchet could speak, waved him to silence as though he might be Grimaud. "Patience still," said she. "One of our party is yet to be collected."

The other three looked on in surprise as Athos leaped lightly into the saddle, for they sought vainly in their minds to know who this other person could be.

"Wait for me," said she, taking the reins of the second horse to draw it behind her. "I will soon be back." And she set off at a gallop.

In but a quarter of an hour, Athos returned, accompanied by a tall figure riding the second horse, hooded and masked and wrapped in a large red cloak. No soldier's badge nor uniform did this person display, but a heavy sword hung at their hip. The other three musketeers looked at one another questioningly. None could give the others any information, though, for all were ignorant of who this stranger could be. Planchet also appeared uncertain as regards this person, which told d'Artagnan that this part of Athos's plan was beyond even the valet's involvement.

All looked to Athos for some word on the identity of the red-cloaked stranger, but the elder musketeer said nothing on the matter. Instead, she rode close to d'Artagnan and the others, and spoke these words: "We ride to Milord this night."

Guided by Planchet, the little cavalcade set out, taking the route the carriage had taken. It was a melancholy sight — that of these four musketeers, galloping in silence, each plunged in their own thoughts, sad as despair, gloomy as chastisement.

— CHAPTER 65 —

THE TRIAL

It was a stormy and dark night. Heavy cloud concealed the stars, and the moon would not rise till midnight. Occasionally, by the glow of a flash of lightning which gleamed along the horizon from an approaching storm, the four musketeers and Planchet at their lead saw the road stretched out before them, white and solitary. Then the flash was extinguished, and all was in darkness again.

Every dozen strides of the horses, Athos was forced to restrain d'Artagnan, who constantly pushed to advance to the front of the little troop. The elder musketeer begged her young friend to keep the line, but each time d'Artagnan did, she would soon depart from it once more. The Gascon had but one thought, which was to go forward — and forward she went.

They passed in silence through the little village of Festubert, where the wounded valet had been, and then skirted the adjacent wood. At a crossroads, Planchet led the column through a turn to the left. Several times, Porthos and Aramis attempted to speak with the person in the red cloak. But to every question which was put to the masked stranger, they only bowed without response.

The storm increased in intensity. The lightning flashed more rapidly, the thunder began to growl, and the wind howled in the ears of the riders like the precursor of a gale. The cavalcade trotted on more sharply, but a little before they came to Fromelles, the storm burst. Athos, Porthos, and Aramis crouched in their cloaks, as the stranger had since the ride began. But d'Artagnan took off her hat, and could not be persuaded to make use of her cloak. She found pleasure in feeling the water trickle over her burning brow and over her body, which was agitated by feverish shudders.

The moment the little troop drew within sight of the lights of Armentieres, a figure sheltered beneath a tree detached themself from the trunk, against which they had been indistinguishable in the darkness. As this person advanced into the middle of the road, putting a finger to their lips, Athos recognized Grimaud.

"What's wrong?" said Athos. "Has Milord left Armentieres?"

Grimaud made a sign in the affirmative. D'Artagnan let out a fierce sound.

"Silence, d'Artagnan!" cried Athos. "For I have charged myself with executing this affair, and I promise you, all is well in hand." Then said she to Grimaud, "Where?"

Grimaud extended her hands in the direction of the River Lys.

"Far from here?" asked Athos. Grimaud showed the musketeer her forefinger, bent.

"Alone?" asked Athos. Grimaud made the sign, 'Yes.'

"Gentles," said Athos, "he is alone within half a league of us, in the direction of the river."

"That had best be truth," said d'Artagnan. "Lead us, Grimaud!"

The silent valet nodded, then set a sprinting course across the fields that abutted the road, acting as guide to the cavalcade.

At the end of a short journey, they came to a stream, which they forded. By the aid of the lightning, all then saw Grimaud extend her arm, and all could distinguish a small, isolated cottage on the banks of the river. It sat between an old abandoned windmill with motionless wings, and closer by, a boat docked at a ferry rope.

One window of the cottage was lighted.

"We are here," said Athos.

At that moment, another figure who had been crouching in a ditch jumped up and came toward them. It was Mousqueton, who pointed their finger to the lighted window.

"He is there," said they.

"And Bazin?" asked Athos.

"While I watched the window, he guarded the door."

"Well done," said Athos. "You are all good and faithful allies."

Athos sprang from her horse and gave the bridle to Grimaud. As the others dismounted, she made a sign for all to go toward the door. D'Artagnan moved at once to do so, and it took Porthos and Aramis to hold her back from running forward to burst through.

The little cottage house was surrounded by a low hawthorn hedge, some three feet high. Athos sprang over it and went up to the window, which was without shutters, but had its half-curtains closely drawn. She mounted the skirting stone, that her eyes might look over the curtain.

By the light of a lamp and a bright-burning fire, she saw a figure wrapped in a dark mantle and seated in a chair. This person's elbows were placed upon a fine table, and they held their head within their two hands, which were white as ivory.

The elder musketeer could not distinguish this person's face. But at that moment, a horse neighed. Milord raised his head, revealing himself. He saw at the window glass the pale face of Athos, and screamed.

Athos pushed against the window with her knee and hand, and it yielded, broken to shivers. Then the musketeer, like a specter of vengeance, leaped into the room. In response, Milord rushed to the door and opened it.

More menacing than Athos, d'Artagnan stood shadowed on the threshold.

Milord recoiled, uttering a cry. D'Artagnan, believing that he might have means of flight and fearing he should escape, drew a pistol from her belt, but Athos raised her hand.

"Put back that weapon, d'Artagnan!" said she. "This one must be tried, not assassinated. Wait but a moment, my friend, and you shall be satisfied. Come in, gentles."

D'Artagnan obeyed, for the voice of Athos carried the solemnity of a judge. Behind her entered Porthos, Aramis, and the person of the red cloak. The four valets guarded the door and the window.

Milord had sunk into a fine armchair with his hands extended, as if to dismiss this terrible apparition. "What do you want?" screamed he.

"We want Charles Backson," said Athos, "who was first called Arne de Breuil, then the Count de Fere, and afterwards Milord de Winter."

"Bravo," murmured Milord in rage. "You know my names. What do you want?"

"We wish to judge you according to your crimes," said Athos. "You are in our custody henceforth, and shall be free to defend yourself. Justify yourself if you can. Madame d'Artagnan, it is for you to accuse the prisoner first."

D'Artagnan stepped forward, trembling. "I am d'Artagnan of Gascony and Bearn, of the queens' musketeers. By my name and before these witnesses," said she, "I accuse this villain of having poisoned Constance Bonacieux, who died yesterday evening."

"I bear witness to this, by my faith," said Aramis, who nodded behind her.

"As do I," said Porthos grimly.

D'Artagnan continued. "Before these witnesses, I accuse Milord de Winter of having attempted to poison me, in wine which he sent me from Villeroi, with a letter forged as if that wine came from my friends. Fate alone saved me, but one named Brisemont died in my place."

"Aramis and I bear witness to this as well," said Porthos, and Aramis nodded in the same manner as before.

"I accuse Milord de Winter of having attempted to conscript me for the murder of the Countess de Wardes. But as no one else here can attest the truth of this accusation, I attest it myself. I have done." And d'Artagnan passed to the other side of the room with Porthos and Aramis.

Milord let his head sink between his two hands and tried to focus his thoughts, which seemed to be whirling in a deadly vertigo.

"And now my turn," said Athos, trembling as the lion trembles at the sight of the serpent. "I married that man when I was young and he younger. I married him in opposition to the wishes of all my family. I gave him my wealth, I gave him my name. And then one day, I discovered that this man was branded. Marked with a fleur-de-lis on his left shoulder, confessed by letter and deed as a felon thief, and worse."

"I am vilified in all this," said Milord, rising from the chair as if he had awaited Athos's pronouncement. "All is lies, and I shall prove it by first establishing the perjury of this witness, who attempted to murder me when I was but a youth and under her sway."

Milord felt all in the room react to his words, and felt the power return to his voice. He directed his thoughts to the tale told to Mistress Felton, and judged that as that lie had broken her resolve, it might well be retold to sway the hearts of these soldiers. For well did Milord judge that he had but one opportunity to save himself.

"Listen," said he, "and I will swear to you that the mark I bear was placed there by an evil and foul creature, who attempted to debase and corrupt me when barely I was a child. A creature you well know. The Cardinal de Richelieu." Skillfully, he directed his gaze to Athos, but tempered his rage with a sudden weakness. "Had you sought word of my alleged crimes, you would know that no court in France records that infamous sentence against me. I defy you to find any tribunal which pronounced it. I defy you to find the justice who executed it."

But Athos only smiled. "There it is," said she, "as expected. And so I have come prepared, for d'Artagnan and I are not the only accusers here this night." And saying so, she stepped back, opening the floor to the stranger in the red cloak, who stepped forward.

"I shall reply to Milord," said the stranger, their heavy voice speaking for the first time in the presence of any but Athos.

Milord's bluster was shaken with this unexpected event, and he stepped back to the table to appraise the person before him. "Who is that?" cried he, defiant and flushed. "Am I now to be accused by masked strangers?"

Approaching Milord with a slow and solemn step, so that the table alone separated them, the stranger took off their mask. Milord's gaze scanned a pale face, framed by graying hair and whiskers, the only expression of which was icy impassibility. Then fear shattered his countenance, and he cried out suddenly, retreating to the wall behind him.

"No, no! It is an infernal apparition! It is not they! Lies! It is lies!" screamed he, slamming both fists against the wall as if he might tear an opening there with his hands.

"Who are you, then?" said d'Artagnan, shocked to see the change that had come over the proud Milord.

"Ask that man," said the person in the red cloak. "For you may plainly see he knows me."

But Milord said nothing, having fallen prey to insensate terror, and clinging with his hands to the wall to avoid falling.

Everyone drew back, and the person in the red cloak remained standing alone in the middle of the room. "Musketeers and others, I introduce myself to you. My name is Maitre Francis d'Agney, once of Lille, retired now to Bethune. This is my history."

D'Artagnan felt her heart racing, seeing that the eyes of Porthos, Aramis, and all the valets were fixed upon the speaker, whose words hung heavy in the small room. But she saw that Athos had cast her face down to the floor.

"Five years ago, that creature you name as Milord de Winter was a young man by the name Arne de Breuil. As cunning and as beautiful as he is today, he was a novitiate in the convent of the Benedictines in Templemars. A young acolyte, with a simple and trustful heart, performed the duties of the church of that convent. De Breuil undertook his seduction of this poor young woman, and succeeded. For his lies would have seduced a saint.

"Their vows were made in secret. De Breuil prevailed upon his young lover to leave their rustic land, and to fly together to reach another part of France where they might live at ease. But to do so, money was necessary. With the acolyte's assistance, de Breuil stole the sacred vessels of the convent and sold them. But as they were preparing to escape together, they were both arrested. Eight days later, de Breuil had corrupted the son of the jailer to believe him innocent, and to aid in his escape. The young acolyte was thus judged alone for the theft, condemned to imprisonment, and to be branded…"

The red-cloaked figure trailed off. All heard the weight their heavy voice carried as they spoke again. "My name, as I have said, is Maitre Francis d'Agney. Five years past, I was executioner of Lille, and it was my jurisdiction that this case fell under. I was obliged to brand the guilty one. And she, gentlefolk, was my daughter."

D'Artagnan saw a fire rising in Milord de Winter's eyes. She understood that she herself might well have quailed beneath that gaze, except that her heart had been numbed by all that was said.

"I then swore," said d'Agney, the red-cloaked executioner, "that this villain who had ruined my daughter, who had urged her to the crime, should at least share her punishment. I suspected where he had gone to hide himself. I followed him, I caught him, I bound him. Then I imprinted the same disgraceful mark upon him that I had imprinted upon my poor girl.

"The day after my return to Lille, my daughter in her turn succeeded in making her escape from prison. My poor girl rejoined this man and both fled north. The two passed as brother and sister among the villages there, to better conceal themselves. Then one of the gentry on whose lands they had settled saw the young Arne de Breuil and became enamored of him. So much so that she proposed to marry him. And so de Breuil abandoned my daughter who he had ruined, to trade her for whom he was destined to ruin, and became the Count de Fere."

D'Artagnan felt sickened to hear once more the details of the story Athos had told in that room of the Golden Lily inn. Aramis and Porthos, who had learned only of Athos's former name in La Rochelle, and who now heard that tale for the first time, looked in shock to the elder musketeer, who nodded to confirm that all was true which the executioner had said.

"Then," continued the figure in red, "mad, desperate, determined to flee an existence from which this villain had stolen all honor and happiness, my poor daughter returned to Lille. And there she hanged herself. These are the crimes of which I accuse Milord de Winter, who is Arne de Breuil. These are the crimes for which he was branded."

Silence settled in the cottage, broken only by Milord's harsh breathing. His bloodied fingers had streaked the wall. He looked with longing from window to door, but all egress from the room was barred.

Athos spoke. "When I saw the name of Armentieres on the note of the Count de Rochefort, I inferred with dread the plan of Milord which has brought us here. He knew these lands of old for their nearness to my estates that were his home, and knowing that I had fled those lands, assumed it would be the one place I would be afraid to seek him."

Milord said nothing to that, but his furious look told all that Athos had guessed at the truth.

"Four years ago," said the elder musketeer, "I had sought and found Maitre d'Agney in Bethune to hear their daughter's story. No doubt more there are who would have charges to lay at Milord's feet were they here. Perhaps in England?"

Milord only laughed in response, bringing his hands to his face, and leaving blood on his pale cheeks.

"Is it so, then?" Porthos murmured. "The Duke of Buckingham?"

"Dead," said Milord. "An enemy of France, assassinated. Will you call me hero, musketeers?"

A shudder crept through all the witnesses at the revelation of this crime. Aramis placed their hand to their heart. Porthos shook his head.

"Madame d'Artagnan," said Athos. "For the murder of Constance Bonacieux, what is the penalty you demand against this man?"

"The punishment of death," whispered d'Artagnan.

"Porthos and Aramis," said Athos, "you who are his judges. What is the sentence you pronounce upon this man?"

"The punishment of death," said Aramis, in a hollow voice.

"Death," said Porthos, simply.

Milord then uttered a frightful scream, and drawing his poniard, he threw himself across the table toward his judges. Athos it was who caught and disarmed him, and held him fast.

"Charles Backson, Milord de Winter, Count de Fere, Arne de Breuil," said she. "Your crimes have tormented good folk on this earth and all the forces of the heavens. If you know a prayer, say it — for you are condemned for the murder of Constance Bonacieux, and you shall die."

At these words, which left no hope, Athos released her hold and Milord lurched free. He raised himself up in all his pride, and made as if to speak. But his strength failed him. He felt that a powerful and implacable hand had seized him with a great finality. He did not, therefore, attempt even the least resistance as the four musketeers surrounded him, and all went forth from the cottage. The room was left empty, with its broken window, its open door, and its bright fire burning slowly down to ash.

CHAPTER 66

MILORD'S END

It was near midnight. The moon, waning past half and reddened by the last traces of the storm, arose behind the little village of Armentieres in the distance, which showed against its pale light the dark outline of its houses and the skeleton of its high belfry.

In front of the party of the musketeers as they walked from the cottage toward the Lys, the river rolled its waters like molten tin. On the far bank was a black mass of trees, profiled against a stormy sky and buffeted by large coppery clouds, which created a sort of twilight amid the night. To the party's left, from the ruins of the windmill, an owl threw out its shrill, periodical, and monotonous cry. On the right and on the left of the path which the dismal procession pursued, a few low, stunted trees appeared as deformed figures crouching down to watch those foolish enough to be traveling at this sinister hour.

It was the executioner in red who had directed the party toward the river, though none had asked their reasons. From time to time, a broad sheet of lightning opened the horizon in its whole width, darting like a serpent over the black mass of trees, and like a terrible sword, dividing the heavens and the waters into two parts. Not a breath of wind now disturbed the heavy atmosphere. A deathlike silence oppressed all nature. The soil was humid and glittering with the rain which had recently fallen, and the refreshed herbs sent forth their scent with additional vigor.

Grimaud and Mousqueton now did close escort for Milord, whom each held by one arm. The executioner walked behind them. Athos, d'Artagnan, Porthos, and Aramis walked behind the executioner. Planchet and Bazin came last. Step by step, all drew closer to the boat moored at the ferry rope. Milord's mouth was mute, but his eyes spoke with their inexpressible eloquence, imploring by turns each of those on whom he looked as he cast his head behind him.

At a point when the path brought them through brambles whose noise would obscure his voice from those who followed, Milord whispered to Grimaud and Mousqueton. "A thousand pistoles to each of you," said he, "if you will assist my escape. But if you deliver me up for your masters, I have near at hand forces loyal to me who will make you pay dearly for my death."

Grimaud stumbled. Mousqueton showed a tremor in their arm.

Athos, who saw this, came sharply up. D'Artagnan did the same.

"He has spoken his poison to Grimaud and Mousqueton," said Athos. "They can no longer be trusted."

Planchet and Bazin were called, and took the places of the other two valets for the remainder of the journey.

On the bank of the river, they stopped. The executioner approached Milord, and began to bind his hands and feet. Then Milord broke the silence to cry out, "You are cowards! Miserable assassins! Nine of you it takes to murder one person, bound and defenseless."

"Do not call yourself a person," said Athos, coldly and sternly. "For you do not belong to the human species. You are a fiend escaped from the shadow-realm, whither we send you back again."

"Ah, you virtuous musketeers," sneered Milord. "I pray you remember that whichever of you takes my life is yourself an assassin. I will leave your soul tainted, and thus take my revenge."

"But the executioner may kill, without being on that account an assassin," said Maitre d'Agney as they stood, with Milord now bound. They rapped upon the heavy sword still at their hip. "This is the last judge. That is all."

On hearing these words, Milord uttered three savage cries, which produced a strange and melancholy effect in flying away into the night, and losing themselves in the depths of the woods.

"If I am guilty, if I have committed the crimes you accuse me of," shouted he, "take me before a tribunal. You are not judges! You cannot condemn me!"

"Your whole life, you might have sought repentance or exile," said Athos. You might have confessed your crimes, but did not. Why plead for judges now?"

"Because I am not willing to die!" cried Milord, struggling. "Because I am too young to die!"

"The innocent you poisoned at Bethune was still younger than you, villain," said d'Artagnan bitterly. "And yet she is dead."

"I will swear my penitence before all gods. I will seek sanctuary in faith and trouble no one again," said Milord.

"You had taken sanctuary in faith," said the executioner. "And you left it to ruin my only child."

Milord uttered a cry of terror and sank upon his knees. The tall executioner took him up in their arms as though he weighed nothing, and carried him toward the ferry boat.

"Oh, gods!" cried he. "You mean to drown me!" And his voice was a wail of fear.

Milord's cries had something so heartrending in them that d'Artagnan, despite the sorrow and abhorrence that was in her, sat down on the stump of a tree and hung her head, covering her ears so she need not hear.

Aramis though, was the gentlest soul of all those assembled, and on hearing Milord's pleas, their heart failed them.

"Oh, I cannot behold this frightful spectacle," said they. "Though I know this just, I cannot consent that anyone die thus!"

Milord heard these few words and caught at a shadow of hope. If he could win but a moment's doubt from two of the four, he might be saved.

"D'Artagnan!" called he, and he saw the young musketeer press her hands harder to her ears, even as she was driven to turn to see him. "Truly, I loved you! But I was driven mad by the pain you dealt me. Forgive me, I beg you!"

But Athos rose, drew her rapier, and placed herself between Milord and the others.

"If anyone here take one step farther," said she, "we shall cross swords together." Her hand was deadly calm.

Porthos moved across to Aramis, and helped them turn away. D'Artagnan sank on her knees, her back to Milord, and closed her eyes.

"Come," said Athos to Maitre d'Agney. "Do your duty."

"Willingly, madame," said the executioner.

Athos then made a step toward Milord. "I pardon you," said she, "the ill you have done me. I pardon you for my blasted future, my lost honor, my defiled love, and my salvation forever compromised by the despair into which you have cast me. Die in peace."

"I am lost," murmured Milord. "I must die…"

Then he cast around himself one of those piercing looks which seemed to dart from an eye of flame. But he saw nothing. He listened, and he heard nothing.

"Where am I to die?" said he.

"On the other bank of the river," said the executioner, "which marks the lands of Belgium. For I will not defile the soil of France with your blood."

Then d'Agney placed Milord in the boat, and as they were going to set foot in it themself, Athos handed them a purse of coins.

"Here," said she, "is the price of the execution, that it may be plain we act as judges."

"As it should be," said the executioner. "And now in his turn, let the condemned see that I am not fulfilling my trade, but paying my debt." And so saying, they threw the money into the river.

The boat moved off toward the far shore of the Lys, bearing Milord and the executioner. All the others remained on the near bank. Alongside d'Artagnan, Athos and Bazin fell to their knees.

The boat glided along the ferry rope under the shadow of a pale cloud that hung over the moonlit water. The troop of friends saw it gain the opposite bank. The executioner and Milord as they stepped forth, the one carrying the other once more, were defined like black shadows on the red-tinted horizon.

They saw from the other bank Milord slip to his knees. They then saw the executioner raise both their arms slowly. A moonbeam fell upon the blade of the heavy sword, and then the two arms fell with a sudden force.

Across the water, they heard the hissing of the sword and the cry of the victim. Then a truncated mass sank beneath the blow.

D'Agney took off their red cloak and spread it upon the ground. They laid the body in it, threw in the head, tied all up by the four corners, lifted it on their back, and entered the boat again.

In the middle of the stream, the executioner stopped the boat, and suspending their burden over the water, they cried in a loud voice, "Let justice be done!" Then they let the corpse drop into the depths of the waters, which closed over it.

— CHAPTER 67 —

THE CARDINAL'S OFFER

our days afterward, the musketeers arrived back in Paris on the final day of their furlough. That same evening, they went to pay a visit to Monsieur de Treville.

"Well, gentles," said the brave captain, "I hope you found what you sought on your excursion."

"Prodigiously," replied Athos in the name of herself and her comrades, who all were uncommonly quiet that night.

⚜

Three days later, the Queen Louise, in compliance with the promise she had made the cardinal to return to La Rochelle, left Paris — which by that point was all in amazement at the news which had begun to spread of the Duke of Buckingham's assassination. That news had first been heard the day of the four musketeers' return to Paris by the Cardinal de Richelieu, who received their letter from Milord against a backdrop of rumors that the English ports must be closed, for no ship had set sail or returned across the channel in over a week. Word of Buckingham's death was immediately announced in La Rochelle, then sent forth by courier to all corners of the realm. Thus was their eminence able to at last set their mind at ease in the matter of the future of the siege, and of Milord's fate — while having no idea of the turn that fate had taken.

Although warned that the man she had secretly loved so much was in great danger, the Queen Anne, when Buckingham's death was announced to her, would not believe the fact, and even imprudently exclaimed, "It is false. For he has just written to me!" But the very next day, she was obliged to believe this fatal intelligence. Laporte, detained in England as everyone else had been by the orders of the English royals, arrived having secured passage on a smugglers' ship, and was the bearer to Anne of Austria of the duke's dying gift.

Fresh on the heels of this heartbreak, the Queen Anne was advised by messenger sent by Aramis of the death of Constance Bonacieux. And so the tears she was able to publicly shed for her brave tailor sufficed to serve also as mourning for the Duke of Buckingham, whose grief she would carry in secret and silence for the rest of her life.

The joy of the Queen Louise in response to the news of Buckingham's death was well noticed before her departure from the city. She did not even give trouble herself to dissemble, and displayed her mood with much affectation before the Queen Anne. For Louise, like all those of weak heart, was most wanting in generosity. Still, she soon tired even of that satisfaction, and the return to La Rochelle was profoundly dull.

Our four friends, in particular, astonished their comrades with the sorrow of their mood, for they traveled together, side by side, with sad eyes and heads lowered. Athos alone from time to time raised her expansive brow, a flash kindling in her eyes and a bitter smile passing over her lips. Then, like her comrades, she sank again to be lost in her own thoughts.

Each time the escort arrived in any stopping place, after they had conducted the Queen Louise to her lodgings, the four friends either withdrew to their own quarters or to some secluded cabaret, where they neither drank nor gamed. They only conversed in low voices, looking around attentively to see that no one overheard them.

On the fifth day of the journey, the Queen Louise had halted for an hour to hunt the magpie, a pastime for which she had always preserved a great predilection. The four musketeers, instead of following the sport, stopped at a cabaret on the high road as was their custom. A group of soldiers coming from La Rochelle on horseback pulled up a short while behind them, alighting to water their mounts, and for their leader to enter the cabaret and seek a glass of wine. As the stern and pale figure did so, they darted a searching glance into the room where the four friends were sitting.

"Ho! Madame d'Artagnan," said they. "Is not that you whom I see yonder?"

The young musketeer raised her head and uttered a cry of rage. For this soldier was the Count de Rochefort — her villain of Meung, and the architect alongside Milord of Constance Bonacieux's abductions.

D'Artagnan drew her sword and sprang toward the bar. But instead of falling back, Rochefort advanced to meet her.

"Ah, monsieur," said she, "I meet you again at last. This time you shall not escape me."

"Escaping you is not my intention, madame," said Rochefort, neither drawing his sword nor showing any concern for d'Artagnan's blade, stopped now a hand's breadth from his heart. "For I am, in fact, seeking you. In the name of the queens, I arrest you."

"Fie! What do you mean?" cried d'Artagnan.

"I mean that you must surrender your sword to me, madame, and without resistance. Your very life is at stake, I warn you."

"We have not yet met," said a calm voice from behind d'Artagnan. Athos stepped forth, with Aramis and Porthos moving past her to both sides. All had hands on their swords.

"I am Monsieur the Count de Rochefort," said he of that name, "esquire of Cardinal de Richelieu. And I have orders to conduct the Gascon musketeer named d'Artagnan to their eminence in La Rochelle."

"We are, in fact, returning to La Rochelle, Monsieur Esquire," said Athos, stopping beside d'Artagnan. "And you will please accept the word of Madame d'Artagnan that she will go straight to their eminence when we do."

"I must place her in the hands of these guards with me, who will take her into camp."

"We will be her guards, monsieur, upon our word as musketeers. But likewise, upon our word as musketeers," added Athos, knitting her brow, "Madame d'Artagnan shall not leave us."

Rochefort cast a glance backward, and saw that Porthos and Aramis had placed themselves between him and the door. The cabaret was otherwise deserted. He understood that well before he could make any cry to his troop, he would be completely at the mercy of the four.

"Gentles," said he, "if Madame d'Artagnan will surrender her sword to me and join her word to yours, I shall be satisfied with your promise to convey her to the quarters of the cardinal."

"You have my word, monsieur," said d'Artagnan, "and you shall discover what my word is worth. Here is my sword."

"Frankly, this suits me the better," said Rochefort as he claimed d'Artagnan's blade, "as I wish to continue my journey north. Good day to you, musketeers."

Athos waited until Rochefort had stepped into the yard once more before she called to him. "If your journey north is for the purpose of rejoining Milord," said she coolly, "it is useless. You will not find him."

Rochefort turned back, ill hiding his surprise at the elder musketeer guessing at his business. "What has become of him, then?" asked he, as if without care.

"Return to La Rochelle and you shall know."

Rochefort remained for a moment in thought. Then he nodded, and he and his riders were ready to rejoin the musketeers as they mounted up again to make their way back to the Queen Louise's troop, then to resume the journey south.

On the ninth day since Paris, as three o'clock was sounding, all arrived once more at the camp at La Rochelle. The cardinal there awaited the Queen Louise, and the minister and the queen exchanged numerous felicitations upon the fortune which had freed France from the Duke of Buckingham, that inveterate enemy who had threatened to set all Europe against queens and country.

When all was done, Rochefort slipped close to the cardinal to inform them that d'Artagnan was arrested, and was given word in return that the young musketeer should be brought to their eminence's quarters at Pont-de-Pierre the next morning. But on returning in the evening to their quarters, the cardinal found d'Artagnan, Athos, Porthos, and Aramis already standing before the house their eminence occupied.

D'Artagnan was without her sword. The other three musketeers were armed. The cardinal, of course, was well attended with guards, and their eminence looked at the musketeers sternly. They then made a sign with their eye and hand for d'Artagnan to follow them.

The young musketeer obeyed.

"We shall wait for you, d'Artagnan," said Athos, loud enough for the cardinal to hear her.

Their eminence stopped for a moment, and then kept on their way without uttering a single word.

D'Artagnan entered after the cardinal, and behind her, the door was closed by the guards who waited there. One of those guards was Rochefort, who showed surprise to see d'Artagnan accompanying their eminence, but said nothing.

Richelieu entered the chamber which served them as a study, and made a sign to Rochefort to bring in the young musketeer. Rochefort obeyed, walking with d'Artagnan to the door and within. He then nodded and returned to the entrance hall, closing the study door behind him.

D'Artagnan was alone in the study for her second interview with the cardinal — a second interview that she felt well assured might be her last. Richelieu remained standing, leaning against the mantelpiece. A table stood between their eminence and d'Artagnan.

"Madame," said the cardinal, "you have been arrested on my orders."

"So they tell me, maitre."

"Do you know why?"

"No, maitre. For the only thing for which I might be arrested is still unknown to your eminence."

Richelieu looked steadfastly at the young musketeer. "And what," said they, "does that mean?"

"If maitre will have the goodness to tell me firstly what crimes are imputed to me, I will then tell their eminence the deeds I have truly done."

"Crimes are imputed to you which would bring down far loftier heads than yours, my bold madame," said the cardinal.

"Name them, maitre," said d'Artagnan, with a calmness which astonished even Richelieu as they appraised her.

"You are charged with having corresponded with the enemies of France. You are charged with having sought out state secrets. You are charged with having tried to thwart the plans of your superiors."

"And who charges me with these crimes, maitre?" said d'Artagnan.

"Agents of the crown, madame, whose names are known to me and are none of your concern."

"Ah, but I believe I know those agents, maitre," said d'Artagnan, who had no doubt that all the cardinal's accusations came only from Milord de Winter. "For was one not branded by the justice of France? And another engaged in execrating the laws of marriage and inheritance by claiming one wife in France and another in England? And was there one who attempted both to poison and assassinate me, and who has engaged in assassinations which, if revealed, could well lead to war?"

"Think carefully of what you say here, madame," said the cardinal, flushing with anger.

"I will say the name of Milord de Winter," replied d'Artagnan. "Of whose crimes your eminence was doubtless ignorant on all those occasions when you honored him with your confidence."

"Madame," said the cardinal, "if Milord de Winter has committed any crimes you lay to his charge, he shall be punished."

"He has been punished, maitre."

"And who has punished him?"

"We four musketeers. Athos, Porthos, Aramis, and myself."

"He is imprisoned, then?"

"He is dead."

A silence hung for a long moment, as the cardinal could not believe what they heard. They stepped forward to the table. "Dead," repeated their eminence. "Do you attempt to delude me, musketeer?"

"No, maitre. For three times, Milord attempted to kill me, and I pardoned him. But then he murdered the one I loved, and my friends and I took him, tried him, and condemned him."

As she said these words, d'Artagnan began to weep with the memory of that grievous day at the convent of Bethune. She knew she had no need to relate the name of Constance Bonacieux to the cardinal. By their eminence's silence, d'Artagnan understood that they would not ask.

A shudder crept through the body of the cardinal, who did not shudder readily. Then all at once, as if undergoing the influence of an unspoken thought, Richelieu's uncertain expression recovered its perfect serenity.

"So," said their eminence, in a tone that contrasted strongly with the severity of their words, "you four have constituted yourselves judges and executioners, without remembering that they who execute without license are murderers in their own right?"

"*For myself, I willingly submit to any punishment your eminence may please to inflict upon me. I do not hold life dear enough to be afraid of death…*"

"Maitre, I swear to you that neither I nor my friends ever for an instant had the intention of defending our actions to you. For myself, I willingly submit to any punishment your eminence may please to inflict upon me. I do not hold life dear enough to be afraid of death."

"Yes, I know you are a person of stout heart, madame," said the cardinal, with a voice almost affectionate. "I do not fear to therefore tell you beforehand that you four shall all be tried, and condemned, and thereafter put to death. Unless…"

And at that, Cardinal de Richelieu assessed d'Artagnan with all the weight of their piercing eyes, and their close-set lips hinted at a smile. "You will pledge to me your absolute loyalty, not only on your own behalf but for your three friends. You will all join the ranks of the cardinal's guards. From this point hereafter, you will all serve me, for without any debate, your lives are mine."

D'Artagnan was silent a moment, as if in thought. "Against such learned judgement," said she at length, "I might normally content myself with saying, 'Command, maitre, for I am ready.' But I fear that the pardon I possess will set aside that judgement. For which, my apology, your eminence."

"The pardon you possess?" said Richelieu, astonished.

"Yes, maitre," said d'Artagnan.

"A pardon signed by whom? The queens?" And the cardinal pronounced those words as a singular expression of contempt. "Louise would not dare without my leave. A pardon from Anne, I will make worthless within an hour."

"No, your eminence. Signed by you."

"By me? You are insane, madame."

"But maitre will doubtless recognize their own handwriting."

And d'Artagnan presented to the cardinal the precious piece of paper which Athos had forced from Milord, and which she had given to d'Artagnan upon their return to La Rochelle, to serve her as a safeguard.

Richelieu took the paper, which they read in a slow voice, dwelling upon every syllable:

By my order, and for the good of the state, the bearer of this has done what they have done.

— Richelieu

The cardinal, after having read these lines, sank down into the chair behind the desk, and into a state of deep thought. But they did not return the paper to d'Artagnan.

After a moment of waiting, and seeing no sign that the cardinal would speak, the young musketeer spoke instead. "Maitre, are you meditating by what sort of punishment you shall cause me to die? For by my faith, I am willing to show you how a musketeer and a Gascon can die." By the tenor of her voice, d'Artagnan showed that she was in an excellent disposition to die heroically.

Richelieu, though, only continued thinking, rolling and unrolling the paper in their hands.

At length, their eminence raised their head, fixing their eagle-eyed look upon the young musketeer. The cardinal read upon her face, furrowed with tears, all the sufferings its possessor had endured, and reflected not for the first time how much there was in that youth not yet of twenty years now standing before them, and what resources her activity, her courage, and her shrewdness might be put to under proper control.

Not for the first time, the cardinal also reflected on the crimes, the power, and the infernal genius of Milord, and how that genius had more than once terrified them. With Buckingham now dead, their eminence registered a feeling something like a secret joy at being forever relieved of that dangerous accomplice.

Richelieu slowly tore in half the pardon which d'Artagnan had generously relinquished.

With a sinking heart, d'Artagnan could only imagine that she was lost. "I take that as my condemnation," said she, quietly but bravely. "Pray, maitre, will you be kind enough to spare me the ennui of the Bastille, or the tediousness of a trial? That would be most kind of you."

The cardinal drew more paper from across the table, and wrote a few lines upon a sheet of which two-thirds were already filled. They then affixed their seal.

"Here, madame," said the cardinal to the young musketeer, ignoring her words. "I have taken from you one blank slate to give you another. The name is missing in this commission. You may write it yourself."

In confusion, d'Artagnan took the paper hesitatingly and cast her eyes over it.

It was a lieutenant's commission in the queens' musketeers.

D'Artagnan felt her anger rise, and worked to keep her voice even. "Maitre, if you presume that this offer binds me to your service, I invite you to recall our conversation of the Place de Palais-Cardinal. My friends remain in the service of the queens, and my enemies in the service of your eminence. Nothing has changed on that account…"

"You are a brave youth, d'Artagnan," interrupted the cardinal, with impatience in their tone. "Do with this commission what you will. Only remember, though the name be blank, it is to you I give it." Then the cardinal turned and called in a loud voice, "Rochefort!"

The Count de Rochefort, who had clearly lingered near the door to hear all, entered immediately.

"Rochefort," said the cardinal, "you will please see Madame d'Artagnan out. Be aware both of you that I know your quarrels and have no patience with them. And I would urge you both be wise in your conduct toward each other if you wish to preserve your heads."

Rochefort coolly nodded to d'Artagnan, and both left the chamber at the same time.

"We shall meet again, madame," said Rochefort as he escorted d'Artagnan to the door.

"When you please," said d'Artagnan coolly. "I do not forget your role in the events that led to Constance Bonacieux's death, ser."

"And I do not forget the insults of a country vagabond, ser, no matter her uniform," replied Rochefort. "An opportunity will come."

D'Artagnan said nothing as she pushed through the door and left Rochefort behind her, stepping past the guards there and toward where Athos, Porthos, and Aramis still waited.

"Here I am, my friends," said she. "Not only free, but in favor."

"Tell us all," said Athos as all embraced the young musketeer.

"This evening," said d'Artagnan. "But for the moment, let us separate. I will come to you when the time is right." And so saying, all embraced again, then departed.

⚜

Accordingly, at eight o'clock that evening, d'Artagnan went to the quarters of Athos, whom she found well on the way to emptying a bottle of a fine Spanish Malaga — an occupation which the elder musketeer had religiously accomplished every night since Bethune. While d'Artagnan joined her in the assault on the wine, she related at length what had taken place between the cardinal and herself, to Athos's great delight.

"The cardinal seeks to keep their enemies close," said she.

"Indeed," answered d'Artagnan. "And of all those enemies, I know the one who most deserves this honor." Drawing the nameless commission from her pocket, she added, "Here, my dear Athos. This naturally belongs to you."

But Athos only smiled with one of her sweet and gentle smiles.

"Friend," said she, "for Athos, this honor is too much. For the Countess de Fere, it is too little. Keep the commission, for it is yours. Alas, you have earned it dearly enough."

Though d'Artagnan attempted to argue, Athos would not hear it. So in the end, the young musketeer left the elder musketeer's chamber, and next went to the quarters of Porthos. She found the tall musketeer clothed in a magnificent surcoat covered with splendid embroidery, admiring himself before a mirror.

"Ah, is that you, dear friend?" exclaimed Porthos. "How do you think this finery suits me?"

"Wonderfully," said d'Artagnan. "But I come to offer you a uniform which will become you still better."

"Indeed?" asked Porthos. "And what uniform is that?"

"That of a lieutenant of the musketeers."

D'Artagnan then related to Porthos the substance of her interview with the cardinal, and said, taking the commission from her pocket, "Here, my friend. Write your name upon it and I will follow your command."

Porthos cast his eyes over the commission with astonishment — and then returned it to d'Artagnan, to the even greater astonishment of the young Gascon.

"Yes," said he, soberly. "Yes, that would flatter me very much. But I should not have time enough to enjoy the distinction. In Paris after our expedition to Bethune, I received word that the husband of my duchess had died. So, my dear, with both a fine lady and the coffer of her inheritance holding out their arms to me, I must decline."

"Both rich and in love!" d'Artagnan cried. "Your patience in this affair has served you well, then."

"Indeed," said the tall musketeer. "For this surcoat is to be my wedding suit! Keep the lieutenancy, my dear. Keep it."

D'Artagnan then entered the apartment of Aramis, finding the gentle musketeer kneeling before a prayer bench with their head leaning on an open hymnal.

After Aramis cheerfully bid her join them, the young musketeer for the third time described her interview with the cardinal. Aramis was thoughtful afterward, and d'Artagnan for the third time drew the commission from her pocket, saying, "You, our friend, our intelligence, our invisible protector. Accept this commission. You have merited it more than any of us by your wisdom and your counsels, always followed by such happy results."

"Alas, dear friend," said Aramis, "our late adventures have exhausted me of military life. This time, my determination is irrevocably taken. After the siege of La Rochelle is ended, I shall finally seek my calling as a cleric among the order of the Lazarists. Keep the commission, d'Artagnan. The profession of arms suits you. You will be a brave and adventurous lieutenant, and then a captain beyond."

D'Artagnan, her eyes wet with gratitude though she beamed with joy, went back to Athos, whom she found still at table, contemplating the charms of her last glass of Malaga by the light of her lamp.

"Well," said the young Gascon, "Porthos and Aramis have likewise refused me."

"That, dear friend, is because no one is more worthy than yourself." Athos then took the commission, grabbed up a quill, wrote the name of d'Artagnan on the paper in the appropriate spot, and returned it to her.

"I shall then have no more compatriots among my friends," said the young musketeer, "with Porthos and Aramis retired, and me your commander, Athos. Alas, I shall be left with nothing but bitter memories."

And she let her head sink upon her hands, while tears once more rolled down her cheeks.

"Not so," said Athos, as she embraced her friend. "For you are young, and you are brave, and you are true. And thus your bitter memories will change themselves into sweet celebrations, in time."

EPILOGUE

La Rochelle, deprived of the assistance of the English fleet and of the diversion promised by Buckingham, surrendered as expected after two additional months of campaign and siege. When the city's capitulation was signed, the Queen Louise made her return into Paris. As the Queen Anne noted in a most cold and public way, she was received in triumph as if she came from conquering an enemy, rather than her own citizens.

D'Artagnan took her promotion, and was soon given her first command under Monsieur de Treville. She quickly proved herself an adept leader, though many who served under her would note the grief she seemed always to carry. Until late the following spring, when the young lieutenant was surprised at a visit from a certain valet, newly returned to Paris from the service of a gentry of Tours. Then in the company of Kitty, with whom she lived long thereafter, the noble d'Artagnan in time set her sadness aside.

Planchet remained at d'Artagnan's side for many a year, but in time returned to Picardy, his home. In the regiment there, with glowing references provided by d'Artagnan, he obtained the rank of sergeant.

As he had promised, Porthos left the queens' musketeers, and in the course of the following year, he married Madame Coquenard, and both were much contented. In the end, the attorneys' strongbox so much coveted contained eight hundred thousand livres. Remaining in Porthos and Madame Coquenard's service, Mousqueton had a magnificent livery, and enjoyed the satisfaction of which they had been ambitious all their life — that of standing behind a gilded carriage.

Aramis, after a journey into Lorraine, disappeared all at once, and ceased to write to their friends. Those friends learned at a later period through Madame de Chevreuse that the gentle musketeer had held to their word and yielded at last to their true vocation, retiring into a convent. Bazin had accompanied them, taking vows alongside Aramis — but which convent the two had dedicated themselves to, not even Madame de Chevreuse knew.

Athos remained a musketeer under the command of d'Artagnan for more than ten years, at which time, after a journey she made to Touraine, she also left the service, letting it be known that she had inherited a small estate in Roussillon. Grimaud followed her, and managed the retired musketeer's lands and affairs with a deft — though still silent — hand.

The Count de Rochefort was killed in a duel with an unknown assailant, within one month of his return to Paris after the ending of the campaign at La Rochelle. Lieutenant d'Artagnan was questioned by agents of the Cardinal de Richelieu in the matter, but her placement elsewhere in the city on the night was proved by the testimony of Athos, Porthos, Monsieur de Treville, the Queen Anne, and others.

Monsieur Bouquet lived on very quietly, pleased that d'Artagnan never returned to the Rue de Fossoyeurs, wholly ignorant of what had become of Constance Bonacieux his wife, and caring very little about either. One day, he had the sudden urge and indiscretion to recall himself to the memory of the Cardinal de Richelieu, sending messages asking for certain favors he felt humbly owed for past service to their eminence. The cardinal responded to tell Bouquet that his service was well remembered, and that they would provide for him so that he should never want for anything in future.

In fact, Monsieur Bouquet, having left his house the following evening to go to the Place de Palais-Cardinal, never appeared again in the Rue de Fossoyeurs. The opinion of those who seemed to be best informed was that he was fed and lodged in some royal castle, at their eminence's generous expense.

EDITOR'S POSTFACE

All right, a little more seriously this time. I thought I would talk a bit about why this book actually exists — which, it turns out, is kind of a longish story.

⚜

I'm extremely fortunate to be able to spend my days working as an editor, a writer, a story editor, and a game designer. I spend my life working with incredible stories and characters, and amazing worlds of adventure. And it would be absolutely impossible for me to overstate how important *The Three Musketeers* was to shaping and defining my imagination and my love of story.

"Where do you get your ideas?" writers are often asked. And just as often, it turns out to be an impossible question to answer. Or sometimes there is an answer, but it has all kinds of levels and layers and nuances, and the person asking regrets doing so an hour into the writer trying to formulate a response.

Other times, knowing where an idea comes from is extraordinarily clear.

⚜

The first time I fell in love with *The Three Musketeers* was 1969. I'm four years old. One of my earliest memories. I'm watching *The Banana Splits Adventure Hour*, which had a couple of cartoon serials that ran alongside the live-action Sid and Marty Krofft costume stuff. And one of those serials was *The Three Musketeers*. This was my first experience of those characters, and that world of swordplay and horses and swashbuckling adventure.

I remember collecting the musketeer figures that came with Kellogg's cereal at one point. I remember my mom helping me cut out and build a French castle diorama from the back of a Rice Krispies box. Back before we had role-playing games, we were stuck with make-believe. And the world of *The Three Musketeers*, with imaginary horses and my friends and I bashing each other with wooden swords, was where that first came to life for me.

Since that first time, I've fallen in love with this story over and over again. The 1973 and 1974 films *The Three Musketeers* and *The Four Musketeers*. Kids' versions of the original story. *Three Musketeers* comics. The original novel by

Alexandre Dumas and Auguste Maquet in full, read for the first time when I was twelve — one of the William Robson translations.

Then much more recently, I fell very much in love with the 2014 BBC series *The Musketeers*. This was a show that didn't tell the story of the novel, but which built the world and the characters out into something new, something different — but something with all the same qualities of heroism and intrigue and heartbreaking romance that I first fell in love with when I was four.

But even before I saw my first episode of the series, something interesting happened.

As you'll know if you've seen the show (and you should, because it's awesome), the producers of *The Musketeers* did something really cool when they cast Howard Charles, a Black actor, as Porthos. In doing so, they adopted for him a piece of Alexandre Dumas's own family story, making Porthos the son of a white French noble and a Black mother who was a freed slave. And so naturally, even before I first watched the show, I became aware of the wailing hue and cry that arose from that certain little group of people who like to scream about historical accuracy in fiction, and about how historical accuracy in fiction means we should only ever tell stories about straight white men, because that's what history is really all about.

I remember reading multiple articles about all this manufactured outrage, and idiots crying about political correctness run amok, and how social justice warriors were just going to keep ruining everyone's fun, and I remember getting as ticked off as I usually do about that sort of thing. But I also remember a particular thought popping into my head while I was processing all that ranting, and which just kind of hung there.

That was the thought that if I'd been the show runner on *The Musketeers*, I not only would have cast Howard Charles as Porthos, I would have made two of the other musketeers women. And I would have made half the characters across the entire show people of color. And I would have made half of all those men, women, POC, and white characters LGTBQ+. And then I would have just sat back and watched those "But historical accuracy!!!" jackasses while their heads exploded.

And six-odd years later, here we are.

I'm really happy to be able to share this book, and to work with the amazing Aviv Or on bringing this unusual version of seventeenth-century France to life. I honestly wish someone else had edited this version of the original *Three Musketeers* a long time ago. I wish this was a book I could have read with my daughters back in the day. When those daughters were younger, I remember sharing with them so many of the stories that I loved as a kid (including the 1973 and 1974 *Three Musketeers* and *Four Musketeers* films at one point). I remember sharing lots of other cool stuff with them that featured characters they could relate to, and in whom they could see themselves. But I also remember being very cognizant that so many of the stories I loved when I was their age wouldn't feel the same to them as they did to me, because so many of those stories had been written primarily for people like me.

That's also a big part of where the idea for this book came from, and I wish that idea had come to me sooner.

I'm hoping that a large number of people ultimately enjoy this new edition. I'm hoping that this silly little project allows this book that meant so much to me to resonate with people who might normally not be able to see themselves in its characters and its world.

But at the same time, I'm also kind of hoping it makes at least a couple of jackasses' heads explode.

So thanks for helping with both those things.

— Scott Fitzgerald Gray

ABOUT THE CREATORS

Scott Fitzgerald Gray (he/him; 9th-level layabout, vindictive good) is a writer of fantasy and speculative fiction, a fiction editor, a story editor, and an editor and designer of roleplaying games — all of which means he finally has the job he really wanted when he was sixteen. He shares his life in the Canadian hinterland with a schoolteacher, two itinerant daughters, and a number of animal companions. More info on him and his work (some of it occasionally truthful) can be found by reading between the lines at insaneangel.com.

Aviv Or (she/her) is a UK-based freelance illustrator with a passion for character art. Her work in the tabletop game industry includes titles like Thornwatch, Acquisitions Incorporated, and the Jane Austen roleplaying game Good Society, and she is the co-creator of the webcomic and RPG Crystal Heart. She doesn't know much about nineteenth-century literature, but enjoys a good swashing of buckles. You can see her work at www.avivor.com, and at the webcomic uptofourplayers.com.

Alexandre Dumas, pere (he/him), was a French playwright, travel writer, and novelist whose works have been translated into dozens of languages, and who has been one of the most recognizable authors in the world for nearly two hundred years. He is best known for his novels of high adventure, including *The Three Musketeers* and *The Count of Monte Cristo,* and for the hundreds of film, television, and fiction adaptations those works have inspired.

Auguste Maquet (he/him) was a French playwright and novelist, and the long-term collaborator of Alexandre Dumas, pere. Author of more than twelve novels under his own name, Maquet co-wrote eighteen novels with Dumas, including the world-famous works *The Count of Monte Cristo* and *The Three Musketeers*.

William Robson (he/him) was British educator, writer, and translator. The author of numerous nonfiction works, including a biography of the Cardinal de Richelieu, Robson produced one of the earliest English translations of Dumas and Maquet's *The Three Musketeers*.

COLOPHON

For inspiration, assistance, and general awesomeness,
thanks et la gratitude are owed to the following.

House Guards of the Louvre
Colleen, Shvaugn, and Caitlin

Directors of the Royal Academy
Gabriel Duclair, Shvaugn Craig, Christine Sandquist,
Maple Intersectionality Consulting, Colleen Craig

Acolytes of the Convent at Bethune
John P. Roberts III, Roger Labbe, Scott David Gray, Sue Asscher,
Anita Martin, David Muller, David Widger

Gemsmiths of the Buckingham Estate
Aviv Or, (studio)Effigy

Orchestra of *La Merlaison*
Leigh Bardugo, Johnny Clegg, Fire From the Gods, Steve Jablonsky,
Guy Gavriel Kay, Nnedi Okorafor, Freya Ridings, Sofia Samatar,
Samantha Shannon, Devin Townsend, Benjamin Wallfisch,
Within Temptation, Hans Zimmer

THE THREE MUSKETEERS

Published by Insane Angel Studios
insaneangel.com

Text copyright © 2020–2021 Scott Fitzgerald Gray
Illustrations copyright © 2020–2021 Aviv Or
All rights reserved

Cover, Design, and Typography
by (studio)Effigy

v1.1
May 2021

We try to make sure that no errors creep into our work, but publishing is a chaotic enterprise at the best of times. If you spot a typo or a formatting glitch in an Insane Angel Studios book, email insaneangel@insaneangel.com with details (including which e-book version you're reading, if applicable). If any errors you spot are ones we haven't yet caught and are in the process of fixing, we'd be very happy to send you another of our e-books of your choice for free.

www.ingramcontent.com/pod-product-compliance
Lightning Source LLC
Chambersburg PA
CBHW040510170726
48295CB00012B/146